BRAIDING
OF
DARKNESS

ANOTHER BEAST'S SKIN, BOOK 2,

JESSIKA
GREWE GLOVER

GenZ
The Future of Publishing

Cover Designer: Lauren Johnson
Supervising Editor: Shannon Marks
Design Assistants: Fiona Suherman
Editing Assistant: Megan Peterson
Publishing Assistants: Amit Dey and Lisa Wood

Please write to the publisher at info@genzpublishing.org

ISBN: 979-8-437086-97-1 (paperback)
ISBN: 978-1-952919-85-5 (ebook)

DEDICATION

For My family of hooligans,
Damian, India, Phineas, and CocoMonster
My *Wonderwalls*

TABLE OF CONTENTS

Acknowledgements. viii

PART I 1

Chapter 1 3

Chapter 2 17

Chapter 3 23

Chapter 4 30

Chapter 5 43

Chapter 6 61

Chapter 7 72

Chapter 8 78

Chapter 9 90

Chapter 10 106

Chapter 11 123

Chapter 12 127

Chapter 13 132

Chapter 14 143

Chapter 15 156

Chapter 16 174

PART II **183**

Chapter 17 185

Chapter 18 203

Chapter 19 224

Chapter 20 233

Chapter 21 238

Chapter 22 247

Chapter 23 250

Chapter 24 257

Chapter 25 262

Chapter 26 267

Chapter 27 284

Chapter 28 288

Chapter 29 301

Chapter 30 309

Chapter 31 322

Chapter 32 329

Chapter 33 336

Chapter 34 342

PART III **349**

Chapter 35 351

Chapter 36 354

Chapter 37 367

Chapter 38 375

Chapter 39 381

Chapter 40. 386

Chapter 41 388

Chapter 42. 395

Chapter 43 402

Chapter 44. 410

Chapter 45 421

Chapter 46. 427

Chapter 47. 433

Chapter 48. 450

Chapter 49. 463

Chapter 50. 473

Chapter 51 485

Chapter 52 499

Chapter 53 502

ACKNOWLEDGEMENTS

S hout out to Matt Wallace for taking a couple hours to help me understand magnetic fields, some basic physics, and how one might use crystals and temperature variations to create a weaponized magnetic field. Definitely flexing that I have a JPL rocket scientist on speed dial.

Aoifsing

<u>Former Elders by province:</u>
Faestara: Paschale
Saarlaiche: Turuín
Veruni: Analisse
Maesarra: Feynser
Laorinaghe: Lorelei
Dunstainaiche: Soren
Naenire: Camua
Prinaer: Nanua

Characters by province:

Saarlaiche
Cadeyrn
Corraidhín
Silas
Magnus
Lina
Rhia

Maesarra
Saski
Ewan
Reynard
Cyrranus
Arneau
Etienne
Francois
Alan

Laorinaghe
Yva
Arturus
Farus
Xaograos

Faestara
Petyr
Tuso
Bestía
Kíra
Olek
Sergo

Veruni
Analissse
Julissa
Lord Dockman

Heilig
King Konstantín
Queen Marja
Saski (crown princess)
Arik
Ludek
Pavla (deceased)
Basz
Eamon

PART I

CHAPTER 1

Neysa

Occasionally, I would catch his scent. A light layer of his rain essence around me, catching my breath every time. Most instances, the essence would disappear as soon as it appeared. Weeks of following mere mentions of a beast had us downcast. Many times, my *baethaache*, the beast within me—like the one Analisse forced from Cadeyrn—would become restless and seem to sense him. I willed her to come out as I did when I was a child, but somehow, she refused. The day of the summit, I had a split second to decide how to act. How to play the events that unfolded once my mate became a monstrous version of our innate selves. Many pledged allegiances. Bestía, the platinum-haired general from Festaera, Kasseik of Neanire, Soren of Dunstanaich, Turuin of Saarlaiche. They all witnessed the dark magics used to tear Cadeyrn's self from its beast. Though my body wanted to wrap itself in despair and seek revenge, I knew that was why Analisse had done it. She wanted to show the delegates that we were monsters who would turn on them, and I refused to give her the satisfaction. So, I walked out of the palace with Corra and Silas, having entombed my grief and become purpose driven. I barely spoke. Basic functions were automatic, and my interaction with people was warm only when I had to represent our cause. In the evenings, I descended to a depth of grief too lightless and cold to support life.

Corra began to materialize before Silas and me as we sat around the fire. The days were getting longer, allowing more time to hunt him. Or at least what was left of him.

"I had a hawk come to me," Corra reported. "Messengers reported him in the north of Dunstanaich." We never said his name, I realized. "Him" or "It." Perhaps trying to objectify this whole mess for us all. "Oddly enough, some have reported seeing the male. Someone recognized his markings."

That gave me pause.

"Do you think," I stammered, my voice like sandpaper from disuse. "He is fighting it and winning?"

"Perhaps," Corra said. "One farmer claimed a sheep was stolen by the beast. This is the first we have heard. Could be a load of rubbish, but it's worth taking into account. If the countryside starts getting razed, then we have bigger problems."

I asked how far we were from Dustanaich, and Corra told me to wait for the next update. That update was from two days ago and the beast moves. We would head further north and see.

A week later had us in the center of Prinaer. I knew the quarries of stone here were immense and the gemstones harvested were said to be the most powerful in the realm. The *adairch dorhdj*, or double horn, I wore thrummed against me in a constant rhythm, like a second heartbeat. Corra had given it to me for Yule. It was once a present to her from Cadeyrn—a talisman of amethyst on one side, black tourmaline on the other. Corra claimed she realized it must have been given to her for safe keeping until Cadeyrn and I met. Met and fell in love. And mated. Before he was torn from me.

A hawk landed near Corraidhín as we cleaned up after a meager evening meal of river fish and cheese received from a sympathetic farmer. She read the encoded message and told us the Queen had a contingent of support from every province, but seers warned of a darkness moving in. The beast was spotted in Laorinaghe. Children happened upon it while it was sleeping, and they said it opened its eyes and stared at them as they backed away and it growled to the sky. Yet, it didn't attack.

My magic was in tatters, whether from the blight on our bond or from my own self-inflicted damper, I didn't know. I barely saw a hint of the white light, the electricity, the heightened senses. It was almost as though I had shoved that cloaking back over me. Once again, I was wearing the skin of another beast. I couldn't even bring myself to try to speak to him through our *Cuira*íbh *Enaíde*, the braiding of our souls that made us more than lovers, more than mates.

Corra said she would go to Laorinaghe ahead of us, and we could head out in the morning, as she would follow the river in her dematerialized form. Corra and Silas could both dissolve into any moisture, allowing them to travel faster through their gifts than on land. Silas stayed with me, allowing his sister to move faster without us. She gave me one small, defeated glance as she became mist. I shucked off my boots, jacket, and various weapons, then slid into my bedroll. For hours it seemed, I laid there thinking and not thinking in turn, trying to sort out what to do next. We couldn't stay in the countryside forever. In fact, we all knew that it was time to think about heading back to civilization. We needed to be present in the cities and towns. Needed to be amongst our folk, with or without him. My solitary life in the human realm wasn't looking so bad anymore. I would trade my anxiety attacks for this numbness. Loneliness for this abyss of helplessness.

Silas and I sparred every day to keep up our strength. He taught me archery as well. His hands adjusted my hips, directing my body's angle for aiming my bow. Each kick of his boot against my heel, a gentle indication of proper foot placement for the method of combat I was yet untrained. I did as I was told and became proficient, arrows flying true. He was patient and gentle, never pushing for me to snap out of it, unlike his sister. Corra lost her cool with me one day after being fed up with my vacant company. She yelled and shoved me, telling me to get a grip. I simply shrugged and walked away.

Corra's leaving felt like a chapter's end. We would no doubt go to Laorinaghe, and from there, begin our migration back to Saarlaiche or Eíleín Reínhe. The night pressed in on me and I began to hate the looming dawn. My breathing hitched and I started to feel my anxiety rising. It was better than nothing, I supposed. Buzzing filled my ears. Shuffling sounded behind me and Silas' warmth pressed against my back. His arms circled around me and he tucked his head onto my shoulder, offering the comfort of a friend. For a moment, it felt like that hotel in Varna so long ago with Cadeyrn. I struggled for breath. As heat pricked up my spine and scalp, a light, misting rain began falling on us, cooling me down. I always overheated during my anxiety attacks, then was left shaking and cold in the aftermath.

For the first time in three weeks, I sagged. Exhaustion and misery finally had my eyes filling and a great sob came out. Silas' arms tightened around me. I felt his floppy brown hair against my face as he pressed his own into my shoulder. Ugly, racking sobs came out of me, churning my stomach. Still, he held on, as if grief weighed heavy on him as well.

"This is it, isn't it?" I managed. He knew what I meant.

"Yes."

"Where will we go? I don't know where to go, Silas," I admitted.

"Your mother will want you with her," he answered quietly.

"I don't want to be there. I am not *that* princess. I don't know who I am anymore." I pressed my hands into my eyes.

"You are that princess. You are still his mate. You are who you always have been, *Allaíne Trubaíste*."

"In the stories," I said softly, "the ones Cadeyrn's mother told him, *baethaache* could only be expelled if the male died." I swallowed. "Mine feels different. As a child I could summon her. He never could. Is his different? Is there any hope, Silas?" I asked.

"There's always hope, *Trubaíste*," he answered. "His power is different. Perhaps he needs to learn to separate his magic from that of the *baethaache*."

"I can't use my magic," I admitted to him.

"I know." He kissed the back of my head. "We could sense its absence."

"Is it gone? Am I...broken?"

"No! Dammit!" He turned me towards him and grabbed my chin. His face, shadowed from the dim fire light, was awash in anger. "You are not broken. By the fucking gods and *moinchai* shite. You have been through so much in such a short time. Your body is trying to protect itself. You have cloaked yourself," he said, staring into my eyes. "That's all."

"You have been through a lot too, Silas," I said, staring right back. "How do you not fall apart?"

He considered for a moment, then cupped the side of my face. "I let my purpose be my shield. Instead of ducking behind it, I thrust it forward and move on."

"I heard you bedded your way across the battle camps. Is that what you mean?"

He rasped a laughed and pressed his forehead to mine.

"That's one way. I could help you with that aspect if you insist," he joked. I smiled. Smiled. He felt the lifting of my cheek and poked me in the stomach. "See, you're in there, *Trubaíste*." I whacked his arm.

"I do love you, Silas." I said it in an amused way, but meant it. He snorted. "I do. If it were the end of battle and I had to choose, I would save you over saving myself. Over saving the world, even." Well, that sounded really dumb. Thunder rumbled overhead.

"It's because of my glorious male body as you said. I know."

I laughed and laid my head against his chest, watching a streak of lightning cross the night sky.

"Yes, certainly it's because of that. That and the fact that every time I've fallen, it's you alone who has picked my sorry ass up."

"Weeel, you're so snotty when you fall apart. Someone has to do it. It's embarrassing."

I laughed again into his chest and breathed in his woodsy scent. A flash of lightning brightened the forest around us, and I felt a fluttering in my stomach. My magic.

"Silas," I whispered.

"I felt it," he said. I clutched his arm and there was another flutter. The sky flashed bright again, and my beastie purred. I smiled, looking at my friend, and touched my stomach. The brightest flash yet illuminated the sky, night turning to day. I counted to three and the thunder shook the ground. Electricity sparked through me, and I sat upright, Silas with me. White light surrounded us as I concentrated and reached at the sky just as lightning flashed again. The bolt met with my hand and the electricity danced at my fingertips before fading away. I grinned like an idiot and tackled Silas to the ground and kissed his cheek over and over like an enthusiastic puppy. He laughed, then stilled. Oh. I had forgotten all the things he had admitted to me. His feelings for me.

"I'm sorry," I said, ducking my head.

"No. I am. It's just...Sometimes it's harder than others." Shit. Needles of guilt crawled through my mind. Reminding me of how new this all still was for us all. Silas made space for me and my grief, regardless of his own.

"Thank you. For helping me. For always helping me." Like stars blinking in the sky, thoughts and ideas floated around my mind.

"I have an idea," I said, alighting on a thread. "You said there were temples to each element. I would like to forge my own."

WE CLEARED our camp, leaving only the fire. Around it, we dug five additional holes and built a small fire in each. Silas gathered six stones from the riverbed and dried them off. He sketched rudimentary representations of the element to which each fire would be dedicated. I copied each symbol onto a river rock, scratching it with my dagger, along with the symbols I had carved in the stones while left in my captivity. From a piece of parchment we carried, I wrote a blessing to the elements and a promise to care for each. On the sixth stone, I scratched the same eye and dagger, and a heart with beastly wings, "C & N" carved in the center. I had no real crystals to add to the makeshift temple, but I had my engagement ring with its large diamond and eight embedded gems: aquamarine sitting under the center diamond, emerald, amethyst, topaz, sapphire, moonstone pearl, peridot, and black tourmaline, which was on the underside of the band.

"These gems are the symbols of each province," Silas told me. I had known that, yet didn't know which stone represented which province. Hadn't had time to find out. "Moonstone pearl is Maesarra. Aquamarine is Saarlaiche. Amethyst for Veruni, emerald and topaz are Neanire and Prinaer. Sapphire is Laorinaghe. Peridot is Dunstanaich, and black tourmaline is Festaera, because we all need protection from those fuckers," he explained. I placed my ring just before the center fire, hoping no harm would come to it.

One by one, I walked from each fire, placing its stone and the written message in the flames and reciting a prayer to find him and bring him home. Safely home. When I reached the center fire, I placed both the heart carved stone and the stone he had saved from my antics. Impulsively, I flicked out my dagger—the one Cade had given me for Yule—and sliced my palm. I heard Silas' sharp intake of breath and his extra plea to the gods. As I dripped my blood over the fire and over my ring, I recited my last entreaty to the elements, spirits who care for this realm, old gods, and whomever chose to listen at the moment.

"There was a time," I said aloud, facing the flames, "that nothing kept me tethered to life. I had lost all that I thought I'd had, and I had no purpose. When I met my mate and his cousins, seeds of life were planted in my soul. I breathed freely for the first time since I was a child. They are my family. I fell in love with my mate in a slow tangle of not understanding how deeply I could care for someone. I never knew," I sobbed. "I never knew I could feel like that. To want and be wanted and need him and have the barest touch make me come alive. I wanted years with him. I wanted..." My voice cracked, and I felt Silas behind me, placing his hand on my lower back. "I wanted children." I took a deep breath. "I am pleading with who or whatever is listening to help me find my mate, and I swear I will work to make this world a better place. I swear it." I squeezed my fist, and blood dripped out. I smelled the copper of Silas slicing his hand as well, dripping it in the flames.

"I swore months ago that you two would be together again," Silas began. "I swore to make that happen and twice now, you have been robbed of time. By my blood, Neysa, I swear we will get him back, and you will have your years together. On my life. By my love."

I pressed his palm to mine. The fires grew and burned ferociously for a moment, then settled. Rain began again overhead, sending smoke in every direction, and I knew in my heart that it was searching for him. I leaned my head against Silas, our palms still together. As dawn tiptoed across the sky, the fires burnt to embers. I retrieved my ring, which was covered in ash and blood but not worse for wear. We went to each fire, and the ashes in each were concentrated on the same side. South. In the center fire, our rock with the heart glowed like a coal.

"You called me Neysa," I said.

"It is your name, is it not?"

"Yeah, but you never use it."

"Eh. Seemed like an occasion to be formal, what with the creepy blood-letting and all." I burst out laughing and, after replaying the scene in my head, laughed even harder.

"It was a bit dramatic, huh?"

"Let's just say, if I go missing, you had better think of something fucking memorable to top this."

"Don't go missing, my friend," I told him.

"Oh, I may, just to mess with you and see what you come up with. Maybe add costumes and such." I hit him on the leg.

We cleared our things and set off to Laorinaghe to find Corra.

LAORINAGHE WAS mostly peaceful, I had been led to believe, so we hadn't anticipated the threat. Lorelei had seemed incensed by Analisse at the summit. The summit where it all gone to hell. I wondered often at the severity of the wound my mate took in throwing himself in front of my mother. Had he healed in his usual way, even though he was trapped as the beast? Silas and I met Corra at the rendezvous point we had discussed prior to her departure. It was on the edge of the city, on a hilltop that had a vantage point of the city proper and the sea beyond. Even from up here, we could spot it. Past the white buildings topped with blue and green roofs, which looked as if the city was a part of the sea itself, there were torches and soldiers along the coast. Boats were moored in a blockade.

Initially, we had thought this was in our favour—Lorelei amassing her forces to stand with us.

"There are wards as soon as one enters the city," Corra chimed, not bothering with pleasantries once we had caught up with her. "I figured out where the border of the wards is, and Silas, you and I can slip through. Neysa, you will have to stay out here."

"She can't stay alone. If there are wards and all that," Silas said, pointing to the soldiers. "Then there will be scouts up here. They are not ignorant of this landscape."

"I can stay hidden," I protested.

"You stand out like a dancing monkey in a public toilet," Silas commented.

"Where do you come up with this shit?" I asked.

"They were two incongruous things that came to mind. You understand the meaning."

"I agree with the sentiment," Corra said. "Though perhaps not the phrase. Especially without your magic, Neysa. What happened to you lot, anyway? What's with the scars on your palms?"

I hadn't noticed the scars. It was odd neither of ours had healed completely.

"*Trubaíste*, as you have your full magic back," Silas began, turning a pointed glance in his sister's direction. "I want you to stay hidden, near a bright, sunny place, aye? Should it seem that your hiding place becomes compromised, move to the bright spot and release the white light. We will make a run of the city and see if we can find out anything more. Meet you back here in two hours' time. If we do not return, you leave. Two hours, *Trubaíste*. Understand?"

I nodded, knowing he didn't believe me for a second.

He swore and grabbed my chin. "You go to Maesarra. Find Ewan. You go where it is safe. Do not come after us. Once you are within those wards, you are trapped." His sea glass eyes shot daggers into my eyes.

"He is right," Corra said, adjusting her scabbard and daggers. "You are needed. Especially if we are all gone. Without you—"

"Without me, there's Ewan."

"I need you to see him safe," she whispered. "Don't ever tell him that or there will be hell to pay. Stay hidden. Stay safe. Two hours." They dissolved into mist, and only a smudge on the horizon told me they were moving into the city.

I ducked into a thicket of rosemary which butted up against both a large tree and a boulder. And there I sat, shifting from leg to leg, waiting and watching the time. There were scouts. I could hear them mostly in the distance. The sun began dipping low, and ever-increasing shadows fell over the wilderness above the city. I fished through my pack and quickly ate a piece of cheese and dried meat, really wanting the apple but knowing it would have made too much noise. I checked and rechecked my weapons. Two daggers sheathed on my gauntlets, short sword and scythe on either thigh, throwing knives on my bootstraps, long sword down my spine, and bow over a shoulder. Just before the two hours were up and I began to get twitchy, scouts started yelling to one another. I couldn't tell what they were saying, but there seemed to be a scramble to reach the city. The minutes clicked by, and at two hours the twins were nowhere to be seen. I unfolded from my rosemary hideout only to find a uniformed female stood directly in front of me. I covered up a gasp and a stumble.

She seemed just as surprised to see me. We faced one another.

"Who are you?" she demanded.

"Neysa."

Her eyes went wide.

"The princess?" She shifted on her feet, and my hands shot to my weapons.

"What is the commotion down there? Why are there wards on the city?" I demanded of her.

"You shouldn't be here," she said quietly. "We are ordered to kill you. All of you."

"Ordered by whom? My mother is Queen. There is no law beyond that at the moment."

"Lady Lorelei. I will not kill you now, but I beg of you to leave." Crashing sounded behind us, and two guards appeared.

I tensed, and the female guard gave me a sharp, warning glance before turning back to them. "I have found a straggler from that caravan from yesterday," she announced to them.

"Kill her," one said. "I can't be assed to bring another one in for questioning. Plus, I want those weapons."

"Come and get them then," I purred, spinning and flicking two of my throwing knives at them. Each found their mark in the hip crease of either guard. This was beginning to be my signature move. They yelled and yanked the knives out, then sloppily launched themselves at me, swords swinging. My own sword came free of its scabbard, and I ducked and slashed, steel hitting steel.

"Yva!" One yelled to the guard. "Kill her!"

"Yva," I said, knocking my sword into the exposed armpit of the mouthy guard. He screamed and swore at me. "Either help me or attack me." She seemed to consider, honey-coloured eyes mapping the scene. She even so far as took a step toward me with her blade.

I was nicked on the inside of my arm. Blood ran freely into my gauntlet. Her face seemed too open for deceit as she watched my injuries with something like fear on her face. She tipped her chin slightly, a barely noticeable movement, and I knew she would side with her queen. Yva joined the fight and pushed against her comrades.

"Traitorous filth!" the quiet one finally chimed in.

"I will not follow orders that go against my Queen," she answered, and I saw her spin to gain momentum. Yva became a whirling dervish of movement before slamming into the quiet guard, knocking him into the next. Her movement reminded me of dust devils dancing on the side of the freeway in California. She drew back to spin again, and I allowed my electricity to surge through me into my sword and watched as the metal conducted the power through the guard's sword into his body. Because his compatriot had fallen against his shoulder, it took him too. They turned to ash. I stepped back, sword high.

"Swear your allegiance," I demanded, sounding nothing like the half-broken woman I was when I first came to Barlowe Combe. She sank to a knee and held her sword to me.

"I swear allegiance to Queen Saskeia and, by default, Her Highness, Princess Neysa." I gave her a quick nod and sheathed my blade.

"Why the wards?" I asked again. A roar so loud it made the trees tremble sounded from the city below. A roar that I had heard only once, right before powerful wings beat across the sea. He was here. I knew then why the wards. To keep him in. He could not change, could not access his non-corporeal magic. Prickles of the magic connecting me with Cadeyrn quickened my heartrate. Was it possible he was so near? Could I rely on my faulty heart as compass? "Do you know where he is?" I asked, voice shaky.

"He?" she asked.

"The creature," I said, and swallowed. "My mate."

"There are caves. By the beach. You won't be able to leave if you go in there," she warned.

"Then I will stay with him," I said, and took off at a sprint.

CHAPTER 2

Silas

O f course he would have landed himself here. Cadeyrn said I was always getting into trouble, yet when he got himself in it, he was neck-deep in poisonous shite. I scented him as soon as we crossed the wards. Corraidhín and I got as far as the city center when we saw a protective circle. Salt and crystal dotted the streets. For just a moment, our magic vanished, leaving us heaving on the cobbled streets, and the light from the setting sun glared off the too-white buildings, blinding us. That was all it took to catch us. They knew they couldn't stifle our magic for more than a split second. A contingent of hundreds of guards surrounded the square.

"Any brilliant ideas, sister?" I asked, unsheathing my twin swords.

"None you're going to like."

It was too close quarters to lose our forms now. We would be more vulnerable during the dissolution. So, we held our weapons high.

"We are emissaries from Her Majesty the Queen," I said, my voice carrying. "We bear no threat to you."

"You trespass on the Sacred City. We have orders to dispose of you. Lady Lorelei does not recognize Saskeia as Queen," claimed a voice from the center of the lineup.

"Surely her lack of recognition is not shared by all of you?" I smirked, trying to catch a few shifty eyes. The whine of steel being drawn pierced my ears. "We are not alone, and your Sacred City will be a battle ground if you keep your loyalties to this insurgence. If you value your city and are for the good of all of Aoifsing, stand with us."

For a second there, I really thought most of the little fuckers would stand behind us. Gods know what they had been promised. A good half moved to face their peers in defiance.

"Yeah, well, that'll do," I said, and whirled, Corraidhín and I fighting back-to-back. I knew damn well we wouldn't make the two hours just as I knew Neysa wouldn't leave.

I had no idea how long we moved through the guards, but I was tiring and I knew my sister's magic was sputtering. I transferred some of my energy to her, the electricity in me vaulting from my veins to hers. In doing so, each pixel of the fae female dripped into salt water, building higher and more violent. She became the sea. A rogue wave, washing forty or so insurgents from the battle. I dissolved myself a bit and was able to move quickly through the confused lines of the onslaught, slicing and stabbing as quickly as picking weeds. Which I had never done, but in my blood-addled mind, it seemed about accurate. Bells began tolling, more soldiers rushing into the square. My sister's corporeal absence left another wall of sea water which took down hundreds more.

Then I heard him. That beastly little hellion roared so loud the whole godsdamned city shook. Blue roof tiles crashed down, and people ran screaming from their homes. I had no plan at this point. My magic was fizzling, Corraidhín's was as well, and my sword arm was nearly useless. The slice on my palm where I had sworn to Neysa to bring my cousin to her had ripped open, and the hilt of my sword bit into the opening. Blood ran down my arm.

Neysa, get the hell out of here, I thought to myself, wishing I had that connection she had with my cousin. For about a million different reasons.

"Cadeyrn!" I yelled, amplifying my voice so it carried across the city. There was a pause, then the battle commenced. Thundering footsteps sounded. The boots of a thousand soldiers. For fuck's sake. How big of a regiment did Lorelei have? Up through the streets, knocking buildings and soldiers down, I realized it wasn't a thousand soldiers, but one pissed off beast, dragging chains, headed right for us.

Fuck the gods, he was hideous. I was a bit envious. Especially as, even though he was bound and his wings looked as though many arrows had pierced them, he pushed through the crowd, culling soldiers until the remaining ones who stood against us fled. The beast looked at us, and I wasn't sure either Corraidhín or I was breathing,

"You do have a flair for the dramatic, cousin," I said before I could think of something better to say. My sister swore and shook her head. The beast huffed. Its eyes glowed and nostrils flared. It stepped closer to me and thrust his fucking great head into my bleeding hand and licked at it. I puked. Right there. Maybe because of the battle high or the fact that my cousin was now a bloody great monster, or maybe just the fact that the monster had licked my godsdamned hand. Once the purge settled, I saw that the cut had healed. His eyes were wild, casting about for... oh. Looking for *Trubaíste*. Her blood had mingled with mine.

"Do you know us, cousin?" my sister asked. His giant head cocked to the side. He huffed and sunk down. I wanted to take those fucking chains off him. I stepped forward and he growled. I held up my hands.

"Silas," Corra warned. I knew if the situation were reversed, Cadeyrn would risk everything to free me of chains.

"Cousin, I want to remove the chains. Will you let me? So you can get to Neysa." He became agitated and started whipping the chains around as though to break them. I ducked, covering my head.

"Stop this," my sister scolded him as she always did to us. "That's enough, Cadeyrn. Settle yourself and we can fix this."

He lay down, defeated. I snorted, and those huge eyes, the same colour as my own, narrowed at me. I walked to him and lifted the chain. I knew he was a split second away from gnashing those fangs at me, but I ignored him, looking to the cuffs and the chains themselves to see where the weak spot would be. I brought my sword down on the chain and released the weight. He didn't move. The cuffs needed to come off, and we were on borrowed time out in the open city. Dredging up the last scraps of my power, I shoved most of what I had left of my power into the metal, filling them with enough exposure and mist to rust them completely.

"You can stop looking at me like that, you great shite." I spoke while I worked, just as he always did for me when he healed me. "I swore an oath to your mate." He thrashed a bit, knocking me down. "Calm down. Stop thinking with your cock. She nearly lost herself over you, you know. Lost her magic for a long while. I tried to convince her I would be much more suitable..."

"Holy fucking gods, brother," my sister swore. The beast narrowed those eyes again and snorted a great nasty sound that may have been a laugh.

"But, *Trubaíste* that she is, she decided that rather than spend her days with me in the forest," I continued, even though both he and Corraidhín growled, "she would build her own gods-damned temples in the middle of the forest. Temples, brother. She had me digging fire pits in the middle of the night, and called upon the Aulde Gods, the elements, the ghosts of the past, and everything in between to help her find you. You, you great hulk-ing sack of shite." I could hear my sister sniffle a little. She never cried. I rusted one cuff so thoroughly that it broke apart as soon as my dagger tapped it. On to the next. "Do you know what she said—apart from that she loved me too?" I winked at him, and he snapped his teeth at me. Eh, too far, then. "She said that in her whole life—" I pointed at him. "Are you paying attention? In her whole life, she never thought she could feel the way she feels with you, you stupid arse. She said she wanted so many years with you and…maybe I shouldn't be the one telling you…"

"Then, perhaps don't, brother," Corraidhín said, low and viscous. I ignored her.

"She said that she wants children with you. And she swore on her blood that she would do what is in her power to protect the realm if she could have you back." He swung his back as the cuff fell away and his chains were released. His great beastly head, nearly the size of my whole body, pinned me down on the cobbled streets. I probably shouldn't have said that about her loving me. Even though it was true.

"The thing is, cousin," I said, poking my finger into his leathery scaled chest. "She wants Cadeyrn back. So get your godsdamned shit back together and separate the beast from the male!" I screamed in his face, not caring by then if he ripped me apart. I swore an oath. He snarled, dripping bloody spit onto me. I thought I might puke again. It was that spit. By the gods, it was rank.

It was then that a rain of arrows fired down on us. I took one in the shoulder as I rolled, shield up. Corraidhín waved her arm and drowned the archers in the mist from the gathering night. I knew she was as spent as I was. We needed to get out of there. My cousin lay there, thirty or so arrows sticking out of him at various spots. Most through his wings, one in his chest, though it still rose and fell. There was one through the side of his face. Visions of when our parents were killed shot through my mind like moving pictures, giving me a last burst of strength.

"Fucking hell," I yelled. I tried to push him over. Tried to move him, but he was solid. Suddenly, he stood up and took off toward the water. We followed behind. He rounded on the beach where hundreds of soldiers lay drowned, victims of my sister's waves, then banked and headed for the cliffs. Eventually, we followed him into a cave. Torches lined the walls, and the brackets remained where his chains had been hung on the stone walls. This is where he'd been confined.

"Bloody hell," Corraidhín swore. "Silas, he needs healing."

He collapsed onto the sandy ground and passed out.

"He needs me," *Trubaíste* said from the cave mouth. Of course she bloody found us.

CHAPTER 3

Neysa

T here were so many arrows in him that I didn't know where to start. The twins were breaking them off and pulling them out as I applied pressure to the wounds. The one in his cheek made my heart hurt. Each shimmering scale reflected the last dying light of day. Our *baethaache* reminded me of the mythical beasts depicted in idyllic medieval tapestries. Wyvern-like with our leathery wings, yet almost softer in the face like a dog. Cadeyrn's spiked terror in others, with the deep inkwell of its colouring and double rows of teeth which resembled glass shards. The injuries had him smeared in blood, panting and unconscious, and I sunk down and placed my hand on his face, my beastie growling in response, beating her wings. I let them flare out from me, shielding him. The twins barked at me as the wings pushed them back. I covered him with my wings and laid down on the sand along his side. Had it been me, battleworn and bloody, his presence would have done more than any bandage could. After weeks of sleeping on the ground, the fact that it was sand did nothing to staunch the exhaustion pulling at me. I drifted asleep, my magic spooling from me in threads and ribbons, winding into my mate as he laid unconscious beside me, no longer a fae male, but a beast.

No dreams marred my sleep. I started coming to before opening my eyes and felt that Corra and Silas were not in the cave. Deep, even breathing sounded beside me. My wings had faded back into me, and I breathed in. My eyes sprung open.

Peridot eyes looked back at me. Not the eyes of a beast. The watercoloured eyes of themale who was my mate. Drawn cheeks and thumbprints of shadow smudged under those eyes in stark contrast to his too pale skin and raven hair. A painful lump caught in my throat.

"Cadeyrn?" I asked so quietly. I reached a hand up slowly to touch him.

Please tell me you haven't forgotten me, I said to his mind, brushing the tip of his ear with my fingers, and his eyes closed. A sound came out of him that was more of a croak. Red stained his cheeks. I had never seen him blush. The colour lit his eyes aflame.

I haven't used my voice in so long.

There are vocal warmups you could do. Like A-E-I-O-U. Red leather, yellow leather. It helps your singing voice...

His mouth was on mine.

That's not a vocal warmup per se.

To hell with the vocal warmup, he said, keeping his lips crushed against mine.

Silas rounded the corner then.

"Is everything...Oh. Well, that's a change," he said. "I'm not sure you're in any shape for any of that, cousin," he teased. A snarl ripped from Cadeyrn.

"I'm in fine shape...cousin," he managed to choke out, though his voice was grainy and rough. Silas snickered, and Corra walked in.

"Sorry to interrupt, but we are in an enemy city and there is a female dressed in the livery of Lorelei's guards saying she knows Neysa and swore allegiance to her. Am I killing her or is she telling the truth?"

"Yva. Yes, she fought her kinfolk with me."

Corra made an agreeable sound and left.

"We have sent hawks warning our known allies and have called for aid," Silas informed us as he tossed clothes at Cadeyrn.

"Lorelei was here," my mate said. "She personally set up the wards. I couldn't get out and I was injured enough for them to shackle me. She sat by me for days. Time was difficult. I was me but not. How long has it been?"

"Nearly a month," I said softly, my voice hingin on a sob. He swore, low and vicious. I watched as he pulled on the trousers and tunic, strapping weapons to himself. "What now?"

"Do you remember the story I told you? The one my mother used to tell about the *baethaache* who flew all over playing spy?"

"What have you been up to?" I asked. His answering smile was devilish.

He had visited the domain of each representative, individual of influence—whether financial or political—and military personnel. Information gleaned in his shadowed *baethaache* persona from those visits would clue us in as to where we could place our trust in the coming conflict. He had been planning to take to the seas and monitor Dockman's marine affairs when magically launched spears and arrows brought his beast down just off the coast of Laorinaghe. My hand stayed over his heart, fingers feeling every beat, almost uncaring of the success he had.

AN OFFICIAL audience was requested with Lorelei and her ministry. Yva gathered known resistance to the Elders. Most residents did not understand what their representative was doing in sealing off the city. Having her guards under instruction to kill the royal family was a surprising and unprecedented course of action. We walked through the streets offering warmth to people and speaking of an Aoifsing with representation from the people. By noon, a messenger found us with an invitation to join Lady Lorelei for dinner. Our hawks had come back as well, bringing news of forces at the ready in other cities and a regiment on the way to us. They wouldn't arrive until tomorrow or the following day, so we were on our own until then.

There was an inn near the sea where we settled for the afternoon, Yva agreeing to bring us clothing to wear to the dinner meeting.

"What did I look like?" Cadeyrn asked after bathing. He stood in front of a clouded mirror, a worn towel wrapped about his hips. "I know I had wings. And I saw talons."

I stopped finger combing my wet hair and walked to him, tucking my own towel in under my arms.

"You were magnificent." I looked into his eyes. "Shall I show you?" He took my hand and I pressed it to his face, showing him my vision of him.

"What if I hadn't been able to change back?" A weighted question. One which I didn't know how to answer. So, of course, my lacking social skills cracked a joke. A bad joke.

"I would have had a pet all the other kids would be envious of." He frowned, and I held onto his hand even as he turned away. "There is no magic stronger than this," I said, my electricity crackling between us, meeting his heat. "What's between us can shatter this realm if we let it. And if I had to let my beastie take over, then so be it." He stilled and focused his eyes on me.

"No. You do not change for me. You do not change for any-one. Silas said..." He coughed. "He told me about the oath you swore." My eyes were clear and met his as he held up my palm, grasp gentle, voice knowing. "He told me some of what you said...during the oath, I suppose. It's foggy as I was not exactly me. I smelled you on him—your blood, that is, and he was able to bring me back." He stopped and fidgeted with the thigh hol-ster that was sitting on the wooden table beside us.

"What did he tell you?" I asked softly.

"He said you wanted children. With me." He didn't quite meet my eyes.

"I want everything with you. I understand if you don't—or can't." Slowly, he turned back to me, a crooked smile softening his face.

"Don't be stupid, Neysa," he said with a twinkle in his eye. "Shall we get a head start on that now?" he asked, pointing to the bed. I tugged him closer using his towel, but then there came a knock at the door. We laughed.

"Typical."

YVA BROUGHT us two options each to wear. She included old livery underpinnings to stash in our packs in case we had to take off, plus formal wear and something casual.

"I didn't know what royals might want to wear," she admitted.

"Oh, Yva, we aren't picky." I told her. Cadeyrn changed into the formal wear, which was a cobalt blue jacket that buttoned up the front with black trousers that tucked into his boots. I saw Yva out and turned to begin dressing myself but stopped dead looking at Cadeyrn. I had never seen him wear colour. Ever. Not that I was complaining. I could live my life and enjoy him in his black, grey, and white, but the cobalt on him was striking. He finished buckling on his various weapons and caught me staring, slack-mouthed.

"What?" he asked, confused. I shook my head and ducked behind a screen to slip my dress overhead.

"I have never seen you wear colour," I called while doing up little gold buttons here and there all over the top of the gold dress.

"I have worn colour...just...not often."

"Well, it suits you. Although, really, what doesn't? It must be hard being so gorgeous," I teased him. He snorted and muttered something I couldn't hear.

The dress itself was ankle length with slits up the side to mid-thigh. The bodice came up in two separate pieces to cover my assets, while buttoning in four spots between my ribs, then more little buttons under the arms, linking the bust to the back of the dress. I knew Yva was my sort of girl when she said she threw in some bronze gauntlets she "found along the way." I slipped them on and moved from behind the screen to tend to my hair in front of the tiny mirror. It was still mostly damp, but the temperate air was letting the waves form without frizz. I twisted small sections back away from my face, and, as I lacked pins to secure it, I tied the length of my hair in a low knot. It wouldn't last the evening, but that didn't worry me. I turned to grab my own sword belt and daggers, but Cadeyrn stood right behind me.

"This dress is fit for a queen," he said, running a finger down the material, making me shiver. I cleared my throat.

"If we weren't running late, I would show you how the skirt splits." I lifted my leg and propped it on the table to strap on a couple more daggers. The material fell away. He growled. "Oh, look. That's how."

"I think I'm closer to my beast than I knew. We really should have taken a bit more time alone before all hell breaks loose."

I laughed and pushed onto my tiptoes to kiss him quickly before pulling him out the door. The twins were waiting outside the door, dressed similarly to us. It was Silas who spoke up.

"You two will never be able to fight in those dresses."

"I can fight in anything," I answered. "My boobs might come out; but I can still fight."

Silas and Corra roared and Cadeyrn rolled his eyes, which made me laugh. He then smirked at me.

"That's the spirit."

CHAPTER 4

C ypress trees lined the road leading to the palace in the Sacred City of Laorinaghe. As we neared, palace guards lined the drive and steps into the building. The gate rolled up, and we were admitted, walking four abreast through an open-air atrium with potted citrus and olive trees sprinkled around merrily bubbling fountains. A guard asked us to follow him up a wide, winding staircase to the next level, quite a ways up. We followed further into the palace, along the terracotta floor, through arched doorways lined with flowering climbing vines, and into a dimly lit dining room.

"Welcome to my home," a voice called from the archway. Lorelei stood, a half-smile on her face. She tsked. "It is generally regarded as poor form to upstage the host with your attire. Or do they not teach that in the human realm?" she asked, clearly speaking to me. Her eye zeroed in on my engagement ring and narrowed, though she had seen it at the summit last month.

"I was limited in my selection at such short notice and wanted to be sure to honor, not upstage, my host, my lady."

She laughed at my response. "You're learning to play the game quite well, it seems. Such a change from the last time I saw you." She walked around us in a predatory circle, running a finger along Silas and Cadeyrn's shoulders.

"Corraidhín," Lorelei said. "You are looking well. You have been sneaking around my city for the past few days, my spies tell me. Find anything of interest?"

"I am happy to begin that part of the discussion, my lady," Cadeyrn spoke with dangerous quiet. "Though we were under the impression that this was a dinner."

"Ah, the *cuídvsite*," she said to him, walking over. She placed a finger on his jacket, and it took everything in me not to rip it off her for calling him a monster. "I miss my pet." She pouted and turned away, walking to Silas. Cadeyrn stiffened beside me.

"You may sit by me. Your reputation precedes you." With that she walked to the table. I was ready to rip out every honey-coloured hair on her head and peel the golden-brown skin from her face. Cadeyrn's hand shot to mine and squeezed before speaking mind to mind through our bond.

Control it, Neysa. She's baiting us all.

I'm going to kill her for the pet comment alone.

That's only because you wanted me for a pet first. It's pet-ty jealousy.

Oh. My. God. That was the worst joke in the history of jokes.

It certainly was. I may throw myself from the parapet over there because of it.

I stifled a laugh and sat down next to Silas, Cadeyrn coming to sit across from me. A salad with hard cheese and dates topped with marinated olives was brought out and placed before us. We picked at the course for a few minutes, and I was almost embarrassed by the amount of bread I was eating.

"Lorelei," Corra spoke. "I do love that gown. The colour suits you very well." The mint green chiffon did look lovely on her skin. I would admit it even though she had had hundreds of guards attack us and kept my mate as a pet. Right now, I just pictured a slowly spreading stain of blood across the material. "I like it almost as much as that yellow you wore on summer solstice all those years ago. That yellow was..." Corra let her voice get a bit smoky.

"Hmm. Yes. Thank you, Corraidhín." Lorelei turned to us.

Salad plates were cleared, and a terrine of ground meat and potato was brought out. We ate again in silence.

What do you think she's doing? Stalling for time? I asked Cadeyrn in my mind.

I am not sure. I think Corraidhín is sussing it out.

Silas has been unusually quiet as well.

I agree. Let's sit tight and see what happens. His eyes met mine across the table.

Good, because this is the first meal I've had in ages that didn't need to be skinned first and I really want dessert.

You know what I want? My mate's voice darkened, and I looked up, but he continued pushing the meat and potato onto the back of his fork.

Couldn't imagine. Ugh, I couldn't even pretend to say that without a shiver.

I'm sure you could. Watercolour eyes met mine as I saw his throat bob with his swallow.

Peanut butter cookies?

Yes. We both smiled, a shy smile meeting me across the platters of food. I'd wished he had sat beside me.

"So, Lorelei," Silas crooned, leaning toward her. She pushed her ringlets back over a shoulder and cocked an eyebrow at him. "Do you not have an entourage? We dine alone with you."

"I thought it best to have you all to myself," she purred, placing her hand on the table between them.

"I'm not complaining," he drawled. "I was just wondering if we could have a private tour of...the palace." Something changed in her face, and I wondered if he pushed his leg into hers. She flushed.

"We shall see," she said, her voice rough.

I felt Corra's magic slip out in drops and beadlets. I sensed I was missing dessert. Cadeyrn shifted, and an ember of his power slipped around me like a second skin.

Did you just shield me? I asked him.

Something is up. Are you ready to engage her in conversation?

"Lorelei," I said. "While I am glad you enjoy my friend's company, tell me. What are you trying to do here? There was no ultimate rule over Aoifsing. The provinces were still going to run mostly independent of one another. Why put a death order on my family?"

"Better question," Corra chirped in. "Where is Lorelei?"

Cadeyrn swore, and I could feel his power snaking toward her, unraveling whatever spell was there.

She laughed nervously and rang a bell. Three chairs shot back, and I followed suit. Guards entered the room, effectively cornering us.

"Do not come closer," Cadeyrn said to them in a voice that promised death. "She is not your Lady Lorelei, and she threatens the life of your queen and princess."

"Kill them all," Lorelei, who was not Lorelei, ordered. They stepped closer, faltering a bit.

"For centuries, this province has lived in peace. Why now would your representative choose to sever ties with the rest of Aoifsing?" my mate asked them. One bloodthirsty guard charged from the back, and it set them all off like a pack. The four of us slammed our power into them. A relative hurricane of force took out the whole lot of them. More boots pounded down the hall. Silas threw the table against the door, blocking it for the moment.

"Who are you?" Corra demanded.

"She is Julissa, Analisse's sister," Silas offered. "I knew her scent was different from Analisse. I knew hers rather intimately." His words sent a shot of raw anger through me.

"Where is Lorelei? Have you killed her?" I asked.

"Bah. No, no. She's too useful. I bound her tongue and powers. She was so frightened of you, *cuídvsite*," Julissa said, pointing at Cadeyrn. "When she slammed around in her cell too much and drew attention to herself, I would dump her in your cave to silence her." Holy shit. "Mostly, though, I need to keep her alive in order to keep the spell going."

The guards were beating against the door.

"You have to know that this won't end well for you," I said.

"For me? Oh, girl, you are sorely outnumbered. Though I was hoping to have a bit of fun with that one." She pouted at Silas. The door broke; the table splintered. She lashed out at Corra, who was nearest, and Corra dissolved before her and spun around the female in a waterspout, trapping her within.

"Guards of the Sacred City!" Cadeyrn called to them to halt. "We have not come to harm anyone here. This female has been impersonating your Lady Lorelei. She is not who she claims to be and is the sister of the witch, Analisse." There was a murmur across the males in front of us. "Stand with us and help to find and free Lorelei. Stand against us and you will be killed. There will not be another warning." Corra's waterspout sputtered out as Julissa's magic pounded against it. The guards took one look at Julissa and saw only Lorelei. They advanced. Cadeyrn moved first and swung his twin swords forward and back, cutting through the soldiers like they were nothing. The movement and speed with which he fought put mine to shame. Nevertheless, I followed him, stabbing and slashing as I went, my skirts swaying. The twins fought behind me, blades, water, and a compound of power that throbbed against me. I reached Cadeyrn, and we pressed our backs against each other, still fighting.

"Princess!" Julissa called. "I thank you for finding a traitor amongst my ranks." I spun and saw that she had a knife at Yva's throat. Silas was closest, and I called to him. He dropped into a slide and kicked the legs out from under both Yva and Julissa. Yva jumped to her knees only to take a sword to her side, making her fall again. I lunged for Yva and tried to staunch her bleeding as I pulled her out of the fray.

Silas had Julissa by the hair and pulled her hands behind her back. He walked backward to the throne room behind us and reversed up the steps to the dais. Corra and Cadeyrn were still taking down soldiers, though I noticed neither were making killing blows.

Get to the dais, Cadeyrn told me. *Stand beside Silas.*

You had better be right behind me. That better not have been a cryptic, last words, 'stand beside Silas' comment.

No, I just meant to literally get your ass up there.

So we did. By the time we had all made it up, Cadeyrn brought up a wall of impenetrable heat between us and the regiment beyond.

"Soldiers of the Sacred City," I called, fumbling and shaking with adrenaline. "This female is not your Lady. She is wearing a cloaking spell to seem like Lorelei. She claims to be keeping your representative captive to keep her spell going. She held my mate captive here as well, forcing him to remain as a *baethaache*. I lay no claim to your lands. Find Lorelei, and we will right this."

Cadeyrn finally unraveled the spell. As it shed, Julissa remained, the dress hanging on her thin frame. Where Lorelei was average height and full figured, Julissa was tall and statuesque. The soldiers all stopped and gasped.

"Find your Lady!" I commanded.

Most of them dispersed to track down Lorelei. Some stormed the dais, eager to get ahold of Julissa.

"It is up to your Lady to decide her fate," I said to them. "If you would assist in keeping her bound?"

"Your Highness," they intoned and bowed. That will never not be weird. I can count on one hand the times my name was said correctly at Starbucks, and here, everyone drops to their knees for me.

We sat there for over an hour waiting. Cadeyrn went to help find Lorelei while the rest of us stayed to contain Julissa. Yva's bleeding stopped as Silas kept a hard pocket of pressure against her wound.

"For the future, soldier," he said to the female, "I'm not one for too much colour in my wardrobe." He gave her a silly smile, gesturing to his dark green jacket and brown pants.

"Duly noted. Next time, you can use your own coin to purchase your colourless wardrobe." Oh, I did like Yva.

"Duly noted," he answered.

I saw Cadeyrn walking up through the hall, Lorelei in his arms. My heart sank. *Please be alive.* At the threshold, I saw movement. He set her down, and she walked, slowly and painfully, toward the dais. Her honey gold ringlets hung limp against her brown skin which was sallow from malnutrition. The dress she wore hung in tatters from her once voluptuous body. Anger flared in me. We stood in waiting before a large set of open windows facing the sea.

"This is the witch," Lorelei stated, voice vacillating between a rasp of what I assumed was her natural voice, and the higher pitch of Juliss's. "Bring her forth. If you please," she added with a slight bow to me. Corra and Silas kept Julissa bound and stepped forward. "You have led my folk to death. You have caused irreparable damage to families and the sacred heart of their city. What have you to say, witch?" Her voice belied a strength I knew was waning.

"My sister brought me with her here before the summit when she was to meet with you. Your trust in her allowed her to take you captive and cloak me to be you. Her imprisonment and the stripping of her lands was unexpected. I am now without a home myself. I was victim here just as you were."

Lorelei tipped her head to the side and studied Julissa. She whipped a hand across the female's cheek and drew blood. Then whipped another across her chest.

"You caused chaos and destruction. You will not live." She swiped once more, and a deep gash lay across Julissa'a throat. Lorelei pulled the imposter off of her feet and threw her through the open window, down to the rocky beach below. The moment was so brutal and drenched in wrath that I looked away. My mate caught the Lady of Laorinaghe as she swayed and nearly fell.

"I apologize for any destruction we have caused when the soldiers attacked us." I put a hand over my heart and faced her. She waved me off.

"It is done, Your Highness," she said softly. "My weakness for a certain woman led to this." She turned to Corra. "Was it you who figured it out?"

"She did not remember the summer solstice," Corra said with a wink. Lorelei chuckled.

"Ah. One could never forget that summer solstice."

"No, lady. I shall always have fond memories of your yellow dress."

The lady blushed, lighting up her sickly pallor.

"I thank you all and bid you to please stay here as long as you need."

"My lady," I called to her. "Yva is one of your guards who was stationed beyond the wards yesterday. She saved my life and helped us today. She is quite loyal."

"Indeed? Your Highness's recommendation bears much weight. I shall see to her promotion myself."

Corra offered to escort the lady to her chambers along with a small contingent of guards. Cadeyrn and Silas walked Yva to the infirmary where another healer was brought to Yva as her injuries were not life-threatening at the moment. The throne room cleared out.

I was tired of these palace battles. Tired of throne room disasters. Just tired. The week I spent in Aemes doing nothing consequential with Cadeyrn before the summit seemed like a distant dream. I slumped onto the ledge of a fountain, facing out toward the sea. Gold satin spilled around me onto the terracotta floor. It was blood-splattered and torn. I looked down and adjusted the bust. I did not come popping out, which was surprising, but the top was soaked in sweat and blood, making me quite indecent. I didn't care. Slices and bruises marred where my arms were exposed, and my elbow ached. An old tendonitis issue had cropped back up. I knew it was because I had been gripping my sword too tight, and in the back of my mind I wondered why my fae body wasn't healing it. I needed to remember to have Cadeyrn tend to it. When he wasn't immersed in healing himself and everyone else.

"Your Highness." A soldier appeared and bowed at the waist. "Are you all right? Might I get you something?" He spoke softly, like I was a wounded animal. I tried to summon a smile, but I'm quite certain it was more of a grimace.

"Thank you, but I just needed to sit. Could...would you get me some water, please?" He started to turn but stopped and offered his own canteen.

"If it doesn't offend, I would offer you mine whilst I fetch a pitcher for Your Highness."

I took the offered canteen with thanks.

"What is your name, sir?" I asked.

"Xaograos, lady," he said with a deep bow.

"Thank you, Xaograos. You are very kind."

"It is my honour to serve." He left his canteen with me and walked through the hall where bodies were still being carried away. So many had to die tonight. For what? They were all loyal to Lorelei and yet they died for that when we were all on the same team. I couldn't let that train of thought continue. As I stared out at the sea, a woman appeared before the alabaster railing. At first, I thought her a servant, as she was dressed in homespun, a kerchief on her head. I wiped at my eyes with the back of my hand, no doubt smearing blood across my face. The woman's form wavered, and I realized she was a spirit. I swallowed, a bit unnerved, and she smiled at me kindly.

"There will be trying times ahead," she said to me. I didn't know if anyone else could see or hear her. "You will face obstacles both friend and foe, but your path does not shift." A monologue so similar to the old woman in Peru last year. "Trust yourself. Do not lose heart, for that is where your true strength lies. Time shall alter you. Time shall wear on you." She began to fade.

"Wait!" I called. "What obstacles?"

"Many trials. If you keep your faith, you will persevere." She faded completely.

"Bloody hell," I muttered, hanging my head. I felt Corra slump next to me.

"My tits came out. Yours?" She asked. I smiled.

"Nope. Yours are bigger, though."

"Huh. Oh, well. You okay?"

"Can I let you know?"

"The others aren't back yet?" She pushed at a large puncture in her thigh. It was healing already, but an inch or so off would have hit an artery. I shook my head. "What did the ghost say?" Trust Corra not to beat about the bush.

"The usual. Trust yourself, blah, blah. You're going to encounter many horrible things, but it's okay because you are warm and fuzzy, etcetera."

"Och, that old chestnut."

"So, summer solstice."

"Lorelei would never have forgotten that."

"How long ago, Corra?"

"Twenty, maybe twenty-five years ago? Not sure."

"You two would have been quite a pair. The eyes on you two alone..." I said, nudging her with an elbow. She chuckled.

"Alas, we were not meant to be."

"What happened?"

"The truth is that I did not love her as she loved me. I loved her, and we were quite compatible in the bedroom, but I was missing something vital. The same feeling that stopped every relationship I have had in three hundred years." She was being so open. Corra rarely spoke of herself. She kept it all tightly sealed despite her intrinsic warmth. I didn't want to press her for details but wondered if she knew how deeply Ewan cared for her. It was not my place to say. He felt she would never settle down. "I am in love with Ewan," she said finally. "I think he is what has been missing, but I don't know if..."

"He was hurting. When we were gone. It took him a while to tell me. But we shared a common grief. He told me that he told you to move on. For your sake."

She stared at me.

"He didn't want you to feel like you owed him anything. But he said he loved you, Corra."

"Well." She sat up straighter. "I shall speak to him, then." She patted my knee. Xaograos brought a pitcher and cups and set them next to us. Corra grabbed the pitcher and chugged from it, then passed it to me. I followed suit, and a distinctly male chuckle sounded.

"You two are quite a sight." Cadeyrn took the pitcher from me and drank as well, then passed it to Silas. "Come, you lot," my mate said, offering his arm to help me up. "You're injured?" he asked, nostrils flaring.

"It's nothing." I turned my arm over and held it out to him. He unclipped the gauntlet, and a gash ran along where the top of the gauntlet met my skin. There was a decent amount of blood, which was likely why I felt as faint as I did. Rumbles of anger flittered through his touch as he held me a little closer. Quickly looking down at me, I caught a flash of that beast, vying for permission to escape. His exhaustion and anger held a tenous chain to that beast. I hooked a foot around his ankle. A slight token of our here and now. An anchor in the tempest.

"I've found us quarters for the night." He covered my arm with his and led us away, his healing magic working its way to pull the skin back together. I turned back to the guard, who waited patiently, and handed him his canteen.

"My gratitude, Xaograos. I hope you can rest this evening."

"Your servant, Your Highness," Xaograos said. Cadeyrn inclined his head to him in thanks.

"You want to tell me about the ghost?" he asked me as we walked through the tiled hall. I knew he would have seen or sensed her through our connection. I always had trouble controlling what I projected when I was exhausted.

"Maybe later. It was all fortune cookie mumbo jumbo."

"I believe that reference is somewhat lost on me, but I assume it was typical oracle perils and heartache ahead but be true to thine self...?"

"Precisely," I told him. I put my head against his shoulder as we walked. "We never do get to just stay in bed as long as we want, do we?"

"It will happen. I promise you."

CHAPTER 5

Another dress ruined. Another night I would spend without clothing. The satchel Yva packed us with the underpinnings was still in that inn by the sea. After bathing and scrubbing the blood from my skin, I thumped my head back onto the pillow and half-heartedly pulled the sheet up. The air was temperate enough that it was cool without being cold, warm without being uncomfortable. I wished Cadeyrn would hurry. After nearly a month without him, all I wanted was to feel his warmth around me. To breathe again with our souls entwined. A year ago, I would have said that was the biggest load of rubbish I had ever heard. A year ago, I would have sworn that love was fickle and insubstantial.

"And now?" my mate asked from the door to the bathing chamber, a blue and white towel slung low across his hips. My mouth went a bit dry.

"Now I know that you are a part of me, and I want and need you as much as I need breath."

He used another towel to rub at his hair, drying it. Every muscle on him was pronounced and cut from his skin, his chest honed like granite.

"High protein diet worked out for you, then?" I teased a little breathlessly.

"Sorry you missed dessert," he said quickly. A little too quickly. I just looked at him and sat up a little, the sheet falling down. His eyes moved from my face and left trails like the sun on my skin. They travelled down my neck and collarbone, to the rise and fall of my chest, my peaked breasts, my stomach. I watched him move a little closer to the bed, the planes and tucks of muscle shifting as he walked. I saw that his hand was shaking a little as he ran it through his hair and reached back to grab the back of his neck, a gesture so familiar to me that my heart ached.

"Are you hurt?" I rasped, suddenly nervous. He gave me a shy, crooked smile, then sat on the edge of the bed next to me. I reached for him, not wanting to be apart any more than absolutely necessary. Our fingers entwined, and something ancient settled in me.

"No, lady," he said in that rough voice that sent me spinning. "A little nervous, I suppose." He huffed a laugh. As tired as I was, I smiled. As beaten down and aching, and hungry again, I smiled. I smiled because we were together here. For all my hoping and praying and searching, I really hadn't been sure it would happen. When I looked into those clear green eyes, I saw every hope and prayer and answer staring back.

"Come here," I whispered and sat back. He scooted further onto the mattress, and I lifted the sheet for him to come under and into my arms. Within the circle of my embrace, I held him against me as he has done for me. When was the last time he slept and felt safe? Certainly not in that prison cave. Likely not the entire time he was trapped as his *baethaache*. His cheek pressed against my chest, and his arms went around my waist. I kissed the top of his head and tightened my own arms, then linked my legs through his. It couldn't have been more than a minute or so before I heard his breathing slow and I felt his heartbeat even out as he fell asleep. I could keep first watch tonight.

TAPPING. TAPPING like a beak on a window pane roused me from a deep sleep. Bright, warm sunlight flooded the room.

"My lady," called a voice behind the door. More tapping. A cough. "My lord?"

Cadeyrn raised his head and grumbled, still half asleep. Normally, any noise would have him up and in a crouch. I brushed my lips across his silken dark hair and began extricating myself from our tangle . He mumbled a protest and tried to hold on. I chuckled and slid from his grasp and edged from the bed. Grabbing the grubby remnants of my dress, I held it in front of me before opening the door slightly. Xaograos stood in a clean uniform, looking fresh, if exhausted.

"Your Highness," he said with a bow. "Apologies for disturbing you. There have been reports of ships. A fleet gathering in the Sea of Saen Daíthaen." The Sea of the Old Gods.

"Not friendly, I take it?"

"Not likely, Your Highness. The Lady of Laorinaghe and your companions are preparing to gather in the council room."

"Please tell them, Xaograos, that we will be there shortly." He bowed and left. *What the hell am I going to do with Cadeyrn?* I stared at him sleeping facedown. His powers must have been in desperate need of recharging. Perhaps shifting back into his fae form really depleted him. I stood, twirling a strand of hair around my finger, trying to figure out what to do about my mate and what to wear. Pulling the sheet from the bed, I wrapped it about myself, toga style. It looked utterly ridiculous, but I wanted to get to the council. Someone could find me clothes then. Cadeyrn was going to be so pissed I didn't wake him. Oh well.

Along the coast between Maesarra and Laorinaghe, near the Ispil of Bogvhi, sat a fleet of ships from Veruni and additional ships, flying an unknown standard. Messengers rode in that morning from the South bearing the news. Corra received a hawk informing her that the naval fleet was preparing to sail and that we should remain here. Shelter in place was the official recommendation. Everyone debated who undersigned the threat. The main players, Paschale, Feynser, and Analisse, were out of the picture. Analisse was imprisoned under the palace on Eíleín Reínhe, the Queen's Isle. Something in my gut sloshed thinking of Reynard's parents and their vehemence towards us. What we faced now seemed to be an enemy standing beside us. Silas scrubbed at his stubbled face and kept blinking his eyes as though he, too, was completely worn down. He asked questions about exact locations, sea depth, known military officers in Veruni, and so on. Yva stood guard near Lorelei and was given instructions to call in commanding officers in her Lady's guard to bring intelligencers, and I finally pulled her aside and asked if she could use her very unmilitaristic skills to bring us clothing again. Corra dissolved momentarily and came back in, having received another message by hawk.

Turuin had raised soldiers (what was left, as Saarlaiche had volunteered so many during the uprising against the Elders since they were fiercely loyal to Cadeyrn) to defend the coastline. Additionally, he stationed ships in formation off the coast, facing off with several craft of unknown origin.

"Fucking hell," Silas swore. "At least between Western Mae-sarra and Saarlaiche, we know there is some defence. Corra, get word to Soren and find out what is going on in Dunstanaich."

"My border guard has neither heard nor seen anything out of the ordinary," Lorelei stated.

"With all due respect, my lady," Corra interjected. "Based on the events of days past, we need to ascertain where loyalties really lie here. As in, in Laorinaghe, outside of the city."

Lorelei swallowed audibly but nodded. I could imagine she was infuriated. Not so much with Corra but with the entire situation. Just as Cadeyrn was infuriated. Cadeyrn, who I could feel coming in at the moment, his heat preceding him. We turned toward him.

"Good morning, princess," Silas teased, winking at his cousin. "Sorry, *Trubaíste*. No offense." He winked at me as well. Cadeyrn came to stand behind me in his blood-stained trousers from last night, no shirt. What a pair we made.

I like the look, I said to him. He leaned down and kissed just behind my ear.

It got cold after you stole the bed sheet for your own fashion needs. You could have woken me.

You clearly needed the rest. I couldn't have you falling asleep on me again today. It's a blow to my self-esteem.

I can assure you, I am fully recharged.

"What have I missed here?" he asked aloud.

I filled him in, and Silas gave him notes we had taken and messages we had received. Lorelei motioned for two guards to come to the table. They twisted two knobs in the center and pulled back leaves of the wood to reveal a map. Compartments on either side held pieces to place on the board like a chess game. Silas moved the pieces into the formations we knew were out there.

"How do you—do we—does one," I stammered, waving my hand, "determine location here? Apart from general magnetic pole directions like North, South, East, West? Is there longitude and latitude? How would one pinpoint exact locations?"

"Do you remember when you asked me if this is an alternate Earth?"

"Quite fondly. I loved watching you squirm."

"I did too. Very entertaining," Silas added. Cadeyrn shot him a half-hearted glare.

"I told you it was the same universe, but a different realm. Well, it is, but it's not. As you may have noticed, the stars are different. We are at a magnetically separate point in the universe."

"So, like a different planet?" I asked.

He pinched his nose. "No. Remember the folds?" he asked. "We are within one of the folds. So rather than being one blip in a plain of vastness, we are a blip within a fold. Does that make sense?"

"Not to me," Lorelei admitted. I smiled at her.

"So, Earth, the solar system, and galaxies I knew growing up are all within one fold? Then here—Aoifsing, the lands across the sea that are so super mysterious that no one really knows them, the stars above that are somehow written upon our skin—these are all within a different fold? And the universe itself is the folded blanket?"

He agreed with my assessment.

"So, what does that have to do with positioning?" I asked, looking to the map.

"Magnetically, it is different here. In terms of true north, the pole shifts. We have different magnetic fields and, while overall it stays the same, the grid system we use loosely cannot be relied on one hundred percent."

"So, there is no equator because the demarcation line bounces in a sense?"

"Yes."

"So, it's a crap shoot as to how you would place armies on this board?"

"Oh! I watched a documentary on casino games!" Corra exclaimed. "In this case, it would be more of a roulette shoot. Or game? I don't remember. However, the magnetic fields here tip and rock, so where a continent is may change based on how the magnetism shifts. Like a ball on a roulette wheel. Well, they would be on a map, that is. They don't scoot around on land or sea." She summoned a droplet of water in her hand and let it wobble around before it settled.

I think I followed where she was going with this.

"So, could we make a line grid and use Universal Transverse Mercator coordinates to pinpoint locations if we knew the median magnetism in the area?"

"In theory, yes," Cadeyrn answered. "The grid would shift but we could have a percentage of room for error based on the known magnetism within a given part of the grid." He paused and looked at me. "How do you know about military coordinates?" "Military history analytics helped with my trading. Remember I told you I did a dissertation on it?" I answered. "Anyway, if we knew where a regiment was or would be, I think it may be possible to use the magnetism to contain it to a particular part of the grid, thereby hedging the forces. If we could establish a geographic locator code like the military uses."

"If we could, that could be quite handy," Silas said, pursing his lips.

"What we don't know is the topography of Heilig, the land across the sea," Cadeyrn added.

"Really, I am flabbergasted that no one knows anything about the 'land beyond the sea.' I mean, really. It's irresponsible."

"Well, actually," Lorelei chimed. "We do know a bit." We all turned to her fully. "I have been there with Analisse." She flushed and placed both of her hands on the table and blew out a long breath. "Your mother, Princess," she began, "hails from a family across the sea."

AN AFFINITY for water was not common in Aoifsing, Lorelei explained to us. Those of the mist, like my mate and his cousins, were an isolated group, and as of now, the bloodline had come to a stop. That was the closest that those of Aoifsing come to a water affinity, apart from Feynser, who gained his affinity after being sworn into his Elder position. A half millennia ago, Lorelei explained, a young king and queen were called to Aoifsing. They were drawn here to fulfill a need to balance the *taerra* magic—the magic of growing things—with that of the water running through the world. Aoifsing was stagnant in its growth, and it was felt the gods delivered these monarchs to the lands. Across the sea, fae were known to have a wealth of power in water magic. The royal family set off on a quest of sorts to imbue their gifts to a new land.

"Eíleín Reínhe had been a stone isle," Lorelei continued her history. "It was windswept and covered in rocks and boulders with no wildlife or foliage to speak of."

The newcomers, Lorelei told us, sheltered there during a storm. Once the winds and rain had passed, a wild bloom swept across the rocks and sand-blasted island, as if in welcome. The queen touched the ground, a hand on her swollen belly, as she was near to delivering, and claimed the island was hallowed ground. There they would build a bridge to this new land, keeping the isle close to their hearts. As things didn't always work out the way we would like, the home was not ready for children, and the queen was in need of a midwife. They were summoned to the interior of Maesarra, where the most revered midwives and healers were located. Twins were born, a male and female, who grew up between the Isle and Bistaír, their estate in Maesarra.

This family brought new life in the form of both the children, who possessed powerful gifts for water magic and oraculoís (the ability to use one's mind to communicate). Consequently, the landscape on Aoifsing began to thrive once again as it had in centuries past. Though they had no true claim to rule, it was widely accepted that they held the key to the natural prosperity of the land.

"What happened to their homeland?" I asked Lorelei. "If they were monarchs when they arrived here, who maintained the rule in their lands?"

"I was part of the decision to ask them to come here and help balance our magics. The queen had a sister to whom she handed over her rule. Perhaps fifty or so years ago, Analisse and I were sent by Queen Saskeia to see how the lands were faring. We have very little communication with them, as there are wards stitched throughout the very atmosphere of the archipelago which surrounds the great lands. We carried with us specific instructions and stones to allow our passage."

"When was Saskeia crowned?" Cadeyrn asked. I was wondering the same thing.

"Roughly three centuries ago. Her parents, your grandparents, abdicated the throne when the children were of age.

Your grandmother became very ill. It is widely believed that she was poisoned. When she passed, your grandfather allowed his immortality to wither away. They were both friends to me, and I mourned their passing. Analisse grew up alongside your mother. Her own father was the original Elder from Veruni. Your uncle, Konstantín, became the King of Heilig and your mother's liaison to the lands."

"Why does no one say the name?" Silas asked.

"There is power in knowledge and names, and perhaps your mother and uncle never fully trusted us all—with good reason—so they kept the name secret. Only Analisse and I were given it and permission to travel there."

"And Lord Dockman," Cadeyrn added. She nodded.

"That is more recent. Trade became necessary."

"What did you find on your journey there?" Corra asked.

"I love my lands here. Laorinaghe is my pride and the child I never had. However, I found that I did not want to leave Heilig. The beauty was astounding. It is a land of many rivers and bodies of water where the flora bloom in extravagant explosions of colour. My senses were saturated day and night. It is no great surprise that your mother is as beautiful as she is—as you are as well, Princess. It is as if the land itself is incapable of mediocrity."

"What of Konstantín?" Silas asked.

She sat back. "He is beloved by his people. They have a council similar to that which you are trying to accomplish. We were welcomed to the lands and treated as compatriots. Analisse made many acquaintances."

"We need to pay Analisse a visit," Cadeyrn growled. Deep within me, I snarled, wanting to shred the succubus apart.

Silas was arranging ships on the board. Seeing the known fleet positions and the formation, I reached out and touched the ship at the forefront. A vision barreled into me., sending mind and body into a maelstrom.

Ewan riding to us. Blood. Waves. A hole blown in the archipelago, ghostly soldiers marching through, my mother's eyes looking back at me, glazed over and unseeing. Dead. A hand reaching to me. Analisse sitting on a stone dungeon floor, smiling.

"Shit. Grab her feet, Silas. Neysa. Look at me." Cadeyrn was speaking. I was aware that I was shaking violently with cold, as though ice water ran through my veins. My body arched up and there was a crack in my back. "Look at me, my love." He held my face in his hands and blew. I tried to focus on him.

"Watch her neck, Cadeyrn," Corra warned. "She is shaking too much. Neysa, darling, grab onto Cadeyrn. You need warmth."

I just wanted it stop. Needed it to stop. I ached with the force of the convulsions, and I had never been so cold.

"*Trubaíste*," I heard Silas say. "What did you see? Let us take that away from you."

I sent the images to Cadeyrn. He swore, and I heard the shouts of his cousins as heat flared around us.

"Corraidhín, send a hawk. Tell Ewan to return to the palace and take soldiers. He needs to secure his throne. And by the fucking gods, someone get her some proper clothes."

Gradually, the convulsions eased, my mate's warmth covering me.

Secure his throne. Ewan's throne. The queen was dead. My mother was dead. I could feel it in my bones.

SHUFFLING FEET and a cacophony of voices surrounded me. I was vaguely aware of lying on a velvet bench or chaise. There was a cloak wrapped around me and a blanket draped across my legs. I sat up, grunting in pain.

"Don't move too quickly, darling," Corra said. "We aren't sure what cracked in your back, and Cadeyrn wanted you awake before he healed you."

"Did you send the hawk?" *Ewan's throne.*

"I did." She grabbed my hands. Hers were icy, likely having just shifted from mist. "I am going to leave and try to find Ewan. I want to accompany him back and help in any way I can."

I nodded.

"He's so strong, Corra," I said. "Tell him I'll be there as soon as I can. Give him..." I told her, "give him this." From the center of my palm, I dropped a single aquamarine. "Tell him I found it in my clothes after we collapsed the Veil. Have him add it to his crown."

Corra kissed my head and walked off. We were wasting time. I couldn't keep sitting here like a useless lump while the world was falling apart. The problem was that I couldn't move my legs. Holy shit. Panic crept up. The knot in my chest had me in its vice again. Breathe, Neysa.

Cadeyrn. I called to him. *I can't move my legs. Where are you? I can't move my legs.*

I tried to let an electrical current flow through my legs like a power line. If I could shock them like an AED machine, they might work. Somehow, I managed to send out a simultaneous trickle of electricity and a deluge of water and shocked the hell out of myself. That was the most water I'd ever released. Given my mother was dead, I suppose her power transferred to me as well. Every ounce of the female who I had only just gotten to know, had become a part of me now. Me and Ewan. Once again, my body rocked and slammed back into the bench, vibrating with electricity. Silas started to walk over. I flung my hand out to tell him to stop, and a lash of lightning shot towards him.

"Shi-fuh!" he yelled, diving out of the way. "The fucking gods, *Trubaíste!*"

"Don't come near, Silas. You have too much water. I can't control this." I wrapped my arms around myself.

"What the fucking hell did you do?"

"I tried to shock my legs into working."

Cadeyrn walked in. He raised an eyebrow at me.

"Causing trouble?" he asked with a quirk of his mouth.

"Don't come close. I'm out of control." I stuttered the words, electricity still rocketing through me, water dripping from me as well. I didn't know how much longer I could deal with this without turning my brain to porridge. Cadeyrn stepped closer. "Please. I don't want to hurt you." He stood next to me and started to lean over. I screamed as lightning erupted from me. He caught my arms and pushed his fire into me. Immediately, the powers receded, and I calmed.

"Now, what's this about your legs?" He leaned over me, his hair slipping forward and brushing my forehead. I was trying to let him in. Let him soften me into relaxing, but my panic crept up. Tears slipped out and ran down my face and my lip quivered.

"Hey. None of that. I can fix it. Scoot over, bed hog," he teased. I pushed up onto my hands and shoved myself over. His hands gently rolled me to the side, facing away from him. His deft fingers touched and flicked at my back like he was playing an instrument. When he got to the lower back, I stopped feeling him. My breathing caught. I felt nothing below my lumbar spine area.

"Did you realize that when you first came to Barlowe Combe, I had no idea what to do with you?" he asked, a smile in his voice as he worked on my back. "You infuriated me and made me need a cold shower in the same moment."

"And yet..." I complained, bad-natured.

"I know. I knew, or thought I knew, how you felt, and yet I wouldn't accept it. I thought surely you wouldn't want this life with me. In Rila, when you touched that tree carving..." He trailed off. "I felt you. A longing in you, and the thought that you might never be loved. And I wanted to burn the fucking forest to the ground to spite everything that had made you feel like that. Because I loved you, and I didn't know how to say it. Old as dirt and I felt like I was a lad."

I snorted. Sounds of Silas' footsteps told me he had left the room. From the hall he yelled to call if we needed anything.

"So, while I thought I knew, I am male enough that I was sore that Silas had you. I was pissed he loved you and had you and I was standing in that frozen forest knowing you thought you were unloved and I couldn't make myself tell you otherwise." He stroked my back along my spine, and I let my wings stretch out across us. Prickles of feeling returned. A wash of heat alight at his touch. "Beautiful," he murmured. The wings receded. "You know now?"

I turned and looked up at that world-ending beauty in him.

"I mean, I should hope you are aware of my feelings, mate?" he asked so seriously that I smiled.

"I'm getting the idea." I kissed his chest. "There's always room for enlightenment."

"Neysa," he began. "About your vision."

"Let's wait until we hear from Corra."

"We can't. We have to discuss it." He pulled on a strand of my hair.

"Not yet, okay?" I whispered. His arms slid around me. "Ewan doesn't want to be king."

"Most of us don't want the lot we are given," my mate answered. I looked him in those glassy green eyes. I knew how his fate weighed heavily upon him. Today meant one step further down the road to his birthright. Now our fates were intertwined. Or, always had been. "We make the best of it." He tucked that errant strand of dark hair behind my ear.

"And you?" I asked carefully. "Would you have chosen all this had it been offered to you?"

"Every second of it."

"Can I tell you something? You don't have to say anything. I just want to tell you." He nodded and moved his fingertips up my arm, still testing and firing up the nerves. "When Ewan and I were across the Veil, trying to find a link between the stones, the Veil, and those who could cross, he mentioned bloodlines. He made a comment about you both being from the mist fae, and yet had healing unto yourself. Ewan said that you were the start of a new era and that any offspring you had would likely be so strong they would be the cornerstone for all fae. I held it together fairly well whilst we were there. I really did. But when he said that, I felt like everything living in me was yanked out. I knew..."

Ugh. I stopped and blew out a breath. Get it together, Neysa. "I knew then that you would have to move on. You needed to provide a next generation." He shook his head. I put my fingers to his lips. "I made Ewan swear to keep to the outer crescent of the stones. I had lost too much already," I choked. "I expected it to kill me." There. I'd said it.

He swallowed, and his heart was racing. Anger shone in those eyes. Anger with me, I realized with a bit of a shock.

"I knew based on the chemical constituency of the stones, the Veil, my blood, all of it, that it would be so volatile that it would close the damned Veil. But I knew it would destroy me too. I did it to save him and you, and my friend, Shannon. She was my only friend, and she had a family."

I was blubbering a bit now. Not quite crying, but in hysterics. Tears failed where panic reigned. "It was our only chance to make it right. My mother must have seen it happen—or seen me realize it. Ewan and I both had dreams the night before. That's why she came to us. She gave us all of her magic and that's why I'm alive. And that's why she's dead. She depleted her magic, and because of it, she was murdered." *My fault. It should have been me. She would have lived, and you could have gone on.*

"What is wrong with you?" he barked, pulling away from me. I jerked like I had been slapped. He stood glaring down at me.

"Me?" I felt like a pumpkin that had been scooped out, the innards dumped on the ground. All that I had held in, all that I felt, laid bare.

"You were sacrificing yourself. We could have found another way. I knew it. I *knew* you would do something like that when I let you go."

"You did not *let* me go, Cadeyrn. I decided to. I had to. I was expendable here and needed there."

"Expendable? Bloody fucking hell, Neysa. Survivor's guilt is one thing. You should hear yourself. A little self-worth for fuck's sake. We would have found another way!" He pivoted, heat coming off him in waves. My fingers clutched the sheet.

"You tried to find a way for almost a hundred years, Cade! I found the way. I needed to collapse the damned thing, and you were needed here." He whirled to me. Lights flickered in the room around us.

"To be a prize stallion? Nice. Thanks for that." His hand raked through hair still mussed from sleep. "You gave up. You decided to get it over with and gave up."

"What did you do, huh? You nearly let yourself die on that battlefield. That much you told me. And what I saw for myself, while you slept, is that you got steaming drunk for weeks after. You were letting females all over bloody Laichmonde touch you." I didn't add the one I saw kiss him in that alleyway. He might not have taken another to bed, but there were females following him and Magnus around for weeks. He stood, wide, wild eyes looking at me.

"I wasn't the one out socializing and flirting every night, Cadeyrn." I shouldn't have said that last bit. I didn't even hold it against him, nevertheless, it came out like a slap. His head reared back, eyes wide. "I don't know what I'm supposed to do or say to you," he said, his voice barely audible. "It's never right. It's true, though. I did want to die out there. I only fought to keep everyone else alive."

"What do you think I did?"

"The difference is that I didn't make that final call. You did. You said, 'Fuck it.' And sacrificed yourself. I kept fighting." His arms crossed and uncrossed over his bare chest. "Yes, I got drunk. To get you out of my head. Everyone was telling me to get on with it and take someone to bed. Everyone except Silas. I had wished you loved him and never gave me the time of day so I didn't feel like death was kinder than what I was feeling. How about that?"

"Well, I suppose that would have been easier for everyone, eh? Then you could have got on with it, stud." And that's about when I shoved my foot in my mouth. I was a walking, talking, maelstrom. I stood up, tripping on the stupid sheet around me. What did it take to get clothes in this place? His nostrils flared and chest heaved as he stood stock still. He looked utterly defeated. And I wanted to take it all back.

"Cadeyrn."

"I don't know why we bother," he spat, quietly and viciously. Every thought went out of my head. Nothing but screaming, empty silence filled the space where I should have said something. He turned on a heel and walked away. I dropped the sheet, wrapped the cloak around me, and made my way through the other door. Silas stood there, arms crossed. I braced myself for a snarky comment, but he just stared at me like I was someone else entirely. My traitorous lip wobbled as I looked at him.

"Did you honestly think you were expendable?" he asked in a whisper.

I shrugged.

"You made this mess, *Trubaiste*. You two need to fix it. Stop destroying each other."

I walked past him towards my room, my head hung like a wounded animal. "Maybe we shouldn't fix it. Maybe we shouldn't bother."

Distant, rumbling thunder and a driving rain began outside the balcony doors. I didn't care. In my heart, I knew I had been the one who destroyed everyone. My parents' marriage. My father died protecting me. My brother grew up an orphaned slave because of me. Caleb gave up on me years ago. It wasn't his fault. I was a shell of a person. Not even a person, as it turned out. Even Cyrranus nearly got himself killed for me. And my mother. She gave everything she had for Ewan and me to get back safely. She likely even knew she would be killed. And I never even had the decency to call her mother. Why would anyone bother with me? I was as worthless as they came.

CHAPTER 6

I n my room was a pile of clothes. Everywhere I went, I had to find clothing based on the charity of others. I was sick of it. I didn't have anything of my own, apart from the aphrim skins which I knew Reynard had made for me. I dropped the cloak and slipped into a loose pair of black silk trousers and a matching fitted cami. I snatched up a jug of wine from the table, along with my weapons, and left the room. Yva stumbled as I crashed out the doors to the private apartments.

"My la—Your Highness," she said.

"It's Neysa. That's all. Do you drink?"

"Pardon?"

"Do you drink wine, Yva?"

"Yes, though not on duty."

"Good. You're off duty now. Come with me."

I stalked down to the beach and swigged from the jug, then passed it to her. She took a cautious sip while I picked up my sword.

"Would you like to spar with me? It's not a command. Just a question."

"I would rather not...Neysa. It could cause trouble for me."
Fair enough.

"I'm not holding you here. You have the rest of the afternoon, evening, whatever it is, off. You are welcome to stay and
drink with me, or you can go home to your friends and family."

Spinning my sword felt so good. I lashed and swept, rolled,
flipped, did all the stupid shit my father told me would be the
death of me. Who cared at this point? I chased waves from the
water like a dog and would flip, then throw my dagger into an
escaping glob of seaweed. The seaweed made me think of Ewan.
I didn't know what to think about him. About him and Corra.
That was none of my business, yet I still let the concern get
caught in my tangled web of mental vomit. Yva and I passed
the jug back and forth until it was empty. She was giggly, which
made me laugh, because she seemed like the least giggly person
I had ever met. The legs of my trousers were soaked through,
so I took them off and continued my swordplay in my cami
and black underwear. There was no one around, and my bathing
costumes in the human realm were far more revealing than this.
I wondered if I actually did fit in more there than I did here.

Thwack. I threw another dagger. If there were another Veil,
from what I gathered, I would be the only one with the correct biochemical makeup to pass through it without incident.
Thwack, the dagger hit in the center of the already speared
seaweed ribbon. I could cross back. Let everyone get on with
it. Thwack. I pulled the three daggers out and walked back to
my position. The reality was that I wasn't needed here. I got
Cadeyrn back. He could carry out his birthright. Ewan would
rule. Analisse would die. I had promised the skies that I would
work to make this world better. Running full speed, I did an aer-
ial over a large rock, landing in the calf deep water, then threw
my sword at the shore. It stuck into the ground exactly where

I had been standing. I noticed Yva, swaying a bit on the beach, staring with an open mouth. I bowed. If I left and stopped messing up everyone's lives, I would be making the world a better place.

A wave smacked me on the back and careened me into the rock, face first. My nose exploded in pain. I pulled out of the water, laughing like a lunatic.

"Shit!" Yva yelled, sprinting for me. I waved her off as I made my way out of the shallows.

"I'm fine. It's a nose. It'll heal." She grabbed my wet trousers and held them to my face. There was a lot of blood. I was very drunk. She swayed as well. "That was a lot of wine." I stated the obvious.

"I haven't eaten today. You?" she asked.

I shook my head no.

"Maybe we should go get something."

"I don't feel like going back there." Not to mention there was a copious amount of blood running down my throat into my stomach. Face wounds bled like crazy.

"We could go to a tavern?"

I could just see us in a tavern. Her livery and my being soaked through, drunk as college kids. I wasn't reckless enough to invite that kind of trouble.

"Maybe in a little while."

"I realize I'm overstepping, Your Highness." I glared at her. "Neysa. But may I ask what is wrong? I saw your mate as well. He was...*Aedtine Aimschire*." Fire weather. An accurate description, I'm certain. "Lord Silas as well. I asked him if he needed anything, and he snarled at me. Then apologized." That sounded about right.

"I am a glorious fuck up, Yva. I am ressponssible for countless deaths and the ruin of ssso many lives. All because I exist.

Plus, I'm sssocccially inept." Crap, I'd started slurring. "I shh-hould leave Aoifsssing." She looked alarmed.

"Forgive me, but I see no reason that would rectify anything. Would your mate and friends not find that unbearable?"

I shrugged in answer.

"Perhaps for a time. They are all better off without me. Trust me. I have multiple degrees." I stood and rolled my shoulders. "Okay, I'm ready to go for round two. Sssstand back, please."

Thwack. I tossed the dagger at a plant and pinned the blossom through the pistil into the dune behind it. Not that drunk then. Thwack. I let another fly. Where the hell did it go? My third shot from my hand. I heard it land but couldn't see it. *Okay, I've lost two.* I stumbled up the dune looking for the daggers. Where the—

"You could kill someone like that." Silas had a dagger in each hand, the blades cutting into his palms. Shit.

"Oh my God. SSSilas, I'm ssso sssorry." He passed them back to me and wiped his hands on his pants.

"They'll heal. Who ate your face?"

"Giant shark," I said. He smirked.

"Corraidhín watched this thing called *Shark Week*. She wouldn't go near the water for a year." Corra and her documentaries. "You seem to have lost your trousers too."

I headed back down the dune, weaving back and forth. Yva looked at me in alarm after noticing Silas.

How many weapons had I brought down? One sword...

"Fix it," Silas commanded in a voice he never used with me. Three daggers...

"I can't. I make everything worse. I am better off leaving." No, four daggers. Where was the fourth? Crap. I hoped it wasn't swallowed by the ocean. I dropped to my knees and pushed at the sand.

"Bullshit. Fix it." He toed my foot. *Where is my dagger?* "You two have dealt with so much and are so in love it makes me physically sick."

I wanted to be sick right then.

"Stop, Silas. Leave me alone." *Where's the dagger?* It was the one I threw first then moved towards... Yva held it out to me. I gave her a sheepish smile.

She winked and started jogging up the shore. Silas watched her go. Four daggers, one sword. I could have sworn I had something else. Maybe I shouldn't have drunk that much. With weapons. I sat back on my heels thinking about what I was missing. Silas squatted down next to me.

"He would be better off without me," I admitted. "I shouldn't have come back. It's been nothing but trouble."

He smoothed the salty hair away from my sticky mess of a face.

"You don't believe that."

"No? Then why is it you are always finding me and trying to get me to make it work? I ruin everyone's lives. Everyone I love. You can't deny that." I pointed at him. "I messed you up a little too."

"Of course you did. I jumped in headfirst, though. I'm still alive."

"For now," I grumbled.

He chuckled.

"I'm serious. I needed to die to collapse the Veil. It is a scientific fact. Not Ewan. Not any of you. I did. I was doing it willingly. You all would have been fine. Life would have gone on. It had been over a month. Cadeyrn would have been well into getting over it. Instead, my mother gave us every drop of her magic to keep us alive and get us back over. Everything. And now she's dead. Ewan is probably a target now. It's all because of me."

"One, Cadeyrn would not have been fine. He was getting sloppy in his fighting. He was dying alongside me after facing Paschale. Do you think having a week of binge drinking meant he was getting over you? I fucked half the legion and I still didn't! And you weren't even mine to mourn."

Oh.

"So, no. We are not better off without you. If you don't give a shit about us, then do it for Ewan."

"Ewan was enslaved for thirty years while I had a warm home and a father who loved me. Who died for me. I wouldn't blame Ewan if he decided that his first job as king is to wipe me off the map."

"Oh, please." He waved me off.

"Silas, I don't want to wreck anything else. When Corra said I was an abscess, she was right. I wish...I wish I could have realized how to seal the Veil before everything went to shit. It would have been better for everyone."

"Feeling mighty sorry for yourself, Princess?"

"Don't call me that." I tried to snarl, but it came out as more of a slurp. It felt like my nose was turned inside out, a cartoonish sketch of a female. "I will call you that when you're acting like someone who can't handle her shit. If you don't want to be that person, then get it together and be that troublesome disaster I know and love. Might I remind you that you swore an oath to the gods and fuck knows who and what else? Make it better."

"What if it's better without me?" I looked him in the eyes, my own spilling over. My broken nose wasn't healing due to the seawater. I felt it swelling more as I fought the tears that wouldn't stop coming. My right eye was swelling shut.

I looked down at the ring on my finger. His mother would not have wanted her only son to marry and mate with me, considering the damage I caused. My shoulders were curved inward. I couldn't stop the damned tears, and I wanted Silas to leave. If he was going to call me princess for falling apart, so be it. I could get my shit together later.

"Come, *Trubaíste*," he said softly. "Let me take you back up. It's getting dark." He lifted me. "We wouldn't want any more sharks to come get us." I stopped fighting and let him steer me, picking up my weapons as we went. "You're going to walk through the palace in your knickers?"

I shrugged, but he handed me the wet and bloody pants. Fine.

It seemed a lot further walking back up. Maybe because I just expended roughly the amount of energy I would have when I did MMA fighting. Plus, the wine. Thank the gods for being fae and metabolizing alcohol fairly quickly. We passed through the vine-covered gates to the palace with its hanging blue and white tiles, and into the foyer on the main floor. It was empty, apart from a few guards. Up the stairs into the residential apartments, I hid my bloody face as we passed more and more guards. In the open central room near the corridor to my chamber, Cadeyrn was speaking to two soldiers and Lorelei. He stopped when we walked in. Lorelei gasped and hurried over, clicking her fingers for servants to bring things. I shook my head, which felt like there was an actual shark attached to it for all the weight and swelling.

Cadeyrn stood staring at me, breathing heavily, his jaw tight and ticking.

"What. Happened?" He addressed the question to Silas.

I snorted, which sent a clot of blood flying from my nose onto the lapis medallion inlaid on the tile floor. The blood began running freely again. Cadeyrn stepped closer, as if to heal me. I stepped back even though my face hurt like hell. And my legs. I looked down. Hmm. They were battered as well.

"Shark," Silas reiterated what I had said. He knew it was a load of crap.

"Shark?" Cadeyrn exclaimed. Lorelei yelped.

"Fucking great one at that," Silas said, pressing his lips together.

"No. I was joking," I said, my voice nasally. "It's fine. My face hit a rock. I'll live. Good night."

Servants rushed back in with linen, gauze, and tinctures.

"Thank you," I said to them, taking the supplies.

"I'll take them," Cadeyrn said, his voice strained. I made myself meet his eyes, and I felt like I could die right there.

"I've got it." I turned away, my stomach flipping in on itself.

"Shall I clean your weapons, Your Highness?" Xaograos spoke. He took them from me. I walked slowly on my own, then heard Cadeyrn call after me, not even bothering to speak mind to mind.

"Let me at least heal you. Please." His voice was like a rubber band pulled taut. I stopped, then blew out. "Please, *Caráed.*" *Caráed.* My heart. I squeezed my eyes—my eye—shut.

"Fine." I left the door to my—our—room open. He had to have been spent from healing my back earlier. An abscess. That was what I was. I stripped away everything good from everyone. I was swaying a bit. More from hunger at this point, but I had no real desire to eat. He caught my arm, keeping me upright.

"You were drinking?" An easy question. No judgement.

"Yes."

"Did..." He cleared his throat. "Did someone push you into the rock?" I nearly snorted again but wasn't keen on another clot shooting out.

"No. I managed it all on my own with the help of a wave."

"You were swimming?" He looked confused and concerned. It reminded me of Cuthbert.

"I was…It doesn't matter." His nostrils flared, and he took a deep breath as if to steady himself. Hands were on my face. I closed my eyes. That zapping and tingling sensation wound around my nose and eyes. Then he looked down at my legs and touched them one at a time, knitting the cuts back together. It was done in less than twenty minutes. I supposed our powers worked in tandem.

"Your orbital bones were shattered. You could have lost an eye. Plus, your nose had a lateral fracture. It felt painful."

"It was." I walked to the bathing chamber and began shucking off my clothes. "Thanks for healing me." The door shut, and I ran the bath.

As soon as I lay down in bed and had his scent around me, I couldn't stop the tears. It was the opening of flood gates. The compounding loss I felt and couldn't shake. Night dropped its curtain over the sea. The room was cast in shadows; only three dim lamps were lit. I sobbed into the pillow, wishing the pain to go away. I knew enough from Psych 101 to know I was sinking into a depression. Knew I was enabling it with my self-loathing. The sheet was clutched in my hands so tightly, my nails bit into the skin of my palms. To stifle the sound of my sobs I bit into the pillow, tearing the fabric. Shuffling, like someone standing up from the ground, sounded from the other side of the wall. The door clicked open.

Ugly sobs were flowing, and I tried to reign them in and bury my head deeper into the pillow. The side of the bed depressed. I felt him shift closer to me. The heat from his hand warmed through the sheet and my chemise as he hovered it over my side, like a question. My shoulders rocked through another embarrassing sob. That must have been answer enough, because his hand came down on me and he slid against me, tucking me against him before I had a chance to protest. Our bodies lined up, back to front, and he pressed his face against the back of my head. We stayed that way for an hour, maybe more. I couldn't stop crying. He didn't stop holding me.

"I didn't mean it. Any of it. I'm a shit," his strained voice said to the back of my head.

"I'm…" I sobbed again. I couldn't catch my breath to speak properly. "Corrosive. I strip away everything good."

"Corrosive? No, no, my love. You are everything that matters."

I had my entire face in the pillow.

"Why *do* you bother?" I asked, pulling my knees into my stomach, trying to staunch the ache.

"Because I love you. We love each other more than any-thing else in this life. Your parents, your brother, are not your fault. Terrible things happen. We have each other." I let myself put my hand next to his. He immediately threaded his fingers through mine. "Neysa." There was a catch in his voice. My back pressed into him, and I grabbed his other hand in mine. "You said to me that night in Bulgaria that you hoped that I could find peace and be happy. I have. With you. Only with you. I don't want you to ever question that. No matter how mad you get at me, or how much of a shit I am being. I am happy with you like I have never been in my entire life. And I am old."

"Are you sure?" I whimpered like a child. He laughed.

"Yes, *allaíne caráed*. I am quite sure. You?"

I laughed a little through my seemingly endless tears.

"I am yours alone."

"As I am yours," he said, kissing the back of my neck. "Just so we are clear, I had no intention of furthering my bloodline without you. If I were to have a child, it would be with you only."

"I would say we should start working on that now, but it seems war is upon us."

"Yes, and I would wager you have eaten as little as I have today."

I let him in to see what I had been doing on the beach for hours. He flipped me over on top of him.

"You truly are *Alláine Trubáiste*." A beautiful disaster. He called me the affectionate name Silas had for me. "You didn't show me the wave, though."

I cringed and thought back to it so he could see. He swore and sucked air in through his teeth.

"Bloody hell." He kissed my nose and eyes and ran his mouth down my jaw. "If I promised I would feed you soon, could I steal a few moments of your time, *caráed?*" he asked, moving that mouth along my neck.

"Just a few?"

"Perhaps more. I haven't had the pleasure of your full attention for a month. And I missed you terribly."

"Take your time."

Silken locks of hair trailed across my stomach, following the path his mouth made. I pushed my hips up into him, and he grasped me under my backside, pulling me up to his mouth where he explored before moving back up to my chest and neck. The chemise came off along with his clothes. I pulled him to me and claimed his mouth with mine, nipping hard enough with my sharp incisor to break the skin. My tongue found the drop of blood and sucked at it. He groaned and pushed against me. The month apart, the fighting, word of death, the argument between us, our hunger, and everything else that built like a tidal wave crashing into us today, made us too desperate for one another to take each other any slower. We joined and moved quickly, soaking in all that we had missed and needed while we were apart.

CHAPTER 7

Corraidhín

When I was small, my mother had told me I had a secret gift of knowing someone's heart. She trusted my intuition better than anyone else because I could read intention. Ewan, however, I could not read for so many years, and I wondered if it was because my heart knew his and blocked him out. What I could do, though, was find him anywhere. I could locate him through any drop of water or heaviness in the air. What that meant for us, I did not know and refused to think about. I needed to find him and get him to a secure location to keep him alive. All we knew from Neysa was that the Queen had been murdered and Ewan needed to secure his crown. As I left that palace in the Sacred City, I could hear all hell break loose between my cousin and his mate. I don't know how he didn't know she had prepared to sacrifice herself at the Veil. I suppose that was my gift, though.

As I travelled the skies and waterways, my magic was depleting. I hoped to get to him for long enough to explain.

Once that was done, I could try to recharge. Even though I truly hated seeing Ewan when I was so thoroughly disheveled. Perhaps halfway through Maesarra, I felt my powers spluttering. Awe, hell. He had to be close by. I felt his water affinity. If I could latch onto that, I could release my magic a bit and become a part of his, if only to have enough left in me to speak. It was a long shot, but I could try. Using the gift of sensing Ewan, I found him and tried to attract his magic. I hoped it wasn't an intrusion. Once his magic came close enough, I dissolved into it, like rolling with a wave. Except that I became like a bottle caught in a swell and was tumbled over and over in his magic, dragged under and pulled into him for miles and miles. When I became mist, my body flowed sensually in the water and air, fluid and soft, but in his magic, I was cast into a stormy sea. It was as if Neysa's lightning and his water affinity were awash together—a veritable typhoon. Not even Silas and I had a presence like this. Never in my three centuries had I allowed myself to be given over completely to anyone else's magic. Not once had I become this vulnerable. Fitting that the first time I did so, I became debris in the midst of a shipwreck. Rolling and tumbling and being cast about for countless minutes or hours, I lost my grip on myself and stopped feeling. I was only unarticulated existence, riding his power until I landed atop Ewan, soaking him through in my non-corporeal form.

"What the hell?" he yelled, jumping up. I was a sad little puddle on the ground, and I had regained enough of my true self to realize that I felt truly ridiculous. Additionally, I was having a bit of an issue gathering my power to get my body back. I pulled from the ground. Voices other than Ewan's sounded from around the campfire. *Please don't try to kill me on sight.* Silas and I were always at our most vulnerable as we dissolved and reestablished our bodies. Pulsating power pushed into me, prodding.

"Corraidhín?" he yelled. "Holy gods." His power pulled at me more, and I gained my body and collapsed onto him. Utterly naked and looking like a drowned kitten, I tried to make the best of it and flipped my hair back.

"Hello, darling," I managed before passing out.

Whether Ewan took my news of Neysa's visions well, or if he was spiraling down into a mad fury, I wasn't certain. I still did not know him as well as I would like. Despite his being the first male I had ever wanted to keep. For centuries, I flitted between lovers. Some I loved, of course. Lorelei, for example, was a treasure. Thinking of her still made my toes curl. Yet I knew I could never give myself to her fully. There had been plenty of males who caught my eye for a time, but truly, once the chase was over, I was bored. If I were being completely honest with myself, I was far worse than my brother. He never cared for the chase. He just wanted the catch. Then he would let them go. Like those documentaries about the American men who would go catch and release fishing. They never ate the fish. What was the point of getting dressed up in those hideous outfits to spend a day swatting flies on your neck, and you still didn't eat what you caught? Well, I was quite certain my brother ate before the release, so perhaps not a true analogy. I really didn't care for fishing either way.

Then came Neysa. Poor sod. I had never seen my brother so dumbstruck as he was the day after she had lain with him. Gods. I did wonder when he would get over her. If ever. I had hoped that Lina would help on that front. She always made my own mouth water. Yet he still wasn't quite there. With Ewan, though, I saw a future. I wanted him. I wanted to keep him. I was not liking his silence on the matters afoot. I motioned for him to say something. Anything.

"It still makes more sense for me to head to the Sacred City and present a unified front. Do we even know yet the state of the Isle?" Ewan sat across from me, his elbows braced on his knees. I had dressed in his spare shirt and a pair of breeches, and now sat sharpening my knife. Normally I could change the molecular structure of everything I had on me, like clothing and weapons, but this time I was so fully given over to his power, everything but my dagger dissolved completely.

"I have sent hawks to make sure our fleet is at the ready. There have been more revelations," I told him, willing those bright mossy eyes to look at me. He looked up briefly and scowled.

"Of course, there would be. What now, Corraidhín? My mother is dead. We are under attack from who the hell knows what or who. You came splashing into me, having infiltrated *my* power. So, what else?"

Well then. I was speechless for probably the first time in my life, and so I sat back and bit my lip, staring at him. Infiltrated his power? He thought I had breached his power for my own fun? Gods it was the worst experience of my life. Well, there may have been others, but still.

"Well?" he pressed.

"I tried to get to you as quickly as possible. The situation seemed dire enough to warrant it. I assure you, I meant no offense, Ewan." I spoke quietly, not liking the feeling in my stomach. This was new to me. Perhaps all the water contained an amoeba or parasite that now lived in my stomach. Gods. I wished I had never watched anything on the American South.

"And I appreciate the haste, Corraidhín, but you have yet to elaborate on the latest."

"Your mother descends from a monarchy in the lands across the sea," I began. I told him all of what Lorelei had divulged.

He stood abruptly.

"I can't believe I am hearing this. So, we may be fighting an entire land mass and their armies? We stand no chance of winning. Of surviving. And my sister?"

"I left before she was healed. I am certain she fares well. Ewan, please."

He whirled on me.

"Ewan please, what?" he barked at me.

I growled in his face, teeth bared so hard, my canines tore my lips. I would be godsdamned before I let him speak to me that way. His eyes rose with rage as colour bloomed on his face, reminding me so much of Neysa.

"We move to Laorinaghe. Tonight. Send hawks to gather forces with Soren and Bestía of Festaera. She answers to you lot, does she not?"

I nodded.

"Good. We need their ships and whatever nightmares Paschale has been brewing in that festering cesspool of a province. I want us all together and planning this out. What are you waiting for? Get the damned hawks in the sky!"

I stared him down for another minute, warring with whether I should just leave or tackle him to the ground and ride him until he had a rosier outlook. I decided I was far too upset with him to do that. Shame.

"I will send the hawks and escort you back to Laorinaghe because I promised Neysa I would see you safe..."

"I am not a child. Do what you like." He dismissed me and turned away.

"You are certainly not, Eóghaín, King of Aoifsing." He faced me at that, a distraught look on his face that was shuttered over in a blink. "Yet you are reacting as though you are. I shall keep my word to your sister, whom I love. Know that had I not given my word to her, you would be pouring water from your boots for a month to come, and I would be gone and bedding the first good-looking fae I came across. I do not take well to being spoken down to, boy king."

I knew that had him in a twist as I could hear his heart ticking a thousand beats a minute and his own power casting a grey twilight over the camp. Perhaps this was why I never bothered to get involved with anyone of consequence. I passed Cyrranus and licked my lips while giving him a raised eyebrow. I knew there was no way in Mother Aoifsing he would take the bait, but it was fun to goad them all in my fury. I suddenly remembered something.

"Neysa handed me this." I walked back to him and dropped the aquamarine in his palm. "She said to be strong and put this in your crown. She believes in you. For the record, I did too. I am, as humans say, on the fence now."

He snarled as I stalked off.

CHAPTER 8

Neysa

C orra's hawk arrived within a day of her departure, so
we converged in the Sacred City to present a unified
front. Cadeyrn was in agreement, though we were all
concerned by the tone of Corra's correspondence. She said
Ewan was not himself. She told me to not hold her to oaths
from now on. I hadn't realized I held her to one. Within
another half day, hawks arrived from Bestía in Festaera
and Soren of Dunstanaich. They were all readying forces. I
went to the archery range to meet Silas, but found Yva, not
dressed in her livery, but wearing simple, practical clothing.
Her shots were outstanding, and I stood watching for a few
minutes before approaching her. As with any skill, especially
in weapons training, learning from multiple instructors
garnered more success.

"I know you didn't want to spar with me when I was drunk,
but how about giving me pointers on archery? It's a skill my
father left out of my training."

She lowered her bow at my question, and even from behind I could see her amusement.

"It would be my honor, Princess," she teased. "That flip over the rocks was worthy of a ballad 'round a campfire. Until the wave, of course."

I laughed. "Yes, until the wave. I apologize if I put you in a strange position."

"Not at all, Neysa. I had...fun. It has been a while since I enjoyed myself. My head was pounding a bit this morning, though, and I don't have a healer attached to my hip as you do." She winked, nocked an arrow, and let it fly. Straight into the centre of the target.

A whistle sounded behind us, and we both turned. Silas swaggered over, his bow slung over a shoulder.

"Impressive. Has my *Trubaíste* found a new archery instructor?"

"Great skill comes from many masters. Or so say the cat posters in the human realm."

"I shall take your word for it, but I do relish you calling me master."

I laughed and prepared to take a shot, willing my nerves to quiet.

"Show me, Yva," Silas said, rolling her name off his tongue with just the slightest bit of heat. "How you would correct her stance and form."

She shot her eyebrow up, quirked her mouth as if to say "challenge accepted," and moved to me.

"Neysa, you have the basic stance down. Your feet are parallel to your target, but you tend to let your right foot turn in. It likely doesn't affect you in anything else, but comes from running, I should think. You over pronate because your calves are so tight. You run on your toes?" I nodded in a daze. "It isn't a big deal, and you are quite skilled at self-correction, but it keeps your stance just that bit off. In an ideal situation, you would be lined up perfectly with your target and your feet would be perfectly straight. In real life, however, we would be releasing arrows quickly, at a clip, and on the run. For our purpose today, let's have you line up and really try to pull your feet out of the pronated stance."

I was shocked at her direction and looked to Silas. His mouth was hanging open, his eyes wide.

"Question," I asked both of them. "I have gotten okay at hitting my mark from my normal stance. However, I was practicing from kneeling or an otherwise situational stance and couldn't hit the damned thing for love nor money."

"Show me your kneeling," she said.

Silas muttered something that sounded a lot like "I've tried that one before," but I ignored him. I knelt down on one knee and released my arrows, missing my shot.

"Now, tuck tail," she told me. She walked to Silas and gestured for him to kneel as well. I nearly peed myself as he looked completely confused, kneeling alongside her. She pulled his hips backward and pushed up so his backside was slightly elevated. I copied the stance and released my arrow. It found its mark dead center. I grinned at her and caught Silas' eye as he fixed a bemused, lopsided grin on Yva.

"You can stand up, Lord Silas," she told him before turning back to me.

He looked so flummoxed that I burst out laughing.

"What? Did I do something?" she asked, suddenly less confident.

"No, no," I said, wiping my eyes. "Lord Silas isn't used to being told to kneel then being dismissed." She turned a thousand shades of red and, to my surprise, so did Silas.

"Apologies, my lord," she said to him with a bow. He snorted and waved her off.

"I am not your lord, Yva," he said. "Though I might not be opposed to it." He winked and clapped me on the shoulder before walking away, saying he had to check whether any other messages had come through.

"That was interesting," I told her.

"How so?" she asked, self-consciously tugging on her unbound honey brown hair.

"Oh, nothing." I winked at her and started to nock another arrow when we heard a commotion. "If this is your day off, you might want to leave now before you get sucked into whatever that is about." She narrowed her eyes at me, and we set off at a jog into the palace.

"HE'S HERE, Neysa. It's going to take a hot bath, a full bottle of wine, and quite possibly a willing participant to get me in a better mood." Corra stormed through the courtyard in male clothing, looking much worse for wear. Ewan and three guards, including Cyrranus, were several paces behind. Ewan looked briefly towards Corra and brought his attention back to the rest of us.

"I don't think she will actually find a willing participant..." I started.

"I don't care. Brief me," Ewan said, voice clipped. Cadeyrn and I looked at each other.

"Bestía mobilized forces. Soren set his fleet southward. The guards in Eíleín Reínhe have asked what we plan to do with the island and—" Cadeyrn coughed and held my hand. "Her Majesty. Not to mention Analisse, who is in the dungeon." Shit. I had forgotten that. "We assumed you had gone back. Until Corraidhín sent a hawk."

"As I told Corraidhín," Ewan said hotly, "it made more sense for us to convene here and prepare. I am told there is much to our family history."

I nodded at him and brought him inside to discuss away from the others.

Care to talk about it? I asked him silently.

Not particularly.

Something happen with Corra?

Are you not getting the not particularly part?

Geez.

We have a lot going on. I just want to know what is causing unrest among us. Yesterday it was Cadeyrn and me. You should have seen it. He gave me a side eye. I showed him some of our argument, Silas, the daggers, the beach, the wave. He widened his eyes and smiled slightly. *So, you see, we have to keep each other in check.*

It's just a lot going on. Our mother. Then Corraidhín infiltrated my magic. It's just a lot.

I stopped and turned him to me, which was difficult because he was much taller and broader.

You're going to do just fine. I can't think of a better king. Plus, I'll always be here to annoy you. I mean, have your back. I hugged him though he remained still.

I don't want this, Neyssie. I am a foundling. I wasn't good enough to keep with you or our parents, so how am I good enough to rule? I don't want it. Any of it. I want to be left alone.

Before I could stop him, he walked off. I stood, trying to breathe over the breaking in my heart.

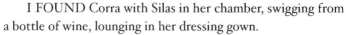

I FOUND Corra with Silas in her chamber, swigging from a bottle of wine, lounging in her dressing gown.

"It seems you had a day yesterday, Neysa," she said in greeting when I walked in. I smirked and squeezed her bare foot, which was propped on an ottoman. "Your brother was a right arse to me. I am releasing myself from keeping watch over him."

"He is having a hard time, Corra. Give him a little bit to sort himself out."

She waved the bottle at me.

"Do you know how many times I have given my heart to another?" she asked. "Never. I have allowed myself to be vulnerable to another and release myself to their power just this once. And it slapped me in the face. Actually, I wanted to slap *him* in the face, but I did not and you understand my meaning."

I sat down next to Silas on the settee.

"I suppose that was an interesting experiment three hundred years in the making. Well, moving along now," Corra chirped. Her forced cheeriness left a sick feeling in my gut.

"Corra," I pleaded. I wouldn't tell her what Ewan had trusted me to know. So, I just patted her foot again and left. What a mess. Neither Corra nor Ewan were any semblance of their usual selves, and my head was pounding on and off since the night on the first floor. Poor Silas having to deal with all of us.

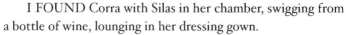

DOCKMAN SENT a hawk informing us of a host of ships moving across *Saen Daíthaen*. Cadeyrn found Ewan training outside and delivered the message. I watched from the terrace above. Corra stepped next to me. She was still in her dressing gown, yet looked perfectly put together otherwise, from her shiny slightly waving hair to her lined eyes and rosebud mouth. I saw Ewan scrub at his face and throw his hands up. Cadeyrn placed a hand on his shoulder, which was shaken off.

"See what I mean?" Corra intoned. "He's an arse."

Of course, with the fae hearing, the two males looked up at us. Ewan stared daggers at Corra.

"I am done with him," she spat and left.

"Have them confront the ships. We need to know what's happening. What would you do, Cadeyrn?" Ewan asked my mate.

"It is not my call, Majesty, but I would have one or two of Dockman's ships confront the fleet. Perhaps have a scout or two in the air if he has them."

"Who the bloody hell would we have as a scout in the air?" Ewan asked.

"A hawk with mind affinity. Or use me."

"No," Ewan and I both said at the same time.

"I could go," Cadeyrn said. "Put me to use."

"You're not going." Ewan said. "Your little beast stunt this past month nearly killed my sister."

Cadeyrn became very still and looked Ewan straight in the eyes.

"Then tell me your plan, Ewan."

"I don't have a plan. We are all fucked. Between my sister's weakness for you and your cousin, your monstrous temper tantrum, that succubus imprisoned near my dead mother's body, and Corraidhín's obnoxious possessiveness, this whole fucking realm is primed to fall. Do any of us have any idea what is going on? I mean, truly. Why again are Neysa and I in line for this throne? We aren't even from this place. Send the hawk. Tell Dockman to figure some of it out and get back to us."

He pivoted to walk away, but Cadeyrn pulled him back. Ewan swung out to hit him. Cadeyrn dodged it, and in one move had Ewan backed against him, arm around his throat and his knees kicked out. I sprinted down. By the time I arrived, Ewan was on his knees and Cadeyrn was talking him down.

"I understand your grief and frustration. I understand your questioning what is happening, because believe me, we all are. What I do not understand, and will not tolerate, is your chastising my mate or my cousins. We were all thrown into this mess. I didn't ask for my birth right any more than you did, and yet here we are. I like you, Ewan. Quite a bit. I will stand beside you and be of service so long as there is mutual respect. That goes for respecting my mate and my cousin as well. Are we clear?"

As I came up behind them, I saw Ewan nod.

"Good." He let him go and offered a hand to my brother. We all looked skyward as a hawk swooped in, no doubt looking for Corra. Rushing to find out the message, the three of us stomped inside. Corra stood scowling.

"I suppose I should get dressed now," she said. "There is a host moving on foot through Prinaer. Bestía said they circumvented Festaera and her border patrol. We aren't sure who it is, but they move aggressively. Bloody hell. Can I get some food around here?"

Lorelei summoned a servant to prepare dinner, giving Corra a quizzical look. I needed to expound on the idea I had yesterday before the visions, so I asked everyone to meet in the war room.

BASED ON the knowledge we had of the hosts being provided to defend Aoifsing, we could be at a serious disadvantage. Especially seeing as there seemed to be an additional force moving against us from the sea. Not knowing our enemy was really starting to piss me off. Cadeyrn sent out messages to all of his contacts to gather forces and store provisions.

"We need to catch them off guard," Silas announced. "They know we know they are coming, and I would bet there are smaller units moving at a quicker pace than the ones we have eyes on."

"Special Forces," Cadeyrn clarified. "Mobilized combat teams that are sent ahead of the host to...lighten the load. Make surgical strikes."

I looked to Cadeyrn.

"I want to look into what Neysa was saying yesterday about hedging the forces in. Silas, do you remember when we had to fight that militant faction that tried to overthrow the Elders?" Silas nodded in confirmation. Cadeyrn turned to the rest of us. "We were sent as a small reconnaissance team to sort out who and what we were facing. It turned out that we had a few hundred militants to contend with, and there were maybe twenty of us?" He addressed the question to Silas.

"I remember hearing this story when I was young. My chambermaid had seen you two after the battle and had quite a crush on you, Cadeyrn," Ewan interjected.

"It's because you walked in all pissy and battered, screaming for ale. All the females swooned." Silas winked at him. I laughed, and my mate quirked a smile at me.

"I digress," Cadeyrn went on. "One of their scouts found us and sent up an alarm. We could either try to retreat and outrun them, allowing their forward progress to the Elders."

"You probably should have," Ewan grumbled. Lorelei snickered.

"Not all of us were evil, your Majesty," she said to him.

"Or," Cadeyrn continued, "we could hedge them in. Silas and I split into two groups and led each around the outer edge of a small valley. Actually, come to think of it, Reynard, that slick weasel, was useful that day as well. Silas and I each sent out our shields away from us, around the perimeter of the valley. Reynard ran like hell toward the center, luring the militants into the valley. We closed the shield and unleashed hell on them where they couldn't escape."

"If I recall, you did sustain some losses and you may have been partially gutted yourself?" Lorelei asked. Cadeyrn waved her off. I blanched thinking of it.

"Point being, we made it out and the faction was eliminated. I see, Cadeyrn, what you are getting at. You want to trap them." Silas strummed the table and looked at the map. I was afraid to touch the pieces again. "We may not be able to rely on the same topographical advantage though, Cadeyrn," he pondered aloud.

"That's why I think we should look into Neysa's idea," he answered.

Everyone turned to me. I took a breath and tried to explain. We would need to mobilize our forces to lure the advancing army to a more reactive area. Prinaer stood out as being a good place if we could get there in time. From what I had been told, it contained many crystal mines. Perhaps we could find one that had magnetic properties like the tourmaline. Regardless of that idea, we could pick an area and set up a magnetic field within it.

"There are mines of hematite in central Prinaer," Ewan blurted. "I saw the location in Saskeia's journals. I remember from our research in the human realm that hematite contains the highest levels of iron out of any terrestrial rock. She also had procured many stones, which she sent with me. Hematite, iron nickel star stones, and peridot. She knew." He shook his head and yanked at the collar of his jacket.

"What are the star stones?" I asked my brother.

"Magnetic rocks. Like chunks of metal that come from the sky," he explained.

"So, we think we could use the stones to generate a current?" Cadeyrn asked.

"Exactly," I answered. "Corra, are you able to decrease temperature?"

"A bit. Not drastic. It's easier if there's moisture involved that I can freeze. I am more of a ceiling fan than an air con." She winked at me. I saw Ewan swallow. "Lorelei can, though. She can drop the temperature even in the hottest moments."

Oh, Corra. Lorelei looked a bit uncomfortable given the company but agreed that she could indeed cool the air. I explained my plan and said we should head out as soon as possible. Ewan was the first to storm out of the room. I looked at Corra and pursed my lips. She lifted her chin and raised a single eyebrow at me. Cadeyrn walked over to her and started to say something but stopped like a wall had been erected between them. She met his eyes and sucked in her cheeks. He cocked his head to the side and backed up a step.

"Corraidhín, would you follow me out for a moment, please?" Cadeyrn asked. She nodded and walked out.

Silas twiddled his thumbs and stared at the war table. I walked over and placed my hand on his back. He smiled and turned to me.

"Clever plan, *Trubaíste*. Don't let it get you killed. Even if you are the only chemically accurate whatever you called it."

"I won't, if you won't," I promised. "Pinky swear?" I held up my pinky to him and hooked his with mine.

"Only if I don't have to admit to saying 'pinky swear,'" he laughed.

Corra and Cadeyrn came back in. She was red faced and looked on the verge of tears, though I'd never seen her cry. She pointed at me.

"Not a word to anyone outside this room," she told me in a tone that brooked no argument.

Corraidhín is with children

I brought my hands to my mouth. Based on the thoughts careening in my head—happiness, fright, questions about her power and being a part of this fight, and finally, her relationship with Ewan—I knew hers must be worse.

"Before you say anything, yes, I am fine to fight. No, I am not telling anyone. I refuse to have this be an inducement. Life goes on. Yes?"

I agreed, feeling my heart ache for my brother who lost everything he ever cared about—from me, to our parents, to Corraidhín—and gained only a crown. The one thing he didn't want.

CHAPTER 9

After a full day and night of travel, Reynard caught up to us in the company of roughly five hundred soldiers from Maesarra. He had left another two thousand to defend the coastline. Units were coming from Saarlaiche, closing in on the time we would likely meet with the opposing force. Soren and Bestía travelled from the north and were planning to arrive behind the enemy. Corra kept close by my side. She and Ewan wouldn't so much as look at one another. I tried to move close to him to chat, but when he saw who kept close to me, he kicked his horse on ahead. I sank onto my bedroll in our tent that first night and groaned. Everything in me ached. I was dreaming of soaking in a large hot bath. The tent flapped back and Cadeyrn ducked in, kicking off his boots. He chuckled seeing me face down.

"Not liking the roughing it part this time around?" he asked.

"I think I'm better at it when I'm trying to find you. My misery and determination alleviated the awfulness."

He sat beside me and ran a hand along my back, then under my jacket and shirt. I made some small sound that had him sniff a laugh.

"Are you worried about the fight?" he asked.

"Yes. What if I was wrong? What if they are expecting the plan? What if it gets one of you killed?"

"Ah. Not yourself then? Just us?"

"Mostly, yes." He snorted and pulled off my boots and began rubbing my feet. Then worked his way up my legs.

"You should probably sleep fully clothed in case we get surprised," he said, his voice getting rougher. I flipped onto my back and looked at him.

"I figured as much." Propping myself on my elbows, I watched as his hands stroked along the length of my leather pants. "Are you worried about anything?"

"Of course. I worry about keeping you safe. About making sure Corraidhín is okay."

"Not yourself? Just us?" I teased him.

"Mostly, yes." He climbed on top of me and claimed my mouth fiercely. I dove my hands into his hair and wrapped my legs around his waist. Stupid leather pants. His palm moved over my arms and chest, fumbling with the hooks on my jacket.

"I thought we should keep our clothes on, general," I breathed. He pulled back and stared at me, those green eyes raking over my face and the open jacket. When he spoke, his voice was several octaves lower and laced with darkness. I shivered.

"I'm certain that would be the safest idea," he said. "I'm willing to risk it if you are."

He unlaced my pants as I fumbled with the toggle on his. Our hands found each other as I slid closer and kissed him. Flipping me over onto my knees, we made use of the cramped space as best we could, and he roared loud enough to wake the camp. I went over the edge at that roar, feeling the heat and power rolling from him into me. I was panting and still pushing back against him as he laughed and kissed up my spine.

Whatever we face, Caráed, we face together. Never doubt that.
I love you, Cadeyrn.
And I you. Always.

AN HOUR or so before dawn, scouts came tearing into the camp. A regiment had moved overnight and taken the high ground that would offer us no advantage. Our plan would never work if we couldn't get them off that ridge. What's more, if we were stuck beneath them, our losses would be catastrophic. Ewan found me as I was strapping on various weapons and sheathing my twin swords across my back. He was bedecked similarly, a shield on his arm as well.

"Well, that was a good idea," I told my brother, pointing to the shield.

He shrugged.

Dammit, Ewan, give me something.

"Can you feel it?" he asked. I stopped and tried to block out the sounds of the camp dismantling, the sing of weapons. It was faint, but I felt it perhaps a couple miles out. A tug on my psyche, like the pull of the tourmaline. I looked to him, eyes wide. "Any idea what it is?"

"No, but I can go see."

"We can both go."

"Ewan," I warned. "You are needed here. Plus, what if it's a trap?"

"This whole thing is a trap. We knew that and have tried to play it to our hand."

"Please stay here," I begged. *Stay and look after Corra.* I guess that was the wrong thing to say. He glared with at me with a simmering rage.

She can take care of herself just fine, Neysa. And she has made it quite clear that she is done with me.

Oh, Ewan. She is not.

"I am coming with you. I want to know exactly what it is. And where you are."

Cadeyrn walked up to us, glancing between the two of us.

"Everything all right?" he asked.

"There's a tug. We both feel it. We need to find out what it is, and if it can help us."

He nodded, meeting Ewan's eyes.

I kissed him quickly and stalked off with my brother toward the direction of the pull. Once we had crossed the tree line and walked into the depths of the forest, the tug became stronger. I grabbed his hand, and the pull was exacerbated with our energies connected. I felt the urge to run towards it, and yet with what the coming days or weeks had in store, I knew it was wise to conserve some energy. Out of all the crystals I had located since I crossed paths with Cadeyrn, the tourmaline was the strongest. It made sense, as it was the protection stone and had pyro-electric properties in line with my own. Tourmaline was called the stone of the goddess Heícate in Aoifsing. The one which could contain and control magic, just like the goddess herself. The further Ewan and I walked toward that draw of power, the more forceful it became. I focused on my *adairch dorhdj,* harnessing the protection in it. Ewan looked at me warily.

"That was from Corraidhín?" he asked, feigning nonchalance. I nodded. "It retains her scent. She...has changed."

"Ewan."

"Don't, Neysa. What shall be, shall be."

I wish I hadn't promised Corra. I wished I could tell him what I suspected was true. I finally understood what Corra meant in the wagon when she told me some things were not for her to tell me. Though we were friends, she had known Cadeyrn and I were mates, or *Cuira*íbh *Enaíde*, and would not tell me. Some truths needed to be heard from the place from where it came. For Ewan and Corra, if they were mates, they needed to realize it on their own. Perhaps Ewan was so much like me that he was blocking it out. Perhaps they too were mates? I could see pain coming off him like drops of sweat. Through whatever bond he and I had from being twins, Ewan's distress was a visible, tangible thing to me. I only hoped we would all live through this battle.

My head was swimming with the effects of whatever was pulling us. The forest was still night dark, though dawn was approaching. No moon or stars lit the oppressiveness around us, but I knew we had found the source of that pull. Standing a hundred or so meters west of the two of us was a cliff face several hundred feet high. At the bottom was a cave mouth. We steeled ourselves and entered. The entirety of the cave pulled at us from every direction. Our weapons strained against the pull.

"Hematite," Ewan breathed, touching the walls. "The entire mountain is hematite." He looked at me. We sprinted for the opening and took stock of the breadth of the mountain side. It stretched for a mile or so north and south, blockading the west. "We need to lure them here."

I agreed and tried to open communication with my mate.

Cadeyrn.

Neysa, we don't have much time. Scouts are reporting forward teams approaching us.

You need to come here, I said. *Lure them here. We have to move our plan. I can explain more when you get here, but I need Silas and Lorelei first. Keep Corra on the fringe. She won't want to be, but the risk is too high for her.*

On my way. Shields are going up.

I was marking positions on the ground using rocks and looked up to find my brother staring at me, lips so tight, they had gone bloodless.

"She's with children," my brother said. His nostrils flared. I saw him straining to breathe. "I heard you tell Cadeyrn to..."

Shit. I bit my lip and opened my palms to him.

"Say something. Yes or no. Please."

"I cannot. I'm sorry."

He slammed his sword into the earth, resulting in a tremor across the forest. Well, that might lure them.

"Why wouldn't she...? Forget it. You won't tell me."

"I swore I would not."

"Fuck it all to never. The only good thing I have ever done in this life and I crushed it."

"It's not gone, Ewan. Go to her. As soon as this is over."

He scrubbed his face and roared, pulling water from the tree roots and causing a few to top over.

"Control it. Use your rage for battle and passion for your mate."

"What did you say?" he asked. I tapped my foot, warring with whether I should just tell him. He stalked closer. "What, Neysa? This is my life we are talking about."

"I think you may be mates," I blurt. "You are so much like me and pushed her away when you lost your sense of self."

He staggered in a circle. A howl sounded from the north. We looked up to see hundreds of yellow eyes glowing in the darkness.

"Shit," we both said.

I could really use some reinforcements right about now, I told Cadeyrn.

What's happened? We are en route.

Lupinus. Hundreds of wolves.

Child's play. You two took them on before. He was joking, yet there was worry in his voice.

Howling resounded from every tree and hollow. Why did they have to be so damned creepy sounding? We began to raise our individual powers. Ewan drew the water he had summoned, and I linked my electricity into it. Threads sparked between us. We held the connection as we separated and backed up, stretching the current between us. A positive and negative. Wasn't that what I learned in physics? When you jump a car battery, opposites attract, right?

I don't understand a single thing you are blathering about in your head, but I trust it will work, Ewan said to my mind. As we stretched the current between us, several hundred meters apart, we both walked perpendicular to how we had been walking, creating a veritable horseshoe of electricity. The current flared, becoming stronger, and from the edges, the magnetic pull of the hematite began to waken. A wolf lunged for Ewan and he swiveled, nearly dropping the connection. I could feel him panting from the exertion, but he carefully slipped a dagger from his thigh, and as the wolf came at him again, he threw it, spearing the animal through the eye. The rest of the wolves howled and descended towards us.

This might not be the right time to tell you this, but your eyes are glowing, he told me. Uh oh. I reached into myself, feeling for a thread to this problem. My beastie fluttered, anxious and ready to be let out. I didn't know if I could hold the charge while letting her fly. But if I had a link to lupinus, then perhaps... I focused on them. Unfortunately, as I started that, three or four decided to attack us. I dropped the connection. Shit. The magnetic power still trembled around us. Ewan pulled out his sword and began slashing at them. At least ten more joined the fray and I was quickly swiping and stabbing with swords.

Arrows began piercing the furred creatures. I didn't have a chance to look around as we fought more and more, but I knew Reynard was around somewhere, backing us up.

"Oddly glad to see you, Reynard. Last time you ambushed a fight of mine, you shot my friend," I heard Ewan snarl and saw him brutally decapitate a wolf. I shuddered. "I like being on the same side."

I heard him chuckle.

"Glad to be of service, little mouse." In a blink, he was standing beside me. Christ, he was fast. With him trading his bow for a sword, we fought together. I spiraled deep into the link I had to lupinus and gave a single command.

STOP. They halted and sat. Okay, that was super strange.

"Whatever you did, it worked. Your eyes are still glowing."

YOU ARE MINE. YOU HEEL TO ME. YOU ALL WILL FIGHT FOR ME. SPREAD OUT AND SERVE. They all listened. Every wolf slunk off and melded into the predawn darkness. I slumped over. Ewan put his hand on my back, then he turned and threw up. I felt sick myself seeing the gore.

As though the forest bowed to him, Silas showed up near us with barely more than a rustle of leaves. Lorelei trailed behind.

"Do the trees do your bidding too, God of the Forest?" Reynard asked Silas. My friend smirked, shoving his sword into the ground as he had that day on the beach in Barlowe Combe. I remember how sexy I had thought he looked. And how much I had wanted to pummel him.

"Only if I ask very nicely," he purred. Pressure built overhead. It was time. Ewan and I took a deep breath. Cadeyrn arrived and began unleashing his shield. Reynard moved to a high tree, still within the boundaries we had marked. Thirty or so other archers moved to similar positions. My brother and I reinstituted our play from earlier, with me harnessing Silas' unstable weather. It would be hard for my mate to keep his heat to a minimum, but for the magnets to be as powerful as possible, we needed the temperature to be low. Soldiers had set the iron nickel star stones on the eastern border. Silas and a few other fae with shielding abilities took to the south to blockade the clearing. The north was open, allowing room for the advancing troops to pass. Once the stones were all in place, plus the extra hematite and peridot Ewan had brought from our mother, I latched onto Silas' power, and we forged the magnetic field that would fence in our enemy. Together, Ewan and I formed an iron core, strengthening the field. The more fae that moved into the field, the stronger the magnetic field would be. Cadeyrn was cloaking the bulk of our army, allowing only a hundred or so to show, inviting the adversaries to the party. We held for another ten minutes or so. Waiting was draining me. Keep it together, Neysa.

Then I locked eyes with my brother. We felt it. Icicles spearing in like daggers. Arrows slamming into the shield.

Paschale had been building a horror show up there. I don't know who is controlling it now, but the ghost soldiers and ice spears were a hit in the last battle, Cadeyrn said to me. Holy fucking hell.

You sure Bestía isn't controlling them? You trust her? I asked.

Um.

Cadeyrn?

I'm sure. She and I...

Oh, for Christ's sake.

It was a very, very long time ago. We fought together and were involved.

Well, maybe she's pissed at me and wants to send some ghostly ice daggers at my ass for having you.

I...don't think so.

No?

Just then one of those ice spears pierced the ground an inch from my foot.

Next time, could I be debriefed prior to the situation?

Yes, Your Highness.

Fuck off.

He laughed.

Hundreds of Festaerans, laden with ice daggers, stampeded into our trap, followed by strange beasts with exposed veins that glowed in the greying dawn. Ewan and I ran the same as we had earlier, creating our horseshoe of electrical current. Lorelei dropped the temperature to unfathomably cold. By my command, the wolves began picking off the enemy as they neared. I felt each of the wolves' losses like a splinter in my finger. We knew the moment the magnetic field had been fashioned completely. Soldiers kept coming, and Cade finally unlocked the full spectrum of our forces. Arrows rained down on the enemy; swords clashed and spun. My brother and I had to keep to the center, yet out of the melee. Most did not get close enough to me for fear of the electricity I harbored. Some tried and died the instant their steel contacted my power. However, each time they did not stay away or die instantly, I sustained another injury. Ewan was dealing with the same thing. Almost like death by repeated paper cut. It was maddening.

All around us, the battle waged on. The stench of death hung over us all, trapped in this vacuum of our own making. Blood and innards, feces and urine. I was freezing and feeling my power splutter here and there. Ewan's eyes went wild for a second, and I knew Corra had appeared.

"Get out of here!" Ewan snarled at her. A wave of warriors launched into us, throwing us all back quite a ways. Corra became mist and drowned the lot of them in one fell swoop.

"Sorry, darling," she said, becoming slightly more corporeal. "What was that?"

I snickered. Ewan had a murderous look on his face, but it broke a bit as he tried not to smile. Thank the gods.

Dawn broke over the eastern front, showcasing the carnage around us. Through the strewn bodies and the clashing steel still going on, came a very not-dead Feynser followed by an equally not-imprisoned Analisse. Feynser locked onto me. Corra tried to come closer, and he sent a wave of water at her, dispersing her mist. Ewan screamed.

A little longer, Ewan. Hold it steady and we can get out of here.

"Did you think you could get rid of us that easily? You are so young, my dear," Analisse cooed. "Sorry about your mum." Analisse began screaming, and I knew a lance of heat hit her. She screeched like a banshee.

Sorry. I couldn't not do it, Cade said to me.

"Many thanks to your papa, Reynard, for my release," Analisse drawled, casting her gaze about in search of the archer. "You two truly aren't on the grandest terms, are you?"

"Perhaps," Reynard hissed from the cover of the tree canopy, "that's because he is a murderous sycophant who delighted in torturing me for a few centuries." An arrow caught her sleeve, pulled her arm back to hit Feynser in the jaw. She snarled and ripped the lance from her shoulder.

The water level began to rise. Our warriors were panicking. There was too much electricity around.

Get everyone out, Cadeyrn. Wait for us on the northern end. Be ready.

Dammit, Neysa, he answered, but moved as many of our fae out as possible. Feynser picked several retreating soldiers to drown as they ran. It was disgusting. I was losing a hold on my power, and I felt my brother in the same predicament. We had to do this quickly.

"There is someone from far, far away who is quite keen to meet you," Feynser said to us. "It's really too bad the ships you thought were protecting you are the very ones that are destroying your hope to hold the throne, young king." He raised his hands and pulled water from every pore in the earth. Rather than a wave as our mother had summoned, Feynser used Silas' weather system against us and caused a super cell. Rain, winds, and pressure collided to form a tornado. Bodies, limbs, blood, and weapons swirled, dancing on a wind driven point near the ground. All around it, particles sucked upwards into the cyclone.

"Silas!" I screamed. "Get out!" I felt him running towards us, spearing for the exit. A knife thrown into his neck knocked him down. I screamed and heard from a distance Corra do the same.

We go now, Neysa, Ewan said to me.

Run for Silas. Drag him out. I will keep the fence up and follow you.

You are not dying in here, Neysa. Do not pull that shit again.

No. But I will hold this as long as possible. Get Silas out. He's dying. I could see blood puddling around my friend as he choked around the knife in his throat. Silas' booted feet were scrambling in the dirt, heels flinging grit in every direction as he kicked. The thought of Silas going down curled its fingers into my windpipe, cutting off air. Not Silas. Ewan sprinted, still keeping his power up. Bloody hell, he was strong. He grabbed a hold of Silas under the arms and dragged him toward the northern opening. Blades were flying. I spun and sent my throwing knives into the bushes. Reynard followed my lead and began picking off more and more hidden threats.

"What do you say, my dear?" Analisse asked, taking a step toward me in the waist-deep water surrounding us, as the winds and rain lashed at everything. "You and me?"

Out of the corner of my eye, I saw Ewan and Silas cross the line. Arrows started spinning in an arch from only a short distance from where Reynard perched. I took my eyes off Analisse to see why. Glimmering in the early light, Corra was spread out on the ground, barely corporeal. Shit.

The look cost me. Analisse lunged. I parried but caught a dagger in my side. Oh fuck, that hurt. She pulled her dagger back, my skin and muscle attached to the blade, and licked the length of it, eyes twinkling in delight. I started to sway, shifting backward. Reynard dropped from the tree, fast as an adder, and grappled for purchase on Corra, trying to pull her away. She couldn't die there. With any last scraps of power I had, I spun the light from myself, casting the scene in complete white out. Another scream sounded and the freezing temperature stopped. The air became heavier and warmer like the late spring morning it was. Lorelei. Her power slipped from the world in the brightness of this nightmare. The atmosphere was a phone line gone dead. A soul had been removed. Guilt riddled me for her people losing her. Still, I ran for Corra, blood gushing from my wound. Reynard still struggled with lifting Corra. I spoke to her, trying to get her to hold on. Together we heaved her up and ran for the border. Just at the edge, though no one could see, I was yanked back.

I felt Analisse's mouth on me, pulling blood from my wound. Nails and fingers prised the ragged edges of my laceration, her teeth worrying at the flesh, sucking more and more blood. Agony soared through me everywhere her fingers and mouth dug. Bone and muscle tore, the action audible even in the thick of all that was happening around us. At first there was the warmth of my own blood and her saliva coating my sides and dripping into my waistband. Once she had chewed deep enough, nerves must have severed, because I didn't feel much at all.

I was losing consciousness quickly. *Think, Neysa.* Analisse was so enraptured with drinking from me, I took the moment to release the thin dagger from my wrist and drive it into her temple. She stilled. I pulled it out and stabbed it back in again, and again. Then I rolled and stabbed her through the heart and screamed and thrashed and stabbed her for everyone she had hurt. For my parents. For Cadeyrn. Pulling my sword from my back in a fit of pure rage, I brought it down, severing her head. Meters from the exit seemed like miles.

I don't think I can make it, I said to Cadeyrn through our minds.

Like hell you can't.

Cadeyrn ripped through my magic, tearing across the white out, hefted me over a shoulder, and sprinted out of the field. I brought down the white, and still trapped within was Feynser and a small battalion of his soldiers looking bewildered. Cadeyrn set me down and turned to the force field we had created. His unleashed heat and mist ignited everything at once in the trap. Fiery water spouted like hell geysers, sparking flames and boiling mist in arcs around the enemy. That power. Feynser bowed and began surrounding himself with his own water to fend off the heat. Ewan and I released our hold on our own power, and the heat from my mate warmed the magnets, which destabilized the field. Magnets could not stay stabilized without the cold. Nothing needed to be trapped anymore anyway Nothing would survive. And so, Cadeyrn walked into that firestorm and became the fire and mist itself. He dissolved into it all and incinerated Feynser where he stood in his pocket of steam.

MY BROTHER was crouching over Corra, snarling and trying to figure out where she was injured. I crawled toward Silas. Cadeyrn and another healer pulled out the knife and tried to staunch the bleeding, but he was still choking and spluttering. My mate came back over and dropped to the ground, feeling for my wound. I was rasping for breaths and couldn't see.

"My two troublemakers here," Cadeyrn said to me softly. "Let's get you sorted. Shhh, cousin. Don't be pushy. Your bleeding has stopped, at least." I felt Silas grab my hand and squeeze. I opened my eyes and saw Cadeyrn swallowing repeatedly, his jaw ticking. All three of us were hurt. His whole family. My beast rumbled. I couldn't quiet her. She broke free and separated herself completely from me. Ewan shouted an expletive and watched her soar, then land next to him. He tensed, but she laid her wing over Corra and chirped quietly. The beast was always protective of my brother, so helping his mate must have been in the job description. Slowly, Corra's form appeared. She was stark naked and slightly rounded in the belly. Cadeyrn worked on me, knitting the wound together. I saw Ewan tentatively place a hand over Corra's belly and another hand on her cheek.

"You ridiculous, wild thing," he said to her through tears. "What were you thinking?"

"Oh, you know. A flashy entrance and all that." She tried to wave a hand.

"I am going to marry you and take you away and make you my queen and love you. Even if you protest. I will have my sister's beastie carry you along. Got that, Corraidhín?"

She laughed and patted his cheek.

"Oh, you love me now, do you?" she asked.

"I have always loved you. I just had to convince you that you loved me back. And I was a horrid twat for the way I treated you."

I turned away, giving them privacy in this forest of so many. I could finally breathe, and as my mate worked on Silas, I met his eyes.

"Are there any more coming? Did it work?" I asked.

"Yes, it worked, you silly sausage," Corra piped in. "Gods, you two will give me grey hairs, and fae are not known to get grey hairs, so beware my wrath!" she teased.

"I need a hawk," Ewan spoke. "We need to send word to Turuin. He needs to defend the incoming ships and attack Dockman's fleet." Cadeyrn swore. "I think our world just expanded," Ewan said, hanging his head.

CHAPTER 10

Consciousness was a fleeting thing. Once Cadeyrn had closed my wounds from both Analisse and the incessant slashes from various weapons, I had fallen into a sort of oblivion. A stream or river rushed nearby. As I woke, I heard the water close by and felt Silas asleep next to me. His neck wound was severe. I knew Cadeyrn lingered close and could hear him pacing now and again, speaking heatedly to someone. Why was I still struggling to keep my eyes open? I tried to speak, but nothing came out. What was going on? Burning still pricked in my side where Analisse had torn the dagger wound open. I knew some wounds took longer to heal and some needed more recovery time. However, I felt like tent stakes kept me on the ground. How many godforsaken injuries could I manage in less than a year? There was a damper on my power. I couldn't summon light or open the connection to my mate or brother. My beastie was gone, and come to think of it, and Cadeyrn was unreachable. No breath came easily, and my heart was racing. Dirt scraped under my fingernails. I could move my hands. I slapped them on the ground.

"You're awake?" Cadeyrn knelt beside me. I could see him lower down but couldn't turn my head. "You can't move?"

My hands slapped the earth again. A second set of boots scraped beside his.

"Did she not heal?" A female voice. I knew that voice yet couldn't place it.

"She did. Perhaps I missed something," he mused. Hands moved over me. "Neysa, touch me with your right hand if you can hear me." I did as he asked. "Touch me with your left hand if you cannot speak." I did so again.

"What is the problem, Cadeyrn? We need to move them shortly," that female voice intoned. I wanted to pull her hair. He growled. A fair female came into view. *Bestía.* In my addled state all I could think about was how she and Cadeyrn had been involved, and now she hovered over my compromised body. She had piqued my defenses that first time she opened her mouth at the summit on Eílein Reíne. Had someone told me she was the one to kill my mother, at this point, with her standing so close to Cadeyrn, I wouldn't have questioned it.

"Neysa, I think Analisse tainted your blood. I cannot be sure, but there seems to be a restraint on your power and your body, not allowing mine to fully heal you. Touch my right hand if you understand." I tapped his hand. "Good. I cannot speak to you mind to mind." I tapped his hand and squeezed my eyes shut. That link was based upon our mating. I couldn't feel that either. He touched my hand, brow furrowed in what I took for worry. "I think there may have been a constraint put on our bond. Do you feel that too?" I tapped his hand. "I'll work on it. We need to move you to a secure location. Our forces need to get to the coast. I may need to go as well." I tapped his left hand. *No, no, no.* "What? You don't understand?" Oh, for Christ's sake. *Don't go. Not without me.* He looked up at his companion.

"She's delirious, Cadeyrn. Allow her to convalesce while we see to the coast." Something hot and not at all magical boiled in me at that statement. Pulling her hair out one strand at a time while I poked holes in her seemed like a good idea. I heard a grunt next to me and knew Silas had woken. Cadeyrn scooted over to him and began speaking with his cousin. A shadow passed over me, and a fair female came into view. Her platinum blonde hair was braided and hung over her shoulder, brushing my face, as she bent over me. And she smiled. An adder's smile. I started slamming my hands in the dirt, flicking it from my left hand at her. Her cold thumb pressed into that hollow spot between my collarbones as she winked those glacial, nearly lashless eyes at me. Cadeyrn called over.

"She's having a fit. I'm going to check on my soldiers," Bestía said. As she turned to leave, the Festaeran kicked ground cover onto my hand. This was not good. I scrabbled for Cadeyrn. A hand wrapped around mine. Not my mate's. Silas. I squeezed repeatedly.

"I'll take you both to the wagons," Cadeyrn said to us. "We can travel together into Maesarra. I will leave you in Bistaír and head further." I squeezed my eyes shut. No, no, no. I felt him over me before he lifted me up and carried to the wagon. Cadeyrn looked down at my face, his expression empty and distant. Not like the male whose soul mine knew as its own. As he lay me on the wagon floor, a strange sort of look came over him, and he simply walked away. I was thrashing inside. I needed to figure out what had been done to me. To us. Silas was brought in next. He was walking on his own, albeit slowly. My friend crawled over to me and took my hand as he laid down. I was squeezing as hard as I could and tapping my finger on his.

"Och, *Trubaíste*. I reckon you are trying to tell me something," he said. His voice was a rustle of leaves on concrete. "I don't know what yet, but we will figure it out. I recognize that... the penguinness is gone." I crushed his hand in mine. "I swore an oath, remember. Do not worry too much."

There was nothing to do but worry. However, my body had other ideas, and I slipped back into that odd sleep.

TWO DAYS on my back in the wagon had me wanting to annihilate everyone. Little by little, feeling came back to my extremities, starting with my toes and feet. By the evening of the third day, I could sit up and speak. Weakness wracked every part of me, my disposition suffering right there along with my body. Silas helped out around camp and was even training for short periods of time. He watched Bestía and constantly muttered about her being a Festaeran demon. Cadeyrn brought me meals and offered to help me to see to my basic needs but left me alone beyond that. It humiliated me enough that I refused his help. He became more distant each day.

The stench of old wood and the tang of my unwashed body and dried blood permeated my senses in the wagon. Just as I had felt when word of my mother's murder came, the abyss of emptiness I was encountering had me in a vice grip. I couldn't allow Bestía or Analisse, may she rot in seven realms of hell-fire, the satisfaction of seeing my downward spiral. So, I ate and spoke and walked and tried to retrain myself. It was useless to swing a sword yet. Each morning before dawn, when the world was at its darkest, I strapped on my thin dagger, left the camp, and did endless sets of squats, lunges, army crawls, and the like to strengthen what I had lost. Accessing my full power, like our mating bond, was still out of reach. However, each morning I would make a point to call upon the lupinus. They allowed me to walk amongst them. Even without my cache of power and the benefit of my swordsmanship, I had a small feral army of my own.

A fortnight after the battle in the magnetic field, I attempted pull-ups on a branch perhaps a couple feet above my head. Initially I swung myself up to stare out over the canopy of forest and plains that stretched toward the coastline of Maesarra. These were my lands. I would claim them and hold them with my brother no matter what. Lorelei died defending her lands. My mother dies for hers. If kin had indeed come from across the sea, I would meet that head on as well. There were no birds in song as I sat on my branch like the *paítherre moinchaí* Silas called me, my lupine brethren scattered below, keeping watch.

It was said Analisse was the reason my gifts had abated and my healing compromised, but I was absolutely certain Bestía had more than a little to do with it. In fact, though my fae powers were buried, my female instincts were on high alert. Bestía was trying to ruin me, starting with capturing my mate's attention. I could have my wolves tear her limb from limb to see if that reestablished my magic. However, did that make me a monster akin to her or Analisse? I thought it might. Perhaps soon enough, I wouldn't care. For now, I was better than that. I slipped down the branch and hung, packing my shoulders into place, and began to pull. Four pull-ups in, I felt a slight tearing of my stitched skin, and I dropped to the ground. Too soon. As I made my way back to the wagon, I heard a rustling between the tents and stiffened.

"Your Highness," Cyrranus greeted me. I wondered what he had been doing. Or who, rather. It wasn't my concern. "May

I help you back to your wagon?" No one but Ewan knew I had been trying to retrain myself.

"Thank you, Cyrranus, but I should be fine." I hoped. He leaned in closer. Close enough to share breath.

"You smell of blood. If you are not looking to draw the attention of a certain male, then perhaps get to your wagon quickly." He pointed to my side. I felt it and swore. Indeed, the skin had fully ripped. Shit. "I see that there is a vileness here. Something has settled amongst us, and I know it has frayed your mate as well."

"I have no mate," I spat without wanting to. I had a mate. But he was so distant and unresponsive to me, my grief and anger forced my tongue. I wanted to throw up, but that would just tear my skin more. Plus, I needed every ounce of nutrition I could get.

"Thank you," I forced. "You have always been kind to me," I told him.

"You always have my loyalty. Know that." He turned and walked back between the tents.

I slunk to the wagon and climbed in, hissing from the sting of taking off my jacket. Fae healing, both my own and the extra abilities Cadeyrn offered, had become so commonplace to me that having this wound not heal was humbling. Having my magic cut off felt as though I were constantly chasing phantom limbs. If I could not use my powers as they had been meant to be wielded, then I would train until I was a new sort of beast. I touched my stomach, missing the flutter of my *baethaache*. She had stayed with Corra and Ewan. Was Cadeyrn's still within him? I stifled a sob. Confusion at the mating bond's absence, I could understand. Yet his indifference to me was something else. It was as if he were...oh. Bewitched. As the thought processed, I pulled my shirt off over my head. It would need washing. If he were bewitched, what was her endgame with him? Essential oils next to a small basin of water sat near me. I took two cloths. One I used to quickly wipe myself down and freshen up. The other I used to clean my wound and staunch the bleeding. Lina had told me that using frankincense followed by lavender helped to clot wounds. I dropped each on the torn skin. Circles of possibility ran through my mind of whether Cadeyrn were sentient behind the enchanted wall Bestía had mortared in his mind. Was he tortured and trapped, feeling as hopeless and helpless as I felt?

These physical wounds, as mortal as they were, paled in comparison to my detachment from Cadeyrn. These physical wounds served as mascots of my emotions. Crude representation of an all encompassing love now unattainable. The scar ran the length of my side from the underside of my breast all the way around my rib and into my oblique muscles. Bitter crimson lines streaked like veins from the tear, while red puffiness formed the perimeter of the injury, making every movement hurt. I knew infection when I saw it, yet there was nothing anyone seemed able to do.

As the canvas flap opened, I expected Silas to come through. Where he had been, I didn't want to know. It was Cadeyrn, however. My heartbeat tripped at seeing him. Even now, our bond in shreds, facing all we were, one look at him and my hands started shaking from wanting to touch him.

It might break me. When you pull away, I had said to him that night in Cappadocia. I didn't know how right I had been. Every time we were separated, each time I thought I had lost him. Every fight, misunderstanding, and now this utter disregard for me, pulled at each of my seams. I kept trying to stitch myself back together, but I didn't know if this time it would be possible. Everything was unraveling. I stared at him as I held an arm across my bare chest, the other hand pressing a linen to my wound.

"What have you done?" he asked, his voice like frost. I closed my eyes and counted to five before answering.

"Apart from being stabbed and torn open by a succubus and having my magic ripped from me?" I blinked at him. His eyes were shuttered, then he rolled them. My gut clenched. "The wound reopened. Again."

"Shall I look at it?" he asked. I tensed at the thought of his hands on me, yet I agreed. He slipped into the wagon, and I moved the cloth, still covering myself out of some self-preserving sense of modesty. His nostrils flared as his hands moved along the cut. Memories of sitting in the dining room in Barlowe Combe after Peru rushed at me like a storm surge.

You're like this great ocean...all I want is to drown in you. His words clanked around in my head. Drown in me. Please come back to me. I was shaking as he felt around the torn skin.

"Is it painful?" he asked, eyes on the wound. I didn't answer. I couldn't trust myself to speak. Finally, he looked up for an answer. His eyes met my own which were filling with grief. For a brief second, I thought there was a softening in his. I could have sworn I felt a pulse of wanting. I reached out and touched his face. He jerked back. How the whole camp did not hear the violent break of my heart at that rebuke was beyond me. I quickly scooted back and threw my filthy, bloodstained shirt overhead, hissing with the pain.

"You need to rest and heal," he said.

"No," I answered. "I need you." He started at my statement. "What happened to you, Cadeyrn? To us? Maybe our bond has been smothered for the time being, but my feelings for you haven't changed. You can't say the same, though, can you?"

He looked at me with that impassible face.

"Perhaps a female healer would benefit you." That was all of an answer I received as he left the wagon.

"What were you doing?" I heard Bestía's pinprick voice ask him from a few feet away.

"Nothing."

No, I supposed not. Blood still leaked from my wound. Pain still lanced my side. A female healer. Lina.

"Were you in the trash tent?" Bestía asked, knowing full well it was my wagon. Cadeyrn was silent but for the scuff of his boots on gravel. "Gods she stinks of death."

I jumped from the wagon and ran for Corra's tent. Cadeyrn and Bestía were on my heels.

I turned to them.

"Fuck off, you two," I said, giving them an obscene gesture. Bestía laughed. Silas rounded the corner of Corra's tent, an oatcake in his hand.

"Silas," I called. He shot the others a look and ducked into Corra's tent with me. "Shield, please."

He threw up a cocoon around the four of us. Corra looked at me quizzically as she lounged against my brother on a bedroll. They were beautiful together: Corra's auburn hair and glowing skin and Ewan's bronze-flecked dark hair and liquid emerald eyes. As much as I was hurting, something softened in me that they had each other. Ewan finally had someone to call his own, and Corra had love after centuries of it escaping her. I wished Yva was with us. Another female on our side. She had felt it her duty to return to Laorinaghe and see to her fellow provincials.

"I need to send a hawk to Lina. I need her to figure out a tincture like the one she gave us in Laichmonde. A magic shield or protector. Something that can sort out what is happening to my power and..." I would not cry. I was done with tears. There was no more room for them in my fight. Silas placed his hand on mine.

"I can do it now." Corra sat up.

"Wait a bit. Bestía is watching. We have to be careful."

They nodded.

"I think…" I began, not wanting to sound like I was simply a jealous ex. "She may have bewitched Cadeyrn. Is that even possible?"

"I couldn't understand why she was here to begin with," Silas said. "She pledged loyalty, yet the contingent of soldiers she brought with her have come out relatively unharmed and the Festaeran nightmares we dealt with were independent of her? It stinks of something. I saw her watching you, Trubaíste. I've been around loads of jealous females, but the look on her face was something else entirely."

"Anyone can see there is something off," Corra said with a shrug. "Call it my female intuition, but I think she's been trying to get Neysa out of the way."

"I say we get rid of her," Ewan whispered. "I have no qualms whatsoever. I shall take council on the matter but know that it is my position. She has used aulde magic on you both. I can feel it."

"Did she?" I asked. "Perhaps. Or perhaps Analisse drained me of my magic. Perhaps Bestía is conveniently here at a time when my power is gone, and my bond with Cadeyrn too," I said, the last with more than a little waver to my voice. Rain pattered overhead, ticking on the roof of the tent.

"What is between you and my cousin was not magic. It was you two. Love. It is not natural to go from one breath to the next and have one's heart change completely. Whatever the case may be," Silas added, "Analisse was working with Feynser, and I would put coin on our Festaeran friend being in that happy arrangement too. Magnus sent me a message from the coast of Saarlaiche. He is in position to do whatever we need of him. Including overrunning the Festaeran forces. *Trubaíste*, perhaps it's time we put on a little show like we did in Bania."

The rain strengthened. I knew what he meant, and I knew how hard it had been for him. The show we put on trying to convince Analisse and her loyalists that Silas and I were togther in order to get me out and back to Cadeyrn—back to my mother—altered something in him. The offer meant that much more to me because of it. I leaned my head on his chest in thanks. Knowing they all held suspicion about Bestía calmed the voice in me which said I sounded delusional. There had to be some great plan linking the Festaeran with Analisse and Feynser. But two of that circuit were now dead. The final death. So, who was Bestía working with?"I don't want to put you in that position again, Silas. You are not a pawn, and I refuse to use you. But I love you for offering." I kissed his cheek. Corra bolted upright.

"No, Neysa. I believe we have all been made pawns. It is time to be queen. The queen uses her pawns to protect her king. Plus, you know, Silas and I are knights. But not like Elton John kind of knights. Like the ones in those documentaries I watched on finding the Holy Grail and the order that disappeared. Templars, I think? We should name ourselves. The Knights of something or other. I don't know. You figure it out. Ewan, be a love and fetch me breakfast."

Despite my poor disposition, I had to laugh. Silas was watching me, searching my face for an answer to Corraidhín's statement. I nodded to him, and I knew he understood I would play along again. One more time. To break the spell between us, I turned back to my brother."She hasn't made herself a meal in three hundred years, Ewan. Good luck." He gnashed his teeth at her playfully, then left the tent to do her bidding.

HAWKS ARRIVED from Turuin that Konstantín, the king of Heilig, had made it through his blockade safely. Messages followed Turuin's from Konstantín, that he came as a friend to Aoifsing, requesting an audience with his kin. Both sides agreed to reconnoiter in a small village on the coast of Maesarra. Corra made certain the exact location was not passed on to Bestía and her soldiers, which, at the very least, bought us time in the planned rendezvous point without any diversions. The situation made it so that I was not deposited in Bistaír as planned but travelling along with the campaign to the coast. From the morning we had decided to play our cards differently with Cadeyrn, it took four more days on the road to reach the village where we were to wait for our meeting. Each day I stuck close to Silas, leaning on him and making everyone think I needed more physical support than I did. The longer she believed me infirm, the more leverage we had to pick apart her plan.

Cyrranus sought me out the first night we arrived in the village.

"I have been played for a fool more than I care to think about, and contrary to my history, I am no fool. I recognize your caged animal actions, and I want you to know that I can help in any way you need. I do not care much for your mate, and the way in which he is treating you has not softened my regard for him. However, the situation seems...less than characteristic of your relationship." He held his hand and sliced the palm with his sidearm. "I swear to uphold my loyalty to you and your brother. I repent for my actions earlier in the year and wish to make amends. I am in your service." He knelt on the ground and offered his hand to me, life source running free and dagger held aloft.

What the hell was I supposed to do with it? Shake it?

"Rise, please, Cyrranus. I accept, but quite honestly have no idea what to do with a bleeding hand. Any guidance?" He smirked and took my hand. Kind of gross. I didn't know him that well.

"Your acceptance is sufficient. The land has heard my pledge to you." He stiffened and looked over my shoulder, where foot-falls sounded.

"What's going on here?" Cadeyrn asked. Feeling his heat near me sent my body into a frenzy. I was quite sure everyone could sense it. My cheeks heated.

"Nothing," I answered just as he had that day outside of the wagon.

"It certainly looked like something. Cyrranus, your hand is bleeding. You have gotten it on her Highness." I turned to face him. Cyrranus stepped to my side. Cadeyrn's eyes snapped to the male standing at attention near me.

"Is there something the matter, Cade?" I asked. His eyes narrowed. Since we had been together, I had only called him Cade when I was angry with him. And in that moment, I knew he was not really my Cadeyrn. "You don't seem concerned with my life any other time."

He stared at me, then Cyrranus. For a split second, it was as if the shutters came down in his eyes and I could see the male I loved so fiercely. I fiddled with the engagement ring on my finger, and my hands dropped nervously to my side. He caught the motion and his mouth opened slightly. I couldn't so much as breathe.

Where are you? Then Bestía came up behind him, and the moment passed.

"So cute. Neysa is cavorting with the help." She ran her hand over Cade's chest. I pulled back and hit her straight in the face, then immediately once more. A one-two punch knocking a tooth and crushing her nose. Her slight frame hit the dirt.

"I believe the address you have forgotten is, 'Your Highness,'" I spat at her. "You have been permitted here only because I have not given the order to kill you. Yet. Do not test me further." I turned to leave, but her voice caught me. She raised it.

"Do you not think that killing me because your betrothed no longer wants you is a bit monstrous, *Your Highness?*" she asked with a smirk on her bloody face. The entire camp was watching us now. Silas had come up to me and taken my hand. Ewan's sword was drawn, as were many others. I cocked my head, assessing her, then squatted down to peer into her face.

"You're a witch," I said, low and dangerously. "You stink of deception and rot and everything decaying in this world. If my mate wants me away from him, then so be it. If you threaten me or the integrity of my brother's throne, I will put you down with no regard for my monstrosity. I can be the assassin, the monster, the darkness that one day snuffs you out."

She spat on the ground and smiled.

"Then you will never figure out how I did it," she whispered so low that only I could hear her. I released the dagger at my wrist and pointed it right between her eyes. Cade's hand came down lightly on my shoulder. Briefly, there was a soft zing in the connection. I snarled at him in warning, and he snatched it back.

"You have no mate, Your Highness," she whispered. "Who are you going to be now?"

"I am who I have always been. My own beast. Watch yourself, you sick piece of shit." I walked away, pulling Silas along with me. Not more than two or three paces from where Bestía and Cade were standing, Silas turned me to him and pulled me into an embrace, his hands on my face. My heart was racing. I touched my forehead to his.

"That's my girl," he said to me.

Cadeyrn had said that to me. I wanted to vomit. I wanted to cry. I wanted to stick my blade in my own heart. None of that would do anything for our situation. The air became unbearably hot, and a snarl ripped from Cade as he helped Bestía from the ground. They walked from the center of camp into the village. Bestía's blatant disregard for me, for her king, for the obvious scheme she was pulling was maddening in itself. But she was right. Until we figured out how to undo her damage, our hands were tied. Even Ewan couldn't stop her so long as Bestía's spell—or whatever she was doing—was a mystery. We could only watch and observe her. Make certain she had no access to critical intelligence—but only watch her.

"Cadeyrn seems to be warring with something inside of him," Cyrranus offered.

Silas snarled. There was a whole lot of snarling going on.

"Of course, he is," Silas snapped. "My cousin would rather die for his mate than see her treated this way." He stopped and realized he had put a wrench in our plan. "Fuck it all to never."

I put a hand on him.

"I can play the game, my lord," Cyrranus told Silas. "I understand the play and the risk."

Silas nodded at him and took me to an open field at the edge of camp.

Just as I was about to ask what we were doing, he pulled the twin swords from his back and tossed me one. My side kept splitting open. Almost every morning when I snuck off to train, it ripped. Angry red lines speared from the wound toward my heart, indicating blood poisoning, but there was nothing I could do, so I ignored the pain. I wasn't sure I could even play dress-up with a sword, and I admitted to him that I wasn't sure I could manage it. Silas stalked over to me. Eyes from the camp followed us, many fae following our tracks. He bent over and kissed me. Slow and devilishly. I looked up at him, stunned. Wild wickedness danced in his eyes. I had to laugh. We stepped back from each other and began a dance of swords.

"My lady," he drawled. "I have missed these daily romps with you." He lashed out.

I spun and knocked his sword with mine. Pain lanced up my side. His eyes widened. I shook my head. I would rather put on a good show. Cade's presence came to the line of voyeurs, yet I didn't spare a glance for whether Bestía stood beside him in the place where I should have been. "You do always know how to take the edge off of me, Silas," I crooned back and whirled. Spiraling to the ground with more speed than anticipated, I came up under his sword, flush against his chest. He laughed and leaned down to nip my ear. I ducked and dove between his legs, rolling behind him. The seam of my wound opened completely, the side of my torso feeling like my insides were barely contained. It wouldn't be long until everyone saw the blood seeping down. I winced from the pain.

Silas, his back to the crowd, mouthed whether I was okay. Lips quirked in a forced smile, I ran full speed at him. The side of his blade arm knocked me back several feet. An "oooh" came from the crowd. He stood over me, whispering an apology. Just as he was about to put a boot on me, I rolled, then kipped up to standing. Oh, Christ. I nearly passed out. Fever was overtaking my body, causing shaking and chattering teeth. He crouched, ready for an assault. Prancing and pawing at the ground, I circled him.

"I always look forward to having you under me, *allaíne Trubaíste*. It's always such a pleasure."

"Then come and get me." I kissed at the air and ran the opposite direction, barely able to see. Being fae and worked up, he wouldn't be able to resist giving chase. My wound was bleeding freely, and I suspected if I didn't see to it soon, I might lose consciousness. Again. Boot steps came up and I stopped short, jumping to face him. So quickly I didn't register it happening, Silas picked me up and had me on my back in the grass. His sword stretched from his hand away from us; his other hand pinned my arm.

"Do you yield?" he asked loudly and breathlessly. Then, so quietly, "Gods, *Trubaíste*, you are bleeding. Can you even get up?"

I shook my fuzzy head.

"Wrap your legs around me." I did as he said. "Ready for a good show?"

I smiled weakly as he stood with me wrapped around him and walked us back to the camp, his hands on my face, trying to transfer energy to me. There were mutters of "I thought she and Cadeyrn were mated?" and "Yeah, well, that Festaeran bitch has done something to him."

A trail of warmth followed us.

CHAPTER 11

Ewan stayed in Silas' tent, field stitching on my side while we waited for a healer to come.

"How many times has this opened, Neyssie?" my brother asked softly. Every time it opened, it ripped further. The scar stretched down to my hip now.

"Nearly every day."

He and Silas both hissed. I'd needed to train. Needed to show everyone I was just as good without my magic and without my mate. The healer pushed through the tent. She tsked at me and worked slowly, knitting the skin together, pulling the infection from the tissue. Her dressing worked better than Cade's had on this wound. Whatever magic held our bond at bay kept him from healing me as well. It wasn't the wound itself, but the lack of conductivity between us. The lightning was gone. I was panicking again. Additionally, without my magic, there was not enough siphoning off of my energy and I had no ability to restore my sense of self. Wet rasps of breath racked my lungs like staccato beats of a metronome. The healer shushed me. When in the history of shushing had shushing ever worked? I was ready to punch her in the face as well.

"Now, darling," Corra soothed. "Ama needs to work. You must try to still. Use your clever breathing thingy. I will tell you a secret. I am thrice as powerful now as I was before. When the time comes, you and I can destroy anything and everything you wish. It will be that girls trip we wanted when we so unfortunately ended up in the godsdamned cloud forest eating meat bars and getting shot at. We can raise hell and kill Bestía an inch at a time, starting with her pinky toe. I may even be able to find some wild horses to run with. But for now, lovely, sit still and allow Ama to work."

I knew that name.

"Ama?" I asked, looking to the healer, who pulled back her hood. She smiled at me.

"Always in trouble, I see," she teased. I laid my head back and stilled for her.

The sun close to setting by the time Ama finished. She began dozing in the corner, too spent to make her way back to wherever she slept. Staring at the ceiling, I began singing. Maybe I was delirious, but in that instant I missed music. My father always used to tell me to crank the volume or sing when I was upset. I had forgotten that. He loved off-beat music with strange cords I'd never understood. I'd had bands and songs I loved.

Lyrics, normally sung in low-fi with electric guitars and violins, spilled out of me, telling tales of lovers believing impossible things between them. Songs from a band I used to see in L.A. Alone in that tent, feeling so alone in every aspect of the word, it was as if every lyric of every song I had ever loved applied to my ridiculous life, even though I was sure there was never anything like my life. Still, I kept singing. Song after song. As though music were a stand-in for my powers, giving me release.

Ama woke and checked my wound before leaving. Corra walked in and out. Voices carried through the camp. All the while, I stared at the ceiling, not allowing myself to shed any tears, and I sang. My voice was horrid and scratchy, yet I felt every bass line like the amplifier was next me. The sun had set, and a lamp was lit in the far corner. Sounds from the camp quieted; still I sang these stupid songs. Songs which had filled my days while I studied or commuted or ran or cooked dinner or stood in my shower while I struggled to breathe through countless anxiety attacks. Here I was, in another realm, fighting a war, losing my powers I had worked so hard to master, dealing with Cadeyrn, and wishing I had music beyond what my own parched throat offered me now. I didn't want to think about how much else I could lose.

After what felt like hours, I stopped singing. I pulled my knees into my chest and knew my wound had finally been healed. In turning, I saw Silas sitting in the corner, near the lit lamp, his red-rimmed eyes on me. The tent pushed open, and Cade walked in, seeing us both there. Heat flared around us.

"What is going on?"

"Is that your catchphrase now, Cade?" I asked sourly, voice like fingernails on rust.

"There was blood in here. What has happened?"

Silas unfolded from his seated position and stalked to his cousin, controlled and lethal.

"What happened is that you never healed your mate and didn't realize it. She's had a festering wound for weeks because you are allowing yourself to be bewitched by that *cuídvsite*. You are still rational, Cadeyrn. Use your godsdamned brain."

"She would not have torn the wound had you two not been engaged in such brutal foreplay. Or did it tear in the throws?" Cade asked, a flare of green fire in his eyes.

Silas visibly shuddered, restraining himself from attacking his cousin.

"I hope that question keeps you up at night," he said instead, then walked to me and stroked my face possessively. I leaned into the touch. Cadeyrn's eyes followed the movement. He swallowed.

"Konstantín has arrived. I expect he would like to speak with his kin." Before he left, Cade looked to my hand where my engagement ring still sat. "Unless you want to invite questions, you might want to take that off."

Howling in the distance echoed my feelings. I knew my eyes must be glowing, yet Silas said nothing. I stood from the table where I had been laid and pulled on my boots and jacket. Before leaving the tent, I saw a necklace made of raw rose and clear quartz. Each crystal was left jagged and harsh, hanging like icicles from a silver chain. In touching the crystal, I was shocked that a vision came with it: Ama placing it there and dropping a crystal into the pocket of Cadeyrn's trousers. I clipped the necklace around my neck and left.

CHAPTER 12

Silas

What sick fucking twat would play those games? I had my run of debauchery and enjoyed it very much. But what had Neysa done to deserve all she had gone through? If I didn't know my cousin and all he had withstood, and the fact that I could clearly see that Festaeran demon scrambled his thinking, I would have killed him. Neysa may not have loved me the way I would have liked, but part of me wanted to take her far from that mess. Far from the death and intrigue, and to have kept her quietly with me. But that was a drunken daydream.

Standing by and watching Cadeyrn with Bestía while Neysa hung her head and accepted it was torture. Ewan, the beautiful little sod, had threatened to kill the Festaeran bitch several times. I tended to agree, but my sister and Neysa said to hold out and see how to dismantle the enchantment. Funnily enough, I'd heard rumours that Bestía had been slain in the battle in which I nearly died. Inaccurate dissemination of information, I supposed.

Neysa thought no one saw her as she snuck past me every morning to train on her own. In the beginning I would follow her and watch. Watch her anger over not being able to do what she could months ago. Watch her improve. Watch her bleed and scream and cry out in the woods where no one could see her. Apart from me. I thought I had scented Cadeyrn one morning. In the trees near me. No one knew what to do to wake him from this spell. It was as if his memories had been wiped clean, along with their bond and Neysa's powers.

Once we had decided to play our scheming parts again, I knew deep down that eventually Cadeyrn would be overcome with seeing his mate with me. I knew her scent and desire would wreak havoc on him. So, we played the game. She let me kiss her and hold her and sometimes, I told myself, it seemed like she was okay. Until the night after Ama healed her and she began to sing. Fucking gods, what weepy, emotional songs they had in the mortal realm. She sung for hours about the "*beautiful corpses of this destroyed humanity*" and all that kind of rubbish. Some of those songs she sang would haunt me. Fucking hell.

Reynard, the weaselly little shite, had become my closest ally. His speed allowed him to run messages between towns for me. I had to corral our supporters without Bestía and her legion getting wind of it. Kaseik diverted his regiments, and rather than come to us and deal with the wreckage we were amassing here, I had them reroute and merge with Turuin. Eventually, I'd see us joined, but when the head of our army was enchanted by an enemy posing as ally, I couldn't take the risk.

I hadn't sent for Lina days ago when Neysa asked. I hated to involve her in everything. She would have been taking a great risk, leaving her business, and she was still pissed off at me. It had seemed like every time we had a go, I took off and left her. Not to mention the fact that she blamed Neysa for quite a few of the trials of late—from Cadeyrn's and my injuries to my leaving. Even though there was no one I would have trusted more to figure out this spellbinding bullshit Bestía pulled, I couldn't do it. So, I'd sent for Ama instead.

Our weapons were meticulous, because every frustrating, raging minute when I walked away from Cadeyrn or Neysa, I cleaned them. I even cleaned others' weapons.

"Silas." Neysa snuck up on me. I was so used to her scent from the wagon, I hardly noticed. I set the sword aside and looked at her. I hated how her eyes saw right through me. She had lost so much weight, but still it was that face that undid me. "If I don't hit something right now, someone is going to die a slow and painful death."

"What can I do for you, *Trubaíste?*" I stood and held up my hands for her to punch. She knocked them half-assed.

"That whore keeps making snide remarks about my smelling of blood and sweat. If I kill her now, there may not be a chance to break the spell. So, I need a distraction."

As she spoke, I saw my cousin come around the corner with the whore in question. Every time he saw Neysa, it was like he had never seen her before. I pulled Neysa to me and leaned into her neck and sniffed the length of her. She shivered, and I nearly growled at it. Gods, I wanted her.

"They are coming this way. Are you up for a bit of theatre?" I whispered in her ear.

She answered by putting her arms around me and grabbing my face to kiss. Fucking hell. I wasn't expecting that, and I backed her against the wagon, pressing my body into hers. I knew she felt the heat come off of Cadeyrn. He didn't even seem to notice it, the poor sod. None of us knew whether he was bedding Bestía or not. They had a thing a hundred years ago. It was casual, I remembered. He never seemed bothered about its ending. I pulled away from Neysa's mouth, knowing I had to stay my course, even though reattaching myself to her was the only thing I wanted to do.

"Silas," Cadeyrn called. "I have need of you."

I turned to slowly look at him, my hand twirling in the escaped hair from Neysa's braid. His eyes caught the movement. I saw it then. Another flash.

"It looks as though *she* has need of him as well, my love." Bestía's words could have been a gut punch to me as hard as I felt them hit Neysa. Against me, where they couldn't see her, her shoulder caved, and she bit my shoulder to keep from crying. I wanted to kill them both.

"I can spare you this moment, Silas," Neysa said, rallying herself. "Feel free to bring me back that whore's head. In flames." She beamed an evil, beautiful smile. I walked away, pushing at my trousers.

"WHERE ARE our reinforcements?" Cadeyrn asked. "Turuin was supposed to be here before us."

"As far as I have been told, there was a storm off Saarlaiche, which delayed the travel a few days. Turuin even lost a ship," I lied through my teeth. Normally, my cousin could see right through my lies. This, however, seemed to appease him. I needed Turuin to stay offshore and offer back up of sorts if shit went tits up on our end.

"You need to let them know," Bestía said to me, "that we are being patient, but our patience has its limits."

The flaming head seemed like a bloody great idea right now.

"Pardon me, lady," I answered, gritting my teeth. "But you do not give me orders. Come to think of it, Cadeyrn, why exactly is she here?"

"She aided us in battle and is a part of our collaborative defense."

"She did fuck all, cousin," I barked.

She hissed.

"The battle was a success due to Neysa and Ewan's plan. You go worry about whatever you worry about these days, and I shall uphold my responsibilities. As always."

"Go warm your little bitch's bed, underling," Bestía spat. I started to lose control; rain came down in great sheets.

"I should say the same to you, but gods know, there is no warmth anywhere in your body." I stalked off to find Corraidhín and secure the hawks.

CHAPTER 13

Neysa

Turuin opted to hold the sea line of defense, staying offshore while we all gathered in the village to meet the King of Heilig as he disembarked his ship. Dark mahogany hair like my own and my mother's was in a shaggy crop on his head. Though he had a spray of freckles like Ewan and I, his face was very fair, his eyes large and a deep olive.

As siblings, we faced him and bowed in welcome. He did the same. The meeting was to take place in a private home in the village. Our host graciously offered to vacate completely so we could reside there for the duration of our stay, but we all opted to stay in camp. Bestía walked alongside Cade, her hand on her sword, like his consort or second-in-command. The air was tense as we settled into the drawing room of the comfortably appointed home. Konstantín looked me over, no doubt noting the hollowness in my face, the lack of colour from fever and trauma.

"Are you well, Your Highness?" he asked with what felt like genuine concern.

"I am presently, Your Majesty. I have recently healed from the last battle in which Analisse of Veruni both stabbed and drank from me. The wound was difficult to heal."

His eyes widened as he sat forward.

"I was told you have a mate and are betrothed," he asked me. "Is your mate not present?"

I swallowed. This could have been planned better.

"That would be me, Your Majesty," Cadeyrn answered. I found my voice.

"King Konstantín, my mate, Cadeyrn Bowden of Saarlaiche." The words tasted like ash on my tongue, and to anyone who knew me, sounded much the same. It seemed to placate his curiosity, so he began to tell us of the strife in his lands.

TEN YEARS ago, the ruling party of Heilig decided to allow certain trade ships to enter the archipelago which protected the lands. Heilig was completely surrounded by these enchanted islands, and they served to protect the people for millennia. In recent years, the Lady Analisse, her commander, Lord Dockman, and several others travelled often to Heilig for trade and pleasure. Unrest began in the larger cities, and the fae of Heilig rose up to protest the royal line having been given to Aoifsing. The visitors only recently pledged to bring back their royal heirs and provide the lands with fae who might breed more power in the land.

"I came to beg you to consider establishing a presence in Heilig," King Konstantín began. "While en route, we were ambushed by Lord Dockman and a fleet of ships. We managed to get away, and though the ship with Dockman himself was sunk, I witnessed his being hauled onto another boat."

We sat back. Something didn't sit well with this story. Where would Dockman have gone and where was the seed of deceit? With the Heiligan king or within our own ranks?

"His Majesty and Her Highness must remain in Aoifsing for the time," Cadeyrn spoke up. I looked to him in shock. Why did he feel he needed to answer for me or Ewan?

"I understand this to be quite surprising," Konstantín said, showing us his hands in supplication. "I come bearing no ill will. I left these lands long ago so my sister could rule. She and I were very close, and it was quite hard. You both favour her so much. You, Neysa, remind me of my daughter, Saski. All I ask is that you help to keep the peace in your homeland."

"Who blew through the archipelago?" I asked, remembering my vision.

"Phantomes were called from the darker, aulde magics. Part of the unrest. Phantomes were released in some villages as well. Many lives were lost. You see, it has become quite a problem."

"Those phantomes. Where did they go once they blasted your wards?"

"I don't know," he admitted.

I turned to Cade and reached to show him the vision in my mind, even so far as touching his arm. He looked down at me with indifference, and I withdrew my hand. Bestía snickered, then coughed as though she swallowed water wrong. Thank you, Corra.

"Cadeyrn," I said. "The ghost army you fought. What did they look like?"

He watched me for a hair of a second.

"Wraiths. Barely there, yet capable of tactile assault. They moved through their own army—that of Festaera and those who fought alongside them, without causing harm, yet were as deadly as corporeal warriors against us."

"Phantomes," Konstantín confirmed. Ewan swore.

"And have you any means to dismantle the phantomes? Can they be eradicated beyond killing the one who controls them, like Cadeyrn did?" I asked.

"We have mystics and necromancers who are able to fell many at a time. Though we must find who controls the intent. Our mystics are very skilled, but this type of warfare is older than most." Aulde, dark magic.

"Have you any mystics with you, Your Majesty?" I asked.

"Seven."

"I should like to speak with them directly."

"Of course." He motioned to one of his guards to fetch the mystics.

Having mystics at my disposal sparked a plan in my head. I leaned into Silas and whispered to him so only he could hear. He stood and left, returning with Cyrranus and five guards of our own. Konstantín looked alarmed at first, but the guards all moved to Bestía.

"What is going on?" Cade asked. Honestly if that question came out of his mouth one more bloody time, I was going to hit him.

"Bestía, you are being detained by the rulers of Aoifsing and Heilig." I looked to Konstantín, realizing I might have overstepped his authority. He tucked his chin once. "You will remain in custody until I have deemed you not a threat." Which was not bloody likely. My boots stomped on the rug with enough force to make the mantel vases teeter.

"On what grounds?" she asked haughtily.

"Conspiracy against the crown," I answered, ticking off the offenses on my fingers. "Accessory to murder. Deviant use of dark magic. Shall I go on?"

"This is absurd," Cade remarked.

"I love you more than life itself, Cadeyrn. But so help me God, if you say anything else that makes you look this stupid, I will lose my shit."

"You see, she is just jealous. This is a lovers' spat. She is upset that he chose me," Bestía said. Silas' hand on my back steadied my rage.

The mystics entered the house with a small faction of guards. I thanked them for coming before they looked at me and then to each other. The plan which had formulated in the preceeding moments had so many iffy factors, yet it seemed like my best option.

"What has been done to you, child? Let us look." They spoke as one.

Goosebumps ran up my arms. Silas and Ewan flanked me.

"You have been spelled. Bound by your own magic." They tilted their heads side to side in synchronized creepiness. "It cannot find its way through." They turned their heads to Cadeyrn. "You must see her to release her."

"This is bullshit." Cade stormed out.

"I have one question at the top of my list," I asked. "If I kill the one responsible for spelling me, will the spell be broken?"

They seemed to be having an internal conversation.

"That one has been long dead," they intoned in unison.

Shit. Bestía laughed.

"Stupid girl," she said.

"How do I break the spell?" I begged. Silas threw a shield around Bestía, keeping her from hearing their answer. Bless him for the forethought.

"Face the one who fears you. Be the one who holds you. Embrace that which seems foreign. Speak as though you can be heard. Find those who dance to your song." They quieted and left the room.

"Any code breaking skills on that one, Neysa?" Corra asked.

"Fucking hell," Silas swore.

Bestía laughed from the other side of the room.

"So, may I go now?" she asked. "My lover has left. Analisse is dead. Good luck." She began to choke, water bubbling from her lips. *Lover. My Lover.* Bestía calling my mate her lover created a rising tide of tar like hatred in me. I didn't know if she and Cadeyrn had been together intimately yet. I hoped I would have sensed it. Scented it. Something. Still.

"Corraidhín, love," Ewan remarked.

"Sorry, darling. My hormones are getting the better of me."

"Keep her contained," I commanded. "Your Majesty, I will help in any way I can. As you can see, we face an internal threat. Please know it is sensitive in nature."

"Of course," he answered.

PASSING SMALL shops and homes, I stalked back through the town. It was a quaint, happy village. Cats lounged on balconies; warm light lit the windows. Bistaír, my family's estate, was mere miles inland from here, and I had yet to see it. Tonight, I needed to get to the sea. Just north of the harbour was a beach covered in shells and washed-up coral. I ran to the shore and pulled my boots off to sink my feet in the water. Breathe.

Movement to my right had me spinning, daggers out. Cade raised his hands.

"If you say, 'what is going on' again, I swear I will throw this dagger at you."

He actually chuckled.

"I didn't mean to scare you. I came to breathe in the sea." he said. Of course he did. Just as I had.

"Why don't you see it?" I asked.

"See what? We had a mating bond, I will admit. It is gone now, and I am free to feel as I would like."

I could have eaten hot coals and felt less pain.

"And you as well. You are free to...dally with Silas."

"So, everything. Every feeling we had. Every touch. Every promise. You chalk it all up to a bond that has been removed?"

"Yes."

"Ah. Stupid me. I suppose then that the thought I had in Rila was correct. I will never be loved. As I love you."

"I am sorry. I do not mean to hurt you this way. Truly."

"Will you humour me a moment?" Trying to speak as though every breath hadn't been stolen made my question torpid. Still, I would not cry. He shrugged in the darkness of the beach. I stepped closer to him. Alarm shot to his face. I touched his arm and moved my hand up the length; my other hand moved to his stomach. He tugged at my hand to pull it away, heat flaring slightly. Tightening my grip, I stroked his face and hair. Everything in me was trembling. Rumbling came from deep in him. Whether it was his *baethaache* or just a response, I didn't know. My lips touched his neck as I stood on tip toes. Even with my height, he was at least six inches taller. I kissed his salty skin softly, then pulled away. His hands fisted, and I saw his eyes were closed, but I walked away before he could say anything else.

"I don't know why I bother," I said.

A NECROMANCER, a sparring ring, *Aráiran-aoír* nut flour, sugar, eggs, vanilla, five clear quartz, five rose quartz, and a hot bath. Like the start of a bad joke, I stood in my tent with my knights of whatever and spewed a list of what I needed. On our way to an inn, Silas gave me a searching look. I knew I smelled of Cadeyrn after pressing against him and likely my desire in that horrible moment. I did not want to talk about it. Talk about getting a couple of blocks away and throwing up until my sides ached. I wanted to bathe and wear fresh clothes that were not covered in blood. Yes, I should be sleeping, and I told Silas he should be as well, but I had a plan, and it needed to be done quickly.

Inquiring about a necromancer in a small village was a delicate matter. Of course, no one knew of one. *No, no aulde magic here, Your Highness.* In speaking to the most respected healer, I impressed upon him the need I had for a necromancer to free our realm from a plague. I also asked for groceries, new clothing, and underwear to be sent to the inn. So really, the knock on the door could have been anyone.

A father and sleepy young child stood waiting to be invited into our room. They carried two parcels. The father handed them to me and blurted out that we could not speak to anyone of his child's abilities. I explained that we may be able to cloak the child, but we needed him to help us. They would stay the night at the inn.

I bathed quickly, barely long enough to enjoy the water on my skin. Buckling my weapons over the fresh leathers my mother had made for me gave me a sense of power and purpose.

I lined my eyes with a kohl pencil and braided my wet hair back. Dressed and ready, Silas and I stomped down the stairs of the inn. To the kitchen.

Hours later, a few soldiers dragged the two most ostentatious chairs we could find in the village down to the field I commandeered as a sparring ring. Dawn painted lazy lilac stripes across the sky, dragging its languorous fingers through the horizon in slow, teasing strokes. Dread filled my gut in that early hour. In these muted watercolour minutes, everything could turn around or be blown to hell.

Cadeyrn was standing amongst a few males near the cook's fire, drinking tea and listening to their stories. Bannocks and tea, Neysa. Focus. The morning was warm already with a humid breeze coming off the sea. I left my jacket in my tent, wearing just a fitted cotton tank with my leather pants and boots. The new necklace from Ama hung below my clavicle, above the *adairch dorhdj*, which sat just above my modest cleavage. My hair had dried in waves from the braid, and until I had to get in that ring, I was wearing it down and loose. From the braziers I lifted a kettle and poured into a tin cup. Chatter stopped when I came round, but as I sipped from my cup and waited for the bannocks to cook, the chit-chat resumed.

"It's 'ere," one male pointed to just below his elbow. "It gives me shite whens I use me sword 'an whens I pull sommin' from the wagons." I recognized the soldier and his Dunstanaich accent.

"It's called tendonitis, Griffin," I told him. He looked surprised I knew his name. They all turned to me. "I have it as well. Hurts like hell in your grip, right?" He nodded. "It's very common. For me, it's worse when I grip my weapon too tightly. The bist that hold your muscles and bone together get inflamed— like, they swell, and that's why it hurts. Try some of this on it." I reached into my shirt and pulled out a tin of salve Ama had made for me. It had lemongrass, calendula, lavender, and something else I couldn't place. He caught the tin as I tossed it over.

"Awe, your 'ighness. I couldn't be taking from ye," he said, his cheeks darkening.

"Please. I insist. Can't have my warriors in pain." I winked at him and turned to Cade. "Remember how bad mine got after we sparred that day in the woods? Oh, and then after the fight in Bulgaria?"

He narrowed his eyes at me and blinked several times as though he were trying to remember. Griffin rubbed the salve on his arm before handing it back to me with thanks.

"Let me know when you need it again, Griffin, okay?" I pushed my mass of hair over my shoulder and rubbed some of the salve on my own elbow and shoulder, working it into the kinks there as I drank my tea.

From a distance it was the same Cadeyrn. He was easy and encouraging with his soldiers. Refined elegance and sun-bronzed fair skin. He had trimmed his hair and still shaved every morning. Broad shoulders still pushed at his leathers from centuries of daily training. I noted all the blades he had on him that I had strapped on him myself at times. Even the hidden ones. I guess we hadn't known each other that long, but it had felt so real. It had been so real. It was to me, at least. Every small moment when I stared into those eyes that swallowed me whole. Every touch and tease. The way his heat would rise when I pressed my hand into his back or touched his stomach. The way he made me feel when his hands went into my hair just before he kissed me. The quips and whispers between us. The way we bantered and were content to lay all night, talking of books and nothing consequential. All these little details I catalogued in the short time we had been granted. The last time we slept together, the night before the battle, came to me as vivid as the first time in the hollow. I wasn't hungry anymore and stood holding the warm bread as I stared off in the distance, thinking about the male mere feet away. The soldiers he had been speaking to left, and he turned to me, sensing or scenting a change in me. I glanced his way, then back into nothingness.

"Did I heal your elbow in those times you mentioned?" he asked me.

"Yes. Well, after our fight, I avoided you for a couple of days until Reynard attacked me in the woods. You offered then." I smiled a little. He looked up at me from lowered lashes. I honestly could have had him right there in the middle of the goddamn cooks' area.

"I don't remember. That's odd."

"Do you remember when you healed me after Peru? My broken rib and shoulder?"

He shook his head. "It was kind of you to offer your salve to that male." It seemed like he was avoiding the question.

"I don't like to see anyone in pain."

He nodded.

"I don't remember after Peru. I'm sorry. I suppose things have been busy." It was a gentle let down. I swallowed and set the bannock down for someone else and swigged the rest of my tea before steeling myself.

"Cadeyrn. If there's nothing left between us, then I should give this back to you." I pulled the ring from my finger and placed it in his hand, folding his fingers over it.

"Keep it," he said. I smiled sadly at him.

"I only wanted it for one reason."

"What was that?" he asked quietly.

"To be yours." I walked away before I could say or do else.

CHAPTER 14

Neysa

Today, I would play queen. Today, I would sit beside Ewan in his crown, and I would pretend for the life of me that I was running the show. Today, I would fight like the warrior queen I had to become. Ewan and I lounged in our ostentatious chairs on the field that was laid out with clear and rose quartz outlining the shape of an *adairch dorhdj*. Two thrones borrowed from stately homes. I hadn't seen Reynard in days, yet he sat along the length of my armchair, perched like an elegant cat. We drank wine and called Cadeyrn and the others over. Full fighting leathers completed my get-up with a touch of dark lip stain. Once everyone had been brought down, Cyrranus showed up with Bestía. Cade looked confused and stood before our makeshift dais.

"What is the meaning of this?" he asked.

"Of what?" Ewan asked back with an air of innocence.

"Why have you brought her here?" Cade asked.

I stood, wine in one hand, and came very close to him. "I want to have fun, and we can all spar together and drink wine."

"Are you mad?" he asked me. Likely.

"So, question is. Who fights first? I know. You and Bestía. Silas and me."

"It's a trick. She is going to try to kill me, Cadeyrn," Bestía said.

"Oh, please. Were I to want to kill you outright, you'd be dead. Isn't that right?" I smiled, sick and saccharine. "Let's go. All of us in the ring." I grabbed Silas by his jacket and pulled him along. Cade looked so pissed I nearly laughed. Cadeyrn and Bestía squared off and began to dance around each other—strike and parry, block and thrust. He removed his jacket, the heat getting the better of him. My mouth went dry looking at his chest and back. Wine did not help in this heat. Removing my own jacket and Silas doing the same, we began our own waltz. I was distracted but didn't care much. I wasn't trying to win against Silas. That wasn't the point of this. He managed to get behind me and wrap an arm about my sweat-soaked abdomen and the other held his sword near me. Our bodies were pressed together, sweat slick and panting. I looked at Cadeyrn sweating and caught his eye. Bestía took advantage of his distraction and cut his arm. I hissed and she smiled. Though Silas kept me in check, I stared at Cade. Between the press of Silas and looking at Cade, warmth built in me.

"Do you yield or shall I have you on your back again, Princess?" Silas purred. I moved my free hand up his thigh in answer.

Cadeyrn. I kept trying to reach him. I gave myself over to the warmth building in me from watching him, Silas near me, and I projected that to Cade. *Watch me.* My hand clenched on Silas' thigh. I could feel him pressed against me, his heart racing, though outwardly, Silas remained unruffled.

In two moves Cade had Bestía down and disarmed. Cyrranus and the other guards kept her there. Cadeyrn looked to

Silas and me. I wrapped my leg around my friend and spun in his sweat-soaked arm, then pushed us both down. I sat on top of him and pressed into his chest. Cadeyrn's eyes were on us, I could feel them. The heat was oppressive.

"Do you yield?" I asked Silas, my mouth just above his.

"Whenever you want me to. Shall we do it here?" He cocked an eyebrow at me. I stood and bowed before Cadeyrn.

"Ready?"

"You can't be serious?" he asked. I pushed my lower lip out in a pout.

"Why not? Let's dance."

He moved so fast I didn't see it at all. His sword lay across my chest, his other arm holding a dagger to my throat as I faced him. Hmm. I looked him in the eye and smiled.

You could just take me here.

He shook his head as if to dislodge a fly. His dagger dropped a fraction, and I knocked it away with my elbow, earning a smarting cut, then kicked him backwards. As he stumbled, his hand darted for my arm and pulled me to him. I pushed as hard as I could and knocked him down. My knees were on either side of him, hands on his chest, my thin dagger out. A wicked gleam came into his eyes, and a smile spread across his face. Uh oh. I shoved down harder and pressed myself into his body, my face inches from his. I felt a response in him and a rumble. He flipped me over and had a knee pinning down one of my legs, his mouth latched onto my neck like a wild animal, teeth slowly puncturing the skin. I didn't know what to do. My arms were pinned above my head; his breadth of power poured into me.

Kill me then. I felt a bite that instantly healed, and he slowly slid from me, coming to kneel beside my heaving form.

I knew you'd pull away. Eventually. His head snapped to look at me, my hand shading my eyes from the sun.

"What does that mean?" he asked me. So slowly, I turned to him.

Can you hear me? He gave one curt nod. I couldn't breathe. *I made you cookies.* Holy shit, Neysa, really? That was what you chose to say? *Even though you've been horrible to me.* A smile ghosted his lips.

"Cadeyrn," Bestía called. His head shot up and looked to her. He started to stand. I grabbed his arm, and he tried to yank it away, so I tackled him. Full on, ungraceful, Texas Friday Night Lights-style, headfirst, tackle.

"Now, Ewan!" I screamed. Chanting and a childlike voice rose above the din of onlookers. The crystals surrounding us glowed in the morning light, casting beams of pinkish light between us and Bestía. I hoped I was correct in assuming she had been dead and come back, just as Feynser had. The necromancer was there to unravel the tethers holding Bestía to this realm. What a fate to contend with as a child.

I wrestled with Cadeyrn, who had a solid upper hand, then brought my own mouth onto his neck and bit down with just enough pressure to show I was serious, but not enough to break skin. We were godsdamned fae, and I would claim my mate. I pushed at his arm and set my hand on his stomach. Heat rose between us. The chanting and child singsong voice got louder. Cadeyrn's hands went into my hair, and I still grappled for him, driving my knees into his inner thighs. He took my face and crushed his mouth against mine so hard, my teeth sang. His kiss was nothing I had experienced before. It was animalistic and closer to feeding than desire. As though his very life depended on that kiss. Teeth caught on my lips and tongue. Blood slithered in my mouth. Both his and mine, mingling. I couldn't see or think as I was lifted off the ground and carried away. I knew Silas followed close behind, and Cadeyrn pulled from my mouth to snarl at him loud enough to make the tents shake.

A wall of flame, courtesy of Cadeyrn's gifts, blocked us off from the onlookers, and an avenue in the middle of blue flames opened for us as we rushed along. His hands clawed under my vest and tore at my skin. I dragged my nails down and over every inch of skin I could find purchase. We were covered in each other's blood and sweat and everything came alive in me. Into his tent we crashed and dropped to the ground in a heated tangle. Distantly, there was a screech, and I knew Bestía was succumbing to the necromancer. Cadeyrn tore open my vest and his hands were all over me. We pushed out of our trousers and paused for the slightest second, both crazed and shaking. I launched myself on him and pulled him on top of me. I raised my hips until he was fully sheathed, his growl turning everything in me molten. I went over before I was ready for it to be done. He slowed and brought his lips to my ear, touching the pointed tips with his tongue, then whispered, "I remember all of it now." He slammed his mouth and body into mine again and thundered a moan that reverberated off every tent, wagon, and structure in the vicinity. The beast and Battle King staking his claim.

We were a mess. As much as I knew we had to go back out there and deal with Bestía and the necromancer, I wanted to stay and lick each other's wounds until they healed. Entranced, I watched some of the gashes I caused on Cadeyrn's chest knit back together, leaving just a smear of blood behind. He ran fingers and mouth over my own scratches and gouges, healing them. His long fingers touched the scar from Analisse and ran a trail up the length of it. His skin became hot to the touch, his jaw ticked.

"I couldn't even heal you?" A low, sandpaper rasp of a question. I turned, not knowing if I could even have this conversation. The crystals of my necklace fell to the side of my neck when I shrugged and looked away. He lifted and straightened them across my chest.

I still loved you, I told him. *Every second I watched you not feeling anything for me. Watched you with her. It was cruel. I thought...I thought that surely you could feel me. Feel something for me.* I looked up, the tent ceiling rippling with refracted light. *With or without the bond I thought you'd still at least know me. Want me.* I hated admitting that. That I missed being wanted. *But everything was gone.* I kept talking, his catching breaths the only other sounds.

You didn't feel. Is it... is it just chemical for you? Just a preordained animal need? I asked, still staring away. Because if that was all it was, that was not how I wanted to go on.

I think...that's what she intended it to feel like. So you would always question it. He was able to respond to me again, and he gently turned me to face him.

"All my memories of us were gone," he spoke aloud. "It was like you were just this person who appeared with my cousins. I knew we were supposed to have been mated, and I didn't understand it, because I didn't know you. There were times I would start to...feel something. When I walked into Silas' tent and smelled your blood. On the beach, I wasn't sure what had hit me. When you gave me back the ring, in my head I knew I shouldn't feel anything, but something inside was screaming at me to pull you back, to say something. So, no, it is not just some preordained notion.

"It is a deep, fucking, soul-ending love I have for you." His hand raked through his hair. "Even though the strongest magics were used to tamp down our bonds and feelings—my feelings. I felt myself falling for you over and over again anyway."

I refused to cry. Of course, that meant I had to keep my damned mouth shut. Screams and wails were coming in a constant wave from outside. We really should get out there.

"Say something," he begged me. I turned to look at him. He knelt next to me, fully exposed, head lowered like a weeping angel.

"What flipped the switch finally?" There was a cold note to my voice. I knew it hurt him, but I had tried these past weeks to build a shell around myself in order to survive. He reached forward and touched my stomach.

"When I had you pinned down," he murmured, embarrassed. "I could hear every beat of your heart and heard you speak to me. Then...you said you knew I'd pull away. It was like a bucket of water was thrown on me. Something started screaming at me. So, really just you. You 'flipped the switch,' as you say."

A particularly loud and awful screech sounded. We both sat up and gathered our clothes. Leather pants were horrendously difficult to put on over sweaty legs, but duty called.

"GOOD OF you to join us," Silas yelled over the screaming of the dead who answered to the Fesaeran demon. His chuckle resounded through the high-pitched chanting of a child no one could see. For a split second, I was rooted to the spot, taking in the scene. All over the field, coming up to just beyond the crystals, were reanimated bodies trying to surround Bestía and bolster her reserves. A veritable generator of life from which Bestía was syphoning energy. She knelt with arms flung wide, eyes bleeding, arrested in a state of suspended animation. *You were right,* Ewan said to me, and I heard him. Which meant my magic was fully back.

"I usually am," I yelled back to him smugly. He grinned and tossed me my sword. I spun it gratuitously, making Cadeyrn roll his eyes.

Every now and again, one of the dead would break through the line and one of us would sever head from body. Bestía's platinum hair had turned white and wispy. I walked to her.

"Neysa," Cadeyrn and Ewan both growled.

"Face the one who fears you. Be the one who holds you. Embrace that which seems foreign. Speak as though you can be heard. Find those who dance to your song," I said to both of them in our minds. Darkness was as much a part of me as the light I harbored. From the day I was taken from my mother and brother, I had a heady, nearly impermeable darkness in me. It fed my drive, my soul. It kept me from breaking. I would not apologize for my darkness. I would stroke it and listen to it. I would never again allow myself to be vulnerable to someone or something like Analisse or Bestía. Perhaps that did make me a monster. I stood before the female who had stripped my magic, my light, and my love from me, and gave myself over to my creature tendency. I was fae, not human. I was beast. *Baethaache.* Where was my beastie? I cocked my head to Bestía and knew my eyes cast a yellow glow. Wolves slunk from the tree line and surrounded the field. The onlookers and soldiers were gasping. I commanded the wolves to take down the dead. And they obeyed. Crunching, screeching, wet, ripping sounds drowned any voices as the wolves met with the dead. Splinters of loss hit me from my charges who were killed. In mere moments, however, the corpses were felled. Konstantín and his mystics stepped toward me.

"How long ago was she dead before she came back?" I asked them. In unison, the mystics answered.

"Four cycles of the moon, daughter of the between." That was an interesting answer.

Bestía smiled, blood pouring from her eyes and nose.

"I had him. I nearly freed him from you. Who would want that crown of darkness you possess?" she cooed in a lilting, spun sugar voice.

"Is the necromancer nearly finished unravelling her spells?" I asked. The mystics looked to one another in silent conversation. Good grief, they were unsettling.

"It is done. She is ready to be finished, she who is held in darkness," they sang. Ewan stepped to me, Cadeyrn on my other side, Silas at my back, a host of lupine subjects in the field behind us.

Find those who dance to your song.

My brother, my mate, my Silas, my wolves. They were all my darkness and salvation. Together we would pull ourselves from the catacombs of what we had endured. Together we would forge a new light. Not to drive out our darkness, but to illuminate different paths through. I angled my sword to take out the female who nearly destroyed everything. Part of me hated Cadeyrn for letting her. I knew he was spellbound, but it hurt me.

"So, she is ready to be put down?" Cadeyrn asked all of us.

The mystics all bowed.

"Battle King," they sang. "Consort to the one held by the Goddess of Aulde."

My skin crawled at their deference and implication. Without a moment's delay, Cadeyrn lunged forward and severed Bestía's head from her body and set the corpse aflame in blue fire. Silas sent a wind to scatter the ash. I gasped for air as the last dregs of her spell fled.

The necromancer stopped. I felt the child leave, relief washing over me that the cloaking of the child necromancer worked. No need to destroy another life. Cadeyrn set fire to all the dead who lay across the field, his vast power finding an outlet. My wolves kept at a distance yet held me in their sights. Cadeyrn walked toward them, his weapons sheathed, and he knelt before the line, bowing his head to my charges. They sunk down to their haunches in return. It was an eerie sight to behold; in this field, on this morning, all of my world and particles had come together.

In turning, I saw the seven mystics facing me, each holding out an item. I walked to them. As each handed her item to me, she bowed. A magic coated bean or seed, a wand of selenite, quartz, pyrite, a seed pearl, a gold thread, and a polished red stone like garnet or ruby.

"Daughter of darkness and light. Paladin of the Veil. Queen of *Taeoide Gaellte* and *Aedtine Aimschire*. We honor you and beseech your assistance in the lands beyond the sea. Come to us, across the waves. We will be waiting." Just as they spoke in unison, they turned and walked away. Konstantín looked to me and sunk to a knee.

WE TOOK council once more at the home in which we had met only yesterday. It could have been a lifetime ago. Though we knew the main players and had dealt with them, we had not figured out some of the supporting roles and who held them. Bestía had indeed been killed in the final battle against The Elders. She had been a double agent so to speak for Paschale, yet was working with Feynser and Analisse, eradicating The Elders for their own gain. Who had brought her back, we still did not know. We assumed their ultimate goal was to rule Aoifsing amongst themselves. Why Analisse promised to bring Ewan and me to Heilig was still a mystery. None of us were naive enough to trust Konstantín at his word, however genuine he appeared. I believed the threat against his family—my family—was real, and against it, he sought our help. How closely knit his ambitions were to Analisse's, however, was yet to be determined. I felt so very tired. In five days' time, we would set sail for Heilig. I hated leaving without Ewan and Corra, yet I knew it was the best and safest option. Who I was and had been were spinning around each other like cars on black ice. I left the house, seeking the sea, and stopped to watch a family playing along a beach.

"I want you to know that I am incredibly creeped out by those mystics and the shit they said to you." Corra came up alongside of me and threaded her arm through mine. "However, if it makes you feel any better, I knew you were the heir of Heícate, the Goddess of Aulde, long before today. And it didn't scare me. Even being the goddess of darkness and magic. The mystics, though..." She shuddered.

I laughed, but a loud sob tore through me as well.

"Oh, darling. I know. This has been too much." She pulled her arm from mine and wrapped it around my side.

"Who am I, Corra? That answer has changed six times in the last year. How can I be anything to anyone without knowing who I am?"

"Look at me," she said in the authoritative voice she used on her brother and cousin. "That answer has not changed even once. Only the accessories have changed. You are Neysa. You are your mother's daughter, making you a princess. You are your father's daughter, giving you life and light. You are heir to the goddess of magic and darkness. That's fabulous, by the way. You are Cadeyrn's mate and queen and lover and friend. His world. You are Ewan's sister, and my friend, which is by far the most important." I laughed through my ugly crying. "You are everything to Silas, which is sometimes an issue and may need revisiting. But I feel that you both need one another to traverse this world and the next. None of these things changes *who* you are. Now, go stare at the ocean or whatever it is you lot do. But do be careful of sharks; I watched this documentary on them for a week straight. Ugh. Or, here's an idea. Do everyone a favour and lock yourself away with your mate until you two cannot walk."

"In case you didn't know," I told her, "I love you, Corra. You're quite good at this helping me get my shit together stuff."

"I know. What do you think I've been doing for the lads these past three centuries?" She walked off, her hand upon her tiny, rounded belly.

I sunk down into the shell-covered strand and opened my palm. In it was a seed pearl, given to me by the first mystic. An offering to the Protector of *Verraige*. The sea. Perhaps I was asking for safe passage. Perhaps I was giving thanks for the gift of knowing I could breathe near the ocean. Whatever the case may be, I let the lapping water lick the pearl from my hand and swallow it into the depths of *Verraige*.

Shells crunched behind me. One by one, they will come, I thought to myself with a smile. It was the beginning of a children's story my father used to read me. I couldn't remember the tale itself.

"*Trubaíste*," Silas said. I looked up at him and smiled. "Quite a day."

I stood and hugged him fiercely. He laughed and hugged me back, his scent wrapping about me.

"The cookies we made are in the room. I could get them."

"Promise me something, Silas," I said into his chest, breathing in his woodsmoke scent.

"Anything," he answered, voice gruff.

"That you will always believe in me. Because you have the clearest soul and biggest heart of anyone I've ever met in either realm, and if you believe in me, I know I stand a chance."

"Your mate will always believe in you," he said carefully.

"Silas."

"Of course I will always believe in you, *allaíne Trubaíste*." He kissed the top of my head.

"Corra thinks that, for whatever reason, you and I need each other. Do you believe that? I think we both know I need you. I would have fallen off a cliff of my own making a million times had it not been for you. Do you feel like you need me?"

"Like the air I breathe." His voice was hushed and could have been carried away in the waves. "Your mate is waiting for you. Better hurry, lest I steal you away into the forest and keep you for my bride." I smiled at him and reached up to press a quick kiss on his cheek. "Och, you stink!"

He made a face and waved a hand in front of his nose. I sniffed myself.

"Remember when Corraidhín said you and my cousin were like penguins?" he asked. I did. Before we left for the Isle, she said she saw a documentary on animals who mate for life, and Cadeyrn and I were like badgers and penguins. Silas leaned in and winked at me.

"The penguins are back."

CHAPTER 15

C obbled streets drank in the late afternoon sun as I made my way through town. At first glance, it was a small fishing village, but the further I walked, I realized it must be a resort town. Many shops, cafes, taverns, and boat rentals lined the shore. It could almost be human, but for the way colours danced in dizzying arrays, the spectacles the flowers put on, and the fae I encountered who were equally beautiful and fearsome. I was raised to see people for who they were and appreciate cultures and colours for the beauty in our individuality. In Aoifsing, I saw it as no different. Were we any less lovely because we had pointed ears or elongated canines? Decidedly not. Going back to that inn on the other side of town was what I was supposed to do. What I needed at the moment was to wander. To think without being injured, or scheming or... Christ, I hadn't eaten today. No wonder my leathers were loose. Weeks of anything I ate tasting like dust from the crushing despair had kept me from holding onto any weight.

Polished wood columns and wide shutters opened to the street of the inn I procured on this side of the seaside town. Balconies hung over the water and dripped with climbing vines releasing the intoxicating scent of jasmine. Luxurious and simple in its decor and feeling, it felt like the kind of hidden gem one might find in the Caribbean. Next to the inn was a dressmakers. I ended up purchasing four dresses and sandals. In my head, I was pretending to be on holiday. A careless tourist, spending coin and decompressing. By the time I had eaten my third pastry and bathed, having changed into one of my new dresses, the town's folk were whispering that I was here and patronizing businesses. Everything in my body ached to be by the sea, so even the restaurant in which I chose to eat had tables on the edge of the rocky shore.

Only a tickle of a breeze moved across me as I sat sipping a sparkling rosé, while picking at a breadbasket. The breeze felt heavenly on my bare shoulders. Ribbon-like straps held up my dress, meeting at the fitted bodice, which contoured my torso until it hit at the hips and dropped to the ground with open sides, allowing ventilation in the warm, Maesarra air. Black silk looked dramatic, yet the dress seemed to call to me. I had scooped my hair into a topknot, secured with pins, and still wore the two necklaces.

It wasn't that I was avoiding Cadeyrn, though it may have seemed that way. I needed to be on my own for a bit and not be in a war camp or a palace under siege or on a quest. These last few hours were likely the only time I would have to do this for a long while. Sailing for Heilig was not something I wanted to do. In fact, the thought angered and exhausted me. I wanted to just be for a while. Wanted to figure out what being me was. Especially in this place. As that thought presented itself to me, I realized I did want Cadeyrn to be a part of this discovery process. Admitting to myself that I hadn't been entirely sure after the days' events made my stomach clench in consternation. Really, I was a mess of confusion and self doubt. He was my mate. Even when the bond was stripped and he didn't know me, I felt him. I always felt him and knew. So, after keeping my thoughts closed off all day, I sat back at my little table by the sea and opened them back up, reaching out to find him.

There was a restaurant in Malibu that everyone used to go to, I said to him. It was a touristy place with buckets of shrimp and slices of pie the size of my head. An awakening, softly amused acknowledgment of my words came across. It was where people in L.A. took out-of-town guests because it was on the ocean and all that. My dad and I had another little place we liked to go a little farther north. It was less crowded, and I think it was really only patronized by the people who lived in the vicinity, because it was tucked kind of behind houses and hung over the Pacific. It felt a little bit like the cafes in the South of France.

It sounds lovely. His response had a smile in the tone, though his voice was rough.

We would go often, and they knew us there, I continued. *It was the first place I went after my divorce. They didn't say anything to me but gave me a small slice of chocolate mousse cake. Then Dad died, and I went there again. They gave me that cake again. Well, I assume it was a different cake, but the same type, you see. I realized after that, ever since I was little, whenever Dad or I had a rough day when we were in California, that's when we would go there. And so often, Dad ordered the chocolate mousse cake. He likely had quite a few rough days. So, intermittently, for twenty-five years or so, this little place north of Malibu was where Dad would take us when things got heavy.*

Did you go there when you went back to fetch the amethyst dagger? Cadeyrn asked.

No. I just got tacos. A soft chuckle came through. *Because all I wanted at the time was to get home to you lot in England. The only thing that really weighed heavy on me was who I am or was becoming and how you fit in that picture.* Silence. Then a rough answer.

And all I have given you are more weighted questions.

Do you have questions for me? I asked, thinking he may question the ruse with Silas.

Only if you want to answer them. I am certain I have many to answer for you.

Would you have dinner with me? I showed him where I was, further opening up the link.

Give me a few more minutes. I'm finishing up here. He showed me what he was doing. A group of ten or so children stood around him in a courtyard while he showed them how to properly hold and swing a sword. Their eyes were bright, and they were soaking in being given lessons by Cadeyrn. I missed seeing that softness in him.

Take your time. I'll be here.

PACING MYSELF on the wine while I sat waiting was a bit of a problem. Staring at the sea, piercing my second sight into the depths, spun me away from this picturesque town, and I saw the colours below the surface and could feel the varying pockets of warmth and cold. Felt the soft cloud of sand on the sea floor and the ripples from the bump of waves. As though I were swimming for the surface, I pulled up from the sea to growing warmth around me. Cadeyrn stood a few feet from the table, watching me. He had changed from what I had seen him wearing. He was now clad in a simple white shirt with his sleeves rolled up in the heat, and black trousers shoved into boots. I smiled at him in the coral-tinged light of sunset, and he sat in the chair across from me. Everywhere his eyes hit on me I felt a trail of warmth and a whisper of his rainlike scent as though it were a scarf being teased over my skin. After a time, his eyes found mine.

"You are so beautiful," he said finally.

"Having a bath and fresh clothing makes a difference."

"It doesn't matter what you're wearing."

I looked down at the table and fiddled with my glass. A server came over and bowed to Cadeyrn, filling a glass for him. I had ordered a plethora of dishes, from pasta covered in shellfish to mussels in a lemongrass broth. We ate until near bursting. Though our conversation wasn't deep or meaningful, we chatted about little things, and I realized these were more of those small moments I craved.

The dishes were cleared, another bottle brought out.

"I heard your singing in the tent. I sat outside for quite some time, thinking you must be a siren and that's why I kept getting pulled to you even though I didn't know you. How ridiculous is that?" His eyes were so wide, and his mouth was quirked comically. I laughed.

"With my voice? Especially last night? I'm the worst siren ever. Lure unsuspecting warriors with my scratchy emo rock songs."

He snickered and finished his glass.

"Smelling the amount of blood that came out of that tent had me in a blind rage."

"Yes," I drawled, wine easing my nerves. "'What is going on?'" I teased, mocking his voice and accent with those words. "Holy smokes. You kept asking that over and over. Drove me mad."

"I was a lost puppy. I truly had no idea what was going on." He smothered his own laugh. "It feels so stupid now. I feel so stupid." He scrubbed at his face.

"You were violated," I said seriously. Though for some sick reason, I just burst out laughing. Horrified, I covered my mouth with my hands and ducked my head into my napkin but still laughed hysterically. The table shook a bit, and I looked up to see him laughing.

"I'm sorry. This is so inappropriate." It took me three times to say that, my eyes streaming tears from giggling. His mouth was trembling at the corners, and his face was flushed from laughing so hard. I took a deep breath, attempting to quell the outburst, then sipped my wine, but it ripped from me again and I sprayed the wine across the table, narrowly missing Cadeyrn.

"It's like an affliction," I gasped, my cheeks hurting. I hadn't laughed in months. Not really.

Our server brought a third bottle of wine out and set it down saying it was on the house. He also set down a small silver bowl of chocolate mousse.

"They didn't have mousse cake," Cadeyrn explained, sobering slightly from our fit.

"Chocolate mousse is actually my favourite dessert. In Paris, I would order one in every single restaurant. I gained like ten pounds every trip."

"I want to know everything about you." He looked to me, still flushed. "If that's okay with you? I want to know your favourite foods and scents and songs. Everything you think is important and likely what you find trivial."

"And will you tell me about yourself?" I asked, raising an eyebrow.

"Anything you want to know." We both sat back and sipped from our fresh glasses of wine. I wasn't ready to spoil the mood with questions about the past few weeks.

"I miss music," I said, looking out at the calm water. "I never realized what a big part of my life it is. I always used to have it on at home. Dad and I used to play it all the time growing up. I went to concerts regularly. L.A. has all these small theaters where bands played, and I liked doing that. There were three or four bands I saw every time they toured. So, while I don't necessarily miss doing that—they were all good memories. Well, not all, but most."

I thought of the night I had gone alone to a show because Caleb was busy. He ended up following me and made a scene outside of the El Rey theater. The worst part was, that as embarrassing as it was that he caused so much drama, he had actually come with a girlfriend. I had enough wine in me now to where I wasn't sure if I had projected that memory. From the look on Cadeyrn's face, I suspected so.

"Anyway, what I miss is the music itself."

A group of fae walked by, dressed up and happy. Males and females, heading out for the night. They smiled at us and continued down the boulevard. I wondered where they were going.

There are taverns and nightclub-like places that way. We could go if you want, he offered.

In a little while. I'm happy sitting here for now. A breeze blew in, cooling my sun-warmed skin. I closed my eyes and let it flow over me. The sun was nearly set, the world darkening slightly. The past month I had spent dreading the darkness. I hated being in my tent or in the wagon, not knowing where Cadeyrn was or what he was doing. The worst part was knowing he had not cared where I was. It took me a minute to restructure my feelings on the oncoming dark. When I opened my eyes again and took in the soft lights twinkling on the bay, the townsfolk coming out to dine or dance, the warm lights in windows, the male before me, there was a shift. Like the darkness inside me, the night was nothing to fear anymore.

"You figured out the riddle the mystics told you. May I ask how?"

I sat forward and looked at his face in the dying light.

"It wasn't exact. I kind of guessed and took chances. 'Face the one who fears you.' I figured it was Bestía. After all, I was the only one who could bring an end to her. 'Be the one who holds you,' I had to keep it together. Myself. Keep myself together. If I didn't think objectively, and it was hard, nothing would change. 'Embrace that which seems foreign.' Using my lupinus gifts. It was the only power that remained in me." I mused over that to myself for a moment. Perhaps my lupinus gift was a link to both realms. A power existing within me which kept me toeing the line of the fae and human realms. I pulled my eyes from where they looked down at fidgeting fingers.

"Plus," I continued, "we had decided as a group that Silas and I would... pretend. I hadn't wanted to, but Corra told me it was time to be queen and protect my king. So I had to use my knights." I smiled a little.

He did as well but looked unsettled. I continued.

"The next one was easy. 'Speak as though you can be heard.' I kept trying to talk to you. In my mind or in person. I just kept trying. For so long it had been like speaking in a vacuum, but I kept trying. 'Find those who dance to your song.' I have my fair share of darkness in me, Cadeyrn. I know that. It makes me volatile and emotional. It protects me. Ewan has it too. Perhaps we all do. When I looked at us standing there in that field, I knew Silas accepted my darkness, and I hoped you would too. So, I used that hope and knowledge and I just went for it." My voice was a little raw. It had been such a long day, and I was fully drunk. Yet I didn't want this to end.

"You did well." We were silent. My head buzzed, and my limbs felt liquid. "When we were younger, Silas, Magnus, and

I used to go out to the clubs. It's not too different than in the human realm. We..." He paused and coughed a laugh, giving me a sidelong glance. "We were quite a trio. I think that's why Magnus tried to get me to be that male again when you were gone. We drank until we were sick—which is saying something. We can handle our alcohol fairly well. We had companionship. It was next-level debauchery."

He rolled his eyes gloriously. I gave him a look that said I wasn't surprised. By God, he was something to look at.

"There was this one night." He ran his hand through his hair, then grabbed at the back of his neck and looked to me. I bit my lip. "I have no idea how much we drank. Gods. Magnus got this idea—he was always shit stirring—to replace the musicians. I don't play anything. Silas really doesn't either. He was schooled on the viola, yet all he really did was cause the livestock to run."

I laughed.

"So, we got up into the little box where the musicians play, and handed them our drinks, telling them to take a walk."

"What did you play?" I leaned forward, chin on my hands.

"This instrument called a síarnan. It's similar to a guitar but plays deeply like a bass, and you keep beat on a skin on the back like a drum. It's well complicated, and I was horribly drunk. We did a whole set of shit music like that until we were kicked out. For whatever reason, a whole gaggle of folk followed us—males and females fighting for our attention. It turned into a full-on brawl because males and females were upset that their partners wanted to come home with us. Turns out, Magnus took some half-cocked love potion he stole from Lina and put it in our drinks. It took us all night to lose the following."

I was laughing openly. "I'm quite sure you would have had some offers regardless."

"Not with how poorly we played," he laughed.

"Let's go find one of those clubs," I said. We paid for the meal and took to the streets, following some of the folk along the boulevard. A block or so after the restaurant, Cadeyrn's fingers brushed mine in question. I walked a little closer to him, feeling my blood spike, and touched his fingers back. He laced his long, calloused, beautiful fingers through mine. Holy God, just his hand in mine made me dizzy.

The interior of the club was dark with small fae lights bobbing from the ceiling and in corners. Instruments played songs that were upbeat and entrancing. I smiled, bright and happy for Cadeyrn. He answered mine with one of his own, and I swear my heart stopped completely. Not that we needed any more, but he left to get drinks. Others were on the dance floor, and I joined in, moving to the music. I had to pick up my skirts so they wouldn't get stepped on, and tied the sides in a knot, exposing my legs. Cadeyrn stood at a table, watching me dance.

Come here, I said to him.

I rather like watching you. I am not the only one, either. I laughed aloud because just as he said that, a female came up to him and placed her hand on his arm.

"You have beautiful eyes!" she yelled over the music and din of voices. He smirked.

"That's what my mate tells me." He pointed to me. She pressed her lips together in embarrassment and mouthed an "I'm sorry" to me. I waved a "no big deal" and kept dancing, moving with the crowd across the floor. I lost sight of Cadeyrn as the crowd shifted, and then I was on the opposite side of the room. My skin was getting sticky with sweat from dancing. I found him again; he was still standing against the high table with untouched drinks. A lazy smile greeted me, and he blew slightly, sending icy wind at my neck and chest. I moaned a bit.

"What do you want to do?" I yelled over the music. Though there was no stereo or DJ, the music was loud and permeated the establishment just as much as any human club. He shook his head. I stepped closer to him, instantly wishing we were somewhere more private. Instead, I wrapped my arms about him and pulled him to dance. We moved to the music and let it hold us in its trance for a few songs. He leaned into me and took my hand.

"I didn't do anything with her," he yelled. He knew I knew who he meant. "She was persistent. Called me 'lover.' I didn't do anything. I want you to know."

I pressed my head to his and nodded. He caught my bottom lip in his and pulled at it.

"I know how it looked with Silas," I said. "I know you saw us kiss. It was to try..." I smoothed at his collar and ran my hands along his broad shoulders. "To wake you up."

His eyes found mine, amused.

"It worked."

We made it about half of a block after leaving the club before I pushed him against the wall of a building and kissed him senseless. My skirts were still tied up, and the heat around us was near suffocating. I drew back and gulped down air. He was breathing hard and exhaled theatrically.

"Wait. Before we go any further. I have a confession," he told me. My hands stilled on him. "I hope that tray of biscuits was for me, because I ate the whole thing." I yanked him to me and fastened my lips to his, walking backward towards my inn. An inn further from the others. We backed into the doorway and pulled apart, as a couple exited, chuckling.

"This isn't even our inn," Cadeyrn said, making to turn. Pulling a key from the folds of my dress, I grabbed him and pulled him further in the building and up to our room. He marveled at the room that hung over the water. The dark wood floors and white linens matched the woodwork and jasmine on the balcony. A fountain bubbled in the corner of the room, and the breeze danced through the curtained windows.

"Nicer than the other, I thought." He walked to me slowly. I drank in his powerful body and the way it shifted as he moved. Heavy-lidded mountain stream eyes raked over me as he moved closer still. "My favourite song is about a letter being written to a lover saying he wished she could have been the one—thought she was the girl he'd always dreamed about, but the make believe ran out," I told him, swirling my finger in his palm.

"That's... very depressing," he said.

I laughed.

"Yes, I told you I was dark. My favourite scent, apart from the ocean, is the smell of rain. Whether it's the way it smells coming down in winter and mingles with woodsmoke, or how it smells steaming from a thunderstorm in summer when the world needs to cool down. It smells like you."

He stepped closer still, standing just in front of me, and put his hands into my hair and pulled the pins holding the top knot. My hair fell, and his hands dove through it and ran down the length.

"Tell me more."

I closed my eyes, trying to think, and leaned into his hand on my cheek.

"When I was seventeen, I had a boyfriend who wasn't very nice to me. He wore this horrible cologne—something or other 'Noir,' and I will always associate it with him. That is my least favourite scent."

"Did he hurt you?"

"He pushed me once. I slammed an elbow into his face and kicked him in the chest, breaking a rib. So, no."

Cadeyrn chuckled. Fingers trailed over my collarbone and touched the crystals at my throat. He leaned down and kissed my shoulder. I brought my hand to the back of his head and twined my fingers in his dark hair.

"More. Please."

"I ran away from home once. Not to get away from my father. I felt bad about that. But I was sick of the kids in school. Sick of the boys who stared at my chest and made up stories and the girls who believed them. I was fifteen and looked older."

"How far did you get?" he asked, kissing my other shoulder and lifting the strap on my dress, simply running a finger under it.

"Spain." He snorted and had me confirm it. "We lived in England that year."

"Why Spain? Why not France, since you have a clear problem with chocolate mousse?"

"We had been on holiday in Spain the previous summer, and there was a boy who worked near the house we rented."

"Completely ridiculous," he said, smiling against my ear. "Who follows someone to another country?"

I whacked him.

"He had this black hair that fell into his bright blue eyes..."

"And did you find him?" Hands trailed down my back and along my waist, as his mouth moved along the side of my neck. I leaned my head back, giving him access to my throat.

"Yes. It took me forever to get to Barcelona. My flight connected in Brussels, which was dumb. Anyway, I looked like a bedraggled cuddly toy when I arrived. He said he didn't remember me and introduced me to his girlfriend."

"Ouch." Teeth scraped my throat. The memory of his teeth at my throat hours earlier had me arching to him. "What did you do?"

His heart was racing, and the colours of the room and the lights from outside were swirling in my vision.

"I called my dad to pick me up."

"From Spain." Not even a question.

"From Spain. He did. My swords were taken away for a month."

Cadeyrn laughed again, lifting both straps and pulling them slowly from my shoulders.

"Tell me about you," I said breathlessly, undoing the buttons of his shirt from the bottom up. Sea breeze blew in the balcony doors, momentarily cooling our heated skin.

"I trained Magnus on the sword," he began, undoing the tiny buttons on my back. "His and Lina's father died when they were very young, and I am maybe a hundred years older."

"Negligible age difference to be sure," I teased, bringing my hand round to his backside. He growled.

"So, I think, and I never found out for sure, but I think Silas put them up to this. We had been training for a few hours one day at their home outside of Laichmonde. I was a bit of a hard ass on Magnus." He drew a line down my arm and held my hand to his mouth.

"You? Can't imagine." He nipped my finger and promptly had it in his mouth. I gasped and pushed against him.

"Magnus was perhaps twelve or thirteen at the time. He asked me if I wanted to see his father's swords. He said his mother told them they could use them if they learned properly. So, I agreed and followed him to a woodshed at the edge of their property." He lifted the dress by the shoulders and pulled it off my arms, letting the silk swish over my arms as it laid me bare for him. I was thankful I had gotten new undergarments. He stopped talking for a moment and stared at me. I put a finger under his chin and lifted it, meeting his eyes, and nearly getting lost in them.

"Keep going," I whispered. His hands traced my new scar, and heat flared around us. Lace ties held my underwear together at the hips, and he looped a finger through the tie and cocked an eyebrow at me. "What was in the shed?" I asked, breathing so hard, spots were forming. His chest rose and fell as often.

"Swords. As he said. But there was another door, and Lina opened it and told me that inside it was the best one of all. So, like an idiot, I walked in. And they shut the door and barred it. It was a safe room of sorts."

I started laughing, my chest bouncing against his. "How long did it take for someone to find you?" I asked through giggles. He was laughing and brought his hands up to the lace bralette and removed it.

"Two days." He ran a thumb around the edge of my chest. I undid another button on his shirt.

"You must have been very hungry."

"Starved. Eventually, Corraidhín dragged Silas by the ear and had him let me out." Another button. I lifted the shirt open a bit more, running my thumb over the bumps of his abdominal muscles.

"Did they get in trouble with their mother?" I asked.

"No, no." He shot me a cat-with-a-canary grin. "I upped their training and made Lina join too. It was far worse a punishment. I don't think either has forgiven me."

I answered his grin with one of my own.

"I want to see you smile for as long as I live," he told me. I undid the last button and pulled his shirt off completely. On a silver chain around his neck hung my engagement ring. I touched it lightly. I hadn't seen him wear it earlier today.

"I cloaked it. When you gave it back to me. I told you it had felt wrong. So I wore it, but cloaked it so she wouldn't see."

I leaned my head against his chest and pressed a kiss to him, then smoothed my hands down his sides and wrapped my arms around him. He held me.

"What is your favourite anything?" I asked. He rumbled against me. "Apart from *that*?"

"The scent of crushed leaves in autumn when the sea air blows through the trees. That sounds a bit sad. The way your skin smells when you get out of a hot bath. Reading. The time to read and sit. Peanut butter cookies, thanks to you. Those pork dumplings you get in Hong Kong. The sea and everything about it." I nestled my head against him and ran my hand along the inside of his waistband. He traced circles on my lower back and pulled the tie from my underwear. I backed up and sat on the bed.

"You boots are still on," I said, low and gravely. As I blinked, they were off and in the corner. I sat up, stunned, and pushed at his trousers as he climbed over me. "However did you do that, mate?"

"Particle transference," he growled. He tugged open the other tie.

We moved together slowly, and I left strokes of electricity along his face as we rocked. He shuddered and had alternating blankets of warmth and cool mist laying over our bodies. Pushing up on my elbows, I kissed his eyelids and along his cheekbones. He held my face in his hands and kissed me, stopping all movement and just relishing in the kiss itself.

"I told you that no matter what happened, to know that I love you and you are my mate," he said, voice thick. "Never doubt that. I am sorry for what happened."

"It was... harder than I could handle. I thought I was tough and could keep going. I kept trying to be strong and hear you say to never doubt you. Yet... you didn't even know me. I couldn't even eat. Stupid girl, right?"

He ran a hand along my ribs and shook his head.

"Never stupid. Just... mine," he said softly. I staked claim to his lips and brought him further to me until there was nothing in the world but the two of us and the magic between us.

ONE DAY we would sit on a balcony and it would be ours. It would be where we settled or where we were for lengths of time. Above all, it would be where we chose to be. Sleep was so needed, but I felt panic at having this night end. This was how I wanted us to be. This was what we deserved to have together. When I first attempted to open up to Cadeyrn and let him in my mind to see the visions I initially had, I started by picturing myself sitting with him and telling him inconsequential bits and pieces from my life. As though I knew what I longed for. I had felt so much in those moments that it scared the hell out of us both. Here we were on the coast of Maesarra, pretending to be on holiday, and not awaiting a sea voyage to an unknown land. Our bodies were pressed in close, squeezing onto the chaise on the balcony, surrounded by jasmine. *We might need a beach house*, I thought with a yawn. A rumble of laughter jostled me.

"I wouldn't mind that," Cadeyrn answered. "You're tired. We can sleep."

"No." I said it too quickly.

"I won't go anywhere."

"I know. I just don't want this night to end." He pulled my hand from under the sheet that wrapped us together and held out the ring he removed from around his neck. I held out my finger and sniffed a restrained cry. The metal slid over my finger and settled in. My mate took my hand and kissed the knuckle above the ring.

"Let's not wait. On anything."

I turned in his arms and looked into those eyes.

"I'll need a dress."

He smiled against my mouth.

CHAPTER 16

Setting sail across an unknown ocean, for an unspecified task and an unspecified length of time, made me more than unsettled. This was not the honeymoon either of us would have chosen, and leaving behind Corra and Ewan made my heart ache. Silas swore that Turuin and Kaseik would defend, and that the forces gathered amassed to far over a million. He was confident enough in them that he felt comfortable leaving with us. Even still, the previous days passed far quicker than I would have liked.

The morning after the defeat of Bestía and her ill begotten army, Cadeyrn and I found the others and announced our plans to wed that day.

"You need a dress," was the first thing that came out of Corra's mouth. Cadeyrn rolled his eyes at us and murmured something like "she could stand there in a fishing net and still be beautiful." Corra splashed water in his face and told him he would acquiesce to every wish I would ever make because he caused hell for me for weeks.

"I'll do my best," he said, and flashed me a grin, dimpling.

Once the town caught wind of our planned nuptials, there was a bustle. The dressmaker I shopped with the previous day tracked me down and insisted she be the one who provided my dress. Children covered the sidewalks of the boulevard in flower petals, and local vintners scrambled over our wedding wines.

"And here I thought we were doing the equivalent of eloping and not making fuss," I grumbled as I was pulled away from discussing with Cyrranus whether he would be staying on with Ewan and Corra or whether he was planning to accompany us across the sea. Silas sauntered up behind us and poked me in the ribs.

"Did you truly mean to keep a low profile? In their eyes, royalty is marrying in their town. The bunting is stringing as we speak," he teased me.

"It seems like a lot of hoopla when there are so many pressing matters at hand."

"That, *Trubaíste*, is exactly why it should be celebrated. As you did for my cousin, you both are bringing light upon a dark time. They want to set up this hoopla, as you call it, though I have no idea what that means."

"Oh, you make pretty speeches too, my Silas." I nudged him with my shoulder. "Cyrranus was saying that he will stay on with Corra and Ewan."

Silas nodded.

"Gratitude, man," Silas said to the male. Cyrranus sketched a quick bow and left us. "I wonder, *Trubaíste*, should I do the same?"

I started to panic. He held up a finger and raised both eyebrows.

"Before you say anything, just listen."

I pressed my lips together and was breathing from my nose. He explained that there would be a time in the coming months that Corra would be more vulnerable, and Ewan would be preoccupied with her, his crown, and the new babes. Silas felt as though he may be of more help with them than he would be with us. Especially now that Cadeyrn and I would be wed. I loosed a breath and took his hand.

"I will support whichever decision you make. I see a definite advantage to your staying on. But, Silas," I continued though he was looking off a ways, "don't leave because of me. Especially since we don't know what we are facing. Who we are facing."

"Are you worried?" he asked.

"Listen. It seems to me that every time I turn around, something awful presents itself. By my count, each and every time that has happened since I came to meet you lot, you, Silas, have held me together. I am worried. I'm terrified."

He pulled his hand from mine and scrubbed at his stubbled face, then looked at me sidelong. The weight of that gaze, his measured countenance, had me fidgeting.

"So, you are asking me to stay? With you?" Yes. No. Ugh.

"I'm asking you to consider both options. Perhaps with a little bit of sympathy for my tendency to attract trouble." I wasn't being fair, and I said as much. He laughed but it was forced. Those glass green eyes narrowed at me, and he began tapping his booted foot. My heart matched the beat, waiting for his response.

"You are aware that I could never deny you?" I wasn't, but now I felt really guilty. "I told Cadeyrn. You two will certainly be the death of me."

"You don't have to answer right now. Think it over. Speak to Cadeyrn and Corra." He agreed, and we walked together to the inn so I could get ready. I stopped short outside the doors to the inn and turned to Silas.

"It's tradition in the human realm for the bride's father to give her away to the groom. Would you.... Can I ask for you to do that? For me?" His mouth popped open in a little *O*, voice rough with emotion when he answered.

"It would be my honor, Neysa." I hugged him tightly, and in touching his jacket, a vision swam into my head. It was of Cadeyrn, telling Silas that if it was my choice, and I did not wish to take him back, he would not stand in the way of Silas and me being together. I gasped for air, pulling from the vision.

"*Trubaiste?*" Silas asked me, worry clouding his face. "A vision?" I nodded. "Anything I should know?"

I kissed his stubbled cheek and made for the door. "Only that you and Cadeyrn are hands down the most admirable, true-hearted, and beautiful males ever." I had to walk away before he saw the tears coming down my face.

Is everything okay, Neysa? Cadeyrn's voice.

I believe so. I want you to know that I love everything about you.
Silence.

That's oddly cryptic; but okay. May I mirror the sentiment?
I'll see you in a little bit.

I WORE white for my marriage to Caleb. My father was unimpressed by my choice of fiancé from the beginning, and even so much as asked me if I was quite certain of marrying Caleb just as we were about to walk down the aisle. Doubt made my knees weak the entire walk.

This time around, with my mate and the surety of what I was going through with, not only did I choose to forgo the aisle bit—it wasn't a custom here anyway—I wore a dress that was the colour of candlelight, embroidered with gold. The shoulders had capped tiny sleeves made entirely of dripping gold and silver beads and crystals. The beading travelled across the chest and dove down into the gathered satin of the bodice. The silk satin dress skimmed across my midsection and dropped to a puddling mermaid train befitting of the seaside venue. Ama curled my hair and left it half down, fastening in combs and barrettes that gave the illusion of being a chandelier in an art nouveau French nightclub. In a last-minute decision, I pulled the ostentatious diaspore earbobs from the satchel I carried everywhere. When I was taken in Cappadocia, they were in the pocket of my dressing gown. Somehow, seeing them on me in this dress, they seemed to fit. If nothing else, it would make Cadeyrn laugh. All in all, I was pleased with how I looked, and was in a bit of a mad tumble to be with my mate and soon-to-be husband.

Silas fetched me from the inn, and a carriage brought me to the beach where we had stood not two nights earlier. As I came across the shell-encrusted beach, a large crowd gathered both on the shore and along the boulevard in either direction. I had eyes only for Cadeyrn. He was dressed in a fitted black suit, still a few weapons bumping out from the fabric. I smiled at him.

"I believe this is where I give you up, *Trubaíste*," Silas said roughly, kissing my cheek and once more on my hand as he passed it to Cadeyrn. A thrumming of electricity passed swiftly between my friend and me.

"Thank you, brother," my mate said to his cousin and took my hand. "Perfect," he said to me. "Everything about you is perfect."

"Down to your blood type?" I said nervously, then giggled.

He looked at me oddly.

"It's a line from a song. Sorry." I smirked at him, and he chuckled.

"Have you met the wood sprite in the earrings yet?" he whispered.

I leaned in and whispered back. "She's a right little mischief maker."

Oh?

Hid my underpinnings so I was forced to forgo any at all. Oops. Heat flared around us.

"Are you lot finished with the innuendo?" Corra called over.

And so we were wed by the captain of a ship from Saar-laiche, presided over by Ewan, and sealed with a meeting of lips which sang a hundred songs of hope in my blood. After the brief ceremony, we all descended on a large restaurant and drank sparkling wine until the effervescence permeated the atmosphere. Cadeyrn and I held our glasses to toast, our matching silver bands glittering in the soft lights. As the wine touched my lips, I was once again struck with an immersive vision.

Beasts swarming an area. A discarded and dented crown, splattered in blood. Lands with rivers and small inland seas. Energy. So much energy. A pull to me. To Cadeyrn. Rippling in the air. A Veil, clouded like looking through fumes—but it was failing. Allowing things to pass into this realm, but not from the human realm. I slumped forward in my seat, and Cadeyrn caught me before my head smacked the table. Folk around us gasped. Our family surrounded us in a protective circle. I looked to my husband in shock, then sought the eyes of Ewan, Corra, and Silas.

"There's another Veil. In Heilig. Something is wrong with it."

Ewan swore viciously.

"It is not your sacrifice to make, Neysa," Ewan said, swirling grey building in the air. "Not this time."

"No, it is not," Cadeyrn agreed. "We will figure it out and deal with it."

Corra whimpered. A sound I would never have thought could come out of her.

"I will be back here, and I will meet my little niece and nephew or whatever they may be. I promise you. We will all be back here." While I didn't know if it was a promise I could indeed keep, I knew that keeping my family together was my top priority. To do that, though, we needed to sort out this new Veil.

TWO DAYS after our wedding, Silas and Reynard joined us aboard our vessel headed for the land of my mother's parents. Many trials ahead indeed. On this voyage, I planned to take advantage of every moment in the suspended time frame that was sea travel to be with my mate. Whatever waited for us in this land of beauty and water magic, our purpose there would imbue us with obstacles and peril. I stood at the helm of the ship and cut my palm, allowing my blood to drip into the sea. An offering and an oath.

The blood ran freely. Cadeyrn and Silas rushed to meet me.

"I swore once to do what is in my power to protect these lands, and I will uphold my promise as I swear to the elements that I will return safely with my family." Both cousins pulled my dagger from me and sliced it across their own palms in turn, echoing my pledge to return.

"Fucking hell, *Trubaíste*. What did I tell you about the theatrics?"

"Only that they had better be spectacular if you went missing. I'm just proactively dramatizing things. Besides, it's fun to see Cadeyrn get all hot and bothered when my blood is shed."

From the depths of the sea to the skies above came a long sigh and a feeling as though the world itself were bracing for theatrics of its own.

PART II

CHAPTER 17

Neysa

A green so green, it was blue. The entirety of the coast had a scarf of opalescent green, which met the shoreline in a majestic kiss of colour like the scales on a mythical beast. Passage through the archipelago had been a harrowing marathon of moving within the parameters of the natural wards imposed upon the landmass itself. Konstantín gave us strict instructions on how to make the passage, which involved invoking both mine and Cadeyrn's magic. The power I was able to draw from the sea itself had strengthened throughout the course of the voyage. Yet my inherent raw power seemed to need both my mate and Silas to harness it. Since that night by the campfire while we searched Aoifsing for Cadeyrn's beast form, my magic seemed to require Silas' nearness to function optimally. Nearly a month passed since we set sail from Maesarra. Though the time on the ship was a borrowed pause in the chaos that we had been thrust into, the wounds of what we endured were still a bit jagged.

Cadeyrn's power burned in a steady throb around him almost constantly. As we neared the archipelago, he released the damper and was a stanchion of heat and flame. Tendrils of my power found his and latched on, fusing together as a part of our *Cuiraíbh Enaíde*, the braiding of our souls that lived deeper in us than even our mating bond. What none of us had anticipated was that my power seemed to request buttressing from Silas' own now. As Cadeyrn stood on the prow of the ship, my magic twisted and curled with his. Silas stood near me as well, his magic looping and stitching itself through mine. During the first week of being in close quarters on the ship, the males were butting heads over this new revelation. I myself had always felt that though Cadeyrn was my husband and mate, I was connected to both his cousins almost as strongly. By the second week aboard the ship, Silas could barely look me in the eye. Our past, our closeness, his guilt with Cadeyrn, all built to an uncomfortable reality we would all need to address once off this blasted vessel.

Similar to the haze of the Veil, the forcefield of magic around the archipelago that surrounded Heilig was a murky, tangible thing. With our three powers synched, the ward admitted us, allowing a slow crossing through the haze. Months ago, in that war room in Laorinaghe, before Bestía, before Lorelei had been killed in the battle on that magnetic field, I had a vision of these lands. Of this archipelago. Between the fortifying islands and the shoreline of Heilig, the waters were placid and clear. Our ship glided noiselessly through the straights toward that teal shore.

Twinges of apprehension fluttered in my stomach. Cadeyrn slipped his arm around my waist and drew me closer. His scent wrapped around me like a blanket as I lay my head against his chest. He knew I resented having to come here. What I wished for us was to be able to live in peace in Aoifsing and perhaps start a family as my brother and Corra were doing. Though, Ewan now had the responsibility of the crown he resented as much as I resented coming to Heilig. What a pair we were. Breathing deeply, I tried to quell the rising anxiety in me; my mate pressed a kiss to my head.

"We have made it through worse," he said quietly. I tightened my arms around him.

"Technically, we have no idea what we are about to encounter so it's quite possible this will be much worse than what we've dealt with in the past," I countered. He chuckled and made small circles on my side with his thumb.

"I suppose. Though it will have to top murderous ambushes in jungles, Bulgarian dams, kidnappings across realms, near ablation of your body in a magical and chemical explosion, attacking aphrim, battling Elders, having our souls torn apart— twice—lupinus attacks, magical impotence, impalement, blood poisoning, deaths of our parents...Am I missing anything?"

"Cracking my spine from a violent vision?" I grumbled, nestling closer to him. His thumb stroked up my side and brought my face closer to his. I looked up into his watercolour eyes, the shade between an aquamarine and a peridot, and felt my stomach flip over. My hand went to the flat of his abdomen, and an answering rumble came from his *baethaache*. His face came down to mine, lips parting to kiss me softly. I turned to him and wrapped my arms around his neck, holding on for perhaps the last time before we disembarked.

You're stronger than anyone I've ever known, Neysa, my mate said to my mind. *I don't believe this ordeal will change that. If you need reminding of that strength, feel free to exert your dominance over me any time.*

I laughed against him and pinched his backside.

I will hold you to that, Mate.

We have some time before landfall...

"It will be a blessing to get off this floating stink boat and be away from you lot for an extended period of time," Reynard drawled from the cabin door. "Gods above, I hope the males of Heilig are as good-looking as your family, Little Mouse."

"A compliment, Reynard?" I gasped. "From you? I'm shocked."

"Mm. Don't let it go to your head, Mousey." He winked and strode for the helm. The captain announced land fall, so we began to gather our belongings in preparation for this journey to the lands of my grandparents.

Silas

A TASK. I needed a job to do, if only to get my mind off what we had dealt with the past months and the mental mayhem from being on the bloody ship for three weeks. Stepping onto dry land made me want to run for miles to get out of my head. My cousin and *Trubaíste* likely felt the same.

The day after our tryst, we agreed to put it all behind us. The day I knew, without a doubt, that she was Cadeyrn's mate—even before he did, the poor sod, I made the mental note to get on with it. That day in Bania after Analisse, when I knew—I knew she wanted me, and I don't know which of us it killed more. Then she kissed me goodbye. It was the longest I had ever been out of control with my magic. Lina wasn't stupid.

She still took me, knowing full well I could never love her as I loved my cousin's mate. My sister knew there was a connection between Neysa and me that was more than my simply being a stupid bastard who couldn't get past wanting to bed my own damned cousin's mate. Neysa couldn't leave it alone any more than I could. I had thought the answer was in staying behind and looking after Corraidhín and Ewan and the babes. Until *Trubaíste* begged me to stay with her.

The night in the forest when I swore on my blood to bring back my cousin, Neysa's magic came back when she connected to mine. At the time, I couldn't bring myself to say anything, but the pull we always had to each other turned to a solid, necessary element in that single moment. Fucking hell. It wasn't until we were all stuck on the godsdamned boat for weeks that there was no way around our bond. Cadeyrn tried to ignore it. He did a bloody great job of it, but his mate was connected to me, and I loved her as though she were my own. How was any male supposed to get past that? How was I supposed to get past the only female I had ever really loved being mated and married to my cousin? My brother, really. Where did that put me? I couldn't very well walk away when our powers were connected. I hadn't even been able to look at her this past week. By the time we disembarked the boat, I was out of my mind needing to get away from her. Thank the gods that Konstantín's envoy, whom we had dealt with in Aoifsing, was waiting with wagons just off the dock.

"Basz," I greeted him, grasping elbows. Cadeyrn and Neysa came up behind me. Reynard was no doubt scouting up ahead. I wouldn't be surprised if the little weasel jumped ship and swam ahead just to show his speed.

"Lord Silas. Your Highness." Basz inclined his head to us all.

"Bah. I'm no lord. Just Silas."

"I'm afraid your journey to Kutja includes another boat. The wagon shall take us just up the road where we shall take the river barge inland."

All of us groaned.

Neysa

WHILE THE thought of another boat made me want to hide and refuse to come out, once on the barge, it was clear that this experience would be a far cry from that of the sea voyage. Polished wood decks surrounded the vessel in three levels, punctuated with copper pillars. Seating areas dotted around the main deck, and it looked as though there were covered dining set ups on the next. Basz explained that we would be on the barge for two nights as we moved inland toward the capitol of Kutja. Then he said the magic words: bathing chamber. Not chamber pot, privy, or bucket. Basz gestured to it with irreverence, yet as soon as I saw where it was, I passed my weapons to my mate and walked directly in. Behind me, Cadeyrn and Silas snickered. A servant was already filling the large copper tub, steam billowing out in glorious, humid puffs. As Ama had done for me the first day in Bania when I was covered in a hundred different kinds of filth, I grabbed a flannel and wet it, scrubbing my skin raw and cleaning my nails before I sunk into the glorious heat of the tub. I covered my face with my hands, attempting to quell the rising panic about being in Heilig, dealing with phantomes, and figuring out what was going on with Silas and me. And my mate. Holy burning hell I had a real problem. We hadn't all spoken about it in detail. It was uncomfortable for each of us, yet at some point we needed to assess this. Just not yet.

TWILIGHT WAS falling when I made my way to the dining area on the second level of the barge. Staircases twined from the starboard side, opening up onto a spacious deck with a large round table set with baskets of bread and bottles of wine. Once out of the bath, I had donned a simple white slip of a gown, needing to be out of restrictive clothing. A stunning female poured my wine as Reynard slipped into the chair next to me. He had regained so much colour in the past weeks. Cadeyrn worked to heal in him what Paschale destroyed. Weeks at sea under the sun had even bronzed his skin. With his colour returned, the fine-boned structure of his face was revealed.

"Mousey," he said, sipping from my glass before his was poured.

"Look at you, Reynard, all clean and handsome."

He started, not expecting that. I wondered briefly if he had ever really been complimented. The more time I spent with him, the more I realized I liked him. He was witty and fun, and seemed to genuinely enjoy being with us all.

"What must it be like, Mousey, having those two males ripe for the taking?" And then he said stuff like that, and I wanted to drop kick him. However, I knew a diversion when I heard one. He was embarrassed by my compliment and tried to deflect it.

So, I leaned toward him and whispered, "It can be quite... hard, at times." I winked at him, and he snorted. "In fact, it is quite a...slippery situation if you...come to my meaning."

He clinked glasses with me and laughed heartily. It wasn't a laugh I had heard from him before.

"I guess you are more fun than I thought. I'd still take them both, though."

It wasn't his fault. He didn't quite understand the situation, so I ducked my head while I sipped the light white wine. Of course, both of the males being drooled over happened to crest the staircase at that moment, and Cadeyrn coughed.

"Not going to happen, Weasel," Silas said, plucking a bread roll from the plate before he sat opposite to me. Cadeyrn slid onto the seat on my other side and trailed a finger down my arm in greeting. I leaned into him, breathing in his rain scent.

Basz joined us and began a debrief on what had transpired since we last spoke with Konstantín, who left after arriving in Aoifsing. We had entered Heilig from the south and were travelling northeast to Kutja. Along the west coast, and further north, there was more unrest brewing, yet it hadn't made its way this far south. We could convene with the royal family and begin to travel round, doing a show of face. Between the wine and the low light, my mind drifted whilst I stared out of the open sides of the barge. Trees of varying species and size banked the river, small waterfalls and boulders littered about. Lights of colours I couldn't catalogue were shining from the trees and water, reflecting off the river current in a mad frenzy. It was hypnotic. I stood and walked to the railing, holding my wine.

"What are they?" I asked aloud, not bothering to turn to anyone. Basz came alongside me and pointed outward.

"In essence, they are simply pockets of light. Energies converge in this land. When the air and atmosphere itself cannot hold onto it any longer, pockets of light and colour burst, shining for days at a time. It is seen more in the less populated areas, as energy transfers between fae when we are together. Therefore, it is absorbed rather than it bursting."

Awe must have shown on my face. Basz smiled, pleased that his land had elicited my reaction. I looked to the male beside me, feeling the eyes of the three at the table. Basz had a serious face, with golden eyes setting an amber glow to his ebony skin. Every angle, from his cheekbones to his chin, was sharp and chiseled, making him look like a digitalized rendering of a beautiful male.

Lorelei wasn't lying when she said this land was full of beauty. Thinking of the Lady of Laorinaghe, my heart gave a great thump. New representatives must be chosen to spear the provinces onward. I left a letter of recommendation for Yva, the Sacred City of Laorinaghe guard who had fought for me. Cadeyrn and I agreed that she would be a fair delegate should she wish to embroil herself in politics. In the distance, a few pairs of glowing eyes stared at me across the river. I inclined my head to the lupine creatures. Warmth neared me, and I smiled over my shoulder as Cadeyrn came to stand beside me, an arm about my waist. Whether he was clean and polished as he was now, or roughed up and war-torn, my husband was breathtaking. I pressed a kiss to his shoulder. His peridot eyes smiled down at me. Every time we had a moment of relief or rest, some disaster showed up knocking.

"Tell me, Basz," Cadeyrn began. "How does Konstantín fair?"

Silas shuffled to us, his woodsmoke scent pulling at my senses.

"Well, Majesty. He has kept his immediate family—your family, Your Highness," he added with a nod to me, "within the palace and grounds. Just precautions."

"And you, Basz?" Silas asked. "Have you seen the trouble areas yourself?"

Basz regarded Silas. "Some, my lord. I was sent with a group of soldiers when we heard of the phantomes in the north. I witnessed the destruction they caused, and upon taking our leave of the areas, we were blockaded by mobs angry over the dwindling protection magic."

Perhaps, like the crystals needed to diffuse the Veil in Aoifsing, there was a more concrete reason for the release of the aulde dark powers. I touched the raw rose quartz shards hanging on my chest below the *adairch dorhdj*, the double-horn pendant I wore. The crystals warmed to my touch—and with a pulsing beat, I was thrust into a vision. The first I'd had since our wedding night nearly a month ago.

Haze and grey-tinged air clouding a tree canopy. A dented crown laying amongst the ashes and ruin of a structure. Blood. So much blood. Phantomes moving across the barrier to the human realm. Winds and waves. Cadeyrn on his knees in battle black, head hung in grief. A sword stretched from another hand coated in blood and filth. The sword is etched with rune-like markings—one I saw in Barlowe Combe. The cuff of the jacket is ruched up to reveal a tattoo of a single marking that looked like an arch with a looped squiggle bisecting it, a single star in the middle.

I choked on my breath, feeling my dinner rise up in me. Cadeyrn's arms grabbed my shoulders and brought me to the railing. The nausea subsided but the vice around my chest clenched.

"Let it out," my mate said softly, his healing gift trying to feel for the anxiety's cause.

White lights spun from my body, bathing the deck in an incandescence. Basz swore. Just as quick, the light spiraled into me. Black spots danced in my vision. Just as I began to pass out, Cadeyrn called to Silas for help. Soft mist blew around while my mate's cousin wrapped an arm about my middle. Lightning shot from us both. I heard Basz exclaim as he drew a shield around himself. Finally, my breathing opened up, and I collapsed on Silas. Turning in his arms, I yanked at his sleeve, needing to see for myself. He attempted to push my hand away, but I snarled, and he stopped resisting and looked away. Just above the inside of his wrist was the tattoo in my vision. Both of my hands covered my mouth as I stumbled back into Cadeyrn. Silas was still looking away. I looked to my mate and pleaded with my eyes.

"What does it mean?" I asked Silas. He still looked away and shook his head once and looked to his cousin, cocking his head to the side. Their eyes locked and Cadeyrn nodded. Some unspoken conversation that their centuries together made possible.

"Please," I begged and grabbed at his jacket, pulling him closer and pounding on his chest. His head still turned from me, he embraced me, and I felt his breathing quicken. Seeing his arm on the ground, covered in blood, and Cadeyrn kneeling on a battlefield, I understood what I had seen. And as the realization dawned, I knew I had projected the vision to Cadeyrn. His heat flared and he dropped his wine glass, the smashing glass a distant bell toll.

No. A single denial from Cadeyrn. His own thoughts blowing through my mind.

Cadeyrn, Silas, and I excused ourselves from the company and walked to our rooms. Once the door clicked shut, Silas' shield came up around us, barring any listening ears from eavesdropping. I slumped against the desk.

"Where was it?" Cadeyrn asked, a cold steel note in his voice. The assessing general.

"Are one of you going to tell me what this is about?" All humour in my friend had gone.

"I don't know," I said. "I feel like it must be here, yet I'm not sure."

"Fucking gods, you lot," Silas swore. "Tell me."

I yanked him to me and placed both hands on his face, about to tell him to go somewhere safe. His eyes widened; his mouth gaped like a fish.

"I saw it. I could see it. Your vision." He pulled my hands from his face and stormed out of the room.

I slid to the ground and placed my head in my hands. Cadeyrn sat beside me.

"I'm sorry," I whispered. "I didn't mean to...I don't try." I looked at my mate, his dark brows drawn together, eyes somber. He touched his forehead to mine and kissed me.

"Don't apologize. I understand. I mean, I don't. I really bloody don't understand what is happening. But I know you don't either."

This male beside me meant the world to me. His nearness sent jolts of wanting through me. I wanted nothing more than to be with him for as long as we could live. Yet, I could not live without Silas. Physically. My power was linked to his. What did that make me? In my vision, I saw him dead. If he were dead, then surely I would not survive long. Where did that put us?

"As my cousin would say, 'knee-deep in poisonous shite.'"

SUNLIGHT STREAMED in the small windows of our room, waking me with the dawn. I stretched and rolled to Cadeyrn. His eyes opened, sleepy and unfocused. The sight of him in the morning, tousled and warm, had me writhing against him. Slow and tauntingly, he moved his hands up and down my back.

"You should go to him," he said softly, running his hands through my hair. "He likely needs you."

"Cadeyrn."

"We'll figure it out, Neysa. We will. Go to him. I can't imagine what it must be like for him. Perhaps for you as well." I swallowed and kissed his chest once. Twice. "For the record, this is my favourite way to wake up," he told me, matter of fact.

IT ALWAYS seemed redundant to knock on a door with fae. Between the hearing and scenting, chances were they knew who was coming. Silas, I knew, could sense me from a distance. It was a part of whatever was between us. I still wished we weren't on a boat. As luxurious as this one was, none of us could get away. Though with the vision I had, I didn't want to let him go far at all. He scoffed when he answered the door and turned back into the chamber. Perhaps I woke him as it was still early. He stood in loose pants and no shirt, his brown waves in a bit of a mad tangle. I thought about pulling my fingers through them to detangle, but quickly shook off the thought. He poured water from an ewer and swished his mouth before swallowing.

"What can I do for you, *Trubaíste?*" he asked, folding his solid, ripped arms across his chest, tattooed side facing inward. "Did you not get quite enough this morning?"

A slap. That's what it felt like. My lip curled and wobbled at the same time, pissing me off. He hadn't asked in a teasing manner like he might have another time. It was a barbed question. One I resented.

"Piss off, Silas."

"I would, but I'm stuck on a fucking barge." The glass crashed onto the wooden side table. Never had Silas spoken to me like this. My nostrils flared in and out as I weighed whether to walk out. Then the vision came back to me.

"What is the tattoo?"

He filled another glass of water, draining it. "A symbol from the aulde language."

"I gathered as much. What does it mean?"

He scrubbed at his face and looked out the small window. I backed up a step. Maybe I shouldn't have come. Maybe he didn't want me to be here. Really, why would he? Maybe Cadeyrn knew that and was a bit sneaky in ushering me out. Maybe—

"Stop, *Trubaíste*," he said roughly. You're sending all that mental vomit to me."

"Oh, fabulous. Do I get any privacy in my own head these days?" I leaned my forehead against the wood paneled wall. He chuckled.

"Though if you must brush my hair out, I wouldn't say no."

I smiled. "Shithead."

"Always." He held a hand out to me. "Come here. I'm a bit worse for the wear this morning, Princess. Took a bottle of wine to bed last night."

"Did it treat you well?" I stood in front of him.

"Took full advantage of me and left. And now I've a pounding head."

I wet a flannel, then rummaged through his pack to pull out a bottle of peppermint oil that Lina had given us months ago. Three drops on the wet flannel soaked in, and I touched it to his forehead and temples, then the back of his neck.

"That's what you get for taking strangers to your bed," I teased. The peppermint was bracing and helped wake me up more. His eyes watched me, throat bobbing before pulling my hand away.

"Thank you. That helps," he said roughly.

"Tell me." He knew what I meant, but I turned his arm over to look at the tattoo. My thumb brushed it, making him shudder.

"Destruction or disaster. It's the same word. And love." He looked at me sidelong, sea glass eyes narrowed. I exhaled, not knowing what to do. "Tosser who did it fucked up. Was supposed to be the symbol for 'bloody great warrior.'" He gave me a lopsided smile. I choked a laugh. Disaster. *Trubaiste*.

"When?" I breathed.

"The day of the..." He waved his free hand. "Thing with Bestía." I nodded absently.

"You were planning to stay." He made an agreeable sound. "I asked you to stay with me instead. I'm horrible."

He laughed and kissed my hands.

"*Trubaíste*, I don't know what the hell is happening here, but I don't want to cause trouble for you both." Stay, I thought. Stay and be safe. The thoughts popped in my head like directives. Stay with me.

"I will." He answered what I hadn't said aloud. I stepped to him and wrapped my arms around him tightly. "I knew you couldn't be near me without wanting to jump my—"

I whacked him on the arm. "Cad."

He chuckled against my hair.

NOTHING WAS ordinary in this place. Lorelei's description was correct. Even the rock faces through which the river wound had swaths of flowering vines and ivy draped here and there like accessories. Just before moonrise on our last night aboard the boat, I took supplies to an isolated part of the observation deck, hoping to be alone. From my basket I pulled a small copper bowl, gems, smudging sticks, and frankincense oil. The barge had emerged a few hours ago into a wide section of the River Matta. Basz explained that the waterway we had started on merged from the narrow mountain pass with the River Matta, and where the leg we were on flowed to the capitol, the leg we moved away from headed to the sea in the northwest.

The seven mystics who sailed with King Konstantín revealed that I was the heir to the Goddess Heícate, guardian of magic and darkness. Each mystic gifted me an item. The seed pearl I released to the sea before leaving Aoifsing. I knew each additional gift would have its own indicative feel for how and when it should be used. Under the full moon, I felt the need to scry for a vision using the golden thread one of the mystics gave me. The air was chillier as we made our way further into the center of Heilig. Small pillars of clear quartz surrounded me where I sat cross-legged. Seven drops of frankincense fell onto the glassy surface of the copper bowl of water. Calling on my gifts, I isolated the electric charge I carried with me and concentrated on willing the charge to my fingers to spark the sage smudge stick. Around me, the crystals wobbled and vibrated, filling with energy. As though a small window opened in me, a jolt sparked from my fingers, dancing atop the sage until the smudge stick caught fire. I smiled, pleased with myself. For a few short moments, my hands moved the bundle through the air around my circle, and then I blew the fire out, dropping ash into the bowl.

Concentrating on my heartbeat, the rhythmic thump set the tone as I peered into the water, allowing my mind to wander. Questions popped in and out, and I let them flow. In the ripples of water I saw faces. *My brother and Corra; Bixby and Cuthbert; my mate, walking away, smiling back at me. My own face, turning and crumpling. A female with dark hair like mine. Basz shielding me from something. Lances of pain. That dented, bloody crown again. Looking down at myself with a rounded belly, strong hands covering mine. Fingers entwined, above two heads on a pillow, that tattoo showing.*

Distantly noting my body in the here and now, I lifted the golden thread from the mystics and dropped it into my palm. I called out to Silas in my mind, then hands were upon mine. Electricity and mist swirled, lightning brightening the skies around us.

My cheek scraped against Silas' stubbled face. His woodsmoke scent heightened my senses. It was still fully dark. For a short moment I held my breath before opening my eyes, hoping Cadeyrn wasn't here. God only knew how this looked. No one but us, I confirmed. I lifted myself from the male under me and held my pounding head.

Cadeyrn. I was scrying and released a bit of energy. Silas found me. I'm fine.

Be careful. Come back to bed soon.

"You know how some people are messy eaters?" Silas asked from the wood deck. He propped himself up onto his elbows, stomach muscles rippling with the movement. "I've come to think that perhaps you are a messy magic wielder. You can't help it. You just explode like the sad bastards who get food everywhere." I picked up bits of ashy sage and flicked them at him. He lifted an arm, and his power dissolved the sage midair. I dove forward and straddled him, grabbing his arm.

"Oh my God, Silas," I said, holding up his forearm. I felt him breathing under me and knew I should move but couldn't make myself. Above the tattoo marking on him, perhaps two inches in length, was a single gold line. The metallic of it shone even in the darkness. He stared at it.

"It's the thread from the mystic," I said, though he knew that. Tingling electricity still surged through me, running through the veins in my arms. His eyes zeroed in on my right forearm, and he pushed up the sleeve of my sweater. In the same place as it was on him, a gold thread stretched across my skin. A snapshot in my mind of a squiggle—the same squiggle as Silas had inside the arch on his arm, etched onto a stone and into the dirt in that forest in Prinaer. The symbol for the *Taempchal a Caráed*. The temple for the element of love. The face of the mystic who had given me the thread showed in my mind, smiling, knowing I understood now. I looked to Silas. Emotions ran across his face like credits on a screen.

Cat-soft footfalls sounded, and warmth entered as Cadeyrn came over to us.

"I have it as well." He lifted his arm. He was in pajama trousers and no shirt or shoes, as though he jumped from bed and came to us. We three sat, knees bent, looking at our matching golden lines, wondering what in all the realms to do now. Silas broke the silence.

"I came out because it seemed like there was a request for my power. Like a knocking at the door in my mind. I knew it was Neysa, so I allowed her to take it." Ah. The window opening, allowing electricity to come through.

"I came out to make sure she was okay, Cadeyrn." He turned pleading eyes at his cousin. Cadeyrn patted his hand.

"I need to write down what I saw." I stood. Perhaps it made me a coward for walking away when we should all be addressing this, but I couldn't sit there with my husband and talk about a thread of love that imprinted itself upon me and another male. I simply couldn't.

CHAPTER 18

Palaces made me jumpy. There. I said it. This past year, every palace we had been in, including my childhood home on *Eileín Reínhe*, we had to engage in a battle of sorts. Whether it was having my arm torn open by Paschale in Festaera, the full-scale mayhem at the Elder Palace, the battle with Analisse's sister, Julissa, pretending to be Lorelei in Laorinaghe, or the night of the summit when Cadeyrn's *baethaache* was forced to emerge and he disappeared in the skies. It seemed well within my rights to be twitchy about entering another palace. Especially in a foreign land with questionable allies and formidable dark magical enemies.

Basz and his guards led the way forward from the barge onto the walkway into the palace. The building itself sprawled for acres. It seemed to be more of a walled city than a palace with fully separate keeps and ramparts. The overall facade was not of a fortified castle, however, but of a majestic property with serious attention to detail. Guards lined the walkway, shields and weapons at the ready. They had been under attack, I reminded myself as my adrenaline spiked. I felt my mate's hand move toward mine as he brushed my fingers once. Near the walls, foliage spilled along the banks of the loveliest moat I could have imagined, glowing with orange flowers. We continued walking in, Basz leading the way. Once we crossed a grassy plain inside the walls and came to the steps leading to the palace itself, he turned to us, gesturing upward.

"For the time being this is the only entrance to the palace itself. There are wards on all other exits. You understand the reason behind it, I'm sure."

I'm calling bullshit, I said to both Cadeyrn and Silas. I assumed they could both hear me. I still couldn't hear Silas speak mind to mind, but at least he could hear me.

Yes, my delicate princess, Cadeyrn responded with a smile in his voice. *I'm quite certain this is the only exit they have* allowed *us to use.* A brief flare of light and electricity surged through me. Luckily Basz had his back to me, though I'm sure he felt the flare, so I quickly kissed my mate to cover it up.

Stealthy, mate. The old kissing in an alley cover up? I touched his stomach in response, which made his heat flare.

"Oh, for the love of males in armor," Reynard exclaimed. "Spare us all. Or at the very least, include us all."

Basz laughed good-naturedly.

"Sorry, Basz," I said to him. "It's all still a bit new." He only smiled and said he and his mate likely acted the same in the beginning. As we walked up the slate stairs to the main palace door, I shot my hand back and squeezed Silas'.

He hesitated, then squeezed back.

SWEAT AND grit covering him, Konstantín and four others rushed towards us from a balustrade just inside the building. The three males with me tightened in a protective blockade, which might have pissed me off had it not been kind of sweet.

"Your Highness," Konstantín called, out of breath. "We weren't expecting you until much later. I apologize for my appearance. We were in the training ring when I heard you had arrived."

"Not at all, Your Majesty. I'm sure we are looking a bit ragged ourselves."

"May I present my children." He turned, revealing two males and a female, all dark-haired and olive-eyed like Ewan and me. "Arik, my son. Saski, my daughter and the heir to my throne." We bowed to them. "My son and intelligencer, Ludek." He bowed to us and smiled at Basz. There was a tangible connection between the two, and I guessed he was Basz's mate. "My wife, Marja, you shall meet later. She was married before me and birthed two children; Ludek being her eldest. Pavla was killed leading scouts in the north this past autumn. My wife still mourns."

"Our condolences, Your Majesty," Cadeyrn said to the king, his hand over his heart. The others were looking at us like we were their next meal.

Konstantín sighed.

"The rumour is that you lot are impressive in the training ring. Might we get a glimpse of that whilst you're here?" Arik said to us with a wicked gleam in his eye.

I grinned at him. "As soon as I've slept on solid ground and had a few full meals, Your Highness, I would be happy to stretch my limbs."

He said he would show us to our chambers himself so that we could get started on the rest.

NOTHING WAS helping me sleep. The breeze coming in through the windows, as chilled and perfectly night-kissed as it was, felt wrong. The wards on the balcony door and windows let the air in and out, but I knew we had no access to the night itself. Trying not to panic when sleep-deprived, more or less trapped, built itself into a bubbling angst. Cadeyrn fell asleep beside me, and I stared at him, bitter he found it so easy. Did he not feel trapped? What about Reynard and Silas? They were probably all asleep, not bothered by the sensation of being stuck.

Breathe, Neysa. Inhale for five, hold for seven, exhale for nine. I repeated the sequence four or five times, then willed a soft projection of light to the tin tiled ceiling. Using the cadence of my breathing, I watched the light expand and contract as though it breathed along with me. It slowed my heart rate after a time, and the anxiety subsided slightly. Turning to my sleeping husband, I watched his breathing as though it were my own. Gazing at his chest as it rose and fell, my eyes trailed the scars that showed in certain light. Injuries that he never properly healed or allowed to scar, like the split on his lip from when Silas hit him. In sleep, his full bottom lip pouted and made him look almost childlike with his long dark lashes fanned against angled cheekbones. So much for controlling my breathing. It hitched watching him, so I scowled at him for being able to sleep and for being so beautiful it made my breathing trick useless.

"You could wake the dead with the intensity of that scowl," he said without so much as moving. I stuck out my tongue at him, and a small smile played at his lips. "If it makes you feel any better, I've sussed out how to dismantle the wards on our windows, the rear gate to the training ring that leads to the stables, and the door to the kitchen garden. I wouldn't suggest trying unless we are in check, as there will be a big fuss. But it can be done."

"How?" I didn't even know when he had time to figure it out. Dinner directly followed our arrival. A taxing few hours of wherein Queen Marja blamed me and Ewan for the death of her daughter. She stated in no uncertain terms that had my mother sent us there years ago, the blight on their land would never have happened.

"She could not be bothered to travel here once. Not once! Our gifts need tethers. We need to often be in close proximity to those with whom we share bonds," she said, breathless and rushed. My eyes caught Silas' and shifted away quickly. Konstantín coverfed his wife's hand with his own, giving it a squeeze. Her face pinched and I saw Ludek's gaze shoot to his mother's hand. Her long, dark fingers tangled in a grip far tighter than a loving gesture would require.

"I dare say," Konstantín beamed, voice and smile brighter than the overall mood. Dirt and sweat still clung to his face from his sparring, and had he not been crushing Marja's hand, I may have liked him for the casual statement he made in welcoming us with no pomp and circumstance. "Enough talk of bygones. We have welcomed a new era. Niece, I am so pleased to have you here assisting us in our plight." Marja scowled at him, her dark eyes narrowed to slits. He may be using excess force, but she was not laying down for it.

That is a dynamic I would rather not have to endure for very long, Cadeyrn said to me through our bond.

Tell me about it. Seems like Ludek is the only one who reacts. The male cattycorner from Marja watched his mother until she gave a barely perceptible nod. She immediately turned her ire for her king back to me. *Great.*

"I will say this once," she began. "My husband is not over fond of displays of emotion." With all eyes on the king, he sat back, drinking from a blown glass goblet of wine. Ludek sat up taller, as though preparing for something. I wondered what his gifts were. "My Pavla died. A violent, lonely death. She died because of the blight on these lands. Saskeia could have built upon my king's magics. Possibly even Saski and Arik's magics. Together they could have *helped us*," she sobbed. "Instead, she sent you to hide in another realm and refused to reveal her heritage."

Uncharacteristically, I kept my mouth shut and allowed the implications. Her children eventually stepped in and apologized, but it did absolutely nothing to improve my feeling about being here.

"The wards are tied to individual spell casters, so my gift was able to see a spell signature on each we passed. The training ring and likely a few in that vicinity are linked to Arik. Our windows are linked to the queen. The kitchen was linked to someone we haven't met yet. There is a heavy spell signature of Basz, but I haven't been able to isolate what and where."

I sunk back onto my pillow and exhaled.

"The idea being that should one of them leave or be harmed, the other signatures are different?" I asked into the darkness.

"One would assume." I made a silent snooty mimic of his tone and vernacular. He reached over and flicked my nose. "Does it make you feel better to make fun of me?"

I made a noncommittal sound. His arm reached over and pulled me against him, where I laid my head in the crook of his neck and shoulder, breathing him in. I traced my finger on his chest in a small circle, listening to his breathing and letting his scent dance with mine until sleep finally found me.

DAWN SAW me up and out in the training ring, trying to get in a few circuits before everyone else came out. While the ground of the ring was gravely dirt, the walls surrounding it were ivy-covered and glowed blue in the predawn light. An iron gate closed off the far side, beyond which was more foliage and the sounds of rushing water. That must be the gate Cadeyrn said had Arik's signature.

Setting stones at various angles and tracing lines into the dirt, I used the lines and stones for agility drills. My feet hopped and scooted, shimmied and pounced from one stone or line to the next over and over again. Once done, I sprinted across the ring, jumped into a handstand against the wall, and threw my torso into handstand push-ups. On the boat we trained daily, but freedom of movement was not a benefit of sea travel.

Slow, melodramatic clapping sounded from the gate where Arik stood leaning, his sword belt hanging from a hip. Long sword, two daggers, throwing knife in his boot. Likely a hidden weapon or two.

"I see you're waiting for me, then?" he asked. I bowed quickly, and he waved me off. "Let's be done with the titles, shall we? I couldn't care less, and I have a mind that you feel the same."

"Good morning, Arik," I said with a smile.

He grinned back and unsheathed his sword. I did the same, pulling twin swords from my back. We walked a circle around one another, taking our measure.

"What is breakfast like here?" I asked.

"You seem quite invested in your meals." He lashed out. I turned slightly out of the way.

"I am. One of life's greatest pleasures." I stabbed forward. He easily slid away.

"What, may I ask, are the others?" He stroked the trimmed beard on his strong jaw.

"Oh, I'm sure you can guess. Dogs, wine, sleep, sex."

He barked a laugh, and I caught his sword between my two and arced all three to the right. His eyes went wide as he attempted to step back. I moved forward and caused him to stumble. Seizing my advantage, I opened my swords and rolled so I was back-to-back with him, then turned and held my forearm dagger to his throat.

"So, about breakfast, cousin?" I released him. He was laughing and panting a bit. Silas and Saski stepped from the shadows of the doorway into the palace.

"Did you let her win, brother?" Saski called over, a slight sneer on her face. She too was wearing black flighting leathers, and I made a mental note to see if I could order a set like hers. They had ventilation patches like fish gills, under the arms and behind the knees. She carried a curved blade sword, similar to a scimitar, with a hilt fashioned to look like a great bird with open wings. She was taking stock of my weapons and stance, looking eager to try her luck.

"She bested me, sister. Perhaps our conversation took a distracting turn." He winked at me, and I bowed. Silas snorted and tugged on the braid I had pulled my hair into.

"*Trubaíste*," he said. "Ready for me?" I nodded, and we started our typical dance around each other. The same we had done nearly every day we had seen each other since that first little spar on the beach in Barlowe Combe. His twin swords kissed mine, and our energies struck through them. Above us, clouds rolled in and thunder boomed. There was a collective gasp from our audience, which seemed to have grown by a few, but I wouldn't turn to see.

Show off, I said to Silas in my mind. He smirked and raised an eyebrow at me. I did the same as our blades came together, crisscrossed to the point of having to call a draw. His left hip dipped ever so slightly, and as I was keenly aware of his body tells at this point, I knew he was about to drop down. As he tilted, I let go of my swords and flipped sideways over his back, wrapping my legs around his waist, and reached for my short sword. Silas' hand beat me to it and pulled my sword from its thigh holster, tossing it away with a growl. The growl had my toes curl in my boots, and light spilled from me, meeting with the yawning light of early dawn.

His back straightened, and I let myself drop from him, hitting the ground hard, then rolled. He picked up his sword again and tossed me mine. I kissed the air between us and heard chuckles from the outskirts of the ring. The morning dew seemed to inch its way into every crevice of my leathers. Taking a minute to pull off my jacket while Silas did the same, I whooshed a breath as he charged me. He was in a battle crouch, pushing forward with his head. I jumped to the side, and he caught me around the hips, pulling me down under him, laying my arms straight above my head. I inched my knee up slowly as I had in my chamber in Bania.

"Ah, ah, *Trubaíste*. Not falling for that one again." We were both breathing in great gasps. "Yield?"

I thought I needed to still show a thing or two to this audience. My partner smirked, sensing or hearing my thought, and gave me the slightest give as he deliberately slid his bare chest off me. Holy gods. Cadeyrn was off riding with Konstantín, or this could have been awkward. Silas' smoky scent was like incense around me. I took a pause, then quickly shrunk into a tight fetal position before rolling out from under him, then flipped him on his back. My nails drove into his palms, right on top of the scar we both still had.

"Do you?" I asked. His fingers curled into mine. Though he laughed and agreed, I saw a burning intensity in those sea glass eyes. Saski walked to us, a sly smile on her olive-skinned face. Her face that was much like mine yet slightly darker. There was really no question we were related.

"That was quite a performance," she said. I pulled my knee over Silas to stand, straightening my tank top. I felt Saski's eyes go to my arm. "What does it mean?" She pointed to the golden thread imprinted on my forearm and the matching one on Silas'. I cleared my throat, looking around for water.

"The thread was gifted to me by one of your mystics. It found its way onto my skin."

"And his as well. Curious." She walked to Silas and touched his arm. I could see on his face that he was not happy to have been touched casually like that. Yet we were guests in this castle. I stepped between them and answered.

"Yes. On Cadeyrn too. It is a bond between the three of us."

"The three of you? Or between you and both males? Interesting."

"I wouldn't touch that, Your Highness," Reynard said from the shadows. "Trust me. I've tried."

I winked at him. Saski's mouth curved into a viperlike smile. Oh, lovely. Another one like that.

"It would never work between us, Weasel," Silas said, brushing dust from his thighs.

"Come, sister," Arik called. "I've promised our cousin a breakfast fit for royalty."

Everyone began filing out as I picked up my weapons and dusted them off. Silas handed me my jacket and said into my ear, lips grazing the shell, "Good match."

My blood heated, and suddenly I wasn't hungry. I was nauseous and needed to bathe. And perhaps find my mate. So, I stomped off to my chamber.

Cadeyrn had returned and was finishing cleaning himself up as they had gone riding through boggy forest plains. I tossed my blades down when I entered and made a straight line for him. He laughed and let me push him against the wall.

"Did you lose?" he asked.

"No." I pulled his clothes from him with a marked growl and toed off my boots and trousers. He pulled me in, and I claimed his mouth while I yanked his backside to me. He kissed me fiercely and started to move against me, then stopped. I lurched forward, trying to keep going. His eyes narrowed and mouth pressed into a thin line. I made an impatient sound, but he shook his head, nostrils flaring.

"I think perhaps not," was all he said before turning away.

"Cadeyrn."

No. He pulled his shirt overhead and buttoned up his jacket. I stood against the wall, mostly naked, burning with desire, and shaking from cold rejection. He paused before walking out of the room.

"I won't touch you if your lust is for someone else." Each word was slow, quiet, and decisive.

"YOU NEEDN'T pretty yourself for us, cousin," Arik called as I walked into the dining room. I had taken a very cold bath and dressed in my aphrim skin pants and a grey on black damask patterned jacket. The jacket had a stand-up collar with full length tails and skirt split and opened in the front. Perhaps because I was in a mood to be reckoned with, I lined my eyes with a rim of kohl and stained my lips darker. Reynard muttered a plea when I walked in.

"I hope I didn't keep you waiting. I was filthy."

Reynard leaned to me and whispered, "You look more like the heir to the Goddess of War and Death than the Goddess of Magic. Tone it down, Mousey."

I nodded once and accepted a plate to fill with pastries and bacon, fruit, and something that looked like the love child of Greek yogurt and whipped cream, dusted with cinnamon. Cadeyrn was seated near Basz and Ludek, on the opposite side of me. Saski was next to Silas, engaging him in conversation.

"It intrigues me that you were trained to fight as a human," Ludek said to me. His voice was almost delicate, like movement in the night. I wasn't dumb enough to think it made him less formidable a character. He had a deeper olive skin than his half siblings, and warm, rich brown eyes that seemed to be everywhere at once yet felt concentrated on me.

"My father saw to my training from a young age. I took to it well enough."

"I like the way you moved. It was like...controlled chaos. A beautiful destruction."

Silas and Cadeyrn both coughed.

"I'm sorry. Was that out of line?"

"No. No. Thank you. I think. I'm sure the males who spend time with me would tend to agree with you. About the chaos part, at least." I grinned to put him at ease. "Were you born in this area, Ludek?"

"Far from here, actually. My father was a council head in our land. Heilig is broken into lands rather than provinces, but it is essentially the same as Aoifsing. The land we are from is called Sot. I can show you a map later if you'd like. I hear you are somewhat of a scholar."

I told him I would love that.

"I will be in the library in the afternoon. Join me. Unless, of course, you need as much time to get ready for the party as my sister does." He saluted his sister with his juice glass. Confusion must have shown on my face, as it did on my mate's.

"Our father has arranged a party tonight with our trusted friends and courtiers. It won't be too formal. Entertainment, dancing, and surprises," Saski explained. I wanted to groan. I didn't like surprises.

Cadeyrn left the room with Basz and Arik without so much as a thought to me, though both males accompanying him bowed to me.

"So, it does bother him, then?" Saski asked.

Whipping my head round in shock, I looked at her. Electricity crackled in my extremities and the water glass on the table boiled, shattering the glass. She laughed and clapped, reminding me of Reynard when I'd first met him.

"I did wonder."

"I know I am a guest here, yet I would advise against any remarks like that or assumptions about my mate and me." I crossed my arms on the table and leaned forward. She was openly smiling at me, lighting her eyes and freckles. "I have come here at an inconvenient time, having endured more than you may know. If at any time this arrangement does not suit me, I will leave and let you sort out the problems internally. Understood?"

"She means no harm, Neysa," Ludek assured me. "She tries to push the limits with everyone. We understand your terms. Don't we, Saski?" She was still smiling but agreed. Silas held a hand for me to follow him out.

"What?" I snarled at him once we were in a private courtyard.

"What happened?" he asked.

"She pushed me."

"You've been pushed before. That's not what I mean. What happened when you left?" he asked. I couldn't meet his eyes. He opened his mouth to ask again, so I started talking.

"He wouldn't touch me. Because...because I guess, he scented..." I flapped my hand. "And you." I covered my face with my hands, utterly embarrassed. He swore. "I wish Corra were here."

"Me too."

BASZ FOUND me wandering the inside grounds of the castle an hour or so after breakfast. It was so unlike castles in the human realm and most of what I had seen in Aoifsing. Plaques along the walls of an exterior wall told tales of kings and queens, warriors, and villains throughout Heilig history. Etched in bronze was a depiction of a woman holding a book while waters rose around her. When I felt Basz near me, I asked about the plaque, as it had no explanation.

"She was a great queen from many generations ago. A different bloodline from you, I believe. These lands were in peril. Her people hungered and sickened. An entire generation had gone without reproduction—which, in our terms, was a few hundred years. Magics died, and eventually the plant life grew tired." He had a voice for tales. Deep and musical with the slight slip and shuffle of his Heiligan accent.

The queen ascended her throne after her parents slipped into the next life. The population was dwindling, and she felt she must try to do something. Her gift was considered useless to most, as she could turn foliage to metal—gold, silver, bronze, copper. No one cared for a monarch with only the ability to make more riches. Left on her own, she fled the castle to find an answer.

Trails of the plague led her. She followed the path of hungry people, drooping flora, and parched ground. In the center of Heilig she found a cave. Deep within the cave was an ancient pond. After months of searching and on the verge of death herself, the young queen sat by the pond in the cave and submitted to an exhaustion beyond any she had ever known. Glinting images on the pond surface came to her. In the surface of the water, she saw the future of her kingdom. It flourished and prospered with her and her family alive and well. She at first thought it a cruel joke. She couldn't imagine being well enough to walk out of the cave, let alone stand for generations as figurehead. When she raged, her gifts manifested into something greater than she had imagined. The queen threw herself into the pond, distraught and alone. The water evaporated around her, turning into silver along the shores. Within a short time, all that was left was a veritable tub of silver, holding a queen and a book. She picked up the book and, at her touch, words appeared. Sitting on the metal bottom of the pond, the queen read for days, absorbing knowledge and prophecy. In the power of written words, her magic grew. As she read, veins of silver rushed through the lands, purifying the ground water. After, the queen stepped from the cave, squinting in the dim light of dusk, and held her hands aloft. From the depths of the ground rose a well of water. Two trees beside her turned to metal and attracted an oncoming lightning storm. The elements met, and within the storm, the queen submitted to her lands, pleading with the elements to save her people. In the silver soaked flood, she was drowned and flushed from the center of the land mass. Some say she was found dead by a young necromancer, who couldn't bear the thought of losing her. Others say the necromancer was her soul partner, hidden within the drying lands until their powers needed to be braided together.

"Either way, no one knew for certain, but the young queen returned to her palace with a mate, finding the paths leading her home, alive and thriving. Though she had no remarkable gift, somehow, through that which she did possess, and her sheer will alone, she saved the lands. She is Heilig. The heart of our lands. Its life blood." Basz finished the tale, and I was lost in the story.

"Did she ever find out what caused the sickness?" I asked, turning to the bronze rendering of her story.

"Some say a curse. A mystic who turned against the people. Others say a natural way for things to start anew. An unpopular opinion is that the boundaries between this world and the next thinned, allowing elements on either side to convene and attempt to eradicate each other." Like the Veil. I turned to him, wide-eyed.

"What do you believe, Basz?"

"I have never been one for popular opinion." He gave me a small smile.

I touched the bronze, feeling its smooth bumps and reliefs. As though drifting on the sea, I was cast into a vision.

Reading until my eyes burned. Elemental symbols swirling in the air like snowflakes. Electricity crackling through a forest. A box, sacred and old. Within the box, photos of visions past—Silas' dead arm. Cadeyrn kneeling in the dirt of a battlefield. The dented crown. A hand closing the box. Rushing water. A hawk.

Slumping against the wall, I came out of the vision. Basz crouched near me, asking if he should get Cadeyrn. I told him I was fine, though I felt far from it.

"I think Ludek is waiting for me," I told Basz. He looked at me skeptically, yet offered his arm, leading me away from the hall of history.

LUDEK WAS in the library with his mother. I swallowed, steeling myself for her thorny remarks.

"My Queen," Basz greeted her with a bow.

"The young heir. I hear you have been playing in dirt and stirring up trouble." And here we go.

"Mother," Ludek warned. She waved him off and stood in front of me.

"Sshh, *allaíne balaíche*," she said to him. "I want to hear from the princess why she thinks it was acceptable to hold a knife to your brother's throat."

"They were sparring, Mother," he said with impatience.

"My mother used to call my brother her beautiful boy as well." I met her eyes. "When Ewan and I were reunited, I remembered that. She was always smoothing his hair, and I remember thinking, as a child, that the stars shone in her eyes when she looked at him." I was speaking familiarly yet felt nearly entranced. "So many years had us separated. I can't imagine what she went through losing us all. The loss I felt was nothing compared to hers." I covered my heart with my hands. "Your loss is greater than I want to imagine. I am more than sorry for it, and I intend to help prevent any further pain for your family."

The room had fallen silent.

It was Ludek who whispered, "Your family too, Neysa. We are all one. My sister was a warrior heart like you. We are all family, even though I may not be your blood."

"Family is more than blood," I said. "Family is in the small moments. The ties that bind us. Threads that connect. Family is in the intention to protect."

Tears streamed down the queen's round, sun-kissed face. She looked at me once more and rushed from the library.

Ludek had a shine in his eyes. His mate stood beside him, a hand at his back. How handsome they looked together. Needing a show of strength, I pushed back thoughts of my mate who wouldn't touch me. How much easier his life would have been had he found a normal mate or even just a wife. Not some monster bound to both him and his cousin. A monster incapable of harnessing her powers alone.

On the wall was a map of Heilig. Ludek began to explain the different lands within it. He pointed out Sot, far to the southeast. A land of black sand beaches and plants which made their own water. The land from which we entered was Manu. It was the largest seaport, yet largely unpopulated beyond the port, as the jungles and forest converged there, making it difficult to maintain a settlement. Along the coast was a long land known as Biancos. The land was heavily populated, as many small cities were there, and it stretched inland for hundreds of miles, where it met with Ech, the central land in Heilig, largest of all. The palace sat in the very center, in a place known as Kutja. Kutja meant "box," he explained. It was said that the secrets to the heart of Heilig were here. The only land left to show me was

Annos in the north. That was where much of the turmoil was happening—where his sister had been killed.

"Am I correct in thinking that you and I will be working together to figure out the course of action to take?" I asked Ludek.

"I believe I may be of use, yes. Arik likes to take action before it is wise to do so. I would feel more comfortable laying out the scene before any of you leave here." As he spoke, he walked around, tidying up things he had left in different places. Against the far wall, a curtain behind it, shielding it from the sunny window, was a book encased in glass. I walked to it and looked in. Symbols were drawn on the open pages.

"This is the book," I said, tapping my chin. "The Heilig queen's." Ludek strode to me, his long legs crossing the distance in a flash.

"It is. Basz told you the story then."

"May I look through it at some point?" He tipped his head side to side. "I don't see why not. We need all the assistance we can get. I can have it taken out tomorrow morning if that suits you?" I nodded, wondering whether I could interpret anything in it. "They are mostly elemental symbols. Those for things like water, silver, and such."

"Tell me honestly. Will I hate this party tonight?" Both males huffed.

"It really just depends. Some like it because it is an opportunity to let go and just...be. Basz is not a fan. I don't mind it much, so he puts up with it."

I blew out a breath and touched his shoulder in thanks. A snapshot of him as a child flashed. He was standing with his sister, both identical in their dark olive skin and molten chocolate eyes. I looked up at the grown version of that boy.

"Pavla was beautiful. She looked just like you. I am so sorry for your loss."

He leaned over and kissed my cheek.

"Thank you. And I am sorry for all that you have endured as well. It is never easy."

"Nothing worth fighting for is."

Cadeyrn said that to me so very long ago on that terrace at the Elder Palace. My heart ached for him, but I knew he needed time. I knew, perhaps, we all did. Tomorrow I would work on this new puzzle. It may just take more of me then I had anticipated.

REYNARD WAS lounging atop a curved stone railing on the furthest edge of the formal gardens. As his head was tilted back, allowing his creamed honey hair to brush the railing, I saw his eyes were closed, letting the sun warm his face. I jumped up onto the railing myself and leaned against the opposite curve. From the pocket on my jacket, I pulled a small journal and pen and began writing down the visions I'd had today. Something about the box I saw piqued my curiosity. I knew that whatever happened, I had to save Silas. The crown wasn't Ewan's, and though that gave me a sense of peace, the fact was that I saw Silas dead and Cadeyrn distraught, and that was a fate with which I simply refused to comply.

"Whatever you're planning, Little Mouse, count me in."

"Not planning anything, Reynard. Yet. But I shall let you know. Do I really look like war and death?"

"Not war and death. The goddess of such. Your lips have faded and the murderous scowl with them. But let's just say, that had you looked like that when we first met, I may have thought twice."

"About biting me?"

"Mmm. Maybe."

I chuckled. He hopped from the railing and was gone. Good gods, he was fast.

The gardens were peaceful. Where I sat was hidden in ferns and summer blooms, and the only sounds were that of birdsong and trickling water from the fountain that ran the length of the garden itself.

Who was behind the blight here? Was it a Veil issue again? Regardless of that, someone had to physically control the phantomes. Who was it? Whoever had taken up Analisse's mantel was who needed to find. Reluctantly, I made my way back through the gardens, enjoying the late afternoon golden hour of sunshine. I had planned to wear the black gown I purchased in the seaside village in Maesarra, yet Reynard's warning to "tone it down" rang in my head. Ahead of me, sharpening her knife on a fountain side bench, was Saski.

"Hello, cousin," she purred. Keep it together, Neysa.

"Saski. I meant to tell you that I like those leathers. Might I be able to order myself some before I leave?" There. I complimented her. She smirked at me.

"Of course. On the subject of clothes, I've left you a present. I guessed that perhaps you mightn't have anything suitable with you, so I left a gown for you in your chamber." I wasn't sure how I felt about that, but I thanked her anyway. "If it's not right or doesn't fit, feel free to send it back with your handmaiden. She will find a replacement."

"I'm sure it will be perfect. I look forward to tonight."

A creeping, wicked smile appeared on her face that sent chills up my spine.

CHAPTER 19

Gertie, my handmaiden, was a chatterbox and gossiped until I had forgotten the fact that Cadeyrn had not returned to our chamber. What was more, his clothes had been moved. How I was going to get through this party without losing my shit was starting to worry me. Gertie made me look in the mirror on my way out the door. The cut lines of my shoulder muscles and thighs were back. I regained some of the weight I'd lost. Once upon a time, I may have felt too prudish to wear this dress. I could bet money that Saski picked it just to see if it rankled me. Gertie curled and glossed my hair, pulling the voluminous barrel curls forward so they framed my face and spilled over my shimmering, oiled shoulders. The dress tied behind the neck with thin straps, which led to a skintight sheer black panel embroidered with copper and rose gold flowering vines that strategically covered my breasts. Well, part of them. The sheer panel stopped in a vee below my navel and became the flowering vines again as they fell in hundreds of swishing rose gold blooms, bracketed by the softest black silk which split at mid-thigh, putting my legs on display as I walked in four-inch copper heels that laced up the legs. Gold climbing vines started at the top of my ears, down through my lobes where they dropped to shoulder-skimming chandeliers. She pinched my cheeks until I threatened her, and while my skin smarted, she applied a gooey blush and gold shimmer powder before making my eyes smoky and dark. I applied a soft lip balm to my lips in lieu of lip colour and thanked her for her help. Here we go.

Potted plants marked the entrance to the ballroom. They towered above, creating canopies within the room, small lights twinkling amongst the leaves. Cushions were all along the floors, small tables set amongst them. Servants meandered, pouring drinks and passing food. What I assumed would be a small party for the family alone was, in fact, a large to-do filled with fae. Many stopped to watch as I walked in. Alone. Without my mate.

Why do we bother? I remember him saying. Stop it, Neysa. Shut it down. I needed to remember that I was here to fulfill a request for aid. A job to do. Still, it would have been nice to walk in with someone. An arm linked through mine.

"My sister sent the dress, didn't she?" Arik asked.

I nodded, still a bit too nervous to speak.

"Say what you want about her, but she definitely has good taste. You look lovely, cousin." Everyone did. There was not an unattractive face in the room. "I'll get you a drink and you can relax. I'm sure it's a bit much." He steered us toward a servant and pulled a crystal goblet from the tray for each of us. Arik released my arm and turned to face me while I sipped. "You really are nervous. I'm sorry. I should have told you it would be like this."

"It's okay. I just take a while to warm up at parties. Plus, the last few I've been to ended in full-scale battle."

He howled a laugh and drank his wine to the dregs. I took a few more sips as well, wondering where everyone else was.

"Well, not to worry tonight. I promise you it is just a party. Perhaps wild. But just a party. And you are certainly dressed for it."

"Don't you look the part?" Saski said, coming up behind her brother, Silas and Cadeyrn on either arm. They were both impeccably suited in black on black. I wanted to reach for Cadeyrn and tell him how good he looked. Saski angled herself in front of him. She wore a one-shouldered fiery red gown that barely covered her chest and, like mine, opened mid-thigh to show her legs. It was obviously a favourite style of hers. She looked incredible.

"What part might that be?"

"The heir of darkness." Ah, so that's what this was about. Making me feel off balance in front of people.

"I shall take that as a compliment, then." I knew full well it was not meant to be, but the wine loosened my tongue. She giggled slightly. Cadeyrn and Silas must have been drinking already, as they were swaying slightly.

In that moment, I recalled a question I had for Ludek, and I suspected I would be in no state to ask later, so I walked to him and Basz where they lay against cushions, chatting with a few other fae. They all looked up at my approach. This was an odd seating arrangement for formal wear, yet I squatted down to speak to them. Ludek introduced me to their friends. One female began playing with a vine on my skirt. She smiled sleepily at me. This would be a long night. I explained that I had a question for Ludek, and Basz threw up a shield around the three of us without so much as taking his hand from his mate's chest. He nodded at me, eyes much clearer than anyone else around us.

"I was told I am the Heir to the Goddess Heícate. I really don't know what that will mean for me, but I was wondering..." The same female had two vines twirling in her grasp, and her fingers found their way into the folds of my skirts, moving upward. I gently removed them and kept talking, Basz and Ludek softly laughing. "Could that mean anything in regard to the story you told me today, Basz?"

It was Ludek who answered.

"The thought did cross my mind. All the pieces seem to have come together at the same time. Whether you have a con-nection to only the lands or their intrinsic powers, we will have to see."

"What is your gift, Ludek?" I asked. Basz smiled and kissed his mate's earlobe, making Ludek blush fiercely.

"I am able to...understand things. That which others will not or cannot. And I am an oraculois. That gift runs in both our bloodlines."

"That sounds like a beautiful gift," I said, finishing my wine. A servant appeared, replacing it. "I find it hard to read people. Silas' sister, Corraidhín, sees intent. It seems similar. I feel I am always adrift." Oh, I must have been a bit drunk to have admit-ted that.

"I know you do. You're doing well, cousin." He turned to his mate, who caught his mouth in a gut-twisting kiss. I had to look away. Cadeyrn sat maybe ten feet away, sprawled like my companions, on rugs and cushions, Saski, Silas, and Kon-stantín sitting with him. He didn't catch my eye, so I searched the room for Reynard. In the far corner, speaking with a small group, he raised his glass to me. I hated parties. Konstantín called me over.

"Niece, how lovely you look this evening." I didn't like admitting that something in his voice made my skin crawl. Though he looked much like Saskeia, I was not finding that warmth and sincerity my mother possessed. His hand crushing Marja's flashed in my mind.

"I heard you gave Arik a beating this morning," Konstantín continued. "I would have paid good money to see that. Please. Sit. I will be leaving the young to the festivities shortly. These parties get a bit wilder than an old man such as I can abide." He winked at me, looking no older than myself. I suddenly missed my mother.

"Was Saski named after my mother?" I had been meaning to ask, but it never felt right.

"Oh, yes. My beloved daughter to carry on the name of my beloved sister." I hung my head a bit, sipping my wine. Konstantín left us with a hearty good night and signaled for more wine to be brought over. Looking around, I had the feeling that it was not ordinary wine we were drinking. Everyone was in some state of being atop one another, dancing, kissing, or leaving, semi-attached. It wasn't offensive or crude, only very open. Saski toed at my heeled foot, and I looked up at her, sitting between my mate and Silas. None of us had regarded each other, causing the ever-lurking hollowness in my chest to claw and throttle me.

"You seem to be having no"—she poked my foot— "fun." She poked it again and draped an exposed leg over my mate's. "At." Her hand was on Silas' thigh. I was seeing red. I met Cadeyrn's eyes, imploring him. This was more than enough of this bullshit. "All."

Her other leg crossed over Cadeyrn, and she turned into Silas' face, nuzzling him. He was fully drunk, eyes clouded and lust addled. I couldn't tell if Cadeyrn was so drunk on this drugged wine that he didn't care or notice the female's attention, or if he was challenging me. She reached back and touched his stomach. Had I not been drunk and trying to prevent another palace battle, I would have ripped her hand off with my teeth. She inched her legs further up onto his lap, and I saw his breathing hitch. Everything in the room deadened to the sound of his heartbeat in my ears. As she wiggled her legs atop my mate, her hands were on Silas' chest and face, and she began kissing him. His hands went into her hair and down her back. Tears were pricking behind my eyes, but I would be goddamned if I allowed them to fall. Arik came behind me laughing and lifted me up.

"Princess Neysa," he introduced me to a male dressed in fighting leathers, though otherwise polished. "This is my very best friend, Lord Eamon of Kutja." He bowed to me, ebony skin glowing in the low lighting.

"Pleasure, Lord Eamon."

Arik brought us to a low sofa away from the males I loved.

"I'm saving you from my sister. She really knows how to provoke, does she not?"

"She's fondling my mate and my—" Shit, Neysa. "Silas."

He made a dismissive gesture. Eamon turned to me.

"Will you be training tomorrow?" he asked me. "I would be honored to spar with you. I don't know how you beat Arik, but I'd like to find out. I've been trying to for years."

I grinned at him and agreed to meet him before breakfast.

"You certainly have the shoulders of a fighter." He ran a finger along my collarbone and down my shoulder muscle and bicep. I shivered and swallowed.

"And what is your weapon of choice, Lord Eamon?" He raised an eyebrow at me, and I laughed. Cadeyrn was watching with sleepy eyes, Saski's bare legs pushing into his lap, her chest and lips all over Silas. What made me feel even more sick was that she looked like me. Eamon leaned into me as Saski looked over.

"You are more than welcome to join me in my rooms." Eamon's mouth met the shell of my ear.

"I think not." I laughed and gently pushed him away with an eyeroll.

Saski looked over, I opened my legs wide enough to show off the dagger I had strapped high on my upper thigh. With a feeling like a knock to my chest, I saw Cadeyrn's hand come down onto her legs and stay there. I excused myself from Arik and his playboy friend, making for the garden doors. Reynard caught up to me.

"Mousey."

"Go enjoy yourself, Reynard."

"Oh, I will. I'm just worried about you."

"I'll be fine. My cousin seems to be making headway with both Silas and my husband, so I refuse to sit around and watch."

The entire party was lost in a daze of partnering up. I did not like parties full stop and with this string of events, I was not happy. I didn't know where to go either. Back to my chamber to be drunk and alone with my thoughts? Even if I could scream at Cadeyrn at the top of my lugs, I wouldn't do that here. That old, sour question came back again. Where did I go? Where did I belong? If I didn't need to see the book in the library, I would have left this very evening to check on the Veil in the north.

Oh, Ewan, I wish you were here. I knew he couldn't hear me. In a blinding moment I thought of what needed to be done. I would send a hawk to Corra tonight and look through the book tomorrow morning, then leave by nightfall. I couldn't spend another night here with Saski and even Arik, who was sweet, if not a little on the arrogant side. My hawk waited patiently outside my chamber door. I sent her off with a note to Corra and Ewan, then made for the garden again.

The serenity of the place in the day turned to a ghostly calm at night. Leaves blew in swirls; roses scraped their thorns against the stone walls, like nails along a hallway. The very rear of the garden, where I sat earlier, had stone benches and gazebos. I made for one, thinking I could even fall asleep in there. Turning the corner, I saw movement and was about to turn around but caught sight of a swath of red fabric. Grunts and moans carried on the breeze. Like a train wreck, I couldn't look away. Heart hammering in my chest, I walked closer. Silas had Saski backed against the lip of a large planter, her skirts open, both of them moving together. Quietly, I backed away.

God, I fucking hate parties, I said to myself. The sound of a grunt and female swear sounded behind me, and feet began to hurry in my direction. I ducked behind a hedge and tried to make my way back without being seen. *Oh, bloody great, I'm in a maze. Of bloody course.* Drunk, drugged, mind on everything it shouldn't be, in four-inch heels, on the verge of tears, and stuck in a fucking maze. *Think, Neysa.* Where was my beastie when I needed her? Turn right. Keep turning right. How did I get through the one at Hampton Court? I tripped over a bramble and stumbled, catching myself before going headfirst into the juniper. Turning right again, I was face to face with Silas, whose trousers weren't even done up all the way. I pushed past him and kept storming off but ended up in the same spot. I growled, lower and more viciously than an angry dog.

"*Trubaíste*, wait." Okay, so maybe the right turn thing wasn't working out for me. "Please." I heard him stumble. I couldn't stand the smell of him. Of her on him. It was too close to me.

"Back off," I snarled.

"Or what?" he snarled back, turning me.

"No. You don't get to dictate this scene. I am trying to walk away. From you."

"Just me?"

"Stop it!" I yelled in his face. I pulled the dagger from my thigh, which made his eyes widen in shock. Two quick slices through the laces on my shoes allowed me to kick them off and keep walking. Godsdamned heels.

"Why are you running?"

"I'm walking. You left your plaything back there. Go play." I looked up and spotted a lowish branch, so I jumped and swung over the hedgerow into the center of the maze.

"Fucking *paítherre moinchaí*," he swore and followed, dropping like a cat in front of me.

"I will say this once more, before it becomes a real problem between us. You know I don't play nice when I'm cornered. Leave me alone."

"I know it bothers you. I know this night was a fucking disaster."

"I am a fucking disaster, Silas! I am! Don't you see that? Run away from me! That little bitch knows it and couldn't wait to get her hands on you both." I was screaming now. With fae hearing, I was sure everyone could hear us. Though most were likely too drunk to care. "When we left Aoifsing, I needed to sleep for a month and take a vacation. Not deal with this shit! Go, have fun. The last thing I want is to stop you. I'm a horrible, selfish, stupid asshole, whose mate won't even touch her now. Why would I wish anyone else to be as miserable as I am? Especially someone I love as much as I love you. Just leave me alone." I wasn't even crying. I was raging. Why were mazes a thing? Who enjoyed this shit?

I stalked off, leaving him in the center alone. Basz was waiting at the end, Ludek by his side.

"If you're going to leave, you will need an escort. And a shield," Ludek said. I stared at them. "Reynard was worried and thought you were leaving." Great. I probably ruined his night too.

"Please don't say anything to anyone else. Is there another chamber I could use tonight?"

CHAPTER 20

Cadeyrn

I must have walked the halls of this godsdamned palace for hours trying to find her. I hadn't meant to be so harsh, but I couldn't in good conscience take her to bed, when I knew my cousin had gotten her worked up. I just couldn't. I didn't understand what it was between my mate and my cousin. I didn't and I hated it. It might be the death of me.

So, I stayed away, even though I had wanted to be with her at the party. Saski intercepted Silas and me on our way, saying Neysa had been in the library with Ludek for hours and was running late getting dressed. I should have known. When I saw her walk in looking terrified, it clicked. At that point the wine, or whatever was in that wine, had my mind lusty and fucked. Even the movement of my hands lifting my glass caused colour trails, which were mesmerizing. I had tried to ask Silas if he felt just as strange, and he gave me some stupid look and a gorilla-like chuckle. I guessed that was a yes, but his chuckle sent me into a giggle, holding onto Saski's arm like she was the last column of reality. Neysa sat watching Saski fondle Silas, and her expression was so murderous, I was back where I was earlier, not giving in, and letting the viper wiggle her legs on me. The sick part was that Saski looked so much like Neysa, it was bizarre.Somewhere on the fourth floor of this monstrously large castle, I picked up on her scent, mixed with that of Basz. I would bet she had them find her quarters for the night. I opened my mind to her, but she had shut hers down completely. Each time I tried to say something, I couldn't make it come out. I was still pissed. She was still pissed. We were still in this impossible situation, and once again, I'd made Neysa feel like I didn't want her. If I could bury myself in her and stay there forever, I would. If only I could find her.

A NOTE laid atop of the table in our chamber the next morning, weighed down with a rock. Somehow seeing it had my legs feeling as though they were about to give out.

Cadeyrn,

I sent a hawk to Corra and Ewan last night explaining things. I can understand why you won't touch me. I don't know what to do about it because I love you and it hurts to be near you if you won't touch me. Regardless, there was a tale in the histories here that I felt held a key. Ludek and I spent the morning perusing a book that could help, and I think I know a way to fix the Veil. I am armed and prepared. Basz and Reynard are with me. I will try to be back in three months' time. It's something I must do and it's not worth causing you and Silas more pain. I know I am a monster. What did Bestía say? "Who would want that crown of darkness?"

I love you more than life itself. Please don't blame Ludek.
Neysa

I quite literally couldn't breathe.

"Silas," I wheezed, trying to be louder but not finding the air. "Silas." The door opened and he came in angry. I thrust the letter at him. Muscles ticked over and over in his jaw as he read. Our eyes met.

"Go," he rasped. "Go, you fucking twat! Or I will go."

"Find Ludek." I needed to see the only member of this household I trusted before I set the place aflame in fury.

"You stupid bastard." He had my shirt in his hands, face inches from mine. "She's out of her fucking head. Either you go or I will. Choose, brother."

Ludek appeared in the doorway. I didn't know who summoned him or if his gift alone had him come to us.

"I was sworn to secrecy. I'm sorry. Know that my mate will protect her with his life."

"What was the story?" I asked him. He looked repentant. "What. Was. It? Was it a prophecy? If you have sent her there to die, there will be more hell unleashed on this fucking land than you have ever seen." My quiet seething had heat building in the room. A storm was mounting outside, rain lashing at the windows. The rest of the family members gathered, no doubt drawn by our shouts.

"It was the story of the namesake of Heilig," the queen said. "The heart of our land. I saw in your mate's mind that she believed there was a way to close the Veil. She believes it is a Veil between the realm of the living and dead. I watched her walk out of the palace." There was at least truth in her story, and for that reason alone, I heeded her. I briefly wondered about the dynamic between her and the king. A tangent of disassociation in my rage.

Silas swore, thunder echoing it.

"Did you see how she planned to close the Veil?" I asked, dangerously soft. She shook her head and said something about elements. "My mate and her brother closed the Veil between the human realm and Aoifsing. Do you know how she did it?" I could see the royal family take a collective breath. "She sacrificed herself. Did you know that? She crossed over and used human magic to close the Veil. The only reason—" I snarled and pinched my nose. "The only reason she didn't die was because your sister"—I pointed to Konstantín— "had a vision and gave every single drop of her power to her children so they didn't combust in the explosion. Did you know that, Your Majesty? Saskeia was murdered because she had nothing left. And you." I pointed to Saski. "You thought it would be funny to play with a female who had been beaten and torn apart."

"I'm sorry," Saski said.

"I don't care if you're sorry." I looked around the room, noting what Neysa took. "I need a fucking hawk. I want to know every single thing you know about this mess. I want a guide, a scout."

Everyone scrambled. Silas stood, arms crossed.

"Cadeyrn, I had meant to be there for her, and the night... went differently."

"Don't you think I know that? Why do you think I wasn't there? Do you think I gave a shit about what happened this morning? I fail her time and again, and she thinks *she's* the monster." I laughed, dark and sick. "I'm a worthless piece of shit. And she is willing to die for all of us. You know as well as I do that if there is something in that bullshit story they fed her about giving yourself over to the elements or some shit, she will do it. Neither Basz nor Reynard will be able to stop her." I was shaking.

"So when do we go?"

"Now." He nodded and left the chamber.

Saski spoke to Silas in the hall. "I truly did not mean to cause such a stir."

"Of course you did. But this is not about you. You would like to think so, though. You want help getting rid of those ghostly bastards? Find my cousin's mate. Otherwise, when we do, we will get the hell out of here and let you lot rot. The only reason I fucked you is because you look enough like her and I was drugged with that swill you had at the party."

His bootsteps stomped away. I stood momentarily staring at the dress Neysa wore last night, draped across the chair. The dress that looked beautiful, but it wasn't at all her.

Neysa. Everything in my head is empty.

CHAPTER 21

Neysa

The beauty of Heilig was wearing off. The ground was sodden, and leaves dripped on me all day and night. On a scale of stupidity, I was quite sure this adventure tipped the scale to monumentally asinine. So here I was without either Silas or Cadeyrn. Without Silas, I didn't know if my powers would behave. Without Cadeyrn, my soul was brittle. My mate and his wealth of gifts could have warmed my frozen feet by now and healed the massive cut I got from a thorn. That was, if he weren't still pissed at me.

The fire was low and comfortable, given the night wasn't terribly cold yet. According to Basz, as soon as we crossed the gorge tomorrow, we would be in Annos. I stared into the glow, getting lost in the dancing flames.

"I know I always tease you about it, Mousey, but help me understand the dynamic between you and both males." I hung my head.

"Silas and I had a thing before Cadeyrn would even look at me. I was attracted to him. I mean, who wouldn't be?" Both males around the fire snorted. "Silas and I get along well. It's easy with him, and I didn't know he loved me. Until Bania. I fell in love with Cadeyrn slowly, and I am...quite stubborn. So is he. I thought I could never be loved liked that. To love like that. The feeling of him being in a room with me makes me crazed." I looked to Basz, who gave me a small, understanding smile. "We want a life together. Without all this bullshit." I swiped at my face where tears were falling. "There is something between Silas and me, though. None of us understands it. There's an emotive drive that links us. The mystics gifted me this thread of love, and it wound into the skin of the three of us. I don't know what that means. I only know that it causes pain. I don't want Silas to be alone and unhappy, but when I see him with a female, I want to rip her heart out like I would for my mate. It makes no sense. I feel that I must be some sort of monster. To do this to them."

Surprising me, Reynard took my hand. The males were quiet, giving me room to finish my story while a chittering of insects harmonized with the crimped edges of my breathing.

"I could have killed Saski last night. I very nearly did. I could have dealt with her being all over Silas. But when she was writhing on Cadeyrn...then she touched his stomach."

"By the gods," Reynard gasped. "I've watched what that does to him when you touch his stomach. Even when he was spelled by Bestía." I laughed a little and squeezed his hand.

"There was very nearly a diplomatic incident in that party," I said. Basz kept sharpening his sword.

"I believe, Your Highness, that the entire party was a diplomatic incident. You two get some sleep. I'll keep watch."

THE SCENT of rotting flesh permeated the air as soon as we crossed the gorge. An entire village had been overrun by phantomes. Children laid dead on the streets, parents half draped over their small bodies. Fires smoldered in cottages. There was a silence like the atmosphere itself refused to allow for breath. We three were shaking. No one escaped, it seemed. I understood then, soldiers coming home from wars where they witnessed atrocities. I understood the trauma and stress that could follow. The shapes of fae who were murdered in that village would haunt me forever.

I felt for a link. A tug. Something to tell me where the Veil was. I pulled on my magic, regardless of the distance. Something to make this senseless violence stop. According to the map, Annos wasn't a very large land. As we walked through the village, a desperate feeling of hopelessness overcame me. What if in leaving, I caused Silas to die?

We walked for hours until I suggested we make camp. I offered to take watch as they slept, and in the silence, I tried to scry in the flames. From the bag of gifts, I pulled a chunk of pyrite. It was a stone with a fire element. Holding it in my hands, I focused on the flames. After a time, images flickered on the orange. *Ewan with his head hung low, eyes sunken. Cadeyrn, battle ready, standing off with Konstantín and Arik. The prince had thick brows pinched together, eyes remorseful. The king's face was awash with little emotion. In my head I heard Cadeyrn yelling. He very rarely raised his voice. I listened closely.*

"Did you set her up? It's not even there, is it? Where is my wife?"

I was breathing hard, losing my grasp on the images. A land of turquoise waters and white sand. Sea grass and dunes met the water and slunk back into cities and towns. A wobble in the atmosphere near a hidden cove. My eyes sprung open. There was movement around us.

"Basz," I whispered. He was instantly alert. "Movement."
I felt his shield go up. Reynard moved quickly to smother the
fire, so we weren't night blind. Basz was to my left. I walked to
him in a crouch; the three of us stood back to back to back.

As though a curtain were lifted, phantomes spilled from
the woods around us. Gods above. Reynard hopped to the
highest branch and began picking them off with arrows
while Basz and I used blades, cutting off heads. I unleashed
my electricity, and it went straight through them as though
they were nothing. Think. Pyrite, tourmaline, amethyst,
rose quartz, and clear quartz. I had major protection stones.
Yanking the necklaces from my neck, I held all the stones
together and willed my energy into them. The air took a
great pause, and like a light switch, the phantomes blinked
out. We collapsed. That was a lucky break. Had there been
more, I am quite certain my stones would not have been
enough. More movement came from the direction we had
come from. Basz and I readied, and Reynard was still in
his perch. A figure dove forward and rolled. An arrow went
through her hand and she screamed. Reynard dropped down
and aimed at her heart.

"Saski?" Basz asked, trying to remove the arrow.

"Give me one reason to not kill you. It better be fucking
good because you are at the top of my list." My twin swords
were trained on her.

"You're going the wrong way."

"I figured that out, thanks. Not good enough."

"Which hand touched his stomach, Mousey? I could take
the other as well."

She snarled at him.

"I brought you a set of leathers," she offered. Hmm. Maybe.

"Why did you follow us?"

"I owe it to you. I was childish."

"On the contrary. There was nothing at all childish about how you acted. By every law I could have your head for laying your hands on my mate."

She was sweating, and Basz was trying to staunch the bleeding. He looked at me, a plea in his eyes. His mate's other sister. Fine.

"I left as soon as I heard. I thought I could track you here best. I figured," she started and cleared her throat. "You may not want me telling the others where you are."

"Yet you thought she would want to see *you*?" Reynard sneered. Saski gave him a look which could have burned through steel. She was right, though. I had needed out.

I told them that I had seen the Veil. It looked as though it were in Biancos, along the western shores of Heilig. It would be a week's trek into Biancos. From there, as the land was vast, who knows how long it would take to find the Veil. The bag of gifts pulsed as if in answer. We would head southwest in the morning.

As I fell asleep, I opened my mind slightly. The silence had been torture.

Are you okay? His tone was clipped and far away.

The Veil isn't in the north. It's in Biancos. We head out in the morning. Saski found us. I didn't kill her.

See. You're not a monster.

I am, though. And I'm sorry. For everything.

If you're a monster, he said, *Then I am too.* Tears were running freely now. *I don't care what it asks for. I don't want to lose you. Do not make that call, Neysa.*

You can't ask me not to.

I just did. I would rather see the world burn than lose you.

What would that make us?

Monsters in love? he said, and I could hear a slight smile in his voice. I could picture the twinkle in his eyes and his dimple gracing the world.

You realize you just gave me an image of two colourful furry things running towards each other on a beach, right?

Yes, that's clearly what I meant.

Good night, Cadeyrn.

Good night, Caráed.

SASKI WAS still horrible. Perhaps it was a defense mechanism. I knew how those could backfire. But she was still awful, and despite having come to help us, she seemed thoroughly uncontrite over how she acted. Squatting by a stream to fill our water skeins, I washed a bit of grime from my engagement ring. One stone for each province in Aoifsing, a diamond from his mother, large and clear enough to see glinting colour from an aquamarine set beneath it. Our birthstones, our birthrights. Squeaking leather moved next to me.

"You know, you could have had fun at that party."

I glared at Saski. The males were doing their thing further away to give us privacy in our conversation.

"How so? You made sure I arrived without my mate. You were all over both of them fairly quickly."

"It wasn't my fault you two were arguing before. Nor was it my fault that Silas was so worked up by you I could have taken him in that ballroom." Don't hit her, Neysa. Don't be that girl.

"Perhaps not, but you certainly used every bit of opportunity to cause trouble."

"I like a challenge. Surely you can understand that. I have little issue finding male attention. Yours are both so...desirable. I wanted to see just how far I could push it."

The entire stream lit up with electricity. Shit. I sat back and stuck my hands in my armpits.

"I'd say you got your answer. You drugged them and had your legs all over my husband and, fairly soon after, had Silas in the garden. A win for you. Congratulations." I made to stand. Maybe I could sacrifice her at the Veil.

"Mm. Your mate threw my legs off him the minute you walked out. Silas dropped me on the ground when he heard you. I had pebbles in my bum." She shrugged. "You know what he told me?" I rolled my eyes and gathered my things to start back on the path. "He said he only fucked me because I look like you." Oh, Silas. "I really don't think it's fair you have both of them, though."

I laughed a little. "No. It's not. It's not fair to anyone."

"That's for damned sure," Reynard said, sidling up to me, bow over his shoulder. He really had gotten handsome. The first time I met him I thought he looked like a demon. Shades of white and cream with dull eyes. It never occurred to me he had lost his colouring from being tortured. "Ready to go, Mousey?"

I squeezed his shoulder.

Thankfully, we made it out of Annos within a day. Not that it wasn't lovely. I had expected it to look like Festaera, but it was craggy and green with cold streams and wildlife everywhere. However, the draw of Biancos and the sea pulled me away with little thought for the rugged landscape behind. A week passed. Mounting dread filled me the closer we came. Once in Biancos, our path took us along the coast, as I had seen the Veil in a seaside cove.

Nausea woke me the morning of the second week on the road. I ran to the edge of camp to empty my stomach. The vision of the pregnant belly came to mind. Quick calculations in my head had me relaxing a bit. Just terrified, it seemed. Everyone was up with my retching, pointedly not saying anything.

Tall reeds of seagrass swayed as we walked through them along the cliffs and dunes. Even breathing in the sea didn't lighten my heart. I knew Cadeyrn asked me to not give all, but if that's what it would take to close the Veil, then I would give it.

"I don't know why you liked my leathers when you have those," Saski said, pointing to my aphrim skins. "Whatever are they?" She reached over and touched my arm. My first instinct was to twist it back and knock her knees out. Yet I didn't.

"Aphrim skins. Reynard had them made for me."

"Aphrim are great scaly beasts used as disposable infantry. They make phenomenal clothing. Watertight, moveable, almost armor-like. Jealous?" Reynard asked her. I smiled, though the thought of the drooling, scaled creatures made me shudder internally.

"Quite. They also make your ass look amazing."

I burst out laughing. Okay, it was a bit of a hysterical laugh as I was still on the edge of a nervous breakdown.

"No wonder Corra was envious," I replied, wishing Corra were there with me.

Dusk was coming on quick, and though there was a definite pull—a confusion in the atmosphere—it would be risky to keep searching in the dark. We made camp in a small valley of dunes. I forced down the crab we cooked, knowing I needed my strength. I hadn't heard from Cadeyrn since the last night in Annos. It was distant enough that I knew between the wards on the castle, the stones I carried, and now the proximity to the Veil, it was as though we had a wall up between us.

Sea breezes tickled the small hairs that escaped my braid. It was beatific in this land, but then, I thought that of most places near the sea. Then the wind turned icy, and I whipped my head to the others, sitting around the fire. A high-pitched keening wail sounded in the distance.

"Mousey, get your stones ready." Reynard ripped pieces of his handkerchief and wrapped them around the tips of his arrows, dousing them in a bit of liquor from a canteen. He was ready to set them aflame. From the south we saw a fog rolling toward us. Phantomes.

CHAPTER 22

Corraidhín

Oh, I was not at all surprised to receive a hawk from Neysa saying what she did. Ewan wasn't either. Knowing it might happen and receiving it, however, were vastly different.

We had been in meetings with representatives and merchants for weeks. Ewan was utterly exhausted, and these two hooligans in my belly were kicking all night. It never helped having to deal with Etienne and his cronies. That male made every hair on my arm stand on end. Although, admittedly, I hadn't much hair. Actually, I had none on my arms. I suppose that was a human phrase I became accustomed to using. Things were fairly calm here given the extremes we had not long agoWhen the hawk came in, I was running along a path on the estate in Bistaír.

Corra,

I believe the Veil here is a separation between the realms of the living and the dead. Someone has torn it open and is commanding the phantomes. There is a story of a queen from long ago, and a book she used to harness elemental magic. I must go and see if I can close it. I have had visions of Silas dead. Cadeyrn refuses to touch me now, and I am a bit lost as you can imagine. Know that I will travel with Reynard and Basz and I will do my best to come home and kiss those babies. Should I not, please tell Ewan I love him, allaíne balaiche. Never let Cadeyrn doubt that I love him more than the stars could have ever known. Tell Silas he will always have my love. Thank you, Corra.

All my love,

Neysa

Poor sodding hawk. That was a long message. Ewan dismissed everyone from his office and put his face in his hands. I stacked the books he was always perusing on his desk. Aulde magic texts, dark magics, gateway realms, necromancing, all of the frightening things he had been reading lately in his little free time.

"I need to go," he said finally.

"Absolutely not."

"How can you tell me not to save my sister?" His eyes were red from lack of sleep.

"I can tell you that because these little beasties in me need you here. Alive. And if...if she saw Silas die, I cannot be alone, Ewan." I didn't cry, but I was close.

"Beastie." His head snapped up. "Corraidhín, her beastie. She needs her."

Neysa's little rat eater stayed hidden most of the time. She stayed on with us—we assumed to look after the babes once they were born—but she made herself pretty scarce for the most part. I went to the old barn, hoping she was there.

"Halloo, beastie, darling?" Couldn't Neysa have named her? Poor cow. There was a rustle in the moldy hay. Ewan stayed close by. "Neysa is in trouble, you see. She has gone off to deal with dead soldiers and ghosts and close another Veil." At the mention of the Veil, the beastie's head snapped up and looked to Ewan.

"Do you remember when we closed the Veil the last time?" he asked her. She huffed and lay her great head near us. "It nearly killed us. You as well, my friend. Well, I am afraid my sister may be going to get herself killed too. And her mate and his *baethaache* are not with her." Great wings spread wide. Oh, Neysa.

"Will you help her, darling?" I smoothed the scales on her snout. "You will have to fly across a great sea." She looked to me and closed her eyes. It almost looked as though she nodded. "Well then. Let's get you fed and on your way." She stood and followed me out. How does one prepare a *baethaache* for a long journey? Perhaps the same as I would prepare my brother?

Just as we climbed the steps to the house, another hawk landed.

Ewan,

You must have received a hawk from Neysa by now. I have only just found out she left. I cannot hear her in my mind. If you can, please... just tell her to come back. Or wait for me. We are on our way. I'm sorry, Ewan. I have failed you both.

Cadeyrn

Even if we sent a unit to her, it would take weeks to cross the sea. This was a waiting game now, and no one waited worse than I did. We stood and watched as Neysa's beast took flight and disappeared. I wondered if she would find her. And if it would do any good.

CHAPTER 23

Cadeyrn

This was a mistake. Every intention we had in coming here was for the greater good, yet we all felt as though we had been led to slaughter. I was not questioning Neysa's aptitude for what she had embarked upon. I did question her ability to see reason in the face of the scale of what is happening. I might have lost mine as well. However, that was why we were all together here. To keep each other in check. And she left me.

Arik prepared horses and provisions for us to reach them in Biancos, a three-day ride west. He wanted to see his sister safely back and close the Veil. My only reason for keeping faith in him. Perhaps Saski's guilt rode her hard, and that's why she followed Neysa. I hoped so. Konstantín I did not trust. He was Neysa's uncle, and his lands were in peril, but I was under no illusion that he wasn't willing to sacrifice any of us in the process. Seeing as Neysa closed the Veil between Aoifsing and the human realm, he saw that success as his foothold. The only one I trusted—cautiously at that—was Ludek. Not only did he want his mate back safely, but he had spoken plainly to me, and to Neysa it seemed, since we arrived.

"I still don't see what this bullshit queen story has to do with Neysa," Silas said, pacing the floor. The only times I had seen him pacing like this was when our parents were killed and when Neysa was taken in Turkey.

"In her mind, she saw resemblance between her task and the queen's," I said, knowing how stupid it sounded.

"The queen found a fucking book and purified the ground water, then died. How does that relate to this ordeal?"

"The queen gave in to all her power and sacrificed it all to the land."

We were quiet.

"Why does she pull this shit, brother?"

I put my head in my hands and shook it. I didn't know.

"Don't start blaming yourself, either. She's a right pain in my arse. I don't care if she's your mate. Neysa refuses help, then lands herself in deeper shite than she started out in."

"We should have left already. What's taking Arik so long?" We were waiting outside the stables in the courtyard and, just as I asked, there was a commotion from inside. Arik stormed outside, Ludek on his heels.

"A faction has moved north from Manu," he told us, out of breath. "The port has been closed. They move to Biancos. Ships have moved to the coast."

"Where is your fleet?" Silas asked. Ludek looked murderous and fanned his hand to Arik as if to tell him to get on with it.

"It was mostly in Manu. We have a few ships off Sot, but that is too far for aid."

Neysa, we have a problem.

Having a problem of our own at the moment.

She screamed.

What's happening?

Phantomes.

Shit. A regiment is moving towards you. Enemy ships closed the seaport in Manu and are off the coast of Biancos. Konstantín has no fleet available. If you can reach Ewan, tell him to send ships. We are heading out now.

Don't come.

Don't be stupid.

She screamed again, and I saw a flash of what was happening. My heart sank. They were overwhelmed. Four of them against a hundred. I pulled the horse to me.

"We ride. Bring hawks. They are under attack." I was shaking. Silas put his hand on my arm. "They are overrun, Silas. We're going to be too late."

"Like hell we are."

I mounted the horse and kicked it into movement. The sounds of others following behind became a matching beat to my heart.

Stay alive.

Trying. I can barely hear you.

Then she was gone.

ONCE WE reached the city limits, there were soldiers waiting to accompany us. I kept riding, noting the hawks launching into the skies. We scaled the bridge across the Matta River, and Silas disappeared. Bloody hell. He must have given himself over to his power and took the river to the sea. I refused to stop for the night, despite Arik and the others urging us to. It was dusk when we set off, and I saw well enough in the dark to keep going. Ludek, who I got the feeling wasn't much for warfare, was in agreement with me and kicked further forward. Exhaustion pulled at me after a full twenty-four hours of riding. No one would benefit if I couldn't muster my gifts when we arrived, so we camped only as long as necessary to recharge. Maybe Silas would get there. Maybe Ewan sent ships. The odds were against everything working out, and Neysa, bloody hell, I knew, had no intention of not seeing it all through to the end.

WHEN I was young and lived in the forest with my mother, we passed the days with her teaching me. She showed me how to hone my gifts. Even those which were foreign to her, like healing and particle transference—or "that blinking thingy" as Neysa called it. She was proficient on the sword. Not a warrior, but her patience and control allowed for her to give me a foundation for my skills. When I was three or four, we went to live with my aunt and uncle. The twins were a year younger and were not happy about the arrangement. I didn't let that bother me. I always wanted people to like me, and that included them. We three children began training together. Silas, though younger, had always tried to bully me. Until we began really training. Battle skills came so naturally to me that he struggled to keep up. I found him once, late at night, having snuck out of the house to practice. I watched him for hours and finally asked to join him. He was so pissed that I had been watching and nearly refused to let me join until I slunk off, half-defeated already. It was in Silas' nature to help, and when I turned away from him that night, he called me back. From then on, we both trained day and night, getting stronger and feeding off one another's strengths and weaknesses. Corraidhín found out about our nightly training by the time we were eleven. She was in a tip over it. She demanded we show her exactly how to be the best and threatened to tell her parents if we refused.

The three of us worked best together. It has been that way for almost three centuries. When Neysa came into the picture, it was Corraidhín who said she was our missing piece. Even before Neysa and Silas, and well before I pulled my head out of my ass and admitted I hadn't stopped thinking about her since the day we met. Now Corraidhín was half a world away, Neysa was quite literally at death's door, and Silas and I were at two separate points trying to get to her. Neysa was her own animal, and perhaps I was a fool to think she would not go off on her own. Perhaps part of who she was would have to need both my cousin and me for her to be satisfied.

When I was small, my mother soothed me when my cousins wouldn't play with me, telling me to always remember, *Chanè à doinne aech mise fhìne.* I am no one's but my own. It seemed so apropos a phrase for Neysa's personality that I had that dagger made for her with the phrase etched upon it. Plus, the addition of "my own beautiful disaster," as Silas calls her. I debated the dagger for weeks, thinking she would see straight through the gift and know I was out of my mind in love with her. Finally, I gave in. The relief I felt when she opened it—the total wash of heat when she stroked the blade and laid her head on my shoulder—I knew there was no turning back for me. Years of learning to keep myself upright while riding was the only reason I didn't topple off the damned horse. My mate had been hit. I felt it like I had been hit myself. Whether it was an arrow or a blade, I couldn't be sure, but I knew she was down. I whipped my head to Ludek, grabbing at my inner bicep. His eyes were wide, staring at me. We pushed on, and I felt another blow. This time to my stomach and another to my leg. It felt like a puncture. Dammit. I prayed to whatever gods watched over us that at least one of us made it to her in time, and that they both pulled through this. Arik called that we were getting closer. Only a few hours left, he said. We didn't have hours. I reached to Ludek, willing him, with my eyes, to trust me. Hauling my powers from the deep well within me, I invoked my particle transference, and Ludek and I disappeared from our group of riders and landed in a roll, in the midst of a full-scale battle.

Before we could take in the whole scene, a blade came down towards Ludek, and I knocked it away. Perhaps Ludek shouldn't have come, but I wouldn't keep him from his mate. Phantomes were everywhere, confusing the scene. Who were they fighting? In the near distance, a roar sounded, and Ludek blanched. Basz came tearing through a group of the ghostly army, covered in his own blood, and limping.

"Where is she?" I yelled, hacking through the necks and torsos of the phantom soldiers. Ludek swung and used his shield to fend off the creatures. I threw a shield around him, knowing Basz likely used too much of his already. I moved him to the outer rim of the fighting.

"She was close, and we lost her. She has her stones, but they weren't holding up."

"She's down, Basz. Where is the Veil?" He pointed toward the sea. I ran, creating a tunnel of fire to burn through the demons.

Where are you? I'm here. Where are you? A moan. Then the thumping beat of a set of wings. Within me, my *baethaache* pushed, trying to emerge. Neysa's beastie landed on a cluster of phantomes and roared. She charged toward a cove, hidden behind a dune swarming with phantomes. Dammit. Where was she?

Arrows flew, tipped in fire, finding their marks far faster than anyone but Reynard could fire. I sent flares into the oncoming soldiers and they fell. Just beyond the horizon were twenty or so ships heading in. There were rowboats on shore and fae soldiers, both alive and dead, trudging through the sand. Any question I had as to whether they were friendly or not was answered when I saw Saski firing arrows, crouched in front of something. Reynard's shots were from the same direction. They were covering Neysa. Fully encased in a shield of fire, I moved towards my mate. Anything near me incinerated as I made my way to that cove. I saw her crawling further to the cave mouth, blood trailing from her. I was swarmed by enemies, both corporeal and phantasmic, delaying my forward progress. I was screaming and slashing, arrows piercing, supporting my efforts. When the path had cleared again, she was gone.

CHAPTER 24

Neysa

Hearing that the phantomes weren't our only problem really put a damper on my plans. Basz and Saski wanted to know who the insurgents were. I told them that if a news brief containing the name and rank of their leader was sent to me, they'd be the first to know. Then I cut the head off a phantome and caused a white out around us. We held them off for a day, then managed to keep a shield up around us using crystals and the scraps of power the four of us could muster while we slept in shifts. Basz was limping from a blade that met his knee. Reynard tried a field patching of it, but his power was too gutted.

I didn't want Cadeyrn anywhere near this mess. If I tried to open up communication with Ewan, not only would he send ships away from defending Aoifsing, if I knew my brother and Corra, there was a good chance that one or both of them would be on one. And I wasn't willing to risk them. We just had to hold out long enough to bring down the Veil.

The symbols in the book were quite basic, indicating there was a build-up of air and pressure, resulting in a continuous blast that kept the Veil seemingly closed to this realm. If I could get to it and destabilize the compression, the Veil could very well collapse from the force of it. If I were lucky, I could manage it from this side. If not, I may have to stand within. Either way, it had to close, and compared to the main Veil in Aoifsing, this task was elementary. That was, apart from the damned phantomes and insurgents.

Basz carried with him a sheet of paper on which we copied the symbols from the book in the order they were written. The first page of the text looked almost like the Periodic Table of the Elements, though far more simplistic. Elements in the human realm either did not exist here, or did not work the same. The knowledge I had used to close the Veil months ago was useless here, because though my crystals worked in protection, their chemical makeup and mine were scrambled here. We had to rely on magic and strength alone. Kind of a letdown, really.

As I tried to get to sleep, I thought of my brother and the life he should have had. The love between him and Corra and the babies they waited on. My family. They were the reason this had to work. I drifted off, clutching the *adairch dorhdj,* and saw, amongst the ghostly fog of phantomes, my mother standing on the edge of the water. I tried to sit up, but she put her finger to her mouth and gestured to the sea behind her. Then she was gone. In her place was a vision of her brother, the king of Heilig, wreathed in darkness.

It was roughly eight hundred meters from where we rested to the Veil. If Basz could cover us while I made a run for it, Reynard covering from the high dunes and rock faces, then I might make it.

"I can use the wind," Saski said. We all looked at her, wondering why she hadn't said anything earlier. "To divert them. Blow them off course. With the sand, the fae would find it quite difficult to see as well."

"That was your escape?" I asked.

Basz shook his head, disappointed.

"Why not just go?" I spat. We had fought for two days straight. I was using my left arm only, as my right shoulder was shot, my grip nearly gone, and all of us were actively bleeding, our fae healing nullified. Yet she never indicated any particular powers.

"I considered it," she admitted. I scrubbed at my filthy, blood-caked face.

"Let's get ready, then." I checked my weapons and kissed the *adairch dorhdj,* attempting to program it to help us out and maybe just for luck. I couldn't think about the fact that I had essentially said goodbye to my mate in a letter to Corra. Or that I may never see those babies, much less have my own. I couldn't think about the fact that I was sure Konstantín had willingly led us to slaughter here, unwilling to sacrifice himself. That he was a coward. Unlike my mother, his sister, who sacrificed all of herself for us. Unlike my father who protected us all with his last dying breath. I had a job to do.

So, I ran. The weight of my weapons and the drain on my system from exhaustion and blood loss pulled me back, making me feel like I was running in a dream, never getting anywhere. Off the coast, a beast's roar sounded. My *baethaache* beat her wings furiously, knocking down sails and soldiers alike. She came ashore and tore through insurgents. I sobbed from relief and fear.

An arrow caught me in the soft spot between my neck and shoulder. I went down hard and was covered in phantomes immediately. Basz was yelling, trying to pull his shield up, but I felt him getting further away. Or perhaps I was being pulled. I couldn't tell. The beastie came closer and, siphoning off her link to my power—a storage unit of sorts that had sat, untapped for a few months—I summoned electricity to blast the phantomes away. Clawing at the ground, sand running through my fingers, I managed to stand and bear crawl toward the cove. I felt heat from behind but couldn't turn to see. A swell of phantomes closed around my exit path. Not that I would use it. The throbbing aberration of the Veil loomed before me. I walked closer and heard two voices screaming for me. Silas and Cadeyrn both were trying to get to me. No, no. They weren't supposed to be there yet. My beastie beat her wings like a turbine, keeping everyone back. Almost there. Once the Veil was gone, the fae soldiers would be ripe for killing. It wouldn't be hard. Cadeyrn's power could wipe them out in one fell swoop. I hoped. The skies darkened. A sheet of charcoal smudged over the land. Thunder crackled and heat flared.

Walking into the Veil, there was an audible crack as I crossed into it, not quite crossing over. I was on the threshold of the living and the dead. A release of my white energy was the catalyst I needed to begin to compress the air within the pocket of this in-between. I felt it rise and rise in me, then burst out like the colours that popped in the air while we were on the barge. The white energy pushed all around me, making this pocket of ether between life and death a pressurized capsule. Once I felt as though my head was near to bursting itself, I willed my electricity to come out. Cadeyrn's heat from outside as he neared the Veil pushed at the capsule I had built, causing the pressure to increase further. The dead swarmed against the threshold, mounting the invisible shield I had created. The pressure from Saski's wind, Silas' storm, and Cadeyrn's heat from the opposite side created a negative pressure, preventing them from entering. And me from getting out.

Every warning on an aerosol can or pressurized air canister warned against adding heat or pressure. They explode. That was how I intended to collapse this anomaly in the realm. The pressure from what my mate and the rest were doing outside created a negative pressure like a vacuum seal, keeping the explosion from harming them. Instead of the negative pressure keeping a biological eccentricity like a virus out, it was keeping out the magnitude of the particle explosion I was creating. Being in that moment meant I was past the point of being frightened. All I had left was my drive to end this plague, and a universe full of regret for the life I had started to build.

Once the Veil was fully swelled and pressurized, I felt an uncomfortable pop in my head. Objectively, as though looking from an outside standpoint, I registered that I had a small aneurism due to the effect of the compressed air filtering through my body. With that, I poured all my electricity out of me, releasing everything I had ever known.

CHAPTER 25

Silas

My entire head felt like it was going to blow apart. We all felt and heard the explosion, yet all that remained was a ringing in my ears. I had never been on a human battlefield with the weapons they used. Tanks, missiles, landmines. I knew from reading about it that, oftentimes, the eardrums of those who were nearby would blow. The profound silence around us where there had been noise and chaos a second ago was disorientating. Cadeyrn was kneeling, facedown, blood pouring from every orifice, screaming soundlessly. I looked beyond him, where he stared.

Neysa's beast lay sprawled in the sand, her mistress's arm flung away from her still form. I stumbled toward him, feeling an emptiness in my chest. My first thought was that we needed to keep Cadeyrn calm. I honestly debated knocking him out just to buy us time. The foreseeable problem was that the strongest fae warrior in Aoifsing just lost his mate. If we didn't think of a way to calm Cadeyrn, this world was going to burn to cinders, us along with it. Basz nodded to me as though he followed my train of thought. He wasn't looking so good himself. I risked my ass and walked over to him. He looked up at me, blood running from his eyes, nose, and ears. Complete defeat shone on his face. His body swayed. I knelt in front of him, hoping he wouldn't stick his dagger through my gut, and placed my hands on his shoulders. If I could get him to listen long enough...

"Cadeyrn, listen to me." But I didn't finish because something slammed into my back and I went down. Hard. Cadeyrn incinerated the attacker, then yanked a sword out of me with a bellow that shook sand from the dunes and covered the wound with his hand. It still bled, so something in me knew I was still alive. Cadeyrn held himself over me, attempting to heal me. He hadn't even made a move to walk to *Trubaíste*. He knew she was dead.

"There might be a way to fix it," said a soft voice. Ludek, perhaps.

"If his sister weren't pregnant, this world would already be gone." He spoke with such unnerving quiet, I shivered. I took in a shallow breath. Another healer moved forward to take over for Cadeyrn, but he growled and waved them off.

"In the story of the queen, her mate finds her. He is a necromancer," Ludek said, but my vision was fading.

I watched as Reynard walked to where Neysa's body lay, still and battered. Her cousins stood around on one knee. I wanted to kill them. Her beastie lay just as still, a wing lying atop Neysa's chest. She was burned and bloody, her arms at odd angles. Cadeyrn kneeled, catatonic to everything around him. Reynard lifted her without a thought for permission from any of her family, and somewhere in my consciousness, I applauded the weasel. Neysa had been his friend when no one else had bothered. Across the beach, to a waiting rowboat, he carried her body. Cadeyrn draped me across his shoulder and carried me as well. As he laid me in the boat next to *Trubaíste*, from her bag of gifts fell a wand of selenite. Reynard set it atop her, and it glowed. Other small craft moved onto the beach, and I saw Cyrranus step out with Turuin. They took in the scene. Cyrranus looked daggers around and lunged for Neysa. He placed both her hands on the selenite, making it glow further. Cadeyrn was trying not to look at her face. Trying and failing. Her beautiful face, blue and bloody. I tried to reach out to him but found I couldn't fucking move. I knew pain in its most basic sense. I'd been cut and stabbed and shot with arrows more time than I cared to admit. Seeing *Trubaíste* like that—all but removed from this world—broke something in me I never knew existed. I didn't know whether I hated her for it. All I knew, as I lay dying, was that nothing in me would ever be the same without her.

"We need a necromancer," Reynard rasped.

The others from Aoifsing looked at him like he was stark fucking mad. He repeated himself.

"There was a prophecy. We need a necromancer!" he screamed hysterically, over and over. Cadeyrn joined my hands with Neysa's. An impossible situation. Others came up behind us.

"Where are your mystics?" Cadeyrn asked Arik or Ludek, I couldn't be sure.

"Likely with our father," Arik answered. My cousin nodded absently.

"One day he will burn for this."

"I know," Ludek whispered. His brown eyes went wide. "There is a spark left in her." He stepped forward. "Here." He touched her abdomen. "Where her *baethaache* was. There is a spark. We can keep the spark alive until we find a necromancer."

Cadeyrn scrambled into the boat and placed his hands on her face, her chest, her stomach. His tears mixed with her blood, running along the cold sides of her still lovely face. His body was rumbling, the very ground beneath us responding to his anguish. If it didn't stop, I sensed we might have an issue with the reverberations causing a tidal wave.

"If we can get them to Aoifsing, we can get someone to help," Reynard said, looking at Cyrranus for some reason. I was too fucked to figure out why.

"It's not as far as we assumed," Turuin said. "Take them to the ship. We can be in Saarlaiche within a week."

"I will come. Once I rest, I can force the winds to push us faster. Let me help," the vixen cousin pleaded. Her eyes focused on me with a mix of shame and horror.

"I will as well. I am not as strong as Saski, but I can keep her power going." Arik placed his sword in front of Cadeyrn. A token of deference.

"Then we go," Cadeyrn said, barely above a whisper. He looked up at us all. Flames burned in his eyes, and I knew that if she didn't come back, this world was in for an unleashing of hell.

"MOUSEY."

I woke to Reynard's voice.

"We are headed home," he said to *Trubaiste*. "You will be in Saarlaiche in a few days."

I had a sleep clogged memory of him coming in to tell Cadeyrn to go eat. I'd been in and out of consciousness for two days, and Cadeyrn had been crouched next to his mate's body the whole time. No one needed him sputtering out too. Reynard climbed on the desk in the ship's cabin and spoke to *Trubaíste*, though she was still not of this world.

"I told your mate to eat," he said. "Between you and me, I hope he bathes too. As it stands, you are dead and look better than he does." He touched her hair. "You fought for me. When no one else would. I don't even know why I call you a little mouse. You've never been a mouse. You were like a raging cat, and I thought, no wonder those two male specimens love you. So, hold on. Okay, Kitten?"

"*Paítherre moinchaí*," I rasped from next to Neysa. "She is a *paítherre moinchaí*." A panther monkey.

"So she is. And you, God of the Forest? Feeling alive?"

"No, but apparently I am, Weasel. My cousin?"

"Eating and bathing, I hope. Silas, if this goes poorly and she doesn't make it, Cadeyrn..." He trailed off, and I nodded shallowly. "Keep reminding him that there is good in this world."

I rolled with a grunt and laid both hands on her. The selenite glowed brighter than it had yet. After a time, the selenite glowing brighter and brighter, Cadeyrn walked in. He placed his hands atop mine. A white glow swelled in the cabin. The ship seemed to pick up speed. We were moving like arrows across the sea. Saski and Arik were working tirelessly to move the winds, but it seemed the tides were being pulled as well. I had to hope that between all of us and the company we kept, we could bring her back. Reynard whispered that he was sorry for all he put her through, and all she had endured. That she deserved more. She bloody well did. She always had.

CHAPTER 26

Neysa

Sounds that I knew should be familiar were foreign. If I stayed completely still, the sounds might go away until I figured out where I was. Who I was. Scuttling and humming. In my mind, the sounds were close and invasive. To have gone from complete unconscious existence to heightened senses was frightening. Flowing sounds that stopped and started, whistling, more scuttling. Thumping. Thumping from within me. Rationally, I was aware the thumping was my heartbeat. If there was another thumping sound, further away, it must be someone else's heartbeat. Who? I couldn't recall anything before this moment. The flowing sound became louder, and the scuttling faded away.

I opened my eyes to a box. Closed in. Not a box. A room. Baskets hung from rafters. My mind said the rafters held the ceiling up. Plants spilled from the baskets. There was heat. I looked to the wall, where a fire burned and a kettle hung. I knew heat. I...needed heat. There was little light, yet I could see. Memories came on in a rush. I was in bed and a man—my father—told me stories to drive away the darkness. In my mind, a boy sat next to me, looking out. Looking at the sea. I could breathe thinking of the sea. If I concentrated hard enough, I could hear the sea from this room.

There were warm things on my body. I touched them. Stones? They lined along my midsection, covered my heart, my legs. One on my forehead. It slid off as I touched it, and it clattered to the ground. The flowing stopped, and the scuttling drew close again.

"Ah, *allaíne aoín*," a female voice said. "I wondered when you would wake." I began to shake and shiver. "Slowly, *caráed*. It is a transformation."

She removed the stones, one at a time, then wrapped me in something soft against my skin. My brain noted it was fuzzy and familiar. The only familiar thing, apart from the sound of the sea. There was a scent in it that seemed to merge with my own. Something like the sea, but softer. I closed my eyes again. The fae female, round-faced and dark-skinned, lifted me easily, moving me to a chair near the fire. She placed a stone in my hand to hold, and stones around my neck. Memories came of placing stones around me and fighting. Swinging a sword. I winced, and there was an explosion in my mind. I cried out. Something was pressed to my lips. I drank, and it soothed me, reminding me of quiet nights with dogs. Then a memory of drinking by the sea with another fae. A male. His watery eyes were looking at me. I felt warmth on my face, eyes blurring. The female with me began brushing out my hair and singing. I didn't recognize the tune or words, but it wound around my soul. She stopped singing as she smoothed a sweet-smelling oil into my hair.

"Pl—" I stopped, choking on getting the sound out. "Please," I wheezed. I touched my throat. "Sing."

She smiled at me and patted my shoulder, then began singing anew.

If I loved you more than life itself,
If I brought you brightness to your day,
Would you tell me you would light the skies,
Would you tell me I could stay?
If I stayed with you and made you mine,
If I could braid my soul inside of thine,
Could we stay forever thus entwined?
Could we never see the end of time?

I squeezed my eyes closed, trying to reach for a thread that seemed to dangle tauntingly from that song. The female rubbed the oil on my arms, kneading the flesh and muscle. Dim light caught on a thin band of gold. I touched it, and faces appeared in my mind. Two sets of nearly translucent green eyes and faces so close to the surface of recollection. She continued her ministrations on my arms.

"Trying to get the blood flowing again. You've been through a trial, love." She moved to my hands, pulling the fingers one at time and wiggling them. Atop one hand was a collection of freckles. I knew those. They had always been there. I smoothed the skin over them. A picture formed of the night sky and the same arrangement of stars and the freckles on my hand. Then another picture of a broad, beautiful back with yet again the same constellation of markings. I took a sharp intake of breath as a pang went through me. She smiled. Once done, a dressing gown was brought over, and she helped me into it, then made to take the fuzzy wrapping from me. I protested, keeping it with me. The scent kept me from wanting to run. My legs felt the urge to sprint. I didn't even know where I would run and that scared me more. There was a shuffle from beyond a door, then a tapping.

"Rhia, It's Ewan." I knew that name. The picture of the boy flashed before me again.

"Come then, *balaíche*." The door opened, a waft of sea air following the man inside. Something cracked in my chest, and I squeaked.

"Hallo, *áoín baege*." Little one, I knew it meant. "I've missed you." He sat on a stool facing me and took my hands.

"She's only just awoken. Have a care. Everything is new again." I looked into his eyes, a deep, warm, brownish green, and knew he was my brother.

"Yes, madam. Do you know me, Neyssie?" I nodded and squeezed his hands. Tears slipped from his eyes. "I knew you would. Corraidhín warned that you might not. I told her we would always know each other." That name he said sounded so...right.

"Corra?" I managed to get out.

"Yes. Corra. My wife and your friend. She is with children, do you remember? You promised to come back and kiss them. And here you are. Rhia tells me it may be quite some time to be back to yourself, but she doesn't know you, does she?" I didn't know me either. "Can I give you something?" I nodded. My voice was so harsh, and I didn't want to keep barking at him.

I don't mind you barking. I've missed having a dog. My mouth dropped open hearing him speak to my mind.

I had a dog. Two. Bixs—Bixby. And Cuthbert.

He wiped at his eyes with the back of his hand and reached into the pocket of his jacket.

"This is yours. You may not remember it yet, so he asked me to give it to you. He said to take your time, and when you remember, he will be here. May I?" He slipped a ring onto my finger. I knew this ring. It had stones hammered into a white gold band, a large diamond shining from the top. It slid onto my finger, and a name came to mind.

Cadeyrn.

Yes. Cadeyrn gave this to you. I could see his face in my mind, and touching the ring made my stomach flutter. I knew it was his scent that covered the fuzzy wrap around me, and I knew I wanted him near, but he said to wait until I remember him. And I didn't. Not really.

"It will take time. Do you recall when we were reunited at the Elder Palace?" I did. "Cadeyrn was there. He freed me from them. I knew when I saw you two together that he loved you. I don't even think you knew. He looked at you like you could make it rain sausages and it would be fine by him."

I coughed.

"So, think on it. And when you remember, call upon me. Or him. I must go, but I shall be back soon. I love you, Neyssie. Thank you for coming back."

I was so tired that I closed my eyes as he kissed my forehead. When I woke, there were two cold things pushed up against either of my bare calves. I moved my legs, and the cold things were replaced by wetness. Dogs. I sat forward and hugged them, sobbing. They stayed by me the rest of the night as I slept. When I awoke, Rhia was there making a ruckus with cooking and changing this and that. I stood and walked around, legs as shaky as a newborn fawn.

"Good morning. This was left for you." On the counter where she cooked was a slice of cake. It was yellow and spongy with a ribbon of red in the middle, and what looked like cream on top. On the plate next to it lay an amethyst. I touched it and recalled it floating from my hand. Then felt the memory of hands on me—in my hair and on my arms. I turned from Rhia, who had smothered a cough, and started in on the cake.

The dogs and I walked along the sea, and through a grove of gold and silver trees. The leaves caught the light, and I remembered walking through these with both males whose faces appeared in my mind. There was a wall at the end of the grove. I sat on it, the stone giving me visions of sitting there, my legs over the legs of Cadeyrn, my head on his shoulder. Suddenly it was so hard to breathe. I panicked. I knew him. I knew all of him, and maybe I didn't know how to love him, but I knew my soul knew him. Yet I couldn't breathe. The dogs pawed me with concern on their shaggy faces.

I know you, I said, hoping he could hear me. *I remember you. Would you be okay if I came to see you?*

Please. Do. A feeling of relief came through. I swear it was less than a few minutes when a figure came through the grove. His head was hung, night-dark hair crested up like the wing of a great bird. I stood and smoothed down the light dress I wore. My stomach clenched, and my body felt like it was on fire from within. I didn't know where to look. Surely, he could sense how I felt. I was nervous. Finally, his eyes met mine, and his hands reached out to touch mine, asking a question with his fingers. I closed my fingers around his and held them against me.

"I don't remember everything. But I know you."

"It's okay. We can take it slow. These two," he said, scratching the ears closest to his feet, "were convinced I was keeping you hidden. I guess their assumptions were correct and they shall never trust me again."

I smiled at him. The first smile. His neutral expression broke, and a look like he lost something crossed his face. I touched it, unable to keep my hands from him. His eyes closed, and a hand went around my back. I had flashes of memory. Kissing on a balcony in a cave. Fighting in a palace. Laying on a bed of ferns near here. The visions faded, but I wanted more of them. I wanted more of him. I let myself fall against his body, looking up into his face. With one hand I traced the lines of cheekbones and jaw. With the other, I touched his stomach over the fabric of his shirt. His head turned down and he bent, slowly, a question in his eyes, and touched his lips to my cheek. Then my eyelids. My hand went around the back of his neck and stroked his hair. His lips moved along my jaw and finally found my lips, where they kissed me so hesitantly. I shuddered and clenched my hand on his stomach. His hand shot into my hair, and he kissed me more thoroughly. I couldn't get enough. The dogs started whining, and we pulled away at the sound of others approaching.

"So that's where you ran off to," Rhia called. "I suppose things are getting clearer, then? Majesty," she intoned to Cadeyrn and bowed. He bowed in return.

"Thank you, Rhia." Tears were streaming from his eyes. I nearly looked away; the pain from those tears was almost unbearable. Behind her, my brother stood, shifting from foot to foot. I stepped forward and hugged him. With a force like rushing water, our lives together as children came back to me, then my life as a child without him. Memories of fighting alongside one another. The death of our mother. The death of our father. I hugged him tighter, and he wrapped his own arms around me. It wasn't everything yet, but this—my brother—was the foundation for my memories. My life. The circumstances surrounding what happened to me were just out of reach, but I could grasp the feeling behind both Ewan's and Cadeyrn's mannerisms and Rhia's ministrations, and it all pointed toward my having died. Flashes of another female who should have been dead came before my eyes. Platinum hair and her hands on my mate. I tried to shake the images out. Memories of hitting her. Of feeling a fault line in my soul rip open from not having my mate.

Of fighting him and loving him. Of a necromancer unravelling the threads that bound the female to reanimation. I looked at Cadeyrn, who I knew had seen the images in my head. I couldn't control them yet. Then I turned to Rhia.

"You are a necromancer? And you brought me back?"

"I am, and the answer to the second question is a bit more complicated, *allaíne colleíne*." I implored her with my eyes and turned to the two males with me. "Perhaps you would like to hear your tale in your home? Your mate can tell it better. I must get to cleaning my cottage." She stroked my hair and tucked it behind my ear, then made a symbolic sweep of her thumbs across my forehead and chest. "Remember, it is not our memories alone that indicate our happiness. It is the emotion behind them. Some things may have lost their clarity, but nothing stands between the notion of two souls entwined. Good day."

Flagstones with tiny fossils made up the extended patio at the back of the manse. Home, Rhia called it. I knew it here. As soon as I touched the stone walls I remembered being here. Perhaps the happiest I remembered being. Cadeyrn suggested we sit out back where we could see the horizon over the sea. A low wall had chairs atop and cushions on the ground beneath that looked far more comfortable. My legs still ached enough that I chose to stretch out on them. He sat next to me and held out a glass of wine.

"Where shall I begin?" he asked, taking a sip. I was back on that cave balcony again, and the emotion behind that memory was a wave of granite against my mind. Without thinking, I turned and kissed him, needing that emotion to have a buoy to hang on to. Pulling back, he looked at me with heavily lidded eyes and a dumbfounded expression.

"I died?"

He stared out at the vastness of open water. It was still warm enough to sit outside in the gilded light of early evening, though a chill went straight through me.

"We were in Heilig." He touched my arm and showed me images of being there. Even that of a party. Through his eyes, I saw me looking uncomfortable and angry. I could remember feeling destroyed. "You found a story of a queen who was able to save her kingdom and its lands, and it gave you the idea that you could do it too. Only, you had been given only half the story. The lands in the story were not plagued. They were cursed. It required a sacrifice to lift the curse. The legend was a prophecy doctored over centuries, and you arrived and fit the requirements of the prophecy." I heard a soft voice in my head retelling the tale, notes of regret in his voice. "You and I, we were at odds that day. You figured out what needed to be done to close the Veil between the living and the dead, and you left."

He yanked at the back of his neck and shot a hand through his hair, making it stand up. I touched it. He smiled at me, small and sad.

"I knew what you would do. You willful, beautiful creature. I guess you realized I would have done anything to stop you. I still got there too late. You closed the Veil, but it exploded and stopped your heart and burst your brain." He tripped over his words, a sob coming out. "You were dead. I felt...nothing. There was nothing. You were gone, and Silas nearly died. A sword was in his back. I don't even know how anyone was able to get that close to him. Ludek realized there was a spark left in you. Between Silas and me, we kept the spark alive until we got here. Your brother pulled the tides to get our ship here faster. He has so much power, Neysa, and it's all good in him. I've never seen someone so powerful and yet uncompromised."

"You," I breathed. "You are the same."

"No," he laughed. "I have done terrible things in the name of what I think is right. I nearly..." He drank the rest of his glass. "I nearly set the world aflame. When you were gone. Out of spite. Only the fact that Corraidhín is pregnant kept it intact. So, no. I am far worse."

"How long was I...gone?"

"A week? I think. It has been another three that Rhia kept you asleep to recover. Had you awoken when you were first brought back, things wouldn't have gone so well."

"Did you come to see me?" He nodded and fiddled with the fabric of my dress. It was an ugly dress. I must have sent that thought along because he chuckled.

"Hmm."

"What?"

"It's humiliating. I must have looked a sight laying there all..." I made an eyes rolled back, tongue out face. He laughed.

The three siblings from Heilig and Basz were staying in Laichmonde, under watch from Turuin's soldiers. They were welcome dignitaries, and it was because of them that I was here. I knew Saski came to my aid. I knew she pulled me out from under phantomes. I knew she pushed the winds to get the ship to move faster. I knew it all, and my head forgave her. However, she took advantage of me and Cadeyrn.

"Should I stay here?" I asked, sipping from my glass, keeping my eyes down. He looked to me, and I could see from my peripheral wetness on his cheeks.

"I would very much like that. This." He swiped at his eyes. "This is your home. I know you don't remember everything. I understand. But do you remember being my wife? My mate?"

I set the glass aside and took his away. Making to touch him, I didn't know where to start. Clumsy hands scrunched the fabric of his shirt and tried pulling him closer. He watched me and drew a thumb across my lips where they parted for him.

"Help me remember everything. I know that you belong inside me." My face instantly heated. "I meant, my heart, like..." He laughed and crushed his mouth to mine, then laid me down on the cushions. As he hovered above me, his hair fell forward, tickling my chest, and I arched up into him. Behind his ribs a fluttering had him growling and sweeping across my mouth with his tongue. I raked my nails up under his shirt and down his rippled back.

"I take it back. I meant inside me."

Chuckling against my mouth, he teased his fingers along the neckline of my dress. I pulled his shirt over his head and stopped to stare at his chest before fastening my mouth to it. His hands dove in my hair and moved down my sides before lifting my ugly dress overhead. The breeze blew in and had us moan from the feeling of a thousand fingers tickling our heated skin. His mouth moved down my stomach, stopped by my navel and circled it with his tongue as his fingers leisurely slipped along my body. I pulled my feet high up and pushed at his trousers with them until he was as bare to me as I was to him. He looked at me with eyes that were nearly in an alternate plane of existence. My hips rolled back and forth over him, his hands making their way up to my breasts and pushing them together. I arched into the touch. He sat up, his full lips on my chest, as I kept rolling over him. I moved back incrementally and pushed further. He swore and scraped fingers through my hair. With him holding my back, pressing my chest to his, I kept moving until I was gasping for air.

We laid there, the night falling around us, chilling our overheated skin, still joined.

"Don't even think about moving," I said, so tired yet content.

"Not for the world." He kissed my temple and ran his hands along my arms and back.

"I feel like I remember everything. I know I remember loving you. Feeling like I could die from wanting you or being apart."

His hands stilled on me.

"I lost you. It was bloody great luck that had you back with us. I keep thinking. If the same thing had happened the way you thought it might, when you and Ewan collapsed the Veil in Aoifsing, there would not have been a way to save you in the human realm. I wake up from nightmares screaming sometimes. I'm sorry. I am not sure I was myself at all when you were gone. If I'm

different—if you find me unappealing, I will understand."

I pulled my head back to look at him, my hair falling over my shoulder onto his.

"You told me once that the only thing about me that was unsavory to you was my lack of self-preservation," I began, and he snorted. Okay, he had a point. Or two. I was a train wreck in that department. I must have been remembering everything, because a pain akin to a wave slamming my face into a rock came back.

"You have, historically speaking, because I am perhaps still waking up, you see..." I chattered nervously and he rumbled a laugh into my hair. "...pissed me off when you try too hard to keep me from doing reckless things. And when you pull the overbearing male thing. Unappealing, though, is a word that could never be used about you." I pursed my lips and stared at his face with those cheekbones and full lips, the strong brow and green eyes that had little lines at the corners which deepened when he smiled. I cocked my head to the side and touched the hair just above his forehead. There was a tiny sliver of a silver streak in his dark locks.

"Corra told me I would give her grey hair," I said. "It seems as though your death took its toll on me as well." A lopsided smile.

"It just makes you more ravishing," I told him, smoothing the hair with my thumb. "I love you. I was hurt. I know you were too. I'm sorry. I just wanted you. Know that I came to you, wanting you. That party. I hate parties." He snickered. "She was very lucky. I was going over the laws of Aoifsing in my head while I sat there staring at her legs on you. I knew I had license to kill her for touching either of you."

"I know. We were so drugged, you sent those thoughts to me. I also seem to remember thoughts about you knocking her out of the way and taking up Reynard's persistent suggestion."

Er, well...

"No comment."

THE DOGS woke me just after dawn. Cadeyrn threw a pillow at them and hid us under the covers. I wanted to start training again, so I tried to push out of the duvet. Strong hands pulled me back and asked me to wait a little while longer. I gave in but made him promise to properly spar with me after breakfast. After breakfast, we were still wrapped in blankets, lounging on the couch, when someone came up the steps to the front door. I tried to sneak off to get clothes on, but Reynard appeared in the living room before I made it off the couch.

"Really? No clothes again, Kitten?" he said with a half-smile.

"I only dress up when things are scheduled to go to hell."

He fidgeted. I tucked the sheet under my arms and moved to hug him.

"What have you been doing with yourself, Reynard? Surely things are slow when you're not sweeping up my messes."

"Dreadfully. Have you got any famine or floods with which to contend?"

Cadeyrn returned with tea and a dressing gown I could slip around myself.

"No one was sure you would remember any of us. Apart from this beautiful beast." He gestured to my mate, who rolled his eyes.

"Apparently I am too stubborn to abide by the rules of nature. Some things are foggy, but we've been...clearing the cobwebs."

"Yes, it certainly seems so," he teased. "Not to spoil your homecoming, but I've been to see my parents." We all groaned. "Your cousin joined me on his way to Bistaír."

"Silas is in Bistaír?" I asked.

Cadeyrn nodded. Disappointment pierced through me.

"My father is vying for the position of a representative of Maesarra. He has been campaigning."

"Why am I not surprised?" Cadeyrn said, handing us all plates for the pastries he set down. I smirked at him, and he rolled his eyes at me.

"Where is your apron?" I asked. He reached over and flicked my nose.

"Apron?" Reynard asked.

"Mm. Yes, it's pink and green with little flowers. I gave it to him for Yule."

"I would pay to see that on him."

"I don't share, unfortunately."

"We know. So, I asked for a rundown of what my lovely father would like to accomplish as a representative, and it's quite a list. First and foremost, he wants to allow the establishment of personal militia. Followed by a class-based system of government. That's the start of the fun. He has some support, Cadeyrn."

"No doubt. Money is power. Has there been any word from Naenire or Prinaer since the uprising?"

"Ainsley Mads would like to speak with you and Ewan." I didn't know if he was referring to Cadeyrn or me. "She has taken over the family mines since her father and brother were killed in the battle of Prinaer. She has ideas for a unified territory of both Naenire and Prinaer, as they have worked in tandem for a millennium."

"I knew of her family. They fought alongside us. Has she elaborated on her ideas?"

"She wished to speak with you lot. I'm just the messenger."

"I've no desire to travel yet. Either we wait, or she can come here once Neysa is ready."

"If we need to go, or you need to go, I can be ready," I said. He stood and knelt in front of me, putting a hand on my face.

"I know you would be, *caráed*, but I am pulling the overbearing fae male card now. I am sick of running around the world to do others' bidding. Right now, we stay here. I would assume we would both like to be in Bistaír when the babies are born, so let that be the time frame we plan to leave here. If anyone wishes to speak to us, they can come to Saarlaiche. I am quite sure the reason we have is sufficient."

Reynard was looking away.

"I don't want to seem weak," I told Cadeyrn. "I don't want you to look like you would put me before what needs to get done."

"I will put you before anything. It's not weakness. You come first."

"No one would think you weak, Kitten. Not you." Reynard put his hand on my arm, and I was struck with a vision so clear it was as though I were standing in the scene. *The male next to me, fine and golden as he is now. Holding another male who had tanned skin and brown hair. They were speaking quietly and laughing with playfulness glinting in their eyes. Solange walking into the room and seeing them together. She smiles and leaves. The piazza at The Elder Palace, Solange speaking to the Elders. Reynard's partner standing between Elder Guards. Nanua's eyes glowing, and Reynard screaming and fighting to get to the male.* With a lurch of nausea, I was thrust from the vision.

"He was taken from you. She had him taken from you," I said to him. Horror showed in Reynard's eyes. He snatched his hand back.

"He was my world. That is why I couldn't let either of you lose each other. Love is drowning, and it is pleasure spiked with pain. Loss of a love like yours is drowning for eternity. There is no breath that doesn't burn. No night short enough to lessen the crushing weight."

I left the room and came back, dropping a crystal into my friend's hand. He looked at the rose quartz and gave me quizzical look.

"It is the stone of love. Maybe that part is far-fetched, but Ama gave me the necklace when she healed me, and she dropped one—this one—in Cadeyrn's pocket when he wasn't looking. What I want is for you to know love again. Perhaps not the same, but something wonderful. Then we can drink wine and chat about boys." I winked at him. He sniffed a laugh.

So, Reynard would dispatch messages to all the candidates for representatives, stating that they could meet in Saarlaiche in a month's time if it was their desire to help lead Aoifsing. No large summit. No palace ordeal. Small meetings. Corra was due in three months, putting us all together at Bistair for Yule. It seemed so long ago. So distant a place when we celebrated Yule together in that manor in Barlow Combe. It was one of the most wonderful nights I had spent. I was so in love with Cadeyrn and terrified to be going to Bulgaria with him. What a turn of events. I touched the gauntlet on my right arm which hid the forearm holster for my dagger. The words etched on it seemed to glow through the gauntlet. It felt good to be putting weapons on. After clicking the eyes of my training jacket, I braided my hair before a large mirror in our bedroom. I needed to see Silas. I needed him to know I was never angry with him. I just needed to see him. And that made me horrible.

You can't speak back to me, and maybe you can't hear me anymore either. Since, you know, I was dead and all that nonsense. But I was wondering if I really had to wait until Yule to see you. It's okay if that's the case. But I miss you. Did I mention the thing about me having been dead? Because that's a pretty big deal, and sometimes that trumps other bullshit. If you do hear this, give Corra a kiss for me. There was a quick feeling, like touching hands through a glass window, then it fled.

CHAPTER 27

Silas

This was a shitehole. The entire town stunk of piss and ale, and somehow this was where I chose to be for a week. When Corraidhín asked me to dispatch messages, I took leave of the estate and all the feel-good coziness she and Ewan put off and found the worst cesspool in Maesarra. Comparatively, it was still not quite as bad as the Ukrainian tavern where I found my cousin after he slaughtered hundreds of human slave runners. That was worse. There was ice on every surface of that tavern, and not the kind in the ice bars in Scandinavia where there are blond gods and goddesses walking around in knickers and fur. No, this was puke and piss iced over on the floor. I knew Cadeyrn had gone off on a rage bender when we hadn't heard from him for a couple of months. A search for the crystals turned into vigilantism. I would have done the same, sure. But it was hell to clean up.

This piss shed in the north of Maesarra seemed like a good idea at the time. The messenger I was waiting on staggered through the door and nervously handed me a slip of paper. I dropped a coin in his palm, one on the filthy table, and left. It was all but five minutes of being inside the home of the wealthiest merchant in the area before I had his daughter—or was it his wife—spread across the bed, begging me for more. She found me the day before and offered information on...oh, it was on her husband. Shite, I must need sleep. Anyway, she said he wanted to assist Etienne, Reynard's bastard of a father, in becoming a representative. I asked her price and there we were. Sad part was, I didn't care. She was pretty enough, and I was bored. So it went, pretty much everywhere I heard a buzz of who wanted to fund, support, arm, whatever, any particular male or female. My sister must know this was how I was sending back so much intelligence. I'd hardly been in the state to be sweet-talking my way through things.

This particular day, there was a noise as I slid off the female I was whorring myself to get information from. A door clicked quietly downstairs. Fuck it all to never. She pointed to the window. I grabbed the ledger she pulled for me and slid out, jumping down at least five godsdamned metres. My legs were burning as I ran full-speed three or four towns away, until I found a stream to dissolve into. Thank the fucking gods for this power. It was the only time I had any peace of mind.

Just as I started to pull back into my corporeal self, nearing Bistaír, Neysa's voice sounded in my head. She always had a way that made me crazed. If she weren't mated to my cousin, I would have sworn she was my mate. I didn't understand it. So, she wanted to see me before Yule. I pinched the bridge of my nose and kicked the root of a big fucking tree. Thunder rumbled overhead. I yanked my boots off as I stormed in the main house of the estate. I didn't know where my sister was, and at the moment she would see right through me.

"How many was it this trip, brother?" I tossed the ledger, files, notes, and sworn statements. "You don't have to do this anymore. I know why you are doing it."

"Not now, Corraidhín," I said, the pull of a bath and clean bed too strong.

"Silas," she said. Her hand was always on her belly. I wondered when Neysa would be with children. "Go see her."

"No."

"You're destroying yourself."

"She destroyed me."

"Then get your shit together and saddle that horse. Or whatever the saying is. Listen, brother. This will get you killed, and I can't have that."

"Cadeyrn threatens to burn the realm to ash without an intervention, but I fuck a few bastards for information about their sorry ass lives and I'm the greater threat?"

"Do you remember the story our aunt used to tell us?"

I was impatient with her now. I had been on my feet for two full days and nights.

"The brothers who shared the apple tree?" she prodded.

I scrubbed at my face. "Say whatever you want to say, Corraidhín, and let me leave."

"The brothers grew up dreaming of having the apple tree to share between their families for their whole lives. Then as they got older, the one brother gave apples to friends and neighbors, blossoms to pretty females, and built a house that looked upon the tree. He grew up to have a wife and children, and they played around the tree and climbed the branches. The other brother took his apples to the next town and sold them. He built a house that looked away from the tree and would sneak the apples from his brother's side in the middle of the night so he could sell more. Eventually, the tree stopped producing.

There was one apple that grew slowly at the top of the tree. They all watched it for weeks and weeks. Then one night the family-minded brother was out walking, and he spotted his brother climbing the tree, taking the last apple. He realized then where all the fruit had gone. All he said to his brother as he looked upon their beloved tree, as it withered away, was, 'I would have given you my apples if you had asked.'"

"That has nothing at all to do with me, Corraidhín." I was out of patience.

"Oh. Perhaps not then. I thought it did—wait! No, it does. Sorry, darling, these babies are making my mind flaky. I am not saying you don't share well. However, Cadeyrn understands there is something between you and Neysa that is not ordinary. Perhaps just ask him."

"That was a fucking long way to get to that point, sister. Good night." I kissed her cheek. Like *Trubaíste* had asked me to. I could do that for her.

CHAPTER 28

Neysa

Admittedly, I was running myself into the ground. I took the afternoon to work on sprints. Estimating distances, I laid rocks at different points and would sprint between them, practicing turning and rolling from the run. Eventually that got boring, so I would sprint and run up a tree to back flip. Really, it was impressive that I could still do these things. There was an excellent tree for pull ups and hauling myself between branches to work on balance and coordination while I slashed with my sword. I hung upside down from a high branch and began sit ups from the hang, using my sword to reach up each time touch a higher branch.

"For someone who was just dead, you seem to be fairly energized," a female voice called from below. I flung my sword down and it pierced the ground about a foot from her, then I flipped from branch to branch until I was on the grassy ground, facing Saski.

"More energy than ever," I responded.

"Want to play?" She smirked.

I still wanted to rip her to shreds. So, I bowed in invitation. She unsheathed her curved blade with the bird hilt and tapped from side to side. I moved in a semi-circle around her, then lashed and ducked. She easily avoided it and slashed her own blade, which I met with a ringing of steel. We both pushed at the position, grunting.

"Thank you for helping me. I still want to put depilatory cream in your shampoo for touching my mates but thank you."

"I don't know what that is."

"It makes your hair fall out." Her face blanched, and I laughed.

"Your mates?"

Oh, shit. I did say that. I didn't even know why I said it. My tongue was certainly forked these days. My eyes darted around, making sure no one else heard. She used my distraction and swiped my blade out of my hand. I released my arm dagger and pulled a short sword from my thigh, jabbing and slashing.

"Saski, I am going to ask you, as a female. As a family member. As a decent individual. Do not repeat what I said. It was an accident. Truly. I'm still figuring things out, and I don't remember half of my life." That wasn't exactly the truth.

"I won't. But I think it's true. That was one reason I tried so hard to push you."

"Then you thought it would be funny to bed someone you thought was my mate?" I scream-whispered at her.

"Good point. However, if you would stop trying to take my head off, perhaps we could have a real conversation? Ludek would like to speak to you as well." I stopped launching at her and stared, nostrils flaring. "I think that maybe we could help." I snorted. "I apologize. It was reckless. Just please, speak with us. Cadeyrn can be there too. Please."

Cadeyrn entered the clearing then with Ludek and Arik in tow. I nodded.

A hawk landed next to my mate. He pulled a note from its underbelly and looked to me.

Silas asked to come see you.

And?

Is that okay with you?

Of course. Why wouldn't it be?

I heard you had words. Before you left.

Tell him to come, I snapped, and he looked stung. I took off at a sprint again and flung myself higher into the tree, landing on one foot. Arik swore.

"I brought your leathers and wine. See you at the house," Saski called. Though it must have looked like a circus act, I couldn't come down. Not from the tree, nor my own manic behavior. What I realized was that I felt like I was on a constant battle high. I couldn't release enough. Personally speaking, that was never a good thing.

Silas. I am going assume you can hear me. Because otherwise I'm the once-dead girl who talks to herself. That's weird even for me. I told Cadeyrn I wanted you to come. So, get up here. Please.

LUDEK BEGAN by explaining that they wanted to talk about our families. Konstantín manipulated us into coming and beguiled me into willingly sacrificing myself for his lands. I was past the point of being able to forgive that. What they brought up additionally was the subject of their mother. She birthed two sets of twins. I had wondered about that.

I did as well. I've never heard of that in this realm.

She married Ludek and Pavla's father when she was young. The children were born a few decades into their marriage. Konstantín met her while on a campaign around the lands. They recognized each other and mated, immediately impregnating her with Saski and Arik. The sets of twins were merely five years apart. Ludek's father killed himself from the grief of losing his mate. I sat back abruptly. Cadeyrn leaned forward and pinched his nose. There was an awful, festering silence.

"Is that possible?" I asked. Cadeyrn looked at me, eyes pleading.

"It seems so. Our parents say it was," Ludek told us. "Our mother never got over her mate dying. She loved him. Then when Pavla was killed, she became inconsolable." I was trying to stay normal. I sat closer to Cadeyrn. He flinched, which made me want to scream, but then he picked up my hand and kissed it.

"We will deal with it."

"How?" I asked. He shrugged.

Saski's sword glinted in the light streaming from the windows.

"I've seen those birds," I said. "They were all over the palace in Bania."

"This was a gift from Analisse when she visited."

IN THE interest of being honest with myself, I was aware that it wasn't normal to have made the hasty exit I did when Saski explained that her sword and many others had come from Analisse. As a gift to Heilig, Analisse brought an armory's worth of Festaeran steel welded and etched with the emblems, stories, and symbolism of Veruni. Perhaps I had become like the pockets of energy in Heilig that couldn't contain anything else, so they burst. Only I needed to release my energy. One moment Saski and Ludek were explaining the steel, the next I was in the forest, running at full speed. Wind ripped strands of my hair from my braid, causing them to whip into my eyes. The afternoon turned chilly, and it seemed an early autumn storm may be moving in. Yet still I ran.

Every day in my human life I ran like this. Absolutely given over to the need to be out of my head. It seemed since waking this morning I had been unable to stop moving. Whether losing myself in Cadeyrn or flipping around like a circus monkey in the tree, I needed to move or release magic. As a child, I read the story of the princesses who snuck out night after night to dance until dawn, and literally danced themselves to death. What if I was doing the same? What if however I was brought back was all stored in a well within me, creating a finite sum of life, and I was acting like an immune response and attacking the life force? What if I were dancing myself to death?

The panic and thoughts fired in like a barrage of bullets, yet I ran still. The pressure of the oncoming storm built, and I was sweating from the humidity and expenditure. I knew I was far from the coast at this point and wondered just how far I ran. The soles of my boots were flapping, my heart pounding. If I stopped suddenly, it would likely cause a heart attack. So, I slowed to a jog, albeit a fast jog, then eventually, after perhaps twenty minutes, I stopped. Where. The. Hell. Was. I? I had no watch to tell me how long since I left. It was evening. Birdsong had quieted; the lazy chatter of things snuffling about replaced them. There was a stream nearby I could hear, and gods was I thirsty. I sat and drank my fill, thinking about what a stupid idiot I was to have left like that. But I didn't actually decide. My body just took off. I quickly opened to Cadeyrn and told him what happened. My ego kept me from telling him that I had no idea where I was, so I said I'd be fine and head back soon. Stupid, Neysa. So, I sat on my ass, in the middle of Saarlaiche, likely a hundred miles from home, with soleless boots. What an asshole. Too bad I didn't have my beastie. I couldn't pull that thread. I couldn't seem to remember where she was—was she still with Ewan?

Where is she? I said to anyone in my head. I was feeling hysterical and didn't know who I was asking. Ewan. Ewan would know.

Who? Ewan answered.

My beastie. Where is she? I can't remember.

Oh, little one. She didn't make it.

No. I cried. *No. She...how?*

I wasn't there. I don't know. I pressed my hands into the soft, damp earth next to the stream and tried drawing deep breaths to calm myself. There was a trick I used to do with my breathing, but I couldn't seem to remember. Electricity crackled in my hands, lighting up the stream. Fish and frogs floated to the surface. I vomited, seeing what I'd done, yet the crackling commenced. The storm came in closer, and the sky lit up. I was suddenly wet and shaking on the ground. I jumped and spun in circles, looking around. My heart was racing, and my head urged me to run again, but I wasn't sure what direction. Shit, I could end up in Festaera for all I knew. Had I run north? The only thing I did know was that I didn't come east because the coast was far away. Something was there. I was wet and cold and there was another presence. How did I access my power? Oh, Gods. I was like a child. I couldn't remember. Couldn't make myself be rational. Run. Just as I set off, there was a voice.

"*Trubaíste*, wait."

A smudge along the bank of the stream showed me where he was. That was why I was soaked. I couldn't move. Slowly he gained his body, and I just stood there.

"What in the bloody hell realms are you doing here? Do you have any idea where you are?"

Still, I stood there.

"Are you hurt?"

I just stared at Silas. *Christ, Neysa, say something to him.*

"I can't control it," I blurted.

"What?"

"Anything. I can't stop moving."

"You've stopped now. You haven't moved at all."

I yanked on my jacket, frustrated. "I've been running. I was at home. She said something about Analisse and I ran and couldn't stop."

He stood where he was, as if afraid to come closer.

"You woke yesterday?"

I nodded.

"I felt it," he said. Interesting. "Did it start then?"

"This morning. I woke up needing to move." My cheeks heated thinking about this morning, and he snorted.

"Let's get you home." He began walking, brushing past me, not stopping. I stood stock still, looking at my hands and my boots.

"For someone who says she can't stop moving, you haven't even breathed much. Come."

I pulled the length of leather string from my hair, broke it in two and used each piece to wrap around my boots, attempting to hold the soles together for a short time. Silas watched me, though he said nothing. Once done, I began walking. Run.

Move. My body urged me. My heart beat faster and faster, but I kept walking, thinking maybe, just maybe, he would speak to me. Hours we walked in silence. I knew I'd run in a straight line. If we had been walking in this direction for a couple of hours, then surely, if we kept going the same way, we would be back in Aemes. Run. So, I did. The leather came off my boots; the soles ripped completely. He swore and ran after me.

"Neysa, stop." I couldn't. Especially not now. With everything that happened and my needing to see him, I couldn't contain what was inside me. Magic built within me, an inflamation of strength and plyometrics as though I were filled with helium, and I jumped to a branch, then ran along it and flipped to another tree. Logically, I knew this was ridiculous. Physically, I needed to keep moving. Tree after stupid tree. Finally, I dropped to a crouch and geared to run again, when there were arms around me.

"Stop," he growled, face in my hair. I growled back, trying to move. "You can't keep this up. It will kill you."

"I know." The arms dropped, but I had been pushing so hard to get away that I fell face-first into a root, splitting my lip.

"Shite," he swore.

I waved him off, pressing my hand to my mouth, smearing blood across my face. Silas shuddered and turned away.

"Keep moving, then. Go. Just don't run." He was still looking to the side.

"I'm going to stop and rest. You can go. I'm fine on my own. Goodbye, Silas."

"You're good at that, eh?"

"What is that supposed to mean?" Rain started then, sheets of it, slipping into my collar and waistband, filling my mouth with water and blood. At least it covered the tears coming out. No need for him to see those.

"It means you're a selfish *colleíene, doinne* áech *mas, á miss, á trubaíste,* áech nooooo. *Tus á bás á misse, aech misse cumachnd aimserre.*" He was rambling, shucking weapons down and tearing off his jacket.

"I have no idea what the hell you just said." I walked off and threw up, shaking and cold. The adrenaline was ebbing away. Who knew when it would spike again.

Don't say you're okay. I can feel it's a lie. Where are you? my husband implored me.

I ran. A long way. I'm in the forest. I accidentally killed a bunch of frogs and fish in a stream. I started sobbing. *Silas found me.*

Of course, he did. Bitterness filled his tone.

Don't you start. I don't need both of you being assholes to me.

I suppose I shall see you when you get here, as I'm sure you will just tell me to not come to you. I started throwing up again. Great. Now I was totally empty. *It's the adrenaline. I can see if I can help with the energy thing when you get back. Be careful, caráed.*

I had nothing to say. Like a switch being flipped, my former energy bottomed out. Emotionally and physically, I was just so tired.

"What did Cadeyrn have to say?" Silas asked with a snarky tone. I wiped my mouth and glared at him.

"You obviously don't give a shit, so don't worry about it." My eyes closed wanting to cry, but not having the energy.

"Yeah, clearly I don't give a shit." He turned his back to me.

I fell asleep against the trunk of an overturned tree and didn't wake until the early birdsong of the forest canopy came alive.

Silas handed me his water skein and told me to finish it. We didn't speak; we only walked. I lagged behind, shooting daggers at his back with my eyes. It was midmorning when we passed a stream, and I stopped to drink and wash my face and sweaty body.

"Silas, you don't have to see me back. I am fine on my own. You clearly do not want to be around me. Go back to whatever or whoever you had been doing in Bistaír." Maybe that was the wrong footnote to add. His eyes were like wildfire. His lips pulled back in a feral snarl. I stepped back, darkness rising in me.

"Would you like that? If I said I had someone to go back to? Would that make your life easier? You wouldn't have to ask me to stay with you. 'Please stay,'" he mimicked my voice.

"I begged you to stay because I saw a vision of you lying dead!"

"Did you see one of you dead? Did you know and not tell us? You fucked off out of that palace and went on a suicide mission."

"I did what had to be done."

He snorted and made a motion with his hand that had mist covering the area.

"You always say that. Whether it gets you killed or my sister shot. Doesn't matter to you. You don't care what it does to us. You just go. You're a fucking disaster!"

"Don't you think I know that?" I yelled. "Don't you think I hate myself for it? I said that on that beach in Laorinaghe. I ruin everyone. Then on top of it, I came back wrong. I am an abomination." I walked away. I couldn't keep doing this. I should be dead. They should have let me die.

"Maybe you are."

"Thank you, friend. It's good to see you too."

"We've never been friends, Neysa." The darkness rising wrapped around me like a noose, pulling at my throat.

I had to get away. I wished for my beastie. Her missing piece doubled me over with pain. I screamed at the wind for her. Screamed for my parents. For the mess with my mate and Silas. Screamed for Reynard and all he endured. Darkness wound around me in sparking clouds.

"Fucking hell." Why did he follow me? "When did that start?"

"It started last night. You aren't helping, you asshole. Just go."

"I can't."

"You can. You turn your nice, intact boots around and walk away. I don't hold you to anything. As you say, we aren't friends. Leave."

And let me mourn, I said to myself. *Let me let her go.*

"I'm sorry she died. She saved you. Her spark within you allowed us to bring you back." Oh. I couldn't breathe. One more life to add to the list of those I'd ruined. I laid on the ground and pushed my fingers into the dirt, curling my legs into my stomach.

"You're probably blaming yourself for that too. I guess you'd be right."

Instantly, I was standing and pushing him. He flew back several meters.

"I don't need this. Not from you."

"Why, because I coddle you and save your ass every time you do something stupid?"

"Because I have nothing left in me! So why keep kicking me down? I'm down. I'm there." I shoved him again.

"You're a right pain in the ass."

"What are you trying to do? Say everything, every word you have been afraid to say to me? I know I'm a pain in the ass. Go on then. Send that hate mail my way."

"If I wanted to say everything, we'd be here for years. I hate you." He leaned in close to my face. My stomach flipped over. It was fair. I knew it was fair. Still.

"I hate what you've done to me. I spent the past month gathering the largest compilation of intelligence for your brother. I whored myself for it." I was going to be sick again. The water I'd drunk was sloshing in my guts. "I didn't care."

"Why?" I asked quietly.

"Because you left. You left us and you died." He pressed his lips together and widened his eyes, shaking his head. "And nothing else mattered. I hate you."

I nodded absently like a bobblehead doll.

"I'm sorry. I wanted to say that to you. Doesn't matter, I'm sure. But I'm sorry." I walked the rest of the way home on my own. I knew he was close. But I was alone. *I hate you.* I hated me too. I walked all day and night and arrived back sometime after dawn the next day and went straight to Rhia's cottage.

RHIA HAD porridge on, which she loaded with honey and Araíran-aoír nuts. She thrust tea, ladened with cream, into my hand.

"I think I came back wrong," I admitted to her. Cadeyrn knew I was there. She sent word as soon as she saw me on her doorstep. The dogs were with me, snoring on the ground.

"Why ever do you think that?" She fussed about, feeling my head and glands, lifting my shirt to check on healed wounds. I explained about the need to move. The need to release. The loss of my *baethaache*. Silas. Cadeyrn.

"Ah. You are the heir to the Goddess Heícate. You make your own magic. You can transform that need to move to anything. But, like the Goddess, you have two mates."

"I cannot," I cried, sobbing into my hands.

"Do you not love them?"

"I do. I will destroy them. Silas hates me already, and I won't hurt Cadeyrn that way."

"Ah, you see it differently. In magic there is balance. Strength and weakness, dark and light. To be imbued with such gifts—magic, darkness—one needs support. Even a goddess cannot shoulder it all, and one mate would carry a great burden. Yours carries his own birthright and will need"—Oh please don't say he has another mate. I would die right here— "you to be grounded."

Phew. She explained that the Goddess had her mates not only for her own needs, but to be a part of the realm. The strength of all three together carried the instrument for all magic. She had children by only one.

"Is it mere coincidence that you coupled with He of the Forest on Mabyn, the autumnal equinox? Did you not exchange gifts of the heart and admit to yourself your love for the Battle King on Yule, the Winter Solstice? Did you not officially solidify the *Cuira*íbh *Enaíde* over the celebration of Imbolc? I see much, my lady. You did not come back wrong. You are blessed and perhaps a bit cursed." She winked at me. "It is a burden to carry. For all of you. However, you came back to them. To us all. Live." She made her markings on my forehead again and fussed at me to eat my porridge.

CHAPTER 29

There were things I could do. I knew that. Rather than dancing through my slippers, I could make myself useful. I checked on the grinder for the Araíran-aoír nuts. The tinkerer was excited to show me the beta unit. I sat at the stool in his warm shop and pumped the foot pedal, cranking the handle and grinding them into a thick nut butter. It wasn't completely smooth—crunchy Araíran-aoír nut butter—but it would have to do for now. It was a positive in a mind-numbingly dark time within the confines of my head. If I could contribute something to this realm, why not contribute a substitute for peanut butter cookies?

Warmth spread through my stomach when I thought of Cadeyrn. His shy smile that lit up a room and the way his head tilted just a smidgen when I spoke to him, like every facet of him wanted to focus on me. When we were alone, the world could fade to black, and I might not notice. I wanted only him. I was happy to have him only. I loved Silas, and I knew I always had, but to have them both forced into this seemed torturous. Silas, who held us all together. Every godsdamned time I fell. Silas who never let me doubt Cadeyrn's love for me. My foot came off the pedal as a surge of adrenaline raced through me, demanding I release energy. I thanked the tinkerer and paid him for the unit. Back at the house I sequestered myself in the kitchen and made batch after batch of Araíran-aoír nut butter cookies. I ran. I practiced on my bow. I avoided the males I needed so desperately.

"Have I done something wrong?" Cadeyrn asked, standing at the edge of the grove where I was walking toward the sea. My heart broke.

"No. Not at all." I walked to him and finally let myself hold him.

"I saw Rhia," he said softly. I tightened my arms on him. "I suppose I knew. We will figure it out." He kissed my nose.

"I can't see how. If you had another mate, we wouldn't be figuring it out. It would be a death match. Even if she were my cousin. *Especially* if she were my cousin."

He chuckled. "I'm quite sure it would be. If we need to take time apart I can—"

"No. I don't want time away from you."

"Then we deal."

"It was a catastrophe. Silas finding me. I've never heard him speak that way. To anyone."

"He is not himself at the moment." No. He was not.

I RODE to Laichmonde to see Reynard, who still rented Silas' flat. When I walked in, he was sitting at a low table sorting piles of correspondence and notes written in my brother's hand. I sat and handed him papers, working in silence for a time. I hadn't been there before. It was sleek and simple with clean lined furniture in shades of grey and beige with ebony stained wood floors. Every breath I took sent me spinning, as it filled me with Silas' woodsmoke and cedar scent. A mate I didn't realize I had. Another victim in my massacre.

"Breathe, Kitten. Passing out won't help anything." Reynard explained the different candidates for the positions and who their rivals and supporters were.

"Why can't you hold a position?" I asked.

He giggled maniacally. "No one would want me."

"I would. I will give you my vote right now."

He gave me a sheepish smile, stacking piles of paper.

"You would be in a great minority, darling." His head popped up as the door clicked. "Shite. I forgot."

"Weasel. I have the latest from Festaera to add to that bloody great—oh." Silas came through the doors to the living area, and his face went from surprise to disgust in a millisecond. "Shall I come back?"

"I can go," I said softly, beginning to stand.

"Speaking of Festaera," Reynard said. "Neysa was about to tell me her concerns over some gifted Festaeran steel."

"No one is buying it since word got out that it was spelled, so it's likely an ill concern," Silas countered before hearing me out.

"Analisse gifted the royal family and its guard an entire shipment of Festaeran steel when she was last there. Ten years ago. I recognized the birds on Saski's blade."

"Ah. That could be a problem." The least hostile thing he'd said to me. I pulled out a rough sketch of Saski's blade and smoothed it on the table. The two males looked at it. "I don't need to see it. It is either spelled steel or it isn't. You wasted your time sketching this." Silas' vitriol crawled under my skin like heated barbs.

"There is no reason to speak to her that way," Reynard said in my defense, standing as I was. I touched his arm in thanks.

"Perhaps it was a waste of time, but it gave me a way to focus my thoughts. Things are scrambled most days since I came back," I admitted, not liking that I felt I needed to justify any of my actions. "It let me think more clearly. Plus, when I touched the drawing, I had a vision."

Silas plunked himself on a sofa, stretching his long legs and crossing them at the ankles. He was lying back in a guise of relaxation, but I knew him, and the stiff set of his shoulders told me he was anything but relaxed. He made an obnoxious "get on with it" motion with his hand. I rolled my eyes, then turned to Reynard and told him.

Pavla, Ludek's sister, had her Festaeran steel blade, and it did nothing against the phantomes and the insurgents, allowing her to be killed. The wards around the palace in Heilig were useless due to the presence of the spelled steel. The metal itself was cursed with a kind of reverse *draíchnhud aemdifna*íd. A reverse magical shield. A dismantler. They both swore. We would have to put out the word to have all allies remove the questionable weaponry from their cache.

"Perhaps," I began, "be on your guard during the meetings ahead. All it would take is one spelled blade." Silas scoffed and said something along the lines of what a brilliant idea; he wished he had thought of that.

"Did you then? Think of it? You can hate me all you want, but I am a part of putting this place back together. We are working together. All of us. The least you can do is show me some respect. I won't take your shit anymore than I would take anyone else's. You want to pick a fight again? We can do it elsewhere. Not when the issues here are this serious." That shut him up. I was beginning to dislike the male lately, and that scared the shit out of me. He had always been my closest friend. My staunchest ally. I said Cadeyrn and I could go to the Festaeran mines and see if there was a way we could find the catalyst for the spell. Reynard made a face like I was crazy.

"That is a spectacularly stupid idea. With respect, Princess." Silas sneered at me. "It's a death trap. Though that seems to be your method of operations."

I was off the ground and out the door in a blink. Slamming the damned door so hard it rattled the building, I tromped down the steps onto the street. His flat was the opposite side of town from Cadeyrn's, so I made my way across the vast park, seething as I went. It was quite chilly for early autumn, and I wrapped my black riding jacket tighter around me. I had to stop at Cadeyrn's to retrieve a book he told me was there. I hurried so I could be in and out before I ran into Lina, who lived on that side of town. That was all I needed today: dealing with her. I liked the apothecary, but she really disliked me. And really liked Silas. Though I wondered if she would still with the new brand of asshole he wore like a bad cologne.

Letting myself in, I wiped my boots and was about to go up the stairs when movement had me pulling my dagger.

"Did you know I was staying here?" Silas asked, casually leaning against the door frame into the sitting room. How did he get here before me? "There's a quicker way than through the park." I backed up. I didn't need the book that bad.

"I just came for a book Cadeyrn had on aulde spells and warfare. It's not important." And I couldn't stand another verbal assault.

"Just find the damned book."

"No, thank you." I turned, trying to not sprint, but he was there blocking my way.

"What book is it?"

Breathe, Neysa. I started to duck under his arm.

"I'll go find it for you." His tone was softer. I told him the title and waited in the sitting room. He brought it back and handed it to me. My hands were shaking when I took it; our fingers met. There was a jolt of the electricity we both carried, and I started.

"Apologies, *Trubaiste*," he said, and it felt like a segue to a letdown. I nodded and started to turn, but he grabbed my hand.

"You've been horrible," I said quietly. "I've never been spoken to that way by anyone." Well, I had a professor in my junior year at university who really didn't think highly of me. He was a patronizing, chauvinistic bastard. "Hate me, but have the decency to at least be respectful."

"I do hate you."

"Yes, you have made that abundantly clear. And I'm sorry for eliciting such vehemence. I should go." My chest started to cave. Then I thought of something. "What did you say to me the other night when you rambled on in the aulde language?"

"A load of rubbish and that you're the death of me and I have no power to stop it." I walked to the door and put my head against it. I kind of felt put out because everyone was pissed at me, saying that I'd be the death of them for going off and dying. Yet no one was addressing the fact that I quite literally died for them. The gratitude was astounding.

I miss you. I could hear the rain outside. It would be a miserable ride home. *I miss my friend.* I reached for the door handle, and his hand closed over mine, interlacing our fingers. I felt him step towards me, and I leaned back into him, breathing him in. I wanted to tell him. Everything Rhia told me. But it wasn't fair to do it yet when I had not sorted out how I would deal with it all. So, I turned and let myself lay against his solid chest. He stroked my hair and my cheek, feeling the wetness there.

"Och, *Trubaíste*. Don't cry for me. Cry for the poor dead frogs you electrocuted."

He laughed, and I whacked his arm, but he pulled my face in and kissed me. A slow, tentative exploration of my lips. I held my hand over his as it rested on my face and had my other wrapped around his shoulders. Something manic and jittering settled in me as we stood, suspending time in our kiss.

"Is that what you wanted?" he said with a cruel tilt to his mouth. Confusion must have shown on my face. "A little bit more, maybe? That 'release' you spoke of. Want to use me?"

He pulled me closer. I started to squirm. I felt his heartbeat, his desire. Yet his tone was icy. I squeezed my eyes shut, trying to shake off what he was saying.

"Something you want to say to me, Your Highness?" He released me. I was fully shivering as though my body were in shock. I dropped the book.

"I have nothing left to say, Silas."

I didn't know Laichmonde very well, and it was dark and raining, so finding where I stabled my horse was an effort. Near Reynard's were the mews houses where the animals were kept, yet I couldn't find them, and I ended up back at Reynard's soaking wet and hysterical. He led me back to the mews and helped me saddle up the lovely beast to get me home.

"I'll see you in a few days for the first meeting. Chin up, Kitten. Remember who you are. Go home and let your husband take his time with you. I know that would work for me." He winked and watched as I mounted the horse and set off for home.

MY HUSBAND was waiting up in bed, reading a book. The lights in the house were all out, bar the low lamp he had near the bed. It seemed almost too low to read, but I guess I hadn't read in bed since allowing my fae abilities to manifest. Every inch of me was soggy and wrinkled from the rain. I stripped down and pulled on pyjamas from a drawer, then crawled under the covers. Wrapping my body around Cadeyrn, I buried my face into his chest and cried. He set the book aside and pulled me tighter against him. All I wanted was Cadeyrn. I didn't want to want Silas. I didn't want to need him. I loved and adored him, of course. There used to be an easiness with Silas I never had with anyone. More playful and effortless than even Cadeyrn and me. But to be mated to him? To need both of them seemed cruel and cheap. I didn't ask to be linked to the Goddess.

"I know I've said this before, but we don't always want the lot we are given," Cadeyrn stated. "How are you so calm about this?"

"I'm not. I'm angry. I'm jealous and trying so hard to control myself. But I know it's not your choice. I know it's not his choice—well, not entirely. I suppose I realized that acting upon my contempt would do nothing but make it worse." At least one of us was rational. "I'm sick of dealing with everyone's endless self-important bullshit when all I can think about is you. Us. Me, burying myself inside you."

I tightened my legs around him.

"Well, get on with it then," I said, still sniffling but feeling heat rise between us. I met his heat with a silken darkness that swept over us, removing clothing and thoughts of anything other than the two of us together.

"New trick?" he asked, lying atop me.

"Learning new things every day."

CHAPTER 30

Generally speaking, everyone was impressed at Reynard's quick execution of getting meetings set up for all the potential candidates. Cadeyrn's flat in Laichmonde was the center of activity. Since Lorelei's death, there were many who were still confused about the closing of the Sacred City, and many who questioned the legitimacy of our involvement in her death. Her personal guard and most of the City's defense unit saw what had happened. It was a sad circumstance.

There were a handful of candidates who came forward, Yva being one. She walked in, serious faced, wearing a freshly pressed captain's livery. When our eyes met, hers twinkled and she bowed, golden brown hair shining from its neatly twisted bun. I grasped elbows with her and the three others who came forward. We had met with those from Dunstanaich first. Soren wished to keep his position, opposed only by a male whose platform was solely based on his being as old as dirt. The session went fairly quick, Reynard making notes and trying to not smirk. I saw as they walked out that he was drawing a small flip book of sheep chasing the old fellow. I burst out laughing. Cadeyrn and Silas snapped attention to us. Quickly smothering the laughs with the back of my hand, I cleared my throat. That was when Yva and her contenders entered. Before they had a chance to sit down, the door opened again, and I was immediately there, throwing my arms around Corra.

"Well, halloo, you," she greeted me. I pulled her out onto the porch and hugged her again. She shooed me off, and I looked at her enormous belly. "I'm quite sure you've heard it all from all the males in your life, so I will spare you my verbal lashing. But I don't want a message again like the one you sent. Are we clear?"

I squeaked in response.

"Good, because the poor hawk was limping from the weight of it."

I sobbed a laugh. "I kept my promise, though," I said, wiping at my nose. She straightened my necklace and wound one of my dark waves around her finger.

"My brother? Has he been himself?" she asked in a whisper. My silence must have answered enough. "Have you told him yet?"

She always knew. I shook my head, and she tsked. I bristled.

"Perhaps when there is a break between his verbal abuse. In the meantime, he can kiss my ass." Of course, as soon as I said that, Silas came out to fetch us. I groaned, and Corra laughed, patting her brother's cheek. He shot me a look I couldn't decipher as we walked in.

Two of the Laorinaghan candidates seemed to be on the same page for their vision for the prosperity of the province and seemed interested in what Yva had to say.

"I believe," Yva began, "that we should be more transparent in our leadership, whether I am a representative for my home province or not. It is an age in which we should be able to be open and accept the criticism and suggestions of the folk. Should I not be chosen to help lead, I would like to be considered for a position to perhaps advise or even negotiate between the leadership and the folk." One of the other three was more of the arcane frame of mind and rolled his eyes at her so-called idealism. The other two listened intently. One spoke up. He was Arturus, the main intelligencer for Lorelei.

"I have found in the years I held position with her ladyship that with whom we work is more the guarantor of success. Lady Lorelei had always been transparent, as Yva—Captain Sonnos calls it, and worked with us closely to maintain the peace and prosperity within the province. It was uncharacteristic of her to close us off when she shut the city down. However, because of the system in place, her rule was solid. We had little recourse. Perhaps, we could govern jointly in Laorinaghe, thereby keeping the power dispersed. Would that be an option to consider?" he asked.

"From what I have seen in both ours and the human realm," Silas began, "when a system of government has multiple heads of state, or at the very least more stringent limitations of power on a single head, the system runs better. I think, Arturus, it is a fine idea."

"I agree with Silas," I added. He looked at me sidelong, and I felt the weight of his eyes. "There may be more bumps in terms of decision-making, but to have a system where there are more than one of you focused on creating a more fair and prosperous province, historically, should be better."

He tipped his head to me in thanks.

"Would you be willing to share the job with those present?" Cadeyrn asked. "And would you, candidates, be in favour of such a system?"

Yva, Arturus, and Farus responded positively. The fourth candidate shook his head and gave a definite no. Within our council, we wrote a decree to instill the three in agreement as representatives for Laorinaghe.

"Yva," Silas said, inclining his head. "Congratulations. May you enjoy your leadership." She bowed to him and smirked, turning to me.

"Are you free this evening, Neysa? I've brought a bottle of Laorinaghan wine and fresh dates. Perhaps we can partake without you losing your trousers and stabbing Lord Silas."

I laughed and muttered that I may stab Silas anyway.

"How did I miss out on that fun?" Reynard asked, introducing himself to Yva. Cadeyrn came up behind me and slipped his arm through mine. In my peripheral I noticed the amused half-smile playing at his lips. I reached up and ran my fingertips over his night dark hair.

"I can tell you, Lady, you were the topic of tavern chatter for months after." Reynard looked affronted. I giggled and told him I would tell the tale later on.

"Make sure you don't leave out the part about you losing your shit and your weapons like a child," Silas added.

The room fell silent. Cords of muscles in Cadeyrn's arm went taught as he tensed. Ewan began walking over, looking like death incarnate, but Corra put a hand on him. Instead, she faced her brother and punched him square in the jaw. He saw it coming and took it, rubbing the spot where a huge bruise bloomed. Fae healing had the blood rushing to the surface quickly. I knew by morning it would be gone. Cadeyrn's nostrils flared, and he told him to go find another healer.

YVA WAS staying in the city, and though we had planned to go back to Aemes for the night, I told Cadeyrn I'd stay with Reynard so I could spend time with Yva and Corra.

If I kiss you goodbye here, do I have to be chaste? Cadeyrn asked me, his long fingers twisting under the hem of my jacket.

If I pushed you against a building and marked your neck with my teeth, would you object? I answered. He swallowed and turned pink. Ha. Score one for me. He put his hands into my unbound hair and gave me that unchaste kiss, so I returned the favour and pushed him against the building, but stopped short of the marking.

We parted ways, and I headed off to enjoy Laorinaghan wine. On a large terrace overlooking a private back garden, Yva laid out the dates and cheese to stuff inside. Reynard howled at the tale of us drinking on the beach and said the realm needed more leaders like us.

"Help me, Yva. I believe Reynard would be a fine candidate for Maesarra."

Corra looked surprised but agreed.

"Thank you, Kitten, but truthfully, I would rather not go up against my father. I would be happier serving in a different capacity." Fair enough.

"Would you be our intelligencer? In an official capacity?" Corra asked him. He looked down, and I knew he was shocked. I put a hand on his back.

"It would be my honor, Lady," he said. I filled our glasses (apart from Corra, though she insisted that fae metabolized alcohol differently so it was not forbidden whilst pregnant) and toasted to his new position. We turned our heads to the sound of boots coming up the stairs in the house. Corra smiled at my brother when he came through the double doors to the terrace, Silas behind him. It was late and time that everyone made their way out. Yva pulled another bottle from her satchel and left it for me with a wink.

"Until next time," she said to me. She walked out with Ewan and Corra. Silas was speaking to Reynard, relaying some information Ewan gave him regarding the Festaeran steel. Normally, I would not hesitate to include myself in the conversation, but I was so out of sorts with Silas' attitude, I hung back awkwardly and poured myself another glass of wine, topping up Reynard's.

"Wine, Silas?" I asked. He paused, mid-sentence, and took the offered glass. It was my own as there wasn't an extra goblet. He sipped at it and kept speaking. I sat back in the cushioned chair and propped my feet on a massive planter that held a tree of some sort. Not caring much in the present company, I toed off my flat slippers, stretching out my feet. It was quite chilly, but with drinking the rich red wine, and my cashmere wrap around my shoulders, I was comfortable. This city felt at once urban and country. Not for the first time did I think it reminded me of Corra—and a bit of Cadeyrn. Silas must have noted that he drank from my glass, because he handed it back to me after refilling it, then went back to his discussion with my friend.

I pondered to myself the issue of the enchanted steel. Wouldn't someone need to be extraordinarily powerful to spell all the steel in a province? Wouldn't that technically be averse to the laws of nature, even here? Shields, whether inherent to an individual like Silas or Basz, or a manufactured one, like the tonic Lina made us, had to have a degree of maintenance. The tonic ran its course. The inherent shield dropped when the magic wielder was burned out. Magic and power were not depthless. They needed rest and replenishment like physical strength did. How would weaponry that had been distributed be able to maintain its spell? I sat up slowly and opened my mind to the thoughts. The inspections Paschale inflicted on his people. On Reynard.

Silas turned his head to me in stunned acknowledgement. His rugged features went slack at my projected realization.

"Care to let me in on what you just figured out, Kitten?"

"Why have you switched from calling me Mousey to Kitten?" I asked, a bit drunk.

"You're no one's prey, gorgeous, and I've seen those claws when you're ready to use them. So, tell me what I'm missing."

I patted the seat next to me.

"Can you tell me anything about the so-called inspections Paschale ran?"

He paled, and I could feel rage and distress seeping through Silas' pores. The memory of his telling me about what he'd endured with Analisse came back to me, and I realized I'd left my mind open to him. He took the glass from my hand and downed it.

"They wanted to see how much of my power they could extract, and whether it could be replaced with something else. Using me like a vessel."

Oh Gods. I grabbed his hand.

"I was there for a month—months—I don't know. After the initial three days of pure torture, they realized I could erect a wall within me that kept the vessel from being filled. Once it seemed impossible, they tried to wipe my memory of the time I spent there. They couldn't kill me like so many others, you see, because, *weel*, at the end of the day, my parents knew I was up there. While they don't love me, it would look bad if they let me die. Especially right before their daughter was married."

Oh my God.

Silas, oh my God.

Reynard chewed at his lip, staring at the tiles.

"So, we know that for over 150 years they have been doing this. Who knows how many 'vessels' they have managed to fill." Just saying that out loud made me sick to my stomach.

I kissed Reynard's icy hands. How could his parents be so callous? Why favour one child over another and be so caustic to him even now?

"You're exceptional, Reynard. I am proud to call you my friend."

He smiled at me, and I was struck again by how dapper he was.

"I think it's time for me to be off to bed." Exhaustion pulled at his every word, as though admitting what had happened cost him. He leaned down, kissed my cheek, and walked off.

"Does anyone else know or suspect, Reynard?" Silas asked, voice rough. Reynard turned to us from the doorway.

"Cyrranus does. I'm sure many others do, though no one wanted to come forward." He ducked through the doors and into the house.

Silas sat hard on the chair that Reynard vacated. I filled the glass we shared and handed it to him.

"Tomorrow should be fun," I said with absolutely no humour. He blew out a breath and took a sip, then passed it to me. I didn't need to be drinking any more tonight, but I couldn't sleep with all of this on my mind. "I kept thinking that maybe there was someone with more power than most of us, who was controlling the spell. It requires too much power. Even Paschale didn't have that. But really, all it took was someone clever enough to forge a plan to contain that kind of power. Over time. I wonder when it really started." I took a sip and passed the wine back. Paschale had torn my arm open and seen just how much power I could contain. I shivered.

"I would have found you," Silas said, after being quiet for so long. "If Reynard hadn't managed to get you out. I would have found you."

I shrugged.

So, we would have to convene in the morning and let every-one know what we figured out before meeting with the Festaer-ans and Maesarrans. It was going to be an awful day.

"This is good wine," he said, looking at the half-empty bottle. "Is this what you two were drinking on that beach?" I was trying not to gape at the attempt at friendly conversation. Tried not to suspect he was leading me to another round of humiliation.

"I really have no idea what we drank. It was in a jug, so per-haps not the best quality?"

He chuckled and gave me a half smile.

"Well, perhaps the ill quality attracted the shark," he joked. I rolled my eyes and flicked a piece of cork at him. He caught it and flicked it back. "I shouldn't have said what I said."

If we were going to go there, then I wasn't lying down for it.

"Which time?" He still had a nasty bruise on his jaw from Corra's fist. He was lucky it wasn't Ewan, as I didn't think my brother would have pulled the punch as Corra did. His eyes slid to mine, narrowed in their glassy depths.

"I divulged a confidence we had between us, and it was unsavoury of me."

"Unsavoury is when something reflects poorly on your own character. Are you apologizing because it made you look like a dick, or because you realize you were one, and that every fuck-ing thing you have said to me since we have seen each other again has been brutal?" He just sat there. "You could have just said, 'Hey Neysa. Look, I hate you and it would be fantastic if I never had to see your stupid face again,' then left it at that. Not this peeling away of everything I know and feel about myself. Then kissing me? Is that part of this apology?"

"Yes."

I sat back, hard enough that it almost knocked the wind out of me.

"Everything. I apologize for everything."

"But you meant it all," I whispered. "It's all true."

"It's not," he barked. "Fuck it all to never."

I was so cold my teeth were chattering. I gave a half smile that was anything but happy and nodded.

"Do you know?" I guessed it was time to ask. My shoulders were rocking from cold and apprehension.

"What?" He sat forward, arms braced on his knees. I tucked my own feet under my legs and took a deep breath. "Do I know what, *Trubaíste*?"

I nearly threw up from the nerves. Something in his face I recognized but couldn't read.

"You're..." I choked on the word. "We're..." Ugh. Dammit, Neysa.

"Mates?" he asked. I covered my face with my hands and asked him how long he had known. "I could have sworn it forever, but you're mated to my cousin. It just kept getting stronger." He scrubbed at his face. "How I feel."

"How you hate me?"

"Yes, that too," he laughed. I didn't. "The night you left. When you died. Still, it didn't make sense. You don't want me, though. Not really. You want your life with Cadeyrn. I knew that. I know that. You married him. You love him."

"I love you too," I said tacitly. "I hate myself more than you ever could because I love you both. Rhia said..."

"I went to see her yesterday. It's some woo woo goddess shite. Yeah, I know. Apparently, you and I enacted something on Mabyn last year."

He waggled his eyebrows, and I laughed.

"It's been a year," I breathed. "Tonight is Mabyn. So much has happened in a year."

"Och, yeah. Something about time changing everything, yet nothing, and shattered remains, or some such depressing words in the songs you sing."

"Something like that," I answered with a smile. In my head I heard the song Rhia had sung me.

If I loved you more than life itself
If I brought you brightness to your day
Would you tell me you would light the skies
Would you tell me I could stay?
If I stayed with you and made you mine
If I could braid my soul inside of thine
Could we stay forever thus entwined?
Could we never see the end of time?

He looked a bit pale.

Is that better? I asked, half kidding.

He cleared his throat and said, roughly, "I don't know." He held his hands out, and I took them, feeling the rough callouses and the warmth. "Come here, *Trubaíste,* and let me say hello properly."

Pulling my feet from under me, I scooted myself off the chair, and he gathered me up in an embrace. I pushed my face into his neck and breathed him in, calming. It seemed like ages that we sat there. His hands made circles on my back and pulled through my hair. I threaded my own through his hair and held his face against mine. His body shuddered against me, and I pressed closer, kissing just under his ear. Hands stilled, then moved to pull my arms down, holding me just in front of him.

"So, you're a goddess now?" he asked. Wow, that sounded so dumb.

"Heir. Heir to the Goddess. How, I don't know. But like the Goddess, I need you both, it seems."

"Because you're sooooo special and powerful?" I punched his shoulder lightly. "What is it you need from me, *Trubaíste?*" He put his mouth on the base of my throat and moved up toward my chin.

"A friend?" His mouth moved to the corner of mine as he spoke.

"A bodyguard?" He pulled my hips further onto him as his mouth travelled along my cheekbone. I had drawn equal parts darkness and light down, casting the atmosphere around the terrace in odd shadow play. His mouth moved to my ear and touched with his tongue the same spot where I had kissed him. Shaking, I drew my fingers along the muscles of his arms, feeling the strength in them. The command of them that moved his sword and bow, that had held me, and hidden me. While I stroked languorous fingers along his arms and sides, he slid his just under my waistband in the back and pushed me even further against him. I made a small sound and felt him smile against my ear.

"What do you need? From me."

I don't know. Because I didn't understand why any Goddess would put us in this position. I just didn't know, and it made me want to cry.

His mouth teased at my neck, teeth scraping down along the soft part of my neck where I was hit with an arrow. His tongue circled the scar and moved over my shoulder, down my arm where a sword had slashed, and the explosion broke it. He kissed the faint scars there. I stared into his sea glass green eyes and felt my world sliding into place. My hand touched his shoulder blade, which struck me with a vision of him being run through with a sword. I gasped. I hadn't known how close he'd come on that battlefield. We both made it back. I loved him. Yet, even mated to both, I couldn't bring myself to take the next step and do that to Cadeyrn. To us. I didn't want it. Silas had loved me like no one else, and yet I couldn't give all of myself to him. I took his face in my hands, kissed him, and said to him in my mind that I will love him forever, but I could not make love to him. He kissed me back, desperately. For ages. I drew him inside, to the room I was staying in, and had him lie with me. I entangled myself with him and faced him, stroking his arms and back, feeling him against me. He drew hands over my skin and never pressed for more than I was giving. After a time, we slept. I woke and found his eyes on me, and I lost myself for a moment in the clear depths, wondering how I could be so blessed and cursed at the same time. Wondering how I could not give him my all. Wondering how I could stomach breaking his heart as I kept doing. Breaking both their hearts.

"I promised to always see who you are," he said, voice scratchy from sleep. "So, I know. I know what troubles you. I won't ruin you and him."

You deserve more.

"I've had centuries of mindless sex, *Trubaíste*. I would rather wake like this once in a while than destroy what you have. Mates or no."

I traced the tattoo on his arm and kissed it. "I'd like to get one as well."

He swallowed and kissed the same spot on my arm.

"I could even add a little tree and woodland animals that embody the whole He of the Forest thing," I snickered. He pushed on top of me, his hair tumbling over his eyes.

"Terribly cruel to me. Maybe I'll add a *paítherre moinchaí* to represent you. Forked tongue and all." Hmph. "Are you ready to see everyone?" I took a deep breath and said I was. I needed a few moments to talk to my husband before we all met.

CHAPTER 31

Cadeyrn

Before Corraidhín became a connoisseur of documentaries on television in the human realm, she made me watch some science fiction show with her. In the episode I suffered through, the characters stumbled into a wormhole in the space-time continuum, and it triggered a time loop. They constantly revisited the same events in the same day, time and again. By the end of the show, I was pacing and wanting to throw axes at things. Somehow the events we had all endured in the past year felt like that. A loop of death and separation, misunderstandings, and chaos. So, my mate had her own birthright to contend with. One that included having another mate. How was I supposed to feel about that? The thought of someone else touching her in that way lended a homicidal rage to my demeanour. Neysa told me she did not take the final step. That she wouldn't, because she loved us. Our life. She chose us. Sometimes, though, choices were made for us. It would only be a matter of time. I knew Silas, and he wouldn't push her, though he must have known since they coupled last year. Neysa, by the gods, was so stubborn. She bit back at the laws of nature. And I was totally bloody smitten by her.

Festaeran steel being spelled by using gods knew how many helpless fae bodies as power vessels was brilliant in its vileness. I looked forward to dismantling it and freeing those poor souls. Once we got through the meetings today. It felt prudent to bring the Heilig contingent along today as they had been victimized as well. When I explained Neysa's theory to Ludek, he became silent, and I could scent a rising rage in him that I would put money on being a rare occurrence indeed. His gift saw and understood what laid beneath the surface of an individual. I could kick myself for not thinking to have him sit in on the meetings from the beginning. I supposed my mind had been elsewhere.

Neysa was sitting on the steps to my flat when we arrived. The others went in ahead of us, and she asked me to walk with her. We stood near the mews, fumbling around for something to say. She asked if I'd eaten breakfast because I got cranky when I didn't. That was it. I had us in the hay, getting thoroughly rumpled, and she made good on a promise from yesterday and tore her teeth down my neck. It was ghastly, and if there hadn't been centuries of innocent fae being tortured in Festaera, I would have called off the meeting and given the horses more of a show. Especially since it would have pissed off Etienne.

As we entered the flat, hoping to have more time to discuss amongst our family the course of action for today, I pulled stray bits of grass and hay from Neysa's hair and clothing. She turned and smiled in thanks, picking some off my own jacket. Etienne had arrived early. As had—and truly, I could throttle myself for not thinking of this—Bestía's brother and mother. They shouldn't have all been here at the same time, so alarm bells began ringing in my head. Silas nodded to me. He grabbed Arik and Saski, then they fanned out, checking wards and defenses. We greeted them tersely, saying we needed a moment. It wasn't surprising to hear coughing and snide remarks as Neysa and I ducked into the kitchen to clean up my neck. She looked at me and burst out laughing while she wiped the blood from my neck. I rolled my eyes at her and wiped a bit of blood from the corner of her mouth, catching her lips in mine.

"When did you two find the time for that?" Silas slammed into the kitchen. "Stinking up the place and looking like something from the other realm. We do have serious matters here to deal with." His tone was light and joking as always, but I felt the pain underneath. And I hated it.

The wards were intact, and Silas had Magnus pull his men from around the city to stand guard. I wasn't going take any chances this time. While they were all there at once, I pulled files on each of them, sliding them across the table between us all, and took a moment to allow everyone to settle. Etienne initially paled at seeing the intelligence we had on him and his supporters but reorganized his features and had the nerve to look into my eyes and sneer while casting a glance at Neysa.

"So, the bastard son-in-law acquires a mate who has another mate. That must make you feel insufficient." Before any of us could react, Reynard had his knife at his father's throat, pulling him to his feet.

"Unless you would like us to give you to the Festaerans to see if they have more luck with you than they had with me, I would suggest keeping your misinformed assumptions to yourself."

Etienne had the gall to smirk. I reached out with my powers and used particle distribution, then reversed my healing gift to release his urine from his body, making it seem as though he pissed himself.

Did you do that? Neysa asked, surprised.

I am not proud of it. She squeezed my knee under the table. *Okay, perhaps a bit proud.* I knew I had let just enough out to show through his trousers, but my cousins must have thought it great fun, as the poor old bastard kept wetting himself. *I believe your other mate is having a go at him as well.* She smothered a laugh and put her hand on Silas.

Three candidates were here from Maesarra, including Etienne and, after encouragement from my sister, Cyrranus. He would have a tough run against the others as they had money to influence people. All we could hope to do was release the dirt we had gleaned. Deep down, I knew Silas must have been debasing himself to gather the intelligence amassed, but I hadn't paid much attention. We weren't speaking after Neysa's death. Neither of us could bear the conversation. Neither of us could come to terms with losing her, and, ultimately, sharing her.

Cyrranus spoke of leading and protecting a province of people who were kind and hardworking. He was a good male. The other candidate, Arneau, piqued my suspicions. He countered each and every thing Etienne said, from personal militia to class-based rule to slavery. I pulled a file and held it up, pointing to particulars written, and asked Neysa, mind to mind, to confirm with Silas through their connection whether this was the last male he had investigated. She paused and looked to Silas, turning his head to hers. Sometimes I forgot he could not answer. It only happened between us after the *Cuira*íbh *Enaíde* clicked into place. So, she had his lips next to her ear, and she touched the file and his hand at the same time. Clever girl. Saski groaned from the charged air.

"Don't pout, cousin," Neysa said to her. Then to me she sent images of Silas bedding a female against a wall and finding ledgers and files sitting, waiting for him. Then he jumped from a window and ran. Holy bloody Mother Aoifsing.

"While I'm glad to hear you disagreeing with Etienne on these matters which we in the bulk of Aoifsing abhor, I have a few questions."

"Of course, my lord," he answered mildly.

"We have taken the liberty of running checks and intelligence on all candidates. After all, the goal here is for an Aoifsing that prospers. In this file, we have sworn statements from former servants, fellow merchants, bank managers, and blacksmiths, all saying you regularly involve yourself in each activity and institution you opposed within Etienne's platform."

"With respect, Cadeyrn," he said nervously. "Surely the word of a former servant—likely one whom I fired for theft—"

"She was fired after you beat her," Silas interjected.

"Lies. Regardless, it is not an indication of collusion. Whatever a blacksmith has to say seems amusing at best."

"One," Neysa began. I smiled slightly, knowing it was about to get lively. "What it is is an indication of is your character. Which clearly is lacking in integrity, if not a basic sense of right and wrong."

"Says the female with two mates," Etienne spat.

"Excuse me, my love," I interrupted. "Speak to my mate like that again and you will be shitting your pants as well as wetting them. Continue, *Caráed*."

She kissed my cheek.

"Two," she kept ticking off her fingers, "the amusing thing about blacksmiths and swordsmiths is that they make weapons. So, when a small-time merchant such as yourself orders the production of a thousand swords with your household insignia on them, plus two ballistae to sit on your sad little roof, it raises suspicion."

"This is a set up. You have no proof of any of this."

I plunked the ledger down in front of him and flicked through to the past three months.

"As we can all see, all of these expenses are listed in this household ledger."

"You broke into my home?"

"Your wife invited me for tea," Silas said.

Saski choked and cleared her throat. Arneau turned red, and anger had him cracking the arms of his chair,"While we can safely say your bid for candidacy is rejected, I'd like to point out what the situation seems like to me," I said. "Etienne was aware of our reluctance to have him lead a province, given his previous involvement in supporting the massacre of our soldiers. Plus, I truly do not care for him. As such, he reached out to you, knowing you share a similar desire for corruption and domination. If you were to make a plea to lead Maesarra from a platform in opposition to Etienne's, we would support your candidacy. Once established, you would be a puppet for Etienne. Have I missed anything?"

"So, who will lead Maesarra?" Etienne seethed.

"Cyrranus," I announced. Surprise, shock, and disgust limned the features of the three males sitting across from us. Two of them stood abruptly, sending chairs flying.

"Etienne," I said, dangerously quiet. "You're a sneaky bastard. Don't give us any more reasons to fertilize the fields with your ashes. For what you allowed to happen to your son, I could have you imprisoned or killed. Tread carefully."

He spat and left the room with Arneau.

We all collapsed back, steeling ourselves for the Festaerans who were waiting in the next room. Neysa left the room, a trail of darkness like a dust cloud behind her. I turned to the others and saw Silas looking down, fiddling with his hands. I pinched my nose and elbowed him, mouthing for him to go after her. He slowly rose from the seat and made his way out of the room.

"Don't, Corraidhín," I said to her, feeling her keen eyes on me. "Not now. Please."

"I was just going to say you should count your blessings that she wasn't mated to all three of us. I wouldn't share nearly as well as either of you."

I thumped my head on the table as the rest of the room gave in to laughter they were trying to hide.

"I can share," Saski said, ruffling my hair. "If you ever need to get away." She winked at me. Ludek growled.

CHAPTER 32

Neysa

I made my way toward the back stairs to sit in the quiet of the bedroom and think for a few moments before the shit hit the fan with the next lot. Wine in such generous amounts still left my head sore in the morning. I heard Reynard's voice. He followed the Maesarrans out, and as I came closer, I saw Cyrranus stroking his face and speaking intimately close. In the same instant I saw them, they knew I was there, and I felt like an intruder. I made a show of covering my eyes with my hands as I turned to go up the stairs. Well, I didn't see that one coming. Cyrranus said a hasty goodbye to my friend, and the back door shut. Closing the bedroom door behind me, I plunked down on the bed.

It was the vision of Silas and that lonely woman that sent me over. Gods, my head was pounding. I know he told me he whored himself. It was just seeing the amount of intelligence he gathered from those trysts seemed staggering. Bootsteps came down the hall. A quick knock preceded Silas slipping in the room. I patted the bed beside me, lying back, my hand over my head. He laid next to me and rested his hand on mine.

"How many?" I asked him.

He shrugged.

"Why?"

"I was being useful."

I pressed my hands into my eyes, no doubt smearing my makeup. After Analisse, I thought he wouldn't put himself into that position. I went to the adjacent bathing chamber and used a flannel to put cool water on my head.

"You took a stranger to bed last night?" he asked, a smile in his voice. Standing by me and taking the cloth from my hands, he wiped my brow as I had done for him.

"You're not a stranger. You're mine." I put my arms around him and held tight. "No matter what. Even if you hate me. Even when the next realm claims us."

"Weeeell, you disposed of the gateway to that realm, so fuck knows what's going to happen now."

I looked up at him, trying not to think of how the male felt his worth was best placed in whoring himself. He hadn't shaved, the shadowy scruff on his face lending him a darker quality which suited him. Within that brooding handsome face were the eyes that looked just like Cadeyrn's. They stared down at me with a world of intensity. It was time to get back down there. I was sure there would be snide remarks and inferences, and if I were to let those get to me, the flat would be abuzz with electricity.

JUST THE sight of Bestía's kin sitting there, facing Cadeyrn, had my powers rising. It was as though my whole body filled with a roadmap of options to vanquish the two fae before me. Every ounce of focus in my being zeroed in on them. I shook off the hand Silas had at my back as I walked to the two. There was nothing at all to say to them, so I stared them down like an angry dog.

Hey, I'm here, Cadeyrn said. *She's gone. Come sit, Caráed.* I shook my head. He was right. Starting out like this would do nothing for us. Sometimes I wished I could kill her over and over again. I wished I could have been the necromancer who stripped away that which kept her alive, if only to see her wither away slowly. In the back of my mind, there was a whisper telling me I could have been. I had that power. That darkness. Cadeyrn was looking at me, and in his eyes, I knew he understood.

I may not be colourful and furry, but I guarantee you I am monster enough to remove their every last breath if you wish it. Say the word, he said to me, squeezing my hand.

Then we'd be just as bad as they all are. We would need to go live in some tall tower covered in thorns where the sun doesn't shine, and the food probably sucks.

It's always about the food with you, isn't it?

I have very basic needs. He projected a quick snapshot of our morning tussle in the hay, and exactly what needs were met when I marked his neck. Just as quick, he brought the meeting to order and there was the slightest, self-satisfied male lilt to his voice which I quite liked to hear.

None of us beat about the bush. We were aware of the depth and magnitude of what had been happening in Festaera for many years. Alongside Bestía's brother, Olek, and her mother, Kíra, there were three there from the province. A set of twins, Tuso and Petyr, and a male whose skin was at once dark and light, as though perhaps a deep brown that had been drained of colour. Like Reynard. He introduced himself as Sergo.

Slight pressure on my aching head gave me pause. Ludek lifted a single finger, as if to signal it was his doing. I allowed the pressure again, and he spoke to me through an oraculoís connection.

Though it may be obvious even to the rest of you, the ill intent of a few of those fae is staggering. I see Sergo's need for rectification and healing. He hoped that in coming here your mate would be able to heal him, but he has been kept by Tuso for decades. He is younger than most. Perhaps as young as you and Ewan. There is uncompromised hatred for you and Cadeyrn tainting Olek and Kíra. They weren't always this way, but they seek revenge.

So, just a normal day then. Gods, my head was killing me. Ludek's hand went on Basz's arm, and instantly a shield went up around them and Saski, Silas' covering the rest of us. Spears of power pricked toward us, taunting, but not penetrating the shield.

"Now, I've invited you into my home and given you a chance to speak on behalf of your candidacy, and this is how you want to present yourself?" Cadeyrn asked, his tone tepid. As they were for the last meeting, files and ledgers were spread across the table. The thought of Silas in Festaera doing what he had in Maesarra terrified me. I should have asked to look through the files before today. I was so wrapped up in my own stupid issues that it didn't really occur to me to do so. *Stupid, Neysa.*

"Festaera spent little to no coin in the past fifty years. How is that possible? Yours is a large province," Cadeyrn said.

"I would say to ask its Elder, but he and his mate, alas, are gone," Olek answered.

"Yes, but its treasurer sits before us. Tuso, explain the findings. Also, I was under the impression that Somoían would be here. Admittedly, he is not my favourite, but his absence is noted. He was head of trade."

I touched the ledger, hoping that it would explain something, but there was nothing. It was spelled.

"We are a self-sufficient province, Cadeyrn. You may have influenced my sister's loyalties and mind, but we are not so easily led." Olek spoke with unmasked hatred. Heat flared, and I didn't know which of us was going to lose it first. Cadeyrn stared him down.

"Your sister was a witch," Corra said. "Not only that, but she allied herself with dark-powered individuals who sought to destroy my cousin and his mate."

"From what I hear, she merely was brought back from the other realm and happened upon a lonely male in his time of need."

Something changed in Cadeyrn's face. Where his hand rested next to my arm, I felt a tremor go through him as though vast amounts of power were being expended. Olek flinched, but nothing else seemed amiss.

"Yes, well, if by time of need, you mean when we needed an army to fight phantomes and invading forces, then you would be correct," Cadeyrn said, as though nothing had just happened. Ludek was looking at us.

"The initial matter at hand today," Ewan began, sensing a downward turn this early in the assemblage, "is who will represent Festaera. It is the opinion of my position that both Olek and Kíra have a conflict of interest. Thus, I shall speak plainly in saying that I do not condone either of you as representatives."

Olek slammed his fist on the table, and ice erupted along the top. The room warmed uncomfortably, and Cadeyrn twitched his lips in a half smile.

Ewan told Tuso and Petyr he would hear their platforms. Petyr began to speak, but his sister turned to me.

"I wonder," she said, cool and collected, a cruel uptilt to her mouth, "how did your mate retrieve all this information? This ledger from my office? Have you asked?"

Though I had no idea, I merely smiled, internally wishing we had delayed the meeting to gather our wits regarding the vessels. She let Petyr speak, though I felt her eyes on me while I flipped through the nearly empty ledger and some of the files.

"You will excuse me while I review this," I said, eyes on the book. "I wasn't available of late to do so."

"A getaway with your other mate?" Okay, the two mates barbs were getting really old.

"I was dead," I said sweetly, reading through the information. "Look here. Under the sales heading for Festaeran steel, it lists sales and distribution to swordsmiths throughout the realm. Under some of the entries, there is a small marking." I turned to show the twins. Cadeyrn and Silas peered over my shoulders. "The first one is dated perhaps 200 years ago, with a footnote. Now, I am not yet fully versed in the aulde language, but *draíchnhud llong* means, what, my love? Magical ship? Boat?"

"Vessel," Sergo said. He flinched, his eyes sliding to the twins.

"Do refrain from threatening or hurting any of my guests," Cadeyrn said to Tuso. She inclined her head.

"Under these entries there is no coin recorded. Care to explain, treasurer?" Silas asked. I passed the ledger and files down to Ewan. "Majesty," Silas said to my brother. "We have seen similar markings and entries from other provinces in the reverse, have we not?"

Indications of slave trade. Ewan confirmed what Silas was asking and explained that many of the provinces seemed to have been trading their citizens for Festaeran steel. At first glance, it appeared to be standard, abhorrent slavery. It needed immediate eradication. However, what it showed us here now was that these slaves were being used as vessels to contain the spells cast upon the steel being purchased. Every item made of Festaeran steel was a risk to its bearer.

"So, what, exactly, are you accusing us of?" Petyr asked.

"Slavery, for one. Trafficking of fae. Molestation. Conspiracy both of murder and to the Crown," my brother listed.

I looked to Ludek, who nodded in agreement.

This sounds really bloody familiar, I said to both Cadeyrn and Silas.

"I'm holding you both in contempt." Ewan then addressed my mate. "Cadeyrn, is there anything we need to hear from them at the moment?" Cadeyrn made a dismissive gesture and told him they were all his. "And Kíra and Olek?"

"I would say they are free to go. Sergo, would you mind staying on? We have yet to hear your bid."

"You have no idea what you are disrupting," Tuso spat. She flicked her fingers, and Sergo grabbed at his head. At once, she began choking and gagging. Corra sat, rubbing her belly and grinning like a cat. Guards entered and dragged the twins out. Kíra looked us dead in the eyes.

"We shall meet again."

Oh, for the love of all that's holy. What a load of overused rubbish.

"Quite sure," Cadeyrn said, looping his arm around me.

CHAPTER 33

Had the circumstances been different, it would have been a party. All of my family and friends in one place again with wine and food. Except that the aftermath of the meeting left us drained, Cadeyrn especially. He spoke with Sergo privately regarding what the male had endured, and he began the slow process of healing that he had provided Reynard. Sergo had almost no desire for the position he was now heading into. His initial reason for putting himself in this position, heedless of what Tuso would try to do, was to tell us what was going on up there. Sergo was escorted to an inn, guards stationed outside his door.

Someone passed me a glass of wine, which I refused, stuffing my face with bread and crackers. I quite literally could not see straight. There were blinking lights and a dull throb behind my left eye.

"What's wrong with you?" Corra asked when my males were otherwise occupied.

"My head is killing me."

She narrowed her eyes, making her seem like a dragon in waiting.

"I miss you, Corra."

She handed me another piece of bread. "I do too, darling."

Reynard brought over a cold glass of water and handed it to me with a wink. I gave him a knowing smile.

"Don't start, Kitten."

"Oh no. You are so in for it later."

He laughed at my threat. "Touché. Perhaps over a bottle of wine."

Oh, Gods. I might throw up from the mention of it.

"Yes. Just, not anytime soon. Excuse me." I ran full speed for the bathing chamber and emptied my stomach. Great. Now I'd need more bread. Shutting the door, I sat on the floor with my face pressed to the cool wall. I knew there were two males waiting outside the door.

"Her head is troubling her from the wine," Silas said quietly.

"Why didn't she say anything?" Cadeyrn asked.

Because you're drained. I can see it.

Neysa.

How did you get the ledgers?

The sound of Silas growling and walking off filled the pregnant pause. Warmth came through the door, and I backed away, allowing Cadeyrn in. He squatted down, hiking his trousers up to get down to my level. The chamber was by no means small, but he seemed to take up so much of it. Warm fingers touched my face and stroked it like I was an instrument. One hand held the base of my skull where a thick throbbing ache had centered itself from the migraine; the other hand covered my left eye. After a time, the pain subsided, and I sagged against him. To my mind, he showed me how the ledgers were retrieved.

Silas had gone south. He was in and out of the twin provinces, Maesarra and Laorinaghe. Cadeyrn was waiting for me to wake, feeling useless. He knew where to look in the palace in Laorinaghe, and though Silas was sorting through those who would be allies and who would be foe, it seemed we needed to get a hold of the ledgers. All the files from Lorelei's cabinet, so to speak. He let his rage take over, and he became his *baethaache* form and went to Laorinaghe. It was a successful mission, apart from he and Silas having a throw down in the forest outside of the Sacred City. Cadeyrn used his *baethaache* form to go straight to Festaera and do the same thing. He knew Sergo was being held by Tuso and Petyr and slipped into her office.

Shouting and snarling erupted from the other room. We looked to one another and stood. Saski was in Silas' face, her finger pointing in his chest. Arik threw his hands up when we came in and downed a shot of liquor.

"You knew something was going on up there. What were you lot doing here the past hundred years?" she yelled.

"Sorry, am I being questioned by someone who has sat on her pretty ass her whole life? You don't know what you're on about," he responded, attempting to remove her finger from his chest. She pushed forward and backed him against the wall.

Basz sidled up to us. I raised my eyebrow.

"You lot work in a devious manner," Saski continued. "I don't appreciate having to sit in there not knowing what we are going to be facing."

"What part of our telling you they had phantomes don't you understand? They brought an ex-lover of my cousin's back from the fucking dead to take him away from Neysa. They experimented on Reynard. What more did you want to hear about? Sorry about your favourite toy, Your Highness. We've all lost something lately."

"You fucked your way through three provinces in order to get answers! Who does that?" she screamed. I wondered why that bothered her, and in my mind, seeing her legs wrapped around him gave me pause. Silas was wide-eyed looking at her, his back to the wall, Saski in his face.

"You were the impetus that had Neysa going off to her death. It was you. Your bastard of a father too. But if we are slinging shite at each other, lovely, I blame you. You are provocative, deceitful, and dangerous." He said it with an undertone of thunder.

She breathed heavily but pulled her finger from his chest.

"I do not trust you. Your brothers, maybe. You? No."

"You were more than happy to be between my legs," she said. The room went white. I lost it.

"Saski," Arik warned. "That's enough." The door slammed, and I knew Silas had left, though there was nothing visible in the room itself. Two sets of hands were on me. Ewan and Cadeyrn. My headache was back. I leaned against the back of the sofa as I gradually brought the room back to normal.

"'People never lie so much as after a hunt, during a war, or before an election.'" I quoted Otto Von Bismark. Everyone's eyes were on me, though mine were closed, trying not to move much. "Saski, you are full of shit. You lied to get my mates in bed. You all lied to get us to Heilig. Though perhaps not transparent, we never deceived you about anything here. What we do know is that we need to shut down the operation going on up there."

I groaned and grabbed my head. Ewan put his hand on my face and sat beside me. Cadeyrn was using his gift, fishing around, trying to figure out why the headache came back. The niggling memory of Bestía and Analisse removing my magic and my link to Cadeyrn had a seed of panic forming in my gut. Forcing myself to open my eyes, I stared between the two males with me.

"It's her gifts," Ludek said, his voice like the wind through an open window. "She needs to master them. She needs to release vitality and embrace the darkness in her. She fights it."

Because I don't want to be a monster, I said to Ludek.

"Darkness is not contemptible. It is necessary for balance. If you do not balance yourself, Neysa—"

"How do I do it?" I felt like throwing up again. *Cadeyrn.* He blew lightly in my face, and the nausea eased.

"I can only see so much. Perhaps it will become more obvious to me in the coming days."

I needed this migraine gone now. One minute I was on the sofa, the next I was in a bed. I curled into a ball, pulling at my hair.

"May I make a suggestion?" Cadeyrn asked in a whisper, allowing a cool mist to cover me. I grumbled something that he was going to anyway. He ran a hand along my hip and the outside of my thigh. "Perhaps you must...finish the mating with Silas." I pulled the pillow over my head. "If you are coming into so much power that you need two mates, then it's not like you can give half effort." Like a snail up a hill, I turned to him.

"Half effort?" I glared through one eye as the other was closed in excruciating pain. "Is that what you think?"

"You are acting like I am your only mate, when unfortunately—for me that is—it just isn't true. If you aren't fulfilling the mating requirement, perhaps your balance is off."

"Ugh. Typical male. It's always all about sex."

He laughed.

"I love Silas. As you know. I'm sorry I'm telling you this." I bit my lip. "He and I. It's always been easy between us."

"Yeah," Cadeyrn breathed. His eyes were on the duvet. "And you and I seem to always stagger around a bit, don't we?" No, no.

"What I mean is that it would be so easy to let go and have him. I mean, it's expected." I moved my hand, and the low lamp that was lit dropped to darkness. That was a new one. "But I chose you. Not between the two of you. I chose us. I love you more than anything in any realm. Because I don't care how much we stumble or bite each other's heads off. I want you."

"You may not be at liberty to make that choice." He pulled at a stray thread on the blanket. "Believe me, Neysa. If it could be just the two of us forever, that's all—all I've ever wanted. But we are a part of something bigger, and I won't have you burn out or die because you refuse to hurt me."

"Damn it all," I said through a sniffle. "Just a horrible monster."

"I killed Olek." Pardon? "It wasn't going to end, and I lost my grip. I released a blood clot in his brain. It may have killed him eventually anyway, but I did it. He will likely be dead before they get home. So, you see, if either of us is a monster, my love, it's me."

"Shit."

"Precisely."

I sat up, and though my head felt like there was a team of horses inside it, I crawled onto his lap and took his face in my hands.

"But you're my monster." I kissed him.

CHAPTER 34

Silas

While the others were shocked and feigned disgust at what Cadeyrn had done, I wasn't. I wished I'd done the same damn thing. In fact, I may have taken out Kíra as well. However, the fact of the matter was that whether Olek died today or a week from now, we would get blamed. Funny how, in the human realm, they would have blamed it on something else. A blow to the head. An accident. Here, they would know. And they would hunt us for it. Problem was that my cousin was already on the hunt. The minute we started in on him for it, he walked out. We heard the whip of wings and the flight.

Neysa's head was still pounding, and she grabbed it while we went over our defenses and how to instill Sergo as representative without getting him killed. A coupe. They would say we caused a coupe. I guess we did. Arik suggested he go to Laorinaghe and speak to Yva and her group regarding their take on the matter, then meet back with Ewan and my sister in Maesarra.

Saski had blood lust written on her face. She seemed to need a task. Like me. Working dogs. That was what my mother would have said.

"In 1914," *Trubaíste* spoke up, "in the human realm, an archduke was shot and killed. He was a figurehead of a corroding monarchy and was killed by an idealistic young student, who was a part of an assassination group." Neysa started talking, and everyone quieted down. She spoke to us with her head still in her hands. I was pissed she was still in pain.

"It happens all the time. Figureheads being killed. I could list hundreds in the mortal realm if you want, though I'm sure it's unnecessary." Saski snorted, and I flicked her shoulder. She air kissed me. "The problem with this one wasn't that it was the death of a monarch," Neysa said. "It was the pressure point on a world that was ready to change. The event is known as 'The Shot Heard 'Round the World' because it was what spearheaded World War One. The empire the archduke was heir to fell. The opposing empire fell. Two great empires ended, and it was the birth of the modern world through the blood and politics that followed. The countries who fought and died during that Great War had little to do with the empires that collapsed. It was merely a stone that was set in a downhill motion."

"Blood and politics always follow blood. What is your point here, Neysa?" Saski asked.

Neysa was so fucked with pain, she didn't take the bait.

"I believe," Ludek joined in, "her point falls somewhere along the lines of it not taking much to start a revolt. Cadeyrn's killing Olek could lead to revolt. So could our being here. We could be seen as usurpers. Anything could start it."

Neysa nodded her head in agreement, then stopped, squinting with the pain. I went to get her a flannel with peppermint as she had done for me on the barge. She looked up at me grate-fully. I placed it on her neck.

"So, do we wait?" Arik asked.

"We move," Saski said. Fucking gods, she was just like me.

"We work immediately to put things in place to prevent any retaliation from spreading throughout Aoifsing," Ludek announced. "The uprising in Heilig ceased upon our leave, though one might assume it is in conjunction with the Veil being down. Basz and I can leave to be with Father to organize our own defenses."

"I will leave for the Sacred City in the morning," Arik added.

"Someone has to stay with you lot and shed a little blood," Saski said with a shrug.

Reynard walked in with the layout of the keep in Festaera. He had been mostly absent this evening and, coming in with a scaled sketch of the layout, I could now see why.

"I need air," Neysa said, pushing her way to the door. She wasn't dressed for the cold outside, but I wasn't about to say anything.

Messages went out to my scouts right away. I needed wraiths in and around the compound in Festaera. Eyes needed to be in every stinking shite hole up there to find where the vessels were kept. After an hour, Neysa wasn't back. It was Corraidhín who looked to me with anxious eyes and motioned to the door. I ran my hand through my hair and stood, strapping a sword across my back. A couple of years ago, I would never have walked in Laichmonde dressed for battle. So many changes in a year.

I wandered around, looking for her in the dark streets, catching her scent here and there. Bloody hell, even I was getting cold. It took me longer than it should have to realize I'd scented her in every elemental temple around the city. A right thickheaded twat I was. The last was the temple of weather on the outskirts of the city. I moved quicker, hoping to catch her, as it was a steep climb to the top, and would be very cold up there. Huddled in the corner, where we sent out ashes to find Cadeyrn early this year, was the female I was mated to. But not really. I rushed over like a stupid lad. She was blue and shaking.

"*Trubaiste*, you need to come with me. It's fucking cold up here. What were you doing?"

Her teeth were chattering.

My head feels better in the cold. She couldn't even speak out loud, her body was shaking so hard.

"Yeah, but the rest of you doesn't agree. Come on. Up you go." I took my jacket off and wrapped it around her.

My arm was around her as we walked, and she was leaning into me like she was happy to be there. I had a sinking feeling I knew what was making her head pound, but I wasn't about to make that suggestion. For a fuck tonne of reasons. However, I did hold my hand out, allowing a cyclone of wind to swirl over my palm. She reached for it like it was a gift, hovering her hand over and pulling up, even smiling slightly as she stretched the cyclone between her hand and mine. Midnight darkness showered from her hand, mingling into the mini tempest we shared. It built and we brought our hands together, but instead of it disappearing, our touch made it swirl around us, covering the two of us in a dark cloud.

"This is where a different male might say something about us making beautiful magic together or some shite," I teased her.

She pulled me to her and claimed my mouth. Bloody. Fucking. Hell. I gave it right back to her with the same enthusiasm. We were near my flat, and I was counting on Reynard still being at Cadeyrn's dealing with the children playing war. Part of me knew she was just trying to please that pressure in her head, and part of me knew she had a need of me beyond that. A year ago, I decided that I would give her whatever she wanted. Which made me an arse for so many reasons. Inside, her shivering started to go away; I could tell her head was worse. This whole thing was such a clusterfuck. I couldn't even take her to my bed, as that was what Reynard had been using, so I led us to the room we shared last night and shut the door.

When I turned around, she was looking at me with such determination, I already felt stripped bare. By the gods, I loved that face. That complete fucking destruction of a female. I didn't think I had ever told her that. She unstrapped my scabbard and laid my sword reverently on the floor. I watched every movement, thinking she would walk away.

"I love you," I said, and it came out so quiet, I wasn't sure she had heard me. I felt sick. I'd never told a female that. Her eyes met mine. Tears were streaming from them. "I know you know that," I told her. She just reached up and held my face. I leaned into it while she reached to pull my shirt off. Then I heard it. A catch in her breath. A whispered thought at the back of her mind.

I don't want this. Like a bucket of icy water was thrown on me. I wanted to be angry. I wanted to hit something. But I couldn't blame her. She wanted to be with my cousin. I was the piece of shite coming between them. Whatever was between us was a cruel wickedness. She was still touching me, and I took her hands.

"*Trubaíste*, don't." Confusion. Then she must have realized I heard her. "I understand. I do. We will find a way to sort this out without any…"

I made wiggly eyebrows at her. She made a play at reaching again, and I kissed her. Hard. My hands were on her face, and I wrapped a leg around hers, then told her I would always be here. But I wouldn't do this with her not wanting it. She sagged against me like a ragdoll.

The problem was her head was still a loaded canon that needed firing. I knew how it felt. Perhaps if she and I were to combine our powers, utilizing them in a different fashion, the connection would still work the way it was supposed to. Almost like when she and Ewan formed that magnetic field. We could beat it another way.

We laid on the bed, completely wrapped in each other, much like last night. I wasn't lying when I said I was happy to be with her just like this. But I'd be a lying sack of shite if I didn't say that more anything in this world I wanted her. All of her. So, when I held the little beast, it was the greatest effort of a lifetime not to seduce her. We laid there, and I tried something I had never done with anyone. I let my magic pour into her, bit by bit. She looked at me, startled.

"I can feel it trickling in." She closed her eyes and tipped her head back like there was some sort of relief. Then I felt her open up. "Can I try? To give you mine, I mean?"

I squeezed her back in answer. I didn't know why this made me as nervous as it did. I kept letting my gifts seep into her. When I concentrated, I saw it moving through her like blood in her veins, lighting her up. Pure magic. I tried not to swear when she released the flood gates on her power.

"Fucking hell." I tried and failed.

She glowed white, with night black surrounding us, energy crackling between us. It started tapping at me, looking for a way in. I let go, feeling that darkness slither in me, the light racing along the electricity within her. It mingled with my own, playing within me. I held her as she thrashed against me, distantly aware that my body was moving the same. Pressure built in the room. She cried out, then the storm started outside and she moaned, resting her head against mine, her magic still coursing from her into me. I pressed myself against her, vaguely aware that we were both here and not here. With a final burst, she released a wave of darkness into me, and by the gods, I couldn't stop myself from bellowing and shaking against her. She threw her head back, and a sound like the flight of a hundred birds came out of her. Her body dropped back onto mine, asleep. Gods above, I hoped that helped her head, because I had never experienced anything like what we just did. Ever.

PART III

CHAPTER 35

Neysa
Richmond, England, Eleven Months Later

Six months ago, I stopped being angry. Or at least I stopped acting on it. If I were honest with myself, there had been signs. So many indications that it was primed to fail. Just because something was written in the stars didn't mean it was permanent. Everything was stardust. We saw stars all the time that had long since faded from existence. What was left was the lingering light, the hope of what was out there. Our stardust could only hold together for so long before a strong wind blew it apart, scattering us to the elements, and we became residual energy. Spectres of galaxies long gone.

Residual energy was what I was now. An accumulation of all that made me who and what I was in a volatile package, ready to explode if the pressure wasn't released bit by bit. For six months, I let it build. Let the troposphere of my emotions build within me while I raged and thrashed and destroyed who

I was. Then one day I walked away from it. I was still angry, but I finally felt a budding of myself. From that shoot of self came a little more power. Letting go of my rage as my power, I embraced that bud and tried to nurture it. I was not my anger, my darkness. I was a survivor. A warrior. Even if the battle was in me. Even if I had no real hope of walking off that battlefield.

The streets of London allowed me to be just a face in the crowd. I wasn't an heir to a throne or a goddess, or someone who once had a great love and two mates, but just a pretty face who didn't look out of place in a city that held the past and future in the palm of its hand. Once I started trading again, I was able to leave. I could afford to travel here and there, spending time amongst the people and histories of places I'd always dreamt about. Then I would come home to my flat in Richmond. It felt the most like Laichmonde, with the river and the parks. I made acquaintances and never spoke about my past. They knew I grew up toeing the line between the U.K. and California and knew as far as when I moved from Los Angeles. I couldn't say I was a part of anything bigger. That I'd had more than I ever could have wished for, and watched it leave. Watched him leave. Finally leave me. Because we were all stardust, and as careful as we were with each other, there was a final touch that dispersed what held us together. And so there I was in the mortal realm, an immortal with no real desire to see the years approaching. He hadn't known when he pushed me through that Veil. We had been conflicted for weeks, trying to figure out how to live without one another, I think. He wouldn't have known there was another thread to pull. That there was a choice in that moment. Had he pulled the other thread, we might have held together. I saw it as I crossed. The possibility. And then it was gone. The visions. The connection. The power. All my power. Like my beastie, it was all gone. Even the Veil. Only memories remained like the light of long dead stars. Perhaps one day they would fade too. Perhaps, like stardust, I too would fade.

When I slept at night, those rare times when I didn't lie awake all night, I dreamt of Aoifsing. Sometimes I thought they were visions. Faces I knew and loved. Memories and visions of cities and events. There was blood too. Broken bodies and bird's eye views of things that had happened to me during our many battles. Memories would surface of being with him. Loving him. Of a bond so real and consuming it shook the skies when we let it. Then I would wake, unable to breathe, sweating, barely able to make it out of my flat to run. Run from the ache and the loss and run until I physically couldn't go any further. I was wrong here. Out of place like ghosts in daylight. I went out and drank and worked and trained, but I was wrong. A shell of what and who I was meant to be. And I wished it would kill me quicker than it was. Because as much as I tried, I couldn't fucking live like this.

CHAPTER 36

Eleven Months Ago
Neysa

A rik was in Laorinaghe. The Heiligan prince and the Representative to the Province of Laorinaghe seemed to share a similar outlook on how the realm should run. Arik presented himself as the cocky prince. A laissez-faire attitude belied a determined and definite sense of how the world should be. While we hadn't recognized that determination straight away, it came to light when the situation demanded he show it to us.

Olek of Festaera died less than a week after leaving our meeting in Laichmonde. His mother blamed us, just as we knew she would. Others were skeptical. A hawk was sent the following day.

"Your demise is my debt to my children," it read.

Cadeyrn grabbed at the back of his neck. He blamed himself. Well, I suppose it was his doing, even if I didn't fault him for it. He left that night and was gone for two days. I was hurt. Hurt that he never said goodbye. The pain I had in my head finally let up after Silas and I shared our magic. It was just as intimate as if we had ended it otherwise, but I felt it was less of a betrayal to my relationship with Cadeyrn. When my husband returned, something was different. He was cold and calculating. Three days after he came back, we were readying to go to Prinaer to speak with the Mads family heir about running the twin provinces. Cadeyrn suggested I stay behind. I scoffed at him. He threw up his hands and tromped across the room, grabbing weaponry. We hadn't been together in bed since before everything happened. I felt the strain. He must have as well. I tried to corner him. Tried to force those eyes to look at me. Only briefly did they meet mine before looking across the room where a knock sounded at the door.

"We're leaving, Cadeyrn." Corra's voice. I wanted them to stay. I wanted to have them here. I didn't want to fall apart, because this time, I refused to let Silas pick me up. And I wasn't sure Cadeyrn was in better shape. He moved past me and opened the door. Corra's eyes shot to mine the moment the door opened.

"You okay, darling?" she asked me.

I forced a smile.

She walked to me and lifted her chin. "Don't let them get you down. You are the goddess, Neysa. You."

A jolt of pain lanced through me, and I honestly couldn't tell whether it came from Cadeyrn or me. I kissed her cheek and left the room to say goodbye to my brother. Whispers and the sound of something hitting a wall trailed behind me.

Only Cadeyrn, Reynard, and I went to see Ainsley Mads. It was three nights sleeping in a tent again. Sleeping next to him with not even a scent of desire. The last night, perhaps an hour or so before dawn, I reached over. I couldn't stand it anymore. I put my hand on his stomach. His eyes shot to mine.

Touch me, I begged. He turned, staring into my eyes, and finally lifted a hand and stroked my hair behind my ear. I was dizzy already, needing him. I walked my fingers up his chest and touched the short hairs at the base of his neck.

Where are you lately?

"I'm right here." His voice was sleep-mussed. I pressed closer.

Prove it.

"Neysa," he growled out loud.

"No. Don't Neysa me. Prove to me you are here, because I'm not buying it yet." The quiet in the tent, in my head, in the mountains around us, was deafening. Finally, I dropped my eyes and pulled my hand away, trying not to shake. He reached between us and grabbed my hand, bringing it to his mouth to kiss. Our fingers interlaced, and his other hand began slowly proving to me he wanted to touch me.

AINSLEY WAS as formidable a female as I had ever met. She was taller than me, standing just under Cadeyrn, with jet black hair and russet skin. She had her hair in multiple braids pulled back from her face, leaving the stark countenance of her bare. As soon we walked into the hall of her family compound, she clasped elbows with each of us, her leather gauntlets rough against my skin. She had a gaggle of rather large males and females in the hall, eyes on us.

"Did you kill Olek?" she asked before introductions.

"I did," my mate answered matter-of-factly. No deceptions, no beating about the bush. He was owning up to his actions.

"Was it necessary?"

"It was a quick, hard call on an escalating situation. Necessary? Yes. He was threatening my family. His sister caused enough damage. Once we address the situation in Festaera, we can revisit your question."

"Would you have made that same call?" She faced me, arms crossed.

"I would have," I said, standing just a little taller. It was a rare day when another female made me feel short. She nodded, then led us into the hall.

We all sat along benches at long tables, casually telling our tale. Ainsley explained the way in which she would organize and lead her provinces.

"It has been too long under the thumb of those two Elders and their brutal ways. We are at a time for change." She gestured around her. This place seemed least likely to change, with every fae here dressed for a raid like a Viking village. In the middle of the mountains.

"Are your ways not brutal?" I asked. Not implying. Simply asking. "Allow me to rephrase. You seem less inclined to bullshit and more inclined to plan, assess, contain, execute."

She laughed and drank from her ale.

"My wife has no inclination to bullshit either," Cadeyrn said with pride in his tone. "See it as a compliment."

I nearly kissed him. Instead, I ran a hand along his leg.

"It is a fair assessment of my nature," Ainsley admitted. "As you know, my father and brother died during the battle near here." I hadn't realized we were in such close proximity to the battlefield. "We mourn for a year and day, keeping the fires lit for them. I believe in the world you are trying to create. I believe in keeping power in check. One concern I have is the presence of royalty. I would like to keep the twin provinces' sovereign from the rest of Aoifsing. And I beseech the dismantling of a monarchy."

Cadeyrn did not look phased at all, but I felt a tightening of the muscles in his leg. Reynard laughed and told her she had balls.

"That's quite a list of stipulations," my mate said. "I have no issue with your sovereignty. It really concerns me very little, so long as, as we have discussed, you keep power in check." She pursed her lips and tilted her ahead in agreement. "Neysa, would you care to jump in?"

"From what I have seen and experienced here in Aoifsing, the monarchy is a suggestion. It's a safety net. My family was brought here to balance the magic of the lands and help keep it all running. According to the annals I have read, none of the monarchs who have been here, from my grandparents to my mother, and now, my brother, have enacted a singular rule. It had always been the Elders. Am I correct?"

"Yes," she said carefully. "However, it is the potential for that supremacy of which we are fearful."

"At the moment my brother is working in Maesarra from a position of keeping that province safe. In the bigger picture, we are all trying our damnedest to bring together those who might change the structure of how Aoifsing has been run historically. Giving the fae of this realm more of a say in the day to day of their lives. Had Ewan not stepped in after the murder of our mother, there very well could have been a massive downturn in Aoifsing."

"We shall stand behind your bid as representative," Cadeyrn said. "However, I need your word that you will not make a move against my family nor will you disrupt the monarchy. In return, I will give you my word that apart from protecting the rights of your citizens, the monarchy will not interfere with your undertakings."

She sat back and looked to her flanking behemoths and considered. For long, uncomfortable minutes, she stared between the three of us, then agreed. We shared a meal and ale.

"Our enclave has self sustained us for centuries," Ainsley began, the room falling to a lull. "Most would not be daft enough to disrupt our way of life." She looked to her right, where a female with scars crisscrossing her face and neck closed her eyes in what I took for concession. "Some time ago, Ursa—" she gestured to the scarred female, "was running patrol on the border of Naenire with her two bairns. They were naught but sixteen at the time. Babes. Their unit ran across a pack of lupinus." She took a steadying breath, and I steeled myself for what I thought I knew was coming. Cadeyrn shifted next to me. "They stayed hidden. We are a forest fae, able to become one with the gullies and canopies. We have all seen lupinus train. I have been with Nanua in her selection ceremonies in times past. It is barbaric." Ursa scrubbed a hand over her face as Ainsley spoke. I looked round the hall, noticing the attention of every other large provincial present was focused on Ursa. Eyes all offered regret and sympathy.

"What Ursa and her bairns witnessed that day on the border," Ainsley continued, "was a pitting of children in a ring. Soldiers held lupinus and their lupine charges back until first blood was spilled between the children in the ring. Then they released the lupinus."

My stomach rolled; my hand shot to Cadeyrn's for comfort. For a link to whatever humanity was called in this realm.

"Who was in charge of this?" Cadeyrn asked, his voice tight.

"My lads begged me to go help the children. I knew we were outmatched and so I refused," Ursa told us. "We made camp that night and they snuck out. Always trying to right the world, they were." She swallowed. "Their heads were delivered to my tent just before dawn." Ainsley grabbed her hand. "I took two of my warriors and went to the border. As you can see," she said gestured to her face, "I was unsuccessful. And my lads were gone. You ask who was behind this? It was Etienne of Maesarra and a small group of fae with accents I could not distinguish. That is all I know. But I will fight."

As though her final words were a signal, the hall rose in chatter once again. In the late hours, Ainsley and her top behemoth brought us to a dark office. An ancient map was pulled from a bookshelf and spread atop the desk. Sconces threw amber light across the spread of hide; mountains and roads were inked. We peered closer. With a wave of her hand, markings on the map began to flow, revealing turns and corners that were hidden before. Tiny rivers moved along the map, dim light catching the caps of white water. It seemed as though they flowed...

"Central Prinaer to Festaera. A direct link through the mountains. The mines and caverns in the north can all be accessed from here."

Reynard whistled and clapped her on the back. She glared at him, narrowing her dark, almond-shaped eyes. Cadeyrn ran a finger along the flowing lines, making them glow with light. I reached out, not expecting much as the map was spelled, but images came to mind.

A clock, worn and perhaps broken. Seemingly endless streams of water. Caverns stacked with fae in suspended animation, drained of colour. Light. A goddess, calling to me. Silas and another female, who was pregnant. Cadeyrn, walking away from me, smiling, though I was screaming. City lights. A river. A sunken meadow, damp with leaf rot, wind blowing. I had gotten better at managing the visions. As long as I didn't try to speak yet, I could act as if nothing had happened. A light hand on my back told me he knew.

"You give us permission to use these waterways to liberate the folk being held in Festaera?" Cadeyrn asked.

"And you will allow our return passage as well?" Reynard added. "I was brought there through these. Nanua did it. I don't remember much, but I recall waterways through the mountains. I had thought it a dream as I was beaten."

Anger flared from me, darkness pooling around my feet. Ainsley looked down in interest.

"We will allow passage both directions. I will come as well." She pulled me aside. "We have a temple here. A lesser goddess who has protected us for millennia. She, like Heícate, dwells in both darkness and light. I believe she would be eager to be summoned by you. May I show you to her temple tomorrow?"

Bloody great. Another goddess to deal with. Maybe I would get a third mate, a hellhound, and an extra set of arms.

Let's not tempt that, shall we? Cadeyrn said seriously.

"Thank you," I told Ainsley. "I would like that." Bugger.

BENEATH A wooden pergola was a set of stairs. Ainsley and my mate stood at the top, allowing me privacy. As though following a rope wrapped about my waist, I let it pull me deep into the temple. The walls were lined in gold, its reflection being the only light within. A dark pool was in the middle, clear as glass, daring a dip of fingers.

"Go on, child," came a seraphic voice, urging me to touch my hands to the surface. As the inky water lapped over fingers and palm, I was pulled under.

Do not wish for me, for I may prove less a blessing, more a demand. Call upon me gently, praying in the night, for I am the will of the mother. Wrapping my arms about my children, allowing them to feed themselves with only what their soul truly wants. I see compassion, identity, love without bounds, love without death, love that transcends time and space. I will strip away your ego and allow you to embrace your darkness. So do not call for me should you wish to remain fixed to that which holds you back. Call for me only when you have need of holy wrath and your own beautiful destruction.

I could see her standing, many-limbed, swathed in glittering black, slicing at ties that bind others. Calling me. *Who are you?* I asked.

I am Kalíma, and I am in you, child. I am youth and age. The great dark womb of mother creation. I despise shackles and cages. I permit you to break free of any bind that sours your soul. I tried to carefully keep my mind blank, not wishing anything. She laughed. At once I was out of the pool, coughing up water on the ground of the temple.

When I emerged from the stairs, soaked and shaken, both Ainsley and Cadeyrn gave me a look. I held up my hand, adjusted my sword belt, and walked off.

"Training ring. Now."

BIG, BURLY, dark Vikings. That was what this whole place seemed to be filled with. They wore horned helmets and fur boots. I was tossed a wooden training sword as soon as I stepped into the ring, sodden and utterly needing to release some energy. Thurton, Ainsley's second, paired me with a male who was relatively small compared to the rest of them. Meaning he was roughly the size of my mate, who could take me down in two moves. My blood heated as soon as I thought of being in a ring with him. As I spun my sword, I caught Cadeyrn's eyes, which were sparkling.

You're next, Cadeyrn.

Oh, no. Not here. Maybe in private.

Promise? Silence. *Ah.*

Neysa.

I took off at a stupidly fast run and flipped over my opponent, knocking his elbow with my sword. He dropped his and swore heartily. There was cheering and clapping, ale mugs slapping together. Bunch of bloody Vikings. So, I would be the Valkyrie. With a pang, I missed my *baethaache*. Igmar, my opponent, crouched and launched for me, reaching to grab my waist. I pitted and rolled over his back, landing in a half squat, then stood. We squared off, and he toed a line on the ground. I narrowed my eyes and scratched my own design in the dirt. He looked at it in question and laughed. It was a kissing-faced stick figure with a sword. I shrugged. We knocked swords back and forth, but I was riled up from the goddess, from not having my mate. From needing to run so far, I'd end up in Laorinaghe. Or Maesarra with Corra who would tell me to chin up and fuck them all. Bored and ready to let go, I dove between his legs and slammed both elbows backwards into the backs of his knees, bringing him down, where I sat on him.

"Yield, friend?" I asked.

"Aye." He took my offered hand before I bowed and told him good match.

In the hall, cups of ale were continuously brought to us. Apparently, it went a long way that I was willing to knock swords with one of their own. In a quiet moment, Cadeyrn whispered to me that he sent out hawks telling everyone where we needed to meet. In the meantime, he and I would stay here while Reynard went to Maesarra to stay with Corra. The ale was going to my head, and I felt full and bloated. I touched his lip with my thumb, listening to him talk, wishing we were alone. He stopped and kissed my cheek, walking off. Ah.

"Wait," I said, louder than I'd intended. The room fell silent as Cadeyrn turned around. I turned red and apologized to the hall. Cadeyrn walked back to me, and the room was lit with chatter once again.

"I saw things. When I touched the map. A clock. I think perhaps the spell is linked to time. The Goddess. Kalíma, she is the destroyer of time and ego. She said many things. I saw so many things." He looked around and sat, knees against mine. I explained the look of the clock, the feel. The meadow and the lights. A look of terror washed over his face, and he muttered about finding Reynard, then left.

In our chamber, alone, I sat on the wooden floor, toying with a loose thread on the woven rug, then began to scry with a crystal pendulum. This one was made of tourmaline for protection. As I was asking my basic questions to find the direction it would move, the door flung open.

"What are you doing?" Cadeyrn barked. "Don't do that here." He grabbed the pendulum, breaking my connection.

"Dammit, Cade!"

"Oh, it's Cade, now?" His eyes flared. "There's too much at stake now. I don't want you opening any doors we cannot shut."

I snorted. "Too late for that." I stood, walking to the water ewer to drink a glass. Even though my belly felt full to bursting. I hated ale. "The clock," I started to say.

"Is a relic. It is on the mantel in Bistair. I saw it once, long ago. Solange tried to take it as a wedding gift. It transforms when touched, showing the time left for he who holds it." I shivered. "So, if you think the spell in Festaera is linked to time, then this clock is probably a part of it. Reynard will bring it back."

I dropped the pendulum into a small velvet sack and tucked it in my satchel.

"Do you remember traveling with a suitcase and clean clothes? Waking up in a hotel and not having to get up right away? Room service?"

"Do you miss it? The human realm?" He sat on the chair next to the window, his leather groaning as he stretched his legs. I wanted to climb on top of him. Have him hold me, do whatever I wanted to him, but I knew I couldn't. Again. The ale burned like acid, rising in my throat.

"Sometimes," I said honestly. "Some things, rather." I jumped to the side of the elevated bed and sat, staring at my hands. The constellation of freckles that matched his. "What I miss in either realm is us."

"How's your head been?" My eyes snapped to his. His mouth was pressed into a hard line like it always had been when I met him. I hadn't even known the softness of his mouth until I watched him sleep. He did not realize what happened between his cousin and me. He must have thought...

"I released my gifts," I told him. "We did it together. The darkness and light, everything I know how to control. I gave it to Silas and he gave me his. It was beautiful, and it worked."

"That's good."

"I thought so."

"What do you want me to say, Neysa?"

"I don't. You know what I want? What I always and singularly want? It's you. It's us."

"Us is a multi-leveled operation now. Us is a factor in a plan, a thread in a tapestry. It's not you and me." That he thought that made my body go numb.

I couldn't help the damned tears. "That isn't true. You know it's not true. It's always about you and me."

"We have to get this problem taken care of. Then maybe we can see about..." He started to say something I couldn't listen to. Darkness cocooned me.

Is this about Silas? Because it's a stupid point. There is you and me and a cast of supporting actors. That's. It. I'm going to bed. Feel free to come too.

He left the room.

CHAPTER 37

Cadeyrn

The clock was going to alter time. It would distort our sense of what would happen, and it would ruin us. I saw in her vision the sequencing. I saw the city lights. I knew those, and they weren't in the fae realm. I knew that meadow. Maybe Neysa caught a glimpse of the past as she had done before, but something deep within me knew it was a future. A prospective future, at least. The walkway outside of our chamber had a wooden railing with stars carved into it. I traced the stars with my fingers, wishing I could go back in and run my fingers along Neysa's body. Knowing she would want that, but I was too afraid. For her. For me. Perhaps I was a cold bastard.

I tore apart fae I found doing despicable things. When I went off last week. I found wretched folk and ripped them to shreds using talons and fangs and a sword. Fae and creatures alike who were taking advantage of females. Ones who were beating their dogs. Anyone I could find and justify needing to be eliminated from existence. I killed them. I was not in the right. I knew that. I knew my soul would pay. Monster. If that was what I had become—if I couldn't be myself and separate my actions from that of the *baethaache*—who would I be? I walked down the stairs to the main square of the grounds. Dogs were laying in huddles near a large tree. I squatted down and held my hand to them. They walked over and let me pet them, attempting to calm myself by stroking their long ears. Bixby and Cuthbert would be a wreck when it all happened. However it happened. I was momentarily so glad they were safely home in Aemes with the groundskeeper. The night shifted, sounds approaching from behind.

"Your mate has strong gifts." Ainsley came up to me. "I have never seen Kalíma respond to anyone."

I shook my head. Fucking goddess.

"She is strong across the board."

"This was given to me by a crone. I was barely out of childhood, so it meant nothing, yet I kept it." She held something out to me. It was a small brass arrow, razor thin. "I feel it prudent to give it to you both." At the back of the arrow there was a hole. Turning it this way and that, it became obvious to me what it was. I went back to our room and sat on the bed, looking at the arrow, debating waking Neysa to tell her about it. About everything. She was exhausted. I could see it in the smudges under her eyes. She had taken out her braid to sleep, and her hair fell in structured dark waves that I wanted to touch. I wanted to throw up a wall of fucking fire and keep us together in it forever to stay out of the mess that was building. But that would be a cage. And, ultimately, it would help nothing. The sheet was clutched in her hands in that way she does when she was trying to not cry. If I prised it away, there would be half-moon marks on her palms where her nails pierced the skin.

A breeze smelling of pine and oak blew through the window, and I watched the skin on her bare arm and shoulder rise in bumps. Just like that, I knew I'd lose her. I didn't know how or when, but I knew it was soon. I couldn't fathom how to process the loss. I didn't know how Silas did it—loved her and resigned himself to not having her. Her eyes fluttered open, and she looked over her shoulder at me, holding out her hand. I placed the arrow in it, knowing that was not what she wanted. Monster. Pushing up on her elbows, the sheet barely covered her, and I was nearly blind with wanting her and holding myself back. I felt the same in that hotel in Bulgaria. Then again in Turkey. She set the arrow aside, not caring what it was at the moment, and sat up straighter, the sheet slipping completely. Kneeling on the mattress, she pulled me to her. In her eyes I saw there was no way she would let me say no. She didn't understand what I could see. So, I let her pull me in and take my clothes off until we were both kneeling on that bed, bare to one another. My lips marked every freckle on her shoulder, every scar on her arms, her belly, every warm fold of her. Each place my mouth travelled caused her hands to knead my skin. She needed to know she was all that mattered. Even when I knew that somehow I was losing her to another realm. I lowered her down and sunk myself deep within her, hoping more than anything in this world and the next that I wasn't right.

Neysa

EVERYONE ASSEMBLED four days later. Ainsley prepared water craft and chose two of her trusted males to come along, leaving Thurton behind to hold the fort. By the look in Ewan's eyes, I could see he was half crazed being away from Corra, and I questioned whether he should have come. Saski was laughing as she and Silas emerged from the mountain road. The clock was an odd shape. Silver, brass, and worn wood composed the piece itself, which looked like it would melt from one's hands. As though when Reynard passed it to Cadeyrn, it was a bag of water, awkwardly slumping. It was an illusion of course, as the materials that made up the clock were sturdy. Cadeyrn set it down and gently lifted the glass crystal from the face. He tried to hand me the arm of the clock the other night. It was relevant, important, and might be the key to making this operation work. In that moment, I hadn't cared about anything other than my mate. He placed the arm on the pin through the tiny hole at the back of the arrow. Once the two hands were joined on the tapered pin at the centre of the odd timepiece, they began to spin. A sickly feeling roiled around in my stomach, and by the looks of everyone else, they felt it too. Almost like a drop on a rollercoaster. Cadeyrn warned me that the clock altered senses. Instinct made me want to smash it to pieces right away, but knowing that hundreds, maybe thousands, of lives depended on our breaking the spell kept me from doing so.

Three smaller bezels on the clock face all stopped spinning at the time the main arms did so. I peered closely at them, trying to remember the parts on my chronograph watch. One was a countdown bezel, used for everything from racing to running. Another seemed to be a GMT, telling the time in another time zone. Before this moment I never considered there being different time zones in this realm, but it was so obvious now I could kick myself. Next to me, I must have projected that thought, because Cadeyrn sniffed a chuckle and ever so briefly touched my back. The last bezel looked to me like a telemeter.

"That's interesting," I mused. Saski stepped forward and looked. "These aren't normally used on mantel clocks. It's more on certain chronograph watches."

"Meaning?" Saski asked. Watches. Not a thing here. I explained watches and chronographs.

"This bezel on a chronograph was originally designed to measure the distance of a sound or pressurized event for officers in wartime. It started during the First World War," I explained.

"Is that the one in which the archduke was shot?" Saski asked. I smiled at her, pleased she actually did listen to me.

"It is. Before then, pocket watches were commonly used, but the military found that wearing the watch on one's wrist gave it better protection and stability as magnetic fields changed, and the stability lent itself to water tightness."

Cadeyrn stood up, arms crossed with an amused expression. *What?* I asked him.

Nothing, I just never knew you knew so much about watches.

I like military history. And anything that made money change hands during wartime was a specialty of mine. Plus, watches are lovely.

Would have made a good gift for you.

Still could, I said, scrunching my nose and giving him a half smile, but his faltered, a look of distress covering his face. He turned and asked me to keep going.

"So, what is it used for?" Silas asked. Ewan was looking closely at the bezel, then looking around. His head tilted to the side, and he tapped the knob closest to the telemeter bezel, then waited, tapping it again.

"It measures distance of sound," Ewan said. Gods, I wished we could be around each other more. My brother figured that out without any other indication of its use. He was even more brilliant than our father.

"Correct. However, it measures both sound and light. So, you could see a flash of lightning and set the chrono, as Ewan just did, and measure the time between the flash and the sound of the thunder that follows to calculate the distance between the two. So, Silas, we could finally figure out just how far reaching your temper tantrums can be," I teased him, and he chuckled, pinching me. "It can be used as the military used it, in measuring firing range. When gun flashes were seen, especially in the night, a soldier would measure the time between the flash and sound to determine how far the enemy fire was. Quite handy at the time."

I knew everyone was thinking as I was. How did this help us? This was not a human made clock. It was fae made and old, so all these bezels had functions that were of use here. So how would this chronograph fit into the dismantling of the Festaeran spell?

The passages into the caverns in Festaera were a straight shot, but we knew that once within the network of tunnels, we would be blind to which direction to take. There were hundreds of miles worth of tunnels and caverns in the Vascha Mountain Range in which the vessels could potentially be kept. Perhaps the telemeter would pick up the lights, sounds, or pressure of the magic in constant use to keep the spell going. I said as much. What about the other gauges? I tapped my foot impatiently, looking at the clock.

"The arrow I gave you, Cadeyrn," Ainsley said after a long while. "The crone said it was special because it was the Hand of the Goddess."

My husband excused himself, walked off behind a wooden structure, and threw up. I followed him, panicking about what had him sick. Silas and Ewan were right behind me. Cadeyrn's arm was braced on the structure, his face pale. I placed a hand in the middle of his back and saw it. A blurry snapshot in the mountains. An abhorrent brace between realms.

"The countdown clock. Once we use it, which we have, it imprints itself onto our cause. It will count down the time we have left. It could be the time left to successfully complete what we must. It could be until the death of one of us. It could be...the end of everything." His eyes met mine and held them. I showed him the Veil in my vision. Then the blood and broken crown.

"So how do we know what it's counting down to?" Silas asked from behind me.

"We don't," Ewan answered. "It alters our sense of time and works differently for each of us. Cadeyrn?"

Cadeyrn nodded, glassy eyes still locked on mine. I moved closer to him. He knew. That was why he was so angry. He knew it was all borrowed time.

I'm sorry, Caráed.

"We can fight it. We aren't green youths who allow magic to break us," Silas insisted, pacing and kicking at the grass.

"This kind of magic buried my relationship with my mate. It took away all I knew of her and stripped her powers, Silas. We are as vulnerable as anyone."

"Then we make better choices," Saski added. No shit. "I mean it. I'm the first to act without thinking. We need to go in ready to calculate each and every move we make."

"It's already begun!" Cadeyrn yelled. His face turned bright red, and heat flared from him. "Don't you understand? It began when Neysa saw the clock in her vision. We started the continuum. As soon as we put the fucking hand on the clock, it started. At this point, we should all have a picture in our heads—a sense or feeling for what exactly we are chipping away. What we are losing," he concluded, not quite louder than the autumn breeze in the forest.

Ewan paled. The others fanned out, hands on faces, in hair, growling. Silas was looking between Cadeyrn and me and Saski, shaking his head, nostrils flaring.

Couldn't I refuse to go? Couldn't it be that simple? Choices. Saski had a point. These were all threads. Not scaffolding. Even in the mating bond. Sure, it would be easier to give in and take Silas and let the thread pull tight. But that would unravel what I had made with Cadeyrn, and there was nothing I would fight harder for. So, I refused to give in. I made that choice.

"What's the last bezel? The GMT?" Ewan asked.

"It's the time. In the human realm. In England," Cadeyrn told him, and their eyes locked.

"No," Silas said. "No. Just fucking no."

"We need to go," Ainsley said. Yeah, we were running out of time. How poetic.

CHAPTER 38

I t was early autumn in the mountains, and despite the stark threat ahead, the waterways were stunning. Clear and cold, bordered by moss-covered rock sheer, clear skies overhead. I tried to stay alert, but hours on the water had me laying back, my head against Cadeyrn, drifting off. Daydreaming about the house in Aemes. The dogs. A beach house we would never have. City lights I never again wanted to see, with implications reaching further than I ever wanted to think about. My niece and nephew—or whatever they ended up being. The children I would never have. The pregnant female with Silas I would never see. Would I hate her if I knew? Would it matter?

I will make the right choice. I refuse to make the final call.

We don't always have the luxury of choice, Cadeyrn said to me, stroking my hair.

Well, I'm too stubborn to bend over and let fate make me its bitch.

Such an image, my love.

I turned around and looked at him, those glassy aquamarine eyes and stark cheekbones. I would have liked to have said something poignant or clever. Romantic or anything. There was nothing. He knew it all. I knew it all. All there was left was to fight.

There was a howl. Nearby, wolves were on the prowl. I sat up.

WHERE ARE THEY? HELP US SAVE THEM, I commanded. The howling ensued, every five minutes on the clock. We followed the sound as it banked right, heading further west. Every five minutes for six hours. When more waterways and streams appeared, the howling indicated directions to guide us, until we reached the cavern entrance and the river mouth ended. We disembarked and continued on foot. Even the wolves wouldn't tread in these caverns. I glanced at the clock, the countdown like a sick vice I couldn't unsee. Time was rapidly decreasing. Flitting light like flares from an artificial torch bounced off the walls in the distance. I clicked the knob and waited. Moans followed. Kilometres. Perhaps fifty. The cavern walls would distort the movement of light, so I wasn't sure if the telemeter would be completely accurate, but we had a while of walking to go. In the dark, I saw a glow from Cadeyrn's eyes that had me shiver. He was becoming closer to his beast. I wish I knew what he had seen. I had a feeling, but he would not disclose the whole thing.

A trickle of water from a spring deep within these mountains moved along the ground with us. Silas started to dissolve, and I cried out.

"Not yet. Please."

He took my face in his hands.

"I know how to be careful. Remember, *Trubaíste.* I've sworn an oath." Then he was mist and water. Saski bristled and snarled. I whipped my head to her, and she turned away. We sped up, making double the time we had initially. In the dark there was a clash of swords, and Ainsley was barking at her warriors. Cadeyrn moved me behind him and blocked the scythe of an advancing fae. A small contingent of colourless fae moved on us. Had they lived under the mountains their whole lives? Unlike the phantomes or beasts that Paschale had manufactured up here, these were sentient warriors, grunting, swearing, bleeding like the rest of us. They were just unexposed to sunlight. I took a blade to the shoulder and fell against the slick rock wall, crying out. Cadeyrn swiveled to look at me and narrowly missed a scythe to the neck. I screamed and lunged at the offender, drawing my twin swords across his midsection, splitting the pale warrior in two. Moon white skin rolled into the stream, the warrior's head caught a rock and hung in an eternal grimace between the water and granite.

Reynard's arrows pierced the necks of two waxen fae who had made their way past Ainsley's warriors. Blood warmed my arms, most of it catching in my leathers, making my grip slick. We kept pushing forward. In the dark, Ainsley shrieked, and there was a thud as one of her males landed at our feet, head rolling. A loud, guttural roar sounded, and it took me a heartbeat to realize it was from my mate. He lashed out with his power, incinerating the remaining cadaverous enemy. Without pausing, we pressed forward.

Silas. Where are you? Please. There was an electrical flash like a torchlight on water, and I hit the knob on the clock. Not far. I told them we could make it quickly. Nearly out of breath, we rounded a corner and were in the main section of what looked almost like an enormous incubator. Instead of maintaining life, it was keeping the life sustainably drained in order to contain the magic necessary to maintain the spell.

Not one of us could keep the disgust off our faces. We all spun in an awed circle, trying to process what we were seeing. We knew what we were coming to find. I had seen a picture in my head, yet seeing it in person was sickening.

The countdown bezel was nearly up. We all looked to one another as lines of magic ran along the wall of the cavern, winding in and out of all the vessels as they hung in the air.

From the far side of the room, figures began to emerge. Cadeyrn snarled. Silas was being dragged by the neck. As they all got closer, Saski screamed with a rage that had the vessels trembling. With an iron chain choking him, Silas was dragged towards us by Konstantín, with Kíra, Petyr, and Tuso beside them. I tugged on every tether we had between us to find a weak link so I could get him out of the damned chains. Cadeyrn became his beast, snarling and scratching at the floor, which, honestly, wasn't very helpful at the moment.

"Oh, come, daughter," Konstantín said to Saski. "It's strategy. Beat before being beaten." He addressed me. "Niece."

"Let go of my mate, you stupid prick." There was a loud, ominous tick on the clock. We needed to break the spell and didn't have long.

"It's sovereignty. To be able to have control over the entire realm is quite a thing. Your mother never cared for such things. How about you, young king?"

Ewan was drawing up power. I felt it building in him. Cadeyrn's own power speared from him to the nearest vessels, testing to see if he could heal them. As his magic touched them, the vessels turned to ash. Horror bled from Cadeyrn's emotions. I pulled on the darkness surrounding me, feeding me, and willed it all inside, trying to merge the dark magic with my darkness that was not vile. My mate sensed what I was doing and wrapped his power around mine. I tapped into Ewan's, and the three of us began pulling the ties that bound the vessels, string by string. That was when Silas started screaming. Sweat poured off him while Tuso had a viper-like grin on her face. Saski charged at her father, who held the chains, and attempted to drop into him, but Petyr slashed out with his broadsword. She turned in time and went for him instead, swinging her own blades. Silas was hollering to keep doing what we were doing. Ainsley and Saski held out against the twins, and Tuso was finally distracted enough to drop the pain she had lancing through Silas' head. He slumped to the ground.

"Did you figure it out yet, Cadeyrn?" Kíra asked. "What it would take to break the spell?"

Bestía had said the same thing and I knew—I knew Kíra had been a part of bringing Bestía back. She smiled at him, showing all of her teeth. His beast snarled. We kept pulling on the threads. Some of the vessels started moaning. Some turned to ash. Healing had the opposite effect on them. We had to unravel the darkness and merge it with our own.

Petyr had a dagger at Silas' neck. I met his eyes. He tried to tell me something, but I couldn't see beyond a flash of losing them both. I exploded with power and a bolt of lightning lanced from me, through Silas and into Petyr. He died instantly, Tuso screeching and trying to run, but Saski separated Tuso's head from her body with one well-timed swipe. I had known that my lightning would never harm Silas. It was a part of us both.

From the shadows, Basz and Ludek emerged, a shield around them both. My heart sank, thinking they had betrayed us. Then Ludek gave me a look.

Trust me. Did I really have a choice?

"You could have had it all, Saski," Konstantín said to his daughter. His first in line. He tsked, pulled the wind energy from his daughter, and sent it into Ewan, closing off his breath, keeping him entombed in a tunnel of hard, impenetrable wind. "I'm sorry, nephew. You must understand; you are in the way."

The final tick of the clock sounded, and we paused, horrified. With a last pull of darkness, the vessels awoke, slamming to the ground. Reynard shot an arrow that hit Basz, whose shield had been down in his shock at seeing the vessels, and I screamed. At that moment, Ludek was bellowing, and Konstantín and Reynard realized that I had reacted on behalf of Basz. I ran for the even-tempered guard and put my hands over his wound. Ripping my jacket off, I tore a piece of shirt to make a tourniquet. Ludek turned and stabbed his stepfather through the gut and kicked him to the ground next to where I was kneeling with Basz. Cadeyrn was lunging for Ewan, who had been dropped from the wind, and Saski had herself thrown over Silas. My shoulder wound was still gushing blood, and I saw now how deep the gash had been. Bone shone through, wet and ivory, inches from my neck.

Child. A clear divine voice sounded in my head. *There is so much loss. For whom do you bleed?* I was tying the fabric around Basz, getting Ludek to put pressure on it. Reynard stood, stunned, then looked to me, horrified. Whether horrified at my injuries or at his own misstep in in shooting Basz, I didn't know. Light and darkness swirled.

For whom, child? The voice persisted.

For those I love. For those who were harmed. For love itself. I stepped back from Basz, looking for Cadeyrn. My blood hit the ground next to Konstantín, and there was a rip sounding in the atmosphere. The air rippled, and I heard Silas yell. Cadeyrn spun to me, his beast disappearing. Having cast herself in shadow, Kíra appeared before me, and thrust her narrow sword into me. Rather, it would have gone into me, had Cadeyrn not gotten in front of the blade, taking the length of sword through his abdomen, out his back, and pushing me away. Into the Veil.

CHAPTER 39

Neysa
England, Nine Months Later

J uly 15th, on the train from Richmond to Oxford, I read the biography of the doctor presenting at the Ashmolean Museum. He had studied and worked in India, camped in the Himalayas, and embedded with tribes in remote Pakistan. The doctor taught anthropology at Durham University in England and was visiting Oxford to give a talk on lesser deities of India and the Middle East. I was bored, so when the notification popped up for the talk, I booked the train. I loved Oxford as a city, and I hadn't fully admitted to myself, but I came up half-heartedly looking in terms of moving. I had run out of excuses for not meeting with friends and colleagues in London and Richmond and needed to put some distance between myself and the cities. I hadn't been back to Barlowe Combe in the past year. Why bother? Why open that box when I could just about manage to compartmentalize that part of my life? It was pissing down rain when I arrived, and I tried to keep my laptop dry as I ran to the museum.

Dr. Dean Preston took to the podium with a nervous clearing of his throat. Did anyone ever check the height of microphones in relation to the speaker before the poor sods went up? I laughed to myself, thinking it was something Corra might say.

"The goddess Kali-Ma," he began. I jackknifed forward at the goddess' name. "She is feared and revered. Known as a cruel and fierce deity, culling those who are troublesome or unworthy of her children. We are all her children once we give up our dreaded egos. So, good luck." He paused, and a tremor of polite, academic laughter went through the crowd. I marveled at the coincidence of this presentation being on the one goddess with whom I had most recently interacted. "Like her Egyptian sister in crime, Sekhmet, the goddess of both war and healing, she instills balance to our world. Where would we be should we give up our ego? Would time itself allow us to hold what precious time we have? Kali was once said to hold the thread to all motherhood. In every culture, a personification of the mother, the womb, the fertile darkness, has come to have been penned. Who better to hold the reigns of time than the mother herself?

"What I would like to discuss with you today is the possibility that the holder of time, Kali-Ma, can play with time as we know it. If she were to hold the seed of time in her hand, could she hold infinite possibilities? Would each possibility sprout from the seed to form trunks, branches, and roots? To answer this, we must first delve into whether time is linear. We have always been led to believe that we are born, we live, we die in a linear fashion. Many fellow scholars agree that time is not linear, but in fact layered. If we strip the layers apart, the possibilities of different occurrences and existences is astounding."

People began to shuffle out. This wasn't the talk they were expecting. While it wasn't what I was planning to listen to, a rock-hard feeling in my gut had me glued to my seat. I stayed until his final word. In the end there was just me and two others sitting there, listening to Dr. Preston, who would likely never be invited back to Oxford. I thanked him for his talk, and he shyly inclined his head to me.

"May I ask you a question?" I spoke in a quiet rush, keeping my eye on the time so I would make my train back. It was tempting to book a room at the MacDonald Randolph Hotel across the street, but the last time I stayed there, I had a dream of Cadeyrn so vivid, I awoke breathless and needing him to the point of physical pain.

"Of course. I think we have cleared the room." He shuffled his papers, dropping them into a Tumi messenger bag. He was younger than I expected, with floppy blonde hair and a twinkle in his eye that led me to think he couldn't care less that he emptied the room at the Ashmolean.

"In theory, if Kali were to hold the potential for layered time and threads, would there be a chance..." Oh shit, Neysa, watch your phrasing.

He raised an eyebrow at me. "To earn back unrequited love?" His interruption was as patronizing as they came.

I gave him my best sardonic smile while handing my business card over.

"Never mind. Thanks for the talk."

"Wait. I apologize. I'm often not taken serious in my research, and sometimes I get people who are off their rocker. You are a currency trader?"

"Yes, but my question had nothing to do with that. My father was an anthropologist, and I have been putting together some of his research."

"Ah. Interesting. May I buy you a drink? We can talk then."

I agreed, cursing myself for missing the train. We sat in the bar of a brasserie a couple of blocks away.

"If the spool of time, layers, knots, whatever, were held, would it be possible to revisit an option from a particular thread?"

"I am not a quantum physicist," he remarked with a smirk.

"I am not speaking of time travel." I took a notebook from my handbag and began scribbling, pushing my Pinot Nero out of knocking range. "Not reaching back in time, but rather plucking an option from a sheet of time. If these are the layers of time"— I began with a mess that looked like a ball of yarn, knocked about by an angry cat—"and we have taken one thread"—I drew a line from it—"if that thread was wrong... If it messed up the world or the space-time continuum..." I explained with a grin that I knew made men take pause. Usually, I'd internally roll my eyes, but I was too focused on this. His attention narrowed. "Could we somehow, whether it's calling upon Kali herself"—I grinned again to seem as though I was possibly, maybe, kind of, sort of, joking—"or simply finding a way back to the initial point of pulling the thread... Could we alter the thread taken? Without the potential for disaster, which we all know would occur with time travel." I winked and felt ill for doing so.

"You're assuming there is a tapestry woven. In your lovely diagram here, you have shown me chaos. In chaos we often pick the thread that leads us out. No matter the cost. It is chosen as an escape hatch. The way out can entangle things further." My heart clenched. "Sometimes we are able to exit and reestablish the tapestry. Sometimes, like a missing stitch or a catch in the stitch, pulling harder on it tangles the thread, creating greater chaos. Or it can even snap the stitch." Like a Veil opening and collapsing instantaneously.

"So, if we were to figure out how to back the stitch up, could we get back to the original tapestry?"

"Whatever is your story, love?" he asked me with a lopsided grin. I pointed to the ball of yarn sketch and said that was about the long and short of it. He laughed and signaled for another round. "I would say, that as time is nonlinear, we should be able to reach back and pluck the other thread. You have to know where to look. I will warn, though, that Kali likes balance. If you are reweaving a tapestry out of self-importance or revenge, she will not be so accommodating." He winked.

"But how?" I asked aloud, meaning the question for me alone.

"While I am an academic, and perhaps not of the class of citizen generally regarded as dealing in the occult, I would, perhaps, advise you to try to connect yourself—your being—to the Goddess, and see where that takes you." He leaned in closer and said conspiratorially, "You could try scrying. Or something to that effect."

"Oh, I'm just asking for a friend," I said with a wry twist to my mouth. His eyes twinkled.

"Where are you staying?" he asked, sipping the last of his drink.

I muttered about missing my train and looking at the Randolph. The nicest hotel in town in my opinion. He whistled.

"You could stay with me."

The air went a bit stale.

It wasn't the first proposition I'd had since coming back. Far from it, unfortunately, but it felt more possible, which scared me. He was easy to talk to and cute to look at, but I was not a whole person. I was still in love with a ghost. So, I politely declined, and we parted ways on the street.

CHAPTER 40

Corraidhín

I supposed I understood that we all lost something that day. None of us escaped unscathed. It was nearly a week afterward that I was told all that happened. All that we lost. I didn't think that I had ever met someone who had fought as hard for everything and everyone, the way that Neysa had. I surely hadn't. I would have given up. Had it been between losing my mate and saving the rest of us, I think, honestly, I would have said to hell with the rest. Yet, here we all were, because that beautiful beast fought for us.

Ewan walked in and I knew. Well, I didn't really know, but, you see, I knew there was a problem. He kept saying, "She's gone. I've lost her." Over and over again. He spent weeks not wanting to speak to anyone. My own twin had been injured, but I knew he was safe and cared for, if not destroyed over Neysa. As I said, no one was unscathed. Cadeyrn was in Saarlaiche, being kept sedated. He was run through with a sword, which pierced his liver and spine. Rather than healing himself, he used the last of his gifts to blow Kíra into the nether realm. There was nothing tethering him to this world. It was three months since that day. Silas came to see us, escorted by Saski and her brother. Sometimes I wondered about them. I shouldn't speculate. It was time to begin bringing our cousin back, as I would be godsdamned if he wasn't here to meet my little ones. I read once, in the human realm, a saying: When one door closes, a window opens—or something like that. Perhaps the losses we had endured would be softened by the new arrivals. Though, I would imagine, for Cadeyrn, it would serve only to remind him of the mate he no longer had, and the children he would never father. I knew, as I knew my own mind, that he would never get over Neysa. I just wanted to try to keep him alive.

CHAPTER 41

Neysa

I f the phone would stop buzzing and let me enjoy the rest of this stupidly early morning, that would be fabulous. I groaned and rolled over to see who was calling before answering.

"Perhaps I was a bit forward last night. May I take you to breakfast?" Dean asked.

I rubbed my eyes and fell back on the pillow. I really didn't want to get out of this bed.

"Breakfast is low commitment. You can just order a coffee and lie to me that it's all you have normally, or you can do a full English and we can talk shop."

I smiled despite myself and agreed to meet him downstairs in two hours.

I didn't even have fresh clothes but had the forethought to wash out my underthings and hang my jeans and top in the bathroom to steam. At university, I went on holiday with a friend who would hang her jeans by the ankles every night and spritz them with water to lay the creases flat. She was a total nut job, but her jeans always looked clean. So, I gave it a go. When I came into the dining room of the MacDonald Randolph, Dean was waiting at a table with both coffee and tea.

"Now you're going tell me that because you're from L.A., you don't do caffeine and subsist on green juice and rosé," he said with a smirk.

I sat and poured tea and milk and winked at him. Once a few sips of tea kicked in, I sat back and started to relax. The room was old world elegance with portraits and house crests lining the hunter green walls. Robed scholars rushed down the street outside the large windows.

"You looked me up?" I asked. He scoffed.

"Of course." I raised an eyebrow. "I suppose you're not from L.A., but rather recently from there. Is that right? I am curious. Professionally and personally," he began, "what has occurred in your life in the past two years?"

I had a sharp intake of breath and made myself look at him. I used to be a morning person. When I slept at night. Dean's clean and pressed morning look bugged me. With a pang, I remembered Cadeyrn in the morning, warm and sleep-mussed.

"So, you divorced, and your dad passed. Sorry about that, pet."

I glared at him, and he put his hands up in surrender.

"There is a blank space between then and when you picked up your Forex career ten months ago, living in Richmond. So, what happened?"

I poured more tea and picked at a scone, the liquid curdling. Why on earth did I think having breakfast with an anthropologist was a good idea?

"Well, apart from being in an alternate dimension, getting attacked by a shark, and realizing I was a long-lost princess?" I smiled and took a bite of scone, giving him wide, dramatic eyes. He folded his arms across his chest. "I rented a cottage and took a sabbatical. Not very interesting, I'm afraid."

He looked disappointed. From his ballistic nylon satchel, Dean pulled folders and notes, and scooted his chair next to me. Scents of fresh laundry and soap came off him as he reached across me to point to a notebook.

There were theories listed on borrowed time.

When a layer of time comes to a choice ending, one must collapse the layer or choose a path that takes it either up or down to another layer. Mostly, people make choices that lead to a linear progression. Thereby, it seems as though time runs along a straight and narrow.

"I refuse to entertain any questions regarding time travel. I have done too many late nights with too much gin, where the conversation runs that way, and not only do I find it conceptually frustrating, I am not a quantum physicist. Plus, I'm not quite certain I get on with gin."

"Wasn't going to go there," I said. I forked some eggs and beans into my mouth. "So why the fascination with layered time? Debunking ghosts?"

"That's amusing. No." He drank his coffee and poured another, stirring in sugar, keeping it black. "The fascination lies in the concept of choice and consequence. Is there a point where we just subconsciously stop making real choices? Our parents, authorities, so on, tell us how to do this, that, and the other, so it puts us on a path. When some of us go off the rails and get lost in drugs and sex and thievery, we think, 'Oh, shame about Charlie. He's gotten on the wrong path.' Did he? Or was there a moment when Charlie had no fucking concept of having a choice and stopped making decisions and found himself behind a pub in Crawley with a prostitute and a bag of heroin?" He blew out a breath and tapped his fingers on the table.

"Okay, Doctor. Take a breath, man, and back up."

He burst out laughing.

"Now, do you need to talk about Crawley?"

"Funny. No, pet. I actually thought you would be interested in hearing more about the Goddess." He put on a pair of glasses, making him look endearingly young.

I longed to hear the voice of the Goddess. The voice of Ludek or Ewan. Cadeyrn. Always Cadeyrn. Everything in my head was so empty. I ached to be who I was meant to be. Not this shell. Dean spoke and gesticulated and joked, and I liked being around him. More than anyone I had befriended since I came back. We agreed to see each other again, but I had to catch a train back to Richmond.

Two training gyms politely kicked me out for being too rough. I was on tentative feet with the third, and tried my very best to be on good, human-like behavior. The plan had been simple. However, as with everything I seem to have messed up in my life, this simple plan of mine went awry almost instantly. The first gym I sought was tucked into a fairly rough South London neighbourhood. The comments and innuendos didn't bother me one iota, as I was used to clawing my way up the hierarchy of a sparring session. I was paired with a guy called Baker Mick. He was, alas, not a baker, but had arms that resembled loaves of Challah bread. I let him put me in check once, to the snickers and jeers of the few in the warehouse. Once they'd had their jollies, I turned up the volume of my abilities and showed them some of what I could do. Within a few moves I had Mick pinned, my sword just under his jugular. I was escorted out by five large men and told not to return.

So, for the second facility, I went in talking myself down. The purpose was just to keep up my skill. Hone my strength. Paired with the owner, we joked and sparred for a few sessions.

One particularly bad day, after a night of dreaming about Cadeyrn's death, I couldn't tone down my violence. The singing of the blades and sound of the movement around us brought on memories and feelings I couldn't compartmentalize. Slow motion droplets of my blood meeting Konstantín's, Kíra's wolfish grin, her sword impaling my husband over and over again. The feel of falling back through the Veil as Cadeyrn fell the opposite way. In an ending like the spar with Baker Mick, I was asked to leave the second gym. And to get therapy. For this third gym, I worked very hard to go in pretending to be human. Sane, rational, emotionally stable human.

As I was walking in to train with my new sparring partner, my phone buzzed.

"What are you up to?" Dean asked.

"About to swing a sword with a man who thinks I'm a bit mad. Why?"

"Not what I was expecting, but okay. I'm in London. Well, I was. I'm on my way to Richmond in the hopes that a lovely girl will let me take her to dinner. I know we skipped lunch and tea, but perhaps tapas toe the line? Small plates and all that."

"I can't miss this session, or they will kick me out. So, I won't be very lovely by the time you see me."

"Oh, I wasn't talking about you. But if you insist on my stopping to see you, I don't mind your grubbiness." I could almost hear the twinkle in his eyes.

It couldn't have been more than ten minutes, because as I landed behind my partner and knocked both his knees out and pinned him to the ground, I noticed Dean standing a bit slack jawed by the shoe cubbies at the front. He politely sat and watched while I finished my session. It seemed at one point that my partner had the upper hand, but I pointed my twin swords down and swept out with my right leg, knocking him into me and allowing me to pin him again. My knee was aching, so I called it and left the ring with a handshake to my partner.

At dinner, I was hitting the sangria harder than was necessary. It was a gorgeous August evening, and I'd had a rough week, both financially and emotionally. I laughed at a joke Dean told, and he put his hand over mine. I stiffened, but he didn't seem to notice.

"I like you, Neysa. Quite a bit." No, no, no. Don't say that. I wanted to throw up. As it was, I was going to have a rip-roaring headache in the morning. "Could we see more of each other? Or, maybe—"

"I don't know that I can." It bubbled out from my lips before I could stop it. "I'm in love with someone else."

He snatched his hand back and finally noticed my engagement ring.

"Ah."

"It ended with him." I couldn't say he was dead. "But, I don't think I can ever get over it."

"It's worth a shot, right? We get on well." Shit. We certainly did but...

"Would you like to hear a fairytale?" I asked him. "I have a good one." So, while we sat amongst the Friday night crowds who were drinking and eating and chatting and flirting, I told him my tale. I never used my own name, but as I told the story, I laughed and cried. In conclusion, I described being pushed through the Veil, seeing Cadeyrn run through with Kíra's sword.

"Where did the Veil leave her?" he asked after sitting quietly, drinking his sangria, then ordering us coffees.

"In the middle of the woods in a small town in northern Germany, called Bad Schwartau. She made her way to Lübeck, then took a flight from Hamburg, eventually making it... somewhere else."

"London?" he asked, not taking his eyes off of me. I gave a curt nod. "That was a hell of an anecdote. Where in England did she originally come to stay?" It was so Dean that he was still asking questions.

"Barlowe Combe. It's in the—"

"I know Barlowe Combe," he said quietly. "I was born there. My mum still lives there. Runs a tea shop." Oh, dear gods. I put my head in my hands.

"Tilly?" I asked.

He looked like the wind was knocked out of him.

"Your mum tried to hoist me on you a couple of years ago."

"Perhaps I should pay more attention to who she tries to set me up with then. You truly believe all this happened?"

"Dean, I have told you a tale. Respect that I have shared it with you."

He walked me back to my flat, where we stood outside chatting. The air blew cool, though the evening was warm. I was looking forward to cold nights. The dark days when rain kept sentry at the windows, giving me the grace not to have to see another soul. I said goodnight and started to walk into my building when he called after me.

"How do you know he didn't heal?"

I stopped short and grabbed the wall, unable to breathe. "Because I know he would have used every last scrap he had to burn her to ash."

"I don't know. I think you may have another thread to pull."

I let myself into my building and spent the night trying not to scream into my pillow.

CHAPTER 42

Corraidhín

The healer pulled me aside when they arrived and said he hadn't spoken the whole journey but got up at dawn each day to train. We should have woken him earlier. Regardless, I wanted us all together for Yule, and I had two little ones now, and I wanted them to see their family. And I made a point of getting what I want. However, when they arrived, Magnus gave me eyes suggesting we were in for a treat. I met the carriage as it came up the drive and threw my arms around my cousin. He barely touched my back in greeting. I dragged him inside, where my brother waited with Ewan. It was as strange a greeting as we had ever had. Cadeyrn's eyes kept roving the room, taking in the pine boughs and candles, the scent of cloves and mint. Laughter trickled in from the back, and Reynard and Saski came into the room. Cadeyrn was standing, looking like he had been punched in the gut. I should have thought of that. She looked so similar to Neysa. If I had to compare, I didn't favour her as much as Neysa, but maybe that was because she still pissed me off every now and again. The babes had been sleeping, but I heard their banshee-like cries from upstairs and went to fetch them.

He might have been trying not to look at my children. I understood. Really. But sometimes, we needed to saddle that horse and ride. Was that the expression? I didn't know. In any case, Cadeyrn was like my brother, and my children were to know their uncle. Silas had been here since their birth. I'd found him quite a few times, sitting and telling them stories, even though the little *moinchai* had no blasted idea what their big oaf of an uncle was on about. Ewan took the lass from me, and we walked in to sit. I wouldn't force them in his face. Gods know I hated when people did that to me with their children. He watched us sit and took his attention back to Saski and Silas, who always seemed to be sitting close. Cadeyrn smirked and shook his head.

"Something to say, brother?" Silas asked. Cadeyrn met his eyes, and the haunted look in them had Silas regretting opening his fat mouth. I could read him like a book. Cadeyrn just pinched his nose and sat there, his hair shooting up like hands in surrender.

"Cadeyrn, tomorrow you and I are going climbing. There's a mountain nearby, and Ewan has all the ropes and such. Might freeze our balls off, but it's worth it."

Cadeyrn agreed without saying more. We had our traditional Yule dinner with spiced wine. It was dark but not nearly as late as we normally stretched the festivities. Last year, the four of us were eating and drinking until nearly four in the morning.

The babes were in their cradles on the other side of the room when they started wiggling. Not the screeching that made me want to go climb a mountain myself, but the sweet funny sounds that I never thought I would love hearing. Cadeyrn looked over and got up.

"May I?" he asked. Ewan smiled at him. My cousin walked slowly over and looked into the cradles. There was a softness in his expression that broke my heart. He reached a hand in, and as I came up next to him, I saw that Efa was holding his finger, looking up at him with her father's olive-green eyes. Silas scooped up his niece and held her out to Cadeyrn, who had a look of terror.

"Go on. Just make sure you hold the head, aye?" He transferred Efa to Cadeyrn. Their eyes met. I knew he was seeing Neysa's eyes in her.

"Hello, *aoín baege*," he whispered, calling her "little one". Ewan turned away and scrubbed his face. Silas held Pim, allowing Cadeyrn to look upon his little elfin features. He carefully touched a finger to my son's tiny ear. "And you, *allaine balaíche*? You have your mummy's mouth. Will you use it to torment us as she does?"

Ewan chuckled. "They are calm with you," my husband said to his sister's mate.

"I think...I am calmer with them." He passed me Efa, then bowed deeply. "Blessings to you both. I will protect them as my own." He knelt down, Silas following suit. Well, I wasn't expecting that. I leaned into the buttery warmth of my daughter and kissed her soft cheek. I didn't know how Saskeia could have let her children go. I would sooner jump out of my window. Granted, there were times when they were screaming and I needed to sleep, that I did actually feel like jumping out of my wiendow, but I digressed. I had found a perfection in this great cruel world, and I only wished my brother and cousin could find the same.

TWO MONTHS later, I noticed Cadeyrn was larger than he had been. He and my brother were always formidable in their strength and size, but even Ewan commented on the breadth of muscle that built on Cadeyrn. He spent his days building and climbing, training and running. I came back to the house after a run myself. Ama was waiting with Pim, who had started giggling, smiling, and, less amusingly, pulling my hair out at the roots. Cadeyrn was swinging an axe, splitting wood and separating piles to deliver to different areas of the province.

"You won't sit still these days, cousin," I said. "Just like Neysa."

He stopped and dropped the axe. He never spoke of her. Never said her name. Silas did. In the beginning especially. He would sit and tell me stories that left a hole in my chest. Ewan, I knew, was always trying to speak to her in his mind. I could see on his face when he was doing it. As though there would be a time when it would work.

Cadeyrn glared at me. Well, I supposed now was as good a time as ever to step in some deep, deep shite.

"Darling," I said, meeting his eyes. Pim started to wiggle at my tone, so I did that funny swaying thing with my hips I never did before I had these little monsters. "Perhaps being able to say her name without growling might allow you some peace?" Pim grabbed at my hair, and I pulled his little fingers away and kissed them one by one before blowing on his little nose.

"I don't see how that would bring peace, Corraidhín." He folded his arms across his chest.

"I don't know. I suppose I see you building such a wall around yourself that no one will ever be able to get past."

"I don't need anyone to get past," he said, starting to turn, but Pim's little arm reached to him, and he didn't resist reaching back. It was sweet, really. I handed my son to him.

"I watched this documentary once," I told him, and he groaned, growling my name. Pim's eyes went wide at the sound, so Cadeyrn looked down at him and smiled. "Scientists in Switzerland were studying waves. Giant ones that smash ships. I can't think of what they are called."

"Tsunamis," he said, bored.

"Ah, yes. So, they were looking into the cause, and how to prepare for such things. They happen on islands when there are earthquakes in the ocean and the poor little sods who live on islands can get washed away. Horrible, really," I mused.

"Corraidhín," he said, pleading me to get on with it. I thought of Neysa and how she loved to stir up Cadeyrn's annoyance. I missed her too. I never had a female friend like her. But my grief was less to contend with than the rest of these moping males.

"Earthquakes and explosions can cause these large waves, but there is something called a mega tsunami that happens every few hundred or thousand years. I can't quite remember. Watched something on meteorites after, and the timeline on both got mixed up. These scientists figured out that something big falling in the water can create a wave that splashes up hundreds of meters to wipe out coastlines."

"Yes, cousin," he said. "I should think that was obvious. When you sit the children in the bath, does the water not rise and splash?"

I waved him off. "Pshaw. Listen. There was a rock that fell into a bay in Alaska, I think. One of those freezing bloody places. It caused not only a splash, but the water built and built, and the wave that it created rose over five hundred meters. It took out trees and such on cliff tops."

"While devastating, I'm sure, I have no idea where you are going with this story." Pim was swatting at his uncle's face, vying for attention. "You, lad, are just like your mummy and uncle. Always needing attention," Cadeyrn said to my son. Gods, he would be a lovely father.

"Okay, okay. So, some years ago, this phenomenon was being studied, and the scientists realized there is a place off Africa—islands called toucans or sparrows."

"The Canary Islands?" he asked with a patronizing smirk. At least the little shit was listening.

"Ah, thank you, darling. Yes. There is an island there. La Palma? Perhaps. If an earthquake were to hit under the water there, or a volcano were to erupt, a piece of the island, a cliff, I think—Gods, I don't know—it would plunk into the sea and the size of that plunk would cause a ripple. The ripple would cause a rise in the water. The rise in water would create a wave. The wave would get larger and larger and move across the sea, spreading out, and growing taller. They think that, within days, it would be travelling as fast as an aeroplane and be hundreds of feet tall. But instead of taking out trees on a cliff lining a bay, the tsunami would hit the East Coast of the United States and take out the coast from Nova Scotia down to the Caribbean. It would reach like ten or fifteen miles inland. Nothing would survive. Gods. Can you imagine?" He looked at me like I was raving. Oh, point to the story. Right. "I think you are like the mega tsunami," I said. He rolled his eyes and groaned. "Neysa going through the Veil was the island breaking apart. I think. Wait. Yes, it was. Now you are building and building walls around you, making you impenetrable, and the destruction within you is going to cause you to explode."

"If I were a mega tsunami, wouldn't this bullshit building metaphor be me destroying everyone else?"

"What do you think would happen to all of us, my darling, if you were gone?" I asked him softly. He breathed deeply and squeezed his eyes shut before kissing Pim and handing him back.

"I can't stop what's building in me, Corraidhín."

"I miss her too. No one has asked me if I am okay, but I miss her. Ewan, Silas..."

"I don't just miss her. She's *my* wife, and I did it. I pushed her through the Veil. I did. We don't even know where she ended up. It could be another time. It could be the middle of the fucking ocean. She could have landed in bloody La Palma. Or the desert. She hates the desert. So, you see, Corraidhín, if I talk about her—if I think about her, that's when this wave gets bigger. That's when I become a threat. I hate this fucking analogy. Gods, Corraidhín." He stomped off, and Pim started to cry. I did the bouncing sway thing to calm him and went to look for Ewan and Efa.

CHAPTER 43

Cadeyrn

J ust past the summer solstice was Aedtine Day in Aoifsing. According to Saski, it was celebrated in Heilig as well. We lit bonfires and paid tribute to the elements of fire and weather, for the summer harvest to be good. Ewan was sitting on the far side of one of the bonfires, staring into the flames. Silas and I had been in conversation for a great long while. I thought it might have been the first real conversation we'd had since...everything. It looked as if Ewan wanted to come over and talk. I knew he felt much the same as I did. Losing Neysa was like losing half of himself. When they were finally reunited last year, it was as though a seam on them which was always open had been stitched up like new. Now it was ripped open again. Except he had Corraidhín and his children. I really had nothing. I knew that when I looked at him, he could see the void in me. Sometimes I thought I would have faded away completely. Just let my immortality flake and die. In fact, I wasn't so sure it hadn't been happening anyway.

As Silas left, I sat staring into the flames. Ewan walked over to sit beside me, staring as well into the taunting lights and crackling sounds of the fire.

"What's next?" he asked.

"You're the king."

"Ah, about that. I think, perhaps, I am ready to dissolve the monarchy," he admitted. I turned to him, eyebrows raised. "I would rather not have that hanging over all of our heads. I would like to perhaps be a representative and help restructure. I am not a king in my heart, Cadeyrn."

We looked out to the masses of fae enjoying the holiday.

"I grew up in the Elders' Palace," he said, pulling at a blade of grass. "Constantly surrounded by others. I dreamt my whole life of having a quiet home, perhaps a family, and not having so many fae underfoot." He looked at me—his sister's husband, pale and withdrawn, from my pointed ears to the silver streak in my dark hair.

"Whatever you decide, Ewan. Like your sister, you are the embodiment of intelligence and strength." It shocked me mentioning Neysa. I could never bring myself to say her name. Barely recognizing the compliment, I could tell he was just as surprised.

"So, I hear you're a tsunami," he said to me. I snorted. A sound so similar to laughter it caught me off guard as well.

"Apparently so. It's probably a good thing there aren't documentaries here, Ewan. Surely at some point Corraidhín will have run out of references for ones she's watched in the past."

"Sometimes," Ewan said carefully, "I feel like the ceiling has come down on the world and it's crushing me. Not knowing where she went, but knowing she's gone. I come out of it because I have Corraidhín," he said. "And Pim and Efa."

I kept staring into the glow of the fire while he spoke.

"So, I can assure you, that what you feel—how you feel—is warranted. Because when I feel like I can't breathe, I know it's worse for you."

"Silas is bedding Saski," I remarked needlessly. We all knew that. Why I felt I had to bloody say it was beyond me.

"That's good," I said, rambling more. "That's his way. Of coping. She, though. She may love him. You will understand if I leave? That I cannot be around that?"

He nodded at me. Corraidhín was waiting for it, I knew.

"Where is she, Ewan?" I asked. "Is she okay?"

Silence answered me. We watched the dance of the flames. They swayed and tipped and flickered, looking like dancers in the sunset. The orange glow parted, revealing shades of yellow and blue, the temperatures showing up in varying colours. Low blue flames looked almost like sky. Sky over water, rippling. The orange touched upon it like blood. I couldn't peel my eyes from the flames. White swirled around the orange, a silken wash of brightness, muting the bloody tones of the drips of orange falling onto the watery azure. Behind the flames was a constellation of stars. A layer of stars upon the *Adairch a Taeoide Gaellte,* the constellation that was written upon my back and Neysa's hand. I blinked, trying to focus. Neysa's freckled hand held a stone, matching the flames. No, it reflected the flames, and pendulumed over a handwritten note, splashed with blood.

"What are you lot doing over here?" Corraidhín came over to us, shaking me from the vision. I looked at Ewan's spectral face.

"A moment, please, my love?" he asked her, voice barely audible. She saw our expressions and walked away.

"Did you see…"

"I think so. Ewan. I wonder if the blood—if we can open a Veil. I think that's what she did. I think that's what happened. Her power reaches between realms. She bled and sacrificed in that cavern. Then Konstantín died at her feet, and the Veil opened."

He swore at my logic, twitching his face.

I had planned to leave the next day. I was heading to Prinaer to check in with Ainsley and her lot. I had been in Laorinaghe with the representatives there for a week or so around mine and Neysa'a birthday. It was an easy escape then, everyone knew. I often went to Laorinaghe. Maybe they wondered if I had been seeing another female. I didn't think Ewan believed I had that sort of constitution. I did think he had other thoughts regarding what I might have been doing in that coastal province.

"Would you be willing to sacrifice someone to open a Veil?" he asked me.

I looked him in the eyes. I knew mine blazed with the fire behind them. The fire inside me.

"For her? Gladly. Though I do not think it's necessary. Will you help me?"

"Whatever you need, brother," he said as we clasped elbows.

CORRAIDHÍN NEARLY tore her husband apart when I explained that we were leaving in the morning. I said we were checking in on Prinaer, but she saw us last night. With that gift of hers, she could easily discern our intentions from the looks on our faces. He closed himself off to her yelling and scratching. She clawed at him and said it couldn't be done, saying he wasn't stable enough to do this and he was New York and would be crushed by a tidal wave, and if there were a virus that killed the human population, the people would throw the weaker ones to the zombies and run. Eventually, he exploded with laughter, standing there, holding her hands away from his scratched-up face in the sitting room. Even I laughed until my cheeks hurt. She pulled her hands back and growled, hands on hips.

"I have no idea what kind of animal a zombie is or what it has to do with a virus," he said through a fit of giggles. "So, my love. You think that I am the weak one to throw to the zombie animals?"

She pursed her lips and splashed water in his face. I hated when she did that. It used to happen to Silas and me all the bloody time.

"Hmph. A zombie is not an animal," she answered. "Although, I suppose it sort of is. Or once was. Doesn't matter."

"And I am the sacrificial weak lamb?" Ewan asked her, smiling, prowling closer. She stepped back a bit and lifted her slightly pointed chin.

"Cadeyrn is even larger now. Though I suppose you are of equal height."

I was trying to disappear to the recesses of the room. Ewan stood before her, looking down at her face where it was lit from the low sconce and last shards of sunset.

"I will be back within a couple of weeks. I promise. I will not leave you and the babes. I thank merciful Mother Aoifsing every day for you."

She looked away and bit her lip. I slipped out the archway and made my way to my chamber.

TRUTHFULLY, I hadn't told Ewan why we were in Prinaer. He didn't particularly like that province, I knew. As a child, he was scared to death of the Elders from there. I believed now it held memories of both the battle in which he and Neysa fashioned a magnetic field to entrap the enemy, and of setting off for Festaera with that wretched clock. Ainsley welcomed us both in her strange hall filled with ale and cider and bearded males with braided hair. It was a look, I must say. Over our third or fourth ale, I asked Ainsley—and by asked, I mean I explained to her that I would appreciate her agreement in my doing so—to visit their sacred temple to the Goddess Kalíma. She looked at me, long and hard.

"Though a lesser goddess, Cadeyrn, Kalíma is powerful. She does not take lightly to being summoned."

"Neither do I," I snarled, fire burning behind my eyes, likely changing them from green to blue and back again. "My mate was tapped by a goddess, infiltrated by this goddess, and taken from this realm. I reserve the right to summon her."

"Ah, but the ego in that statement alone will incur her wrath," Ainsley pointed out.

I slammed my hand down on the table. The hall quieted, a silence filled with the hard stares of a hundred or so fae who were built like bears. Ainsley's slow smile spread across her chestnut face.

"Perhaps look within a bit more and see where your link to Kalíma may lie."

I tore a hand through my hair and grabbed the back of my neck viciously. She looked to me in a rare display of sympathy. There was no masking the sorrow in my eyes these days, I knew. Ewan and Corraidhín kept commenting on what they thought was a rather impressive gain of muscle and strength in me, but anyone could see the underlying promise of a soul ready to flee its home.

"I give you my blessing to go to the temple," Ainsley Mads told me. "Be wise, Battle King."

I KNELT in the temple with its walls of pure gold and still, black pool in the center. I had told Ewan that I would require only his energy and connection to Neysa to bolster my efforts. So, he stood, waiting. The air was thick with rot and something overly sweet I couldn't place. From a sack, I pulled the smoky quartz. I released my gift, and warmth, mist, pure magic, and the light of healing swirled in clouds around us. He knew my power. Knew I exuded it even when I kept it all in check. It was something I had to contend with in my long life. Something that always set me apart in the loneliest of ways. The very walls pulsed with my power, and Ewan's responded in turn. I looked to him over my shoulder to say it was time. The juxtaposition in our powers, the situation, and my age versus the haunted, childlike look I knew I wore at that moment must have been amusing at best. He touched my shoulder and allowed his strength to seep into me. Then I touched the water and was gone. Blasted hell and shite. It was like being ripped through the ashes in a hearth. The things I saw and felt. Though the goddess never appeared to me herself as she had done for Neysa, I knew when she approved of why I had come. I could see out of the wretched dark and could see Ewan pacing, saying aloud that he never wanted to be bloody king and would burn the world to keep his family safe.

I was cast from the pool, wet and gasping. He clasped elbows with me, and I turned back to the stone on the ground and sliced my palm open. The blood dripped onto the stone, causing it to glow and reflect in the gold of the temple. Ewan pulled his own knife and sliced his palm. My eyes widened, but I knew he would blood let to find his sister. They were part of one another, and as such, it might help find her. As my blood dripped in time with his, there was a quiver in the air. A visible thread, golden and thin, shone in the expanse before us. I held my forearm out and pushed his sleeve up, revealing a matching thread. The aura around us grew hazy and soon was very clearly a Veil.

"Step away please, Ewan."

"Fair travels, brother," he told me. Corraidhín was surely going to throttle him for this. Had there been enough of my soul to care at that point, I might have said something. I stepped through, and while I expected the Veil to close as it had after Neysa passed through, it stayed, abhorrent behind me.

CHAPTER 44

Neysa

The top of Dean's package opened, revealing what looked to be a sort of rocket ship. He had it cradled against him, a smug look on his face. I shook my head and turned back to the counter where I was purchasing my perfume. After our initial tapas dinner, we began seeing each other regularly. As friends. It was simple and comfortable to be with him. He wanted more from me than I was able to give, but for now, I enjoyed our time together.

"I thought you were buying gin?" I asked him, paying for the atomizer.

"It's a limited edition rare gin." He pulled the bottle half out and showed it to me. "My superior collects gins, and this designer launched a limited edition gin collection."

"And can you afford to pay rent now?"

"I can if this helps me keep my job after my reprimand." He winked at me and I laughed. We walked out of the back of Liberty's London and headed toward Carnaby Street. Summer was in full swing despite the rain pummeling us as we ran between overhangs, carefully angling our umbrellas to avoid the crowds.

"God, I hate Carnaby Street. Can we get this over with so we can go get a proper drink?"

I said he didn't have to come along, but he tsked. I turned right onto a side street and walked straight into a tall, broad-shouldered man. He grabbed my shoulders to right me and picked up my package. I looked up and caught my breath when I saw nearly black hair and light eyes looking at me.

"Sorry. You alright?" I nodded silently as he walked away. Dean put a hand to my back and moved us further along. I could see the store front where I was headed, off in the distance, but had to pause before going in, my insides warring with their state of matter.

"I'm fine," I mumbled to Dean. He pursed his lips and sucked in his cheeks. "Just caught off guard." Tentative fingers reached out and stroked my face. I wanted to swat at them. I wanted to rip them off and tell him to get away. I wanted to lean into the touch and be held by someone who cared about me. Instead, I turned and made my way to the shop.

There wasn't anything remarkable about the store. It was dim and jumbled, smelling of incense. Crystals glittered from every angle. Some seemed to vibrate towards my energy; others must have been fondled and exposed to so much they were unresponsive. An older man pushed from the back and scratched his head at us. I looked at Dean, who was standing with arms crossed, not meeting my eyes.

"Help you?" the old fellow asked. I walked to the counter and pushed over my dad's journal. The address of the shop and a name was written in the middle of one page, watercolour crystals painted over the rest of the page. The shopkeep peered at the page through bifocals.

"That's me." He tapped the page.

"Did you know Elías Obecan?" I asked him softly. He started and looked directly at me.

"Of course I knew Elías. We were friends for many years."

I exhaled, feeling suddenly very tired and very encouraged at the same time. Dean made his way over to us.

"I am his daughter." I cleared my throat.

"Neysa." His face opened in a smile which faded as soon as it had appeared. "If you are here, then my friend has passed on." As though only just noting Dean, the old man narrowed his eyes at my friend. "Come closer, lad. I'm old and infirm and cannot see from this far."

Dean looked to me as though heading to the gauntlet yet stepped forward. The old man looked directly into Dean's brown eyes and scoffed.

"You can wait outside."

"Pardon me, sir, but I am not inclined to leave."

The shopkeep wheezed a laugh and slapped the counter, saying he would wager Elías' daughter could fend for herself better than any schoolboy could protect her. Colour crept up Dean's face, and I had the urge to touch his cheek, yet refrained.

"You are not the right one," the man told him. He walked away, shuffled through things in the back, and we waited.

"He seems a few marbles short, pet. Do you want me to go?"

"My marbles are all stacked, lad. Here," he announced, and set a sketch atop the counter next to a moleskin sack. "These," he said, pointing to the sketch, "are not your eyes, lad."

I clenched my fists together, counting my breaths. On the paper, outlined in charcoal, and filled in with watercolour the shade somewhere between an aquamarine and a peridot, were Cadeyrn's eyes.

"No," I whispered, touching the sketch. "They aren't. They are my husband's." The sketch did not bring any visions as I hoped it would. Likely because the bearer of those magnificent eyes was dead.

"Ah. I see. Well, I suppose you can stay. Tea?"

THE CLEAR quartz pendulum that came out of the sack pulsed in my hand. Along with the crystal, the sack contained a torn piece of paper, yellowed with time. On the paper were two words: *Baege Maanlach*.

"Little Moon." Dean smiled, knowing it had been Dad's nickname for me. Sensing I might need to speak to the fellow on my own, my friend excused himself to drown his buyer's remorse over a pint. We sat back and sipped the proffered tea.

"In a different time, I was known as an emissary," the old man began. "My family is an ancient line who have always sworn to protect the Veil." Why was I not surprised to hear this? "My name is Percival Bryan, and I met your father about thirty years ago, when I tried to kill him."

I pitched forward in my seat. The cup rattled, sloshing tea. From boyhood, he told me, the men of his family were taught to fight and protect the Veil at all costs. Curiosity had me asking what the women did.

"They learn to summon, scry, and shield," he said, as though I were a bit thick. Long ago, a pact was made between the fae who crossed and the humans receptive to magic. Within that agreement, the humans promised to guard the Veil and dispose of any who sought to shatter the stability. Percival had been spending time around the Veil in Barlowe Combe. He witnessed my father exiting the grotto near the Veil and would have killed him outright if not for the small child he held by the hand. Because of that child, he bided his time and followed my father. Once Elías was finally alone, Percival confronted him. They fought for a time, my father eventually shoving Percival's head into a tree, face first.

"He said, 'Do not presume to know what I am doing to help the Veil. Many know the whereabouts of the stones and are readying crossing-compatible teams to seek them out. This cannot happen. Do you understand that, human?'" Percival chuckled retelling the story. "As I was a clever chap, I agreed to listen to him. I thought that either he had a good point, or that hearing him out would help me be able to kill him. So, we became friends. After about two years, I decided not to off him."

"Two years!" I spluttered. He chuckled again and wiped the lenses on his glasses.

"Oh, he knew. Your dad didn't miss a trick. Although, when you pulled that stunt in going to Spain, he was quite blindsided. Had me fly to Barcelona to keep an eye on you until he got there."

I must have looked shocked because he smirked.

Dad became sick much earlier than I had thought. He confided in Percival sometime around my university graduation. They continued to work together to secure the Veil when Dad had a vision. It was the only one he had ever had, and he guessed it had been sent to him by Saskeia.

"He loved that one fiercely, he did. I myself never married. Never saw the point. But your dad? He went to his grave with his heart across the Veil, I reckon." Once again, my heart broke for them. I told myself over and over that at least Ewan and Corra had one another. At least they were happy. I hoped.

The vision was of a man with those eyes. He said Dad didn't see much beyond the face, but the constellation of stars appeared with a braided rope. He knew the soul behind those eyes would one day belong to me, and that I would need to cross the Veil. So, they set about gathering items to help.

"I assume you crossed?" It was a simple question, yet I gripped the arms of my chair and snapped them in half from the pain in my chest. Percival didn't so much as flinch but stood and went about the shop pulling items. Small crystals, candles of varying colours, a pack of Jaffa Cakes, with a muttering of my being too thin. By the end of our visit, I was emotionally drained.

Finding Dean took me all of five minutes. There was an antiquarian bookstore a few doors down. The bell jingled when I walked in, yet no one greeted me. My friend sat on the floor at the back, a book cradled in his lap. His glasses had slid down his nose, and by the look of him biting his thumb, he was too immersed in the tome to notice. I sat next to him, keeping the silence. Without looking up, he looped an arm around my shoulders.

"Okay, pet?"

I shrugged in answer. He nodded and placed a slip of paper between the pages, closing the book.

"Want to talk?"

I pushed at my nose and shook my head. He stood and held a hand out to me.

"Then let's get you something to eat. I'm sure a plate of cheesy chips will help."

I sniffed and took his hand.

STORIES AND songs of heartbreak tended to say that the quiet moments were the worst. The in between times when there was nothing to think about but the profound loss you felt. I wouldn't argue that, because all I had done since crossing back here was try to avoid those times. I would panic in the evening, knowing that within the sleeplessness that awaited me, there would be the serration of my soul as the dark minutes passed, allowing the unsolicited thoughts of my mate to infiltrate my restless mind. So, I worked and filled my head with numbers and headlines, news tickers and investments. I ran, blasting music I had missed in Aoifsing. I trained and sparred and hoped that pushing my body to the brink of exhaustion each night would allow me to fall into slumber. However, in all those tomes of love lost, it never mentioned the fact that I could hear him speaking when my sword whined through the air in the training ring. I could hear the music of Corra's laughter in the din of a restaurant and feel the weight of Silas' gaze when the rain pounded on the roof of my flat. The louder the sounds, the faster the movement, the less control I had over the memories that would wash in, stealing my breath and leaving me stunned.

In these loud moments, I felt pain lance through me as though I were taking the sword that killed Cadeyrn. Over and over again. I walked through towns and cities, the more unfamiliar the better, attempting to keep at bay any recognition of my previous life. More often than not, it didn't work. I longed for every small moment I would never find again. The heat of his feet curled around my legs at night. The childish gleam in his eyes when he ate biscuits. The feel of having someone so imbedded in my being, I would never walk away from the loss.

I thought of the children Corra and Ewan had, and that not only would I not have any of my own, I would never meet my niece and nephew. Never see my brother again. I thought of Silas. How I hurt him over and over again and still he loved me. Perhaps he would find love again. I had to believe one of us could be happy. The times I would have dinner with Dean, or make plans to drive out to the country, I convinced myself I was hanging on okay. And he would kiss my cheek goodnight, knowing I wouldn't offer more, and I would fall against the back of my door, tearing at my hair and pressing my nails into my palms to keep from screaming. The mask of efficiency I wore for the outside world crumbled from my face as I stepped inside my bare flat. In its place was the face of a female utterly devoid of the ability to carry on as half of what she should have been.

Waking in the predawn hours from another dream so real, I begged to get back to sleep. In the dream, my brother was pounding a pane of glass, soundlessly screaming for me. I couldn't make my limbs move to get to him, and I realized he was underwater, not behind glass. I tried to pound the ice separating him from me, but my blows were slow and soft, unable to make a difference. I cried and yelled until my eyes opened. When it was clear I was awake, my feet freezing after I kicked off my socks, I got up and showered. In my flat, with its scarce furniture and too many blankets, I had one bistro-sized dining table. I lit a red candle. It was the colour for fire. For blood. Passion. Power.

Dean had stayed in town the night before. Richmond was several hours by train back to Durham. My friend planned to head up to see his mum the next day and begged me to come along. I was still deciding.

With my rose quartz pendulum, I sat near the candle's flame and wrote symbols. Nonsense and words, song lyrics, and Cadeyrn's name. Using the dagger he had given me, I sliced my palm and let the blood flow onto the paper. I had no idea what I was doing but begged the Goddess Kalíma. Begged Heícate, to whom I was heir, to help me. It wasn't that I was no one without my mate. It was that I was somewhere wrong. I was trapped. This world was a cage. It shackled my gifts, my light, my heart. Plus, I missed him. I missed them all. My family. With my pendulum, I held still and watched as it swung back and forth without my having asked a question. *Haven't you?* asked a voice in my head. *Is this all not one great question?* If so, then what is the answer? The pendulum stopped, and much like the amethyst two years ago in my cottage, the rose quartz, the stone of love, burst from its binding and dropped onto the paper. It rolled onto its chiseled side, getting stained with blood, and the tip pointed to a drawing of an eye overlapping the lyrics to a song I had stuck in my head. *"Seems like forever when I'm near you, longer when we're apart."* The candle blew out, and I sat in darkness, wondering what the hell that meant. Padding back to the bedroom, I reached into my closet and touched the fighting leathers I had worn when I crossed. They were clean now. Shoved to the back of my clothes. No, I wouldn't go to Barlowe Combe. Not yet. I texted Dean, knowing he wouldn't see it until later, and made a cup of tea.

At exactly 8:15, there was a buzz of my phone as I descended the steps to the street in front of my building. It was supposed to be hot today, and while I wasn't going to Barlowe Combe, I needed to be out of the flat which had no air con. A halter style maxi dress made of gauzy off-white cotton dropped to my feet. Ginger coloured ankle strap flat sandals completed the ensemble. I told myself I could wander the city. Perhaps get a Pimm's in a cafe, or stock up on books from a book shop. It was too hot to train, and I wasn't in the mood to work. My head wasn't in the game. I didn't have to check my phone to see that it was the persistent Dr. Preston, because he was standing against the street sign outside my building.

"Before you say no again, I want to point out that it is cooler by the sea. Plus, mum will have cake. And you look gorgeous. Good morning."

He had a way about him, I had to admit.

"Tell her I say hello. I need to be on my own today, Dean." He tried once more, but I shot him down again, yet gave him a kiss on his cheek and quick hug, before walking away. His arms went around me briefly, like he might have tried to hold on. Often I felt guilty about it, but my friendship with Dean felt like my relationship with my brother or with Reynard. Not at all romantic, but lovely just the same.

The shops opened later, so I wandered about the streets seeing mums with babies in prams, people out for a morning run, and I must have stopped to say hello to ten dogs out for a walk. Eventually I wandered into a shop that had bed linens and candles that smelled of paper whites and sandy shores. I held a cashmere dressing gown in my hands. I never replaced the one I was wearing when Reynard abducted me from Cappadocia. I hoped he was well. Making my way to the checkout, there was a small section of children's clothes and linens. My heart felt like there was a bubble in it. The babies would be seven or eight months old by now. I never kept my promise. As though an escalator were pulling my feet, I gravitated to the children's section. Everything was white with classic little patterns and soft materials. On the shelf above the toddler quilts was a basket of cuddly toys, two having fallen out, landing on their heads. Smiling, I picked them up and had a flash in my mind. I whimpered and held on. Two small faces swam to the surface. A boy with eyes exactly like Corra's, even her rosebud mouth. A girl with peachy skin and olive eyes like Ewan's. Like mine. Both with tiny pointed tipped ears. Tears were freely flowing. They were real. Healthy. I rushed back to the cash register and placed the dressing gown on the counter.

"And will you be purchasing the rabbits as well?" She pointed to the two bunnies clasped in my hands, one pink, one taupe, barely sacks of velour with embroidered eyes and small grins, yet tall ears. I swallowed and said of course. Really, considering the amount of money I spent, I should have stayed home to work. It was early evening, seven or eight, when I sat down to have a Pimm's and cheesy chips. Knowing the babies were fine made me feel lighter. That vision was a gift, and I sent a thank you to the Goddesses who blessed me with them. While I was still encaged in this realm, half of who I really was, just knowing those two perfect beings were thriving was a beautiful thing indeed.

CHAPTER 45

Cadeyrn

Landing smack on my face in the dirt, in what appeared to be a vineyard, threw me. My clothes were still soaked from the temple pool, my palm was healed, yet covered in dried blood. Where was I? I walked through the vineyard, hoping I wasn't in America, where I'd be shot as a trespasser. It had occurred to me to wear a fitted hat that covered my ears, as I had left the smoky quartz in the temple, so there was nothing to cloak me. At the edge of the vineyard was a sign pointing into town written in French. So, I assumed I was somewhere in France. With no money, pointed ears, and soaking wet. Fantastic. In town, attached to a gambling counter, was a money wiring window. Thank the gods. Problem was that it would take a week to receive it. So in this tiny town I stayed, being a farm hand and working behind the bar at the local tavern, just to have a place to stay. Utterly ridiculous to have been able to cross realms, yet I was stuck in bloody France because I had no funds.

On the first day, I asked the owner of the bar if I could use his internet. In a brief search, Neysa was nowhere, but I saw mention of her trading. The barman kicked me off the computer shortly thereafter. A few days later, I tried calling Neysa's old number, but it was already linked to someone else. After a week of wearing my same clothes that I washed out each night, my funds were finally transferred. I took a taxi into Bordeaux and got on a train to Paris so I could connect to London. The rail journey slid me back into memories of the train we took from Madrid after Neysa and Corraidhín had gone off to Peru. Gods those two. Though my cousin had sustained a grave injury, the memory sent pangs through me of a time when there was more possibility. She wasn't mine back then, even though I was hers. But she was safe. This abyss of hell I'd been going through for a year—more, even— hadn't opened up yet. It wasn't just that I missed her, or that I was pissed off with myself for pushing her through the damned Veil. It was that every sound, every action, reminded me of her laugh, her evergreen eyes, and her freckled nose. Every time I smelled the sea and the wild open water, I was crippled with remembering the way she told me stories with her head on my stomach, kissing my chest each time the story paused. I missed my best friend. My mate. My own soul living outside my body.

From London I went straight to Barlowe Combe, half hoping Neysa wasn't at the house so I could at least bathe and change before I saw her. I was going to burn these clothes. Upon arriving at the manor that used to be my home, I saw the dark windows, felt the emptiness, and immediately regretted hoping she wasn't home.

Remnants of when she and Ewan lived in the house remained. Wellies by the door, raincoats, lists and journals, chemical equations. I hadn't realized the work they put into fig-uring out how to collapse the Veil. She explained the chemical makeup, but the amount of notes I could see indicated far more than I gave them credit for. Those two were brilliant.

Among the scattered notes was a dead phone. Once I plugged it in, hoping for some sort of clue, and knowing full well I'd not get one, I looked up Neysa's recently played music. I knew she missed it while in the fae realm, so I was curious what she listened to whilst she and Ewan had been here. What had she last listened to when she assumed she was heading to the Veil to die? The tune was a rasping emotional voice paired with a strumming guitar. Some male singing about the end of a relationship that had been wrong from the start. The singer seemed to have fucked up as massively as I had, repeatedly say-ing he was picturing her there in her wedding dress. "The Fall of Rome." Bloody hell, Neysa.

My laptop was dead. The electricity worked, so I hoped that all the bills were still being paid. It was mid-afternoon by the time I got in, and I realized that bar a half-empty jar of pea-nut butter that probably wasn't safe to eat, there was nothing in the house. I showered and shaved quickly, then changed to run into town and see what I could find to eat, and maybe see if my wife had been back at all.

She always teased me that no matter what I was dressed for, or where we were, my attire was the same. I pulled on a pair of trousers that I used for everyday wear, as well as training, and paired them with a light grey button-down shirt. It was stuffy and hot everywhere this time of year, so I rolled up my sleeves and grabbed the other smoky quartz before walking into town. Time didn't change much here. I'd lived in this village the better part of a century, and it bumbled along with the world, not quite growing up. I supposed that was why I loved it.

Tilly's shop hadn't changed at all either, except she had the door wide open to get some air inside. When I walked in she beamed.

"As I live and breathe, Cade! Where have you been, love?" I smiled back at her. A man, sandy blond with glasses and a pompous smirk, snapped his attention to me. For some reason I found myself checking my dagger, though he seemed more the academic type.

"Hiya, ma'm. I've had business overseas. Just got in today and found I'm out of food. How's the shop? You alright?" Cloaking stones worked on my appearance, but my accent was something else entirely. And the English could always sniff out a false accent, so I had to focus.

"'Course. Yeah, yeah. Sit down and let me fix you something. Been loads of commotion here in town. Marriages and babies. Mike the taxi driver died. Heart attack. Shame." She was rambling, and I could barely breathe. She hadn't been here then.

"Don't fuss about for me, Tilly. Truly." I was so tired, it was hard to keep my accent in place. I kept slipping, and it lilted ever so slightly. The sandy-haired fellow was still staring at me. His eyebrows were up, mouth a bit agape. I turned my full attention to him whilst Tilly heated up something for me. I didn't care what. I had bloody cheese and bread every single day in France. He shrunk a bit when I met his gaze, then pushed his glasses on his nose and sat up. Something about him piqued memories of a gangly teenager running into me full speed whilst playing football.

"Hiya," I said, trying to be polite. "You okay, mate?"

"Och! Cade, this is my son. My youngest, Dean." She came round and gave him a pat on the cheek before bringing me my plate. I sniffed and my eyes met his. He smelled of Neysa.

"You'll never guess who he has come across," she said like a child on Yule morning.

"Can't imagine," I answered, still locking eyes with the fellow, who was sweating now. I could smell the fear enrobing him. He was several inches shorter than I was and didn't seem like he did much in the way of training. I bet he did that cycle class nonsense I'd seen. Or yoga.

"That tenant of yours, Neysa. She's been gone too, and I missed seeing her face around here."

"Yes, I understand how you would." I took bite after bite, keeping my eyes on the man.

"Dean met her in Oxford when he was doing a lecture. He's a professor, you know. They have become close. I do wish you could have brought her today, Dean. How lovely it would have been to see her, don't you think, Cade?" I ate the entire gods-damned meat pie and bread roll in less than two minutes and felt like I was going throw up. What did I do now? Did I want to ask if they were together? Was it something I could handle knowing without burning this place to the ground? *You're not a monster*. I left money on the table, thanked Tilly, and jerked my chin to the man to follow me out. We walked a block or so to where there was a gap in the buildings along the High Street.

"Cadeyrn?" he asked. My shoulders ached from the way my body shook.

"She's okay?" I asked.

"She is. Rather, she has a lot to get through. I believed her. But it still seemed impossible. You healed?"

She told him then. Our story. I pinched my nose, squeezing my eyes shut. She would only tell him—

"She thinks you're dead," he blurted.

"You're close? To her, I mean." Of course they were.

"Not like that. I would like that. But she...loves you, mate."

It was as if I couldn't get enough air in my lungs. I supposed this was how Neysa felt when she had her anxiety attacks.

"Where is she?"

"Lives in Richmond. Want to call?" He pulled his phone and thrust it at me.

"No. I want to see her. Would you mind giving me her address? Please." I felt like a child. He did, and I set off at a run to drive into the city and catch a train to Richmond. It took me another three hours until I got off the train. I didn't know Richmond well and wandered, following the directions on my phone. I turned down one particular street, as it was supposed to cross with the street on which she lived, and there were shops and cafes all along. It seemed like a nice place to live. Perhaps the closest I had seen to Laichmonde. It was eight o'clock or so, and the sun was in that low place that seemed to dust everything in a fair light. I slowed my walk and came to a complete and sudden stop, someone slamming into me from behind. He muttered an apology and moved on. I stood staring. She was sitting at a table. Alone. Drinking what looked to be a Pimm's, an empty plate beside the glass. I would bet there had been cheesy chips on it. I was more or less behind her about ten metres or so, staring at her bare shoulders where the sun was hitting. The breeze blew in from behind me, and I saw goose bumps rise on her arms and back. She stiffened and looked around. I couldn't move. Fucking hell; I couldn't move. Then she turned and saw me, and I noticed she still wore her ring. Her hands went to her mouth, and her nose became swollen and red. I walked over and asked if I could sit. I'm not sure if what came out was English or Aoifsing, or some degenerate mix of both, but she whimpered and stood, throwing her arms around me.

CHAPTER 46

Neysa

For a minute I really thought it was another vision. I thought they had started back up again and here was a vision of him. It honestly took me looking at his clothes to realize he was real. Whatever he said when he walked over was gibberish, but it didn't matter, because I wanted to feel him. His hands scraped against my bare back and my blood heated.

"You're bigger," I said stupidly, running my hands over his arms and chest.

Those eyes I missed raked all over me. I put my hand flat against his stomach, and his mouth was on mine. He lifted me from the ground, my legs locking around his waist. Whistles and cheers, hoots and whoops came from all around us, and we didn't care. We were lost in the shared breath and pull of my lip between his incisors. After finally breaking apart, I dragged him to my dumb little flat with its negligent amount of furniture and stuffy air.

"I thought—thought you were dead. Say something. You're making me nervous."

"Are you happy here?" he asked me, eyebrows pinched together. I knew he didn't fully mean in this flat.

"No." I didn't even have a real couch to sit on. It was embarrassing. We perched on two dumb chairs, one of which was a desk chair where I worked. "Were you happy?" I asked, unable to look at him. He snorted.

"Corraidhín called me a mega tsunami. She said I was building like a giant wave that would destroy them all."

"That's a very serious accusation. The mega tsunami is supposed to take out the entire Eastern Seaboard."

"So I've heard."

"Was she right?"

"Well, I wasn't in the Atlantic, so it wasn't a perfect analogy." My phone buzzed. I ignored it, but a text came through as well. "Check it. It's okay." I looked. Dean, of course. He had been texting for a few hours now. No one else really contacted me. Just asking if I was okay.

"Just a friend checking in," I said, texting back a quick *Yes*.

"Tilly's son?"

I nearly choked.

"He's nice. Likes you. Knew who I was, which threw me." He was looking down at his hands. I understood now.

"He's very nice and we get on well. He's not you. No one else is you. Now tell me how you got here before I stop listening."

Arms locked around me while he spoke, not letting either of us move an inch. I sat on his lap on the chair that seemed like it was going to break.

"You're tired, Cadeyrn." I traced under his eyes with my finger and kissed his eyelids. "Want to sleep?"

He rumbled a laugh against me. His hand sat on my lap, atop my gauzy cotton dress. I touched his wedding band and couldn't help a sob that ripped out. Cadeyrn kissed my shoulder.

"I'm sorry," he said. "I'm so sorry."

I turned to him. "For what?"

"I pushed you through. The worst part was that I knew that somehow it would happen, that's why I was so horrible. I kept trying to get you away. It was too fast. Kíra and the sword. It was too fast."

I unbuttoned his shirt and ran my hands along the scar on his stomach. I knew it wouldn't have healed completely. Knew there had to be a scar. Just as there was a nasty scar on my shoulder where I had been cut.

"How long did it take to heal?" He looked down, then back to me.

"Not sure exactly. They kept me asleep for almost three months." He placed his head in his hands.

"I'm sorry," I said, still touching that scar, smoothing over his stomach with my hands. He caught my lip, his incisor nicking me. I smiled against him. His hand moved to scrunch my dress until his hands were sliding along the inside of my thighs. Though any magic we had was muted, heat pulsed between us, throbbing in time to our hearts and movements.

"It's so hot in here," he murmured.

"Mmm, yes, and you've just made it worse." I was already slick with sweat as his hand slid up the sensitive inner part of my thigh then up my hip. The other hand moved along my ribs and the sides of my breasts. I laid my hand on him, stroking through the fabric of his trousers.

"Did you miss these?" I was touching the outside of his training trousers.

"Comfort is unparalleled. Fae activewear is lacking." I laughed, tracing him with my thumb. "And far too thick." He groaned. So did the rickety chair under us. I stood, pulling him to me. He untied my dress from the neck and watched it drop. I pulled his trousers off and looked at him in his undershorts, the vee of muscles pointing exactly where I was thinking I wanted to go. Every inch of him seemed bigger, cut with muscle. I wasn't complaining one bit. His hands wrenched me forward by the hips, callouses scraping against my skin. We walked, uncharacteristically calm, to the bedroom, and he laughed at my twin bed. Before I was able to lay down, he stopped, kneeling in front of me. Oh gods. When he looked up at me, those eyes shadowed from his dark brows and lashes, I had to lean against the wall. He hoisted my leg over his shoulder and fastened his mouth to me. A thousand lights exploded in my vision, the room fully black with pulsating white lights. Heat rose off his skin in waves, coating him and me both. My hands were buried in his hair, pushing him closer, but I was losing my ability to stand. We moved to the bed, giggling like teenagers. Once he was seated inside me, our bodies slippery in the heat, I took his face in my hands.

"I want to go home. With you. I never want to have to leave you," I told him, kissing the corners of his mouth.

He moved inside me, rocking us together slowly. I lifted my hips, grabbing his backside. We dragged it out as long as possible, kissing, touching, moving, sweating, until the pressure that built was so intense, I went over the edge, crying out his name. He kept moving, lifting my legs up, moving his mouth down the inside of my raised calves. I grabbed the headboard and pushed up my hips until he growled my name, his eyes lighting up with peridot fire.

"My God, I've missed you," I said, not letting him move.

"You have no idea." He drew lazy lines along my arms and into my hair.

"ADMIT IT. You thought I was crazy," I said to Dean a couple days later as we sat in Tilly's shop.

"Not crazy per se, pet. There was a question in my mind though. You're different now. Happy."

I grabbed his hand and kissed it. "I am. Thank you. For being my friend."

"Your servant, ma'am." He gave me his signature roguish smirk.

"You are a handsome thing. Go get yourself a girl, for God's sake." Tilly came by and was glum. "She's not happy with me, I'm afraid." I quirked my mouth to the side.

"Yeah, well. She'll get over it. Now, give us a kiss, pet, and go live your life while we mortals slug through the daily, gloriously unaware of the lost princess." I rolled my eyes and kissed his cheek before leaving. "I will miss you," he called after me. "You know I was falling for you." He winked, making my heart clench.

"I think it's because of you, Dean. Meeting you. It all came together. I'll always be grateful." I ducked out of the shop and headed back to the estate to ready myself.

FRANCE WAS, for all intents and purposes, a pain in the ass to get to. The hope was that we could open the Veil here in the grotto, close to where the original one had been. After promising not to wear a grey jumper, I put on my leathers, and we each packed a bag as though going on holiday. From the bag of gifts the mystic had given me, I pulled a green agate that was fused together with clear quartz. We stood in the grotto, the light glowing ephemeral blue, and sliced our palms. Blood rushed to the stones waiting under us, swirling around the crystals and the etchings we had made in the dirt. I thought of home. My brother and Corra, the babies, Silas. We pressed our palms together, blood mingling, and kissed.

Take us home, I thought.

Home is us, Cadeyrn responded, though I hadn't realized our connection was intact again. I knelt down and placed my free hand on the ground, the other still holding my mate's. Allowing a surge of power to release, it went into the earth. As though waking at my touch, a shimmer in the air told us the Veil had opened. Keeping our hands and arms clasped together, we stepped through.

CHAPTER 47

Silas

Somebody let a herd of wild boar in the house. That was the only explanation for the amount of noise that woke me. My first instinct was to put the pillow over my head. This manor was large, but when the babies kicked off, the sound still travelled. However, this wasn't the little ones. This was my sister, and she was raging. Cadeyrn and Ewan left a week ago to check in with Ainsley Mads and her crew of hairy citizens. I consider myself a fairly rugged chap, but the amount of hair and girth on those males was astounding. Corraidhín was unusually quiet in Ewan's absence, but I suppose that was to be expected. She wasn't entirely pleased that I was bedding Saski either, so oftentimes our conversations were short.

Once I realized the noise wasn't ceasing, I pulled on a shirt and headed down the hall. Ewan had barely come in the front door, his face and hair windblown. And he was spooked. Cadeyrn wasn't with him. Corraidhín was banging him on the chest and screaming in the aulde language. He stood taking it, which had me worried. Saski came up behind me, closer than casual. Ewan looked up the stairs to where we stood and met my eyes.

"He opened a Veil," Ewan said to me.

"You helped him!" my sister screamed. "You let him go gods know where. We don't even know if she is in the same place! He could be lost, Ewan!" He grabbed her hands to keep her from beating him. He had to be fairly bruised by now.

"You knew he was going, Corraidhín," he said to her in a placating manner.

She laid her head against his chest and cried. Actually cried. She hadn't wept since...I couldn't remember. Not even after our parents were killed.

"I didn't think it would work," she whimpered. I didn't know what to do. I wanted to go to her, but she had her husband. I wanted to hit something. I didn't know if I was more pissed that he did it, or that he didn't ask me to help him. I knew he was bothered by this thing with Saski. Perhaps that was why, but I just didn't know.

"When, Ewan?" I asked.

"I stayed one night there, and I came straight back. So, four days. I rode hard. I don't know if you knew, but Neysa had gone to the Goddess Kalima's temple in Prinaer. The Goddess accepted her. That's where Cadeyrn went. She must have done the same."

"He offered himself to the Goddess?" I yelled.

Saski tugged at my arm and I snarled, pulling out of her grasp. She hissed.

"No. I think he called upon her for advice. She must have answered, because he came out of the pool and we bled and opened the Veil."

"You? You bled?" Corraidhín was thrumming, pulling in and out of her corporeal self. Ewan slumped to the floor where he stood and put his head between his knees. "You are lucky you didn't get thrust through with him. Did it close?"

"No," he whispered.

I walked down the stairs barefoot. They could be anywhere. The house was mostly dark; only the sconces by the door were lit. My sister was totally mist. Likely gone outside in my storm. The rain was falling in thick sheets.

"On Aedtine Day, he and I saw her," he began. I clenched my fists. "We were staring into the flames talking about her. He never did, and we spoke about her. He was almost gone, Silas. He was letting go. I could feel it. Then we both saw her, scrying and using her blood. He realized that's how she opened the Veil. Her power transcends realms much like his. It doesn't seek full authority from one realm or another. So, he thought if he did the same that he could try to find her. I helped, seeing as she and I are blood. He didn't tell you because—"

"Because of me," Saski said.

"Not everything is about you," I snapped, feeling like a toe rag for doing so.

"Because of you, yes," Ewan said. Well, fuck. Saski made an obscene gesture at me. "He didn't understand how you were able to move on."

"I haven't fucking moved on! She's my mate too!" I barked, and once again, felt like a piece of shite. "Saski," I said. She held up a hand.

"I'm not thick, Silas. You don't think I know who you want when you're with me?" She walked back through the hallway, and a door clicked shut behind her.

"Fucking hell, Ewan."

He nodded. We had no idea where either of them would have crossed, or where they would even cross back as it wasn't clear if the Veil he opened would have held. What a cluster. If only there were a topographical link to the human realm. If we could lay a map of here over a map of there and have points match up, but it simply did not work that way. When Neysa was taken in Turkey, Cadeyrn and I tried. Even if it lined up, our magnetic pole positions or whatever Neysa had said so long ago, shift. I told Ewan to get some sleep. He was a wreck.

CORRAIDHÍN WAS in the stables where they told me Neysa's *baethaache* had stayed. She was quietly rocking back and forth. By the gods, I had never seen her like this. I put my arms around her. Losing them both. I would give up being mated to Neysa for them to be safe. To return, yes, but mostly just to know that they were safe. I had likely erased any chance I had with *Trubaíste* as soon as I began this thing with Saski. I was a fool, but I was unable to stop myself. We stayed in the stables until morning. Ewan brought Pim and Efa out to us. Efa was already starting to crawl, and she was all over Ewan, trying to scramble down to her mum. I was never a baby type of male, yet these two had me wrapped round their little fingers. I liked to tell them stories about their parents and their brave auntie who had a fierce beastie. I was sure I sounded like a right tosser doing it, but it made me happy to share with them, and they babbled and smacked kisses at me, so I couldn't be that bad, I supposed.

We headed inside, and I made for my room, hoping to sleep for an hour or so before meeting with Cyrranus. Saski was coming out of her room, ready for the day. As she was passing me, I reached for her. She stopped.

"Why do you bother with me?" I asked her. "You're so beautiful. You're a queen. You should find someone less..." I pointed to my head as though it were exploding. She moved to me.

"I should. You're a shit to me. Well, sometimes. But I like a challenge." She leaned in and kissed me. It wasn't really Neysa I wanted when we were together. Saski was wild and hungry, and it loosened something inside of me. Had I not been spent physically and emotionally, I might have pulled her back to her room. Instead, I just kissed her back and said I would see her later.

CONVINCING EVERYONE that it was safe again to use their Festaeran steel was proving to be tricky. I felt bad for Cyrranus taking on this position. Arneau did not go quietly into the night. We found folk who had sworn against him dead or incapacitated. There was nothing concrete to pin on him. I was getting frustrated; I knew Cyrranus must be tearing his hair out. We met in his new residence in Craghen, the coastal village where Cadeyrn and Neysa were married. Reynard was there too, having taken up a home nearby. They both could sense that something was up with me, but it wasn't the time to share. Especially since we didn't have a real idea of what was happening.

The day of the meeting, when Cadeyrn made Etienne piss himself, and Corraidhín and I made it all the worse, set us on a dangerous path with these two Maesarrans. They were out for blood. Cyrranus showed me notes from spies we had on the two sketchy bastards. They both were still fortifying their homes and would not let any servants outside. I felt bad for

Arneau's wife. She must have been thoroughly unhappy to have brought me into their home and willingly sold out her husband. I couldn't save everyone, I knew. However, if she were being mistreated before, then surely, it was far worse now. Perhaps I could get her out. Mentioning it to Cyrranus, he said it would likely make things far worse.

"Think about it, Silas. He sees her as his property. If you make any sort of move to help her, you will have taken from him. More so than you have already. He could strike back hard and we don't need that."

"A wife is not property," I countered.

"Yes, you and I know that. But Arneau is a prick. If you want to see it in a different light, think about it like this. I never really cared for Cadeyrn. He thinks it's because of Solange. Perhaps once it was, but I always saw him as feeling entitled," he said.

Cadeyrn never felt entitled to anything his entire existence. Even as children, he moped about, trying not to get under foot.

"Though he loved Neysa, and I know he never mistreated her, if based on how I felt about him, I felt like I should go in and rescue her, what would he do? What would you do?" This was a stupid point. We'd kill the little shite.

"I understand what you are getting at, Cyrranus, but everything you've just alluded to is a bunch of old wank. Yeah, it's diplomatically unsound to pull the wife. I get it."

I couldn't leave it alone. I knew you couldn't have everyone like you and all that, but I couldn't have Cyrranus, who always risked himself for *Trubaíste*, thinking poorly of my cousin.

"Cadeyrn was the least entitled male I've ever met, Cyrranus. I know you never saw eye to eye with him, and he puts up that wall, but I want you to know. Cadeyrn always contended with his birthright. Never relished it. And he never thought he deserved Neysa. You should know that."

Reynard came in with a book in hand, bow slung on his shoulder. His brows were pinched together, locking eyes with me.

"What do you mean *was*?" he asked, quiet as the grave. I looked up at him. Cyrranus raised his eyebrows. "Silas." Reynard stalked closer, going a bit pale. Cyrranus stood and felt Reynard's face. That was odd. "What do you mean, Cadeyrn *was* always the least entitled male? What has happened?" Ah, fuck it all. The weasel never missed a beat.

I felt like old fabric that's been pulled and scratched and worn down to its barest threads. Looking up at these two, I saw that I had missed the very obvious fact that they were a couple. I closed my eyes, then told them about Cadeyrn.

I DIDN'T know if Saski was speaking to me or not. I never knew with females whether I should make myself scarce or chase them about. Most of my life, I would seek and destroy, as my sister would say. It was quick and fun and done. Then, after three hundred years of that, Neysa came in like a battering ram to the head. Saski, I didn't know. Maybe it was because she was still bloody here under the same roof, or because she looked so much like *Trubaíste*, but what little we had between us was still there. In any case, I had to seek her out and speak of bigger issues. I found her in her room. It was late in the evening when I returned from Craghen, two days after Ewan told us about Cadeyrn. I knocked, and heard the whoosh of wind, and the door opened, though she stood on the opposite side of the room.

"We need to talk," I said. I could have kicked myself. Never a good way to begin. She smirked and flipped her hair back in the way Corraidhín did when she was ready to take on anything slung at her.

"I suppose we do." I stepped further in, and the wind shut the heavy door behind me. She had on a silk dressing gown that wasn't fully done up, likely having just bathed by the heat coming off her skin.

"I've just been to see Cyrranus and Reynard. All the subterfuge we have been expecting is starting to come to a head. With Cadeyrn's possible..." I swallowed and couldn't bring myself to say it. I literally stood there for a moment trying to breathe and reorganize my thoughts. She stepped closer to me and grabbed my hand. "Things could get testy. And you are heir to Heilig."

"Ah." She dropped my hand and turned to the window. "What would you have me do?"

"Are you ready to take your throne? I've sent a hawk to Basz informing him of what's happening here. I haven't mentioned my cousin. Not yet. But it may be time to take what's yours."

"Mine," she murmured. "What's really mine? I wasn't born to rule, Silas. Arik, maybe. Ludek, he wouldn't want it, but you can see how he would be the best of us. Pavla adored him, and he her. She was wilder than I am. Can you imagine that?" She looked over her shoulder with a small smile. I touched her face. She had never spoken of Pavla. "Pavla would take on the bloodiest fight. Like your Neysa, I suppose. Never asked permission. Just went in. Our mother hated it. Father treated us all equal, but when Pavla died, I swore there was a relief in father. I saw it in glimpses, and it scared me. As though he always feared that one day, she would take his throne. Or mine. If I saw it, then Ludek must have. And mother. Arik and I just kept on. Like spoiled children. Though we mourned as well. Differently. She was my sister. I know you see me as wicked." She sniffed a laugh. I didn't laugh. I went closer to her. "But I can love. I love my siblings, Silas. I would do anything for them. If Ludek hadn't killed father, I would have. Because father killed Pavla. With what he involved himself in. He killed her, and I would have killed him. What does that make me?"

I placed my hands on her hips and turned her to me, my hand going to the back of her head.

"Loyal. Determined."

"Not wicked?" she asked. I was taking in her eyes, dim and sad.

"Wicked? Surely. Evil? No. Your wickedness is what I like." I had my mouth close to hers.

"Do you? Like me?" Her voice was so small. I smiled.

"Occasionally. When you're not trying to crush my balls for one thing or another." I touched my lips to hers. "Perhaps then as well. Sometimes." I felt her smile against me.

"I don't know whether I should go back. I don't wish to take the throne. I don't want it."

"My cousin always told me we don't always want the lot we are given. We make the best of it." She pulled back and had a knowing look on her face.

"That's what you're doing, is it not?" she asked. "Making the best of wanting what you have?" Hell. This was why I didn't do relationships. Fuck.

"What do you want me to say, Saski? That I don't still love Neysa? That I don't think about her all the time? That I don't know if she's dead or if she will come back with Cadeyrn and that might kill me more? She is my mate, whom I cannot truly have when she is the only thing in my life I have ever wanted. Is that what you wanted me to say?"

Corraidhín would have kicked my ass for that, but it just came out.

"I am a broken male, Saski. Utterly destroyed, and there is something in me that will never be whole because I am a part of a bond that she doesn't want. You could have everything. I do like you. I like being with you. I like your wicked mouth and your wicked body, and the time we spend. But you could have someone who can love you completely. Not this." I gestured to myself. She cocked her head to the side and looked at me like a contemplative firedrake.

"I don't want anyone else," she said at last. "I want you, no matter how broken. If you truly do not want me, then I shall go. But I think you might want me and are just a bit afraid of what that might mean. Think about it."

I turned to leave, knowing a dismissal when I heard one.

"I didn't say to leave." So, maybe it wasn't a dismissal. Gods-damned females and their mixed messages. I turned back to her, and she had dropped her dressing gown.

"My wicked mouth and wicked body want to play."

Deep, poisonous shite.

BACK IN Craghen, I met with Cyrranus, attempting to sort out trade details between Maesarra and Saarlaiche for Ewan. At some point I needed to get back home and look into readying for the autumn harvest. It was time to take on new workers. I had tried to get more of those grinder machines built. A sort of tribute to Neysa. They needed checking in on. I hadn't told

Cadeyrn about them, not sure how he would feel. The village here in Craghen was in full season, as it was a draw for wealthy travellers and those who would travel to sell their goods. I wandered the boulevard before seeking out Cyrranus at the tavern he had indicated. A family, obviously not very well off, had set up a stall across from the harbour, selling jewelry and trinkets. I gravitated towards it. There was a necklace, silver with a delicate bird stretched from one end of the chain to the next. When I looked closer, the bird had a dagger in its beak, tiny chips of topaz for eyes. It reminded me of Saski's sword. I purchased the necklace before I thought better of it, not even bothering to haggle. I walked briskly off, shoving the thing in my satchel. I had never seen Neysa on her birthday. Never gave her a gift apart from the stupid Christmas tree. I used to get gifts for females all the time. Tokens of lacking affection, apologies, parting gifts. Lina had received three or four herself. The last, she left back on my doorstep. I didn't blame her. Neysa, I would have given the world, and yet, there was nothing I had bothered to get her. Time. There was never time. And she was never really mine.

Cyrranus was meeting with Alan, his minister of trade, trying to establish a presence while we worked out how many local tradesmen and seasonal workers we could take on to Saarlaiche to work the *araíran-aoír* nut orchard. I slid into the table with the two males and pulled the list they were compiling.

"Five hundred more trees were planted last spring. They may not be producing yet, but they will need tending. Perhaps part-time workers would do. Let's pull another twenty."

I had another job that needed workers, but there were many in Saarlaiche after the rebellion who were in need of income. Widows and children coming of age. I could not outsource anymore positions yet. We had always taken care of our own. Our orchards had sustained generations and I intended to keep that going. My heart was not in war. My heart was in Saarlaiche and taking care of its fae. Cyrranus seemed twitchy. I waited until Alan left and asked him why.

"Reynard has gone to check on his mother."

I drank from my ale and waited.

"He thinks that perhaps she would like to leave his father." Oh gods. "You can see why I might worry."

"He's a quick weasel, Cyrranus. I'm certain he will be in and out without incident." He nodded. "It isn't my business, but I'm curious. How long has it been going on?" I asked him. "Between you two." His smile was sly.

"Things were set into motion when you lot were in Laori-naghe last year." He answered with a flick of his wrist like it was old news. They suited each other. "He had a lot to sort through, though. Hasn't had an easy life, that one."

"I always thought you might have had a thing for Neysa," I said, tapping my chin. He laughed.

"Nothing beyond my thinking she was worth saving. I liked her heart. Her spirit, you get?"

"I do," I said, but it came out like a scuffle of feet on base boards. We wrapped up the meeting, and I went back with him to wait on Reynard at his home on the outskirts of town. My mind kept wandering to my cousin. I hadn't known. What Ewan said about him letting his immortality wither away. I hadn't seen it, and I should have. After that brawl we had in the hills above Laorinaghe whilst Neysa was still kept under, we hadn't been close. It was torture. He was moving through the provinces like some fire beast from the hell realms, and I confronted him. What was it doing to his soul? If Neysa woke and he was ash or unrecognizable, what would it do to her? He threw it back in my face. He said he knew what was between us; what would it do to her when she found out I was dropping my trousers for bits of information? We screamed and hit and slammed each other around until we called it quits. He was my brother, and we were at odds for a year. So, I wasn't paying attention enough to realize he was letting go.

Reynard didn't return that evening. A message was sent saying he was staying on with his mother whilst his father was away for the night. Solid worry settled in my gut. Though the weasel knew how to play a game of courts and pawns, I worried he might have been blind-sided by his parents. By his mother rather. The same message came the following night. On the third evening, there was no note and no sign of Cyrranus' partner. As there was little for me to do, and Cyrranus was pacing and snapping, I slipped out and made my way to Reynard's parents' estate.

One window was lit, the rest of the house dark. I snuck in the back garden gate and was face to face with a great, drooling, long-toothed aphrim. Fuck it all. You'd think in three centuries, I would have gotten used to the stench of these fuckers. It was amazing that they made such enviable clothing and such when every bit of their body—from their palm-sized black and brown scales to their sword-length snouts—stunk of rotten fruit and diseased shite. I didn't want to kill it and leave evidence that I was there, but I really didn't want to be dinner for this slick-skinned monstrosity. It growled and sniffed, moving slowly. I put my shield up, as I should have done earlier, blocking it from scenting or hearing me. They were blind and relied only on other senses. It was confused and went a bit wild eyed, then took off away from me. I exhaled, bending over. The kitchen door was on a latch, so I slid my dagger in and up, unhooking it to let myself in. The kitchen was still warm, so someone had made a meal. The light was likely for a servant who was still here. I opened myself to my emotions and had a light rain falling outside, then dissolved into the moisture in the air. In the daylight, I would have been visible, but in this darkened house, I was a wraith.

Room after room, there was no sign of anyone. It looked as though the lady of the house had her own sleeping quarters. I wasn't surprised. I'd seen plenty of similar situations in other houses. Especially after hundreds of years. I couldn't imagine being stuck with Etienne for that amount of time. It actually made me want to gag. His mother wasn't a pearl; don't get me wrong. From what I've heard, she had always been a thorny bramble, but Etienne was a fine example of a tainted soul. I moved around the lady's room, looking—looking for what, I don't know. I felt her bed linen and pulled back the duvet. A note. The size of two fingers. "*Ballaíche,*"—*boy*—was all it said. Was she leaving a clue? Was the clue for me or bait for Reyanrd? I realized then how tired I was. How little I slept lately. If Francois left more clues, they might be hidden deeper. A crystal jar sat upon her bedside table. The kind that holds creams and such. I unscrewed the lid and lifted the inner layer. Another line of script: "*Aídech á caráed*"—*help my love*. I guessed I had to keep looking. I had nothing else to do tonight anyway. It still felt like murky water. The second clue, like the first, and the notes could have been a lure for my friend just as easily as it could have been a plea for help in saving her. In her wardrobe were loads of shoes. She could never have worn that many. I touched a golden pair, embroidered with arrows and trees. Stuffed into the toe was another paper. "*Maíth mise*"—*forgive me*. Well, that didn't make me feel any less confuckingfuddled. I searched for a length of time and found nothing else. Slipping from the house, careful not to attract another aphrim, I made my way back across the countryside to Cyrranus.

THE TRUTH was that we didn't know anything yet. Francois was never what I would call a full quiver. Perhaps Reynard pulled her out while his father was still gone. Where Etienne slithered off to begged more of a question in my mind. Cyrranus and I had both sent hawks to find the two of them, but there was a block on their magic. If my friend had been trying to hide his mother, that made sense. Etienne was a shady arse, so it didn't surprise me at all the hawk came back to us. It took me until midmorning to reach Craghen. Cyrranus was out, which gave me time to figure out whether it was worth telling him. If it were my family, I would want to know. Even if it made me crazed. Even if it were nothing to be concerned about. Though, deep down, I felt it was a concern. I sent messages to my shadows to keep an eye out for Etienne or anything amiss that could be linked to him or Arneau. When Cyrranus didn't return that night, I started to panic. So, I waited. I asked his servants where he had gone, and they didn't know. I sent a male out to search for him—check taverns and inns. I called on Alan, though it was well into the evening by this point.

"Apologies, my lord," I greeted him as he stood, obviously ready for bed. Gods, I wished I were too. "I was wondering if you had seen or heard from Cyrranus since our last meeting. I am planning to set off in the morning and he hasn't returned with the information I requested."

Alan ushered me in his home. It felt empty and old. He was a decent-looking chap, and nice enough, if not a bit boring, but there was no hint of a partner here, male nor female. I wondered if that's how I might seem to some. Fuck, I needed sleep.

"I've not heard from him, Silas," he began. "But I received these. The first was yesterday, the second just this evening." He handed me slips of paper. "The first was stuck to my shed with an arrow. The second was delivered with a parcel I had ordered from a clothier in town." He turned a shade of red, and I decided I really didn't want to know what the parcel was.

Don't let it break the system. Follow the money. Shite. Reynard. The second was penned differently. The same hand that penned the notes in Francois' room.

It is for time he will exchange my heart. Where was Neysa and her riddle skills when you needed her? I pulled at my chin and asked to see where the shed was. Surely enough, it was just off a small road at the edge of his property. The shot could have been made by a skilled archer, and I didn't know of any better than Reynard. There were tracks. Horse and perhaps a small wagon as the indentations weren't very deep despite the layer of packed mud that seemed to hold every imprint. All I could see was that they headed north.

Dawn light had me waking in the parlour of Cyrranus' home, where I fell asleep against the wall, thinking that something about the clothier didn't sit well. Sometime around midday, the clop of hooves sounded up the drive. My host appeared, looking haggard and hopeless. I didn't have to ask whether he had found anything. Without a word, he thrust a note to me.

Aídech á caráed, was all its said. I followed him into the house, where he immediately made for the kitchen to stuff his face with whatever food was lying around. I showed him the notes. He was devastated. I saw the look. I knew the feeling. I lived with it every single godsdamned day. So, I put a hand on his shoulder.

"I'll go. I'll look for him."

"When we took Neysa," he said, "from the human realm, I could see beyond what he presented. He was an ass," he laughed. "But he never let her suffer. I tried to help her. The others were cruel, but I stayed with her, and Reynard wouldn't let her out of his sight. I knew she was trying to contact you lot. It didn't matter to me, so I said nothing. Reynard saw her and said nothing as well. He gave her his own coin for ale. I don't know why I'm telling you this. I just...I need to go. I need to look for him, Silas."

"I can stay here another day or so before I head back to Bistaír. From there we can dispatch more eyes. Yeah?" He agreed and went up to sleep for a bit before setting off.

I pulled out the stupid bird necklace and watched the light glint from the topaz eyes and thought that it was probably a naff gift anyway.

CHAPTER 48

Neysa

When I emerged from the Veil in the German woods a year ago, I was stunned. It had happened so much faster than I thought. My body stayed on the ground, frozen and bloody, seeing my husband's face as a sword was rammed through his stomach. The gush of blood that instantly flowed from his nose and mouth. Not being there. Hours I must have laid in those woods. It grew darker, and I was covered in blood. Many things would start to come check out the smell of death and weakness upon me. What was more, I didn't know how much I would fight when they did. So, I made myself get up, and begin to hide the weapons on myself.

The first place I happened on was a fish farm. I used a tank to wash up, though I didn't smell much better for it. I had no money, and no chance at this point of charming anyone into helping me when I looked like a homeless drug addict. The first thing I needed was to figure out where the bleeding hell I was. The fish farm had little signage. Some instructions in

German, but that didn't mean much. I could have been in Germany, Austria, Switzerland or even middle of nowhere Iowa. Stumbling from the forest, along a street named Kirschblütenweg, I made my way through the neighbourhood into town. Night was falling. I sought out a Kneipe, which was a pub for all intents and purposes, and sat down hard on a wooden chair. The server was a young woman with a brusque manner who, I noticed, didn't look anyone in the eye. It was a very small town, so most eyes were on me. She knelt in front of me and asked what she could bring me.

"Bitte, aber wo bin ich?" I asked quietly. Where am I? My German was rudimentary at best.

"Bad Schwartau, Schatz. Soll ich jemanden für dich anrufen?" Should she call someone for me? No. No one. I shook my head and looked up at her, not bothering to hide my face anymore. It was bruised, I knew. Most of the blood I thought I washed off, but there were bruises and lacerations from the fight. She scowled, anger flashing in her eyes. I was told to wait. After a few minutes, she came back with a plate of food and a beer.

"Kostenlos," she said. *On the house.*

She asked me where I needed to go. I didn't know. My first thought was London, but that necessitated money and a passport. The copper-haired waitress said she would drive me to the next larger town, Lübeck, where I could take a train to Hamburg. My passport was in the cottage in Barlowe Combe. If I went to the embassy in Hamburg, I would have to construct a story about being attacked, and I would be taken for medical questioning, which would be an issue as I was not human and not at all cloaked at the moment. Luckily, my hair was long enough that it covered my ears. I was so tired. If I rested, I could try to use some of my gifts. Something to get me through.

In Lübeck, I found a bar and let someone buy me a drink. After a few, he was pawing at me, so I lifted his phone from his pocket and slipped outside to make a phone call to an old colleague in London.

"Tom," I said, relief washing over me to hear his voice.

"Neysa. For what do I owe this honour? Last time we spoke I was groveling for forgiveness for throwing up on your husband's shoes."

"Well, we're divorced now," I laughed. "So, we don't have to worry about that incident. It was a good concert, though." He chuckled and asked how I had been. "I hate to ask this, but I need a favour. A really big favour."

"All right. Let's see if I can help."

"I've been through something lately. I can't tell you the whole story, and I am sorry for it, but I am stuck in Germany, and my passport is in a small village a few hours north of you. It's in a cottage I let. I need it sent to me as soon as possible. Once I have it, I can wire money and get to London. I will buy you a case of wine and tickets to whatever show you want to see."

"Christ, Neysa. What's happened? I know you said you can't tell me, but it seems bad."

"I'll be fine. I'm just stuck at the moment. It's safe," I added, as it occurred to me that he might be worried about getting involved. "No one is after me or anything like that."

After a long exhale, Tom agreed. So, I explained where it was and where I would be, needing to get out of this town. I left the phone in the bar. On the street, I lifted the wallet of a young woman too drunk to notice. I was not proud of myself, and I left my crystal necklace in its place in her handbag. I needed to get to Hamburg where I could pick up my passport, wire money, and get the hell off the continent. What could have been a cush hour-long train ride took me nearly four and a half on a stolen bicycle.

I scraped by for two days while I waited for the passport and wire transfer. I could go without eating. I had dealt with plenty of that in the past year. Once I had money, I bought clothes from the nearest shop and got a cheap hotel room to wash up. Holy Christ, I looked a sight. Bruises marred my neck and shoulders, my eye. The sword wound left a three-inch scar on my shoulder, but it had healed slightly before I crossed. In a panic, I took off my clothes and looked at my forearm. The gold thread was still there. Shaky fingers traced it, wondering where Silas was. Knowing Cadeyrn was dead. Wondering if there was any reality in which I could survive being here. Being without them.

London was the vortex it had always been. My first crush. It lured with its history and glamour. Its decay and growth. In my ulcerative state of being, it was perfect. A way to immerse and disappear. It took me a month to be able to cloak myself. Well, my ears only. Every other semblance of my gifts was gone. Every link I had to my true self. To my mates and family. Gone. All I had was a gold thread. I was drinking and not sleeping. Going out and meeting men, leading them on until the last possible minute, then leaving. Never intending to so much as let any of them kiss me. I was cruel and promiscuous. It took one final night of stupid amounts of alcohol and too much flirting and innuendos. I led one man on too much, and he followed me home, pushing me into my flat. As he laid his hand into the door and shoved me backwards, I took it. For the slightest of pauses, I stood there waiting for it. I had brought all this violence on myself, hadn't I?

Then, in my head I heard Reynard's voice saying I was no one's prey, and Corra's voice telling me I was a hellcat like her. All it took was a few well-placed moves and a flick of my small knife across his face and hands to have him backing off. I called 999 and had the man restrained while I waited on the police.

The next day, I left that flat in central London and moved out to Richmond. Living a putrefying existence such as I had been was not helping, not sustainable. Once I settled, I opened my trade accounts back up and jumped back into the market as my funds would run out sooner or later. With my first big paycheck, I got a tattoo matching Silas' just under the gold thread. As promised, I added a beastly wing arcing over the top of the original arch, a single pine bough resting on one side. It embodied who we were to each other, a disastrous love. My mates and me.

CADEYRN HADN'T said anything about the tattoo since he found me. I waited for it. I wanted to hear something, but he hadn't said anything in regard to Silas either. As we crashed onto the hard floor of Kalíma's temple, I panicked.

"Is he okay?" I pleaded with Cadeyrn with my eyes. "Silas. You haven't said." He traced my face.

"He's fine. Working with Reynard and Cyrranus." Relief washed over me. We stood in the temple, looking around. I pulled a tiger's eye stone from my pocket and left it with a thanks to the Goddess. We emerged from the temple to a small crowd of horned and hairy warriors with their imposing female leader at the center. Every single one of them had shock on their face—from their pointed ears to their dark, glowing eyes. Ainsley held her broad sword aloft and knelt on the leafy ground, immediately followed by all of her compatriots. Cadeyrn and I looked at one another in confusion.

The hall was bustling with chatter and ale. We wanted to get home. To get somewhere. We were told that the Goddess had never appeared there before and to have both gone and crossed back across realms was a benediction. We were revered and waited upon, and all we wanted to do was leave. Cadeyrn explained to Ainsley that we were in need of horses and it was pertinent that we get back to Bistaír.

I wasn't aware that's where we were going, I said to him. *I have never been.*

He paused.

Sorry. Didn't think that far to tell you. I'm not running at full force right now. Is that okay with you? It had been only two days since he found me. Ten since he left here and scrounged for work and food in France. I threaded my fingers through his.

Of course.

Ainsley finally let us go with repealing her bid for the dissolution of the monarchy. We rode off at a clip and began to slow by nightfall. I had been gone a year. There were babies and politics, likely lovers, and changed dynamics. My breathing sped up, heart rate following suit.

"What's wrong?" Cadeyrn asked, coming closer to me as we rode.

I wasn't entirely sure how to express my concerns without sounding like I was afraid of being kicked out of the junior high lunch table. Except that was not dissimilar to how I felt. What if they didn't want me back? Not really. Surely it was easier without me. Less complicated. I should think the memory of me would be better than the reality. It was still unbelievable that I was able to sleep beside him again. Curling my legs and body into his delicious warmth when we made camp, I closed my eyes. He traced the tattoo as I started to fall asleep.

Do you like it? I asked. I heard him swallow. *All I had left of us was the gold thread. I was afraid, every day, that it would disappear one day. So, I had this done. It's all of us.*

It's beautiful. You're...so beautiful.

I kissed his shoulder and allowed myself to fall asleep with our gifts intermingling between us.

I COULD feel Bistaír as we neared. The pull of a place that held the memory of my parents. Held the imprint of my brother. Nerves fired in me, tumbling my stomach in a washer of fear. Outright fear of seeing everyone. Oh, God. Before we reached the cypress-lined drive leading into the estate, my brother was there, wild-eyed and reaching for the reins. I slid from the horse and embraced him. Pictures in his mind. I saw pictures. As though he were too overcome with emotion to speak to me. In the pictures, I saw the children. Corra. Cadeyrn had the horses and walked alongside us as my brother led me up the drive to the house. Ewan called for Corra. She popped round the wall to the foyer and clutched a baby closer to her than might, perhaps, be comfortable for the poor thing. I covered my mouth and smiled, reaching for her.

"By the gods, Ama! Take the children. Cannot force them on Neysa straight away. It's uncouth!"

Ama came in, shocked, and took the child from Corra.

"Come, darling. Thank the gods you're still you. And Cadeyrn. I thought I'd lost you both." To my eternal surprise, tears rolled down her face. She swatted herself and stood straighter, grabbing me and smacking my cheeks with kisses.

From the top of the grand staircase, Saski's face appeared, and I knew. I knew she and Silas had been together. She greeted me politely, but fear was rolling off her. My eyes must have been darting around, because Corra told me Silas was in Craghen with Reynard and Cyrranus. My heart sunk a little. I needed to see him too. But I was here and could wait. We sat in the drawing room, Corra insisting I did not have to see the babies yet.

"Don't be stupid, Corra." I held my hands out to Ama, who obliged and placed a squirming child in my arms. She looked at me like I was glowing and grabbed at my hair. I held her little fingers and saw Cadeyrn lift a sleeping child from his cradle. Until this moment I could never have imagined him with a baby. Yet, in this moment, I couldn't imagine why I hadn't. I leaned into the milk warm scent of the one I held and kissed her. Tears fell freely, and she wiggled and babbled.

"I don't know their names," I whispered, ashamed. Ewan walked over.

"This young lass is Efa." He touched her nose, and she giggled. "And this one," he said, tickling the foot flopping in my mate's arms, "is Pim." Pim picked at his uncle's face, and Cadeyrn bent to blow a raspberry on the boy's cheek.

"I had a vision. The only one. The day you came to me, Cadeyrn. I was shopping. I saw their faces. I saw them and I knew they were okay. I thought...that it was a gift. To have seen them. Know that they were safe."

Feeling the solid weight of the child in my arms, I thought it might just be the most wonderful feeling in the world.

OUTSIDE, ON the edge of the kitchen garden, I sat marveling at the property, and just being back in Aoifsing. Feeling like the shell I had been was gradually filling back up. I knew I shouldn't bother Silas, but I had been gone a year, and that entitled me to a few annoyances. Although the last time I'd felt entitled to such, our reunion wasn't so pleasant.

You're probably going to say something along the lines of, "Holy fucking hell." I hope you don't hate me, and I know you're busy, but when you have a moment, it would be nice to see you. I left it at that. I didn't want to rush him. I was here. I was content to be here, breathing in the air I never knew was so different. Early evening breezes blew, balmy and calm. Things snuffled around in the garden. I walked in to look. To see what grew here when what was inside of me had weathered away systematically while I was gone. Potato vines climbed, and tomatoes grew over a trellis heavy with fruit. Late summer berries and aubergines all filled the space. The palm-sized velvet leaves rustled in the increasing night breeze.

"Nice?" Silas asked, a smirk in his voice. I moved so fast, I tripped on a cluster of courgette vines. "Just nice to see me? I did not say what you said I would. Mine was far more colourful."

I literally ran and jumped on him, sobbing. Not the silent tears that fell when I saw everyone else. Deep, embarrassing, sobs.

"So snotty, *Trubaíste.* Good to know some things never change." He held me against him, his face in my neck and hair. Moments we stood, creating a cage of arms around each other.

"You're okay?" I pulled back, looking my fill, patting his arms and shoulders. He laughed, then grabbed at my arm.

"This is new." He barked a laugh and brushed his thumb over the tattoo. "I like the additions." Then I let it all out. I told him about London and the would-be rapist, Reynard's voice in my head, my drinking and being awful. Finally, getting away from it and trying to settle. About Dean and Tilly and thinking

I was in a collision course with letting go. I hadn't told Cadeyrn yet. As though I hadn't wanted to spoil being together. I was ashamed at my behaviour in London. Silas just sat me on his lap, holding my hands while I told him.

"There is nothing at all to be ashamed about." He grabbed my chin. "Nothing."

"There is. I was...a different person, Silas. Horrible. I got kicked out of training gyms! I was leading men on and walking away just because I could. Who does that?"

He looked skyward and shrugged.

"I couldn't feel anything of myself."

"And now?"

"It's like I was a shell and being back here...Being with you lot, with my own gifts...The shell is filling back up."

"You haven't told him? Any of it?"

I shook my head, and he took a deep breath, pressing his forehead to mine.

"You should. Tonight. Don't wait. You don't want your shell to fill then you crack like a splattered egg."

I pinched him. He kissed me once. A brush of lips against mine.

"I am very glad you're home." Home. Yes, I was home.

"You've been with Saski," I said. I couldn't judge. "I understand."

"I thought you might."

I rested my head on his shoulder. Footsteps sounded, and I knew from his scent that it was Cadeyrn.

"I can go if you need..." he said to us, at a bit of a loss. I held my hand out to him and smiled, standing. Silas smiled as well, then wrapped Cadeyrn in a bear hug, pounding on his back. They stood like that for a minute or so. I didn't know what had happened while I was gone, or even before that, as things had been different between them. But it seemed that here, now, it was mending. Because they were the most beautiful males, because they were mine, because I needed them, and just because I could, I ducked under one of their arms and included myself in the embrace, pulling them both in as tight as I could possibly get.

"Reynard should be here for this," Cadeyrn said, and I laughed because it didn't seem like something he would say.

"Ah, about our friend," Silas said, pulling away, though I refused to let him go just yet. "Och, I love you too, *allaíne Trubaíste*," he said, kissing my head. "But we do have a problem. Let's go in so I can tell everyone at once." I groaned but let him go.

NO ONE dared speak as Silas told us what he and Cyrranus had been dealing with the past week. We were all in a state of shock. I was in no shape to go after him yet but offered immediately as Reynard was my friend. What was more, it was his voice that had me fighting back in London. Silas had hawks to his wraiths all over Aoifsing. We sent a hawk to Ainsley, letting her know of the situation. I sat, breathing slowly, holding both Silas and Cadeyrn's hands, not wanting to let them go. Wanting to rage at Reynard being in his father's hands. I stood and asked quietly where I would be sleeping. Another home that wasn't mine. Everyone looked at one another.

To Cadeyrn, I asked where I would be sleeping. Everyone looked at each other, causing my fingers to tingle, my stomach to slosh.

"Let's get a fresh room made up for you," Corraidhín said. Cadeyrn's eyes met mine, and I didn't understand the look. "That way you two can start over with your own space."

I followed her up, a housekeeper joining us. Corra stood with me in the bedroom that was being fluffed and readied. The room had two large bay windows, a tufted seat beneath each. In the center of the room was a canopied dark wood bed, covered in layers of white linens. The housekeeper left to run a bath for me, and I slumped into a settee.

"He's quieter," I said to Corra. "Should I worry?"

"He was fading, Neysa," she said quickly, kneeling before me. I sat up.

"I thought he was getting better. Then Ewan told us. Silas and I didn't realize. I think he was giving up. Then they saw a vision of you and then they left. So, yes. He's quieter. For now. He'll be back to normal, I'm sure." She left the room, and I undressed for my bath, pondering what she had said. We had both started to fade, then. I came out of the bath in my cashmere dressing gown. It was too warm for the balmy night, but it was all I had with me. Once again, a vagabond with no clothing. My husband was sitting on the settee, wine in hand, in fresh clothes and damp hair. He must have bathed in his previous chamber. I sat next to him and couldn't resist leaning over for a kiss.

"I have to tell you something." Then I began the horrid details I had given to Silas. After I finished, he set his wine down and took my face in his hands, pressing his cheek to mine, much like that first time I let him in to my visions and memories so long ago. I held on like letting go would have me adrift forever.

"I have a question." He looked at me with those aquamarine eyes aflame. "Did you ever get Tom tickets?"

I pushed him back and laid on top of him, relishing that lazy smile and the smokiness in his eyes.

"Quite good ones. Cost me a bomb. Plus the case of wine."

"Do you need to talk to anyone? About anything?"

"I'm okay talking to you."

"I want to start over. I want us to have a home. Not somewhere I have lived, or we get stuck. A proper home, where your clothes are. And the dogs. I just want to start over with you."

"I love Saarlaiche. I would be happy there. Make that our home."

He looked as though he were wrestling with whether to say something. In the end, he put his hands into my hair and pulled my face in to his.

CHAPTER 49

Neysa

The clues were mostly a mother's plea for her son. None of us knew how to take them. Francois never seemed less than frigid with her son, and she had let him suffer for so many years. Centuries, even. The main question I had was, could we trust her? Were they pleas for us to find her or her son, or were they a horrid manipulation of Reynard's complicated feelings for his mother?

"It is for time he will exchange my heart." I read it out loud to the room.

Silas and Corra were staring at me, which had me twitchy.

"Yes?" I asked. Everyone in the room turned to me.

"Weeell, it's just that you figured out the note from Cadeyrn here. We thought you might have some insight on this one," Silas said with a clap on my back.

I groaned, but Cadeyrn snickered.

Don't laugh, I told him. *I still have nightmares about all that nonsense.*

Apologies. I thought you needed a project. His answer barely controlled the amusement underneath.

Yes, because I didn't have one already.

I'll give you a project later. He laughed into my neck, wrapping his arms around me.

I reached for the notes and touched the one Silas was holding. Our gifts intermingled, playing and zapping at each other, and then I was thrust into a vision.

Spinning arrows. Time counting down. Pale eyes being covered with a blindfold. Francois holding Reynard's hand as he bled in a wagon. Cyrranus walking into a room with at least twenty guards, preparing to fight.

"We have to get to Cyrranus," I blurted. "He won't hold out against all of them. Something keeps blocking his magic." They were all looking at me for more information. I grabbed both Cadeyrn's and Silas' hands and projected the vision to them. They swore.

"Etienne wants the clock." Yeah, not a chance. I turned to Silas, a question in my eyes. "I sent it with Ludek. He seemed the most able to get rid of it. It's in Heilig with him."

"I'll go back." Saski spoke up for the first time. "I'll make sure he knows it's being hunted. I suppose it's time for me to go."

She was looking at Silas. He was staring at the notes, pointedly not looking at her.

Silas, I said to him mind to mind. *Say something to her.*

He exhaled slowly.

"You're ready then?" he asked, not quite meeting her eyes. She just watched him curiously.

"I've been here long enough." She left the room, and we heard her go upstairs. Silas muttered about getting ready to go after Cyrranus.

BISTAÍR WAS my family's home. This place—more than a manor, not quite a palace—was similar, I thought, to Hever Castle in Kent. Corra and Ewan seemed to be happy here. White-washed plaster walls and large bay windows made it so that the place was always shining and bright. A lovely place for the babies to grow up. A library covered the third floor, and I walked the packed bookshelves. From the window I could have sworn I saw movement in the trees, but it faded as soon as I focused. Being back here, all my senses were on overdrive. The basic ones like sight and scent had me spinning. Perhaps it was the light playing as the sun dappled through the branches. Stacks of books sat on a desk in the corner. All magical texts. I touched them and saw Ewan pouring over them, most likely when I was in Heilig. A year. Nearly a full year passed since that day in Festaera. Before that, it hadn't been so long since I died. What an absolute mess. Pulling a book on time and another on goddesses of the realm, I claimed a seat nearest the window.

For time he will exchange my heart.

We all knew what Etienne wanted. However, what he planned to do with the blasted clock was beyond me. We needed to get to Cyrranus and not let him enter that trap. I wasn't ready, and if I were honest, I was terrified of Cadeyrn going, but we owed it to Reynard.

"From chaos we make haste, thus erring in the thread that we pull from the tapestry of time itself..." I read. Then reread. Holy burning hell. Dean said nearly the exact same thing. "It is from discord that we choose a path which follows simplicity in its linear progression. One might halt, digressing in his escape from upheaval, to make the decision to move away from the linear segmentation of his existence. It should be noted that once a linear cord is in motion, it is predisposed to stay in motion along that linear progression. However, time itself does not move in and of a singular dimension. It adheres to no realm or rule. We observe time and events differently from our particular standpoints. We are but moving timepieces, altering the shape and furtherance of our development. Who is to say that we have no mechanics intrinsic to our being, to alter the threads we choose? Time itself is relative."

Magic, physics, philosophy, and a bloody great headache all wrapped up in one maddening ancient fae text. There. Out past the trees. There was motion. It was a man, stumbling. I stood and looked out and he was gone. Head throbbing, I turned back to the text but found my head pounding even more. The room felt stuffier, and I tried to angle my head away from the sunlight. What catalyst pushed me to attend Dean's lecture that day in Oxford? Even though the topic of discussion wasn't exactly what had been disclosed. He had even received an official reprimand from his employer for the deviation. My eyes popped open, sending a searing pain through my head. I ran from the library, looking for a toilet. Shit. I didn't know the layout of the place. I began flinging doors open, trying to push the nausea away. Out of options, I hurdled for the window at the end of the hall, swung the latch out and vomited from the third-floor window. God, I hoped no one was under me.

"*Trubaíste?*" Silas asked from behind me. He came to stand next to me, a hand at my back. I vomited again, the pain in my head lancing. His hand steadied me. I pulled a handkerchief from my pocket and wiped my mouth.

"Your head?"

Yes.

I was afraid if I spoke out loud, the pain would worsen. He steered me away from the window and down the hall. I noticed he was dressed to leave, swords strapped and weapons all visible, but he brought me to a room and sat me on a bed. I laid back, and he brought a cool cloth for my forehead, then laid beside me, a hand over my heart. Cool power flowed into me, coiling and nudging at mine. I let go, allowing it to intertwine with my power. Already the pain was lessening. I looked at him.

"Where are you going?"

He brought his face to mine, close enough to kiss if he dared. "To find Cyrranus."

Oh, no, you aren't. Not without me. His power trailed through me, lighting my veins and filling my empty shell. I turned to him and wrapped my limbs around him, getting frustrated at all the weaponry to get around. We were glowing in an ombre of light and dark. Distantly, I registered his breathing being ragged and strained, and I clutched him closer. Energy shot from us both, and we arched off the bed together. The pain ebbed away like a retreating tide.

"There is a dagger digging into my groin," I said after a time. He huffed and murmured that it might not be a dagger, and I pinched him, which did no good because he was covered in fighting leathers.

"Were you in pain like this while you were away?" he asked quietly.

"No. I felt nothing. Just hollow. I would have relished the pain if it meant...I was connected to you." He squeezed my hands. "It doesn't smell like her in here."

"I never brought her in my room." Yet I was here. "Before I head out." He got up and pulled papers and ledgers from a drawer and sat next to me with them.

"First of all, you aren't going without me. I owe it to Reynard."

He nodded, not insulting me by insisting I stay.

"I have a present for you." He ran a hand through his hair. "It's probably a stupid present. Like the damned Christmas tree, but still."

I smiled at him and kissed his cheek. He laid a palm on the papers and pointed to them. I looked down and recognized the blueprints for the grinders for the araíran-aoír nuts. On the sheets and ledgers were listings for manufacturing of thousands of the machines, a warehouse to house them, and purchases for the machines from both private residents and provincial officials. He even sent one back with Arik. I covered my mouth with my hand.

"I couldn't put a ring on your finger, or give you anything really special, but this seemed important to do. Because I thought I'd never see you again. You were still a living thing in me, and I needed to have that thing represented, aye?" I just gaped at him, tears spilling over. "Now that you are back..." His voice stuttered, and he took a breath. "It's all yours. The plans are in your name. You can do with them what you want."

I looked them over and saw how it brought more jobs to the people. More revenue to the province. Words failed me completely. I stared at him, feeling that thread we wore on our arms pulsing between us. A living thing indeed.

"Know that if I could have...If things were different...I would have given you a ring. Because there has been no one who has ruined me so thoroughly as you, and I wouldn't trade that ruination for a thousand years of peace."

"I want so much to kiss you until you can't see straight, but I was just throwing up and I'm so gross."

He roared a laugh, pulling me in for an embrace instead, and kissed my cheeks.

"Thank you, Silas."

Once the crushing pain had subsided, I remembered that I needed to speak to everyone regarding that antiquated text. We left the room hand in hand, and I ducked into my chamber to freshen up before meeting them downstairs.

CORRA WAS staying on with the babies, which made her testy and bitter. We all met in the sitting room downstairs. The late summer heat had me plucking at my shirt, not looking forward to being in leathers. Explaining the text I'd found and the discussion I had multiple times with my human friend, I elaborated on the parts I thought had been relevant to my finding a way home—or at least a way back to Cadeyrn.

"It doesn't entirely make sense to me," Cadeyrn began, his voice haughty and cool. "You say that you aren't speaking of time travel, yet this pulling of a different thread seems to do just that. What is it that Dean knew that relates to this realm and to the issue at hand?"

I leveled a stare at him, wondering why the frostiness, but Ewan spoke up.

"Starting from the point of the linear progression, the author speaks of an event that occurs, causing the forward progress to be on a roll, so to speak—"

"Oh! That is the first law of physics," Corra said. "Like the meteorite documentary I watched. An object set in motion stays in motion unless an outside force steps in to stop it. Like a meteor hitting a planet."

Ewan smiled at her and bent over to kiss her so thoroughly we all looked away and at each other. She was right, though. It was the same for an object at rest. I said the same, stating that if a thread hadn't been chosen, or there was a suspension in the weaving in the tapestry, things would be stagnant.

"It doesn't make sense," Cadeyrn spoke up, reiterating his previous sentiment. "So what you are saying is that a suspension in a decision can alter the progression of reality? Then how would we all not be living in separate continuums?"

I said that in essence we were, and he pinched his nose in annoyance. My own head was spinning, but thankfully the headache was gone, thanks to Silas.

"Two or more events that occur simultaneously for one of us, may not be simultaneous for another if we are in a different progression or chose a different layer within the continuum."

Everyone groaned. I stopped speaking for a moment, honestly thinking I might just go run and leave them to it for a while. But Reynard and Cyrranus needed us. So, I walked to a pitcher of cool water on a pedestal table and poured a glass, nearly moaning at the feeling of the liquid in my throat. Cadeyrn's eyes were on me, and I met his stare, feeling bare. For a moment, I stood sorting out how to explain what I was thinking, almost wishing Dean were here to help me out.

"The clock," Cadeyrn said after a time. "That's what you're getting at." I nodded. "We all felt different pressure within the headway we had to make. The countdown was different for all of us. I thought it was just an aulde spell. You're saying differently?"

"I'm sure it was an aulde spell, as the reality of it couldn't be perennial without magic. Which is why it works here. It is a harbinger of options for our own tapestries. A relic of both realms as it functions on both human physics within the space-time continuum and the magic here. A bridge of sorts. Hence the GMT on the chronograph. We all saw the same time as it was in the human realm. Or at least where I came through."

"That's why it seemed to be moving," Ewan noted. "It looked fluid."

"It was moving," Cadeyrn said, paling. "It only stopped once we all chose a thread." He looked like he was going to be sick. I felt much the same. "We chose the events that came to pass. In a normal circumstance, things would have played out as the events dictated. When we brought the damned clock in, it became its own—"

"Gravitational force," I said, looking directly at him.

We let the clock be its own dimension, making us all work independent of one another. I had seen the Veil. Cadeyrn saw his pushing me through the Veil. Ewan seemed to think he saw himself not returning. I turned to Silas.

What was your countdown? What did you feel? I asked him.

"Nothing at all," he answered, face slightly green. "Just nothing." He walked outside, barely making it from the room before dissolving.

There was silence amongst us. I noted Saski's absence and realized she must have left as there was no feeling of her in the house. She was in love with Silas. I could sense it. The four of us in the room were looking in different directions, trying to figure out how to process the information. I walked to Cadeyrn and took his hand. His clenched in mine, face looking out the window.

Together, remember?

Neysa, what we are saying is with that damned clock, we chose what happened. I chose to push you through. Because of what you saw, it was a Veil. But I chose to send you there. How do we get past that?

I turned him to me, holding on with both hands.

You made a decision based on slivers of information. What you chose to do was push me away from Kíra. You chose to see me while I was away. You chose to find me. Look at me. His eyes shifted but settled on mine. Gods those eyes. I had missed them. I put my hand on his cheek and lifted on my toes to kiss him. *We always choose each other. I chose you. I will always choose us.*

Scuffling and a door thrown open pulled us out of our little bubble. Silas entered and tossed a heap of a male onto the rug in front of Ewan.

"Found this wandering the woods, Majesty," Silas said in a growl. My eyes nearly popped out of my head as I dove for the heap. "I take it you know the human, *Trubaíste?*"

Holy shit. Semi-conscious, laying there, he looked like a man who had been singing through a beating. Blood ran from his nose and mouth, but his lips puckered in a lopsided grin. He adjusted his glasses.

"Halloo, pet."

CHAPTER 50

Neysa

Dean's eyes looked to Cadeyrn, who was visibly counting breaths.

"Really, it's uncanny how well you described them all."

"Neysa?" Ewan asked.

Helping Dean to his feet, I stood, an arm around his waist, which was marked by both my mates.

"Oh, please you two. Take the threatening male vibe down a few notches," I said to them.

Silas came to stand in front of us and made a show of bending over into Dean's face. A slow, devious smile spread across his stubbled face.

"He has that boyish charm, *Trubaíste*," Silas said, sniffing from Dean's shoulder to his neck. The boyish charmer stiffened at the fae warrior so close to his throat. He heard my stories of Silas and Cadeyrn and what they were capable of. Especially when it came to me. I rolled my eyes at Silas.

"He does, doesn't he? And you are being a pig. You can admire him from the other side of the room. Now, before *I* start threatening you. Dean. What the hell are you doing here?"

Could he cross? Was he going to get sick? Cadeyrn moved to my side with the speed and grace of a wraith and looped an arm around me.

You. Don't forget that you only found me because of Dean. So don't be a pisshead now.

I would have found you. It may have taken longer, but I would have found you. His thumb swept over my lip.

"Was that just a conversation?" Dean asked. I raised an eyebrow at him. "Okay. So, I kept thinking about the threads. Your yarn ball drawing, and the different realms, and that clock you mentioned. They kept nagging me. Then the Goddess. I wanted to see how it all really connected."

"Funny, we were just putting all this together ourselves," Corra said, circling Dean. He looked even more unsettled than he had with Silas. I smothered a laugh and felt Cadeyrn rumble a bit behind me.

"I followed you. When you lot crossed. I know. I'm a complete nutter for doing so. I didn't really think. I just went through once you had opened it."

"You didn't come out when we did—or where we did."

"I came out in a field. It was on the edge of a seaside village not too far from here. Landed right on my face. I walked into town and asked where I was. Dropped a few of your names."

"Someone just told you to come here?" Cadeyrn asked, deathly quiet. Ewan folded his arms over his chest.

"I was held in a storeroom for a...clothing shop, perhaps? Someone called Arneau told me and said to give you his regards. He told me how to get here."

Ewan swore. Silas snarled, the sound making Dean jump. Silas dispatched a hawk to Craghen to track down Arneau. He had to be within a day and half's ride from there.

I moved to the shelves near Corra and opened a bottle of wine. I didn't care that it was early afternoon. Once I poured my own, everyone else came to join in. Dean stood awkwardly until Ewan waved to him to help himself. On the light caramel leather sofa, I pulled my feet under me and sipped at my wine, my knees pressed against Cadeyrn. He angled his head so that it tucked over my own, and our sides fit together. A sigh escaped me, answered by my husband's free hand covering my knee and stroking the underside through my leggings. Ewan asked Dean to continue why he was here.

"That clock. I know, Neysa, you didn't know what became of it whilst you were with me," he began.

There was a snap of electricity in the room, and a flash of heat. I didn't really blame them on this one. Dean was too bright a guy to not have realized what he said. The implication of it—however innocent the reality was.

"I think it needs to be destroyed. Or somehow dismantled. I think it is an object in constant motion, making the choices you make irrelevant."

We all sat drinking. Dean wasn't used to the stillness we could all adapt, so he was shifting foot to foot. Ewan asked him to explain further.

"When I first met Neysa in Oxford, she asked whether it would be possible to back track on a thread within the layers of time."

Next to me, Cadeyrn inhaled sharply.

"Yes, and he made fun of me for wanting to regain unrequited love."

Silas snorted at me and patted my shoulder, leaving his hand there. I shot Corra a look as if to say, "What is with these males?" She gave me a shit-eating grin back.

"Sorry, pet. Well, I wasn't totally off though." He winked. "It did get me thinking. From her questions to what she described in the events that led to her being pushed through the Veil."

The pusher himself on my right went rigid. I smoothed a hand down his leg to calm him.

"It seemed like while the clock led you to the vessels—is that what you called them?—it had begun a systematic configuration of a separate time dimension."

"Fucking hell, man. Are you saying we are in a separate dimension? That everything that has happened, hasn't really happened?" Silas asked. I was wondering the same.

"Not really, no." We all exhaled audibly, making us chuckle. Dean pushed his glasses up and ran a hand through his hair. He was filthy and looked exhausted. We hadn't even offered him the toilet, for God's sake. "I think that because the clock is its own gravitational force, and it is always in a state of motion, teetering on the edge of both realms, instead of there being a tightly woven tapestry from which to pull threads, it's like a sieve or a screen."

"Our decisions transfer back and forth?" Ewan asked. "So, the clock, in its movement, causes time to be different for each of us. Our sense of urgency thus scripted by the differences we experience. Neysa has visions and sees glimpses of things, past and present. Because of her link to Cadeyrn, he can often see what she sees. However, due to the clock, what they saw, though perhaps the same exact images, caused an aberration in how they saw them?"

"Making us victims of our own selves?" I asked. Cadeyrn leaned forward and put his face in his hands.

"I think it can be weaponized," Dean announced.

"It helped us in finding the vessels," Silas stated.

"Maybe...it really didn't," I said. "Maybe, because I had seen it in my vision, we—I—assumed it would help us, so we used it. Perhaps my vision was a warning. It was leading us to the clock to get rid of it. Perhaps Etienne was already trying to claim it. It must have been spelled—"

"It has the same spell signature as the vessels," Cadeyrn said, looking at the floor. "I hadn't noticed it. It was all too much. Everything. Once we had the clock, I should have noticed it and put it all together, but I was distracted."

I got up, filled our glasses and sat for the moment. How could we dismantle the clock without reactivating it? Not to mention, it was all the way in bloody Heilig. All we had going for us was that Etienne didn't know where the clock was. Ama came in and showed Dean to a room for him to clean up. I disappeared into the kitchen and was shooed away by the cook, so I stood by the door waiting as he piled trays of cheeses and summer berries, a danafruit paste, nuts, oysters on ice, and iced white wine. Once the cook and I were laden with food, I called everyone in. Cadeyrn was outside.

"Her answer to everything is food," Corra said to Dean as we sat on the rug next to the coffee table.

"I noticed," he replied. I shrugged and squeezed lemon over my oyster, slurping it down. Corra was staring daggers at me. I finally met those daggers head on and asked point blank if there was something she wanted to know. Ewan pinched his nose the way Cadeyrn does.

She's wondering if you and Dean....

I know exactly what she's wondering.

He threw his hands up.

"Okay, for the record, busy bodies. Dean and I did not date. We never slept together, and there is nothing more to say."

"Well, we sort of dated," Dean dared, likely emboldened by the two very large fae males of mine being out of the room. I groaned and shot him a look.

"Excuse me, Dr. Preston, but I was quite clear about our friendship."

He laughed and said he was messing with me.

"Och oysters. Can't hack them," Silas said, coming into the room and picking up a nub of cheese. "What's got you pissed off, *Trubaiste*?" He handed me a deep red strawberry and sat behind me, legs on either side of mine.

Ewan began asking Dean questions about his life and such, saying how much he enjoyed Tilly's shop. Once they were speaking, Silas put his lips to my ear and used his hand to press my face closer.

"Cadeyrn has gone to intercept Saski. I think she wouldn't listen to me right now. He has a force following Cyrranus' tracks, and we will meet them on the road tomorrow. Not sure I trust your friend here, but if what he's saying is true..." I turned, pushing my face closer, angling away from Dean. I felt Silas' heartbeat against my back.

"We need to move quickly and come up with a fucking good plan." His fingers curled into my hair where he held my face.

Anything else, or do you just want to cuddle with me? I teased. He smiled against my ear and wrapped arms around me to reach for more food. I drank my wine and slurped more oysters. As the light dimmed in the window-bright room, most of the food had been cleared, the wine drunk, and Cadeyrn was not back. Corra and Ewan left to be with the babies, as they had been away from them most of the day. I was wine addled, still lounging against Silas. As I brushed my fingers against the oyster shells, pictures formed in my mind of the ocean floor, the sway of seaweed and tides pulling back and forth. Reaching up, I touched Silas' face and showed him what I saw. His lungs filled, and I felt him smile before kissing my head. Opening my eyes, I saw Dean looking at us. He blinked slowly and gave me a small, lopsided smile as if to say he understood now. Reaching out with my gifts, I sent the images from the ocean to Cadeyrn. I felt a relieved, soft amusement come through.

One of the servants came in and began lighting sconces, washing the room and all of us in a warm glow. Before the last sconce was lit, I tapped into my gifts, willing a glow of white light to come out and darkness to glitter from my feet. Dean's eyes went wide. Finally. Finally, I could use my magic. Release that built-up pressure. Silas reached out like we had done on the street in Laichmonde; we created a cyclone of light, dark, mist, and electricity.

"She's showing off for your benefit, lad," Silas said to Dean.

I snapped my teeth at him playfully. Dean reached out tentatively. Silas pulled back, and I offered my magic to Dean, caressing him. He looked like fingers ran down his arm. Silas chuckled. One sconce above a desk in the corner illuminated a stack of books and ledgers. I tried to stand to walk to it, but Silas growled softly, holding onto me.

"I'll get it. Which one?"

"The top three." He waved his hand, and the books appeared before me. I turned, stunned. He shrugged. They were provincial ledgers and trade agreements. Silas said he had brought them back from his meeting with Cyrranus and Alan. While I waited for Cadeyrn to come back, Dean excused himself to go to his chamber, and I sat with Silas flicking through the ledgers.

"Is he full of shite?" Silas asked after a time. I didn't think so and said as much. Dean couldn't let things go. It was his personality and nature. Following us because he had to offer us his theory fit in his method of operations.

"Do you remember when we were looking for clues in the library at your mum's?" Silas asked. I did and nodded. "I know you always say that I pick you up...and I said some horrible, fucking horrible"—he scrubbed his face— "things to you back after Heilig. But you picked me up that night. It was a complete clusterfuck what happened after with Cadeyrn, but...yeah."

Closing my eyes, I leaned back against him.

"Are you in love with Saski?" A whoosh of air as he stroked my hair.

"Maybe? I like her. I do. I really do."

"Maybe...that's worth exploring further?" I stroked his arm. "I mean, you were involved this whole time? A year?"

"Yeah, more or less. If you call involved just...you know." We threaded our fingers together. "Still, it was longer than I've ever stuck to one female."

A sharp pain lanced through me, and I doubled over. Silas asked if I was okay, and the pain happened again. Cadeyrn had been hit with something. He wasn't responding to me. Silas was pacing and snarling, saying he should track him, which I thought would take time away if he didn't find him and we needed Silas here. We faced off in the foyer of the receiving room, snarling in each other's faces, as the door banged open and Cadeyrn shouldered through, holding his side. Both of us turned to him, our teeth still bared.

"Gods, you two. Stop snarling," Corra called from behind us, Pim on her hip. Silas pulled his cousin to the sitting room. I unstrapped his weapons and opened his jacket. Pim was squawking in Corra's arms, wiggling to get out. I pressed my hands against a stab wound in my mate's side, meeting his eyes.

"It's healing, but the blade was rusty, so I'll have to clean it out before it closes."

I wanted to scream and throw things. Ama came in and waved at us all to move away. We followed them to our bedroom, where Ama had Cadeyrn lay down. She wiped at the wounds—there were two— and used a scalpel-like knife to open the wound where it had healed.

"Stop fussing, you lot. I'm fine." I saw his lip was a bit swollen as well. I leaned down, touched it, and he winced. Yep, definitely a bruise.

You're actually pissed off at me? I just glared back. He rolled his eyes and stared at the ceiling while Ama dug out bits of rusted metal.

"Saski is fine." He looked to Silas, who nodded curtly. "Alan is dead."

"Fucking hell," Ewan swore. I didn't think I've ever heard him swear that much. I felt like a sailor in comparison. "Who?"

"Arneau's henchmen. They cornered me in Alan's house. I stopped to check in after seeing Saski. I knew something was wrong and perhaps I shouldn't have gone in." He hissed as Ama dragged a long shard from his side. I grabbed his hand. "I smelled blood. I found Alan in his toilet chamber, throat cut. They pushed me in then. There were five of them. One was able to cut off my air supply, so I wasn't fighting well."

The healer took a long thin spoon-like utensil and began scraping the shallow bits of the wound. His face was calm, but I could tell by the set of his mouth that the pain was considerable. Ama gave him the all-clear to let his gift take over and motioned for me to step closer to him. I laid beside him on the bed and let my mind and magic open up to him. Let that same unspooling as I had done with Silas, that healed my headache and released my tension, flow into Cadeyrn. The others left the room. Watching the wound stitch itself back together was mesmerizing.

I can't lose you. I just can't. His answering squeeze on my hand didn't reassure me. "I'm serious. Don't go off like that." He was falling asleep, but his lips twitched upward. I gave a mighty humph and placed my hand over his wound.

EWAN WAS in his study when I slipped out of my bedroom in the middle of the night. I'd been thinking of how we could curtail the escalating violence. As I approached my brother, he was looking at Alan's ledgers. The same ones I'd perused earlier.

"A trade embargo," I said. He looked up with red rimmed eyes. Between the situations he had been dealing with, the babies, and me, I was sure his sleep was minimal. "You should impose an embargo on all trade from any of Etienne's holdings. Even seize whatever assets he has in a bank—I don't know how it works here."

He turned a paper to me, written in his hand, of all representatives in Aoifsing and Heilig. It declared trade with Etienne and Arneau an act of war. Any holdings either of them had in another province would be seized and trade with Festaera heavily sanctioned. I sunk into a chair, too exhausted to stand anymore. At least we were on the same page. Earlier he sent another letter, which turned out to be a disclosure to Ainsley Mads requesting her support in the embargo. As she operated as a sovereign province, it seemed in bad faith to declare sanctions and embargoes without consulting her.

Etienne's operations included aphrim skin clothing and wagon coverings and aphrim themselves, which should have been noted as a red flag much earlier as it was, in essence, a militia, or, at the very least, a weapon. He and Arneau jointly manufactured weaponry from Festaeran steel. In closing off trade, no one would purchase from him, and he could not purchase steel from Festaera. In fact, Sergo would now be required to pay heavy tax on exporting the steel. In an effort not to sink the entire province, fluid trade will be opened for Festaera's other resources. Like Prinaer, it had many mines, Festaera's being rich with granite, slate, and marble.

The goal, as my brother and I sat through that long night, was to ensure the self-sufficiency of every province while keeping trade open. Additionally, since our visit to Heilig and the eradication of Konstantín, Ewan and Arik had been in talks about trade agreements. The idea being that trade with Heilig would broaden the reach of each province's cash crop.

"Gods, you two." I struggled to open my eyes in the watery morning light coming in through the study window. I must have fallen asleep with my head against the bottom of the settee in Ewan's office. He was across from me, barely awake with his head tipped back against the polished wood of his desk. Ledgers and trade agreements were spread across the floor. The babies were in Corra's arms, trying to get down. Ewan reached for Pim, his eyes still closed. I sat up, rubbing my own eyes, not quite awake. Efa crawled to me, pushing her little hands on my thighs. I lifted her and brought her to my chest for a hug. She looked at me and put her head against my shoulder, her thumb in her mouth, and stilled. I closed my eyes again and leaned back, holding her. Images of me, of Ewan, of Cadeyrn making faces at her, swam into focus. Silas talking, waving his hands around in an animated story. It took me a sleepy minute, but I realized that my little niece was projecting to me what she saw. Or what made her happy. I tried to show her images as well. Ewan and me as children, my beastie snuggling Ewan, the dogs, the sea. We both must have fallen back to sleep sharing our thoughts, because the next thing I knew was Cadeyrn touching my shoulder. I blinked at him and saw the most beautiful smile across his face, lifting all the way to his eyes, where they shone in the morning light. He leaned in and kissed my cheek and the top of Efa's head on her mop of dark hair.

How are you feeling? I asked him. He lifted his shirt to show me the healed wounds, only a faint pink line where they had been.

Back to normal. Shall I take her so you can get some tea? I debated it. She seemed awake but still clung to me. Until she turned and saw her uncle and began scrambling for him. I laughed and passed her off with a kiss.

Oh, I found these. They tumbled from your satchel. I figured you might want them. He handed over the two bunnies. I held them out to Efa, asking her which she would like. Pim, who had crawled from Ewan to us, was pointing. I held them to him as well. I tried to hand him the pinkish one, but he was saying, "Uddah, uddah," making me giggle. So, I gave him the taupe, and Efa took the pinky, immediately shoving the bum end to her mouth.

As I stood amongst the mess Ewan and I had created last night, I sighed. First tea, then explanations.

CHAPTER 51

In Greek mythology, Achilles was sent by his father, Peleus, to train with the great centaur warrior, Chiron, in the foothills of Mount Pelion. Trudging though the northern part of Maesarra, en route to intercept Cyrranus, I felt like Achilles making his way through Thessaly to get to the cave of the famed Chiron. The landscape here was of rocky forest and unforgiving foliage. Plants looked close to juniper, cypress, and rosemary. The trek north started after breakfast and a rundown of what Ewan and I had managed to lay out the night before. With Etienne's assets tied up, we already had a foothold. Though it was around seven or eight at night, the golden hour of sunshine was only starting, indicating that nightfall was still a couple of hours off. Rocks and boulders became more plentiful, the tree thicket greater, as we climbed the rising elevation. Brambles had scratched my face and neck incessantly, making my mood sour with every footfall.

Ewan was pissed at me. I refused to let him come along. He tried pulling the king card, which I laughed at, and he stormed off. Perhaps I was barely up for the task, but there was no question as to my going, especially since Silas and Cadeyrn were suited up and ready. Corra, who had been slightly frosty with me after our initial reunion, privately thanked me for insisting he stay. However, walking out of that home with my brother stewing in anger with me and Corra less than friendly had me unsettled.

Five guards accompanied us. A company of twenty went ahead, a separate unit of spies fanning out in a large perimeter, and a host of twenty, a half day behind us. We had to move as swiftly and silently as possible, while covering our backs. And fronts, as it were. Lifting a conifer branch to duck under, I was whacked in the face by another, and swore colourfully before tripping over a rock. Cadeyrn caught my elbow just as my knees hit the ground, taking a bit of sting from the fall. Silas paused ahead and looked back with an "uh-oh" look on his face. He was wearing a third or fourth day of stubble, making his features darker, but I saw the look nonetheless. Cadeyrn came round the front of me where I knelt, holding my eye.

"Bloody hell," he said under his breath. I held up my hand in annoyance and waved him off, fumbling blindly through my pack for a handkerchief. "Don't be stupid. Let me see it."

"I'm fine. Keep going; I'll catch up." I pressed the cloth to my eye and saw it came away with blood and sap. Fabulous. He rolled his eyes, kneeling in front of me.

"Not in the mood to be patronized, so give me a second and I'll catch up."

He quirked his lips to the side and knit his dark brows together.

"What? I'm fine. Just go. I'm not a damsel in distress."

His mouth was twitching. My temper flared seeing it. I stood quickly and stomped off, only one eye working at the moment, which started to feel like I was in a strobe light from the sun dappling through the trees.

"I know you've been mountain man gym rat for a year, and maybe you think I've been sitting on my ass for a year, but I have been training. Not in this blasted man-eating forest, but don't treat me like a child." An amused cough sounded behind me.

"Your pyre," Silas muttered to him as I pushed past him and led them both. Cadeyrn chuckled. Boots caught up to me.

"Saski wanted aphrim skins like yours, by the way. She said they did your ass a great favour." I growled, glaring at him through one eye. One, because I didn't even want to think about her right then. I felt like her scent was everywhere. All over both of them. Two, because my aphrim skins died when I had. Three:

"So, is the implication that these leathers do no such favours, or that generally speaking, my ass is in need of such dispensations?" I bit out at him.

There was a very male silence since I knew there was no right answer to that. As I kept walking off, I kissed my fingers and touched them to my ass for good measure. Both males chuckled behind me. Okay, the sap was stinging. Nothing was improving my mood. Every stupid branch and thorn bush I stepped over lent itself to greater moodiness. I wouldn't admit that a year back in the human realm softened me. As I had suspected, after an hour or so, the sun dipped lower, crouching under clouds and slipping behind the mountain. We made camp near a cave mouth within. which Cadeyrn searched for any hiding beasts. Or fae.

"Chiron's cave indeed," I muttered, gnawing on some bread and cheese.

"Is it the time of night we start associating our woes with human mythology?" Cadeyrn asked, cleaning his blade. "Are we theorizing that we all have an Achilles' heel?"

I scoffed.

"That is below my pay grade," I sneered. Silas smirked, munching an apple. "Though true, I was more thinking of the presumption of men."

Both males raised an eyebrow at me, which would have been quite cute had I not been in a horrible disposition. Cadeyrn urged me to elaborate. The wry smile he gave me was like a warm arrow to my core, but I was too nettled to give in to my better nature.

"Achilles' mother, Thetis," I began, "and his father, Peleus, assured he trained with Chiron to be the legendary warrior it had been prophesied he would become."

"If memory serves," Cadeyrn drawled, interrupting me, "Peleus was rather self-serving, and Thetis a tad overbearing." I glowered at him, still pressing the cloth to my eye. "Thetis was impossible to be around, always in a fit, shifting this way and that, making trouble for people and gods alike." Oh, he was pressing his luck. "In fact, wasn't she always that little bit unhappy about having to have just Peleus after Zeus and his ilk had originally been courting her?"

The little shit was baiting me. Silas was smothering a laugh, and my temper was rising.

"Zeus and 'his ilk' rejected her because they couldn't handle the prophecy that her son would be stronger than his father. Typical male bullshit. I wouldn't have put up with it either if I were Thetis."

"As a sea nymph," he said. "She was likely used to having both men and gods at her disposal. To be stuck with just Peleus must have really vexed her." In the flickering firelight I could see him trying not to smile as my fingers crackled with energy.

"Watch yourself, brother," Silas warned.

"Who is to say she was stuck with just Peleus? He was mortal and she was a daughter of a god. She married him, yes," I said sweetly. "Mythology doesn't follow her story much past the Trojan War." He stiffened ever so slightly. "The reason Thetis chose Peleus was because he was told he would have to accept her many forms. So, he called her from the sea and held her."

I opened up my thoughts to both shit stirrers sitting with me and allowed images of how I pictured it going down with Thetis and Peleus.

"As he held her, she became water, slipping through him as he lay there, trying to grasp her." In my mental snap shots, she looked like Corra and Silas in their mist forms. "Then fire burst forth and still he held her flaming skin, accepting her wrathful nature."

Thetis' fiery manifestation recalled Cadeyrn, when he encapsulated the camp with his fire so that he could carry me to his tent after the spar with Bestía. Cadeyrn swallowed, looking at me, his hands stilling on the knife he had been cleaning.

"She became beast," I continued. "Snarling and turning hideous and unforgiving." It was not a stretch that my mind's eye produced a beast much like my *baethaache*. "Yet he held on, pulling her beast closer to his mortal body, wounding him even, until she became fluid once more, washing over Peleus with the salty kiss of the ocean and all its violence, serenity, and unpredictability. Once she became a beautiful nymph once more, he made love to her against the lap of the ocean, and they married."

Both males were looking a bit peaky.

"So, you see, she was quite thorough in choosing Peleus. Christian scholars like to suggest that she was subservient, and Peleus asserted his male dominance over her." I smirked, though I was quite sure it looked dumb because I was still one-eyed Neysa. "I should think it quite obvious that Thetis would never be tamed. She was her own beast. It was only a question of whether Peleus could handle it."

"Holy bleeding hell realm, *Trubaiste*. Now I need a cold bath." I laughed at Silas as he thumped over on his side, facing away from the fire. Cadeyrn's eyes were glued to me. He came over deliberately slow and forcefully turned me to him. Raising both eyebrows, he pulled the cloth from my eye. His nostrils flared as he brushed a thumb over my eye and moved it down my face. It tingled where he touched, all the minor scratches healing, the eye stinging less and less.

Perhaps we should see if Master Chiron is in his cave?

It would be rude, I answered truthfully, though I really, really wanted to go into that cave with him.

Ah.

Don't "Ah" me.

Hmmm. There will be payback, Neysa, he said with a whisper of mischief, brushing a kiss to my eyelid.

Quite sure. Looking forward to it. He got up to pick up his weapons and rearrange the sleeping area.

In my head to Silas I said, *I'm sure there will be payback on your end as well.*

A crackle of his power shot through me, alighting my own magic. Yeesh. Sensitive males.

MAESARRA WAS much larger than I'd anticipated. Ewan's intelligencers had spies who located Cyrranus in northern Maesarra and had spotted Etienne on the border of Veruni. Making our descent from the mountains, everyone was pissy. Silas seemed twitchy about Saski, Cadeyrn was acting pompous, and I wished I were alone with him to warm that frost. The guards with us tried to keep it in check, whereas the three of us made no such effort. My knee was killing me. I twisted it in a throw at the second training gym I went to in England. It had never been the same, but I ignored it most of the time. Until hiking for hundreds of miles. Downhill. With weapons.

Silas was scratching at his face, complaining of the heat, though the temperature dropped the further north we came. Cadeyrn commented that perhaps the scruffy beard wasn't working for him. His cousin got in his face and said he didn't feel like making the effort to shave on a rescue mission. So it went for the entire next day. And night. Waking that third morning, my knee was so stiff I could barely stand from my bedroll. The males were off taking care of their own business, our guards already waiting as I sat, acting like a damned princess. Which I was, but still. Finally, I stood and yelped with the pain, my leg wobbling. Crap.

I didn't want to make a fuss, but I pulled my husband to the side and asked him to look at my knee.

"I can't seem to activate the quadricep muscles," I said. Behind a tree where there was a bit more privacy, he told me to take down my trousers. I did, holding on to his shoulder for support as he knelt before me, feeling the knee and surrounding muscle. His fingers felt upwards into the wobbly quadriceps and stopped just above the kneecap.

"There," he mumbled, his gift seeping in. My gift responded, braiding itself with Cadeyrn's. He looked up, confused, and I shrugged. White light shone around us as he prodded the knee and muscles.

"There's a detachment in one of the quadriceps, and there is fluid under the kneecap. When did it happen?" He stayed kneeling, his hands wrapped around my leg.

"Maybe six months ago?" He choked, asking why I hadn't said anything earlier. I waved my hand. "I got used to it."

He was taking longer than usual to heal the knee, and I wondered if he was drained. Back against the tree, my arm braced on his shoulder, he brought his lips to the inside of my knee, a zinging sensation going all the way through me. Silas appeared from the copse of trees just in front of me. He stopped dead, eyes wide. I knew how this looked. Though I was with Cadeyrn, who was my husband, and even if it were less innocent a situation, it would be appropriate. He silently walked off, dissolving into mist. Cadeyrn stood and motioned for me to pull up my pants. I cocked my head to the side and looked at him. Really looked at him.

"That was for a show?" He grabbed the back of his neck and looked at me sidelong, green eyes burning. "To make him feel jealous? You don't think he feels like shit anyway? You're an asshole." I tromped off, gloriously pain free, and told the guards to follow. Another day in discord then. Great.

Cadeyrn was absolutely unrepentant, wearing a smug male look all day. Silas was mostly mist, moving along the streams and ponds we passed. There was a flicker in the light. Silas appeared, searching the area, when Corra moved in.

"Fucking hell, sister," Silas yelled. For a second I was so worried I couldn't feel my legs from the adrenaline rushing through me. Cadeyrn reached for my hand and I pulled away. Then Corra smiled and flipped her hair back over a shoulder.

"Halloo, darlings. Thought I'd drop in to help."

I flopped to the ground in a languid heap. "

"Sorry, Neysa. Everyone is fine. Well, except poor Reynard, but that's what this about. See, I was faster than you lot, and caught up with Cyrranus just inside Veruni. Our hawks all found him, but he's a stubborn arse, determined to find Reynard. I told him he must wait for us to get to him or else he would die a bloody death at the hands of twenty backwoods soldiers just as Alan had."

"Delicately put, Corraidhín," Cadeyrn said, voice flat.

"Yes, well, he is hiding out in a hunting lodge. I can show you when we get there. What's with you all? Everyone looks like shit and smells like frustration." We all groaned and began walking again. The twins went on ahead, heads together in conversation too quiet for even our fae hearing. Silas shook her off, and she glared back at me or Cadeyrn, I don't know. I looked away.

As we camped that night, Corra explained that Etienne took a stronghold in Bania, usurping Analisse's manor house. I was breathing through my nose to calm down. We would have to go back there. Catching Silas' eye, I could see he was thinking the same. Slipping between the trees to have some privacy before settling down for the night, Corra intercepted me, wrapping a slender hand around my arm and towing me further away without saying anything. A rushing stream drowned out our voices when she rounded on me.

"Listen, I am so very glad you are home, Neysa."

"But?"

"You're making a muck of things, darling," she stated simply. I barked a laugh which contained no humour whatsoever.

"Yes, well, I'm sorry to have interrupted your perfect life, Corra."

"Pshaw. It's not that," she waved, mist streaking through the air. "The children love you. Thank you for the bunnies. They are positively disgusting with dribble, but Efa won't let hers go." My heart ached hearing that. "You have to figure out this thing with my brother. It's going to kill him."

I was silent.

"So?"

I met her eyes, the same as her brother's, and stayed silent. "What will you say?"

I crossed my arms and shook my head. "Tell me you didn't come all this way to bully me."

"I'm not bullying you, darling. I'm informing you of a crisis situation within our family and asking what you intend to do about it. My cousin and brother are both hurting because of you. Cadeyrn was letting go, and he and Silas were so distant for so long. Silas was getting on with Saski. Not that I love her, but..."

"But maybe if I had stayed gone, he would have gotten over me?" That was the question that hung in the air. The question that followed me day and night. "Perhaps you would have found another look-alike for Cadeyrn to bang for a few years until he got over me too?"

She slapped me, and a rush of darkness cocooned me, moving me back from her.

"That is what you meant, wasn't it? I was stuck in that realm long enough to give you all just enough space to deal with me being gone. Appreciate a lag in my chaos? Maybe had I faded completely it might have released them both from our bond and they could have been free. That would have been ideal really." I raised my voice slightly, darkness and light twirling around me.

"That's...not what I meant," she said. I snarled.

"Of course it was. You just didn't want to say it in so many words. I'm sure each one of you has thought it, if only briefly. Well, I'm sorry. I came back, which likely saved me from fading. If it's such an inconvenience to have me around, I can leave once I find Reynard. Do you think I meant for any of this? God, Corra! I would take a knife to my own heart right now if it would spare either of them from dealing with me. Even godsdamned Dean got sucked into my vortex. So just as I said to Silas after I was brought back from the fucking dead, there is nothing you are saying that shocks me, because I know it all. I. Am. A. Nightmare. Slap me again. Hit me. Drop kick me. I don't care. I love them. I am married to Cadeyrn and I want to stay that way forever if he can handle me. I love Silas and want him be happy too. I am mated to them both, Corra. I didn't do it. It was done to us. Yet, somehow, it's my fault? What do you want me to say? I would leave if I thought they would be truly happy. I would. It would kill me, but I would do it. So if you really think they could be happier, then ask it of me."

She stood, chewing her lip and tapping her foot. I walked away, noting the yellow eyes watching me from a distance. Bowing my head, I bid the wolves watch over the camp while I made my way out. Really, I got about a half mile before I realized what a dumbass I was being and stopped. Truly, Neysa, get a grip. Steeling myself to walk back, I was greeted with a sound kick in my ribs. Another blow missed my head when I blocked it with my forearm. Dazed, my forearm barking, I flipped in a crouch, one leg out. No one. Where did it come from? A blink, and a golden-haired male appeared before me, no weapon in sight. I knew him. He had attacked us in Bulgaria. Two others filed in behind him, swords at the ready. Shit. All I had on me was my forearm dagger. What was I thinking in leaving without my swords? The golden male blinked behind me. I felt his magic as it moved through the particles of the atmosphere. Just before he could be out of reach, I swirled my darkness around him, trapping him in a sort of particle vacuum. The other two advanced. Bloody great. Keeping the golden boy trapped, I was able to fight the others. As they rushed me, I dropped and rolled to the right. Jumping up, I released my dagger and ran at them. When it seemed I was going to meet my end on their swords, I caught a tree branch overhead and swung over it, dropping onto one's shoulders. He didn't have time to react as I stabbed the dagger into his neck. I willed a jolt of electricity into the other, dropping him to the ground, unconscious.

Of course, the kilometre back to camp took forever pulling an unconscious male and one wrapped in magical darkness. When I made it to the edge of camp, I dropped the male and electrocuted the golden one for good measure because I needed to sit down. All eight fae in our camp were at attention, wondering what the hell had happened. I said there was one dead a half mile out, and to deal with these two, as I was going to sleep.

Replenishing my magic didn't take very long. It seemed like it was heightened by my adrenaline and general mood, so I felt like it was depleted more than its actually was. I found myself joining my mates and the others as they interrogated the two I dragged over.

Golden boy liked his face and broke every time Cadeyrn brought his knife to the male's face. The other told us that Reynard would be killed if they didn't return.

"He's lying," I said. "That would have been voiced only if they had been sent to negotiate or retrieve one of us. They tracked me, and their only intent was to kill me. Not a word was exchanged. Gut him."

"Wait! I know where he's being kept," the assassin said, shooting a sidelong glance at his companion. From the look in golden's eyes, I knew the assassin was lying. So did Corra.

He's lying. That fast, Silas put a dagger through his temple. I turned away.

"You?" I addressed golden boy.

"It's a job. I don't care about the particulars of who does what. I can give you information in exchange for sparing my life. Etienne is a bastard anyway, so it doesn't worry me."

We gave our word, and for that he divulged where everyone was, and what was happening.

"If I catch a whiff of your worthless mercenary ass again—ever—you will see that what I did to your friend here was a mercy." Silas leaned closer. "Starting with that pretty face of yours." The male swallowed and agreed before disappearing. Everyone turned to me. I gave a nonchalant gesture and swigged from my water skein.

THEIR CHATTER was like the buzz of cicadas from where I sat, still holding that darkness around me. I wondered what it really was. I pulled it around me like a shield, but it wasn't one. Perhaps it was a way for me to recognize my need to protect myself. Fairly certain my rib was broken, and something was damaged in my arm, I pulled a tonic from my bag and drank it to ease the pain. Cadeyrn's face turned, likely from the smell of the tonic. He started to come over, but Corra put an arm on him, saying to leave me alone. Instead, she walked to me and sat beside me on a tree stump.

"I would never ask that of you." She twirled a lock of my hair around her finger. "Foremost because I do not think it necessary. Loads of other reasons as well. But, selfishly, I would not ask it because while you were gone, I missed you too. A great deal. We are friends and we are sisters. My concern lies for all of you. Do not think for one second that there would ever be a time that you wouldn't be missed. Do not think there is any amount of time that shall pass in which either of your mates would be free of you. I simply ask that you make up your mind as to how to be at peace with both. Now, I could wager a full set of aphrim skins that the male contingent has been doing a fabulous job of pretending to not listen to this conversation. I suppose I have been the only one speaking, so it's more of a lecture, but I needed to say that to you. If you need to talk, you can seek me out. I saw this documentary about this woman who always felt that she was being watched and followed, and she started seeing a psychologist, and after a time—wait. No, she killed the doctor. Don't do that. Let's just be sisters, yes?"

I nodded, still in my swaddling blanket of dusk. Dawn was a few hours off, and we all needed sleep. Who knew what tomorrow would bring. As I slid into my bedroll, I felt Cadeyrn lay behind me and put a hand on my ribs, allowing them to heal. I breathed in fully, allowing the murkiness clouding me to subside. With a kiss pressed just under my ear, he left.

CHAPTER 52

Silas

Looking like a trapped beast, Cyrranus was where my sister left him. The cabin was small, only large enough for a couple of males to grunt and piss in. This had been one of the worst treks I had had to make, between the terrain, the heat, and our personal situation. Still not sure if my sister showing up caused more trouble or helped. Ultimately, it helped flush out those mercenary bastards, though it showed how thick we all were that *Trubaíste* had left. Gods that one. The death of me for sure.

Cyrranus paced the cabin while we told him what we knew. Once we had all rested properly and eaten, we set back off for Bania. Truthfully, if I never had to be in that fucking manor house again, I would have been grateful. I should have known Etienne, that sneaky shite, would go there. Just one more god-sawful night sleeping on the road until I could shed a little blood. Saski would have enjoyed sorting the place with us. I probably should have gone to get her rather than sending my cousin, but I honestly thought she would have maimed me. Plus, it was time she got back to her lands. She was to be queen after all. Not a country squire like me.

We sent a hawk both forward and backward to our soldiers, telling them where we were going to enter the city limits. There would likely be all sorts of obstacles, but at this point, I welcomed them. It might make me the basest of creatures, but I needed to run, kill, and fuck until the heat on my skin went away. At least I'd be doing one of the three shortly.

Shields and wards were up over the grounds of Analisse's compound. The orchard seemed unfazed, which meant that it was teeming with snipers in trees and likely some sort of magical traps here and there. Cadeyrn could sense the abhorrence in the atmosphere as though it were a virus in the air itself. Once he knew where and what we were dealing with, he could begin to dismantle it. While he worked, my sister and I dissolved into the omnipresent mist in Veruni and moved through the orchard. I hated to say it, but it felt good putting my dagger through every piece of shite who was guarding this place. Dissolve, reestablish self, gut the fucker, dissolve. That was our course of action for an hour or so, trying to not raise any alarms before Cadeyrn had a chance to break the spells.

Once we cleared the orchard, there was a straight shot to the back of the manor, lined on either side with a smaller grove of trees, full of their late summer leaves. Corraidhín and I moved back through and reappeared at the back edge where everyone awaited our task. She was grinning like a mad hatter, almost as crazed as I felt. The slightest sound of grass underfoot had me dissolving again and retreating into the orchard after a straggler. He loosed an arrow at me which missed, then another that hit me as I was coming to my corporeal self. I kept pace after him, and just as he flung open the door to the house, I drowned the shite before he could call out. Now I was inside. Fuck it all to never, I wished I could speak to *Trubaiste* the way she could speak to me. Making the best of the situation, I moved through the bottom of the house, the way we had the night we escaped. The night Reynard helped us. Now it was our turn to get him out. Slipping in and out of rooms, under cracks and through pipes, I searched for our friend.

Of fucking course he had to be in the room I had shared with Neysa. Reynard's attention snapped to the door as I drifted in. As I came to my form, I saw him staring wide-eyed and battered, bound to the bedposts with aphrim skin ropes. Careful not to make any noise, I made my way across the room. As I pulled the gag from his mouth, I knew my mistake.

"It's all spelled," he choked. The golden-haired teleporter I let go last night appeared beside me, and knocked me upside the head.

CHAPTER 53

Neysa

As an experiment to see if my touch heightened his power, I laid my hand on Cadeyrn's back and willed the slumbering magic from deep within me, where a beast should be, to transfer to him. Ripples flowed between us then. As he unwound the spells warding the grounds of the compound, my power separated the strands of darkness and light, willing them to do my bidding. Corra and Silas came back and appeared before us, smiling as though a bit mad with bloodlust. Silas' eyes found mine, but then he tore back into the orchard where he sprinted after a straggling guard. Corra called after, but he was gone. We heard the whizz of arrows and the thump of one hitting just as I felt a knock to my left arm. Silas was hit.

Are you okay? Just a moment longer and we could all converge on the place. My impatience was making me jumpy, and Cadeyrn growled at me to calm before it undid what we were attempting. But Silas was hurt, and he wasn't back yet.

Then the wards dropped and like puppies, we all ran through the orchard, weapons at the ready. Corra reached the doors fastest, and I went down hard as everyone began filing in. Cadeyrn was ahead, but Cyrranus yanked me up. My head was spinning like I had been knocked.

"Go!" I yelled at him. "I'm fine. Get everyone in and find them." He saluted me and ran after the small group of soldiers who went in. The rest stayed outside, where there was now an entire regiment of aphrim closing in around the perimeter of the house. By my estimate, there were at least two hundred of the feral infantry, moving on us in their clumsy, laboured way, each of the large scales on them shifting with the movement. Our follow up regiment was close behind, moving through Bania, but for these beasts, we had roughly fifteen soldiers, and me with a dodgy head.

Reeking, eye-watering slobber sprayed everywhere when the aphrim moved. It was a wonder they made such enviable clothing, because these creatures were downright nasty. Slow moving and mostly blind, they were simply a means to slow us down and wear us out. As long as the others could get Reynard and now Silas out. A long saliva-covered tooth caught my arm before the beast it belonged to met its end on my sword. I yanked my arm back, pulling the wound open. Disgusting. That would need tending quickly. I was sure the bacterial levels in the spit was insane.

You're hurt. A statement. His voice in my head was clipped, so I knew he was fighting as well. I spun between two aphrim, then crouched down, causing them to crash into each other and angrily battle between them.

Aphrim. I'll be fine. Get them out.

Bloody hell. Pretty much. Losing the strength in my injured arm, I kept swinging and slashing, felling the beasts as I went.

Our soldiers made a point to keep me flanked. There was a sound to my right, a spray of blood. The solider next to me crumpled under the jaws of a huge aphrim. My knees wobbled slightly, yet I rammed my dagger straight through its eye. Distantly I could feel blows to my ribs and chest, and I knew Silas was taking them wherever he was.

Silas, I know you're probably fine, bloody great warrior and all that, but on the off chance the blows I'm feeling are finding their mark, just hang in there. Doubled over in pain, I had to swipe out maniacally to kill an aphrim. *The good news is that we are killing so many aphrim, I can get some new skins made so my unremarkable ass can look better.* There was a brief, painful sliver of amusement on the other end.

The tail regiment broke the boundary on the property and were within view. Somehow the sixteen of us managed to get though most of the oily beasts, with only ten or so more left. I was drained and needed water desperately. My relief was short lived as ballistae started firing arrows and spears into our soldiers, taking them down in impressive numbers. I ran toward the ballistae and the accompanying fae who manned them, spearing my own power into them. A couple fell as my electricity hit them and the metal of the unit. Reaching the unit itself, I tried willing more power to my body to release the energy and take out the other gunners, but simultaneous blows to my mates had me falling over. I was hauled up and slammed into the wall of the house, my teeth singing with the contact. The male wrenched my arm behind my back, tearing the aphrim wound. I screamed and kicked back, making him bark and back hand me, my head bouncing off the concrete wall again, one of the carved bird reliefs dancing in my vision.

"Got me a prize," he whispered in my ear, kneeing me in the kidney. I vomited with the pain and went slack. He sniggered, grabbing my other arm back. My shoulder jolted with pain and I grunted, but he had me bound and was pulling me away. I'd taken out one of the ballistae, though I wished I had managed both before getting caught.

What's happened? Where are you? Cadeyrn questioned through our connection.

I'll be fine.

Damn it, Neysa. Where are you?

Where are you?

That's not funny. Fuck. Ugh. Then the sound of a sword singing and the roar of fire in close quarters. I wished I were there to see it. *They aren't here. Silas and Reynard aren't in this house. He went in but he's not here.* A feeling of cold dread went through me as the guard who had me bound dragged me away from the property towards the city proper.

Cadeyrn, get out of there. Get everyone out. Now. Hysterics began walking in my mind as I kept yelling at him to get out. I tried turning around to see back, but the guard elbowed me in the ear. Christ, I was going to have a compound concussion.

Where. Are. You? he demanded.

Get out of there! I kept screaming at him. Then the entire manor disintegrated like it had been a house of ash, touched by a mighty finger. All that was left of the plaster and birds, the wooden shutters, the stones, was ash on the wind. I couldn't think straight. *Cadeyrn—*

I threw up again, and the guard swore and kicked at me. Had he made it out? Had any of them?

Cadeyrn.

I reached in myself, searching for a tether and finding nothing but a spark of our bond.

We dropped through the ground into what must have been a root cellar. Once at the bottom, there was a tunnel leading deeper to the east. We walked maybe a mile or so, every part of me aching. Though my aphrim wound had stopped bleeding, it stung and felt puffy. I would worry about that later. After a time, a doorway led to a steep ramp with a wooden grate overhead. The guard used my head to push it open, which, if he hadn't been on my to-kill priority list before, he was riding shotgun with Etienne now. Dim light greeted us as we emerged into the kitchen of a modest house. Through another set of doors, flash bulbs pulsed behind my eyes, distorting my vision from the concussion. Then we stopped. He tossed me to the ground like a sack and put a boot on my back. A surge of power went through the room and knocked at my battered self. I looked up to see Etienne standing before me, his son and Silas behind him, both barely conscious.

"You stink of sick, Princess," Etienne sneered.

"Blame the guard," I spat, head throbbing. I was so out of practice, I wanted to punch myself for letting these two-bit guards take me. Don't pass out. Whatever you do, Neysa, don't pass out. I looked at Reynard, his clothes torn, face slashed and bruised. They must have kept beating him as he healed. His own father. Silas' eyes found mine. He was enraged, eyes wild and translucent, as though it were the only part of him that had turned to mist. Gags filled their mouths, and they hung from shackles on the wall.

"You'll find that in this room I've suspended access to all your gifts. Though my son is fairly useless to begin with, being that he has no real gift, apart from speed." Bastard. Goddamn bastard. "Now, what I want is simple. How this shall play out is simple. What you need to do to survive and to save your mate is simple."

He walked to Silas and grabbed his throat. I opened my mind, trying to let my power come to me, despite the restrictive feeling.

"Give me the clock, and together we can use it. Tell your brother to abdicate. There. Simple, no?"

"What do you want with the clock? Surely, you must know it doesn't play to your own agenda."

"For starters, I plan to bring my daughter back."

Oh.

Printed in Great Britain
by Amazon

79911010R00295

Inside the Microsoft® Windows® 98 Registry

Günter Born

PUBLISHED BY
Microsoft Press
A Division of Microsoft Corporation
One Microsoft Way
Redmond, Washington 98052-6399

Library of Congress Cataloging-in-Publication Data
Born, Günter, 1955-
    Inside the Microsoft Windows 98 Registry / Günter Born.
        p.   cm.
    Includes index.
    ISBN 1-57231-824-4
    1. Microsoft Windows (Computer file)   2. Operating systems
(Computers)   I. Title.
QA76.76.O63B64297   1998
005.4'469--dc21   98-25678
                                                         CIP

Printed and bound in the United States of America.

1 2 3 4 5 6 7 8 9   MLML   3 2 1 0 9 8

Distributed in Canada by ITP Nelson, a division of Thomson Canada Limited.

A CIP catalogue record for this book is available from the British Library.

Microsoft Press books are available through booksellers and distributors worldwide. For further
information about international editions, contact your local Microsoft Corporation office or
contact Microsoft Press International directly at fax (425) 936-7329. Visit our Web site at
mspress.microsoft.com.

Acquisitions Editor: Stephen G. Guty
Project Editor: Devon Musgrave
Technical Editor: Jean Ross

CONTENTS

Acknowledgments ix

Introduction xi

CHAPTER ONE

The Basics   1
Why Abandon INI Files for the Registry? 1
The Registry Architecture 3
How Can I Access the Registry Database? 9
The INI Files in Windows 98 11
When Should the Registry Be Modified? 13
How Should the Registry Be Modified? 13
Why Do My Registry Entries Differ from Those in the Book? 14

CHAPTER TWO

The Registry Editor and Other Registry Tools   15
The Registry Editor 15
Importing and Exporting Registry Data 25
Remote Access to the Registry 32
Backing Up and Recovering Your Registry 36
The System Policy Editor 49
Other Tools for Changing Registry Settings 53

CHAPTER THREE

Registering Filename Extensions   55
The *HKEY_CLASSES_ROOT* Structure 55
Registering New File Types and Modifying Existing Ones 62
Techniques for Extending Registered File Types 87
Conclusion 118

CHAPTER FOUR

Customizing the Desktop, Start Menu, and Control Panel Properties   **119**

Customizing the Open With List 119

Modifying the Desktop Items 129

Changing the Start Menu Options 197

Modifying Miscellaneous Keys Containing Shell Data 216

CHAPTER FIVE

Customizing Windows Explorer and Shell Settings   **219**

Modifying Windows Explorer's Context Menu 219

Modifying Miscellaneous System Settings 239

Modifying Miscellaneous Network Keys 252

Registering a New Template for the New Command 253

Modifying the Shell Icons 258

CHAPTER SIX

Miscellaneous Registry Settings   **267**

Sound Events in the Registry 267

Setting Up Application Paths in the Registry 275

Launching Programs During Windows Startup 281

Settings for Signature Checking and Error Logging 284

Settings for the File System 285

System Properties in the Registry 292

Settings for System Software 303

CHAPTER SEVEN

Programming Issues   **315**

Registering Version and Status Information 315

Application-Specific Registry Entries 317

Using a Program to Access the Registry 321

More About INF Files 339

Advanced INF Files 366

Creating Policy Editor Template Files 375

Conclusion 380

APPENDIX A

Icons Contained in SHELL32.DLL   **381**

APPENDIX B

Values for the *International* Key   **389**

APPENDIX C

The Registry in Windows NT 4.0 Workstation   **393**

The Role of INI Files 393

The Windows NT Registry Architecture 394

Tools for Accessing the Windows NT Registry 400

Backing Up and Recovering the Windows NT 4.0 Registry 410

Windows NT 4.0 Workstation Registry Entries 414

APPENDIX D

Canonical Verbs   **423**

APPENDIX E

The Windows INF File Format   **425**

Windows 95 Device Information Files Overview 425

General INF File Format 426

[Version] Section 428

[Manufacturer] Section 429

[*Manufacturer Name*] Section 430

[*Install*] Section 431

[ClassInstall] Section 448

[Strings] Section 448

[Optional Components] Section 449

Sample INF Files 453

Advanced INF Files 457

Using RunDLL32 to Launch Advanced INF Files 460

Advanced INF File Options 461

Sample Advanced INF 469

Index 473

ACKNOWLEDGMENTS

This book could not have been finished without the help of many people, to whom I want to say thank you. First of all I have to mention Thomas Pohlmann and Stephen Guty (my acquisition editors at Microsoft Press Germany and USA, respectively). Both editors encouraged me to develop my initial ideas into a book, and Stephen gave me a chance to actually publish the book—even though I am living in Germany, my native language isn't English, and the schedule for writing the manuscript was pretty short (excellent conditions for a project). I want to give my special thanks to Devon Musgrave and Jean Ross, my editors at Microsoft Press. They spent many hours editing and polishing my text. I also want to thank my wife and my children Kati and Benjamin, who supported me during the time the book was written.

Günter Born

INTRODUCTION

Why I Wrote This Book

This book is the end of a long story. A few years ago I received an early copy of Chicago (the press called it Windows 4.0 at that time). I wasn't exactly ecstatic about the software, but after playing with it for two days, I was convinced. Time went by, and I installed new builds of this software (named Chicago, Microsoft Windows 95 Preview, and Microsoft Windows 95 Retail). I also installed and uninstalled many other preliminary software packages for test purposes and realized that my Registry was cluttered with a lot of unused entries. I wrote two books about Windows 95 and learned how to customize Windows—hacking in the Registry a little bit to troubleshoot and get my old settings back.

Some months later, I translated Nancy Cluts's book *Programming the Windows 95 User Interface* and wondered why some examples that shipped with the book didn't work on my system. After a few hours of debugging, I found the culprit—an incorrect Registry setting. I surfed the World Wide Web to glean tricks and learn how to hack in the Registry, but most of the tricks didn't work properly on my computer. During the hours I spent exploring why, I became more familiar with Registry issues. One important lesson I learned was that I didn't need to hack directly in the Registry; often it was smarter to set an option on a property page to get the same results. (I *always* came to this conclusion after spending unproductive hours in the Registry Editor.)

So I decided that a book about the Windows 95 Registry and related topics was really needed. I started writing down the knowledge I had gained while troubleshooting, customizing, and programming with Windows 95. The result was *Inside the Registry for Microsoft Windows 95*.

The overwhelming feedback about that book motivated me to write a version for Microsoft Windows 98. While many similarities exist between the Registries of Windows 95, Windows 98, and Windows NT 4.0, some structures and settings are completely different. And I discovered many new entries in the Windows 98 Registry.

The Goals of This Book

Of course, this book is not a complete reference to all entries in the Registry, although we'd all like such a reference. Such a book simply can't be written. Because the Registry is used by so many hardware and software components, everybody's Registry is different. My goals in this book were to examine the most important parts of the Registry, to show how to back up and recover the Registry, and to provide some background knowledge about related topics. This book will be helpful for system administrators, troubleshooters, programmers, and users who want to customize Windows 98.

> NOTE: Keep in mind that you can seriously damage your system when you alter Registry settings. Always back up your system before you attempt to modify the Registry. (See pages 36–49 to learn how to back up your system files.) Any change you make is at your own risk—neither Microsoft nor I (the author) can support you with Registry issues. So proceed with modifications cautiously.

Using the Companion CD

Throughout this book, you will find listings for sample files that you can either type in or copy from the companion CD located at the back of this book. To copy the sample files to your hard drive, run the Setup program from the root of the CD. Setup will create a directory on your hard drive, named Win98Reg by default, and copy the sample files into that directory. You can also run the Setup program from the README.HTM file (located in the root directory of the CD) that opens automatically when you insert the CD into your CD drive.

Also located on the CD are useful tools and information. Please read the Microsoft License Agreement (at the back of this book) pertaining to the contents of the CD. See the README.TXT file located in the root directory of the CD for more information on these resources.

Getting in Touch with the Author

If you'd like to get in touch with me regarding the book, feel free to visit my home page at this address:

http://ourworld.compuserve.com/homepages/Guenter_Born

Support Information

Every effort has been made to ensure the accuracy of this book and the contents of the companion CD. Microsoft Press provides corrections for books through the World Wide Web at the following address:

http://mspress.microsoft.com/mspress/support/

If you have comments, questions, or ideas regarding this book or the companion CD, please send them to Microsoft Press using either of the following methods.

Postal mail:

Microsoft Press
Attn: *Inside the Microsoft Windows 98 Registry* Editor
One Microsoft Way
Redmond, WA 98052-6399

E-mail:

MSPINPUT@MICROSOFT.COM

Please note that Windows 98 product support is not offered through the above addresses.

CHAPTER ONE

The Basics

The Registry is the central database in Microsoft Windows 98 that stores and maintains configuration information. It is thus one of the most interesting and important components of Windows 98. Until now, details about the Windows 98 Registry haven't been readily available—developers, administrators, and end users have all faced the challenge of trying to find information about it. This book brings together many of the scattered details about the Windows 98 Registry and provides a comprehensive look at how it works and how you can use it. Fortunately, the concept of the Registry is pretty straightforward, and with a little help you can decipher the database entries.

This chapter discusses the Registry's basic architecture and explains why the Registry (since the release of Microsoft Windows 95) has replaced the old INI (initialization) files found in versions of Windows prior to Windows 95. We'll also examine when—and how—you should modify the Registry.

Why Abandon INI Files for the Registry?

If you were accustomed to using INI files, you've probably asked this question: why did the Windows developers drop the INI files and create the Registry? After all, the INI files were printable, and you needed only a simple text editor to change initialization settings. To understand why the Registry was developed, let's take a look at the old INI structure by examining a small section of the WIN.INI file:

```
[windows]
load=...
NullPort=None
run=...
device=HP Deskjet
⋮
```

Each section in an INI file begins with a keyword enclosed in brackets (such as *[windows]* in the WIN.INI file) followed by several lines of settings. Although

1

this approach worked well enough in earlier, less complicated versions of Windows, it caused problems in Windows 3.1 and Windows 3.11. The disadvantages are apparent if you take a closer look at the INI file concept:

- INI files are text-based, so their size is limited to 64 KB. As you install programs on your PC, the WIN.INI file gets longer, restricting the number of programs you can install—again, because you can't exceed 64 KB in the INI file. In addition, programs often have problems properly reading entries beyond the first 32 KB. So, despite the system limitation of 64 KB, to be sure all your programs run properly your INI file shouldn't be larger than 32 KB.

- All information stored in INI files is nonhierarchical—files contain only section headers and some additional text lines—so accessing lengthy INI files is a slow process. To keep their programs from being slowed by lengthy INI files, software developers started creating a separate INI file for each program they wrote. As a result, each tested program leaves an unused INI file in the Windows directory. Such a disorganized file structure can't be managed easily by the user.

- Each INI file initializes settings that affect the computer as a whole, so user-specific information can't be stored easily in a single INI file. Also, remote access from other network devices to the INI files of a local machine is not possible (nor is it available from the APIs).

These issues became more and more critical in Windows 3.1. Because of these restrictions and the complexity of OLE, Microsoft developers created a different structure to store the information necessary for OLE in Windows 3.1: REG files. Information was stored in REG files by using a registration editor or during the installation of new software. (The REG file feature seemed to be overlooked by many people; I, for one, never played with the REG files in Windows 3.1.) As you can see, the Registry wasn't a new concept for Windows 95. And, because the Windows 95 Registry was used as a foundation for the Windows 98 Registry, the Windows 3.1 REG file structure was the parent of the Windows 95 and Windows 98 Registries.

Requirements for the Registry

The design goals of Windows 98 included continued support for many Windows 95 features, including Plug & Play, remote access to system settings, multiple-user configurations, and so on. During the development of Windows 95, it was clear that a new hierarchical database was necessary to meet all of these requirements. The developers of Windows 95 based their hierarchical centralized configuration database on an advanced version of the Windows 3.1 REG structure, which met the following objectives:

- All configuration information (user and system data) can be stored in a single (logical) source.

- Multiple configurations of user and system data can be stored in one database.

- Hardware and operating system parameters can be stored in a single database.

- The database is recoverable after a system crash.

- The size of this database is not limited to 64 KB.

- Administrators can configure this database with Control Panel tools or other utilities.

- A set of network-independent functions allows examination of the Registry locally or remotely (over a network).

- Developers can access Registry entries by using a set of API calls.

Supporting many of the same features as Windows 95, Windows 98 required the same objectives to be met, and therefore the Windows 95 Registry structure was maintained in Windows 98. (But take care—many specific Registry entries have changed between the two versions of Windows.)

The Registry Architecture

The information stored in the Registry's hierarchical database is organized in keys, where each key contains one or more subkeys and each subkey contains a value, unless a subkey's value is not set, as shown here:

```
key
    subkey 1 | value
    subkey 2
    subkey 3 | value
```

Multiple subkeys allow for the grouping of settings. This results in a hierarchical tree, which you can see in the Registry Editor, as shown in Figure 1-1 on the following page. A branch represents a type of information about the user, the hardware, the application, and so on.

NOTE: The Microsoft Windows Explorer uses a similar structure to show the directory hierarchy. The Registry can be compared with a directory tree: The keys are similar to the directories in the file system. Key values are comparable to files in a directory.

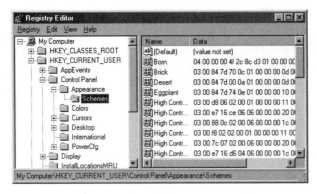

Figure 1-1.
An example of a Registry branch.

The Six Root Keys

The Windows 98 Registry consists of six root keys, each of which reflects a different aspect of configuration data (that is, user data and machine-dependent settings). Each root key's name begins with *HKEY_*, and each of the root keys is followed by several subkeys. The root keys are shown in Figure 1-2.

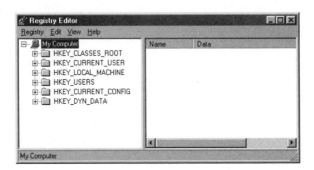

Figure 1-2.
The six root keys of the Windows 98 Registry.

NOTE: This structure is also used in Windows 95, Microsoft Windows NT 3.51, and Windows NT 4.0. However, the Registry in Windows NT 3.51 uses only four *HKEY_* root keys. Also, the tools for editing and displaying the Registry are different in Windows NT 3.51, while Windows NT 4.0 provides two Registry Editors, the Windows NT 3.51 and the Windows 95 versions of the editor.

What Does Each Root Key Contain?

Each branch of the Registry contains information that logically belongs together. Following is a description of the contents of the six main branches within the Registry.

HKEY_CLASSES_ROOT This branch contains all data used in Windows 98 for OLE and drag-and-drop operations, including the names of all registered file types and their properties. Registered file types enable the user to open a file by double-clicking. Properties of registered file types include the icons shown in Windows 98 and the commands (Open, Print, etc.) that users can apply to files of those types. This branch also contains information about Quick Viewers, property sheet handlers, copy hook handlers, and other OLE components (such as OLE servers).

NOTE: Windows 98 offers the option to open files and applications with a single click rather than a double click. Any reference in this book to double-clicking a desktop file or application is equivalent to a reference to single-clicking when you have set your folder options in Windows 98 to Web Style.

Many subkeys (*.bat*, *.bmp*, and so on) pertain to file extensions. For most of these file type subkeys, a second subkey exists (*batfile*, *exefile*, and so on) in *HKEY_CLASSES_ROOT*. This second subkey contains properties such as the icon, Class ID, and commands.

Most of the entries in *HKEY_CLASSES_ROOT* can also be found in *HKEY_LOCAL_MACHINE\SOFTWARE\Classes*. We look more closely at the structure of *HKEY_CLASSES_ROOT* in Chapter 3.

This branch of the Registry was derived from the Windows 3.1 Registry structure (although the formats differ) and is also available in Windows 95, Windows NT 3.51, and Windows NT 4.0.

HKEY_USERS Any user-specific information (customized desktop settings, for example) is located in *HKEY_USERS*. The branch contains the default settings (*HKEY_USERS\.Default*) for the desktop, Start menu, applications, and so on. When a new user logs on to the system, the default settings are copied to a separate subkey that is identified with the user's name (*HKEY_USERS\Born*, for example). All changes that the user then makes to these settings are stored in this subkey. Windows 95, Windows NT 3.51, and Windows NT 4.0 also support the *HKEY_USERS* root key.

The *HKEY_USERS* branch also contains a subkey named *Software*. This key is new to Windows 98, so it is currently used only by Microsoft software. Microsoft uses this key to store user-dependent telephony settings.

HKEY_CURRENT_USER   User settings are built from *HKEY_USERS* during the login process, so all information found in *HKEY_CURRENT_USER* is a copy of the subkey *HKEY_USERS\name*, where *name* is the name of the active user or a copy of *HKEY_USERS\.Default*. *HKEY_CURRENT_USER* contains several subkeys:

- *AppEvents*   Contains paths to sound files that are loaded for particular system events (for example, when an error message occurs).

- *Control Panel*   Contains data that can be altered in the Control Panel window (for example, display settings).

- *Display*   Contains data for the display settings of the current user. (This key is available only when a user is logged on with user profiles enabled.)

- *InstallLocationsMRU*   Contains values defining the paths used during the last install processes. The values named *a*, *b*, *c*, and so on define the paths, and *MRUList* contains the order of these entries. The paths defined in *a*, *b*, *c*, and so on will be used in the list box of the Install From Disk dialog box.

- *keyboard layout*   Contains information about the keyboard layout (that is, the current active keyboard layout, the layout scheme, and optional dynamic-link libraries to load). The current keyboard layout is set by using the Keyboard option in Control Panel.

- *Network*   Contains subkeys describing persistent and recent network connections and the network state (if available).

- *RemoteAccess*   Optional subkey available only if the Remote Access service is installed. It defines the Remote Access settings (such as that for CompuServe).

■ *Software*   Describes the user-specific properties of user-installed software. (This information was previously stored in WIN.INI.) This branch also references *HKEY_LOCAL_MACHINE*. User-specific application settings are stored in here. (Application settings stored in *HKEY_CURRENT_USER* define the options for the current user. Application-specific options for this application that are available on the whole machine are stored in *HKEY_LOCAL_MACHINE* settings.)

These subkeys are discussed further in other chapters of this book. The *HKEY_CURRENT_USER* entry is also available in Windows 95, Windows NT 3.51, and Windows NT 4.0.

HKEY_LOCAL_MACHINE   This branch defines all specific information for the local machine, such as drivers, installed hardware, port mappings, and software configuration. This information is valid for all users logged on to the system. This branch is also available in Windows NT 3.51.

The *HKEY_LOCAL_MACHINE* key has several subkeys:

■ *Config*   Machine configuration is maintained in this subkey. This information is necessary for docking stations with varying hardware and is updated during Windows 98 setup and during Windows 98 startup. The subkey contains two entries: one for display settings and one for available system printers.

■ *Driver*   A key containing only empty subkeys with names like 4 and 11. (Please note that I've been unable to determine the purpose of these subkeys.)

■ *Enum*   Windows uses a feature called *Bus Enumeration* for the bookkeeping of all installed hardware components. The data for these components is stored in this subkey and can be used to build the "hardware tree" shown in the Device Manager. (To view this tree, select System from the Control Panel.)

■ *HARDWARE*   This subkey contains the settings for the serial ports (in the *DeviceMap* subkey) available on the local machine. The subkey *DESCRIPTION* contains entries for devices (such as the labels used to describe the central processor, the floating-point processor, and the multifunction adapter) installed in the system.

■ *Network*   When Windows 98 runs in a network, this subkey contains user-login information (that is, user name, network provider, logon validation, policy information, and so on).

■ *Security*   This subkey is available for networked computers and contains information about the security provider.

■ *SOFTWARE*   All information about the software installed on the machine is stored here. A subkey in this branch (*Classes*) is used to construct *HKEY_CLASSES_ROOT*.

■ *System*   This subkey contains all data that is required for Windows 98 to start. The subkey contains the key *CurrentControlSet*, which contains the subkeys *control* and *Services*. The *control* subkey contains such information as the computer name, the settings for the file system, and so on. *Services* lists the services used in Windows 98.

NOTE: Whenever similar data exists in *HKEY_CURRENT_USER* and *HKEY_LOCAL_MACHINE*, the data in *HKEY_CURRENT_USER* takes precedence. (User-defined data overwrites settings defined for all users of a machine.)

HKEY_CURRENT_CONFIG   This branch handles Plug & Play and contains information about the current configuration of a multiple hardware configuration computer (such as a dockable station). The settings in this branch match one set of configuration settings stored in the *HKEY_LOCAL_MACHINE\Config* key.

HKEY_DYN_DATA   This branch contains the keys that store the dynamic status information of multiple devices. This data can be used by monitoring programs to detect hardware problems, device status, or changing configurations. The Device Manager, available on the System Properties property sheet, uses this data to show the current hardware configuration.

All data in this root key is read and modified by the system. Some data can also be altered by the user, whereas other data can be updated only by the system itself. Details about the altering of data in this key are reviewed in later chapters.

Why Do Identical Keys Appear in Different Branches?

You've probably noticed that in the Registry, key names can appear in more than one branch. This is because certain keys are built from keys in other branches. The Windows operating system automatically stores any modification made by the user in all of the related keys. So, for example, a change in *HKEY_LOCAL_MACHINE\SOFTWARE\ Classes* would also appear in the *HKEY_CLASSES_ROOT* key because *HKEY_CLASSES_ROOT* is built from *HKEY_LOCAL_MACHINE\ SOFTWARE\Classes*. Likewise, because the contents of *HKEY_ CURRENT_USER* are built from *HKEY_USERS\name* (again, *name* refers to the user's name) when a user logs on, the keys would share the same user information.

An exception to this is the *\Software\Microsoft\Windows\ CurrentVersion* branch, which is available both in *HKEY_CURRENT_ USER* and *HKEY_LOCAL_MACHINE*. (The subkeys *\SOFTWARE* and *\Software* are identical, by the way. Registry entries are not case-sensitive. You should worry about correctly identifying upper and lowercase letters only when you are referring to entries that are part of the user interface.) Although the name of the branch beneath the two root keys is identical, the content of each complete branch is distinct. Entries in the *HKEY_CURRENT_USER\Software\Microsoft\Windows\ CurrentVersion* branch contain user-specific settings (recent file lists, for example), while entries in the *HKEY_LOCAL_MACHINE\ Software\Microsoft\Windows\CurrentVersion* branch contain settings that are global for the local machine, the software, or all users (for example, application paths, the Windows tip list, and so on). These issues are discussed in more detail in later chapters.

How Can I Access the Registry Database?

You can access the Registry database from within a program by using the Windows API calls or through a tool called the Registry Editor with which you can display, print, and modify the Registry database. (The Registry Editor is discussed in more detail in Chapter 2.) The Registry is also modified by each new software installation. Following is an explanation of the files that are affected.

SYSTEM.DAT and USER.DAT

For an independent computer user, a single file is adequate to store the Registry. In a network, however, a single file would enable an individual user to modify not only typical user-specific data but also system configuration data—and with settings that might be quite different from the settings that the network administrator prefers. To prevent end users from reconfiguring the system and to maintain some global settings for all users, Windows 98 separates the two types of Registry data and stores the information in two files: SYSTEM.DAT and USER.DAT.

- SYSTEM.DAT contains the system configuration and settings of data (for example, hardware configuration, Plug & Play settings, and application settings). These settings are required during system startup to load the device drivers and to determine what hardware is available. SYSTEM.DAT is always located on the local machine in the Windows 98 directory.

- USER.DAT contains user-specific data (for example, login names, desktop settings, Start menu settings, and so on). During the Windows setup, USER.DAT is automatically stored in the \Windows directory, but the file doesn't have to remain there. If user profiles are enabled, an individual user can have personal settings stored in a directory structure under the \Windows\Profiles subdirectory, which contains a copy of the USER.DAT file for the user. See Figure 1-3 for the location of the USER.DAT file in a case like this. In a network environment, this file can be located on a central server for roving users and can be downloaded if necessary.

NOTE: Windows 95 uses DA0 files (such as USER.DA0) as a backup set of Registry files. (Readers of *Inside the Registry for Microsoft Windows 95* [Microsoft Press, 1997] will remember DA0 files.) These files are not used in Windows 98. The new operating system uses a different backup strategy, which provides several backup copies of the Registry instead of only one. Further information about these backup sets can be found in Chapter 2.

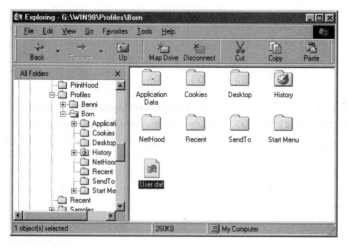

Figure 1-3.
The location of the USER.DAT file.

The INI Files in Windows 98

When we examine the \Windows directory in Windows 98, we still find
WIN.INI and SYSTEM.INI, as well as other INI files. For compatibility reasons, Windows 98 maintains the WIN.INI and SYSTEM.INI files, just as the
Windows 95 operating system did. These settings are used for Win16 applications. When a Win16-based application is installed, its setup program creates
INI settings but doesn't update the Registry because Win16 applications were
designed to be compatible with earlier pre-Registry versions of Windows.

During an upgrade from Windows 3.10 or Windows 3.11, the Windows 98 Setup program deletes several entries from the old WIN.INI and
SYSTEM.INI files and adds these entries to the Registry. Table 1-1 on the
following page describes these entries.

> NOTE: After the Windows 98 setup, you will find the
> SETUPC.INF file in the \Windows\Inf folder. This file contains en-
> tries for manipulating INI settings during setup.

Entries Moved from the INI Files into the Registry

Key	Entry	Subkey Location
[*Desktop*]	*GridGranularity*	*HKEY_CURRENT_USER\Control Panel\ desktop*
[*Desktop*]	*Pattern*	*HKEY_CURRENT_USER\Control Panel\ desktop*
[*Desktop*]	*TileWallpaper*	*HKEY_CURRENT_USER\Control Panel\ desktop*
[*Windows*]	*ScreenSaveActive*	*HKEY_CURRENT_USER\Control Panel\ desktop*
[*Windows*]	*ScreenSaveTimeout*	*HKEY_CURRENT_USER\Control Panel\ desktop*
[*Sound*]	*event*	*HKEY_CURRENT_USER\AppEvents\ Schemes\Apps\event\current*
[*Network*]	*MaintainServerList*	*HKEY_LOCAL_MACHINE\System\ CurrentControlSet\Services\VxD\VNETSUP*
[*Network*]	*LogonDomain*	*HKEY_LOCAL_MACHINE\Network\Logon*
[*Network*]	*LogonValidated*	*HKEY_LOCAL_MACHINE\Network\Logon*
[*Network*]	*Comment*	*HKEY_LOCAL_MACHINE\System\ CurrentControlSet\Services\VxD\VNETSUP*
[*Network*]	*LMAnnounce*	*HKEY_LOCAL_MACHINE\System\ CurrentControlSet\Services\VxD\VNETSUP*
[*Network*]	*LMLogon*	*HKEY_LOCAL_MACHINE\Network\Logon*
[*Network*]	*Username*	*HKEY_LOCAL_MACHINE\Network\Logon*
[*Network*]	*WorkGroup*	*HKEY_LOCAL_MACHINE\System\ CurrentControlSet\Services\VxD\VNETSUP*
[*Network*]	*EnableSharing*	*HKEY_LOCAL_MACHINE\Services\VxD\ VNETSUP*
[*Network*]	*ComputerName*	*HKEY_LOCAL_MACHINE\System\ CurrentControlSet\control\ComputerName\ ComputerName*
[*386Enh*]	*Transport*	*HKEY_LOCAL_MACHINE\Services\VxD\ transport_entry*
[*386Enh*]	*Network*	*HKEY_LOCAL_MACHINE\Services\VxD\ VNETSUP*

Table 1-1.
Entries that move to the Registry when upgrading from Windows 3.x.

Conflicting Parameters

After the Windows 98 installation, you (or some install programs) can add entries to the INI files. However, changing INI files can sometimes lead to a curious situation. Suppose you (or an install program) change some settings in an INI file. You then alter Registry settings with the Registry Editor, test the result, and find that everything seems to be okay. But when you restart the system, the new configuration is lost. Your inspection of the Registry reveals that the old settings are back.

What has happened? Well, there is a big trap in the system: Windows keeps data consistent in the INI files and in the Registry. During each system reboot, Windows examines the INI settings and checks each entry against the Registry entries. If an entry is available in the INI file and in the Registry, the value from the INI file is sometimes copied over the Registry value. This will overwrite entries previously altered in the Registry. The only way to fix this problem is to manually change the entries in both the INI file and the Registry.

> NOTE: The best solution to conflicting parameters in INI files and the Registry is to remove all entries from the INI files that are also available in the Registry. Win32 applications don't use INI files, and Microsoft discourages developers from using INI files for future projects.

When Should the Registry Be Modified?

The safest answer to the question above is "Never!" Modifying the Registry can be dangerous—you have the critical responsibility of storing all values in a consistent manner or your system could crash permanently. But the safest answer is not always the most realistic, so if you have to modify the Registry, let installation routines, setup programs, and utilities do it for you whenever possible.

How Should the Registry Be Modified?

The way you modify the Registry depends on what you need to modify. Most of the time, your safest and simplest bet will be to use the Display Properties property sheet, the Control Panel, the System Policy Editor, or other third-party utilities that enable you to modify Registry settings—for example, customizing the appearance of screen elements, establishing screen saver parameters, and fine-tuning certain parts of the Windows operating system. These methods (described in Table 1-2) are all pretty risk-free and are discussed later in the book.

Safe Methods for Modifying the Registry

Modification Method	Settings to Be Modified
Control Panel	Most of the system settings
Display Properties property sheet	Background, appearance of screen elements, graphic adapter, screen saver parameters
System Policy Editor	User access to settings, several system settings
Third-party utilities	Application-specific settings, mouse, menus, and many others

Table 1-2.
Some of the safest methods of changing Registry settings.

You can also modify the Registry by using the Registry Editor, which is a powerful (and thus potentially dangerous) tool that allows you to modify *any* entry in the Registry. Using the Registry Editor should really be your last resort—use it only when you can't get results via property sheets or other tools. (Whenever I've forgotten that rule in the past, I've spent hours digging inside the Registry. I finally figured out that I can get the same effect simply by checking a box on a property sheet.)

Whichever method you use, always back up the Registry before you change anything. Modifying the Registry is discussed at length in Chapter 2.

Why Do My Registry Entries Differ from Those in the Book?

Throughout this book, the subkeys and values listed (in tables, mostly) might not exactly match what you see on your computer. Remember that every Registry is different depending on computer configuration and the software that has been installed. The keys, subkeys, and values shown in this book constitute the basic structure of the Windows 98 Registry.

The Registry Editor and Other Registry Tools

This chapter describes how to use the Registry Editor to display, modify, and recover the Registry. You'll also learn about the tools and techniques for backing up your Registry and setting the system and user policies.

The Registry Editor

The Registry Editor is the tool provided by Microsoft for displaying and editing the Registry database. You can't display the contents of the USER.DAT and SYSTEM.DAT files with a simple text editor because Microsoft uses a special format to store these files. The following sections describe how to use the Registry Editor.

Locating the Registry Editor

After installing Microsoft Windows 98, you won't find the Registry Editor in the Start menu or on the desktop. Windows Setup doesn't automatically create a shortcut to the Registry Editor; this is to prevent novice users from using the tool. During installation, however, the REGEDIT.EXE file is copied into the \Windows folder.

Starting the Registry Editor

To start the Registry Editor, do the following:

1. Open the Windows Explorer window, and search for the REGEDIT.EXE file in the \Windows folder.

2. Double-click REGEDIT.EXE. The Registry Editor starts.

If you use the Registry Editor frequently, you might want to create a short-cut on the desktop. This can be accomplished by following these steps:

1. Again, open the Windows Explorer window, and search for the REGEDIT.EXE file in the \Windows folder.

2. While pressing the right mouse button, drag the REGEDIT.EXE icon to a free place on the desktop.

3. Release the right mouse button, and select the Create Shortcut(s) Here option from the context menu. A shortcut to the Registry Editor is established on the desktop.

You can change the icon title if you want to (to Regedit, for example). To start the Registry Editor, double-click this icon on the desktop.

TIP: Some users prefer to start programs from the Start menu. To add the Registry Editor to the Start menu, follow the preceding steps, but instead of dragging the REGEDIT.EXE icon onto the desktop, drag the icon to the Start button.

Editing with the Registry Editor

The Registry Editor displays the Registry contents in a window containing a menu bar, a status bar, and two panes. (See Figure 2-1.)

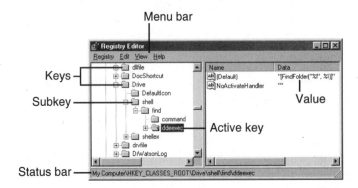

Figure 2-1.
The Registry Editor window.

The menu bar consists of the following commands:

■ Registry, which allows you to print, import, and export the Registry data

■ Edit, which allows you to create, delete, rename, and find keys or values

■ View, which allows you to switch the status bar on and off, to change the pane sizes, and to refresh the display

■ Help, which provides help topics about the functions

In the left pane, the Registry structure, which consists of keys and subkeys, is visible. (When you open the Registry Editor for the first time, the six root keys discussed in Chapter 1 are visible. See Figure 2-2.) Each key and subkey is represented by a folder symbol in the left pane. The active key is indicated with an open folder icon.

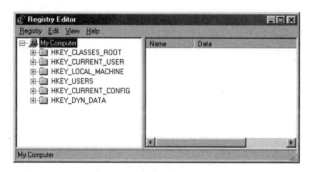

Figure 2-2.
The root keys shown in the Registry Editor.

Displaying Key Values

The values of the active key appear in the right pane of the Registry Editor window. Value names appear in the right pane's first column, which is titled Name. Valid characters to include in a value name are *a* through *z*, *0* through *9*, blank, and underscore (_). Values themselves appear in the second column, which is titled Data. (See Figure 2-1 again.) Every key contains at least one value name, called *Default*, although *Default* need not have its value set. If the *Default* entry contains no value, the string *(value not shown)* is displayed in the Registry Editor. Each additional entry for a key must have both a name and a data value.

> N O T E : The key size limit of 64 KB that existed in Windows 95 has been removed in Windows 98—a key can now contain more than 64 KB of data. An individual value within a key cannot exceed 16 KB, however, so large strings and binary data streams cannot be stored in the Registry. To overcome this limit, use a file to store large amounts of data whose total value exceeds 16 KB and then maintain a pointer to this file as the value for the key.

The Registry Editor can handle string, binary, and DWORD data types:

- **String**   String data types are stored as characters (such as *"C:\WINDOWS\Notepad.exe %1"*). String values are enclosed in quotation marks. An empty string value is indicated as *""*. String values are stored as a null-terminated set of characters.

- **Binary**   Binary data types are represented as a sequence of hexadecimal (or hex) bytes using the digits *0* through *9* and the letters *A* through *F* (for example, *00 03 10 3A*). An empty entry is shown as *(zero-length binary value)* in the Registry Editor. A defined value can be between 1 byte and 16 KB in size.

- **DWORD**   DWORD data types are a special case of a binary value. They are restricted to 4 bytes, and the value is shown in hexadecimals and decimals in the format *0x00000000 (0)*. The first number, *0x00000000*, is the hex representation of the value, whereas the number in brackets, *(0)*, contains the decimal representation.

> **NOTE:**   The data types for key values mentioned above are shown by the Registry Editor. A programmer can also define additional data types as special variants for key values (for example, REG_EXPAND_SZ for a zero-terminated string with Unicode or ANSI characters).

The representation and meaning of the value's data depend on the key. A binary sequence can be interpreted as a single byte, a double byte, or a byte sequence. Some numerical values are stored as strings (for example, those that affect screen resolution).

The entire hierarchy down to and including the active key is shown in the status bar of the Registry Editor. This display can help you keep track of where you are in deeply nested structures when the active key's hierarchy isn't completely visible in the left pane.

Changing an Existing Value

Before you start modifying Registry values, it's a good idea to first read "Backing Up and Recovering Your Registry," beginning on page 36. If you change your Registry's settings and Windows or an application no longer runs correctly, you will at least be able to recover the old Registry settings.

To change any key's values, you must first activate the key and display its values in the Registry Editor's right pane by clicking the key in the left pane. Then you can do one of the following:

- Double-click the value name (in the Name column of the right pane).

- Click the value name, and use the Modify command in the Edit menu.

- Right-click the value name, and select the Modify command from the context menu.

In each of these cases, the Registry Editor opens a dialog box that shows the name and value of the entry you selected. The contents of the dialog box depend on the value's data type. Figure 2-3 shows the Edit String dialog box for a text value.

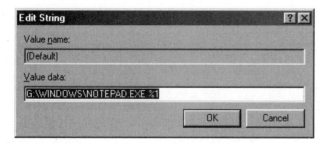

Figure 2-3.
The Edit String dialog box for a text value.

Editing a text value   If you open the Edit String dialog box and the key already contains a value, that value will be highlighted in the Value Data text box. When you type a new value into the Value Data text box and close the dialog box by clicking OK, the new value is immediately stored in the Registry.

> **NOTE:**   Text values are automatically enclosed in quotation marks *("")* by the Registry Editor. You should never enter these quotes in the Value Data text box; if you do, the value will be enclosed in double sets of quotation marks *("" ... "")*, which will cause an error.

Editing a binary value   If you choose to modify a binary value, the Registry Editor opens the Edit Binary Value dialog box (see Figure 2-4 on the following page). The value's name appears in the Value Name text box and cannot be modified.

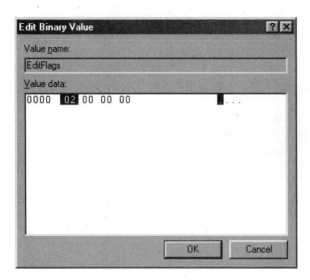

Figure 2-4.
The Edit Binary Value dialog box.

The Value Data text box displays the value in hexadecimal format. The four digits on the left indicate the offset into the data stream. The data itself is shown as a series of byte values (hex digits) followed by their character representations.

To change an existing value, first select it. This highlights the value. Any highlighted portion of the value (as shown in Figure 2-4) can then be overwritten by a new value. Clicking OK closes the dialog box and stores the new value in the Registry. The modified value is displayed in the right pane of the Registry Editor window.

> **NOTE:** Be careful to highlight a portion of the binary value in the Value Data text box before doing any editing. If no portion of the value is highlighted, your insert will be considered new data. For example, suppose you moved the cursor to a new position in the hexadecimal sequence but didn't highlight the adjacent value. If you entered a new value, that value would be inserted as a new byte and wrong data would be stored in the Registry.

Editing a DWORD value A DWORD value is altered in the Edit DWORD Value dialog box (shown in Figure 2-5). You can enter this type of value as a hexadecimal or a decimal number. Select one of the Base options, enter the value in the Value Data text box, and click OK for the new value to be stored in the Registry. A DWORD value can never exceed 32 bits (or 8 hex digits).

NOTE: You cannot change the data type of a value. Instead, you must delete the value and create a new entry with a different data type.

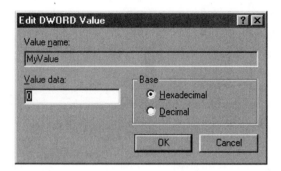

Figure 2-5.
The Edit DWORD Value dialog box.

Adding a New Key or a New Value

A key can have one or more entries in its right pane, each of which is a data value associated with a name. As you know, a key can also branch to one or more entries, or subkeys, in the left pane of the Registry Editor. If you want to add a new key to the active key, you have to define only the key name. If you want to add a new value, you must specify the name and the value. Follow these steps to insert a new entry in the Registry:

1. Right-click the desired key, or right-click anywhere in the right pane of the Registry Editor window to display the context menu.

2. Select New and one of the following commands: Key, String Value, Binary Value, or DWORD Value.

The entry type is defined by the selected command. Choosing Key adds a subkey named *NewKey* in the left pane. Choosing String Value, Binary Value, or DWORD Value creates a value name called *New Value* for the active key and places an associated null value in the Data column. (See Figure 2-6 on the following page.) You should change the default name for the new key or new value by typing over the highlighted entry.

After defining a value name in the right pane, you can enter the value for this new entry. (Follow the procedures on pages 19–21.) A string value initially has no value (""), whereas a binary value is empty and the initial value of a DWORD entry is zero. These initial values are shown in Figure 2-6.

21

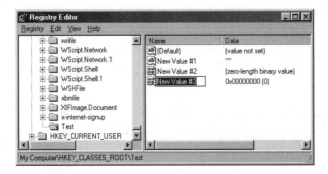

Figure 2-6.
New value entries are displayed as "New Value" in the Registry Editor.

Deleting an Entry

The Registry Editor allows you to delete keys, subkeys, and values. To delete a key or a subkey:

1. Right-click the key in the left pane, and select Delete from the context menu.

2. Click Yes in the Confirm Key Delete dialog box.

The Registry Editor removes the key and all its associated values and subkeys from the Registry. But be careful—you cannot recall the key or any of its subkeys or values once they are deleted.

To delete a value:

1. Right-click the entry in the Name column in the right pane, and select Delete from the context menu.

2. Confirm that you want to delete this value by clicking Yes in the Confirm Value Delete dialog box.

NOTE: The Registry Editor does not have an Undo function. All Registry changes are written directly to the disk. If you want to remove an item in the Registry, consider renaming the key rather than deleting it. If something goes wrong and you can no longer run certain programs or Windows doesn't run correctly, you can simply rename the key to the old name and all the original data becomes available again.

If you accidentally delete the wrong key, you can use the Registry Checker to restore a backup copy of your Registry. This tool is described in the section "Backing Up and Recovering Your Registry," later in this chapter.

The six root keys (*HKEY_XXXX*) can't be deleted.

Renaming a Key or a Value

Rename keys cautiously—a new name can dramatically affect system functionality, particularly if the key is necessary for starting Windows or for some other important task.

To rename a key or a value, right-click the item and select Rename from the context menu. The name you want to modify will be highlighted, and you can type over the string. To write the new name to the Registry, press Return or click outside the highlighted area.

Finding Information in the Registry

The Registry contains thousands of entries, so it can be difficult to find a desired key or value. You could search for it manually by scrolling through the hierarchy, but you'd have to know where the entry is located and how to navigate there to avoid spending a lot of time clicking subkeys to find the entry you're looking for.

The more efficient approach is to delegate this searching job to the Registry Editor, which has a Find command on its Edit menu. When you select this command (by clicking it or by pressing Ctrl-F), the Find dialog box shown in Figure 2-7 opens. In it you can define what you are looking for. Enter a key, a subkey, a value name, or an actual value (text or binary) in the Find What text box.

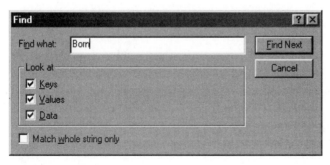

Figure 2-7.
The Find dialog box.

23

The Find function uses a pattern-matching algorithm to find substrings within a string. If you don't know the proper spelling of the value you are searching for, enter only a partial word and leave the Match Whole String Only check box blank. If you know the proper spelling, you can prevent the function from recognizing thousands of potential matches by selecting the Match Whole String Only check box. The Find function will then show only those entries that match the entire pattern. The Find dialog box's Look At options can also help you to restrict your search. All three of these options are activated by default, which means that the Registry Editor searches for matches in the whole Registry. To limit the focus of the Find function, deselect one or two of these options.

- The Keys option finds all key and subkey matches for the pattern.

- The Values option finds all value name matches. Values does not refer to the value of an item; it is the item displayed in the Name column in the right pane of the Registry Editor.

- The Data option extends or restricts the search to the value data of all keys. Data refers to the values shown in the Data column of the Registry Editor.

Click Find Next to start the search. The first match is highlighted by the Registry Editor (see Figure 2-8). As you can see in the figure, if you search for data, the value name for a match—not the matching value data—is highlighted. To find the next match, press F3 or select Find Next from the Edit menu.

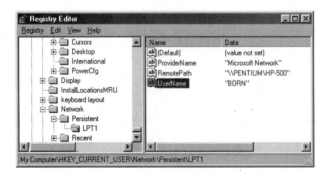

Figure 2-8.
A highlighted match in the Registry Editor.

Printing Parts of the Registry

The Registry Editor provides a function that allows you to print parts or all of the Registry. Open the Registry menu and select the Print command, or press Ctrl-P.

The Registry Editor displays the Print dialog box, like the one shown in Figure 2-9. This dialog box is similar to Print dialog boxes in other Windows 98 applications.

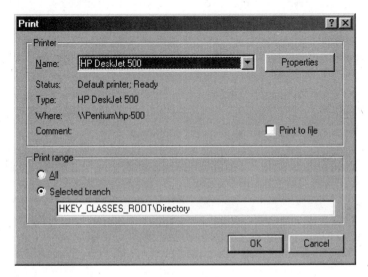

Figure 2-9.
The Print dialog box in the Registry Editor.

Select the range of the Registry Editor that you want to print by clicking one of the two options in the Print Range section of the dialog box. By default, the Selected Branch option is marked. The branch to the active key in the Registry is displayed in the text box in the Print Range group box, so it is handy to select a key in the left pane of the Registry Editor before you invoke the Print command. If you want to print the whole Registry, check the All option box. (Again, however, be careful—you'll be printing several hundred pages.)

Importing and Exporting Registry Data

Depending on the computer, the file size of the Registry database can reach several hundred KB, which is a lot to manage. Based on what you want to do or how the Registry is configured, you should consider storing and reading parts of the Registry in files. For example, if you want to share specific Registry entries (such as the settings for file extensions) between two computers, you can export the entries from one computer into a file and then import that file into the second computer. You can even edit the file and import it back to both computers. You can access import and export functions from the Registry menu.

Importing a REG File into the Registry

There are two ways to import data into the Registry: via the Registry Editor and via ActiveX functions. Both methods need files with the REG extension; REG files are created by the Windows 98 Registry Editor. Both methods produce the same results and are simple to use, so the choice is up to you.

Using the Registry Editor

The first method is implemented by selecting Import Registry File from the Registry Editor's Registry menu. After invoking this function, the Import Registry File dialog box is displayed. (See Figure 2-10.) Select a folder, select a filename (or enter a filename in the File Name text box), and then click Open.

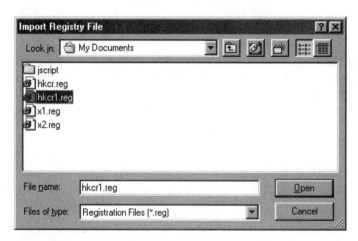

Figure 2-10.
Importing a Registry file.

Using ActiveX Features

The other method of importing REG files takes advantage of ActiveX features included in Windows 98. First you must have a valid REG file stored on your hard disk or on a diskette. Either double-click the file, or right-click the file and select the Merge command from the context menu.

Whichever method you use, all information required to import the data must be in the REG file. The Registry Editor opens this file, reads the information contained in it, and adds this data into the Registry. You cannot select a destination where the data will be stored, so if there are entries in the file that are already defined in the Registry, the Registry keys and values matching the imported keys and values will be overwritten by the new material. No query message warns you before this data is overwritten, so proceed cautiously.

An imported file must have a REG extension and requires a special format. A valid Windows 98 REG file contains only ASCII characters in a predefined format. Its first line must contain the word REGEDIT4, and its second line must be blank. The following format is valid for a REG file:

```
REGEDIT4

[HKEY_CLASSES_ROOT\.bmp]
@="Paint.Picture"

[HKEY_CLASSES_ROOT\.bmp\ShellNew]
"NullFile"=""
```

All the lines that follow the first blank line can contain entries for Registry settings. Each entry starts with the name of the destination key enclosed in square brackets ([ ]). The destination key can already exist in the Registry or can be a new Registry entry. The next line contains the value name of an entry and its associated value data—the material that will be shown later in the right pane of the Registry Editor. The value name is given in quotation marks, while the format of the data being assigned to the name depends on the data type. For example, in the second entry above, NullFile is the value name and "" is its associated string data. Also, some lines start with @= followed by value data. The @ character indicates a default value name for an entry. As we've seen, these entries are marked as *(Default)* in the Registry Editor's Name column.

After a REG file is successfully imported, a message box informs you that the file was valid, indicating that it was a valid Windows 98 REG file, that it was formatted properly, and that all the file's information was included in the Registry. Such a message box, however, does not indicate that the information contained in the file and entered into the Registry is valid. The Registry Editor can't check the contents of a REG file for logical consistency within a system. (Chapter 3 addresses this in more detail.)

Importing REG Files Created in Windows 98

All REG files can be used to change the Registry settings of your own computer or to share the information with other machines. Some software packages come with REG files that modify the Registry after the application files have been installed on the hard disk.

Unfortunately, the REG file extension is used on several Windows platforms for Registry save files. Here are a few guidelines to keep in mind when working with REG files created in Windows 98:

■ Don't import a Windows 98 REG file into older versions of Windows or into Windows NT; or, at least, be extremely careful that the REG file contains valid entries for the destined Windows platform.

■ Import into the Registry only valid Windows 98 REG files, which always contain the REGEDIT4 signature in the first line.

■ Don't import a Windows 95 or Windows NT 4.0 REG file (both of which also contain the REGEDIT4 first line) into Windows 98; or be extremely careful that the REG file contains valid entries for Windows 98.

Exporting a REG File

As we have seen, you can easily import new values from REG files into the Registry. REG files are pure ASCII files that can be created and edited in such text editors as Notepad or WordPad.

REG files can also be created by using the Registry Editor's export function, which allows you to share settings with other computers or to reuse old settings after you've changed them. To export parts of the Registry, follow these steps:

1. In the Registry Editor, select the branch or subkey that you want to export.

2. Open the Registry menu, and select Export Registry File. The Export Registry File dialog box opens. (See Figure 2-11.)

3. Select the location where you want to save the REG file you are creating.

4. Enter a filename for the REG file in the File Name text box.

5. Click Save.

After clicking Save, the Registry Editor creates a REG file containing the information from the selected branch. This REG file can now be imported as described in the previous section.

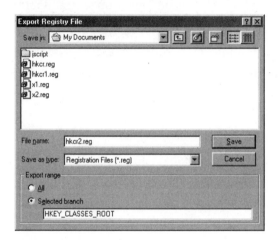

Figure 2-11.
Exporting a Registry branch.

By default, the Registry Editor exports only the active branch, the branch you selected before invoking the export function. You can export the entire Registry by selecting All in the Export Range section, but keep file size in mind. Such a REG file would be too big to edit with Notepad, and in WordPad you would have to be careful to store altered text in the text file format.

Using Export as a Backup Tool

Perhaps I haven't warned you enough to create backup copies of your Registry before you modify any entries. Okay—before you modify, back up the Registry! You can store the DAT files on a separate disk, which allows you to recover the previous Registry settings from the backup files. Again, in the section titled "Backing Up and Recovering Your Registry," I discuss this technique and other related topics.

You may be asking, "Why should I back up the whole Registry if I just want to change one entry?" We have seen that the Registry Editor offers functions that export and import parts of the Registry, so why not save time and disk capacity by creating only a partial backup? The steps for creating a partial backup are straightforward. In the Registry Editor, you select the subkey that you're going to change and then export this part of the Registry to a REG file. All the information contained in the subkey is stored in the REG file, and you can import this file later to recover that particular portion of the Registry.

Unfortunately, this approach has a trap that is still present in Windows 98 (and that caught me off guard several times while I was first working with Windows 95). To illustrate the risks, let's conduct a small experiment. First let's assume we must change an entry in the Registry. The *HKEY_CLASSES_ROOT* branch contains the registration information for file extensions. Let's modify the settings of the BMP file type. Figure 2-12 shows the relevant branch of the Registry with its subkey *ShellNew* chosen as the active key. (In Chapter 3, we'll learn how to register new file types or add commands to a file type.)

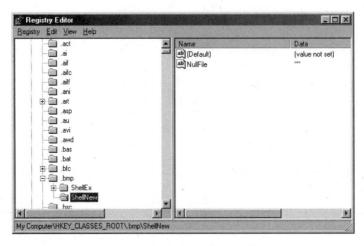

Figure 2-12.
The branch for BMP files with the original data.

Before we modify anything, let's save the information contained in the *.bmp* branch by using the export function. After exporting this branch, we have a REG file with something like the following contents:

```
REGEDIT4

[HKEY_CLASSES_ROOT\.bmp]
@="Paint.Picture"
"Content Type"="image/bmp"
```

```
[HKEY_CLASSES_ROOT\.bmp\ShellNew]
"NullFile"=""

[HKEY_CLASSES_ROOT\.bmp\ShellEx]

[HKEY_CLASSES_ROOT\.bmp\ShellEx\{BB2E617C-0920-11d1-9A0B-    ⤸
00C04FC2D6C1}]
@="{7376D660-C583-11d0-A3A5-00C04FD706EC}"
```

This is the information we find in the two panes of the Registry Editor. Now we are prepared to modify the *.bmp* branch. First I change the value of the *NullFile* entry, and then I add a subkey and another value to the *ShellNew* subkey. I name both the new subkey and the new value *Born* and give *ShellNew*'s data entries (*Born* and *NullFile*) arbitrary values. You can see the resulting Registry structure in Figure 2-13.

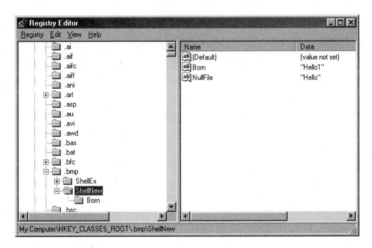

Figure 2-13.
The modified structure of the .bmp *branch.*

Of course, the changes I've made are nonsense, but I use them to illustrate my point. To avoid trouble while running Windows or any applications, we want to remove these nonsensical changes from the Registry, so we should import the REG file we created that contains the previous data (expecting the modifications to be deleted during the import). No problem—the old settings are only a mouse click away. We simply use the Import Registry File command to import the REG file.

The result is shown in Figure 2-14 on the following page: the value for *NullFile* is set back to its previous value, but neither the new subkey *Born* nor the new value *Born* are deleted. What's wrong with our REG file? Well, there's nothing wrong. Importing a REG file does not replace the data in the Registry—it adds to it. If an entry (a value name or a key name) that is not in the Registry exists in the REG file, that entry is added to the Registry. If an entry is in both the Registry and the REG file, the entry in the REG file overwrites the data of the matching entry in the Registry. So entries that are in the Registry but not in the REG file, such as our *Born* value and *Born* subkey, are left untouched in the Registry. (The word "Merge" on the REG file's context menu expresses this.)

> **WARNING:** The import function does not delete or reset new entries in the Registry. Because you can change only previously existing entries, it is not safe to back up the Registry with the export function of the Registry Editor and then attempt to recover the old hierarchy and settings with the import function!

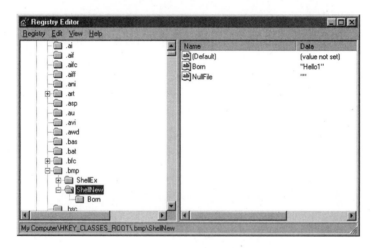

Figure 2-14.
The branch after importing the old values.

Remote Access to the Registry

Windows 98 provides a feature to allow remote Registry access from other computers. This feature, called the Microsoft Remote Registry service, is helpful in networking environments where the network administrator might need to change Registry entries on several PCs.

Installing the Remote Registry Service

The Remote Registry feature isn't installed during the standard Windows setup. This feature can be enabled only in networks that support user-level access control with a server such as Microsoft Windows NT or Novell NetWare. (Windows 98 clients don't have a user-level access control.) To access the Connect Network Registry command from the Registry menu, you must install the Remote Registry service on both the client and the server.

To install this service, do the following:

1. Select the Network icon in the Control Panel.

2. Click Add on the Configuration property page.

3. Select the Service icon in the Select Network Component Type dialog box, and click Add.

4. In the Select Network Service dialog box, click Have Disk.

5. Insert the Windows 98 CD-ROM, and then enter the CD-ROM drive letter and the path \tools\reskit\netadmin\Remotreg.

6. Click OK in the Install From Disk dialog box.

Windows installs the necessary components. After a successful installation, select the Access Control property page on the Network property sheet and set the option box to User-Level Access Control. To access the Registry of a remote computer, open the Registry Editor's Registry menu and select Connect Network Registry (see Figure 2-15).

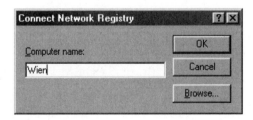

Figure 2-15.
The Connect Network Registry dialog box.

Enter the name of the remote computer, or click the Browse button to scan the whole network. After successfully connecting to the remote computer, you can alter its Registry.

Accessing the Registry in Real Mode

Suppose the Registry is completely corrupted and Windows 98 won't start. You can't start the Windows version of the Registry Editor. How can you inspect the Registry under such circumstances?

The answer is pretty simple: the Registry Editor also runs in MS-DOS real mode, so if you can boot your computer and enter DOS mode, you can access the Registry Editor. You can find a copy of the Registry Editor (REGEDIT.EXE) in the \Windows folder. If you invoke REGEDIT.EXE under Windows 98, the Registry Editor window is displayed. Under DOS, the Registry Editor will have only a command line interface.

When you run REGEDIT.EXE from the DOS prompt without any command line options, a help screen advising you how to use this tool appears. To import a REG file into the Registry, use the following command:

```
REGEDIT /L:system /R:user filename
```

The first switch, */L:system*, is optional and specifies the location of the SYSTEM.DAT file. This file is always located in the Windows folder. The second switch, */R:user*, is also optional and specifies the location of the USER.DAT file. This file can be located in the Windows folder or in another folder. Its location depends on the configuration of your computer, as you saw in Chapter 1. *Filename* is the name of the REG file that will be imported. For example, the following command will import the contents of GLOBAL.REG into USER.DAT and SYSTEM.DAT:

```
REGEDIT /L:C:\Windows\System.dat ⟶
/R:C:\Windows\Profiles\Born\User.dat A:Global.REG
```

This command can be used to add keys to the Registry and overwrite data in existing keys.

NOTE: In the command above, I assumed that user profiles are enabled and that one of the users is Born. SYSTEM.DAT and USER.DAT are system-protected files. To use REGEDIT from the command line, you must first use the *attrib* command to change the permissions on these files: *attrib -s -h system.dat*.

If you want to create a new Registry database, you must use the /C switch. The following command will create two new files, USER.DAT and SYSTEM.DAT, in the Windows folder from the GLOBAL.REG file located on the A: drive:

```
REGEDIT /C A:Global.REG
```

This command is completely different from the previous example because the whole Registry is re-created from GLOBAL.REG, rather than being only modified.

NOTE: Using the /C option to rebuild the Registry database is dangerous. When you import the REG file, if the REG file contains only one branch of the Registry, the complete SYSTEM.DAT and USER.DAT files will contain only this branch. Always be sure that you have a REG file containing the entire Registry database before you use this option.

You can also export some parts of the Registry in DOS mode:

```
REGEDIT /L:System /R:User /E filename
```

The /L and /R switches specify the location of the SYSTEM.DAT and USER.DAT files. The /E switch advises REGEDIT.EXE to export the Registry into a new file, which is named in the last parameter as *filename*. This creates a copy of the whole Registry.

You can also specify a Registry key to export:

```
REGEDIT /E filename regkey
```

The parameter *regkey* defines the Registry key that will be exported into the REG file.

Another action you can perform from the command line is to delete a key from the Registry. Use the following command to delete a key (along with all its subkeys and values):

```
REGEDIT /D regkey
```

NOTE: I don't recommend that you use REGEDIT.EXE within the DOS command prompt. There are too many parameters, and the risk is high that you will destroy part or all of the Registry. The real-mode version of REGEDIT.EXE also has problems importing large keys. (You'll often get an error message.) Using the real-mode version should be the last choice to recover the Registry.

I've used real mode only when I need to update the Registry during a system startup, in which case I included a REGEDIT command in AUTOEXEC.BAT.

Backing Up and Recovering Your Registry

A corrupted Registry prevents the system from starting properly, so backing up and recovering the Registry are two important tasks you need to know how to perform. You can perform these tasks in several ways, but some methods are riskier than others. Also, Windows 98 uses a new tool called Registry Checker to scan (and fix) the Registry during each system start. In this section I will discuss how to use backup and recovery tools for the Registry.

> WARNING: Two Registry recovery tools, the Error Recovery Utility (ERU/ERD) that ships with Windows 95 and the CFGBack utility that ships with the Windows 95 Resource Kit, are not available in Windows 98. *Do not use these tools to create and restore Registry backups in Windows 98.* Doing so will corrupt your system. Windows 98 provides its own Registry tools, described below.

Manually Backing Up

Suppose you would like to keep the current version of your Registry for future reference. The simplest way to create a backup of your Registry is manually—by starting Windows Explorer and copying the SYSTEM.DAT and USER.DAT files onto a bootable disk—but this could present a file size problem. I've seen many versions of the Registry that need more than 1 MB of disk space. If you want to store both files on one disk, you must use a compression program such as Nico Mak Computing's WinZip or PKWARE's PKZIP.

If the Registry is corrupted and you want to recover an uncorrupted Registry from a backup disk, you must use the DOS copy command (remember—Windows won't restart properly). The SYSTEM.DAT and USER.DAT files are stored with the attributes Read-Only, Hidden, and System. Reset these before you copy the backup Registry to your hard disk. After you copy the files, you have to set the correct attributes again. You can do all this with a simple batch program:

```
c:
cd \Windows
attrib -h -r -s system.dat
attrib -h -r -s user.dat
copy a:\user.dat
copy a:\system.dat
attrib +h +r +s system.dat
attrib +h +r +s user.dat
```

Once USER.DAT and SYSTEM.DAT are on your hard disk, you can restart the computer or, from MS-DOS mode, start Windows 98 with the WIN command.

NOTE: You can keep a copy of this batch program and a copy of the DOS program ATTRIB.EXE (found in \Windows\Command) on your backup disk. Keep in mind, however, that the batch commands in this program rely on the fact that your hard disk is your C: drive. If not, you must change the drive letter in the commands.

I have seen this backup method published in magazines and on Web pages. And the procedure will work, of course. The risk is that you will back up and recover the wrong data. I mentioned in Chapter 1 that SYSTEM.DAT is always stored in the Windows folder along with a copy of USER.DAT. Unfortunately, Windows can keep several versions of USER.DAT, each in a different location. If you enable user profiles, each user gets his or her own copy of USER.DAT. During user logon, Windows determines which copy to use. This copy is located in the Windows subfolder \Profiles*name*, where *name* is the name of the active user. You should be careful to copy the correct USER.DAT file back to the correct folder.

Using the Windows 98 Startup Disk to Boot Your System

If you're having trouble with your computer, boot your computer in MS-DOS mode. The Windows 98 Setup process creates a startup disk during Windows 98 installation. This disk contains a mini-DOS operating system, which includes a special version of AUTOEXEC.BAT and CONFIG.SYS. The emergency boot disk (as the startup disk is also called) has significantly changed in Windows 98 (when compared to that for Windows 95). The emergency boot disk contains a CAB file (EBD.CAB) with most of the tools, such as ATTRIB.EXE and SCANDISK.EXE, needed to repair your system. Booting the system with this disk also creates a RAM disk to hold these tools. If your computer can't boot with Windows 98, try to restart the system with this startup disk. After doing so, you can access your Windows folder on your hard disk. The Windows folder contains all the tools, including REGEDIT.EXE, and files required to repair your system.

Creating a New Startup Disk

If you received Windows 98 preinstalled and there is no startup disk, you can easily create one. All you need is a spare disk and a few minutes. You can create the disk as follows:

1. Open the Control Panel, and double-click the Add/Remove Programs icon. Windows 98 opens the Add/Remove Programs Properties dialog box shown in Figure 2-16 on the following page.

2. Select the Startup Disk property page, insert a disk in the disk drive, and click Create Disk.

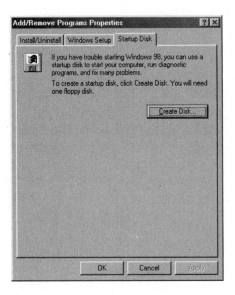

Figure 2-16.
The property page for creating a startup disk.

Follow the Windows 98 prompts to create the new startup disk. Label this copy, and use it later to restart your computer.

NOTE: Although the startup disk contains only a minimal system with the standard files, Microsoft has extended the startup disk to also contain special device drivers to access some hardware (for example, ATAPI drivers and MSCDEX.EXE for a CD-ROM drive). All device drivers are expanded onto the RAM disk after MS-DOS is booted.

Using the Windows Registry Checker

A new enhancement in Windows 98, the Registry Checker is a maintenance program that finds and fixes Registry problems and that regularly backs up the Registry. Windows 98 comes with two versions of this program:

- SCANREG.EXE is the MS-DOS version and is used to restore the Registry.

- SCANREGW.EXE is the Windows 98–based version of the program.

Each time Windows 98 starts, SCANREGW.EXE scans the Registry for inconsistent structures. If no problems are found, Registry Checker makes a backup copy of the Registry (see further explanations below). If a serious problem is found, Windows restarts in real mode and the SCANREG.EXE version of the Registry Checker restores the most recent backup copy or fixes the Registry. Restoring the Registry isn't a problem at this point because the system is in real mode so the Registry isn't in use. If a backup can't be found, Registry Checker attempts to fix the Registry. (You can also use the *ScanReg/FIX* command to perform this step.)

Because unused space is left in Registry files, the Registry can grow to an unnecessary size. The Registry Checker's initial scan also searches for such unused space and removes it, thus reducing the size of the Registry and improving performance.

How to Use SCANREGW.EXE and SCANREG.EXE

Although SCANREG.EXE automatically runs during each system start to maintain the system, you can also use the protected-mode Windows executable SCANREGW.EXE to back up the Registry. This can be helpful if you are installing new software for test purposes, for example, and need a snapshot of the previous system settings. SCANREGW.EXE is located in the Windows directory. To use it to create a Registry backup, open Windows Explorer, search for the Windows folder, and double-click the SCANREGW.EXE file. The program will check the Registry for corruption and determine if it requires optimization. If no problems are detected, the Registry Scan Results dialog box will ask whether to create a backup (see Figure 2-17). To create a new backup, click Yes.

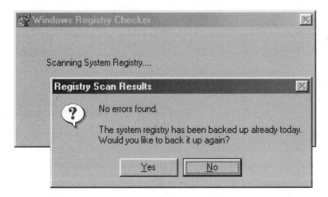

Figure 2-17.
The ScanRegW scan results.

If the Registry Checker detects a problem with the Registry, it offers to restart the computer and fix the problem. This causes SCANREG.EXE to restore the Registry from one of the backups (or, if no backup exists, to repair the Registry). To force a restoration, take the following steps:

1. Restart the computer in MS-DOS mode. (From the Start menu, click Shut Down, select Restart In MS-DOS Mode, and click OK.)

2. From the MS-DOS command prompt, type the command *ScanReg /RESTORE*.

3. Select the latest known good backup.

The *ScanReg /RESTORE* command restores a backup that you choose from the backup files. Those backup files are created each time the computer starts and, as previously mentioned, whenever SCANREGW.EXE is executed.

The DOS version of the Registry Checker can be used in several different ways. (The *ScanReg /?* command displays a help screen showing all available *ScanReg* switches.) To create a Registry backup under MS-DOS, use the following command:

```
ScanReg /BACKUP
```

This command forces the Registry Checker to scan the Registry and to create a backup without prompting the user if no problems are detected. To specify a comment to add to the Registry backup set, use this switch:

```
ScanReg /COMMENT="text string with comment"
```

This comment is displayed with the list of backup files in place of the CAB filename when you run ScanReg with the */RESTORE* command. As described above, to replace a corrupted Registry by restoring a backup, type:

```
ScanReg /RESTORE
```

This command first causes a list of available backup files to be displayed, sorted by date and time of backup. If no Registry backup files are available, you can repair the Registry by using this switch:

```
ScanReg /FIX
```

Both to test whether the Registry is corrupted and to automatically back up the Registry's files, enter:

```
ScanRegW /AUTOSCAN
```

Strictly to test whether the Registry is corrupted, use this switch:

ScanRegW /SCANONLY

NOTE: The AUTOSCAN and SCANONLY options are available for use only with ScanRegW, not with ScanReg.

When you use SCANREG.EXE to scan Registry files, the program returns an error level. Table 2-1 contains the program's error level codes.

Error Level Codes Returned by SCANREG.EXE

Error Level	Remark
0	No problems found
1	Fixable errors found
2	Registry is bad and can't be fixed
-2	Not enough memory; free some conventional memory (HIMEM requested)
-3	File not found (one or both Registry files are missing)
-4	Unable to create USER.DAT or SYSTEM.DAT
-5	Reading the Registry failed

Table 2-1.
The error level codes returned by SCANREG.EXE give you information about the program's Registry scan.

How the Registry Checker
Creates and Maintains Registry Backups

By default, SCANREGW.EXE and SCANREG.EXE create a backup copy of the files USER.DAT, SYSTEM.DAT, WIN.INI, and SYSTEM.INI. These files are stored in a CAB file, which is located in the hidden folder \Windows\SysBckup. Windows 98 uses a simple scheme to create and maintain these backups:

■ On the first successful boot, a CAB file is created and marked as a Registry backup that is capable of booting the system. This file is used by SCANREG.EXE to restore the Registry if a problem is detected during another system startup.

■ Depending on your system's settings, several CAB files containing backups can exist. Each file is named rb*xxx*.cab; where *xxx* stands for a unique number from *000* to *099* (see Figure 2-18 on the following page). By default, Windows 98 creates up to five CAB files, but you have the option to save up to 100 copies. (See the INI file below for instructions on how to change this setting.) Each of these CAB files can be used to restore the Registry and system files.

■ The CAB file used as the current backup is created once per day during the first startup. The new file replaces the oldest CAB file, and the other CAB files are renamed.

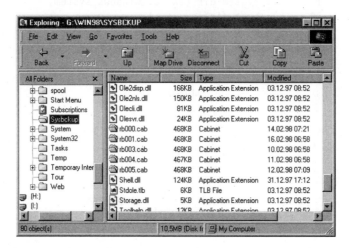

Figure 2-18.
CAB files from Registry backups.

System administrators can customize the Registry Checker by modifying the SCANREG.INI file, shown below, which is located in the Windows folder.

```
;
; Scanreg.ini for making system backups.
;

;Registry backup is skipped altogether if this is set to 0
Backup=1

;Registry automatic optimization is skipped if this is set to 0
Optimize=1

ScanregVersion=0.0001
MaxBackupCopies=5

;Backup directory where the cabs are stored is
; <windir>\sysbckup by default. Value below overrides it.
```

```
; It must be a full path. ex. c:\tmp\backup
;
BackupDirectory=

; Additional system files to back up into cab as follows:
; Filenames are separated by ','
; dir code can be:
;       10        : windir (ex. c:\windows)
;       11        : system dir (ex. c:\windows\system)
;       30        : boot dir (ex. c:\)
;       31        : boot host dir (ex. c:\)
;
;Files=[dir code,]file1,file2,file3
;Files=[dir code,]file1,file2,file3
```

Changing the value of the *Backup* setting to *0* prevents the Registry Checker from creating a Registry backup.

As I mentioned earlier, the number of backup copies is set to *5* by default. You can change this default value by changing the *MaxBackupCopies* setting. You can specify a value from *1* to *99*. A value of *99* allows Windows 98 to keep up to 99 backup copies of your Registry. Each copy contains the Registry snapshot of a single day. When the *MaxBackupCopies* limit is reached, Registry Checker overwrites the oldest CAB file copy. Registry Checker uses the Windows folder \SysBckup as the destination for the CAB files. To set any other folder as the backup destination, change the *BackupDirectory* setting.

> **TIP:** If you want to save a backup copy of the current Registry settings in a separate folder, you can modify the *BackupDirectory* setting, run SCANREGW.EXE to back up the current Registry settings, and then reset the *BackupDirectory* setting. You can restore the Registry from the rb*xxx*.cab file in that directory by renaming the file to rb099.cab, for example, and copying it to the SysBckup folder. Then run ScanReg / RESTORE as described earlier.

By editing the SCANREG.INI file, you can also have the Registry Checker back up more files than USER.DAT, SYSTEM.DAT, SYSTEM.INI, and WIN.INI into the CAB files. If you need a complete system files snapshot, for example, you can also include your AUTOEXEC.BAT and CONFIG.SYS in your backup. You can do this by editing the last lines in the INI file as shown here:

```
Files=30, Autoexec.bat, Config.sys
```

TIP: If you want to see the contents of a CAB file, open the \SysBckup folder, right-click on the CAB file, and select the View command from the context menu. Windows 98 opens a window containing the files that are stored in the CAB archive. Dragging these files from this window into a new folder essentially expands the CAB file and makes the files available for your use.

NOTE: As mentioned in Chapter 1, Windows 95 uses two files, USER.DA0 and SYSTEM.DA0, to keep a backup of the Registry. The CAB archives used in Windows 98 are a more advanced method of keeping Registry backups. Windows NT 4.0 uses its own scheme to keep Registry backups (see Appendix C).

NOTE: During the installation of Windows 98, the Setup program analyzes the system hardware and uses that information to create the SYSTEM.DAT file. After the installation, Setup leaves a copy of this original SYSTEM.DAT file in the root directory of the hard disk in the file SYSTEM.1ST. This file can be helpful if SYSTEM.DAT is destroyed.

Using Microsoft Backup to Save Your Registry

Using SCANREGW.EXE as a backup tool doesn't give you a simple means of fully controlling the backup process, and the old tools from Windows 95, ERU and CFGBack, are no longer supported in Windows 98. Needless to say, I was really unhappy with the process of having to create a Registry backup by using ScanRegW and then restore it later on with ScanReg under MS-DOS. So I began searching for another solution that would be available to all Windows 98 users. As I was writing the German edition of the Windows 98 handbook for Microsoft Press, I found a neat trick.

Windows 98 comes with a new backup tool: Microsoft Backup (MSBACK-UP.EXE). This program is installed as an optional Windows component and is available from the Start menu by selecting Programs/Accessories/System Tools/Backup. My first impression upon starting Backup was that it was only usable if the machine it is running on is equipped with a tape drive. But after further inspection, I found that Backup can also create a backup on a local drive and that the backup can include Registry information.

NOTE: Starting Backup the first time after installing it might display a dialog box reporting a missing tape. Select Cancel to dismiss this dialog box. Backup will accept this and will use a local file as a backup medium.

To create a Registry backup by using the Backup program, you must perform the following steps:

1. Start the Backup program from the Windows Start menu.

2. If the Backup Wizard dialog box is displayed, click Cancel.

3. When prompted, choose Create A New Backup Job and click OK.

4. At this point the Backup Wizard starts. You can select Back Up My Computer or Back Up Selected Files and click Next to continue through the Backup Wizard, or you can click Cancel and perform your backup manually from the Microsoft Backup window, shown in Figure 2-19. We'll choose the second option and click Cancel.

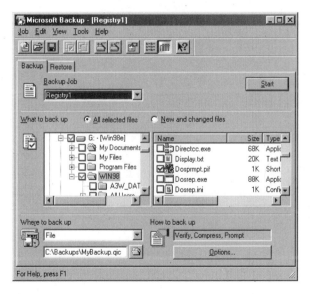

Figure 2-19.
The Microsoft Backup application.

5. Select the Backup property sheet in the Microsoft Backup window.

6. Enter the path and filename for the location where you want the backup to be stored in the Where To Back Up text box. If your machine has a tape drive, select a backup medium.

7. Check the All Selected Files option box in the What To Back Up group.

8. Select a drive and a folder in the left pane of the What To Back Up section. Check the check box of a small file, such as DOSPRMPT.PIF shown in Figure 2-19.

9. Click the Options button. Select the Advanced property page on the Backup Job Options property sheet. Check the check box Back Up Windows Registry, as shown in Figure 2-20. Click OK.

10. Click the Start button. Backup displays a dialog box that reads "This Job Must Be Saved Before Starting. Would You Like To Save This Job Now?" Click Yes, and enter a name for the backup.

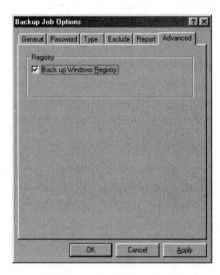

Figure 2-20.
The Advanced property page.

NOTE: In Step 8 above, you need to select at least one file for your backup set for a backup to be created. To keep the backup set with your Registry data as small as possible, select a small file as a "dummy" for your backup. Take care to use a file whose content won't change between backup and restore. If you change your PIF files, use one of the wallpaper bitmaps such as TRIANGLES.BMP instead. You can set the Restore options to skip files that are already available, but it's safer to use a file whose content won't change.

Backup backs up the selected file and includes the Registry in the backup set. After backing up, you can view the backup report by using the Report push button in the Backup Progress dialog box to verify that your Registry has been successfully backed up. (See Figure 2-21.)

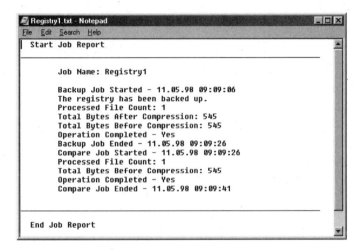

Figure 2-21.
Backup Report window.

> **WARNING:** This method of backing up and restoring your Registry is only available from within Windows. If your Registry has changed and you're unable to start Windows, you won't be able to recover using Microsoft Backup. To protect your computer from major faults that can cause Windows not to start, you should also create a backup by using SCANREGW.EXE. This backup can be used in emergency cases to fix Registry problems and restart the system.

Now it's safe for you to modify some entries in your Registry. If you need to restore the old Registry settings kept in the backup set, follow these steps:

1. Start Backup from the Windows Start menu. If the Backup Wizard dialog box is shown, click Cancel.

2. Select the Restore property sheet in the Microsoft Backup window. (See Figure 2-22 on the next page.)

3. Select a backup set from the Select Backup Sets dialog box, and click OK. From the Restore property page, select the backup medium (if your machine supports a tape drive) and enter the backup path in the Restore From text box.

4. Select the Original Location from the Where To Restore drop-down list.

5. Click Options. Select the Advanced property page on the Restore Options property sheet. Check the check box Restore Windows Registry. Click OK.

6. Select the files to restore from the options in the What To Restore group, and click Start. Backup displays the Media Required dialog box. Click OK.

7. Click Yes in the dialog box that says "This Volume Contains The Windows Registry. Do You Want To Restore The Windows Registry?" Click Yes again in the dialog box that asks "Would You Like To Restore The Hardware And System Settings Contained In The Registry?"

Backup restores the Registry settings kept in the backup set. After restoring the Registry, check the report file by clicking the Report button in the Restore Progress dialog box. Reboot your system to be sure that all old settings take effect.

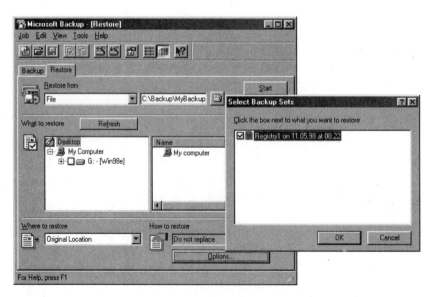

Figure 2-22.
Restore property sheet.

When to Use Which Method?

Maybe now you're wondering when you should use Microsoft Backup and when you should use ScanRegW for a Registry backup. Are ScanReg and ScanRegW sufficient to do the backup job? When should you use which tool?

Please keep in mind that the purpose of the Windows 98 Registry Checker (ScanReg) is different from that of the Backup program mentioned above. The Registry Checker tries to detect Registry problems and repair them with the last known good configuration backup. Therefore, by default, the Registry Checker always keeps up to five backup sets. But remember that each start of SCANREGW.EXE overwrites the daily copies of those backup sets. As a result, there's no simple way to save one known configuration for a special purpose. SCANREG.EXE and SCANREGW.EXE are good as a "life preserver" for your Registry and for your system.

Backup gives you full control over the backup process. It allows you to decide when to create a backup, and it stores the backup in its own folder. Later on you can restore this backup by using the Restore option. This comes in handy if you like to create a snapshot of your current system settings (before you install new software, for instance). If something goes wrong, you're able to roll your system back to its previous state.

The System Policy Editor

During startup, Windows reads the data stored in SYSTEM.DAT and in USER.DAT, which can be different for each user. System administrators customize user settings in USER.DAT. For example, a system administrator might restrict a particular user's access to certain desktop components or Start menu commands or might change the location of the user's USER.DAT file itself. The tool for changing such settings is the System Policy Editor, which is shipped on the Windows 98 CD-ROM. Changing a setting with the System Policy Editor affects the Registry's settings. We'll look at how to install and use the System Policy Editor in this chapter; I'll discuss the different system settings available through the System Policy Editor in later chapters.

Installing the System Policy Editor

The System Policy Editor is available on the Windows CD-ROM in \tools\reskit\ netadmin\Poledit. To install the System Policy Editor on your hard disk, follow the steps on the following page.

1. Open the Control Panel.

2. Double-click the Add/Remove Programs icon.

3. Click the Windows Setup tab.

4. Click Have Disk on the Windows Setup property page. The Install From Disk dialog box is displayed.

5. Enter the path \tools\reskit\netadmin\Poledit. Click OK.

6. Select the System Policy Editor option shown in the Have Disk dialog box (shown in Figure 2-23), and click Install. The files contained in the \Poledit subfolder are installed in the \Windows folder on your hard disk.

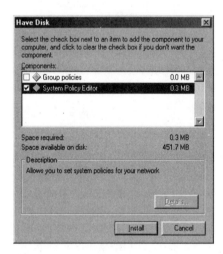

Figure 2-23.
The Have Disk dialog box.

After the files are successfully installed, you can start the program by double-clicking the POLEDIT.EXE file icon.

Enabling User Profiles

Before you can use individual user profiles, you must enable them in Windows 98. To enable user profiles, follow the steps on the following page.

1. Open the Control Panel, and then open Passwords.

2. Select the User Profiles tab (shown in Figure 2-24), and check the second option, which allows users to customize their preferences and desktop settings.

3. Select appropriate options under User Profile Settings, and click OK.

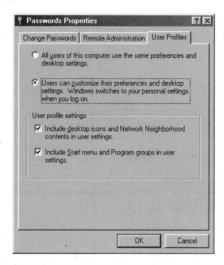

Figure 2-24.
The User Profiles property page.

After restarting the system, individual users can log on with a user name and a password. Now you are prepared to change user profile settings with the System Policy Editor.

Using the System Policy Editor

When you start the System Policy Editor for the first time, a blank window is displayed. You can read the current Registry by selecting Open Registry from the File menu. The System Policy Editor will then show two icons: Local User and Local Computer. (See Figure 2-25 on the following page.)

Double-clicking these icons opens dialog boxes that display the Registry options. Double-clicking the Local Computer icon displays the Local Computer Properties property sheet, which shows system settings. (See Figure 2-26.)

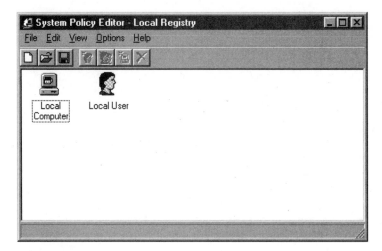

Figure 2-25.
The System Policy Editor.

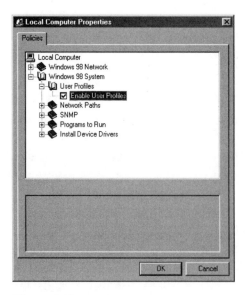

Figure 2-26.
The Local Computer Properties property sheet displays system settings.

Double-clicking the Local User icon displays the Local User Properties property sheet (see Figure 2-27), which allows you to set restrictions for the active user, to customize the shell, and so on. Any values you change here are stored in the Registry. (I will discuss several topics concerning the System Policy Editor in later chapters.)

> NOTE: You can also use the System Policy Editor to set up profiles for other users. More information can be found in the *Microsoft Windows 98 Resource Kit*, which is available from Microsoft Press.

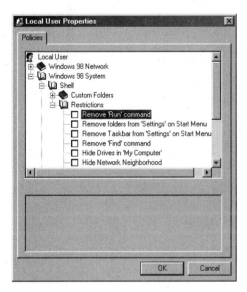

Figure 2-27.
The Local User Properties property sheet displays user-specific settings.

Other Tools for Changing Registry Settings

The Registry Editor and System Policy Editor are only two tools for changing Registry settings. Following is a description of additional tools:

- ■ **The Open With dialog box** Use this tool with the Windows shell to change registered file types. This technique is discussed further in Chapter 3.

- ■ **The File Types property page** Select Options from the Explorer's View menu to access the property page File Types, which allows you to inspect and alter Registry settings for registered file types. This technique is discussed further in Chapter 3.

- **The Control Panel**   The Control Panel contains several icons. Double-clicking an icon will open a property sheet, which contains Registry settings that can be altered.

- **Add-on utilities**   Several add-on utilities (such as Tweak UI) are available for changing Registry settings. Some functions of the Tweak UI utility are discussed in later chapters.

- **Property sheets of applications**   Some application programs store their settings in the Registry. You can update these settings by modifying the options in the appropriate application property sheet.

- **REG and INF files**   REG and INF files are discussed in Chapters 3 through 7.

- **Install programs**   Install programs are discussed briefly in Chapter 7.

CHAPTER THREE

Registering Filename Extensions

When you double-click a filename in Microsoft Windows 98, the file opens in an application associated with that file type. For example, double-clicking a file with a DOC extension opens the file in Microsoft Word (assuming you have Word installed on your machine). The file is opened in the appropriate application because the file extension is stored in the Registry with an association to that application. This chapter describes the different ways to register new file types, extend the commands for registered file types, and delete unnecessary associations. But first we'll discuss the *HKEY_CLASSES_ROOT* Registry structure.

The *HKEY_CLASSES_ROOT* Structure

File types and their associations to specific applications are stored in the Registry during the installation of new software. An application's setup program registers the file extension of the file type and the commands that are applied to this file type. All this information is stored in the *HKEY_CLASSES_ROOT* branch.

Each file type must have two keys in *HKEY_CLASSES_ROOT*. The first key defines the file extension and a name (*name_ID*) for this file type. This name is then used in a second key to define the commands for this file type. The Registry structure for a registered file type is as follows:

```
HKEY_CLASSES_ROOT
    .ext = "name_ID"
    name_ID = <"Description">
        shell
            verb = <menu item text>
                command = command string
            ⋮
```

The text shown in brackets (< >) is optional. Since this generic representation of the structure probably looks a little too abstract, let's examine a particular application of the structure—in this case, for the BAT file extension—and see its appearance in the Registry interface. A BAT file type is registered during the Windows 98 setup, creating two keys in the Registry: the *.bat* key and the *batfile* key. Figure 3-1 shows these keys.

Figure 3-1.
Keys for registering the BAT file type.

The *.bat* key defines the file extension (BAT) and the associated value (*name_ID*). This *name_ID* is set to the string *"batfile"*, which is the unique name identifier for the second key. (You can use any name that is valid for a key. For example, *"batchfile"* would also be valid.)

Although the BAT extension is registered by the inclusion of the *.bat* key, Windows needs some additional information about what to do with a BAT file—in other words, some executable commands that enable the user to double-click and open such a file. This is handled by the second key shown in Figure 3-1, *batfile*. The figure's second *Default* value defines the description text, *"MS-DOS Batch File"*, for the file type. This description is what you see in Windows Explorer in the Type column and in the Registered File Types list on the File Types property page of the Folder Options dialog box. The *EditFlags* value enables and disables the edit options in the Edit File Type dialog box (and is discussed later in this chapter beginning on page 106). More interesting than the values of the *batfile* key, however, are its subkeys.

The *DefaultIcon* Subkey

If you open a window (for example, the My Computer window or the Windows Explorer window), each file appearing in the window is shown with an associated icon. Every registered file type has its own symbol to help simplify the identification of a file's type. Information about each of these icons is defined in the *DefaultIcon* subkey. The *Default* value for this subkey is set to the path and filename that contains the icon. The BAT file value, for example, is set to the SHELL32.DLL file in the \Windows\System folder because that DLL file includes the icon associated with BAT files. Because the DLL file contains a collection of different icons, however, an index is required to select the appropriate icon. (The first icon has the index *0.*) The value for a BAT file, then, is set to something like this:

```
"C:\Windows\System\Shell32.dll,-153"
```

For other file types, this path might address other EXE or DLL files, such as this:

```
"C:\Windows\Notepad.exe, 1"
```

This string uses the Notepad icon as the default icon for a file type. (We'll see further examples of assigning icons in the following chapters.) If the source file for an icon contains only one icon, no comma or index value following the filename is necessary.

> **NOTE:** Depending on the handler for the file type, you can omit the name of the icon file and use *"%1"* instead. This means that the Windows icon handler can use a different symbol for each instance of a file type. In this case, the *IconHandler* key must be added to the *shellex* key. In Chapter 5, I'll show how this can be used to customize the Windows shell.
>
> Another issue concerns the index number given for an icon. As you know, if the icon source (an EXE, DLL, or ICO file) contains more than one icon, you must specify an icon index. Icons are indexed with positive values starting from *0.* However, if you look at the *Default* value for the *DefaultIcon* entry in the *batfile* key (see above), you will notice that the index is a negative value (*−153*). In cases such as this, the icon is designated using a resource contained in an EXE or DLL file. A negative value defines a resource identifier, so the *"C:\Windows\System\Shell32.dll, −153"* value means the resource defined with the identifier *−153* will be used for the icon. To use a resource as an icon source, you must know the resource identifier. Unfortunately, Windows 98 doesn't come with a tool you can use to inspect resource identifiers; you need a resource construction tool found in software packages such as Microsoft Visual C++. Therefore, I haven't used resource identifiers in this book.

The *shell* Subkey

The second subkey under the *batfile* key is named *shell* (as shown in Figure 3-1). This subkey is important because Windows 98 retrieves information from it about what actions the shell (that is, the Windows operating system) can perform on the BAT file type. For example, double-clicking a file of a registered file type causes certain commands to execute: files with the extensions BAT, COM, and EXE are executed, a TXT file is loaded into Notepad, and so on. Figure 3-2 shows how this shell information is stored in the Registry.

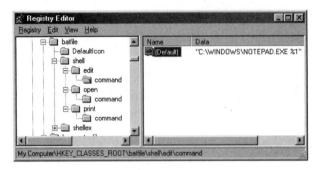

Figure 3-2.
Subkeys of the shell *key.*

The *shell* subkey contains other subkeys defining the actions that can be performed on the given file type—in this example, the BAT file type. (Sometimes these subkeys are called *verbs*.) In Figure 3-2, the subkeys (or verbs) *edit*, *open*, and *print* are shown. If you select a BAT file by right-clicking it, you will find the commands Edit, Open, and Print on the context menu. Double-clicking a BAT file invokes the *open* verb, which is the default in this case. For information on setting the default command, see the section "Defining the Default Command for a Registered File Type" later in this chapter.

Each verb subkey can contain a *command* subkey. This subkey contains the command string in its *Default* value entry. Figure 3-2 shows the *command* subkey for the *edit* verb. The subkeys *open* and *print* also contain *command* subkeys.

The *Default* value of the *command* subkey is set to a string with the name of the executable application that will run when the verb is selected from the context menu. The command string for the *edit* verb in the *batfile* subkey looks like this:

```
"C:\WINDOWS\NOTEPAD.EXE %1"
```

This line is easy to understand—it contains the drive, path, and name of an application. The parameter *%1* is just a placeholder. When the user selects the Edit command from the context menu, the shell invokes the application and replaces the *%1* placeholder with the path and filename of the selected file. If the application needs some optional parameters, you can add these parameters into the command line. The following lines define a Play command for a file that runs in the CD Player application:

```
shell
    play
        command = "C:\WINDOWS\CDPLAYER.EXE /play %1"
```

The *shellex* Subkey

The third subkey in the *batfile* branch shown in Figure 3-2 is named *shellex*. This key is optional and contains information about shell extensions that handle the BAT file type under Windows 98. Windows offers a special property sheet handler for files with this subkey. (See Figure 3-3.)

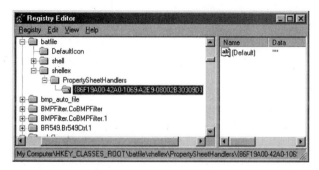

Figure 3-3.
The PropertySheetHandlers *subkey under the* shellex *subkey.*

The subkey under *PropertySheetHandlers* appears to be cryptic, but its function and attributes are fairly straightforward. The subkey defines the Class ID for the property sheet handler. (See Figure 3-3.) This Class ID (or CLSID) is a 16-byte value that identifies the ActiveX class of the handler. As you can see, the value is set in curly brackets, or braces: *{86F19A00-42A0-1069-A2E9-08002B30309D}*. You can interpret this value as you do a phone number. In the same way that a single phone number corresponds to one person, the CLSID number stored in the Registry corresponds to a specific ActiveX module that contains this Class ID code. Only one module (ActiveX server) can contain a particular code, and that module is invoked when you right-click a file of the file type in question and select Properties from the context menu. The module then handles the request and displays the property sheet of the file type. BAT files have property sheets like the one shown in Figure 3-4 on the next page.

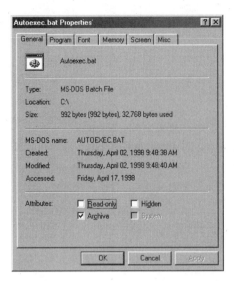

Figure 3-4.
A property sheet for a BAT file.

How Do You Retrieve the CLSID Code for a Module?

To register a new module (ActiveX server), you need a CLSID code that is unique worldwide—no other handler can use the same code or modules will collide. The solution comes from the network computing field, in which the Open Software Foundation developed the unique identifiers for the Distributed Computing Environment (DCE) standard. If you are a programmer, you can use the GUIDGEN (Globally Unique Identifiers) or UUIDGEN (Universally Unique Identifiers) tools to create a unique code for the component class in order to identify your module as an ActiveX server. (More information about the registration of CLSID codes can be found in Charles Petzold's *Programming Windows 95* [1996], published by Microsoft Press.) If you aren't a programmer, you must know only the CLSID code of an existing ActiveX module in order to register that module.

Comparing a BAT file property sheet and the property sheets of other file types—a TXT file, for example—reveals differences. The property sheet of a BAT file contains several pages with information about the file. The property sheet of a TXT file consists of only one page showing the file's general properties. TXT files use the default Windows 98 property sheet.

Combining Branches into a REG File

The previous sections explained how Windows 98 recognizes a registered file type. As we've seen, each file type has two main Registry entries: one that defines its extension and one that contains its properties. These definitions can be combined into a single REG file. In the following lines, I've exported both branches for the BAT file type and merged them into one REG file.

```
REGEDIT4

[HKEY_CLASSES_ROOT\.bat]
@="batfile"

[HKEY_CLASSES_ROOT\batfile]
@="MS-DOS Batch File"
"EditFlags"=hex:d0,04,00,00

[HKEY_CLASSES_ROOT\batfile\shell]
@=""

[HKEY_CLASSES_ROOT\batfile\shell\open]
@=""
"EditFlags"=hex:00,00,00,00

[HKEY_CLASSES_ROOT\batfile\shell\open\command]
@="\"%1\" %*"

[HKEY_CLASSES_ROOT\batfile\shell\print]
@=""

[HKEY_CLASSES_ROOT\batfile\shell\print\command]
@="C:\\WINDOWS\\NOTEPAD.EXE /p %1"

[HKEY_CLASSES_ROOT\batfile\shell\edit]
@="&Edit"

[HKEY_CLASSES_ROOT\batfile\shell\edit\command]
@="C:\\WINDOWS\\NOTEPAD.EXE %1"
```

(continued)

continued

```
[HKEY_CLASSES_ROOT\batfile\shellex]
[HKEY_CLASSES_ROOT\batfile\shellex\PropertySheetHandlers]

[HKEY_CLASSES_ROOT\batfile\shellex\PropertySheetHandlers\      ⇥
{86F19A00-42A0-1069-A2E9-08002B30309D}]
@=""

[HKEY_CLASSES_ROOT\batfile\DefaultIcon]
@="C:\\WINDOWS\\SYSTEM\\shell32.dll,-153"
```

> **NOTE:** This REG file contains all the information you need to register the file type extension, the default icon, the commands, and the shell extensions. We can use this REG file or parts of it as a template for registering other file types. The pitfalls of doing this will be shown later in this chapter.

Registering New File Types and Modifying Existing Ones

Windows offers you several ways to register and modify file types: using the Open With dialog box, using Windows Explorer, using the Registry Editor, and using a REG file.

We've examined the structure of the *HKEY_CLASSES_ROOT* branch, but we haven't really addressed what you can do with this knowledge. Registering a new file type allows you to manipulate how you access and enable functions, applications, and so on. For example, in Windows, all files with an EXE, COM, or BAT extension allow you to double-click them to execute them. When you double-click a data file, its associated application starts and the data file is loaded. Double-clicking a shortcut executes a Windows application. And right-clicking a file opens the context menu, allowing you to select a command.

Unfortunately, many files do not have a registered extension. For example, files downloaded from mailboxes can be simple text files with extensions such as DIZ. These files can be opened with Notepad, but since DIZ isn't a file type registered with Notepad, double-clicking such a file won't open the file in Notepad. (For example, try double-clicking the file README.DIZ in the \chapter3 folder of the sample files.) Other documents are stored in files with names like README.1ST and so on. Programmers use file extensions such as C, BAS, or PAS. Wouldn't it be nice to have quick access to these files? All you have to do is register these extensions as new file types.

Using the Open With Dialog Box to Register a File Type

Before you start the Registry Editor and dig deeply into *HKEY_CLASSES_ROOT*, you should understand the simplest way to register a file type.

Let's register the extension 1ST as a new file type. If no 1ST file is available, create a small TXT file with Notepad and rename it README.1ST. The \chapter3 folder of the sample files also contains a test file with this name. You need this file to execute the next steps.

Before we continue, let's first confirm that the 1ST extension isn't already registered. You can get this information quickly by checking the right pane of the Windows Explorer window (see Figure 3-5). The README.1ST file is described in the Type column as *1ST File*. This is how Windows indicates unregistered file types—by listing the file extension in uppercase letters, followed by a blank and the word File, as the file type. You know that the TXT file extension in Figure 3-5 indicates a registered file type because *Text Document* appears as the type. (See the file README.TXT in the \chapter3 folder of the sample files.) If the file extension were not registered, the default type name *TXT File* would appear instead. The icon in the window's Name column also indicates whether a file type is registered. The standard Windows icon is assigned to files with unregistered types.

> **NOTE:** File types of the "file extension File" type (such as the 1ST File above) aren't always unregistered. Entering a type name when registering a file is optional, so if no name is entered, the default remains the type. Along the same lines, registered files can display the standard Windows icon. You could drive somebody crazy by assigning this icon to a registered file type. Also, Windows itself will sometimes assign the standard Windows icon to registered file types.

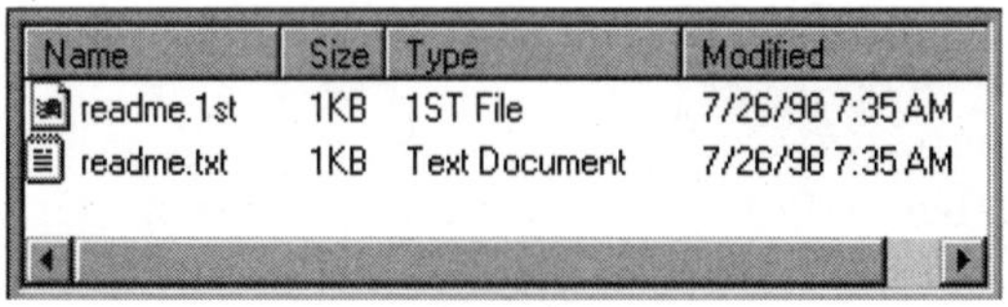

Name	Size	Type	Modified
readme.1st	1KB	1ST File	7/26/98 7:35 AM
readme.txt	1KB	Text Document	7/26/98 7:35 AM

Figure 3-5.
The right pane of Windows Explorer displaying registered and unregistered file types.

Let's register the new 1ST file type. (Remember to back up your Registry before making any changes. See the section "Backing Up and Recovering Your Registry" on page 36 of Chapter 2.)

1. Open Windows Explorer, and double-click the README.1ST file in the \chapter3 folder of the sample files. If the file's extension is unregistered (and it is in our example), Windows (Windows 95, Windows 98, Microsoft Windows NT 4.0, and Windows NT 5.0) invokes the Open With dialog box. (See Figure 3-6.)

2. Enter a short description in the text box. This description will serve as the file type's name and will be used in other places, such as the Type column in the Windows Explorer window, to inform the user about this file type. (See the Tip on the next page for advice about this description text.)

3. Select NOTEPAD from the list box.

4. Activate the Always Use This Program To Open This File check box. This option is selected by default when you open the dialog box by double-clicking a file.

5. Close the dialog box by clicking OK. As Windows opens the README.1ST file with Notepad, the new file type is registered.

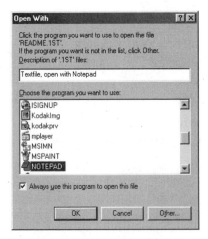

Figure 3-6.
The Open With dialog box.

You can confirm that the file type was registered by closing Notepad and looking at the Windows Explorer window. The entry in the Type column is now set to *Textfile, open with Notepad* (or whatever you entered as the file type's name). If this isn't the case, click in the window's right pane and press F5 to refresh the display. Double-click the README.1ST file again. The text file should be properly loaded into Notepad.

Verifying the Newly Registered File Type

Let's look at what happened in the Registry. Start the Registry Editor, expand the *HKEY_CLASSES_ROOT* branch, and search for the *.1ST* entry. It should be at the top of the hierarchy. If you don't see it, click in the left pane and press F5. (The number *1* is always at the top of the hierarchy because numbers come before letters. See the Tip below.)

Figure 3-7 shows two Registry entries that are relevant for the registered file type 1ST. The first entry is the key *.1ST*. The *Default* value for this key (which I called *name_ID* earlier in this chapter) is set to *1ST_auto_file*. This value was automatically generated by the Open With dialog box in Windows, and it identifies the second key for the registered file type. The algorithm for creating this name is simple: use the file extension (in our example, 1ST), and add "_auto_file".

You will find this second key in the middle of the *HKEY_CLASSES_ROOT* structure. This key contains the *shell* subkey, which contains the subkey *command* under the *open* verb. Figure 3-7 shows that the value of the *command* key is set to the path and filename of the application. That's all you have to do—one keystroke can change your Registry.

Figure 3-7.
New keys created for the registered 1ST file type.

> **TIP:** The file description you enter in the Open With dialog box (see the description I entered in Figure 3-6) is used for many purposes, including to comment the registered file type in the File Types property page of the Folder Options dialog box in Windows Explorer. These registered file types are sorted by comment line, first numerically and then alphabetically. When the registered file types list is huge, you will find it difficult to locate a desired file type unless you use a number as a prefix to your comment. For example, the description I entered in Figure 3-6 appears far down the list in Figure 3-8 (on page 68). If I had entered *1 Textfile, open with Notepad* instead, the file type would have appeared at the top of the list. You should consider adding numerical prefixes to your descriptions to ensure that you can easily locate the file types you define.

Changing the Associated Application of a Registered File Type

Occasionally you'll need to change the association between a certain file type and an application. Consider these scenarios: Suppose an install program overwrites the default file types of your favorite application. Or suppose you inadvertently register a file type with the wrong application. The Open With dialog box is a great feature of Windows 98 because it allows you to quickly register any new file type. There is a risk, however: if you select the wrong application in the Open With dialog box and click OK, the wrong application is registered for the file type and is invoked whenever you double-click a file of that type. How do you change an incorrect association? Don't start the Registry Editor and modify the *HKEY_CLASSES_ROOT* key! Use this process instead:

1. Select the desired file, and then hold down the Shift key and right-click. Select Open With from the context menu so that the Open With dialog box appears on the screen.

2. Select a new application. If the application program you want isn't available in the list, click Other and browse for the application's executable filename. Select the new application.

3. Place a check in the Always Use This Program To Open This Type Of File check box. This check box is always clear when the Open With dialog box is invoked as described in Step 1.

4. Click OK to close the dialog box.

Windows starts the selected application and opens the file. The entries in the Registry are updated, and the name of the new application is set for the Open command.

NOTE: There are several applications that "grab" more than one file extension. For example, many graphics programs register several extensions, such as BMP, PCX, TIF, GIF, JPEG, and so on, for one application. In such a case, however, if you use the Open With dialog box to change the application associated with a file type, all the other file types associated with the original application will also change. This can be risky because the new application might not support all the file formats. I'll discuss this situation further in the section "Registering Several File Types for a Single Application," beginning on page 101.

Disadvantages of Using the Open With Dialog Box

Although the Open With dialog box offers a quick way to register a new file type, using it as an all-purpose tool has the following disadvantages:

- The context menus of other registered file types allow additional commands, such as Print. The Open With dialog box does not offer you a way to define such optional commands for a file type.

- Each registered file type comes with its own icon. You cannot use the Open With dialog box to change the icon for a registered file type. If you associate a Windows application with a file type, the default icon of the application's EXE file (or the default data file icon) will be used. If the program does not contain an icon—let's assume it is a DOS file—Windows sets a default icon, which can be the default icon associated with a DOS application or the default icon for unregistered file types. In the 1ST file example we looked at earlier, we can see the default icon for Notepad text files. This icon is contained in NOTEPAD.EXE.

- You can't define the name for the command shown on the context menu. The Open With dialog box always uses the name Open.

Using Windows Explorer to Change Registry Data for File Types

Given the disadvantages of using the Open With dialog box as an all-purpose tool, you need an alternative method for changing a registered file type. Now do we have to fire up the Registry Editor and jump into the Registry? Not so fast—before I lead you down the "highway to hell," I insist that you fasten your safety belt and consider using Windows Explorer instead.

Removing a Registered File Type

In the beginning of my Windows 95 days, a lot of garbage cluttered my Registry because I kept tampering with the Open With dialog box. My question was: how can I delete an unnecessary entry in the Registry?

Windows 98, as well as Windows 95 or Windows NT 4.0, can do this job for you. Before you delete the key, create your backup as discussed in Chapter 2 and then follow these steps:

1. Start Windows Explorer, and select Folder Options from the View menu. Windows Explorer opens the Folder Options property sheet.

2. Select the File Types property page, and search for the entry of the registered file type. Figure 3-8 shows our previously registered 1ST file type.

3. Be sure you have selected the correct entry! Click Remove.

4. Windows recognizes that you want to clean up the Registry and presents a message box asking whether you're sure you want to remove the file type. Click Yes.

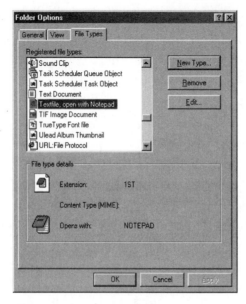

Figure 3-8.
A registered file type on the File Types property page.

Windows will remove from the Registry all keys for this registered file type, so be careful you select the right file type.

NOTE: Just as using Open With for an application that is associated with multiple file types can be risky, so can using the Remove button. If you use Remove, all file types registered for this application will be deleted. A well-behaved application comes with an uninstall feature to roll back the old file type associations.

Registering a New File Type

You can register a new file type by using Windows Explorer rather than the Open With dialog box. Access the Folder Options property sheet, select the File Types property page, and click New Type. Windows Explorer invokes the Add New File Type dialog box shown in Figure 3-9, where you can do nearly everything to register your file extension.

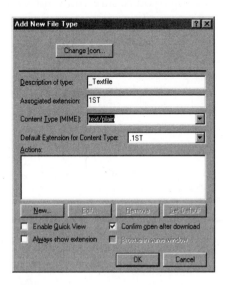

Figure 3-9.
Registering a new file type.

You should enter the information about the new file type according to the following steps:

Step 1: entering the description and extension Enter a description for the file type. A numerical prefix, or any other valid character that comes before letters in a sorted list, ensures that your entry will be shown at the top of the list. An underscore is one of these characters, so I chose the description _Textfile.

Now enter the file extension of your new file type; you do not need to include the dot—for example, *1ST*. Windows Explorer uses this extension as the name of the first key inserted in the *HKEY_CLASSES_ROOT* branch and uses the file extension plus "file"—instead of "_auto_file"—as its *name_ID* value. In our example, then, *name_ID* is set to *1STfile*, as shown in Figure 3-10 on the next page.

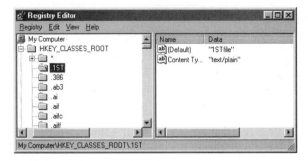

Figure 3-10.
The .1ST key in the Registry.

You must enter a unique, unregistered extension for the file type or you will get an error message and Windows Explorer will refuse to accept your input.

Step 2: defining a command for the file type   Now you need to assign a command to the file type so that when the user double-clicks the file, this command will be invoked.

How MIME Types Are Registered

Windows 98 comes with integrated Internet access functions provided by Microsoft Internet Explorer 4. An important browser feature is MIME Content Type support. If a browser receives a file, it must decide how to use or display the file's content. An HTML file must be shown in the browser window, while other file types require a helper application (a graphic viewer, for example).

To handle downloaded data, a Web browser needs some information about the content of the downloaded data. This information is obtained in two ways. In most cases, the HTTP server transfers the content type of the transmitted file in an HTTP header. If no content type is available in this header, the browser might be able to determine the type by using the file's extension. At this point, the browser searches the Registry for valid MIME types and their extensions. These Registry entries also contain the commands required to handle the received file.

Therefore, to aid Web browsers in identifying the file type you're registering, you should define the MIME type for the registered file type in the Content Type (MIME) list box of the Add New File Type dialog box, which is shown in Figure 3-9. This list box contains a list of predefined MIME types. The MIME type you choose from this list is

1. Click New, which invokes the New Action dialog box, such as the one shown in Figure 3-11 on the next page.

2. Enter the name for the new command in the Action text box. In this example, I use *open*, which will be shown on the context menu of this file type.

3. Click in the second text box, and fill in the path and filename of the application that will perform the command. (If you don't know the exact path, click Browse to browse your system through the Open With dialog box.) After the application name, append a space followed by *%1* as a placeholder for the filename. If you inspect other file types, you will see that many of the commands include this placeholder. If you forget the placeholder, Windows Explorer adds it to the value before storing the value in the Registry.

4. After defining the name and the application, click OK to close the New Action dialog box. (We'll examine the Use DDE option later in this chapter beginning on page 78.)

---

stored in the main Registry key defining the associated file extension (*.1ST*, for example). The MIME type appears in that key as the value data for a value named *Content Type*. (See Figure 3-10.) Also, you should set the default extension for this MIME type in the Default Extension For Content Type list box, also shown in Figure 3-9.

After installing Windows 98 (or after installing Internet Explorer in Windows 95 or Windows NT 4.0), the Registry contains the necessary definitions of MIME types. The MIME content type database can be found in the branch:

HKEY_CLASSES_ROOT\MIME\Database\Content Type

The subkeys under the *Content Type* subkey are named for the MIME type. The values of these subkeys define the content type itself. The subkey *Default* value is always left empty. The *Extension* value specifies the file extension used for this file type (such as *".txt"* for the *Extension* value of the *text/plain* subkey). If the optional *Encoding* value is specified, it contains a code for the data encoding. Another optional value, *CLSID*, specifies the CLSID code of an ActiveX server used to handle this data.

The *HKEY_CLASSES_ROOT\MIME\default* subkey also contains subkeys defining character encoding and the supported code pages.

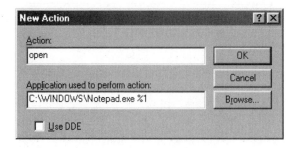

Figure 3-11.
You define a new action for a file type in the New Action dialog box.

Windows now knows a lot more about the file type, so the new command and associated icon are shown in the Add New File Type dialog box. (See Figure 3-12.) You can repeat these steps to define additional commands (such as Print, Edit, and so on).

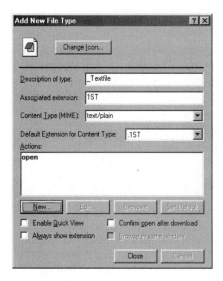

Figure 3-12.
The dialog box after you define the first command.

After you have defined all the commands you want and closed the Add New File Type dialog box, Windows Explorer registers the new file type for you. As you can see in Figure 3-13, the *open* verb is used as a subkey in the

HKEY_CLASSES_ROOT\1stfile\Shell branch and a second subkey, *command*, containing the path to the associated application is also added. You can inspect this branch with the Registry Editor.

Figure 3-13.
The resulting structure in the Registry.

> **N O T E :**   Notice that Figure 3-13 shows the command enclosed in quotes but that these quotes are not shown in Figure 3-11. The quotes are added by the Registry Editor. Only if the path includes a long filename containing blanks (such as *My Editor.exe*) must the user enclose in quotes the path entered in the Application Used To Perform Action text box shown in Figure 3-11. If you omit these quotes, Windows can't find the application and displays an error when you click OK in the New Action dialog box.

Step 3: setting the icon for the file type   To help you distinguish among file types, Windows associates an icon with each registered file type. When you defined the *.1ST* key, the 1ST file type was automatically assigned the default icon for Notepad data files. If you want to change the icon, follow these steps:

1. From the File Types property sheet, select _Textfile and click Edit to open the Edit File Type dialog box.

2. Click Change Icon to invoke the Change Icon dialog box. (See Figure 3-14 on the next page.)

3. Select an icon shown in the Current Icon image list. Figure 3-14 shows the icons available in NOTEPAD.EXE. For an example, select the second icon.

4. If you want to use a different icon source, either you can change the entry in the File Name text box by entering the path and filename of a new file or you can click the Browse button and select a new

filename. Any icons the new file contains will be displayed in the Current Icon image list.

5. Close the dialog box, and confirm your selection by clicking OK. (Or click Cancel to keep the old settings intact.)

6. Close the Edit File Type dialog box to register the new icon.

Figure 3-14.
The Change Icon dialog box.

How is this icon setting represented in the Registry? You will see the *DefaultIcon* key under *HKEY_CLASSES_ROOT\1STfile*. As discussed in the first section of this chapter, the value of the *DefaultIcon* key stores the path and filename of the icon file. If you inspect this branch in the Registry Editor, you will find the *C:\WINDOWS\Notepad.Exe,1* pathname. This means that the second icon will be used for this file type. (Remember that the icon index is counted from 0.)

If you inspect other entries in *HKEY_CLASSES_ROOT*, you might not be able to find a *DefaultIcon* key. The Registry follows these rules:

■ If you don't change the icon in the Add New File Type session, Windows Explorer won't generate *DefaultIcon* in the Registry.

■ If you click the Change Icon button and select a new icon, the *DefaultIcon* key is generated and the *Default* value will be set to the path and filename of the icon source.

■ If no *DefaultIcon* key exists, Windows uses the first icon contained in the application's EXE file.

TIP: Where can you find icons to choose from for new file types? In many cases, the standard application has the right icon for your file type. If you prefer atypical icons, however, you can access other icon sources. Try, for example, the SHELL32.DLL file in the \Windows\System folder. This DLL is an excellent source for many icons. Try also the PIFMGR.DLL file in the \Windows\System folder, which contains icons for DOS applications. MORICONS.DLL in the \Windows folder is also another source. You can inspect the EXE and DLL files found on your computer. Most of these files contain one or more icons.

Step 4: enabling the Quick View command (optional) If you open the context menu by right-clicking the symbol of a registered file type, sometimes you will see the Quick View command. Selecting this command opens the Quick View window, which shows the contents of the selected file. You can enable the Quick View command in the context menu by clicking the Enable Quick View check box in the Add New File Type or Edit File Type dialog box. (See Figure 3-12 on page 72.)

When you enable Quick View for the 1ST file type, the *1STfile* key in *HKEY_CLASSES_ROOT* will contain a *QuickView* subkey. The *Default* value of this subkey is set to "*", which means that the default Quick Viewer will be used. (*HKEY_CLASSES_ROOT* contains its own *QuickView* key that contains subkeys with the various installed Quick Viewers. The subkey * contains the default SCC [Systems Compatibility Corporation] viewer, which automatically detects the right viewing format.)

Step 5: enabling the file extension (optional) Windows hides the file extensions of registered file types by default. If you prefer to see the file extension for a file you've registered even when Windows is set to hide file extensions— as an old DOS freak, I always like to see the extension—you must activate the Always Show Extension option in the Add New File Type or Edit File Type dialog box. If you check this option, Windows Explorer adds the name

AlwaysShowExt as a flag (that is, a value indicating that an option is enabled or disabled), in the *1STfile* key. (See Figure 3-15.) The value for this flag is set to an empty string. (I'll further discuss this option later.)

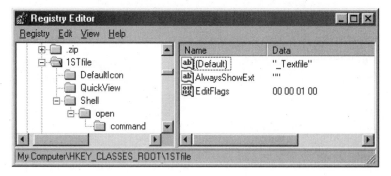

Figure 3-15.
The AlwaysShowExt *flag.*

Step 6: enabling Confirm Open After Download (optional)   The Add New File Type and Edit File Type dialog boxes include a new option in Windows 98: Confirm Open After Download. If this check box is checked, the browser always automatically opens the file after download. You should leave this check box unchecked if you want to have control over whether downloaded files are opened. Leaving this check box unchecked assures that a downloaded file infected with a virus isn't opened automatically.

Windows 98 stores the Confirm Open After Download option information in the *EditFlags* value, which appears in the second key of a registered file type (*1STfile*, for example). If the check box is checked, the *EditFlags* value is set to *00 00 01 00* (see Figure 3-15). (*EditFlags* is stored as a bit field. Setting bit 16 to *0* or deleting *EditFlags* checks the Confirm Open After Download check box.)

Adding a Print Command to a Registered File Type

If you registered a new file type by using the Open With or Add New File Type dialog box, the Registry contains the required settings. But what if you want to change a setting or add a new command? When you right-click a TXT file and select the Print command from the context menu, Windows knows to open Notepad and print the contents of the file. But try to do this with the README.1ST file—you can't because the Print command isn't listed on the context menu. Obviously something is missing in the Registry. Let's try to add this missing Print command to the Registry:

1. Open Windows Explorer, and select Folder Options from the View menu.

2. Select the File Types property page from the Folder Options property sheet.

3. Search for the _Textfile entry in the Registered File Types list, and select it. The extension 1ST is shown in the File Type Details section of the File Types property page (see the left-hand window in Figure 3-16).

4. Click the Edit button. The Edit File Type dialog box appears, as shown in Figure 3-16.

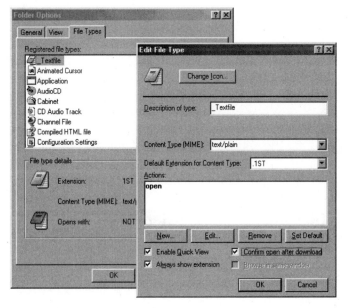

Figure 3-16.
The File Types property page and the Edit File Type dialog box.

5. Click the New button to define a new command for the file type.

6. Enter the print action in the New Action dialog box as shown in Figure 3-17 on the next page.

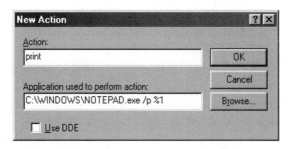

Figure 3-17.
The print command is added to a registered file type in the New Action dialog box.

Notepad uses a simple /p switch in the command line to print the contents of a text file. I have appended this switch to the application name. (Different applications require different methods of controlling internal functions. Some applications recognize switches; others are controlled by DDE messages. It is always a good idea to check how other registered file types use commands so that you can figure out how to start the various programs.) You should also append *%1* to the filename as a placeholder.

Windows will exchange the *%1* placeholder with the current filename if the command for this action is executed. (If you omit this placeholder, Windows Explorer appends *%1* to the command string before this string is stored in the Registry.) The new command is added into the Registry in the *HKEY_ CLASSES_ROOT\1STfile\Shell\print\command* key, which you can examine with the Registry Editor. Now the new Print command is available from the context menu if you right-click the README.1ST file.

Using the DDE Option for a Registered File Type

In the lower left corner of the New Action dialog box is the Use DDE check box (see Figure 3-17). If you know an application accepts DDE (Dynamic Data Exchange) commands, you can go ahead and check this option. When you do, Windows Explorer expands the New Action dialog box to show the following additional text boxes. (See Figure 3-18.)

■ The DDE Message text box contains the command to start an action (for example, opening a file, creating a file, printing a file, and so on).

■ The Application text box contains the name of the DDE application. In Figure 3-18, this is Word for Windows.

■ The DDE Application Not Running text box is optional. In it you can enter a command to start the application and execute an action. This command will be executed if you select the action and the DDE application isn't already running on your PC.

■ The last text box defines the Topic for the DDE conversion.

Your entries will depend on the application used for the DDE conversion. Consult the application manuals to determine the necessary DDE commands.

NOTE: DDE commands entered in the dialog box are inserted in the Registry in the *HKEY_CLASSES_ROOT\...\shell* branch of the file type. For example, if you define a DDE command for *open* you will find two subkeys under *open*: *command* and *ddeexec*. The *command* subkey contains the path and filename of the application. The *ddeexec* subkey contains a *Default* value with the DDE message. Depending on the other options you set in the New Action dialog box, the *ddeexec* subkey can contain other subkeys: *Application*, *Topic*, and *ifexec*. (The *ifexec* subkey contains the value entered in DDE Application Not Running.)

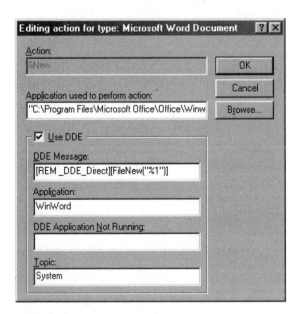

Figure 3-18.
DDE commands for a new action.

Using the Registry Editor to Register a File Type

We have examined several easy, efficient, and nearly foolproof ways to register new file types and define new commands for file types without using the Registry Editor. These methods are real advantages if you like to do tasks quickly and want Windows to keep track of all modifications to the Registry. My suggestion is that you first try the Open With dialog box and Windows Explorer before turning to the Registry Editor. This will save you a lot of trouble and time. For all you masochists, however, here's how you register a new file type with the Registry Editor:

1. Start the Registry Editor, and expand the *HKEY_CLASSES_ROOT* branch.

2. Add a new subkey with the name of the file extension in *HKEY_CLASSES_ROOT*. (You must include the dot, as in *.1ST*.)

3. Set the *Default* value of this key to the *name_ID*, which is the name of the second subkey you will create. (This is the subkey you'll use to define the file type's properties.)

4. Add the second subkey in *HKEY_CLASSES_ROOT*, and name it after the previously defined *name_ID*. (We used the *name_ID* *1STfile*, for example.)

5. Add the *shell* subkey, and expand this branch with the keys (verbs) for the required commands (Open, Print, etc.).

6. Add a *command* key to each verb key.

7. Add the command string (path and filename of the executable) as the *Default* value of each verb's *command* key.

8. Close the Registry Editor, and try to test the registered file type in the Explorer window.

Using a REG File to Register a New File Type

Defining a new file type by using the Registry Editor can seem a complicated process because you must manage every component of the process correctly. One alternative to manually adding keys and values to the Registry Editor is to import Registry settings from REG files, which come with many programs. Simply double-click a REG file, and Windows 98 imports all the file's settings into the Registry. This method is preferable when registering a new file type for users other than yourself. As an example, here is the REG file that adds the 1ST file type to the Registry:

```
REGEDIT4

[HKEY_CLASSES_ROOT\.1st]
@="1stfile"

[HKEY_CLASSES_ROOT\1stfile]
@="_Textfile"
"AlwaysShowExt"=""

[HKEY_CLASSES_ROOT\1stfile\Shell]
@=""

[HKEY_CLASSES_ROOT\1stfile\Shell\print]
@=""

[HKEY_CLASSES_ROOT\1stfile\Shell\print\command]
@="C:\\WINDOWS\\Notepad.exe /p %1"

[HKEY_CLASSES_ROOT\1stfile\Shell\open]
@=""

[HKEY_CLASSES_ROOT\1stfile\Shell\open\command]
@="C:\\WINDOWS\\Notepad.exe \"%1\""

[HKEY_CLASSES_ROOT\1stfile\QuickView]
@="*"

[HKEY_CLASSES_ROOT\1stfile\DefaultIcon]
@="C:\\WINDOWS\\Notepad.exe,1"
```

As you can see and as discussed in Chapter 2, keys are enclosed in brackets. The @ stands for the *Default* value name of a key. A value name other than *Default* is set in quotes at the beginning of a line (such as *"EditFlags"*). The equal sign (=) is always followed by a value (that is, a string, DWORD, or binary value). String values are enclosed in quotation marks:

```
"C:\\WINDOWS\\Notepad.exe,1"
```

Pathnames in a string must follow unique naming conventions. (For example, you must use a double backslash.)

NOTE: If a path includes filenames containing blanks, the path must be enclosed in quotes. These quotes must be preceded by a single backslash to differentiate them from the opening and closing string quotes (such as *"\"C:\\Program Files\\AFile.exe\""*).

Binary values are represented as a byte sequence:

```
"EditFlags"=hex:01,00,00,00
```

The command lines shown above contain the settings to register the file type 1ST with the commands Open and Print. Notepad is used to process these commands. (1ST.REG is available in the \chapter3 folder of the sample files.)

If you plan to register a single file extension on more than one computer, you can use a REG file. For a new file extension, just customize the lines shown in the preceding code. For example, to register a DIZ file, replace all instances of *1st* with *diz*.

> NOTE: You can use the same REG files for registering file types under Windows 95, Windows 98, Windows NT 4.0, and Windows NT 5.0. But take care that the files used on other machines specify valid data for the registered file type. In many cases, the paths to folders and the names of application programs differ from machine to machine. You can find further information about these problems in the next section.

Risks of Using a REG File

As I've said, double-clicking a REG file imports the contents of the file into the Registry. Because this can be risky—a user can accidentally double-click a REG file containing the wrong information—Windows 98 includes a dialog box asking whether the REG file should be imported (see Figure 3-19).

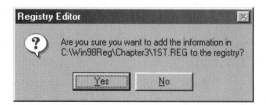

Figure 3-19.
Confirmation before importing a REG file.

If the user clicks the YES button, the contents of the REG file are imported into the Registry. After the data has been imported, the user receives a message saying that the data contained in the REG file has been successfully stored in the Registry. This can be misleading, however—unfortunately, Windows 98 doesn't use a smart algorithm to interpret the information in the REG file. To determine whether a file is valid, Windows tests only the first line of the file. If this line contains the signature REGEDIT4, the rest of the file is read and the information is stored in the Registry. This is a source of many problems. Suppose, for example, that you import a REG file but that the action you wanted to obtain access to by importing the file won't take effect. Let's investigate this scenario by looking at Figure 3-20.

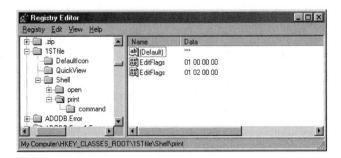

Figure 3-20.
Two entries with the same name?

Two entries with the same name but different values exist in the *print* key. In conformance with the Windows specification, one key can have several values, but a single value name can occur only once in a particular key. However, Figure 3-20 reveals that the *print* key contains the name *EditFlags* twice. What has happened? To find out, we must look at the REG file that created this entry. The REG command that set the second occurrence of *EditFlags* in the *print* key of Figure 3-20 is shown here:

```
[HKEY_CLASSES_ROOT\1stfile\Shell\print]
"EditFlags "=hex:01,02,00,00
```

The second line contains the bug: a blank space follows the name *EditFlags*. Because the name "EditFlags" in the REG file is different from the name "EditFlags" already contained in the Registry, a new entry was generated with apparently the same value name. In this situation, the new setting would never be recognized by Windows as a duplicate setting. In other words, all value names must match the names expected by Windows exactly, or your update will not provide the correct results. If your update fails, load the REG file into Notepad and compare each line for trailing blanks, misspelled keys, missing quotes, and so on. (Don't use Microsoft Word or any other word-processing application to change entries in a REG file. Word, for example, contains an option that can cause you to unintentionally extend an inserted expression with blanks.)

The next problem can be even more difficult to solve. I came across this problem as I was translating Nancy Winnick Cluts's book, *Programming the Windows 95 User Interface* (Microsoft Press, 1995), a few years ago. The book comes with a CD-ROM containing sample programs and REG files. One of the REG files included a line of code similar to the following for registering a new Quick Viewer.

```
[HKEY_CLASSES_ROOT\1stfile\Shell\open\command]
@="C:\\WINDOWS\\Notepad.exe \"%1\""
```

Of course, Cluts's code was a little bit different because its intention was to register a viewer. (I'm using a simplified example to demonstrate the same effect.) After compiling the application and double-clicking the REG file, the viewer wouldn't run for the file type. After spending several hours searching for the bug, I discovered that the second line of the code above was causing the problem.

What's wrong with the command *@="C:\\WINDOWS\\ Notepad.exe \ "%1\""*? At first glance, nothing. Care to take a second look? I guarantee that you won't find anything wrong with the line itself and that it will work on 90 percent of the computers that are running Windows 95 or Windows 98. Still, what explains the fact that some people run into serious trouble with this line?

The name of the Windows folder is incorrect. The path above says that NOTEPAD.EXE is located in the \WINDOWS folder. But on one of my PCs I run Windows 3.1, Windows 95, Windows 98, and Windows NT 4.0 in parallel, and on my other PC I've installed both a German and an English version of Windows 98. On both my PCs, then, I'm using two versions of Windows on the same disk, so I'm unable to use WINDOWS as a name for each of the Windows folders. (Of course, it's possible to keep different Windows versions on separate disk drives and use the folder name \WINDOWS, but I prefer to give the Windows folders specific names such as \Win95, \Win98D, \Win98E, and so on so that I can see which version is kept in each folder.) All attempts to import the REG file above onto a system that has a different name for the Windows folder will fail.

> NOTE: It is also risky to install one Windows version in the folder \WINDOWS and use a different folder name for a second version. If you boot with the second version, the paths in the Registry (set from an imported REG file) will still point to the \WINDOWS folder. If a command is executed, the library modules are loaded in \WINDOWS\SYSTEM. The result is a mix of different modules, which can cause problems.

You can solve this REG file problem in only one way: omit the path to the application. The lines of our code example would be written like this:

```
[HKEY_CLASSES_ROOT\1stfile\Shell\open\command]
@="Notepad.exe \"%1\""
```

With this approach, Windows 98 tries to locate the application after you invoke the Open command. First the \Windows folder is scanned, and if the file is not available, the \Windows\System folder is scanned. If this search isn't successful either, Windows tries to scan the folders set in the PATH environment variable (set in AUTOEXEC.BAT). Finally, Windows checks the following branch in the Registry: *HKEY_LOCAL_MACHINE\SOFTWARE\Microsoft\Windows\CurrentVersion*. This branch contains the paths to various EXE and DLL files for certain applications. Eventually an application found in one of these folders will be loaded.

I don't recommend omitting pathnames from REG files, however, because all other entries in the Registry contain a path description. In the next section, I'll show you how you can use Windows to get around this problem of hard-coded paths.

> TIP: Do you have to use a different name for the \Windows folder? Are you worried about always having to edit the Windows path in REG files obtained from other machines? I felt that way too until I began running Windows 95. Thanks to the ingenious Windows developers, I found a sneaky way to get around that mess. All you need to do is define a folder as a shortcut to your \Windows folder and name it WINDOWS. To do this, open Windows Explorer, hold down the right mouse button while dragging the \Windows folder to the drive icon, release the mouse button, and select the command Create Shortcut(s) Here. Windows will create a shortcut to the \Windows folder. Rename this new folder WINDOWS.
>
> If you use a REG file with \\WINDOWS\\ in a path, the shortcut will direct Windows 98 to the correct folder. Don't forget to delete this shortcut before you boot another copy of Windows 98. Also, this trick won't work if Windows 98 needs data files in a directory (for example, for icons).

Using INF Files to Register a New File Type—A Better Solution than REG Files

The \Windows folder is not always named Windows—each user can change its name during installation. So what we need is a method that lets Windows itself assign the Windows path. Earlier I described how Windows can do this during run time, but you're better off assigning the path during the Registry update. Fortunately, Windows comes with the appropriate tool: the INF files. In an INF file, you can specify a placeholder for a path that will be determined during run time. The following lines, for example, will update the *open* verb for the 1ST file type in your Registry:

```
; File: 1ST.INF
; by Guenter Born
;
; Install script, register the 1ST file type
[version]
signature="$CHICAGO$"

[DefaultInstall]
AddReg = 1st.AddReg

[1st.AddReg]
HKCR,.1st,,,"1stfile"
HKCR,1stfile\Shell\open\command,,,%10%"\NOTEPAD.EXE %1"
; End ***
```

The most important commands are shown in the *[1st.AddReg]* section, which contains statements that add Registry data. Each statement is defined with the following syntax:

```
root-key, [subkey], [value-name], [flag], [value]
```

A statement consists of five parameters separated by commas. Parameters that are shown in brackets are optional. (The brackets do not appear in the INF file.) The root key is identified by one of the following abbreviations:

```
HKCC    for HKEY_CURRENT_CONFIG
HKCR    for HKEY_CLASSES_ROOT
HKCU    for HKEY_CURRENT_USER
HKDD    for HKEY_DYN_DATA
HKLM    for HKEY_LOCAL_MACHINE
HKU     for HKEY_USERS
```

The second parameter defines a subkey. In our example, these are the subkeys *.1ST* and *1stfile*. The name for the value is omitted in the example because we're setting the *Default* value. The flag is also omitted here. The last parameter defines the value that should be updated in the Registry. If you inspect the second-to-last line in the INF file code shown above, you will see the *%10%* string. This is a placeholder for the Windows directory that will be filled with the name of the current Windows directory when the INF file is processed. The INF file above creates (or updates) this Registry entry:

```
HKEY_CLASSES_ROOT\1stfile\Shell\open\command
```

Because of the placeholder, the *Default* value is set to:

```
"drive\windowsfolder\NOTEPAD.EXE %1"
```

This is all we need. To install this INF file, you right-click its name and select the Install command from the context menu. I'll provide additional information about INF files in Chapter 7.

NOTE: You will find the file 1ST.INF in the \chapter3 folder of the sample files.

Techniques for Extending Registered File Types

Earlier in this chapter, I discussed the principles of registering file types. We have seen that we can accomplish a lot by using Windows Explorer and without ever having to examine the Registry. Now I want to show you how to apply these principles.

Using Several Applications for a Single File Type

Opening a file of a registered file type by double-clicking its file icon is handy. When you do this, Windows always registers one application for the Open command. (This command will be executed by default if you double-click a shell object in Windows 98. Exceptions are discussed later in this chapter in the section "Defining the Default Command for a Registered File Type.") Sometimes, however, you need more than one application to load a file type. Here are a few typical situations:

- Loading text files   If you double-click a text file, Windows tries to load it in Notepad. If the file length exceeds 64 KB, Notepad can't load the file so Windows asks you to load the text file with WordPad. In Windows Explorer, you can see the file size and decide ahead of time which application to use to load the file. Perhaps you have a "super-editor" that is able to load text files larger than 64 KB or you want to start WordPad directly for larger files.

- Graphics files   Graphics files are often more conveniently opened with one of several applications (for example, with Paint Shop Pro or with PhotoFinish).

■ **Files with the DOC extension** These files might contain ASCII text or Word documents, so you need several applications to open them.

Typically, with these file types, you start the application and load the data file. In Windows 98, you can select the application by following this shortcut:

1. Click the file to select it.
2. Press the Shift key, and right-click the file icon.
3. Select the Open With command from the context menu.
4. Select the application in the Open With dialog box.

If your favorite application isn't in the Open With list, you have to browse the system for the EXE file. Wouldn't it be nice to save yourself this trouble and have a second or third application available on the context menu with which to open a data file? You can extend the file type properties in this way by using the File Types property page of Windows Explorer, the Registry Editor, or REG files.

First we'll extend the 1ST file type properties. Currently when you right-click a 1ST file, a context menu appears showing only the Open and Print commands (because we have defined only these commands in the Registry). Let's add a third command, Open1, which will start WordPad. The steps are easy:

1. Add a new open1 subkey to *HKEY_CLASSES_ROOT\1stfile\Shell*.
2. Add a *command* subkey to *HKEY_CLASSES_ROOT\1stfile\ Shell\open1*.
3. Set the *Default* value of the *command* subkey to the application name.

You can do this by using Windows Explorer or the Registry Editor (as shown in the steps above). As an alternative, we'll add file type properties to our 1ST file type by using a REG file, which I exported from my Registry:

```
REGEDIT4

[HKEY_CLASSES_ROOT\.1st]
@="1stfile"

[HKEY_CLASSES_ROOT\1stfile]
@="_Textfile"
"AlwaysShowExt"=""
```

```
[HKEY_CLASSES_ROOT\1stfile\Shell]
@=""

[HKEY_CLASSES_ROOT\1stfile\Shell\print]
@=""

[HKEY_CLASSES_ROOT\1stfile\Shell\print\command]
@="C:\\WINDOWS\\Notepad.exe /p %1"

[HKEY_CLASSES_ROOT\1stfile\Shell\open]
@=""

[HKEY_CLASSES_ROOT\1stfile\Shell\open\command]
@="C:\\WINDOWS\\Notepad.exe \"%1\""

[HKEY_CLASSES_ROOT\1stfile\QuickView]
@="*"

[HKEY_CLASSES_ROOT\1stfile\DefaultIcon]
@="C:\\WINDOWS\\Notepad.exe,1"

[HKEY_CLASSES_ROOT\1stfile\Shell\open1]
@=""

[HKEY_CLASSES_ROOT\1stfile\Shell\open1\command]
@="\"C:\\Program Files\\Accessories\\Wordpad.exe\" \"%1\""
```

The last four lines define the new subkeys for the Open1 command. Perhaps you recognized the \"%1\" string in the last line. You can add the %1 placeholder with or without quotation marks. If you decide to add the placeholder with quotation marks, each quotation mark in the text string will be recognized as the start or end signature of a string unless you precede each quotation mark with a backslash (\). So "%1" is inserted as \"%1\" in the REG file. Also, filenames containing blanks must be enclosed in quotation marks (for example, \"My Editor.exe\" \"%1\").

After installing this REG file, the Registry contains a new *open1* subkey, as shown in Figure 3-21 on the next page. (The complete key hierarchy for this entry is shown in the Registry Editor's status bar.)

We now have three commands in the *shell* branch. The *open1* verb defines WordPad as the application, and the context menu of the 1ST file type has been extended with the open1 command (see Figure 3-22). (You can view this by selecting the file README.1ST in the \chapter3 folder of the sample files with a right mouse click.)

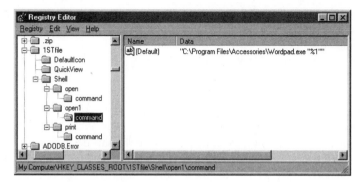

Figure 3-21.
The new open1 *verb in the Registry.*

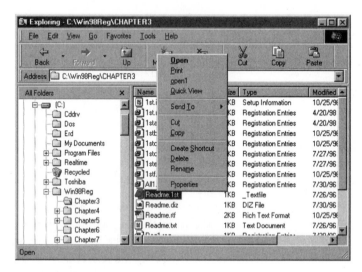

Figure 3-22.
The context menu with the new open1 command.

If you select the Open command, Windows uses Notepad to load the text file. Selecting the open1 command opens WordPad and loads the text file (thus avoiding the warning that the file is too large for Notepad). If you choose Print, Notepad is used to print the text file. (You might also consider extending the context menu with a print1 command that uses WordPad to print a large text file.) You can inspect the *shell**print**command* branch of *Wordpad.Document.1* in the Registry to find out which parameters are necessary for printing a file in WordPad.

You can use this technique for all registered file extensions. I use this technique to open graphics files with the extensions TIF, PCX, BMP, and so on with different applications.

N O T E :   The REG file shown on the preceding pages can be found as 1STA.REG in the \chapter3 folder of the sample files. You can install this REG file by double-clicking the file icon in Windows Explorer. After you confirm the dialog box, the REG file will be imported. Take care! Your folders must have the same names as those defined in the REG file. Otherwise you have to modify all path entries in this file before you import the file! The solution of using INF files to match pathnames, which we examined earlier, isn't possible because I haven't found any way to use a placeholder for the \Program Files\Accessories folder.

Defining the Command Name on the Context Menu

Did you notice a difference between the "open" command names shown on the context menu in Figure 3-22? They are capitalized differently. But if you compare the Registry entries shown in Figure 3-21, the verbs *open* and *open1* are capitalized consistently in the *Shell* branch. Windows obviously uses the name of the verb (key) as an entry on the context menu, but why is the verb *open* shown with an initial capital in the context menu?

This is one of the secrets buried in the Windows architecture (of Windows 95, Windows 98, Windows NT 4.0, and Windows NT 5.0). The general syntax of a Registry entry for a context menu command shown in the shell is defined as:

```
HKEY_CLASSES_ROOT
    .ext = "name_ID"
    name_ID = "description"
        shell
            verb = "menu item text"
                command = "command string"
```

We have seen this structure many times. The *shell* key can contain several subkeys that describe verbs such as *open* and *print*. The syntax above indicates that we can set the value of the verb key to the menu item text, which is what you will see on the context menu. In the *open1* examples, I omitted this optional string to show you the effects. Windows uses the following rules to build the entries for the context menu:

■ If there is a menu item defined as the *Default* value of the verb, that string is used for the context menu entry.

■ If the *Default* value is empty, the verb itself is used as the name for the context menu entry.

These rules imply that we should see the commands open, open1, print, etc., on the context menu, but we don't. That's because Windows also follows these additional rules:

■ Microsoft has invested certain verbs, which can be called canonical verbs, with particular meaning. If you use the names *open*, *print*, and *printto* as verbs in the *shell* key, Windows will insert predefined command names for these canonical verbs into the context menu.

■ The resulting command names depend on the localized Windows 98 (or Windows 95/Windows NT 4.0) version. The U.S. version uses Open and Print in the context menu for the *open* and *print* verbs, while the German version uses *Öffnen* and *Drucken*.

■ The canonical verb *printto* never results in a command being shown on the context menu. This verb is reserved for drag-and-drop operations, as we will see later.

With this knowledge, you can easily rename the context menu entries. You simply enter the command name you want to appear on the context menu as the *Default* value of the verb. For our example, I prepared a short REG file that enables us to rename the context menu entries:

```
REGEDIT4

[HKEY_CLASSES_ROOT\.1st]
@="1stfile"

[HKEY_CLASSES_ROOT\1stfile]
@="_Textfile"
"AlwaysShowExt"=""

[HKEY_CLASSES_ROOT\1stfile\Shell]
@=""

[HKEY_CLASSES_ROOT\1stfile\Shell\print]
@="Print with Notepad"
```

```
[HKEY_CLASSES_ROOT\1stfile\Shell\print\command]
@="C:\\WINDOWS\\Notepad.exe /p %1"

[HKEY_CLASSES_ROOT\1stfile\Shell\open]
@="Edit with Notepad"

[HKEY_CLASSES_ROOT\1stfile\Shell\open\command]
@="C:\\WINDOWS\\Notepad.exe \"%1\""

[HKEY_CLASSES_ROOT\1stfile\Shell\open1]
@="Edit with Wordpad"

[HKEY_CLASSES_ROOT\1stfile\Shell\open1\command]
@="C:\\Program Files\\Accessories\\Wordpad.exe \"%1\""

[HKEY_CLASSES_ROOT\1stfile\QuickView]
@="*"

[HKEY_CLASSES_ROOT\1stfile\DefaultIcon]
@="C:\\WINDOWS\\Notepad.exe,1"
```

If you remove any existing Registry entries for the 1ST file type and import this REG file into the Registry, the context menu will look like that shown in Figure 3-23. The Open command is gone; instead you find more descriptive names for the commands.

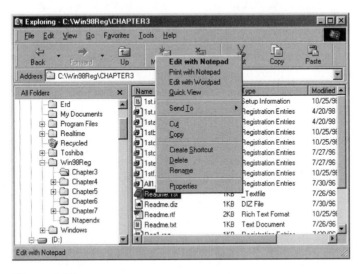

Figure 3-23.
New command names on the context menu.

NOTE: The preceding REG file is named 1STB.REG and is located in the \chapter3 folder of the sample files. You can install this REG file by double-clicking the file icon in Windows Explorer. Name your folders as defined in the REG file. Otherwise you'll have to modify all the path entries in this file before you import it.

Defining Accelerator Keys for Commands

We now have a few options for opening a 1ST file and a few new names on the context menu. Unfortunately, in the process we've lost the ability to select a command with a keystroke. On the context menu shown in Figure 3-22 on page 90, notice that certain letters in the command names are underlined. These underlined characters indicate the accelerator keys for these commands. For example, on the context menu shown in the figure, you can press the *P* key on the keyboard to invoke the Print command and print the selected file.

How can we define accelerator keys? Figure 3-22 should give us a few ideas. The *o* in the open1 command is underlined. By default, when no context menu name has been defined for a verb through its *Default* value and the verb itself is serving as the context menu name, Windows uses the first character of the verb as the accelerator key. Hmm, that's interesting—if we don't set a menu name, we get the verb name and an accelerator key on the context menu. Maybe we could use keys such as *Edit with Notepad* and *Edit with WordPad* instead of *open1*. Well, we could do that, but unfortunately the two commands would each have the letter *E* as an accelerator key.

When I came across this problem years ago in Windows 95, I couldn't believe that Microsoft hadn't provided a solution. But after playing with the Registry a little bit, I figured it out. The solution, buried in the Registry, is actually fairly simple. Let's take a look at the Registry value for the *edit* key in *HKEY_CLASSES_ROOT\batfile\shell* (see Figure 3-24). This part of the Registry is set up during the Windows installation. The *Default* value for the verb *edit* is defined as *"&Edit"*, but if you select a BAT file with a right click, you'll find that E̲dit appears as a command on the context menu. It turns out that the ampersand character (*&*) preceding a character makes that character the accelerator key for the context menu command in question. In other words, if you used the string *"E&dit"* as the *Default* value for the verb, the key *d* would be defined as the accelerator key and the command would be shown as Ed̲it in the context menu. This method also works when naming verbs, not just context menu names. You could produce the same result by naming the verb *E&dit*, rather than *edit*, and not using a *Default* value to define the verb's context menu name.

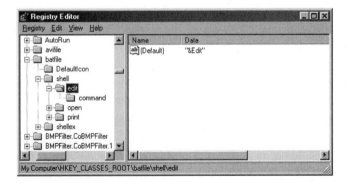

Figure 3-24.
Defining an accelerator key in a command.

My preferred methods for getting ready to create accelerator keys are simple:

■ Use short verbs such as *open*, *edit*, *print*, and *show* as key names.

■ Define different strings for the context menu entries (as I have shown in the previous section).

The following rules for defining accelerator keys for menu commands are a bit more complicated:

■ When a verb is defined without a *Default* value set and without an ampersand in the key name, Windows 98 (and also Windows 95, Windows NT 4.0, and Windows NT 5.0) defaults to displaying the verb on the context menu in a case-sensitive fashion and underlining its first character. (Keep in mind that this is not true for canonical verbs; *open* and *print*, for example, appear as Open and Print).

■ You can use the ampersand in a verb to identify an accelerator character. For example, the verb *Ope&n1* would be shown as Open1 on the context menu. Be careful not to duplicate the Windows accelerator keys used in other commands. If two entries use the same accelerator key, that keystroke would select only the first command using the accelerator key; you would need additional keystrokes to scroll to and invoke the second command.

■ If you add *&* to the canonical verbs *open* and *print*, the verbs would no longer be canonical. For example, the verb *ope&n* would be shown as open on the context menu.

■ If the *Default* value of a verb is set, this string will be used for the context menu entry. If this string does not contain an ampersand, the first character of the string is used as the accelerator key. This character is not shown underlined on the context menu. (Keep in mind that this is poor programming style: all accelerator keys should be underlined.)

■ If you want an accelerator key to be any character other than the first for a verb with a *Default* value, the character in the string must be preceded by an *&*. The string *Open with &WordPad* will be shown on the context menu as Open with WordPad.

A context menu name defined in the *Default* value always has a higher priority than the key name. If you define accelerator keys, avoid duplicating other accelerators defined in Windows. (The context menu might have other commands such as Cut, Paste, Delete, Send To, and Properties). Following is the revised REG file, which defines the file type extensions with accelerators in the context menu.

```
REGEDIT4

[HKEY_CLASSES_ROOT\.1st]
@="1stfile"

[HKEY_CLASSES_ROOT\1stfile]
@="_Textfile"
"AlwaysShowExt"=""

[HKEY_CLASSES_ROOT\1stfile\Shell]
@=""

[HKEY_CLASSES_ROOT\1stfile\Shell\print]
@="&Print with Notepad"

[HKEY_CLASSES_ROOT\1stfile\Shell\print\command]
@="C:\\WINDOWS\\Notepad.exe /p %1"

[HKEY_CLASSES_ROOT\1stfile\Shell\open]
@="Edit with &Notepad"

[HKEY_CLASSES_ROOT\1stfile\Shell\open\command]
@="C:\\WINDOWS\\Notepad.exe \"%1\""

[HKEY_CLASSES_ROOT\1stfile\Shell\open1]
@="Edit with &Wordpad"
```

```
[HKEY_CLASSES_ROOT\1stfile\Shell\open1\command]
@="C:\\Program Files\\Accessories\\Wordpad.exe \"%1\""

[HKEY_CLASSES_ROOT\1stfile\QuickView]
@="*"

[HKEY_CLASSES_ROOT\1stfile\DefaultIcon]
@="C:\\WINDOWS\\Notepad.exe,1"
```

If you import this REG file, the context menu shown in Figure 3-25 will be available. This is a step toward building a customized user shell. We'll look at other examples in Chapter 4.

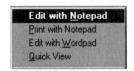

Figure 3-25.
Extended context menu with accelerator keys.

NOTE: The preceding REG file is named 1STC.REG and is located in the \chapter3 folder of the sample files. You can install this REG file by double-clicking the file icon in Windows Explorer. Remember to use the names for your folders as defined in the REG file.

Defining the Default Command for a Registered File Type

Did you notice in Figure 3-25 that one command in the context menu is shown in boldface? The boldface command is the default command, which is activated by double-clicking the file. You can select which command will be the default if you modify the entries of the context menu. At this point, we have not set any parameter that prevents Windows from selecting the default command, so the operating system goes ahead and does so. The rules that Windows follows are pretty simple:

■ If you use one of the canonical verbs (*open*, *print*) as a key name, one of these verbs will be selected. If both verbs are available, *open* is the first priority; *print* is selected next.

■ If none of the canonical verbs are used in the *shell* subkeys, Windows will use the first entry in the *shell* branch as the context menu's default command.

Sometimes you'll want to select alternative default commands. For example, a BAT file is executed if you double-click it, but perhaps you want to open the file in Notepad instead. The Set Default button in the Edit File Type dialog box allows you to change the default command (see Figure 3-16 on page 77). The default command is always shown in boldface in the dialog box's Actions list box. To change the default, select another command in the list box and click the Set Default button; this command will now be shown in boldface, and Windows will use it as the default command when the file is double-clicked.

Inspecting the Registry after you have set the default command for the context menu through the Edit File Type dialog box will give you an idea about how to set a default command by using the Registry. The verb of the command is inserted as the *Default* value of the *shell* key. Figure 3-26 shows this for the registered 1ST file type—the open1 command is used as the default.

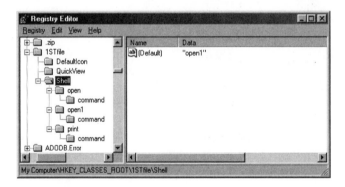

Figure 3-26.
Defining the default command in the Registry.

If you want to use a REG file to set the default command, use these lines:

```
REGEDIT4

[HKEY_CLASSES_ROOT\1stfile\Shell]
@="open1"
```

You will find the 1STD.REG file with these instructions in the \chapter3 folder of the sample files. If there is a *1stfile* key already in the Registry, you can import the new REG file by double-clicking it.

If you run this REG file, two items will change on the context menu: the Edit With WordPad entry will be shown in boldface since it is now the default command, and it will move to the top of the context menu. This is a nice benefit of setting the default command. (We'll work more with default commands in the next section.)

Sequencing the Context Menu Commands

With the one exception of the default command, which is always shown at the top of the context menu, Windows displays the commands on the context menu in the same order that the keys appear in the Registry. (When you're defining many commands for a particular registered file type, consider grouping related entries on the context menu. For example, you might want to list all the Open commands together, then the Print command, and so on. Because the Registry Editor offers no way to move a branch in the Registry hierarchy—that is, you can only delete a branch and then reinsert it at the end of another branch—reordering context menu commands would appear to be a hassle.

Fortunately, the Windows developers have created an easy way to do this within the Registry's user-defined entries. Just list the names of the verbs, separated by commas, in the *Default* value of the *shell* key. For example, for the registered 1ST file type, the *Default* value of the *shell* key should be set in the following order to sequence the commands as suggested above:

```
"open, open1, print"
```

The following lines have the same effect. (This file is available as 1STE.REG in the \chapter3 folder of the sample files.)

```
REGEDIT4

[HKEY_CLASSES_ROOT\1stfile\Shell]
@="open, open1, print"
```

> **NOTE:** This ordering technique for context menu entries has one small disadvantage: when you view the File Types property page, the Opens With information no longer appears.

Defining a *printto* Command Key

Some registered file types come with a *printto* key in the *shell* branch. If you right-click one of these registered files, however, a Print To command isn't available on the context menu. The reason for the *printto* key in the Registry has to do with the Windows 98 drag-and-drop functionality: dragging a data file with a registered extension over a printer icon and releasing the mouse button causes Windows to start the associated application, load the dropped data file, and direct the output to the printer.

If a registered file type supports this feature, a *printto* key is required in the file type's *shell* branch in the Registry. The Registry branch for registering *printto* for WORDPAD.EXE has the following structure:

```
shell
    printto
        command = C:\Progra~1\Access~1\Wordpad.exe /pt "%1" "%2" "%3" "%4"
```

The /pt switch enables WordPad to direct a data file to a selected printer; the other parameters are placeholders. The placeholders function as follows:

- *%1* is used for the name of the data file.

- *%2* is used for the name of the printer.

- *%3* enables WordPad to find the name of the printer driver.

- *%4* contains the printer port.

The *%3* and *%4* parameters are actually superfluous in Windows 98 because printer names are unique in the new operating system.

> **NOTE:** You will find the value above in the following branch of the Registry: *HKEY_CLASSES_ROOT\Wordpad.Document.1\shell\ printto\command*.

Fixing Problems with the File Type Association

Sometimes I experience problems with registered file types, and I've discovered a couple of simple ways to approach them. One way is to delete the Registry data altogether (on Windows Explorer's File Types property page, for example) and then reenter the definition. (You can export the Registry branch for that file type before you delete the key.)

Another approach is to inspect the *HKEY_LOCAL_MACHINE\ SOFTWARE\Microsoft\Windows\CurrentVersion\Extensions* branch. As shown in Figure 3-27, additional information about each file type/application association exists here. Check that these entries are appropriately set to the associations found in the *HKEY_CLASSES_ROOT* key.

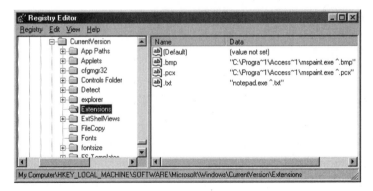

Figure 3-27.
File type associations.

Registering Several File Types for a Single Application

In the sections above, you learned the most straightforward methods of registering file types. Using these methods assures that you won't run into conflicts when you change a file type association by using Windows tools such as Open With or Windows Explorer. However, there still remain a few "not-so-well-behaved" applications that can cause some trouble if a user decides to change a file type association.

I mentioned previously that some applications "grab" several file extensions. If you install a graphic application such as Jasc Paint Shop Pro or Ulead PhotoImpact, several graphic file types will be registered for the one application. For instance, BMP, PCX, and TIF bitmap files will all be opened with the same graphic application.

Extension "grabbing" can cause problems, however, if the user decides to change the association of just one file type. For example, if you change the application associated with the BMP file type, the new association will also affect the other graphic file types that had been associated with the same application as BMP had been. And it's possible that the new application does not support the other file formats! Unfortunately, using Open With or Windows Explorer will not solve this problem. To further analyze this issue, let's look at another example. Figure 3-28 on the next page shows a File Types property page with the registered data of a Text document. The file types TXT, DIZ, and 1ST are associated with the Notepad.exe application. How do we change the association for only the DIZ file type? Good question. There's no simple way to change the association for only one file type. If you use Open With or the Edit button on the File Types property page to select a new application, the association for all three file types changes. The reason for this is the way in which vendors build their install programs.

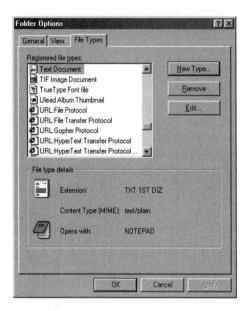

Figure 3-28.
File type associations.

Let's examine how several file types become registered for one application. Registering a file type requires two keys in the Registry. The first key defines the file extension (that is, 1ST, TXT, and DIZ in our example). The second key contains the executable command or commands, the default icon, and so on. The first key keeps the name of the second key as its *Default* value, so you can use only one second key to define the executable commands of the application. As you can see in Figure 3-29, all the keys defining the file types in our example point to this global second key.

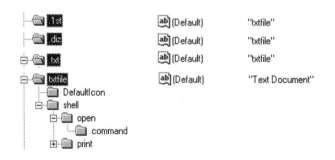

Figure 3-29.
File type associations in the Registry.

Each file type is registered, but only one application is available for all the file types. There are several advantages to this approach. Fewer keys are required to register file types, and the commands for all file types associated with the application are stored in only one *shell* key. Thus, changing a command requires updating the subkeys of only the one *shell* key.

Despite the advantages, I'd like to mention the penalty you have to pay. There is only one way to change a registered file type with this sort of multiple association: the user must fire up the Registry Editor and add a new branch containing all keys required to store executable commands, default icons, and so on. Then the user must redirect the *Default* value of the key defining the file extension to the new branch. Because this is a problem for most users, I don't recommend registering file types in this way. Instead, a vendor can provide several REG or INF files to change file type associations. The following code shows a REG file that registers the file types 1ST, DIZ, and TXT for a single application.

```
REGEDIT4
[HKEY_CLASSES_ROOT\.1st]
@="txtfile"
"Content Type"="text/plain"

[HKEY_CLASSES_ROOT\.diz]
@="txtfile"
"Content Type"="text/plain"

[HKEY_CLASSES_ROOT\.txt]
@="txtfile"
"Content Type"="text/plain"

[HKEY_CLASSES_ROOT\.txt\ShellNew]
"NullFile"=""

[HKEY_CLASSES_ROOT\.txt\ShellEx]

[HKEY_CLASSES_ROOT\.txt\ShellEx\{BB2E617C-0920-11d1-9A0B-    ⌐
00C04FC2D6C1}]
@="{EAB841A0-9550-11cf-8C16-00805F1408F3}"

[HKEY_CLASSES_ROOT\txtfile]
@="Text Document"

[HKEY_CLASSES_ROOT\txtfile\DefaultIcon]
@="shell32.dll,-152"

[HKEY_CLASSES_ROOT\txtfile\shell]
```

(continued)

continued

```
[HKEY_CLASSES_ROOT\txtfile\shell\open]

[HKEY_CLASSES_ROOT\txtfile\shell\open\command]
@="C:\\WINDOWS\\NOTEPAD.EXE %1"

[HKEY_CLASSES_ROOT\txtfile\shell\print]

[HKEY_CLASSES_ROOT\txtfile\shell\print\command]
C:\\WINDOWS\\NOTEPAD.EXE /p %1"
```

You will find this file, TXT.REG, in the sample folder \chapter3. Take care to check the application paths. If your system uses different Windows folder names, you must edit the REG file. If you want to separate the registered file types and avoid the problem I've been describing, you can use the REG file TXT1.REG located in the same folder. TXT1.REG contains the commands shown below. Each registered file type gets its own keys for the file extension and for its commands; therefore, you can change the application association for one file type without changing all the other file type associations.

```
REGEDIT4
[HKEY_CLASSES_ROOT\.1st]
@="txtfile1"
"Content Type"="text/plain"

[HKEY_CLASSES_ROOT\.diz]
@="txtfile2"
"Content Type"="text/plain"

[HKEY_CLASSES_ROOT\.txt]
@="txtfile"
"Content Type"="text/plain"

[HKEY_CLASSES_ROOT\.txt\ShellNew]
"NullFile"=""

[HKEY_CLASSES_ROOT\.txt\ShellEx]

[HKEY_CLASSES_ROOT\.txt\ShellEx\{BB2E617C-0920-11d1-9A0B-    ⟶
00C04FC2D6C1}]
@="{EAB841A0-9550-11cf-8C16-00805F1408F3}"

[HKEY_CLASSES_ROOT\txtfile]
@="Text Document"

[HKEY_CLASSES_ROOT\txtfile\DefaultIcon]
@="shell32.dll,-152"
```

```
[HKEY_CLASSES_ROOT\txtfile\shell]

[HKEY_CLASSES_ROOT\txtfile\shell\open]

[HKEY_CLASSES_ROOT\txtfile\shell\open\command]
@="C:\\WINDOWS\\NOTEPAD.EXE %1"

[HKEY_CLASSES_ROOT\txtfile\shell\print]

[HKEY_CLASSES_ROOT\txtfile\shell\print\command]
C:\\WINDOWS\\NOTEPAD.EXE /p %1"

[HKEY_CLASSES_ROOT\txtfile1]
@="1ST-Document"

[HKEY_CLASSES_ROOT\txtfile1\DefaultIcon]
@="shell32.dll,-152"

[HKEY_CLASSES_ROOT\txtfile1\shell]

[HKEY_CLASSES_ROOT\txtfile1\shell\open]

[HKEY_CLASSES_ROOT\txtfile1\shell\open\command]
@="C:\\WINDOWS\\NOTEPAD.EXE %1"
[HKEY_CLASSES_ROOT\txtfile1\shell\print]

[HKEY_CLASSES_ROOT\txtfile1\shell\print\command]
C:\\WINDOWS\\NOTEPAD.EXE /p %1"

[HKEY_CLASSES_ROOT\txtfile2]
@="DIZ-Document"

[HKEY_CLASSES_ROOT\txtfile2\DefaultIcon]
@="shell32.dll,-152"

[HKEY_CLASSES_ROOT\txtfile2\shell]

[HKEY_CLASSES_ROOT\txtfile2\shell\open]

[HKEY_CLASSES_ROOT\txtfile2\shell\open\command]
@="C:\\WINDOWS\\NOTEPAD.EXE %1"

[HKEY_CLASSES_ROOT\txtfile2\shell\print]

[HKEY_CLASSES_ROOT\txtfile2\shell\print\command]
C:\\WINDOWS\\NOTEPAD.EXE /p %1"
```

Using *EditFlags* to Protect Registered File Types

Having used the Edit File Type dialog box to customize the settings of a registered file type, you can see that the process is straightforward. In the course of modifying these settings, however, you can accidentally delete necessary data. Because the results could be disastrous, system administrators must protect these settings from inadvertent modification. One obvious way to do this is to delete the Registry Editor from each local system—but we've seen how easily the user can change settings with the Edit File Type dialog box available in Windows Explorer. It would be more secure to have methods that disable certain Registry buttons (Edit, Remove, and so on) or lock access to a registered file type's settings. How can we do this? Well, we need the Registry Editor, or we need to use a REG or INF file.

We've seen the *EditFlags* value a number of times in this chapter. This flag is a "gatekeeper" that either allows or prevents a user from changing the settings of a registered file type in the Edit File Type dialog box. If this flag is omitted, the user has access to all options on the File Types property page and in the Edit File Type dialog box. To restrict access, you must insert the *EditFlags* value into the main key of a registered file type. This value is set as a binary value in the format *xx xx 00 00*, where *xx xx* stands for two bytes. Changing the *EditFlags* value data changes how a user is able to access and edit a registered file type's settings.

To hide the name of the registered file type on the File Types property page, insert the following into the main key of the registered file type:

```
EditFlags = 01 00 00 00
```

The main key in our 1ST file type example is the *1stfile* key. Figure 3-30 shows the *EditFlags* value above added to the key.

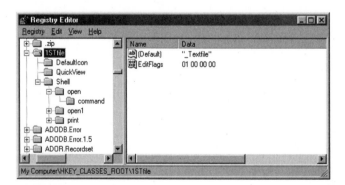

Figure 3-30.
The EditFlags *value.*

The flag value *01* hides the registered file type (that is, _Textfile) in the list of registered file types that appears on the File Types property page. And, of course, if this entry isn't visible, the user can't modify it. Inspecting the Registry will reveal several items with this flag value. Take a look at *dllfile*, for example.

Other values also enable and disable several options on the File Types property page and in the Edit File Type dialog box. To disable the Remove button, use this value:

```
EditFlags = 10 00 00 00
```

If you want to protect the properties of registered file types, use this:

```
EditFlags= 08 00 00 00
```

You can also combine these values in a bitwise OR operation, meaning that *EditFlags* is a bit array that has 16 bits to use to enable or disable options. Table 3-1 shows the coding of these bits. Note that the Registry Editor will display the hex byte sequence of a bit array. For example, the value *0x00000001* will be displayed in the Registry Editor as *01 00 00 00*.

Coding of the *EditFlags* Value

Bit Array	Resultant Coding
Word 0	
0000 0000 0000 0001	Hide the description in the Registered File Types list.
0000 0000 0000 0010	Disable the Content Type (MIME) list box in the Edit File Type dialog box.
0000 0000 0000 0100	N/A
0000 0000 0000 1000	Disable the Edit button on the File Types property page.
0000 0000 0001 0000	Disable the Remove button on the File Types property page.
0000 0000 0010 0000	Disable the New button in the Edit File Type dialog box.
0000 0000 0100 0000	Disable the Edit button in the Edit File Type dialog box.

Table 3-1.   *(continued)*
*The entries shown in the Bit Array column are given as binary values—
a value 0000 0000 0000 0001 is equivalent to the hex value 00 01.*

Coding of the *EditFlags* Value *continued*

Bit Array	Resultant Coding
0000 0000 1000 0000	Disable the Remove button in the Edit File Type dialog box.
0000 0001 0000 0000	Disable the Description Of Type edit box in the Edit File Type dialog box.
0000 0010 0000 0000	Disable the Change Icon button in the Edit File Type dialog box.
0000 0100 0000 0000	Disable the Set Default button in the Edit File Type dialog box.
Word 1	
0000 0000 0000 0001	Suppress the Open/Save dialog box during download in Microsoft Internet Explorer. Files selected are always opened.

Let's try one example. Suppose that you want to disable the Remove button on the File Types property page and the Edit and Remove buttons in the Edit File Type dialog box. You can calculate the *EditFlags* value as shown below:

```
0000 0000 0001 0000 disable Remove on the File Types property page
0000 0000 0100 0000 disable Edit in the Edit File Type dialog box
0000 0000 1000 0000 disable Remove in the Edit File Type dialog box
0000 0000 1101 0000 result
```

The result is the binary value *0000 0000 1101 0000*, or *0x00D0* in hex notation. You must enter this value as *D0 00 00 00* in the Registry Editor.

NOTE: When you change the *EditFlags* value in the Registry, you must close the File Types property page and reopen it before you will see the effect of your change. Also, in Windows 98 the upper bits of *EditFlags* are used for other purposes. The value *xx xx 01 xx* indicates a checked Confirm Open After Download option. (See the section "Registering a New File Type" beginning on page 69.)

Hiding and Showing File Extensions

The View property page on the Folder Options property sheet controls how the shell (including Windows Explorer) shows files and their extensions. This property page is shown in Figure 3-31.

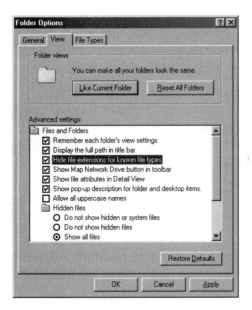

Figure 3-31.
The View property page.

If you activate the Hide File Extensions For Known File Types check box, registered file type extensions are no longer displayed. Why, then, do you sometimes find a registered file type extension in the Windows Explorer window even if this check box is activated?

The Always Show Extension check box in the Edit File Type dialog box has a higher priority than the Hide File Extensions For Known File Types setting, so if you check the Always Show Extension option, file extensions will be shown for that file type. You can also set a particular file type extension to never be visible, regardless of what you set on the View property page. This ability is controlled inside the Registry by two entries in the main key of the registered file type. Here's how it works:

■ If the value named *NeverShowExt* is present in a file type's main key, Windows always hides the extension in the shell. Figure 3-32 on the next page shows this value in the *1stfile* key. The value's data is set to an empty string.

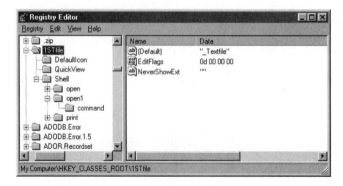

Figure 3-32.
The NeverShowExt flag.

■ If the value named *AlwaysShowExt* is present in this key, Windows always shows the extension in the shell. Figure 3-33 shows this entry for *1stfile*. Its value is also set to an empty string.

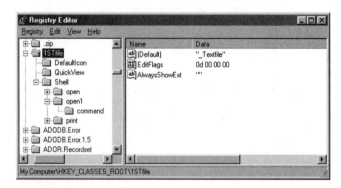

Figure 3-33.
The AlwaysShowExt flag.

You can use these values to overwrite the global settings in the Windows shell and hide or show a registered file type's extension.

NOTE: When you add one of these names in the Registry Editor, it might take a few seconds to flush the new value onto the disk. Close the Windows Explorer window and reopen it to ensure that the new options will be used.

In Chapter 4, I'll show you how Windows stores the Hide File Extensions For Known File Types option in the Registry.

Registering a Quick Viewer for a File Type

As mentioned in the first part of this chapter, you can register a Quick Viewer for a selected file type. This can be done in the Edit File Type dialog box by activating the Enable Quick View check box. Windows Explorer then adds the *QuickView* subkey with its *Default* value set as *"*"* to the file type's settings key in the Registry, as you can see in Figure 3-34.

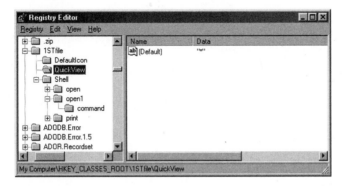

Figure 3-34.
The QuickView *entry in the Registry.*

The Viewer installed in Windows, the SCC viewer, detects a file's format and shows the contents of the file. The text used on the context menu depends on the localized Windows version.

You can extend properties of each file type with a Quick View command, enabling you to right-click the file, select Quick View on the context menu, and get the Quick View display of the file contents on the screen. Figure 3-35 on the next page shows the Quick View window displaying the contents of a REG file.

Although there is no default Quick Viewer for REG files registered in Windows 98, you can use the following lines to extend the REG file type properties. (You can find REG1.REG in the \chapter3 folder of the sample files.)

```
REGEDIT4

[HKEY_CLASSES_ROOT\regfile\QuickView]
@="*"
```

Now, whenever you right-click a REG file, a context menu showing the Quick View entry will appear.

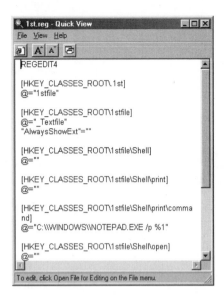

Figure 3-35.
Quick View window with the contents of a REG file.

Defining a Standard *QuickView* Property

After inspecting other branches in the Registry, I originally found it curious that, for example, I couldn't find a *QuickView* key in *HKEY_CLASSES_ROOT* *rtffile*. (See Figure 3-36.)

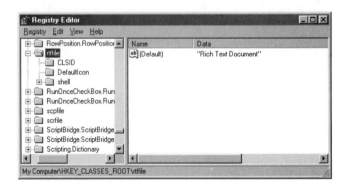

Figure 3-36.
The keys for the RTF file type.

The RTF format is widely supported under Windows 95, Windows 98, and Windows NT 4.0, so I wondered why the key was missing. Then I discovered that right-clicking an RTF file opens the context menu with a Quick

View entry. (Try right-clicking the file README.RTF in the \chapter3 folder of the sample files.)

How could Windows 98 know that the context menu in this case should contain a Quick View command? The other file extensions without a *QuickView* key had no such command on the context menu. The answer can be found in the *HKEY_CLASSES_ROOT* branch, in which a key named *QuickView* defines the properties of the Quick View function. The key contains the extensions of all the registered file types for which the Quick Viewer is available.

Figure 3-37 shows part of this structure. Each file type can be registered by its extension, which is used as the key name. Each of these keys has a subkey that uses the Class ID (CLSID) code value of the Quick Viewer as its name. Windows uses this CLSID value to define the ActiveX server, which will be invoked as a Quick Viewer. Figure 3-37 shows the CLSID of the default Windows 98 Quick Viewer. You can also insert the CLSID of a third-party viewer if you want. The *QuickView* branch contains the file extensions for many file types used in Windows 95, Windows 98, and Windows NT 4.0, so there's no need to add a *QuickView* subkey to the main key of each of these file types.

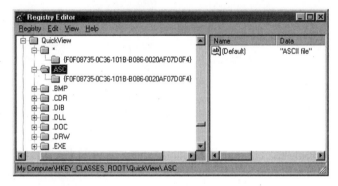

Figure 3-37.
The QuickView *branch in* HKEY_CLASSES_ROOT.

Let's verify this for the REG file type. This file type has no default *QuickView* property. Earlier we registered the *QuickView* key in the *regfile* branch. Delete this key, and try to register a *QuickView* property for REG files in the *HKEY_CLASSES_ROOT\QuickView* branch. Use the following commands for this purpose:

```
REGEDIT4

[HKEY_CLASSES_ROOT\QuickView\.REG]

[HKEY_CLASSES_ROOT\QuickView\.REG\{F0F08735-0C36-101B-B086-0020AF07D0F4}]
@="Born's Quick View Test"
```

After importing this file, the REG file type should have a Quick View property. (This file is available as REG2.REG in the \chapter3 folder of the sample files.)

Information About Viewer Modules

Windows 98 keeps the files for various viewers in the subfolder named \Windows\System\Viewers. Information about the SCC viewer modules can be found in the Registry in this branch:

HKEY_LOCAL_MACHINE\SOFTWARE\SCC\Viewer Technology

By default, this Registry branch has an *OEMMS* subkey containing two subkeys—*Engine List* and *Filter List*—with internal viewer data. The settings for the Quick View windows can be found in the key *HKEY_USERS\xxxx\Software\SCC\QuickViewer\1.00*. The characters *xxxx* stand for a user name or for the default. Entries exist for the fonts (*CurrentFontCharSet, CurrentFontName, CurrentFontSize*), for the options (*Orientation, PageView, Statusbar, Toolbar*), and for the *UseOEMCharSet* flag.

Information about how to write a viewer can be found in Nancy Winnick Cluts's book *Programming the Windows 95 User Interface* (Microsoft Press, 1995).

Using an Application as a Viewer

Would you like to use another application as a Quick Viewer? You can add a *quickview* verb in the *shell* key, name it *QuickView*, and set the *command* key's *Default* value to the application (for example, *"C:\tools\hexview.exe %1"*).

You can also use the QUIKVIEW.EXE file to open a file. For example, if you want to view the contents of a 1ST file with Quick View, use the following REG structure:

```
REGEDIT4

[HKEY_CLASSES_ROOT\1stfile\Shell\view]

[HKEY_CLASSES_ROOT\1stfile\Shell\view\command]
@="C:\\WINDOWS\\SYSTEM\\VIEWERS\\quikview.EXE %1"
```

This REG file, available as 1STF.REG in the \chapter3 folder of the sample files, requires that you have already registered the 1ST file type. After importing the

REG file, you will see the view command on the context menu if you right-click a 1ST file.

> **N O T E :**   If you open the context menu and select the view command, and a message box that tells you that viewers aren't registered for this file type is invoked, then Windows started the Quick Viewer and couldn't find registration information in the Registry. To suppress this message box, you must register the *QuickView* property by using the techniques discussed earlier.

Registering a Command for All File Types

In the previous sections, we have seen how to register a selected file type and its properties (context menu commands, for example). But suppose you want to register a command for all file types. Perhaps you have a hex editor that you want to use to show the internals of any selected file. It can be pretty time-consuming to add the following command to each registered file type to load this hex editor.

```
shell
    openhex
        command = "C:\TOOLS\HEXEDIT.EXE %1"
```

Fortunately, a key in *HKEY_CLASSES_ROOT* for wildcard (*) extensions is available, as shown in Figure 3-38. If you enter a command in this subkey, the command is valid for all registered file types.

Figure 3-38.
*The * branch for wildcard extensions.*

In Figure 3-38, only shell extensions are registered, but we can extend the * key with a *shell* subkey. You can use your own verbs within the *shell* branch to extend the properties of all file types.

Let's have a look at Figure 3-39 on the next page. There I have defined a verb *view* with the *Default* value set to *"&View"*.

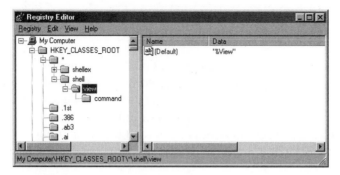

Figure 3-39.
Defining a new command for all file types.

The *command* key is set to the following:

"C:\WINDOWS\SYSTEM\VIEWERS\quikview.exe %1"

The whole structure to register this extension is shown in the following REG file:

```
REGEDIT4

[HKEY_CLASSES_ROOT\*\shell]

[HKEY_CLASSES_ROOT\*\shell\view]
@="&View"

[HKEY_CLASSES_ROOT\*\shell\view\command]
@="C:\\WINDOWS\\SYSTEM\\VIEWERS\\quikview.EXE %1"
```

If your system uses a different folder to store the Quick Viewer, you must edit the path in the last line. You can also exchange QUIKVIEW.EXE with the name of another application. (This REG file is available as ALL1.REG in the \chapter3 folder of the sample files.) If you select a file and right-click, the context menu now contains the new View entry (see Figure 3-40). Notice that the View entry is at the top of the menu. Until now, the default entry, shown in bold-face, was at the top of the context menu. This ordering relates to how Windows 98 scans the Registry.

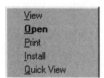

Figure 3-40.
Extending the context menu with a View command.

First the wildcard (*) branch is checked by Windows 98—it detects that we have extended this branch with a new command. The command in the wildcard branch is shown as the top entry on the context menu. Next Windows 98 scans the Registry for the entry matching the file extension. All verbs in the *shell* branch are appended to the context menu. These entries are sorted. (See the section "Sequencing the Context Menu Commands" on page 99 for an explanation.) Then the *QuickView* property for this file type is analyzed, and if the command is available, it is appended to the context menu. After these steps, other entries (Send To, Copy, and so on) are added to the context menu. In Chapter 4, I'll discuss several examples of extending the context menu with new functions.

Getting Your Hands on Unregistered Files

If you double-click an unregistered file, the Open With dialog box opens. Right-clicking such a file brings up a context menu showing the Open With entry. That is all you can do with an unregistered file type. Many unregistered files contain only ASCII text, so it would be helpful to use Notepad to open these files (or to use Quick View to display the contents). One place to add commands to unregistered files is *HKEY_CLASSES_ROOT**, but any command you enter there will be shown for all file types. If you want to display a command for only unregistered file types, you should use the *HKEY_CLASSES_ROOT\Unknown\shell* key. This key contains a subkey named *openas*, which is set as shown in Figure 3-41.

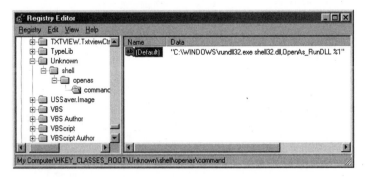

Figure 3-41.
The Unknown *branch in* HKEY_CLASSES_ROOT.

The subkey *openas* is another canonical verb defined in Windows 98. This verb is shown as Open With on the context menu. Examine the *Default* value of the key's *command* subkey to find out how RUNDLL32.EXE is called to invoke the Open With dialog box.

How is it that you can use the *Unknown* branch? Because the branch includes a *shell* key, you can add a new verb and define a *command* key by using a command string. The following REG file contains the command to register NOTEPAD.EXE as the application for opening unregistered file types. (This REG file is available as UNKNOWN1.REG in the \chapter 3 folder of the sample files.) Be sure your system uses the same path as that shown in the preceding REG file.

```
REGEDIT4

[HKEY_CLASSES_ROOT\Unknown\shell\open1]
@="Notepad"

[HKEY_CLASSES_ROOT\Unknown\shell\open1\command]
@="C:\\Windows\\Notepad.exe %1"
```

After importing the REG file by double-clicking, you can open an unregistered file type by right-clicking it and selecting Notepad. The context menu contains the Notepad entry, as you can see in Figure 3-42. If you select this entry, the file will be loaded into Notepad. Also note the Open With entry, which is used to register an application for this file type, and the View command, which is shown in bold. This command was registered in *HKEY_CLASSES_ROOT*\shell*. View has become the default command for the unregistered file type. View appears in bold only if you select an unknown file type because in that case the commands registered in the wildcard branch will be used as the default.

Figure 3-42.
Extended context menu for unregistered file types.

Conclusion

In this chapter, I've shown you how to register file types in Windows 98 (and, therefore, in Windows 95, Windows NT 4.0, and Windows NT 5.0). Now you can fix some problems in your Registry and extend the shell with several new commands. But don't forget the easy way to register file types and modify file type properties! Windows Explorer's File Types property page is a great tool for these purposes. In Chapter 4, I'll show you how to extend the shell further with new commands.

Customizing the Desktop, Start Menu, and Control Panel Properties

Microsoft Windows 98 uses a shell, of which Windows Explorer is a significant feature, to handle all user interface tasks. If you use the Start menu or change the desktop, Windows Explorer is involved. As we have seen in Chapter 3, you can easily register a new file type or change a file type's default icon, but these actions are only two of the ways in which you can customize the Windows 98 shell. You can also do the following:

- Rename title text for desktop icons
- Change the desktop icons themselves
- Change Start menu entries
- Customize Windows Explorer commands

In this chapter, I'll show you several techniques for customizing the desktop, the Start menu, and the Control Panel properties, and I'll discuss how the resulting changes affect the Registry.

Customizing the Open With List

On a freshly installed Windows 98 system, the program list in the Open With dialog box contains only a few entries. After you install additional application programs, this list grows, but it's often too incomplete for many users' purposes.

When I started working with Windows 95 a few years ago, I wondered why some application programs didn't appear in the Open With dialog box and why others were there at all. For example, the list on my system contained install programs, HTML wizards, and so on—unnecessary entries left by application setup programs in violation of the rules of good Windows-based programming. A good setup program should delete entries in the Registry that are used only for installation purposes and should also offer an option to remove the files that deleted these entries, but the world is full of unfriendly programs.

After you've worked with Windows 98 for a while, you'll probably find that your Open With dialog box contains a huge list of application names that aren't helpful anymore. Some entries remain even though you've deleted the related applications. And while you've got many applications you don't need, you don't have many of the ones you do need: some programs (especially shareware) are shipped only as EXE files, and because such programs don't require setup programs, appropriate entries aren't added to the Open With list. The Other button on the Open With dialog box is your only option for accessing these applications. Needless to say, this frustrating situation forced me to think about a solution. Wouldn't it be nice to find a way to add your favorite applications to the Open With list and to delete unnecessary entries?

How the Shell Inserts Applications in the Open With List

Before I dig into the details, let's look at what information is needed to add or remove entries from the Open With list. It took me a long time to find out how Windows 95 manages this list, but the answer is fairly simple and is also valid for Windows 98 and Microsoft Windows NT 4.0. If you look back at Chapter 3, you'll find an explanation of the canonical verbs used to register a command for a new file type. Windows uses those verbs to determine which applications to include in the Open With list. Whenever a user invokes the Open With dialog box, Windows scans the *HKEY_CLASSES_ROOT* key in the Registry. Any application that is defined in the *command* subkey of the *open* verb of a registered file type is added by Windows to the Open With list. If the application contains its own icon, this icon will be shown. The text for the entry is taken from the name of the EXE file or from the *Default* value of the file extension key.

So it's easy to add your favorite application to the Open With list—all you need to do is register a file type with this application. To remove an entry, delete the *open* verb for the registered file type(s) using the application you want to remove. The following sections explain in detail how to add applications to and delete applications from the Open With list.

Adding an Application to the Open With List

First let's register an application for the Open With dialog box. To demonstrate a typical situation, I'll use a new, unregistered file type and application. Here's our situation:

■ The new file extension is set to ASC because many ASCII text files have this extension. You can easily register this file type, as we saw in Chapter 3. (A README.ASC file is provided in the \chapter4 folder of the sample files.)

■ We'll open our ASCII text file with the MS-DOS program EDIT.COM, which is shipped with Windows 98. (You'll find this application in the \Windows\Command subfolder.) We could also open the ASCII text file with Notepad, but NOTEPAD.EXE is already registered for the Open With dialog box.

Registering the ASC file type with the EDIT.COM application will add the application to the Open With list. (You might prefer to register a different application available on your computer. I've chosen to register EDIT.COM because it allows me to show and modify MS-DOS–based files containing the OEM character set. Notepad, besides already being registered, won't let me edit files containing line-drawn characters and umlauts.) Once you add EDIT.COM (or another editor) to the Open With list, you can use this program to load an ASC file instead of using Notepad. You can add the application to the Open With list by using the Open With dialog box or a REG file.

Using the Open With Dialog Box

To add EDIT.COM to the Open With dialog box permanently, we have to register an *open* key for the new file type in *HKEY_CLASSES_ROOT* and enter the command that invokes EDIT.COM in its *command* subkey. Following is the simplest method for adding EDIT.COM to the Open With dialog box:

1. Right-click the unregistered README.ASC file, and select Open With from the context menu. Windows opens the Open With dialog box. The Always Use This Program To Open This File check box must contain a check mark to ensure that the Registry is updated.

2. Enter a description in the Description Of '.ASC' Files text box. (See the Tip on page 65 in Chapter 3 for tips on creating a description.)

3. Click the Other button to invoke another dialog box—the Open With file dialog box. Select All Files in the Files Of Type section, and browse the Windows\Command subfolder.

4. Select EDIT.COM (or the associated PIF file), and click Open. Click OK to close the Open With dialog box.

Windows registers the new ASC file type with an *open* verb and the EDIT.COM command and then opens the MS-DOS Editor. Close the Editor, select the README.ASC file in Windows Explorer, press the Shift key, and right-click the file. Select the Open With command from the context menu to invoke the Open With dialog box (see Figure 4-1). As you can see, the Edit entry is now available in the Open With list. Since EDIT.COM is an MS-DOS application, the default icon for EXE files is used for this entry. The text following the icon is built from the application's filename.

Figure 4-1.
The Open With dialog box with the new Edit entry.

Using a REG File

The second way to add EDIT.COM to the Open With list is to use a REG file to extend the Registry with the necessary entries. Following are the lines necessary to register the ASC file type and to use EDIT.COM as the associated application:

```
REGEDIT4

[HKEY_CLASSES_ROOT\.asc]
@="ascfile"

[HKEY_CLASSES_ROOT\ascfile]
@="_AsciFile"

[HKEY_CLASSES_ROOT\ascfile\Shell]
@=""

[HKEY_CLASSES_ROOT\ascfile\Shell\open]
@="DOS-Edit"

[HKEY_CLASSES_ROOT\ascfile\Shell\open\command]
@="C:\\WINDOWS\\Command\\Edit.com \"%1\""

[HKEY_CLASSES_ROOT\ascfile\DefaultIcon]
@="C:\\WINDOWS\\Notepad.exe,1"
```

All commands in the ASC.REG file are contained in the \chapter4 folder of the sample files. If you double-click this file, all settings are added to the Registry. I used \WINDOWS as the standard name for the \Windows folder, so if you use a different name, you have to modify the preceding code to map the right path to EDIT.COM—before you double-click the REG file.

> **N O T E :** If you plan to ship your application with an installation script, don't use a REG file. If you aren't using a setup program, try to install the application and update the Registry with an INF file. I discussed this topic in Chapter 3 and will show the details of constructing such an INF file in Chapters 5 and 7.

Removing an Application from the Open With List

Removing a superfluous entry from the list can be a simple task, but you should be aware of the potential problems. Following are techniques for removing items from the list.

Removing a Phantom Entry

If you have deleted software from your PC (maybe the package was installed only for test purposes), the Registry could still contain the entries that registered the software's associated file types. Because uninstall features often either are nonexistent or don't work properly, many unused entries can remain in the Registry. Selecting an application associated with these entries in the Open With dialog box invokes the Program Not Found dialog box (see Figure 4-2), which indicates that the application isn't available or at least isn't in the specified folder. The Program Not Found dialog box indicates that it's time to clean your Registry, which you can accomplish in several different ways.

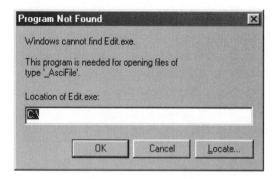

Figure 4-2.
The Program Not Found dialog box.

The most radical solution is to open the Registry Editor and delete the entries for this application. You have to remove two keys in *HKEY_CLASSES_ROOT*: the one that specified the file extension (in our previous example, the *.asc* key) and the one that defined the commands for this file type (the *ascfile* key). If you know which entries have to be modified, this is the best method, and I've used this approach many times.

If you're feeling more cautious, you can use a different approach: redirecting the Open With dialog box to use one of the other installed applications. For example, you can register the ASC file type to use Notepad (or a different application program, depending on your situation). To handle the phantom entry by registering another application for this file type, follow these steps:

1. In Windows Explorer, press the Shift key and right-click the file of the type you want to reassign. Select the Open With command from the context menu to open the dialog box.

2. Check the Always Use This Program To Open This Type Of File check box.

3. Select the application that you want to register for this file type, or click Other to display additional applications that you can choose from.

4. Click OK to close the dialog box.

Windows overwrites the value defined in the *command* subkey with the selected application's path and filename. Double-clicking the file type now opens the new application, and if you open the Open With dialog box again, the old phantom entry will be gone, assuming that no other registered file types are tied to the old application. If you clicked Other to select a new application, you'll see the new entry in the applications list. Even if several file types are registered for a single application, the application will appear only once in the list.

TIP: This trick is handy if the application you're removing has overwritten registered file types of other applications. For example, if the BMP extension has been overwritten by a graphics application, you could use the above steps to reset this extension to open with the Microsoft Paint application.

Using Windows Explorer to Remove an Open With List Entry

Suppose you want to remove some rarely used entries, but you have no idea which file types the Open command is registered under. The application you plan to remove could support several file types. (For example, WordPad supports the DOC, RTF, and TXT file extensions.) If you delete an entire branch for a given file type in the Registry, you will probably disable other functions. Perhaps you'd lose the ability to print with drag-and-drop, or you might lose the Quick View feature for a file type.

You could inspect the *HKEY_CLASSES_ROOT* branch with the Registry Editor and remove all unused entries, but that's time-consuming and you might inadvertently remove or change the wrong keys. Fortunately, there is a less risky way to find out what you need to change in the Registry and to go ahead and alter it. If you want to remove an entry from the Open With list but you're not sure which file types are responsible for the entry, perform the following steps:

1. Open Windows Explorer, click the View menu, and select Folder Options to open the Folder Options property sheet.

2. Select the File Types property page, and click an entry in the Registered File Types list. Windows displays the entry's file type extension and the associated application in the File Type Details section, as shown in Figure 4-3 on the next page.

3. If the Registry contains an *open* verb for this file type, you'll see the icon and the application name in the Opens With line. In Figure 4-3, I chose the *_AsciFile* entry, which I registered earlier with the ASC.REG file. The ASC file extension is associated with the Edit application.

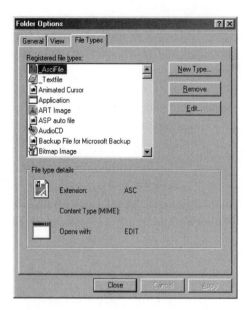

Figure 4-3.
The File Types property page.

4. Click the Edit button to open the Edit File Type dialog box, and check the commands registered for this file type. Here you can select open in the Actions box (or the default name assigned to the *open* key in the Registry—DOS-Edit if you used the ASC.REG file) and then click Edit to bring up the Editing Action For Type dialog box. In this dialog box, you can confirm that the application used for the open action is the one you want to remove. If it is, close the Editing Action For Type dialog box, be sure the open action is still highlighted, and click Remove.

Continue to look for entries on the File Types property page to determine whether other file types exist that contain open actions for this application. You must delete all entries that contain the application's name in the Opens With line on the File Types property page.

This process will work fine as long as you don't need the application to be associated with the registered file types anymore. A problem arises if you want to remove the application's name from the Open With list but still keep the file types registered with that application. In this case, you can't simply delete the *open* verbs in the Action box of the Edit File Type window—you must rename them. I will explain how to do this in the next section.

Using the Registry Editor to Remove an Open With List Entry

Sometimes you don't want to delete a registered file type's *open* verb and its command, because you need this command for that file type. How do you force Windows to prevent an application's name from appearing in the Open With list? As I mentioned earlier, the *open* verb is a canonical verb and is used to build the Open With list. In Chapter 3, I discussed several ways to register a file type without using a canonical verb, such as renaming the *open* verb to *open1*. Doing so prevents the application from being added to the Open With list.

Unfortunately, you can't change an entry in the Action box of the Edit File Type dialog box. In this case, you can use the Registry Editor to solve the problem. Follow these steps:

1. Create a Registry backup so that you can recover the old settings if you fail to alter the Open With list correctly. (See pages 36–49 in Chapter 2 for backup procedures.)

2. Search *HKEY_CLASSES_ROOT* for all *open* keys associated with the application that will be removed from the Open With list. If you don't know the file types, you can identify them by using the File Types property page, as explained in the previous section.

3. Right-click the *open* key in the Registry Editor's left pane, select the Rename option from the context menu, and change the key's name to *open1*. Enter the name you want displayed in the context menu as the *Default* value for this key. As you can see in Figure 4-4, I've used *DOS-Edit*, but you can also use *Open*.

4. Select the *Shell* key (the parent of the *open1* key) of this branch, and set the *Default* value in the right pane to *open1*. This assures that the command will be used when you double-click the file.

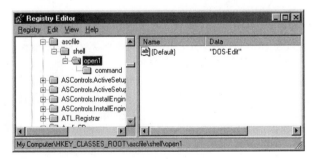

Figure 4-4.
Modified Registry branch.

If the application is registered for several file types, you must repeat these steps for the *open* key of each of these file types. After changing all entries, you should run a test to determine whether the system is still functioning properly. (Perhaps a particular application relies on the *open* verb.) If you've properly renamed all the *open* keys for the file types associated with the specified application, the application's name will no longer appear in the Open With dialog box.

NOTE: Be careful when removing or renaming system-specific entries such as folders, drives, and so on in the Registry. These entries are used by the system, and unpredictable events could occur if their settings are "damaged." (The most serious consequence would be Windows not booting up anymore.) Also be careful deleting entries in *HKEY_CLASSES_ROOT*. Always remember to create a Registry backup before you remove or modify an entry so that you can recover the previous settings.

HKEY_CLASSES_ROOT and HKEY_LOCAL_MACHINE\SOFTWARE\Classes

In Chapter 3, I discussed how to register a file type in *HKEY_CLASSES_ROOT*. The sole purpose of *HKEY_CLASSES_ROOT* is to provide compatibility with the Microsoft Windows 3.1 registration database. If an old 16-bit application inserts entries in the [Extensions] section of the WIN.INI file, these entries will also be stored in the Registry in *HKEY_CLASSES_ROOT*. These entries are available the next time you start Windows 98.

The *HKEY_LOCAL_MACHINE\SOFTWARE\Classes* branch contains the entries for the registered file types. *HKEY_CLASSES_ROOT* always keeps the same data as the *HKEY_LOCAL_MACHINE\SOFTWARE\Classes* key. If you change something in one branch, all modifications are automatically applied to the other branch. I prefer to use only *HKEY_CLASSES_ROOT* to register new file types, as I have explained in Chapter 3.

The *HKEY_LOCAL_MACHINE\SOFTWARE\Microsoft\Windows\CurrentVersion\Extensions* key also contains entries in the WIN.INI [Extensions] style. The *CurrentVersion* subkey contains information about software that supports services built into Windows. As I mentioned in Chapter 3, you must be careful that the settings in the *Extensions* subkey don't contradict the settings defined in *HKEY_CLASSES_ROOT*.

Modifying the Desktop Items

The desktop contains both user-defined and predefined, or system-specific, items. User-defined items, such as a shortcut to an application, can be modified easily. A typical user can change an icon and its title, for example, or delete the item altogether.

The system-specific items, however, which include My Computer, Network Neighborhood, My Documents, and Recycle Bin, are much more difficult to modify. A typical user can change the text associated with a particular icon or the icon itself (for example, the user could change the My Computer icon title to Danny's Computer or use a property page to change the My Computer icon itself), but it's unlikely that the typical user would be able to, say, hide the physical icon without knowing important details about the Registry. In this section, I'll show you how to modify system-specific desktop elements.

Modifying the My Computer Components

The My Computer item is shown by default in the upper left corner of the desktop. The only attributes you can change directly on the desktop are the text below the icon and the icon position. New in Windows 98, however, is the ability to change the icon itself by using the Effects property page. If you know what to edit in the Registry, you can also change the icon that way or hide the displayed drive symbols in the My Computer window.

> **NOTE:** You can also perform the steps described below in Windows NT 4.0 (and in Windows 95 if you have installed the Plus! package), but the property page will be named Plus! instead of Effects.

Changing the My Computer Icon

Use the following steps to change the icon used for My Computer:

1. Right-click a free space on the Desktop.

2. Select the Properties command in the context menu.

3. Select the Effects property page on the Display Properties property sheet (see Figure 4-5 on the next page).

4. Click the My Computer icon in the Desktop Icons group.

5. Click Change Icon. This opens the Change Icon dialog box (see Figure 4-6 on the next page).

6. Select an Icon; click OK.

7. Click OK on the Effects property page.

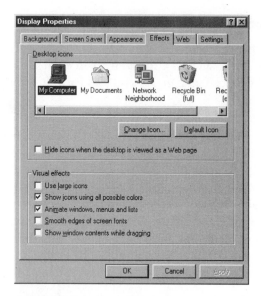

Figure 4-5.
The Effects property page.

Figure 4-6.
The Change Icon dialog box.

These steps assign the new icon to My Computer. How do these steps affect the Registry? The Windows 98 shell is built as a combination of several ActiveX components (formerly known as OLE components). Each shell part, such as My Computer, Network Neighborhood, Recycle Bin, and so on, has its own ActiveX component module. The handlers for all ActiveX modules are registered in the *HKEY_CLASSES_ROOT\CLSID* branch. (See pages 59–60 in Chapter 3 for more information about the CLSID code.) Thus the settings for the My Computer icon, the icon title, and so on are stored in the *CLSID* branch of the Registry. Figure 4-7 shows this branch in the Registry Editor window. The main problem is to find the right key in the *CLSID* branch.

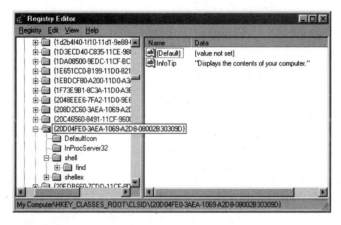

Figure 4-7.
The HKEY_CLASSES_ROOT\CLSID *entries in the Registry Editor.*

Finding and modifying the Registry entries for My Computer   In Windows 95, Windows 98, and Windows NT 4.0, the settings for My Computer are located in this key:

HKEY_CLASSES_ROOT\CLSID\{20D04FE0-3AEA-1069-A2D8-08002B30309D}

As you can see in Figure 4-7, the branch contains several subkeys. The branch's *Default* value and its subkeys define the properties of the ActiveX component.

■ The *Default* value of the ...\{20D04FE0-3AEA-1069-A2D8-08002B30309D} key might contain the icon title. If this value is missing, Windows 98 uses several strategies to determine the icon title (see below).

■ We have seen in Chapter 3 that the *DefaultIcon* key is used to define the icon source of an entry. In this branch, the key defines the icon for the ActiveX component. For My Computer, the first icon in EXPLORER.EXE is used because the Explorer is part of the shell. To change the icon of My Computer, you must alter the *Default* value of the *DefaultIcon* key.

■ The *InProcServer32* key contains two value entries. The *Default* value defines the 32-bit in-process, ActiveX server module (a DLL module), and the *ThreadingModel* value defines the threading model, which is *Apartment* in most cases.

■ The *shell* subkey defines the find command for the shell, and *shellex* can contain shell extensions for this ActiveX module.

Because Windows can use default values and customized values, you won't always find appropriate values in the keys for setting the default icon. The rules applied to the settings are shown below:

■ The *Default* value of the key *HKEY_CLASSES_ROOT\CLSID\ {20D04FE0-3AEA-1069-A2D8-08002B30309D}* might contain the icon's title of My Computer. If this default value is not set (as shown in Figure 4-7), Windows 95 and Windows NT 4.0 use a default icon title. This default icon title depends on the localized Windows version. In the U.S. Windows version, the default is the string My Computer. A German Windows version displays Arbeitsplatz. If you enter a new string (such as Danny's Computer) into the *Default* value of the key mentioned above, the Windows shell shows the string as the old My Computer icon's new title.

■ If the *HKEY_CLASSES_ROOT\CLSID\{20D04FE0-3AEA-1069-A2D8-08002B30309D}* branch's *DefaultIcon* subkey is missing, the Windows shell uses the default icon for My Computer. The *Default* value of the *DefaultIcon* subkey is set to the icon source used in the ActiveX component. If you inspect this key with the Registry Editor, you will find a value such as *C:\WINDOWS\Explorer.exe,0*. This value represents the default icon. You can change the *Default* value (for instance, set the value to *C:\WINDOWS\Explorer.exe,1*), but you must refresh the Desktop to see the new icon.

You can use the Registry Editor and alter the keys and values described above to change the My Computer settings. The My Computer icon and icon title will change as expected under Windows 95 and Windows NT 4.0. However, in Windows 98, the situation is a little bit different. The approach described above will work in a few cases, but on other machines it will have no effect.

Here's what's happening behind the curtains: Each user can have his or her own customized desktop with its own icon and title for My Computer. Windows 98 still keeps an entry as described above for the ActiveX component in *HKEY_CLASSES_ROOT\CLSID\{20D04FE0-3AEA-1069-A2D8-08002B30309D}*. But if you change the icon using the Effects property page (see Figure 4-5 on page 130), the *DefaultIcon* entry of that branch isn't changed. The *DefaultIcon* entry doesn't change either if the user changes the icon title of My Computer on the desktop. I came across this problem after running several tests of Windows 98.

After you've changed the icon title, searching the Registry for the My Computer Class ID leads you to another branch of *HKEY_CURRENT_USER*: *HKEY_CURRENT_USER\Software\Classes\CLSID*. This branch is new in Windows 98. As you can see in Figure 4-8, this branch contains the ClassID code *{20D04FE0-3AEA-1069-A2D8-08002B30309D}*—the Class ID for the My Computer ActiveX handler. Renaming the My Computer icon title on the desktop (using the Rename command in the context menu) changes the *Default* value of this key. Remember that all entries in *HKEY_CURRENT_USER* define settings for the current user logged on to the system. Therefore, if you change the *Default* value of this key, the change affects only the current user's desktop. The same applies to the optional *DefaultIcon* subkey. If you change the icon

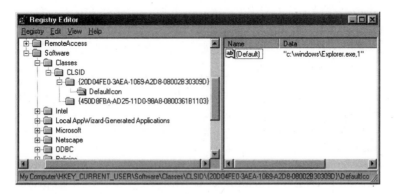

Figure 4-8.
Subkeys for My Computer in
HKEY_CURRENT_USER\Software\Classes\CLSID.

by using the Effects property page, the result is written in the *DefaultIcon* subkey of this branch. You can also set the *Default* value of the *DefaultIcon* subkey to the new icon source. A value of *C:\WINDOWS\Explorer.exe,1* displays the second icon contained in EXPLORER.EXE as the My Computer symbol. After entering this value in the Registry Editor, click a free space on the desktop and press the F5 key to refresh the display and show the new icon for My Computer (see Figure 4-9).

Figure 4-9.
A new icon and title for My Computer.

> NOTE: You can also use other files as sources for icons. For example, all Windows 98 applications come with built-in icons. As well, some DLL files, such as SHELL32.DLL, contain icons. You can also create your own ICO file and associate it with My Computer. You will find some additional information about the requirements for new icons in Chapter 5, in the section "Modifying the Shell Icons" on pages 260–61. This information is important if you use different screen resolutions and color resolutions.

> NOTE: All your changes are going into the *HKEY_CURRENT_USER\Software\Classes\CLSID* branch because changes are valid for only the current user. All *HKEY_CURRENT_USER* entries are created from *HKEY_USERS\name*—where *name* stands for the user name—during user logon. Therefore, you will also find a copy of this data in *HKEY_USERS\name\Software\Classes\CLSID*.

Hiding the Drive Symbols in the My Computer Window

Double-clicking the desktop's My Computer icon opens a window that contains the Printers and Control Panel folders as well as the symbols for all drives and associated network devices. Figure 4-10 shows the My Computer window on my computer.

As you can see, the symbol for the floppy drive A: isn't visible, even though my computer has a floppy disk drive. Obviously, you have the option to hide or show individual drive symbols in this window. Why would you want to hide them? Sometimes you'll need to hide drive symbols for an individual user in order to customize the desktop for special user groups. Suppose, for example, a manager wants access to all drives but needs to prevent an assistant from accessing the CD-ROM drive. Let's take a look at how this is accomplished.

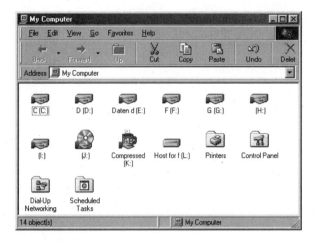

Figure 4-10.
My Computer window, missing the floppy disk drive symbol.

First, for the hide and show options to work, user profiles must be enabled. (Further information on user profiles can be found in the section "The System Policy Editor," beginning on page 49 in Chapter 2.) Then, to activate the hide option, follow these steps:

1. Log on to the system, and start the System Policy Editor.

2. Open the local Registry by clicking the File menu and selecting the Open Registry entry.

3. Double-click the Local User icon in the System Policy Editor window.

4. Under Windows 98 System, select the Shell\Restrictions path on the Policies property page.

5. Check the Hide Drives In 'My Computer' option (see Figure 4-11 on the next page).

6. Click OK to save the settings.

7. Restart your computer, or log off and log on again to reset the Windows shell.

8. Open the My Computer window.

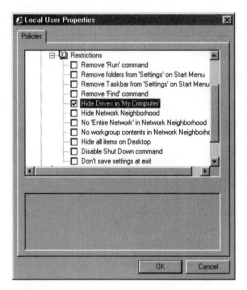

Figure 4-11.
*Using the System Policy Editor's Policies property page to hide
the drive symbols in My Computer.*

All drive symbols are now hidden, and you'll see only folder symbols such
as Printers and Control Panel in the My Computer window. Keep in mind that
this option is valid only for the current user. If you log on again under a new
user name, the drive symbols will again be visible.

> NOTE: Windows 95 and Windows NT 4.0 use the same scheme
> to hide the drive icons in My Computer, but you only need to refresh
> the My Computer window, whereas in Windows 98 you need to re-
> set the shell (per Step 7 above) before the change will take effect.
>
> You can also use the System Policy Editor to hide the drive sym-
> bols from other users or user groups. Consult the *Microsoft Win-
> dows 98 Resource Kit* (Microsoft Press, 1998) for further details about
> the System Policy Editor.

So what does all this have to do with the Registry? Windows (Windows 95,
Windows 98, and Windows NT 4.0) keeps all information about the system in
the Registry key …*Software\\Microsoft\\Windows\\CurrentVersion*. Settings that
are global to the local computer are held in the *HKEY_LOCAL_MACHINE*
branch. User-specific settings of the current system can be found in the
HKEY_CURRENT_USER branch. (There is also a copy in *HKEY_USERS.*)
If you use the System Policy Editor to hide the drives in My Computer, the
following key is updated:

HKEY_CURRENT_USER\Software\Microsoft\Windows\CurrentVersion\Policies\Explorer

The System Policy Editor adds a *NoDrives* value (DWORD) to this key. The value is set to *0x03ffffff* (or, shown differently, *NoDrives = 0x03ffffff*). If this value is found, Windows hides all drive symbols in the My Computer and Windows Explorer windows.

While this is an excellent way to customize the Windows 98 shell and prevent the user from accessing a drive, the System Policy Editor is the wrong tool for fine-tuning these settings. Instead, you should use alternate tools to alter the *NoDrives* value.

One handy tool that hides selected drive icons in My Computer is Tweak UI, which is part of the Microsoft PowerToys, a tool collection created by Windows developers and offered for free to the Windows community. After you install Tweak UI, the tool resides in the Control Panel folder. To use Tweak UI to hide individual drive icons, do the following:

1. Open the Control Panel (that is, click the Start button, select Settings, and then select Control Panel).

2. Double-click the Tweak UI icon in the Control Panel window.

3. Select the My Computer property page (see Figure 4-12).

4. Uncheck the check box of each drive you would like to hide.

5. Click OK or Apply.

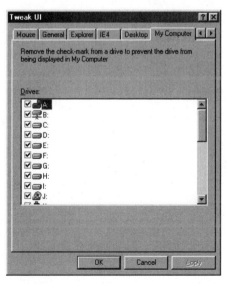

Figure 4-12.
Using Tweak UI to hide the drive symbols in My Computer.

If the My Computer window is open when you complete the steps above, the icons for any drives you chose to hide will be hidden. Unfortunately, the Windows 98 shell differs a bit from the Windows 95 or Windows NT 4.0 shell. Therefore, it isn't sufficient to close the Tweak UI property sheet for your changes to take effect; you must reset the Windows 98 shell, either by restarting Windows or by logging off and on again. If you forget to reset the shell, the drive icons will still be visible in Windows Explorer and will become visible in the My Computer window after you refresh it by pressing the F5 key. After you reset the shell, however, the icons of the drives marked as hidden will remain hidden.

Now let's have a look at what happens in the Registry when you hide all or a selection of the computer's drives. We can do this by using the Registry Editor. Recall that the System Policy Editor adds NoDrives ? 0x03ffffff to the *HKEY_CURRENT_USER\Software\Microsoft\Windows\CurrentVersion\ Policies\Explorer* key if you check the Hide Drives In 'My Computer' option on the Policies property page. The DWORD value is coded as a bit flag, so the value data *0x03ffffff* stands for 26 bits. Each of these bits corresponds to one of the 26 possible drive names. Bit 0 corresponds to drive A:, bit 1 corresponds to drive B:, etc. I set the *NoDrives* value to *00000001* to get the results shown in Figure 4-10 on page 135. In this case, the first drive, which is always the floppy disk A:, is hidden. A bit set to *1* hides the corresponding drive symbol. The trick is to translate the bit pattern into a hex value.

> TIP: You can save the *NoDrives* value in a REG file and create a shortcut to the REG file in the user's Startup folder. Each time the user logs on, this REG file will be imported into the Registry. There's only one disadvantage: the drive containing the REG file remains visible, independent of the *NoDrives* settings. The file NODRIVES.REG is in the \chapter4 folder of the sample files.

> To show all drives, delete the *NoDrives* value. To do this, you can use the Registry Editor or you can use the System Policy Editor and uncheck the option shown in Figure 4-11 on page 136.

Hiding All Desktop Items

If you take a closer look at the Local User Properties of the System Policy Editor in Figure 4-11, you'll find the Hide All Items On Desktop check box. All you have to do to hide desktop items is activate this check box, close the Policies property page by clicking OK, and then save the settings in the Registry. The next time you log on, all items on the desktop will be hidden. Only the taskbar and the Start menu will be accessible.

As we've seen, because shell items are user-specific Windows stores the information about the desktop elements in the following Registry branch: *HKEY_CURRENT_USER\Software\Microsoft\Windows\CurrentVersion\Policies\Explorer*. If you select the Hide All Items On Desktop option, the *NoDesktop* entry is added as a value to the above branch and its DWORD value data is set to *00000001*. The next time you log on, Windows will detect this flag and hide all desktop symbols. If the flag is not available or the value is set to *00000000*, the desktop symbols remain visible.

NOTE: You can disable the Registry Editor for a user. Follow this path: System Policy Editor, Local User, Windows 98 System, Restrictions. Then select the Disable Registry Editing Tools option. Now the user can't go in and change the *NoDesktop* and *NoDrives* entries that you set to limit user access. Still, an experienced user can bypass your settings by creating and running a simple REG file to change the Registry settings. We'll look at a strategy for preventing this technique later in this chapter in the "Restricting Access to the Registry Editing Tools" sidebar on page 209.

Hiding Icons When the Desktop Is Viewed as a Web Page

Windows 98 offers a new feature that enables you to display the desktop as a Web page. To enable Web view and have the channel bar and other Web entries appear on your desktop, follow these steps:

1. Right-click any free space on the desktop to call up the desktop's context menu.

2. Select Active Desktop and then View As Web Page (see Figure 4-13).

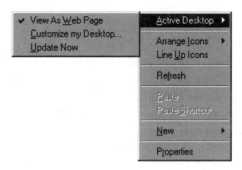

Figure 4-13.
Enabling the desktop's View As Web Page mode.

Switching the desktop to Web page view or vice versa changes a Registry value, the *ShellState* value of the following key:

HKEY_CURRENT_USER\Software\Microsoft\Windows\CurrentVersion\ Explorer

The *ShellState* value in the *Explorer* key is of type Binary and contains a byte stream consisting of six 32-bit values. Changing the desktop mode to Web page view changes the fifth byte (or the second 32-bit value) in the stream. When you first enable Web page view, the value changes from hex *00* to *63*. This means that bit 6 of the 32-bit value is set. If you turn Web page view off again, the value changes to hex *23*.

Take a look again at Figure 4-5 on page 130, and you'll find the Hide Icons When The Desktop Is Viewed As A Web Page check box. Check this box and Windows 98 will hide all desktop icons, allowing you to see only the task bar, the Start menu button, and the Web items (that is, the channel bar and user-defined Web contents).

Checking or unchecking the Hide Icons When The Desktop Is Viewed As A Web Page check box influences the Registry, of course. To store the settings related to Active Desktop mode, Windows 98 employs this key:

HKEY_CURRENT_USER\Software\Microsoft\Windows\CurrentVersion\ Explorer\Advanced

The key contains the flag *HideIcons*, which determines whether desktop icons are hidden during Web page view. If *HideIcons* is set to *0x00000001*, the desktop icons are hidden. Setting *HideIcons* to *0x00000000* reveals the desktop icons again. This setting affects only Web page view; it does not cause icons to be hidden in conventional mode.

Disabling the Active Desktop

As we saw in Figure 4-13, the user can use the Active Desktop command on the desktop's context menu to switch Windows 98 into Active Desktop mode. To disable this command, Tweak UI provides the Active Desktop Enabled check box on the IE4 property page. Unchecking this check box hides the Active Desktop command on the desktop's context menu. The Active Desktop Enabled check box is associated with the Registry key:

HKEY_CURRENT_USER\Software\Microsoft\Windows\CurrentVersion\ Policies\Explorer

Unchecking the check box adds the value *NoActiveDesktop* set to *01 00 00 00* to the key. Removing this value or setting its value to *00 00 00 00* enables the Active Desktop command on the context menu.

NOTE: Customizing other desktop settings is discussed below in the section "Modifying Miscellaneous Desktop and Shell Settings."

Modifying the Network Items

If network services are installed on the local computer, the Network Neighborhood icon is shown on the desktop. You can easily change the icon's title, position, and appearance; hide the icon itself; or hide the icons shown within Network Neighborhood.

Changing the Network Neighborhood Icon

You change the icon for the Network Neighborhood in a way similar to that for changing the My Computer icon:

1. Right-click a free space on the desktop.
2. Select the Properties command on the context menu.
3. Select the Effects property page on the Display Properties property sheet.
4. Select the Network Neighborhood icon in the Desktop Icons group.
5. Click Change Icon to open the Change Icon dialog box (see Figure 4-6 on page 130).
6. Select an icon; click OK.
7. Click OK on the Effects property page.

These steps assign the icon you select as the Network Neighborhood icon.

Changing the Network Neighborhood icon affects the Registry in much the same way as changing the My Computer icon does. Windows 98 uses two Registry entries to store the data related to customizing the Network Neighborhood item. The ActiveX handler for Network Neighborhood has the CLSID code *{208D2C60-3AEA-1069-A2D7-08002B30309D}*.

The following entry defines the global (that is, systemwide) settings of the Network Neighborhood ActiveX module:

HKEY_CLASSES_ROOT\CLSID\{208D2C60-3AEA-1069-A2D7-08002B30309D}

The structure of this branch is similar to the structure of the *CLSID* branch for My Computer. And, as I discussed for My Computer, the default value of the key can be set to a string to define the icon's title. The only difference between the My Computer settings and the Network Neighborhood settings is that your

141

Registry might have a context menu handler for the Network Neighborhood icon defined under the *shellex* subkey. As with My Computer, the icon source is defined in the *Default* value of the *DefaultIcon* key. The *Default* value for this entry is set to *C:\WINDOWS\SYSTEM\shell32.dll,17*, meaning the Network Neighborhood uses the eighteenth icon stored in the SHELL32.DLL file. (Icon indexes are counted from zero.) You can change this entry to *C:\WINDOWS\Explorer.exe,1*, for example, which is the icon shown in Figure 4-9 on page 134. In Figure 4-14, I use the nineteenth icon stored in the SHELL32.DLL file. If after you modify the Registry the icon doesn't change, click anywhere on the desktop and press F5 to refresh the screen. (By the way, this is how the Network Neighborhood icon is customized in Windows 95 and also in Windows NT 4.0.)

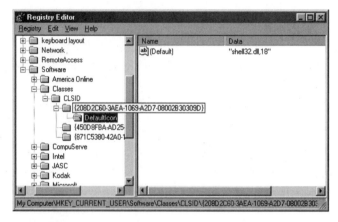

Figure 4-14.
The Registry entry for the Network Neighborhood handler.

Because desktop settings are user-dependent in Windows 98, a second key is used to store the Network Neighborhood settings for the current user logged on to the system:

HKEY_CURRENT_USER\Software\Classes\CLSID\{208D2C60-3AEA-1069-A2D7-08002B30309D}

Renaming the Network Neighborhood icon title on the desktop, by using the Rename command on the context menu, changes the *Default* value of this key. Because *HKEY_CURRENT_USER* is specific to user settings, the change affects only the current user's desktop. The same applies to the optional *DefaultIcon* subkey. And, as before, if you change the icon by using the Effects property page, the result is written in the branch's *DefaultIcon* subkey. You can also set the *Default* value of the *DefaultIcon* subkey to a new icon source. Figure 4-15 shows the icon that results from the settings shown in Figure 4-14.

Figure 4-15.
A new icon and title for Network Neighborhood.

> NOTE: If nothing is changed in the Network Neighborhood icon settings, the key *{208D2C60-3AEA-1069-A2D7-08002B30309D}* isn't available in the *HKEY_CURRENT_USER\Software\Classes\CLSID* branch. But when you change the icon title or the icon itself, the requested keys are created in this branch. Also, Windows 98 keeps a copy of the *HKEY_CURRENT_USER* branch in *HKEY_USERS\xxx*, where *xxx* stands for the name of the current user.
>
>   You can use different files (DLL, EXE, ICO) as icon sources. The icons contained in SHELL32.DLL are shown in Appendix A, "Icons Contained in SHELL32.DLL," which begins on page 381. You can also use your own ICO file, an option that I discuss later in this chapter.

Hiding the Network Neighborhood Icon

If you run a local computer without a network card, the Network Neighborhood icon is hidden. On a network computer, the icon is visible by default, but you have the option to hide it for the current user. You do this with the System Policy Editor.

1. Log on to the system with the user's name and password, and start the System Policy Editor.

2. Open the local Registry (File, Open Registry).

3. Double-click the Local User icon in the System Policy Editor window.

4. Select the Windows 98 System\Shell\Restrictions path on the Policies property page.

5. Check the Hide Network Neighborhood option (see Figure 4-11 on page 136), and click OK.

6. Save the settings in the Registry, and exit the System Policy Editor.

After the next logon, the Network Neighborhood icon is hidden. The information about the visibility of this icon is kept in this Registry key:

HKEY_CURRENT_USER\Software\Microsoft\Windows\CurrentVersion
Policies\Explorer

The System Policy Editor adds the *NoNetHood ? 0x00000001 DWORD value* to the key to hide the icon. If you delete this entry or set the value to 0x00000000, the icon will be shown after the next logon.

> TIP: The Tweak UI utility also allows you to hide or reveal the Network Neighborhood icon. Start Tweak UI by double-clicking its icon in the Control Panel, select the Desktop property page, check the Network Neighborhood option (see Figure 4-23 on page 158), and click OK. Tweak UI will change the Registry settings and inform you that you need to log off and on for the settings to take effect.

Hiding the Icons in Network Neighborhood

When you double-click the Network Neighborhood icon, Windows shows the Entire Network icon and the icons of the current user's workgroup computers (see Figure 4-16).

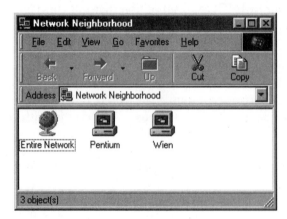

Figure 4-16.
The Network Neighborhood window.

You can hide these symbols for the current user by using the System Policy Editor. Start the System Policy Editor, load the local Registry, and then perform the following steps:

1. Select the Windows 98 System\Shell\Restrictions path on the Policies property page.

2. Check the No 'Entire Network' In Network Neighborhood option to hide the icon.

3. If you want to hide all workgroup computer icons belonging to the user's workgroup, check the No Workgroup Contents In Network Neighborhood option.

4. Close the property page by clicking OK, and save the settings.

When you open the Network Neighborhood window, the icons you specified are hidden.

Windows keeps the information about the visibility of these icons in the following Registry key:

HKEY_CURRENT_USER\Software\Microsoft\Windows\CurrentVersion\Policies\Network

The *NoEntireNetwork* entry, shown in Figure 4-17, controls the visibility of the Entire Network icon. If this flag is set to the DWORD value *0x00000001*, the icon is hidden. Deleting this entry or setting the value to *0x00000000* will display the icon again the next time the screen is refreshed. The *NoWorkgroupContents* entry in Figure 4-17 hides or shows the icons of the workgroup computers within the network. If this flag is set to the DWORD value *0x00000001*, the icons are hidden. Deleting this entry or setting its value to *0x00000000* reveals the icons the next time the screen is refreshed.

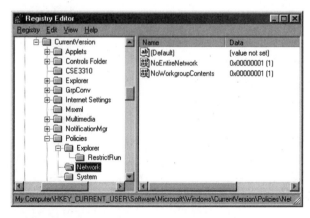

Figure 4-17.
The Network *key.*

Modifying the My Documents Settings

A new Windows 98 feature is the placement and handling of the My Documents folder. This folder is created on the drive where Windows 98 is installed and by default is displayed on the desktop. Several entries in the Registry control the settings of the My Documents folder. Like My Computer and Network Neighborhood, My Documents is controlled by an ActiveX component. You'll find the Class ID of the ActiveX handler as the *Default* value of the key *HKEY_CLASSES_ROOT\.mydocs*. This *Default* value contains the string *CLSID\ {450D8FBA-AD25-11D0-98A8-0800361B1103}*, so the ActiveX handler for My Documents is registered under:

> *HKEY_CLASSES_ROOT\CLSID\{450D8FBA-AD25-11D0-98A8-0800361B1103}*

This key contains several subkeys, as you can see in Figure 4-18. The *Default* value of the key can contain the My Documents icon title. The *DefaultIcon* subkey can be used to customize the icon used for the My Documents folder shown on the desktop and in the Windows Explorer window.

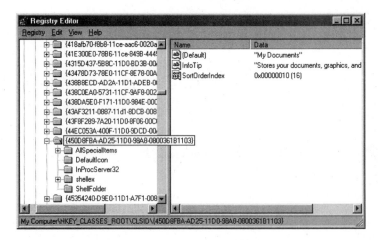

Figure 4-18.
The My Documents *key.*

To allow the My Documents folder to be customized for the current user, Windows 98 also stores the key *HKEY_CURRENT_USER\Software\Classes\CLSID\ {450D8FBA-AD25-11D0-98A8-0800361B1103}*. This entry will exist in the Registry if the user has changed the icon title or the icon itself. (Again, you can use the Effects property page, shown in Figure 4-5 on page 130, to change the icon.) The icon title is stored in the *Default* value of the key mentioned above, while the icon setting is stored in a *DefaultIcon* subkey.

> **NOTE:** In Figure 4-18, notice the value *InfoTip* in the specific Class ID subkey in the *HKEY_CLASSES_ROOT* branch. This value contains the string that is displayed in the QuickInfo window that appears when the mouse cursor is placed over the My Documents icon. The key contains several other subkeys relating to the handler itself. The exact meaning of these settings isn't clear to me.

Hiding and Showing the My Documents Icon

You can hide the My Documents icon on the desktop by right-clicking the My Documents icon and selecting the Remove From Desktop command from the context menu. (See Figure 4-19.) This procedure removes only the Desktop item for My Documents; the folder itself is still accessible through the My Computer folder and through Windows Explorer.

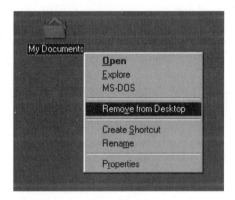

Figure 4-19.
The My Documents context menu.

If you want to restore the My Documents icon to the desktop, perform the following steps:

1. Right-click any free space on the desktop.

2. Select New from the context menu.

3. Select My Documents Folder On Desktop from the New submenu.

To use the Registry to hide the My Documents icon on the desktop, it's sufficient to add the *HideMyDocsFolder* value to the following key:

HKEY_CURRENT_USER\Software\Microsoft\Windows\CurrentVersion\ Explorer\Documents

Set the *HideMyDocsFolder* value to an empty string. If Windows 98 detects this entry, it hides the My Documents icon on the desktop. Deleting this entry forces Windows 98 to show the icon again.

When you hide My Documents by using the context menu, Windows 98 adds more than just the *HideMyDocsFolder* key. Windows 98 gives the user a means of returning the folder to the desktop—the My Documents Folder On Desktop method described above. To do so, it adds several additional entries to the Registry when My Documents is removed. *HKEY_LOCAL_MACHINE\ SOFTWARE\Classes\.mydocs\ShellNew* is added to customize the New command shown in the shell's context menu. The *Command* value of this key is set to *"rundll32 mydocs.dll,RestoreMyDocsFolder"*. This key works with a second key, *HKEY_LOCAL_MACHINE\Software\Classes\My Documents*, whose *Default* value is set to *"My Documents Folder on Desktop"*. If you include the above keys in the Registry, the command to restore the My Documents icon to the desktop will be shown in the shell's context menu. If you choose to restore the icon, the above keys are removed from the Registry.

Modifying the Recycle Bin Settings

The Recycle Bin is shown as an icon on the desktop and in the directory structure of each drive (that is, in the shell and in Windows Explorer). As with the other desktop items, you can rename it, choose a different icon, and hide it.

Renaming the Recycle Bin

Have you ever tried to rename the Recycle Bin? Right-clicking the desktop icon opens a context menu, but the Rename command is missing. So you have to go into the Registry, select the proper key, and change its *Default* value.

The way Windows handles the Recycle Bin is similar to the way it handles other desktop components: The Recycle Bin is an ActiveX component that is registered in the *HKEY_CLASSES_ROOT\CLSID* branch of the Registry. To make a change, you must find the appropriate key in the *CLSID* branch by accessing the Find dialog box in the Registry Editor and entering one of two search patterns:

- Enter the name of the Recycle Bin as it appears on your desktop, and check only the Data and Values check boxes.

■ Enter the key name *{645FF040-5081-101B-9F08-00AA002F954E}* for the ActiveX Server; this key name identifies the Recycle Bin entry in the *CLSID* branch.

A successful search will reveal the *HKEY_CLASSES_ROOT\CLSID\ {645FF040-5081-101B-9F08-00AA002F954E}* branch with a structure similar to that shown in Figure 4-20.

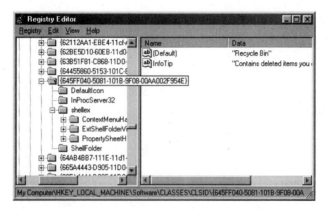

Figure 4-20.
The Class ID entry for the Recycle Bin.

The subkeys shown in Figure 4-20 and described below define the properties of the Recycle Bin.

■ The *DefaultIcon* key sets the icons used by the Recycle Bin handlers.

■ The *InProcServer32* key contains the definition for the server (SHELL32.DLL) and the Threading model (*Apartment*). (Further information about this topic can be found in Charles Petzold's *Programming Windows 95* [Microsoft Press, 1996].)

■ The *shellex* key contains three entries. One entry, *ContextMenu-Handlers*, defines separate context menu handlers, which is the reason you don't see the common context menu that includes the Rename entry when you right-click the Recycle Bin icon. Instead this handler defines commands appropriate for the Recycle Bin (such as Empty Recycle Bin). A second entry, *ExtShellFolderViews*, has to do with the Web View Wizard, available by selecting Customize This Folder from the Windows Explorer View menu. The third entry,

PropertySheetHandlers, defines separate property sheet handlers for the Recycle Bin; these contain the options for configuring the Recycle Bin.

■ The *ShellFolder* key contains the *Attributes* value, which defines the attribute bits for the folder that the Recycle Bin uses to temporarily store deleted files.

To rename the Recycle Bin, select the *CLSID* subkey *{645FF040-5081-101B-9F08-00AA002F954E}* and change its *Default* value to any name you want (to *Trash*, for example). After changing the value, click the desktop and press F5 to refresh the screen and view the new icon name.

You can also customize the QuickInfo text that appears when the mouse cursor is pointing to the Recycle Bin icon. Set the *InfoTip* value shown in Figure 4-20 to the string you would like to see appear in the QuickInfo window. (You'll find this *InfoTip* value in several other keys as well so that you can define the QuickInfo content of other desktop items.)

NOTE: Changing the name of the Recycle Bin does not affect what you see in Windows Explorer. You'll still see the name Recycle Bin there, because this is the name of a folder that keeps deleted files.

The other key that contains Recycle Bin as its Default value is …\explorer\Desktop\NameSpace\{645FF040-5081-101B-9F08-00AA002F954E} in the HKEY_LOCAL_MACHINE\SOFTWARE\-Microsoft\Windows\CurrentVersion branch. Modifications to this value don't affect what you see on the desktop, however, because the value is used as a comment. Refer to the section titled "Hiding and Showing the Recycle Bin Icon," beginning on page 158, for more information.

What's Different in Windows 98?

As described in the previous sections, Windows 98 supports user-specific desktop settings. Therefore, you can find a second key that contains the settings for the Recycle Bin icons and icon title:

HKEY_CURRENT_USER\Software\Classes\CLSID\{645FF040-5081-101B-9F08-00AA002F954E}

If the *Default* value of this key contains a string, the string is displayed as the Recycle Bin icon title. Setting this value to an empty string forces Windows 98 to use the string defined in the *HKEY_CLASSES_ROOT\CLSID* branch. If neither key contains a *Default* value, Windows 98 uses a default icon title for the Recycle Bin, a title that depends on the localized Windows version.

Changing the Recycle Bin Icons

The Recycle Bin uses two icons to indicate its status as empty or full. You can change both these icons by using the Effects property page of the Display Properties property sheet, as described earlier in the section "Changing the My Computer Icon."

The entries used to define these icons are located in the *DefaultIcon* key. As I described above, Windows 98 keeps two branches with entries for the Recycle Bin. The global settings for all users are kept in the *HKEY_CLASSES_ROOT\CLSID\{645FF040-5081-101B-9F08-00AA002F954E}\DefaultIcon* key, while the settings for the current user are stored in the *HKEY_CURRENT_USER\Software\Classes\CLSID\{645FF040-5081-101B-9F08-00AA002F954E}\DefaultIcon* key. The latter key stores the settings entered on the Effects property page in Windows 98. If this key contains an entry, the entry overwrites the machine's global settings specified in the *HKEY_CLASSES_ROOT* branch.

We know that the *DefaultIcon* key typically contains one entry pointing to the icon source. For the Recycle Bin, however, *DefaultIcon* contains three values—*Default*, *empty*, and *full*—as shown in Figure 4-21.

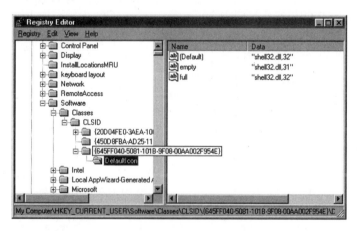

Figure 4-21.
The DefaultIcon *key for the Recycle Bin, which contains three values.*

The handler for the Recycle Bin uses these values to reflect the status of the Recycle Bin:

■ The *Default* value always points to the icon source containing the icon that currently indicates the status of the Recycle Bin. If the user empties the Recycle Bin, the *empty* value's data is copied into *Default*.

151

Each time a file is deleted (which means that the file is moved into the Recycle Bin), the Recycle Bin handler copies the *full* value's data into *Default*. The *Default* value is also updated when you double-click the desktop's Recycle Bin icon, either empty the Recycle Bin or insert a file, and then close the window.

■ The *empty* value points to the icon source that defines the symbol indicating an empty bin. The default for the empty bin symbol is the thirty-second icon in SHELL32.DLL. The value, then, is set to *C:\WINDOWS\SYSTEM\shell32.dll,31.*

■ The *full* value points to the icon source for the icon that represents a Recycle Bin containing at least one entry. This value is set to *C:\WINDOWS\SYSTEM\shell32.dll,32.*

To change the icons for the Recycle Bin, point the values for *full* and *empty* to new icon sources. The file SHELL32.DLL contains additional icons (positions 52 and 53, for example) for the Recycle Bin. (The next chapter addresses the icons stored in SHELL32.DLL in more detail.) You can also use other icon sources, such as EXE or DLL files. In theory, pure ICO files will also work as icon sources, but using ICO files this way is problematic: Windows does not reliably refresh the icons taken from ICO files.

NOTE: As you can see in Figure 4-21, you can define values with or without paths. The *full* entry, for example, doesn't contain a path because the DLL file in question is located in the Windows System folder. Omitting the path is valid only for files stored in the Windows System folder.

TIP: Do you want to inspect the icons contained in the file SHELL32.DLL? Create a shortcut to an application on the desktop, and invoke the icon's property sheet by right-clicking the icon and selecting Properties. Select the Shortcut property page, and click Change Icon to invoke the Change Icon dialog box. Click Browse, and search for the SHELL32.DLL file in the \Windows\System subfolder. Now you can open the file and review the icons.

If you cannot find the SHELL32.DLL file from the Change Icon dialog box, open Windows Explorer and select Folder Options from the View menu. Select the Show All Files option in the Hidden Files section of the View property page, click the Apply button, and then try finding the file again.

Changing the Recycle Bin with a REG File

If you like to change the icons of your Recycle Bin frequently, consider using a REG file. The simplest way to do this is to use the Registry Editor and export the following key, which contains the settings for the Recycle Bin icons:

HKEY_CURRENT_USER\Software\Classes\CLSID\{645FF040-5081-101B-9F08-00AA002F954E}\DefaultIcon

Then set the entries for the *full* and *empty* values to new icon sources. Following is a REG file containing the statements to redefine the Recycle Bin icons:

```
REGEDIT4

[HKEY_CURRENT_USER\Software\Classes\CLSID\      ⇁
{645FF040-5081-101B-9F08-00AA002F954E}\DefaultIcon]
@="C:\\WINDOWS\\SYSTEM\\shell32.dll,31"
"empty"="C:\\WINDOWS\\SYSTEM\\shell32.dll,31"
"full"="C:\\WINDOWS\\SYSTEM\\shell32.dll,56"
```

This REG file sets a full Recycle Bin to the fifty-seventh icon of SHELL-32.DLL and leaves the icon for the empty Recycle Bin set to the original system default value. But before you try to use this REG file, let me point out one problem. Let's assume the Recycle Bin is empty during the export of the Registry branch. If you export the *DefaultIcon* key, the REG file contains the following line:

```
@="C:\\WINDOWS\\SYSTEM\\shell32.dll,31"
```

This line defines the *Default* value for the icon that represents the current status of the Recycle Bin: empty. So when the Recycle Bin is full later on (that is, it contains at least one file) and you try to import the REG file, the *Default* value is set to an empty Recycle Bin icon. Refreshing the screen then reveals an empty bin even though the Recycle Bin is full! After you place another file in the bin or open and close the Recycle Bin window, the icon is set to the correct value, but the initial unexpected result can confuse the user.

To avoid this situation, delete the *Default* entry in the REG file. The resulting file contains the following lines:

```
REGEDIT4

[HKEY_CURRENT_USER\Software\Classes\CLSID\      ⇁
{645FF040-5081-101B-9F08-00AA002F954E}\DefaultIcon]
"empty"="shell32.dll,31"
"full"="shell32.dll,56"
```

This REG file leaves the *Default* setting intact and imports only the new values for *full* and *empty* into the Registry, ensuring that an icon representing the current Recycle Bin state is always displayed. This REG file, which is named RECY98-1.REG, is in the \chapter4 folder of the sample files.

> **NOTE:** Notice that I've removed the path in the REG file shown above. This eliminates the necessity to edit paths if your Windows installation isn't located in a folder named \Windows. But take care: if your icon file isn't in the Windows folder, you must add the paths to the entries. When you add a full path, you're once again faced with the possibility of the user having to edit the REG file before importing it.

To return to the original system default settings, you can use the RECY98-0.REG file in the \chapter4 folder of the sample files.

Sitting Between Two Chairs?

The REG file shown above can be used only for Windows 98 because it uses keys that don't exist in other versions of Windows. I had hoped for the possibility of creating a REG file that would be applicable to Windows 95 and Windows NT 4.0 also, but I discovered two problems.

First, the icons stored in Shell32.DLL differ between Windows 95 and Windows 98. In Windows 95, you must use icon index 53 to get the same icon you get with index 56 under Windows 98. You could solve this problem by using the icon's resource index value (for example, a negative number like -153), which is equivalent in all versions of Windows, but Windows provides no tools for determining this resource index value.

Second, Windows 95 and Windows NT 4.0 use a key in the *HKEY_CLASSES_ROOT\CLSID* branch to store the icon settings. Windows 98 supports this key, but the settings for the same key in the branch *HKEY_CURRENT_USERS\Software\Classes\CLSID* will take precedence over the settings in *HKEY_CLASSES_ROOT*.

Therefore, you'll find the file RECYCLE1.REG in the \chapter4\ Win95 sample folder. Note that if your Windows folder isn't named WINDOWS, you must edit the paths in the REG file before you import the data. After you import the file, you can refresh the Recycle Bin symbol and the appropriate symbol should be displayed. To return to the original system default settings, use the RECYCLE0.REG file in the \chapter4\Win95 folder of the sample files.

Customizing the Recycle Bin with an INF File

To avoid the path problems inherent in using REG files, consider using INF files to set Registry entries. (Remember that I used this technique in Chapter 3 to update the Registry.) The following lines of an INF file set the Recycle Bin full icon to the fifty-seventh icon of SHELL32.DLL.

```
; File: Recy98-1.INF
; Windows 98 only !!!
; By Guenter Born
;
; Set the Recycle Bin Full icon to a new symbol
[version]
signature="$CHICAGO$"

[DefaultInstall]
AddReg = Recycle.AddReg

[Recycle.AddReg]
; Use HKEY_CURRENT_USER\Software\Classes\CLSID\
; Set "Full" to icon number 57 in shell32.dll
HKCU,Software\Classes\CLSID\{645FF040-5081-101B-9F08-00AA002F954E}\  →
DefaultIcon,Empty,,"%11%\\shell32.dll,31"
HKCU,Software\Classes\CLSID\{645FF040-5081-101B-9F08-00AA002F954E}\  →
DefaultIcon,Full,,"%11%\\shell32.dll,56"

; End ***
```

The meat of this code is in the *[Recycle.AddReg]* section. The lines beginning with *HKCU, Software\Classes\CLSID\{645FF040-5081-101B-9F08-00AA002F954E}\DefaultIcon* define the key. The name of the value is defined in the third parameter; the last parameter defines the value itself. The placeholder for the Windows System folder is *%11%*.

To import these settings into the Registry, right-click the INF file and select the Install command from the context menu. (Further details concerning the structure of an INF file are discussed in later chapters.) To help you out, I've provided two INF files in the \chapter4 folder of the sample files. The file RECY98-1.INF contains the lines shown above. The RECY98-0.INF file resets the original system default settings for the full and empty icons.

NOTE: The two INF files mentioned above can be used only with Windows 98. To customize the Recycle Bin icons in Windows 95, use the RECYCLE1.INF and RECYCLE0.INF files contained in the \chapter4\Win95 folder of the sample files. These two INF files use the old keys in HKCR to redefine the icons. These INF files will also work in Windows 98 if the user hasn't customized the icons with entries in the HKCU branch.

Using the Recycle Bin Properties
Property Sheet to Modify Settings

You can change settings for the Recycle Bin by using the Recycle Bin Properties property sheet, shown in Figure 4-22. This sheet allows you to establish global settings for all drives or to define independent values (such as the maximum size of the Recycle Bin) for a particular drive. This property sheet is accessible by right-clicking the Recycle Bin icon and selecting the Properties command from the context menu.

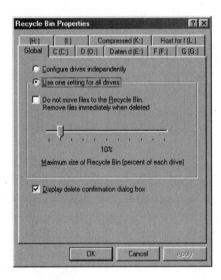

Figure 4-22.
The Recycle Bin Properties property sheet with the Global property page.

The information established on this property sheet is stored in the Registry branch *HKEY_LOCAL_MACHINE\SOFTWARE\Microsoft\Windows\ CurrentVersion\explorer*. Once you have opened the Recycle Bin Properties property sheet at least once and clicked OK, the above branch contains a subkey with the name *BitBucket*. The *Default* value of this key isn't set, but the key's *PurgeInfo* value contains a byte sequence with the Recycle Bin property settings. Table 4-1 contains a brief description of the entries contained in *PurgeInfo*.

Coding of the *PurgeInfo* Value in the *BitBucket* Key

Bytes	Description
4	The value *48 00 00 00*.
4	The flag defining global or individual settings, which is set by selecting one of the two option boxes on the Global property page of the Recycle Bin Properties property sheet (see Figure 4-22). The possible values in the first byte are: *00* Configure drives independently. *01* Use one setting for all entries.
2 * 28	Twenty-eight entries that each define the maximum size of the Recycle Bin in terms of a percentage of the drive's size. This value is set with the slider control contained on each of the drive property pages on the Recycle Bin Properties property sheet. The first entry corresponds to drive A:, the second to drive B:, and so on. Entries for floppy disks are left empty. The twenty-eighth entry contains the value for the global setting (if one setting is used for all drives).
4	Bit field. The bits are set if the Do Not Move Files To Recycle Bin check box is activated on the property page for a particular drive. Each bit corresponds to a drive (Bit 0 = drive A:, Bit 1 = drive B:, and so on). Bit 27 corresponds to the same check box on the Global property page.
4	The values in the last four bytes vary from machine to machine and will not be discussed here.

Table 4-1.
These values are a breakdown of the PurgeInfo *value for the Recycle Bin subkey* BitBucket.

N O T E : In Windows 98, the key *HKEY_LOCAL_MACHINE\ SOFTWARE\Microsoft\Windows\CurrentVersion\explorer\BitBucket* contains not only the *PurgeInfo* value described in Table 4-1 but also an entry for each media drive available on the local computer that has a Recycle Bin folder. These values are named after the drive names— C, D, E, and so on. Each value contains a binary data stream, but I don't know the meaning of these binary data streams.

The value for the Display Delete Confirmation Dialog Box check box located on the Global property page is stored in a curious way. You'll find this value in the key:

HKEY_USERS\xxxx\Software\Microsoft\Windows\CurrentVersion\ Explorer

The characters *xxxx* are used here as a placeholder for the name of the current user. The key has a value named *ShellState*. Its fifth byte is defined as a flag, and Bit 2 (counting starts with Bit 0) of this flag corresponds to the Display Delete Confirmation Dialog Box check box. If this option is checked, the bit is set to *1*. (Remember that values are displayed in the Registry as hex values.)

Hiding and Showing the Recycle Bin Icon

Sometimes you'll want to hide the Recycle Bin icon on the desktop. Windows 98 doesn't offer a feature for hiding the icon, but you can get around this limitation by using the Tweak UI module of Power Toys to modify desktop icons.

Using Tweak UI   You'll find the options for customizing the Windows 98 desktop on the Desktop property page of the Tweak UI property sheet, as shown in Figure 4-23.

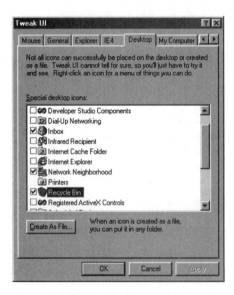

Figure 4-23.
The Tweak UI property sheet.

To hide or show the Recycle Bin icon, follow these steps:

1. From the Control Panel, double-click the Tweak UI icon.

2. Select the Desktop tab on the Tweak UI property sheet.

3. Check (to show the Recycle Bin) or uncheck (to hide it) the check box next to the Recycle Bin entry.

4. Click Apply.

After a few seconds, the icon will be either hidden or displayed, depending on your selection.

> NOTE: If the Recycle Bin icon is hidden and you change its state to visible, the icon will be displayed in a predefined position on the desktop (on the left border). The current position of the icon is stored in *HKEY_CURRENT_USER\Software\Microsoft\Windows\ CurrentVersion\Explorer\Streams*.
>
> One subkey under *Streams* contains the settings for the Desktop folder, but since these values are updated dynamically I can't determine which byte is used for the Recycle Bin's position. However, you can use a shareware tool called EzDesk, created by Melissa Nguyen, to store and restore the positions of all desktop elements. EzDesk uses separate keys to store the desktop icons' positions. This tool is available at *ftp://users.aol.com/EzDesk95/ezde18sw.zip*.

Using Tweak UI to hide or show the Recycle Bin icon modifies the Registry. This "behind-the-scenes" business is pretty interesting because it shows how the Windows architecture handles extensions of the shell's namespace (that is, a collection of symbols used to organize the shell's objects).

Using the Registry Editor   I mentioned earlier that the *HKEY_LOCAL_ MACHINE\SOFTWARE\Microsoft\Windows\CurrentVersion* key contains information about current Windows settings. The properties of the shell (comprising the desktop, taskbar, and so on) are available through Windows Explorer, so you'll find the *...\explorer\Desktop\NameSpace* subkey in this branch. This subkey can contain several entries, each of which is a key containing the CLSID code of an ActiveX component (see Figure 4-24 on the next page). The code for an entry is the same as in *HKEY_CLASSES_ROOT\CLSID*. The Windows shell checks the *NameSpace* key for additional subkeys. If a subkey representing a CLSID code is found, the icon for this ActiveX component is shown on the desktop.

The *Default* value of each subkey in the *NameSpace* key contains a string with the component's name. This name allows you to identify the correct key and is used in the same way as a comment. To hide the Recycle Bin icon on the desktop, you must remove the subkey *{645FF040-5081-101B-9F08-00AA002F954E}* from the *...\explorer\Desktop\NameSpace* branch by using the Registry Editor. The next time you refresh the desktop, the icon will be hidden.

Figure 4-24.
Entries in NameSpace.

Using an INF file   If you don't want to use the Registry Editor, you can create an INF file to hide the Recycle Bin icon. The following lines will remove the Recycle Bin icon from the desktop:

```
; File: DelBin.INF
; By Guenter Born
;
; Remove Recycle Bin icon from desktop
[version]
signature="$CHICAGO$"

[DefaultInstall]
DelReg = BinIcon.DelReg

[BinIcon.DelReg]
; Use HKEY_LOCAL_MACHINE\SOFTWARE\Microsoft\Windows\  ⤚
; CurrentVersion\explorer
; Remove the key {645FF040-5081-101B-9F08-00AA002F954E} from
; \Desktop\NameSpace

HKLM,"SOFTWARE\Microsoft\Windows\CurrentVersion\explorer\  ⤚
Desktop\NameSpace\{645FF040-5081-101B-9F08-00AA002F954E}"

; End ***
```

You will find these statements in the DELBIN.INF file located in the \chapter4 folder of the sample files. Right-click this file, and select the Install command from the context menu. After you refresh the desktop, the icon will be hidden.

To show the Recycle Bin icon again, you must add the previously deleted key into ...*explorer\Desktop\NameSpace*. This can be done with the following REG file:

```
REGEDIT4

[HKEY_LOCAL_MACHINE\SOFTWARE\Microsoft\Windows\CurrentVersion\  ↴
explorer\Desktop\NameSpace\{645FF040-5081-101B-9F08-00AA002F954E}]
@="Recycle Bin"
```

This file, ADDBIN.REG, is also located in the \chapter4 folder of the sample files. Or you can use Tweak UI to show the Recycle Bin icon again.

Hiding and Showing Other Special Desktop Items

You can select other special items, such as the Scheduled Tasks folder, to be displayed on the desktop. As you can see above in Figure 4-23, Tweak UI provides the Desktop property page to hide or show such special desktop items. Follow the instructions above, checking the options on the property page for the items you want to be displayed on the desktop and unchecking the options for those you want to hide.

> NOTE: The positions of the icons are predefined, so they will always appear in the same location on the desktop. See the Note on page 159 for details.

Windows uses the same Registry branch for all the icons displayed on the desktop:

> *HKEY_LOCAL_MACHINE\SOFTWARE\Microsoft\Windows*
> *CurrentVersion\explorer\Desktop\NameSpace*

The CLSID code of the Scheduled Tasks ActiveX component is shown in Figure 4-25 on the next page. If the Registry branch contains this key, the Scheduled Tasks icon is displayed. Delete the key or use Tweak UI to hide the icons.

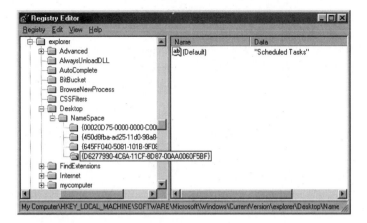

Figure 4-25.
Scheduled Tasks entry in NameSpace.

> NOTE: Windows 95 uses the same scheme for defining desktop
> items, but additional ActiveX components such as Briefcase and Inbox
> are available. Briefcase is implemented in Windows 98, but as a folder
> rather than an ActiveX component, so you won't see an entry in the
> *NameSpace* key. Because it is a folder, you are able to delete Briefcase
> by using the Delete command in the context menu. To create a Brief-
> case icon, right-click anywhere on the desktop and select New, and
> then Briefcase, from the context menu. Again, no entry is made in
> the *NameSpace* key; the Briefcase is created as a simple file in the
> \Windows\Desktop folder.
>
> The \chapter4\Win95 folder of the sample files contains the
> BRIEFON.REG and INBOXON.REG files. Importing these files
> into Windows 95 restores the original system default settings for the
> Briefcase and Inbox icons, respectively, in the *NameSpace* key of the
> Registry. Both the Briefcase and Inbox options must be installed
> before you import these REG files. But be careful—the settings con-
> tained in these REG files are not valid for Windows 98.

Adding the Control Panel Folder to the Desktop

By default, the Control Panel folder is located in the Settings section of the Start
menu, in the My Computer window, and in Windows Explorer. You can also
add the Control Panel folder icon to the desktop if you like. Simply create a new
folder that is recognized by the shell as the Control Panel.

Creating a Folder by Using the Desktop Context Menu

To create a new Control Panel folder, follow these steps:

1. Right-click an empty place on the desktop, and select Folder from the New option in the context menu.

2. Give the folder the following name exactly:
   Control Panel.{21EC2020-3AEA-1069-A2DD-08002B30309D}
   This is the CLSID code of the Control Panel ActiveX module.

3. Click outside the name box of this folder.

The shell creates a new folder using the Control Panel icon and containing the contents of the Control Panel. If you use this method to create the folder, be sure you enter the correct CLSID code for the Control Panel. Also, the dot in front of this CLSID code is important—see the explanation in the sidebar "System Icons as Folders" below. The name before the dot can be set to any string (for example, *Born's Control Panel.{21EC2020-3AEA-1069-A2DD-08002B30309D}*). This information is not stored in the Registry. The Control Panel settings are stored in \Windows\Profiles\usernameDesktop.

System Icons as Folders

The technique of creating a Control Panel folder by creating a new folder that is recognized by the shell as the Control Panel is rather interesting because you begin to understand some of the tricky methods used in Windows (Windows 95, Windows 98, and Windows NT 4.0). If you create a new folder by using the context menu, the shell inspects the name assigned to this folder. The name of a folder follows standard file-naming conventions: A filename consists of a name and an extension; these two components are separated by a dot. Although the extension is rarely used for folder names, you can define such an extension. If the name of the new folder contains an extension (that is, a string after the dot), the shell inspects this extension. If the extension corresponds to a CLSID code of an ActiveX component, the shell tries to assign the properties of this component to this folder. In the naming procedure described in the previous section, the CLSID code for the Control Panel was used to create the extension in the folder's name. The result is obvious: The shell shows the first part of the folder's name

(continued)

System Icons as Folders *continued*

(*Control Panel*) and uses the extension to identify the ActiveX component. If the ActiveX component exists (and if the arrangement makes sense), the icon for this component is shown as the folder's icon.

This technique is not limited to the Control Panel. You can add many other icons (such as the Printers folder, the Inbox, and the Briefcase icons) as new folders to the desktop. The relevant ActiveX codes are given in different sections of this chapter and in the CLSID.TXT file in the \chapter4 folder of the sample files.

What is the advantage of this approach? If you've ever tried to move a desktop item such as My Computer, the Briefcase, or the Inbox into a folder, you've likely received a message saying that you can't do it and that you can only create a shortcut instead. A shortcut provides the same functionality as the folder, but it is only a reference and the icon of the parent component still remains on the desktop. If you create a folder instead, this folder can be moved into other folders and no icon remains on the desktop. You can also change a desktop item into a file by using the Tweak UI utility. Double-click the utility's icon in the Control Panel, select the Desktop property page, select an item, and then click Create As File. Tweak UI removes the item's original icon and creates a file instead.

Adding the Printers Folder to the Desktop

Although the Printers folder icon, by default, is located in the Settings section of the Start menu, in the My Computer window, and in Windows Explorer, you can add a Printers folder to the desktop. The simplest way to do this is to create a shortcut to the Printers folder. The alternative is to create a new folder and assign the following name to it:

Printers.{2227A280-3AEA-1069-A2DE-08002B30309D}

To do so, follow the steps given on page 163.

Adding a Recycle Bin Icon to the My Computer Window

By default, the My Computer window comes without the Recycle Bin icon, and you can't drag the icon into the window. To add the Recycle Bin to the My Computer window, as shown in Figure 4-26, you must extend the shell's namespace.

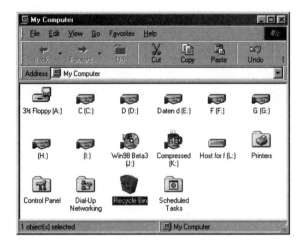

Figure 4-26.
The My Computer window with a Recycle Bin entry.

This must be done in the following key: *HKEY_LOCAL_MACHINE\ SOFTWARE\Microsoft\Windows\CurrentVersion\explorer*

We can't use the …*Desktop\NameSpace* subkey because doing so affects only the desktop entries, so we'll extend the branch …*mycomputer\NameSpace* instead. To add the Recycle Bin to the My Computer window, add a new subkey with the name *{645FF040-5081-101B-9F08-00AA002F954E}* to the …*explorer \mycomputer\NameSpace* key by using the following REG file statements:

```
REGEDIT4

[HKEY_LOCAL_MACHINE\SOFTWARE\Microsoft\Windows\CurrentVersion\  ⇥
explorer\mycomputer\NameSpace\  ⇥
{645FF040-5081-101B-9F08-00AA002F954E}]
@="My Computer Recycle Bin"
```

The string set in the *Default* value is just a comment for the user modifying the Registry. After you have imported the REG file, the My Computer window will show the Recycle Bin icon. To remove this icon, you must delete the *{645FF040-5081-101B-9F08-00AA002F954E}* key in the …*explorer\ mycomputer\NameSpace* branch. You can do so within the Registry Editor, but it's safer to use an INF file like the one on the following page.

```
; File: DelBin1.INF
; By Guenter Born
;
; Remove the Recycle Bin icon from the My Computer window
[version]
signature="$CHICAGO$"

[DefaultInstall]
DelReg = BinIcon.DelReg

[BinIcon.DelReg]
; Use HKEY_LOCAL_MACHINE\SOFTWARE\Microsoft\Windows\    ⌐
; CurrentVersion\explorer
; Remove the key {645FF040-5081-101B-9F08-00AA002F954E} from
; \mycomputer\NameSpace

HKLM,"SOFTWARE\Microsoft\Windows\CurrentVersion\explorer\    ⌐
mycomputer\NameSpace\{645FF040-5081-101B-9F08-00AA002F954E}"

; End ***
```

In this case, you can right-click the INF file and select the Install command from the context menu.

> NOTE: The MYCOMBIN.REG file is located in the \chapter4 folder of the sample files. This file will add the Recycle Bin icon to the My Computer window. The DELBIN1.INF file in the same folder removes the new entry from the Registry. The technique just described can also be used to add other components, such as the Inbox, to My Computer. You can use these files in both Windows 95 and Windows 98.

Modifying Miscellaneous Desktop and Shell Settings

The settings for various Windows elements (such as colors, backgrounds, cursors, and so on) are stored in different places in the Registry. Many settings can be controlled through the desktop's Display Properties property sheet. You can modify others by using the System Policy Editor or the property sheets available through the Control Panel. This section describes how to modify miscellaneous desktop and shell settings within the Registry.

Windows Metrics

The metrics for desktop elements such as icons, fonts, borders, scrollbars, and menus are user-specific and can be controlled through the desktop's Display Properties property sheet. You can search for these related parameters in the

HKEY_CURRENT_USER\Control Panel branch, which contains the ...*desktop\WindowMetrics* key. This key contains the settings for the Windows metrics. Table 4-2 briefly describes some of the values found in this key.

Values for Windows Metrics

Value Name	Description
BorderWidth	Border width of windows shown on the desktop
CaptionFont	Font used in captions
CaptionHeight	Font height of a caption
CaptionWidth	Width of a caption
IconFont	Font used for the icon title
IconSpacing	Horizontal spacing between desktop icons
IconSpacingFactor	Factor used to calculate the icon spacing
IconVerticalSpacing	Vertical spacing between desktop icons
MenuFont	Font parameters (typeface, font name, etc.) used within menu lines
MenuHeight	Height of a character cell used in a menu line
MenuWidth	Width of a character cell used in a menu line
MessageFont	Font used in a message box
ScrollHeight	Height of a horizontal scrollbar
ScrollWidth	Width of a vertical scrollbar
Shell Icon BPP	Number of colors (bits per pixel) used for shell icons
Shell Icon Size	Size of the icons shown on the desktop (and in large mode in Windows Explorer)
SmCaptionFont	Font used in small captions
SmCaptionHeight	Height of a character cell in a small caption
SmCaptionWidth	Width of a character cell in a small caption
StatusFont	Font used in the status bar of a window

Table 4-2.
Entries in the WindowMetrics *key, which is located in* HKEY_CURRENT_ USER\Control Panel\desktop.

Each font data value in the *WindowsMetrics* key consists of a byte sequence representing the font name and several flags, which define the font type, boldface and italic options, and so on. You can modify these options on the Appearance property page of the Display Properties property sheet, shown in Figure 4-27 on the next page. This property page allows you to make and view your modifications.

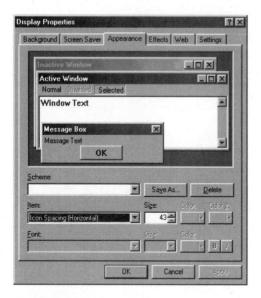

Figure 4-27.
*The Appearance property page of the Display Properties property sheet
allows you to make and view your metrics modifications.*

Windows 98 provides the means to customize certain visual desktop effects. In the Visual Effects group of the Effects property page on the Display Properties property sheet (see Figure 4-28), check boxes allow you to manipulate several values in the Windows 98 Registry.

- Checking the Use Large Icons check box in the Visual Effects group shows all desktop icons at a size of 48 pixels. This option is stored in the Registry key *HKEY_CURRENT_USER\Control Panel\desktop\WindowsMetrics*. The *Shell Icon Size* value is set to 48 (pixels), and the values for the icon spacing are changed. The user can change the same settings by selecting first Icon and then Icon Spacing in the Item list box on the Appearance property page (as shown in Figure 4-27) and changing the value in the Size spin control for each item.

- Checking or unchecking the Show Icons Using All Possible Colors check box modifies the value *Shell Icon BPP* in the *HKEY_CURRENT_USER\Control Panel\desktop\WindowsMetrics* key. If the option is set, *Shell Icon BPP* keeps the number of used colors in a string value (*"4"* for 16 colors, *"16"* for 16-bit, or *"24"* for true color). Unchecking this option changes the *Shell Icon BPP* value to *"4"*. (The value depends on your current color settings for your graphics adapter.)

- Checking or unchecking the Animate Windows, Menus And Lists check box sets or clears bit 1 of the *UserPreferencemask* value in the *HKEY_CURRENT_USER\Control Panel\desktop* key. (See Table 4-3 on page 171.)

- Checking or unchecking the Smooth Edges Of Screen Fonts check box sets the value *FontSmoothing* in the *HKEY_CURRENT_USER\Control Panel\desktop* key to *"0"* or *"1"*.

- Checking or unchecking the Show Window Contents While Dragging check box sets the value *DragFullWindows* in the *HKEY_CURRENT_USER\Control Panel\desktop* key to *"0"* or *"1"*.

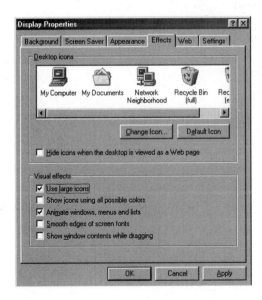

Figure 4-28.
Visual Effects group on the Effects property page.

Can I Disable the Animated Minimize Feature?

Windows animates the process of minimizing windows—as a window is disappearing, you see a sequence of collapsing windows. This can cause problems on a system with a slow video card. To disable this feature, insert the following value in the *HKEY_CURRENT_USER\ ControlPanel\Desktop\WindowMetrics* key: *MinAnimate = "0"*. This turns off the animation feature. You can switch this entry's value between *"0"* and *"1"* by checking or unchecking the Window Animation check box on the General property page of the Tweak UI utility's property sheet, as shown in Figure 4-29.

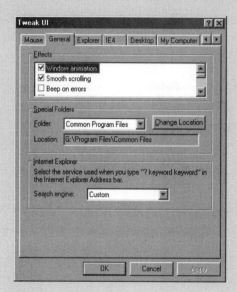

Figure 4-29.
Setting visual effects for the system with the Tweak UI utility.

Switching Smooth Scrolling On/Off

Windows 98 can apply a smooth scrolling feature to windows. You can check or uncheck the Smooth Scrolling check box (see Figure 4-29) on the Tweak UI property sheet's General property page to switch this feature on or off. This check box sets the *SmoothScroll* value in the *HKEY_CURRENT_USER\ ControlPanel\desktop* key to *01 00 00 00* or *00 00 00 00*.

Beep on Errors On/Off

Windows 98 can beep (on the PC speaker) if an error occurs. You can turn this feature on or off using the Beep On Errors check box (see Figure 4-29) on the Tweak UI property sheet's General property page. Checking or unchecking this option sets the *Beep* value in the key *HKEY_CURRENT_USER\ControlPanel\ Sound* to *"Yes"* or *"No"*.

Customizing User Preferences for Visual Effects

Using the General property page in Tweak UI allows you to customize many other visual effects as well, such as animation for menus, list boxes, combo boxes, and so on. Each check box in the Effects list box (see Figure 4-29), as well as some check boxes on other property pages of Tweak UI, corresponds to a bit in the *UserPreferencemask* value, which is available in the key *HKEY_ CURRENT_USER\Control Panel\desktop*. Table 4-3 contains a description of the bits in *UserPreferencemask*.

Bit Values for the Visual Effects Set in *UserPreferencemask*

Bit	Description
0	Activation Follows Mouse (X-Mouse). If this bit is set to 1, each element under the mouse cursor will be activated automatically. This option is on the Tweak UI Mouse property page.
1	Menu Animation. Controls the animation of clicking a menu; can be set on the Tweak UI General property page or with the Animate Windows, Menus And Lists check box on the Effects property page of the Display Properties property sheet (see Figure 4-28 on page 169).
2	Combo Box Animation. Controls the animation of a selected combo box; can be set on the Tweak UI General property page.
3	List Box Animation. Controls the animation of a selected list box; can be set on the Tweak UI General property page.
4	Show Windows Version On Desktop. Can be set on the Tweak UI General property page.
5	Menu Underlines. Hides or shows the underlining for shortcut characters in menus; can be set on the Tweak UI General property page.
6	X-Mouse AutoRaise. Can be set on the Tweak UI General property page.
7	Mouse Hot Tracking Effects. Can be set on the Tweak UI General property page.

Table 4-3.
Bits in the UserPreferencemask *value, which is located in*
HKEY_CURRENT_USER\Control Panel\desktop.

Color Schemes and Custom Colors

Windows 98 maintains a palette of 48 colors, which can be changed through the Color dialog box. Clicking one of the Color buttons on the Appearance property page of the Display Properties property sheet opens a panel showing 20 of the basic colors available in Windows 98. Clicking the Other button in this panel opens the Color dialog box, which reveals all 48 Windows colors. You can redefine the 48 colors as well as define 16 additional custom colors.

The colors used in Windows 98 are stored in schemes. These schemes can be altered on the Appearance property page shown in Figure 4-27 on page 168. Each time you modify a parameter, such as *Font, Size,* or *Color,* for an item—Icon Spacing (Horizontal), Active Title Bar, ToolTip, and so on—the parameter setting is stored in the active scheme. You can save the active color scheme under a new name by using the Save As button. All these color schemes are stored in the Registry in the following key: *HKEY_CURRENT_USER\Control Panel\ Appearance\Schemes.* Within this key you will find the names of all schemes defined on your system. Each scheme is stored as a byte sequence that contains the parameters accessible through the Appearance property page.

The settings for custom colors, on the other hand, are stored in the *CustomColors* value of *HKEY_CURRENT_USER\Control Panel\Appearance.* Each color is defined by 4 bytes. (The last byte of each color is always *00.*) The first 3 bytes define the red, green, and blue parts of the color. The values of a byte can be from *00* through *FF* (hexadecimal). A value of *FF* means 100 percent of the basic color will be used. For example, *FF 00 00 00* creates a pure red color.

Colors for Windows Elements

You can change the colors of some Windows elements (such as buttons, button text, inactive title bars, active title bars, and ToolTips) on the Appearance property page of the Display Properties property sheet. The element names are shown in the Item list box, and you can alter a color by using the Color button to the right of the Item list box (see Figure 4-27 on page 168). The colors defined for each Windows element are stored as values in the *HKEY_ CURRENT_USER\Control Panel\Colors* key. Each element is defined as a value by its name (*ActiveBorder, ActiveTitle, ButtonFace, GrayText,* and so on) and has a string value defining its color. The names of these values are self-explanatory. A color value is a combination of the basic colors red, green, and blue. The values can range from *0* through *255,* which means 0 through 100 percent. Unlike the *CustomColors* value, the colors within the *Colors* key are stored as decimal numbers in strings.

Cursor Schemes

The Pointers property page (accessed by clicking the Mouse icon in the Control Panel, which invokes the Mouse Properties property sheet) allows you to define several cursor schemes. Cursor schemes determine the symbols that represent specific actions, such as Normal Select, Help Select, Busy, and Text Select. Each scheme consists of 14 different cursor symbols, one symbol for each action. Windows has 14 predefined cursor symbols for the standard actions, but you can redefine the cursor symbol for each action and store it in a scheme under a unique name.

Cursor schemes are kept in the *HKEY_CURRENT_USER\Control Panel\ Cursors\Schemes* key. Each value within this key consists of the scheme's name (the name defined by the user) and a value data string containing 14 entries. Each entry in a string corresponds to a cursor symbol, and the entries are separated by commas. An entry defines the path to a cursor file (CUR or ANI). An entry can also be empty, in which case the default cursor symbol defined for the action would be used. The standard cursor scheme definition consists of the *Windows Standard* value with its string set to *",,,,,,,,,,,,,"*. The name of the active scheme is found in the *Default* value of the *Cursors* parent key.

Mouse and Cursor Parameters

The other mouse and cursor parameters (*MouseSpeed*, *MouseThreshold1*, and so on) are changed on the Mouse Properties property sheet (available through the Control Panel). The parameters are stored in the key *HKEY_CURRENT_ USER\ControlPanel\Mouse*. The *Mouse* key can contain any of the values described in Table 4-4.

Mouse and Cursor Parameters

Value Name	Description
MouseSpeed	Defines how the mouse movement is transformed into a cursor movement. The transform factor is not always *1*. When one of the *Threshold* values (*MouseThreshold1*, *MouseThreshold2*) is reached, Windows increases the cursor speed. The values for *MouseSpeed* can be set to the following: *0* Don't increase the cursor speed. *1* Double the cursor speed if *MouseThreshold1* is reached.

Table 4-4. *(continued)*

This table describes mouse/cursor parameters in the Registry, which are stored in the HKEY_CURRENT_USER\Control Panel\Mouse *key.*

Mouse and Cursor Parameters *(continued)*

Value Name	Description
MouseSpeed	*2* Double the cursor speed if *MouseThreshold1* is reached; quadruple the cursor speed if *MouseThreshold2* is reached.
	Both *MouseThreshold* values are established when the user moves the slider control for Pointer Speed on the Motion property page of the Mouse Properties property sheet.
MouseThreshold1	Defines a threshold for the allowable mouse movement (in pixels) between two mouse interrupts.
MouseThreshold2	Defines the second threshold for the mouse movement.
SwapMouseButtons	The values are as follows: *0* Use the original button scheme (right-handed). *1* Swap the left and right mouse button functionality (left-handed).
DoubleClickSpeed	Defines the interval (in milliseconds) between two mouse clicks, which is perceived as a double-click.
DoubleClickHeight, *DoubleClickWidth*	Defines the double-click sensitivity. The values set the height and width limits for mouse movement within a double-click. Two mouse clicks with movement outside these limits will not be accepted as a double-click.

The *MouseTrails* value, which controls the mouse pointer trail, can be altered on the Motion property page of the Mouse Properties property sheet and is stored in the *HKEY_LOCAL_MACHINE\Config\0001\Display\Settings* Registry key. The key *0001* stands for the computer's current configuration scheme and can be *0001, 0002,* and so on. If the *Settings* key contains the *MouseTrails* flag, a mouse pointer trail will be shown. The length of the mouse pointer trail is defined by the value of this flag (*0* through *7*). The *Settings* key also contains thefollowing:

- The current screen resolution—the value is *Resolution*

- The *BitsPerPixel* value for the color resolution (a value of *4* means 16 colors, for example)

- The *DPILogicalX, DPILogicalY, DPIPhysicalX, DPIPhysicalY* parameters, which define the logical and physical screen resolution

- The font files (fixed font, OEM font) used in the MS-DOS window and in older Windows 2.*x* applications

NOTE : If you use a Logitech mouse with three buttons, you can activate the middle button by inserting this key: *HKEY_CURRENT_USER\Software\Logitech\Version*. Then change the double-click value from *0* to *1*, and restart Windows. This key is an example of a key you would use for entries in the Registry related to third-party products. Besides the …*Software\Microsoft* branch, the Registry's basic keys can include …*Software\vendor name* entries. The contents of these branches will be vendor-specific.

Tweak UI also contains a Mouse property page with several options you can use to customize your mouse settings.

Drag Parameters

You can drag a selected object by holding down a mouse button while moving the mouse. Two values in the Registry specify drag sensitivity. These values are optional, and they are kept in the key *HKEY_CURRENT_USER\Control Panel\desktop*. The values *DragWidth* and *DragHeight* specify how far (in pixels) the mouse must move with the button held down before the system decides that you're dragging an object. A value of *DragWidth = "6"* specifies that the mouse must move 6 pixels before dragging is detected. Increase this value if you find that you are dragging objects inadvertently when you click them. You can set these values on the Mouse property page in Tweak UI.

Background Options

You can change the settings for the desktop background (patterns and wallpapers) on the Background property page of the Display Properties property sheet (see Figure 4-30 on the following page). While the solid desktop background color is selected by using the Appearance property page (select Desktop in the Item list box and then choose a color from the color palette), use the Background property page to choose wallpapers and patterns.

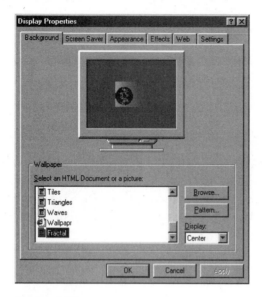

Figure 4-30.
Setting background properties.

You can set an HTML document or a picture file (which can be a BMP, GIF, or JPEG file) as a wallpaper for the desktop background. If you choose an HTML document, you must place the desktop in View As Web Page mode and have Active Desktop enabled. Choosing a picture as a wallpaper enables the Display list box and the Pattern button on the Background property page. Use the Display list box option to center, tile, or stretch the wallpaper picture. If the wallpaper is centered, you can click the Pattern button to select a background pattern to fill the area around the image (see Figure 4-30). All these parameters are user-specific and are stored in the following Registry key:

HKEY_CURRENT_USER\Control Panel\desktop

Table 4-5 describes the Registry entries for the background options.

Again, if you select an HTML document as a wallpaper, this option will be applied only if the display mode is set to View As Web Page and Active Desktop is enabled. Because most Web-related stuff is new to Windows 98, you won't find the options in the *HKEY_CURRENT_USER\Control Panel\desktop* key. I will discuss this topic in the following section.

Values for the Desktop Background

Value Name	Description
Pattern	This entry is available when a pattern is used for the desktop background. The pattern is defined as a string value containing 8 byte values. This defines a pattern of 8×8 pixels.
TileWallpaper	This entry defines whether a wallpaper is tiled (value is set to *1*) or centered (value is set to *0*). If the wallpaper is centered, a defined pattern is applied.
Wallpaper	This entry contains the path to the file with the wallpaper. This file must be a graphics file (that is, in BMP, GIF, or JPEG format). If no wallpaper is defined, the entry is empty (*""*).
WallpaperStyle	Set this value to "2" if you want the wallpaper to be stretched. (This value isn't available in Windows 95.)

Table 4-5.
This table describes possible entries in the Desktop *key.*

NOTE: The Background property page shown in Figure 4-30 is available only if the Active Desktop feature is enabled in Windows 98. If the Active Desktop Changes option is disabled, Windows 98 shows the old Windows 95 style Background property page (see Figure 4-35 on page 186). See also "Modifying Other Desktop Settings," beginning on page 183, to find out how other settings, such as those disabling HTML wallpapers, affect the Background property page.

NOTE: Windows 3.1 uses two entries, WallpaperOffsetX and WallpaperOffsetY, in WIN.INI to set the position of the wallpaper image. I haven't found a way to use these two values under Windows 98. Below I will show you ways to place several background images at any desktop position.

Web Desktop Settings

Windows 98 provides a few new features, such as HTML document wallpapers and Web Page View, with which you can customize the desktop. Web-related desktop elements are customized on the Display Properties property sheet, either on the Background property page (where you can select an HTML document as a background) or on the Web property page, as shown in Figure 4-31 on the next page.

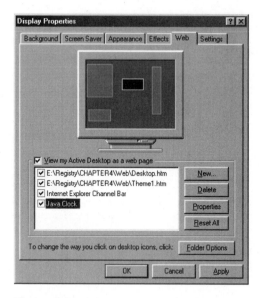

Figure 4-31.
Customizing the desktop by using the Web property page.

Figure 4-31 shows how to add a number of Web pages as windows to your desktop by using the Web property page. To do so, you must select the View My Active Desktop As A Web Page option. Then click New, and select the URL of the HTML file you want to see on the desktop. This URL can point to a Web channel on the Internet, or you can display local HTML files. When you click OK or Apply, the new settings are transferred to the Registry.

NOTE: See the section "Modifying Other Desktop Settings," beginning on page 183, to find out how to disable the New and Delete buttons.

The View My Active Desktop As A Web Page check box (and also the View As Web Page command on the context menu, shown in Figure 4-13 on page 139) is associated with the key:

HKEY_CURRENT_USER\Software\Microsoft\Windows\CurrentVersion\Explorer

This key contains the *ShellState* value, discussed in the section "Hiding Icons When the Desktop Is Viewed as a Web Page," beginning on page 139. Bit 6 (counting from bit 0) in the value's second 32-bit flag (bytes 4 through 7) flags the shell state for Web Page view. If the bit is set to 1, Windows 98 displays Web page contents on the desktop.

I mentioned above that a wallpaper image can be centered, tiled, or stretched. There is no way to move a background image to a user-specified position, and the standard Windows 95 and Windows 98 interfaces allow only one image as a wallpaper. However, as you can see in Figure 4-32 on the next page, using Web view you can customize your desktop to display more than one image. It's also possible to move a "background wallpaper" to any desktop location. (I did use several tricks to demonstrate these new features.) The fractal in the center of Figure 4-32 is just a simple bitmap image that I set with the Background property page. The Registry entries for this image are described in the previous section. The image of the sunset in the upper left corner is defined as a Web page. I created a simple HTML file, shown here, that integrates the image with the background.

```
<html><head>
<title>New Theme</title>
</head>
<body background="Cloud.gif">
</body></html>
```

The <body> tag uses the background attribute to load the CLOUD.GIF image as a background. You can add this HTML file to your desktop by clicking New on the Web property page (see Figure 4-31). You can resize and move this image anywhere you like on the desktop. Windows 98 always places Web content in the background, so you can use your Web image as a pseudowallpaper.

I created the Web page in the lower left corner of Figure 4-32 in the same way. I used a few HTML statements to create a page with a link to another page.

```
<html><head>
<title>Desktop element</title>
</head>
<body text="#000000" bgcolor="#FEFFD7">
<h2>Born's Web Page</h2>
<p><big>Hello there</big>
<a href="Theme1.htm">Background</a></p>
</body>
</html>
```

Here I used the *text* attribute in the <body> tag to define a black color for all text elements in the Web page. The *bgcolor* attribute in the same tag specifies a light yellow background color for this page. The *href* attribute in the <a> tag defines a hyperlink to the THEME1.HTM file. If the user clicks on this hyperlink, Windows 98 opens this page in Microsoft Internet Explorer. This simple HMTL file and the previous one show you how to create your own customized Web pages to be used as desktop content. Again, use the New button in the Web property page (see Figure 4-31) to add the HTML pages to your desktop.

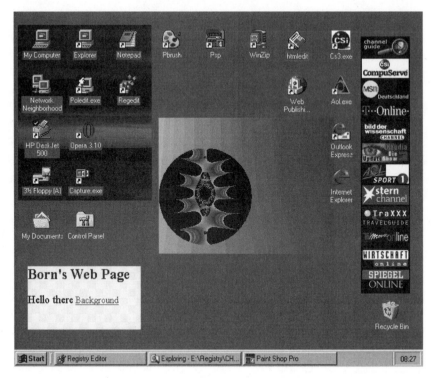

Figure 4-32.
A customized desktop with Web pages as background images.

> **NOTE:** You will find the Web pages and the image files shown in Figure 4-32 in the folder \chapter4\Web of the sample files. The file THEME1.HTM is used for the upper left corner of the figure, and DESKTOP.HTM is used for its lower left corner.

> **TIP:** If you know how to use Cascading Style Sheets to position HTML elements in a page, you can create individual Web pages with several images. You can then use one of these pages as a wallpaper to show several background images at different desktop positions.

Now let's have a closer look at how these settings are stored in the Windows 98 Registry. As I mentioned above, Web pages are new to Windows 98. They are handled by the Active Desktop, which is a part of Internet Explorer. Therefore, a new branch in the Registry stores all the Web settings. Figure 4-33 shows the Registry Editor with the keys relating to the Internet Explorer settings. These settings are kept in the branch:

HKEY_CURRENT_USER\Software\Microsoft\Internet Explorer

Desktop options are located in the *Desktop* subkey. If you select an HTML document as a wallpaper, the path to this document is stored in the key:

HKEY_CURRENT_USER\Software\Microsoft\Internet Explorer\ Desktop\General

The path and filename to the wallpaper document are kept in the value *Wallpaper*. Figure 4-33 shows an HTM file as the wallpaper; this value can also be an image file such as a BMP file. If you use an image file as a wallpaper, the path and filename to the file are always kept in both the value *BackupWallpaper* and the value *Wallpaper*.

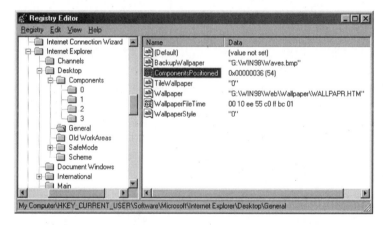

Figure 4-33.
Registry entries for HTML documents used as a wallpaper.

If the user adds Web pages to the desktop, Windows 98 keeps these settings in the branch *HKEY_CURRENT_USER\Software\Microsoft\Internet Explorer\ Desktop\Components*, which includes the following values:

- The *Source* value defines the source used to construct the Web page. This string value can be a path to a local filename (such as *"C:\Web\ Themes1.htm"*) or a CLSID code for an ActiveX component (such as *"131A6951-7F78-11D0-A979-00C04FD705A2"*).

- Web pages can be subscribed Web channels. The *SubscribedURL* value defines the URL to the subscriber. This string value can be a path to a local filename (such as *"C:\Web\Themes1.htm"*), a URL to a Web page containing a channel description file (such as *"http://www.microsoft.com/ie/ie40/gallery/cdf/g_java.cdf"*), or a CLSID code for an ActiveX component (such as *"131A6951-7F78-11D0-A979-00C04FD705A2"*).

■ When you use the Web property page to add a Web page to the desktop based on a local HTML file, the path and filename of the Web page are displayed in the list box. (See Figure 4-31 on page 178.) You can use the value *FriendlyName* to set up a string (such as *"My Desktop Theme"*) to be displayed on the property page instead of the path.

■ *Position* is a Binary byte stream value that defines the position of the Web page on the desktop. This byte stream is interpreted as 32-bit values. The first entry is always set to *2c 00 00 00*. The next four 32-bit values define the x-coordinate, the y-coordinate, the width, and the height of the Web page window in pixels. The other values are used as flags, but I don't know what their meaning is.

NOTE: You will find the file WEBPAGE.REG with the settings for the Web pages shown in Figure 4-31 in the folder \chapter4\Web of the sample files. Use this file to study the settings, but don't import it. Your computer uses different paths, and some of the components in the file won't be available.

Disallowing Active Desktop Changes

Some system administrators prefer to hide the Active Desktop feature in Windows 98 or to prevent the user from making changes to the Active Desktop. You can set these restrictions by using the Tweak UI property sheet's IE4 property page, shown in Figure 4-34.

This property page contains several check boxes that control Active Desktop settings. Unchecking the Active Desktop Enabled check box disables the Active Desktop feature. This check box is associated with the key:

HKEY_CURRENT_USER\Software\Microsoft\Windows\CurrentVersion\Policies\Explorer

If the check box is unchecked, the value *NoActiveDesktop* is set to *01 00 00 00*.

To disable changes in Active Desktop settings, uncheck the Allow Changes To Active Desktop check box. This check box is also associated with the value *NoActiveDesktopChanges* in the same key. Set to *00 00 00 00*, the value indicates that changes are enabled.

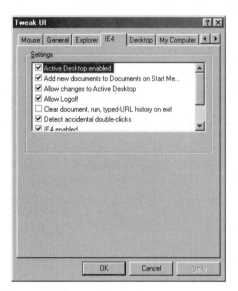

Figure 4-34.
Tweak UI IE4 property page.

Modifying other desktop settings In this chapter, I have discussed how to modify several settings affecting Active Desktop features. Looking at the tools we've used, such as the Display Properties property sheet and Tweak UI, it might appear that there are no more desktop options you can customize in Windows 98. But the Registry contains several more values you can use to further customize desktop settings. The tool Microsoft provides to enable you to set these options is the System Policy Editor, which was introduced in Chapter 3. (Unfortunately, the default templates delivered with the System Policy Editor don't cover all the new Windows 98 shell settings. In Chapter 7, I'll discuss how to extend the templates used in the System Policy Editor in order to extend the System Policy Editor's property pages.) If you load the SHELL98.ADM template file I've provided in the folder \chapter7\adm of the sample files, the System Policy Editor shows a new Windows 98 Shell (Born) branch on the Local User Properties property page. Now proceed with the steps on the following page.

> N O T E : See the section "Customizing the Shell Settings By Using the System Policy Editor," beginning on page 245 in Chapter 5, for further information on loading this template.

1. Load the Shell template by selecting Policy Template from the Options menu in the System Policy Editor.

2. Load the local Registry in the System Policy Editor (File, Open Registry).

3. Double-click the Local User icon. The Local User Properties property page now contains a few additional options under the Windows 98 Shell (Born) branch.

4. Expand this branch and its subbranches on the property sheet. Each subbranch contains several options you can use to customize desktop behavior.

5. Check the check boxes for the requested options.

6. Click OK to close the property page.

7. Save the settings into the Registry (File, Save).

These steps will customize the selected desktop options. Some of these options require you to reset the shell (that is, restart your system or log off and log on again). Below I will discuss a few of the new options available in the Desktop subbranch of the Windows 98 Shell (Born) branch.

The Desktop Restrictions option contains several settings, all of which I discuss elsewhere in this chapter. The Disabling Active Desktop option affects the Registry key:

*HKEY_CURRENT_USER\Software\Microsoft\Windows\CurrentVersion\
Policies\Explorer*

If the option is checked, the value *NoActiveDesktop* is set to *0x00000001*. The Do Not Allow Changes To Active Desktop option sets the flag *NoActiveDesktopChanges* to *0x00000001* in the same key. Further information can be found in the ADM file.

The Active Desktop Items option is of more interest. Here we find a few options that customize the Active Desktop. All check boxes under this option set values in the key:

*HKEY_CURRENT_USER\Software\Microsoft\Windows\CurrentVersion\
Policies\ActiveDesktop*

The Active Desktop Items set of options includes the following options:

- Disable ALL Desktop Items. This option toggles the *NoComponents* value between *0x00000001* and *0x00000000*. All desktop items will be hidden.

■ Disable Adding ANY Desktop Items. This option toggles the *No-AddingComponents* value between *0x00000001* and *0x00000000*. Selecting this option disables the buttons in the Web property page (see Figure 4-31 on page 178).

■ Disable Deleting ANY Desktop Items. This option toggles the *No-DeletingComponents* value between *0x00000001* and *0x00000000*. Selecting this option disables the Delete button in the Web property page (see Figure 4-31).

■ Disable Editing ANY Desktop Items. This option toggles the *No-EditingComponents* value between *0x00000001* and *0x00000000*.

■ Disable Closing ANY Desktop Items. This option toggles the *No-ClosingComponents* value between *0x00000001* and *0x00000000*.

The Desktop Wallpaper Settings option contains two entries to customize the Background property page (see Figure 4-30 on page 176). These two entries also use the key:

HKEY_CURRENT_USER\Software\Microsoft\Windows\CurrentVersion\ Policies\ActiveDesktop

The option's two entries are:

■ No HTML Wallpaper. If this check box is checked, Windows 98 hides all HTML wallpaper entries in the Wallpaper list (see Figure 4-30). The value *NoHTMLWallPaper* is set to *0x00000001*.

■ Disable Changing Wallpaper. If this check box is checked, the value *NoChangingWallPaper* is set to *0x00000001*.

The Desktop Toolbar Settings option contains two entries to customize the options available for the toolbar settings. These two options use the key:

HKEY_CURRENT_USER\Software\Microsoft\Windows\CurrentVersion\ Policies\ActiveDesktop

The Desktop Toolbar Settings option includes these entries:

■ Disable Dragging, Dropping And Closing All Toolbars. If this check box is checked, the value *NoCloseDragDropBands* is set to *0x00000001*.

■ Disable Resizing ALL Toolbars. If this check box is checked, the value *NoMovingBands* is set to *0x00000001*.

NOTE: The Windows 98 Shell (Born) branch also contains entries to customize the Start menu. (See the section "Changing the Start Menu options," beginning on page 197.)

How these options affect display properties   If you deselect either the Active Desktop Enabled option or the Allow Changes To Active Desktop option (see Figure 4-34 on page 183), Windows 98 hides the Web property page on the Display Properties property sheet and significantly changes the Background property page, as shown in Figure 4-35.

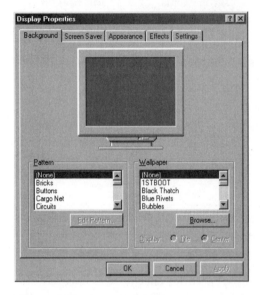

Figure 4-35.
The Windows 95–style Background property page.

If Active Desktop is disabled, Windows 98 uses the old-style Background property page to establish wallpaper and patterns.

Screen Saver Options
You can change the settings for the desktop screen saver on the Screen Saver property page of the Display Properties property sheet, shown in Figure 4-36.

All the parameters entered on the Screen Saver property page are user-specific and are stored in the *HKEY_CURRENT_USER\Control Panel\desktop* key. Each value entry in the key defines a parameter. Table 4-6 describes the Registry entries for the Screen Saver options.

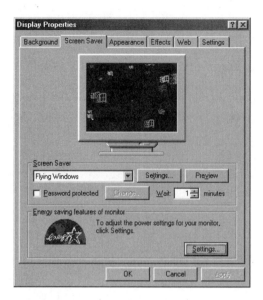

Figure 4-36.
Setting Screen Saver properties.

Values for the Screen Saver

Value Name	Description
ScreenSave_Data	This entry contains the encrypted screen saver password as a byte sequence. This value is available only if a password is set.
ScreenSaveActive	The string value for an active screen saver is set to *1*, which means that the screen saver is activated when the wait time is over. You must select and apply a screen saver to create this entry.
ScreenSaveLowPowerActive	This value is set to *1* when the monitor supports the energy-saving feature and the Low-Power Standby option is set on the Screen Saver property page. (The check box is available only in Windows 95 and Windows NT 4.0. The value will always be set to *1* in Windows 98 if Advanced Power Management is supported.)

Table 4-6. *(continued)*
This table describes possible entries for the Screen Saver in the desktop *key.*

Values for the Screen Saver *(continued)*

Value Name	Description
ScreenSaveLowPowerTimeout	The time-out in seconds. You can change the value by using the Low-Power Standby option on the Screen Saver property page (available only in Windows 95 and Windows NT 4.0).
ScreenSavePowerOffActive	This value is set to *1* when the monitor supports the energy-saving feature and the Shut Off Monitor option is set on the Screen Saver property page. (The check box is available only in Windows 95 and Windows NT 4.0. The value will always be set to *1* in Windows 98 if Advanced Power Management is supported.)
ScreenSavePowerOffTimeout	The time-out in seconds until the monitor shuts off. You can change the value by using the Shut Off Monitor option on the Screen Saver property page (available only in Windows 95 and Windows NT 4.0).
ScreenSaveTimeout	The time-out in seconds until the screen saver starts. You can change the value by using the Wait control on the Screen Saver property page.
ScreenSaveUsePassword	This flag indicates whether the screen saver requires a password. The flag is set to 0x00000001 for an active password.

Advanced Power Management Settings

Windows 98 supports Advanced Power Management. You can invoke the property page for these settings by clicking the Settings button in the Energy Saving Features Of Monitor group of the Screen Saver property page (see Figure 4-36) or by using the Power Management icon in Control Panel.

The Power Management Properties property sheet, shown in Figure 4-37, enables you to set a predefined period of time after which the monitor and the hard disks are turned off and to turn power off on a laptop computer. These settings can be stored together in schemes. Windows 98 uses several keys to store Power Management properties. The subkeys and values storing the Power Management schemes are found in this key:

HKEY_LOCAL_MACHINE\SOFTWARE\Microsoft\Windows\Current-Version\Controls Folder\PowerCfg

The *LastID* value is used to name the subkey for the next Power Management scheme. The values *DiskSpinDownMin* and *DiskSpinDownMax* define the time-out limits for the hard disk power down option.

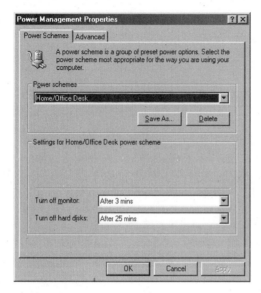

Figure 4-37.
The Power Management Properties property sheet.

The subkey *GlobalPowerPolicy* (in the branch mentioned above) contains a binary byte stream that controls the system's power policies. You can save individual Power Management schemes by using the Save As button on the Power Schemes property page (see Figure 4-37). Each scheme is stored as a subkey in the ...*PowerCfg**PowerPolicies* key. The keys containing the schemes are numbered *0, 1, 2, 3,* and so on. Each key contains a *Policies* value as a binary data stream with the scheme's settings. These keys are used for the machinewide power policy.

User-specific power policy settings are also contained in a second branch:

HKEY_CURRENT_USER*Control Panel**PowerCfg*

The *CurrentPowerPolicy* value of the *PowerCfg* key defines the scheme currently used. Each scheme subkey in the ...*PowerCfg**PowerPolicies* key contains the power settings as a byte stream in the *Policies* value. The *Name* value specifies the string shown in the Power Schemes list box of the Power Schemes property page (see Figure 4-37). The *Description* value contains a simple string with a comment that describes the power scheme.

NOTE: *HKEY_LOCAL_MACHINE\System\CurrentControlSet\ control\Session Manager\Power* contains two values, *AcPolicy* and *Dc-Policy*, that define power policy data. The Power Meter icon can be shown in the Taskbar tray by using the Show Power Meter On Taskbar check box on the Advanced property page of the Power Management Properties property sheet. Checking this check box sets the *Services* value to *DWORD:0x00000007* in the key *HKEY_CURRENT_USER\Software\Microsoft\Windows\CurrentVersion\Applets\Systray*. Some settings for Advanced Power Management are stored in the *HKEY_LOCAL_MACHINE\System\CurrentControlSet\Services\ VXD\VPOWERD* key.

International Settings

International settings are set on the Regional Settings Properties property sheet, which you can access by double-clicking the Regional Settings icon in the Control Panel. On the Regional Settings property page, the user chooses the regional designation (a country code), whose settings will affect how information in many applications is displayed. This country code will be stored in various places in the Registry. The key *HKEY_CURRENT_USER\Control Panel\desktop\ResourceLocale*, for example, contains the country code used for international settings in system resources that require this setting, such as the default keyboard setting (referring to the Windows 98 country code, which is different from the country codes used under MS-DOS and previous Windows versions).

You can modify the settings for international parameters (such as dates, times, currency, and numbers) on the various tabs, or property pages, of the Regional Settings Properties property sheet. These parameters are stored in the Registry key *HKEY_CURRENT_USER\Control Panel\International*. This key contains at least one value with the name *Locale*. This value defines the country code for the selected international setting (*409* for the USA). When you use the standard settings for a selected country, the key contains only the *Locale* value. All settings are predefined for this country. If you change a predefined value on the Regional Settings Properties property sheet, a new value will be stored in the *International* key. Appendix B, "Values for the *International* Key," briefly describes the values used to control international settings.

Settings for the time zone, clock adjustments, locale, and code page can be found in the *HKEY_CURRENT_USER* and *HKEY_LOCAL_MACHINE* root keys. Specifically, the default settings for the time zone are located in the key:

HKEY_LOCAL_MACHINE\SOFTWARE\Microsoft\Windows\Current-Version\Time Zones

The *Default* value of this key contains the current time zone of the user (*"Pacific Standard Time"*, for example). The *Time Zones* key also contains subkeys named after the other time zones (*Eastern*, for example). The values in each subkey of the *Time Zones* key define the display string for the Time Zone property page on the Date/Time Properties property sheet (*Display*), the daylight name (*Dlt*), and the Standard Time (*Std*). The *MapID* value defines the time-zone mapping, and *TZI* (which stands for Time Zone Information) contains the default settings for *Time Zones*. To define user-specific settings, don't modify the *TZI* content; instead, use the keys for the international settings (*HKEY_CURRENT_USER\Control Panel\International*).

The *TimeZoneInformation* key of the *HKEY_LOCAL_MACHINE\System\CurrentControlSet\control* branch contains international settings that control *Bias* values, clock adjustments (*DisableAutoDaylightTimeSet*), and so on. The flag *DisableAutoDaylightTimeSet = 0x00000001* prevents Windows from automatically switching to daylight saving time. (This option is available on the Time Zone property page of the Date/Time Properties property sheet, which can be invoked by double-clicking the time shown in the right corner of the taskbar.) The value *StandardStart* contains a byte sequence representing several entries. The third byte in *StandardStart* defines the month that Windows changes to standard time. A byte set to *0A* defines the end of October for this change. The byte at offset 7 defines the month that Windows switches to daylight saving time (*5 = May*).

Locale options are contained in the *HKEY_LOCAL_MACHINE\System\CurrentControlSet\control\Nls* key. (This key exists only if you have set an option whose value is stored there.) The *Locale* subkey contains entries whose names are locale codes; the value of each entry is set to a string giving the language associated with the locale code (for example, *"0000042D" = "Basque"*). The *Default* value of the *Locale* subkey contains the locale code of the computer's current setting. For example, a *Default* value of *"00000409"* indicates that the computer is set for English (United States). The *Codepage* subkey contains a list of the Windows code-page numbers and their mappings to optional NLS files.

Restricting Access to Display Properties

The System Policy Editor provides several options for restricting access to the Display Properties property sheet. (Right-clicking the desktop and selecting the Properties command from the context menu displays the Display Properties property sheet. This property sheet is also available via the Display icon in the Control Panel.) These access options, including the hiding or revealing of the various property pages when the Display Properties property sheet is enabled, are located on the Policies property page of the System Policy Editor's Local User Properties property sheet under the *Windows 98 System\Control Panel\ Display* option. (See Figure 4-38.)

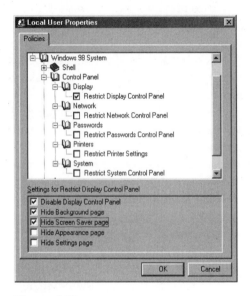

Figure 4-38.
Restricting access to system properties with the Local User Properties property sheet.

These options are placed as values in the Registry in the following key:

HKEY_CURRENT_USER\Software\Microsoft\Windows\CurrentVersion\ Policies\System

This key exists only if you have set an option whose flag is stored in the key. Table 4-7 lists the values available in this key that restrict access to the display properties. (Each value's description begins with the text related to that option on the Local User Properties property sheet.) A value set to *0x00000001* disables access. Deleting a value or setting its data to *0* enables access.

Values Restricting Access to Display Properties

Value Name	Description
NoDispCPL	Disable Display Control Panel. If the value is set to *1*, the Display Properties property sheet is not accessible.
NoDispBackgroundPage	Hide Background Page. If the value is set to *1*, the Background property page on the Display Properties property sheet is hidden.
NoDispScrSavPage	Hide Screen Saver Page. If the value is set to *1*, the Screen Saver property page on the Display Properties property sheet is hidden.
NoDispAppearancePage	Hide Appearance Page. If the value is set to *1*, the Appearance property page on the Display Properties property sheet is hidden.
NoDispSettingsPage	Hide Settings Page. If the value is set to *1*, the Settings property page on the Display Properties property sheet is hidden.

Table 4-7.
These options can be altered with the System Policy Editor's Local User Properties property sheet.

Restricting Access to Network Properties

The Network property sheet is available via the Network icon in the Control Panel. Using the System Policy Editor, you can restrict access to this property sheet. You'll find the option on the Policies property page of the Local User Properties property sheet under the *Windows 98 System\Control Panel\Network* option.

Network options are placed as values in the Registry in the following key:

HKEY_CURRENT_USER\Software\Microsoft\Windows\CurrentVersion\ Policies\Network

Table 4-8, on the next page, shows the values available in this key that restrict access to the network properties. (Each value's description begins with the text related to that option on the Local User Properties property sheet.) A value set to *0x00000001* disables access, while deleting a value or setting its data to *0* enables access.

Values for Restricting Access to Network Properties

Value Name	Description
NoNetSetup	Disable Network Control Panel. If the value is set to *1*, the Network property sheet is not accessible.
NoNetSetupIDPage	Hide Identification Page. If the value is set to *1*, the Identification property page is hidden on the Network property sheet.
NoNetSetupSecurityPage	Hide Access Control Page. If the value is set to *1*, the Access Control property page is hidden on the Network property sheet.

Table 4-8.
Use the System Policy Editor's Local User Properties property sheet to set these options.

Restricting Access to Password Properties

Using the System Policy Editor, you can restrict the access to the Passwords Properties property sheet, which is available via the Passwords icon in the Control Panel. The restriction options are located on the System Policy Editor's Policies property page under the *Windows 98 System\Control Panel\Passwords* option. Options to restrict access to password properties are placed in the Registry in the key:

HKEY_CURRENT_USER\Software\Microsoft\Windows\CurrentVersion\ Policies\System

Table 4-9 shows the values that are available in this key to restrict access to the password properties. (Each value's description begins with the text related to that option on the Local User Properties property sheet.) A value set to *0x00000001* disables access; deleting the value or setting its data to *0* enables access.

Values for Restricting Access to Password Properties

Value Name	Description
NoSecCPL	Disable Passwords Control Panel. If the value is set to *1*, the Passwords Properties property sheet is not accessible.
NoPwdPage	Hide Change Passwords Page. If the value is set to *1*, the Change Passwords property page on the Passwords Properties property sheet is hidden.

Table 4-9. *(continued)*
These options can be altered with the System Policy Editor.

Values for Restricting Access to Password Properties *(continued)*

Value Name	Description
NoAdminPage	Hide Remote Administration Page. If the value is set to *1*, the Remote Administration property page on the Passwords Properties property sheet is hidden.
NoProfilePage	Hide User Profiles Page. If the value is set to *1*, the Profile property page on the Passwords Properties property sheet is hidden.

Restricting Access to Printer Properties

The System Policy Editor allows you to restrict access to the Properties property sheets of each printer. These options are located on the System Policy Editor's Policies property page under the *Windows 98 System\Control Panel\Printers* option. The options are stored in the Registry in the key:

HKEY_CURRENT_USER\Software\Microsoft\Windows\CurrentVersion\Policies\Explorer

Table 4-10 shows the values available in this key that restrict access to the printer properties. (Each value's description begins with the text related to that option on the Local User Properties property sheet.) A value set to *0x00000001* disables access; deleting the value or setting its data to *0* enables access.

Values for Restricting Access to Printer Properties

Value Name	Description
NoPrinterTabs	Hide General and Details Pages. If the value is set to *1*, the pages are hidden on the printer Properties property sheet.
NoDeletePrinter	Disable Deletion of Printers. If the value is set to *1*, the Delete Printer function is disabled.
NoAddPrinter	Disable Addition of Printers. If the value is set to *1*, the Add Printer function is disabled.

Table 4-10.
Set these options in the System Policy Editor.

Restricting Access to System Properties

The System Policy Editor allows you to restrict access to the System Properties property sheet. The options for restricting access are located on the System Policy Editor's Policies property page under the *Windows 98 System\Control Panel\System* option. The options are stored in the Registry in the key:

HKEY_CURRENT_USER\Software\Microsoft\Windows\CurrentVersion\Policies\System

Table 4-11 shows the values available in this key that restrict access to the system properties. (Each value's description begins with the text related to that option on the Local User Properties property sheet.) A value set to *0x00000001* disables access; deleting the value or setting its data to *0* enables access.

Values for Restricting Access to System Properties

Value Name	Description
NoDevMgrPage	Hide Device Manager Page. If the value is set to *1*, the page on the System Properties property sheet is hidden.
NoConfigPage	Hide Hardware Profiles Page. If the value is set to *1*, the page on the System Properties property sheet is hidden.
NoFileSysPage	Hide File System Button. If the value is set to *1*, the File System button on the Performance property page of the System Properties property sheet is hidden.
NoVirtMemPage	Hide Virtual Memory Button. If the value is set to *1*, the Virtual Memory button on the Performance property page of the System Properties property sheet is hidden.

Table 4-11.
Set these options in the System Policy Editor.

NOTE: The contents of the Control Panel folder are built during each system startup. Windows stores the entries in the Registry key:

HKEY_LOCAL_MACHINE\SOFTWARE\Microsoft\Windows\CurrentVersion\Controls Folder

This key contains a record of binary data that points to CPL files found in the Windows\System subfolder. Tweak UI provides a Control Panel property page to hide or show individual Control Panel entries. The options on this Control Panel property page don't change any Registry entries.

Changing the Start Menu Options

The Start menu and the taskbar are also parts of the Windows 98 shell. Customizing the options for these items requires different tools. In this section, I discuss customization choices, required tools, and the behind-the-scenes functionality of these shell features.

Adding a Cascading Control Panel Menu to the Start Menu

Typically, you open the Control Panel window by selecting Control Panel from the Settings option of the Start menu. Often after opening the Control Panel and clicking a few icons, you end up with a series of windows one on top of the other and all on top of any other open Windows-based applications. Wouldn't it be less cumbersome to see a cascading Control Panel menu in the Start menu that closes automatically after you select an option?

Unfortunately, it doesn't do any good to open the My Computer window and drag the Control Panel icon onto the Start button of the taskbar—all that does is create a shortcut to the Control Panel. The Control Panel window will still occupy space on the screen when it is opened, and you save only one mouse click opening it. My solution is based on the technique I used to create a Control Panel folder on the desktop. To add a cascading Control Panel to the Start menu, follow these steps:

1. Right-click the Start button, and select the Open command from the context menu. The Start Menu folder window opens.

2. Create a new folder in the Start Menu window, and name it Control Panel.{21EC2020-3AEA-1069-A2DD-08002B30309D}. Enter the code following the dot carefully; it defines the CLSID code of the Control Panel ActiveX component.

   When you click outside the name box, the shell detects the new definition, Windows changes the folder symbol to the Control Panel icon, and the title is set to Control Panel. (If this didn't happen, you probably entered the folder name incorrectly.)

3. Close the Start Menu window.

4. Click Start on the taskbar. Control Panel is now an option available directly from the Start menu. When you click this option, you will get a cascading menu similar to the one shown in Figure 4-39 on the next page. This menu allows direct access to each entry in the Control Panel.

Figure 4-39.
A cascading Control Panel menu.

Adding a Cascading Printers Menu to the Start Menu

Accessing the printer icons within the Printers folder is as cumbersome as accessing Control Panel options. You have to open the My Computer window, or you have to click the Start menu, then Settings, and then Printers to open the Printers folder. To be able to access the printer icons directly from the Start menu, follow these steps:

1. Open the Start Menu window. (Right-click the Start button, and select Open from the context menu.)

2. Create a new folder in the Start Menu folder, and name it *Printers.{2227A280-3AEA-1069-A2DE-08002B30309D}*.

The Printers folder icon should appear on the Start menu. When you open the Start menu and select the Printers entry, a cascading menu will appear, which will give you quick access to each individual printer.

NOTE: To remove the Printers folder or the Control Panel folder from the Start menu, open the Start Menu window and delete the associated icon.

TIP: If you created a Printers folder or Control Panel folder following the steps in the preceding procedure, you can copy or move this folder into other subfolders of the Start Menu folder. This creates a cascading submenu that reflects these additional Start menu levels.

Removing Entries from the Start Menu's Settings Branch

Clicking the Start button and selecting Settings reveals a cascading submenu with entries for the Control Panel, Printers, Taskbar & Start Menu, Folder Options, and Active Desktop. Allowing you to customize your shell, these entries are user-specific and are customized with the System Policy Editor.

If you want to change the settings for users other than the current user, you must open a profile and select the user or user group. The procedures for defining a user policy are in the *Microsoft Windows 98 Resource Kit* (Microsoft Press, 1998). The advantage of using the System Policy Editor instead of other methods of modifying the Registry is that you can modify the entries for one or more users at one time. In the next procedure, we're going to hide a few entries in the Settings branch of the Start menu for the current user of the system. So start the System Policy Editor, select File, select Open Registry, and then click the Local User option.

1. Open the *Windows 98 System\Shell\Restrictions* branch on the Local User Properties property page (see Figure 4-40 on the next page).

2. To hide the Control Panel and Printers folders, check the Remove Folders From Settings On Start Menu option.

3. To hide the Taskbar & Start Menu option from the Settings submenu, check the Remove Taskbar From Settings On Start Menu option.

4. Close the property page by clicking OK, and save the settings.

The next time the system is started, all System Policy Editor entries you checked above will be hidden in the Settings submenu.

Because the options for hiding and showing the Settings submenu entries are user-specific, and because all desktop elements—including the Start menu and Windows Explorer—belong to the Windows shell, we can search the Registry entries for these options in the *HKEY_CURRENT_USER* branch. We also know that the current settings are always stored in the following key: *...\Software\Microsoft\Windows\CurrentVersion*. And finally, because the entries have something to do with Windows Explorer and user policies, we can guess in which Registry branch the options set in the System Policy Editor will be stored. That's right—it's the *HKEY_CURRENT_USER\Software\Microsoft\ Windows\CurrentVersion\Policies\Explorer* branch, which contains a bunch of values for customizing the Start menu. Table 4-12, on the following page, describes the entries that hide and show the options under Settings.

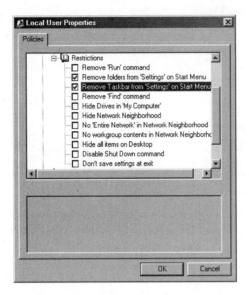

Figure 4-40.
The Windows 98 System\Shell\Restrictions *branch of the System Policy Editor.*

Values for Hiding and Showing Settings Submenu Entries

Value Name	Description
NoSetFolders	Hides the symbols for Printers and Control Panel folders in the Settings submenu when the value is set to *0x00000001*. Deleting the value or setting it to *0x00000000* shows the folders in the Settings submenu.
	If the value is set to *0x00000001*, the Control Panel and Printers folders are also hidden in My Computer. This flag will have no effect on Printers and Control Panel folders that are defined as files or shell extensions. (See pages 162–164 to find out how to define a folder symbol on the desktop and page 197 to find out how to define a cascading submenu in the Start menu.)
NoSetTaskbar	Hides the Taskbar entry in the Settings submenu when the value is set to *0x00000001*. Deleting the value or setting it to *0x00000000* shows the entry in the Settings submenu.

Table 4-12.
These values are contained in the Explorer *subkey.*

Disabling the Run Command

You can start any application program by selecting the Run entry on the Start menu and entering the name of the executable file. The System Policy Editor has a user-specific option to let you disable (or enable) this entry on the Start menu. To hide or show the Run entry on the Start menu, follow these steps:

1. Open the *Windows 98 System\Shell\Restrictions* branch on the Policies property page of the Local User Properties property sheet.

2. Check (to hide) or uncheck (to show) the Remove 'Run' Command option. Close the property sheet by clicking OK, and save the settings.

If you click Run before your next system startup, you'll receive an error message. After you restart the system, the Run option won't be visible.

The flag to remove the Run entry from the Start menu is stored in the *NoRun* value of the following Registry branch:

HKEY_CURRENT_USER\Software\Microsoft\Windows\CurrentVersion\ Policies\Explorer

If this value is set to *0x00000001*, the Run command is removed from the Start menu after the next system startup. Deleting the *NoRun* value or setting its data to *0x00000000* brings the Run entry back to the Start menu.

Resetting the Shell Without Rebooting

Newly selected options take effect after the next system startup because during the startup process the Registry is reorganized—some entries are copied from *HKEY_USERS* to *HKEY_CURRENT_USER*, and other branches are rebuilt to reflect the current state of the system. A complete reboot, however, takes a long time. If you alter shell options and want to reset the shell without a complete reboot, follow these steps:

1. Press Ctrl-Alt-Del. This invokes the Close Program dialog box, which has a list of all active tasks.

2. Click the Explorer entry, and close the dialog box by clicking the End Task button. Windows notifies Windows Explorer about this user request, and since Windows Explorer is an essential part of Windows, the Shut Down Windows dialog box is displayed.

(continued)

Resetting the Shell Without Rebooting *continued*

3. Click Cancel to close this dialog box without shutting down Windows, which prevents Windows Explorer from shutting down too. Windows detects this after a few seconds and displays the Explorer message box notifying you that the program is not responding.

4. Close the Explorer message box by clicking End Task.

NOTE: It might take a few moments for the Explorer message box to appear. If you don't click Cancel in the Shut Down Windows dialog box right away, the Explorer message box will appear anyway. If you click End Task at that point, the Explorer message box and the Shut Down Windows dialog box will both close, shutting down Windows Explorer and invoking your new settings without shutting down Windows.

Clicking End Task drops the Explorer out of memory. Windows then immediately loads a new copy of Windows Explorer to re-create the shell (with the taskbar and the desktop). All previous Registry settings are replaced with any modifications you made. (You should note that this trick can cause problems if the Active Desktop is active. In that case, you might want to log off and log on again to refresh the shell settings.)

NOTE: You might wonder why you can disable some options by either setting the flag value to *0x00000000* or deleting the flag altogether. You will appreciate this feature if you want to alter the settings with a REG file, because you cannot remove an entry from the Registry by using a REG file. For example, if you set the *NoRun* flag once so that it exists in the Registry, you cannot use a REG file to remove it and disable the option. But since you can toggle the value between *0* and *1*, you can still disable the option with the REG file.

Disabling the Find Command

The Windows shell offers you the ability to search for computers, folders, or files. This function is available through the Find command, which is accessed from the Start menu; through the Windows Explorer window (from the Tools menu); or from a context menu when you select a folder, computer, or drive icon. The

System Policy Editor enables you to disable the Find function. To enable or disable the Find command, follow these steps:

1. Open the *Windows 98 System\Shell\Restrictions* branch on the Policies property page of the Local User Properties property sheet.

2. Check (to hide) or uncheck (to show) the Remove Find Command option. Close the property sheet by clicking OK, and save the settings.

After the next system startup, if the Remove Find Command option was checked, the Find command will be removed from the Start menu, the Windows Explorer Tools menu, and the context menu.

The flag that disables the Find function is stored in the *NoFind* value of the *HKEY_CURRENT_USER\Software\Microsoft\Windows\CurrentVersion\ Policies\Explorer* key. Setting the value's data to *0x00000001* disables the Find command after the next system startup. Deleting the *NoFind* value or setting it to *0x00000000* returns the Find function to the menus.

Disabling the Log Off Command

Windows 98 provides a new Log Off command in the Start menu that allows a user to log off and log on again. You can use the Tweak UI IE4 property page to disable this Start menu entry (see Figure 4-34 on page 183). If you uncheck the Allow Logoff check box, the Log Off command in the Start menu will be hidden after the next system start. The check box is associated with the *NoLogOff* value in the key:

HKEY_CURRENT_USER\Software\Microsoft\Windows\CurrentVersion\ Policies\Explorer

If the *NoLogOff* value is set to *01 00 00 00*, the entry will be hidden. Removing the value or setting it to *00 00 00 00* enables the Log Off command again.

NOTE: As discussed in the section "Modifying Other Desktop Settings," beginning on page 183, you can extend the Local User Properties Policies property page by loading the SHELL98.ADM template provided in the folder \chapter7\adm of the sample files. If this template is active, the Desktop branch contains a Start Menu subbranch to customize most of the Start menu settings discussed in this section. All settings are kept in the *Explorer* Registry key mentioned above. See also further discussions below.

Disabling the Documents Command

Windows lists the names of the last 15 opened documents in a submenu of the Start menu's Documents command. Some users don't like to have this entry on the Start menu, but in Windows 95 there's no way to remove it. The Windows 98 version of Tweak UI, however, provides an option on the IE4 property sheet for the removal of the Documents command. If you uncheck or check the Show Documents On Start Menu check box, the *NoRecentDocsMenu* value in the *HKEY_CURRENT_USER\Software\Microsoft\Windows\CurrentVersion\ Policies\Explorer* key is set either to *01 00 00 00* (unchecked) or to *00 00 00 00* (checked). As a result, the Start menu's Documents entry is enabled or disabled after the next system start.

Disabling the Favorites Command

Windows 98 maintains a Favorites list, which is accessible thorough the Favorites command on the Start menu. When you uncheck or check the Show Favorites On Start Menu check box on the Tweak UI IE4 property page, the *NoFavoritesMenu* value in the *HKEY_CURRENT_USER\Software\Microsoft\ Windows\CurrentVersion\Policies\Explorer* key is set either to *01 00 00 00* (unchecked) or to *00 00 00 00* (checked). As a result, the Start menu's Favorites entry is enabled or disabled after the next system start.

Disabling the Shut Down Command

You can shut down Windows in two ways:

- Using the Shut Down command from the Start menu.
- Invoking the Close Program dialog box by pressing Ctrl-Alt-Del and clicking the Shut Down button.

Windows allows you to disable the Shut Down feature, in both of its manifestations, for the current user. The option for disabling Shut Down is available in the System Policy Editor. To enable or disable the Shut Down command, follow these steps:

1. Open the *Windows 98 System\Shell\Restrictions* branch on the Policies property page of the Local User Properties property sheet.

2. Check (to hide) or uncheck (to show) the Disable Shut Down Command option. Close the property sheet by clicking OK, and save the settings.

The Shut Down command is either disabled or enabled immediately after you save the settings in the Registry. Although the Shut Down entry in the Start menu is still available, the user cannot activate it. If the user attempts to use the command, Windows displays a message box explaining that the operation has been canceled for this computer. The Shut Down entry in the Start menu is actually removed or inserted after the next reboot of the shell. If the user invokes the Close Program dialog box while the Shut Down function is disabled, the Shut Down button appears grayed out and is inoperable.

The *NoClose* value of the Registry branch *HKEY_CURRENT_USER\ Software\Microsoft\Windows\CurrentVersion\Policies\Explorer* disables the Shut Down command. Set to *0x00000001*, the value disables the Shut Down command immediately. Deleting the *NoClose* value or setting it to *0x00000000* brings the Shut Down function back to the shell.

> **WARNING:** The *NoClose* flag affects only the Shut Down command provided by the shell. An individual program can still notify Windows about a restart request; many tools allow a "quick Windows exit." You can't block a Shut Down function provided by such a tool by using the *NoClose* flag.

> **NOTE:** The option selected in the Shut Down Windows dialog box is kept in the key:
>
> *HKEY_CURRENT_USER\Software\Microsoft\Windows\ CurrentVersion\Explorer*
>
> This key contains the *Shutdown Setting* value, which is set to *1* (Shut Down), *2* (Restart), or *3* (Restart In MS-DOS Mode), depending on the entry last selected by the user in the Shut Down Windows dialog box.

Disabling Miscellaneous Windows 98 Start Menu Settings

As discussed in the section "Modifying Other Desktop Settings," beginning on page 183, you can extend the Local User Properties Policies property page by loading the SHELL98.ADM template provided in the folder \chapter7\adm of the sample files. If this template is active, the Windows 98 Shell (Born) branch contains a Start Menu subbranch to customize most of the Start menu settings. All settings are kept in the Registry key:

HKEY_CURRENT_USER\Software\Microsoft\Windows\CurrentVersion\ Policies\Explorer

Setting a value to *0x00000001* disables an entry. Removing the value or setting its data to *0x00000000* enables the entry again. The Start Menu subbranch contains several items new to Windows 98 that can be used to customize the Start menu entries:

- Remove The Active Desktop Item From The Settings Menu. This check box is associated with the value *NoSetActiveDesktop*.

- Disable Drag And Drop Context Menus On The Start Menu. This check box is associated with the value *NoChangeStartMenu*.

- Remove The Folder Options Menu Item From The Settings Menu. This check box is associated with the value *NoFolderOptions*.

- Do Not Keep History Of Recently Opened Documents. This check box is associated with the value *NoRecentDocsHistory*.

- Clear History Of Recent Opened Documents. This check box is associated with the value *ClearRecentDocsOnExit*.

- Disable Context Menu For Taskbar. This check box is associated with the value *NoTrayContextMenu*.

Some of these options won't take effect until after the next system start.

Restricting the Executable Application Programs

By default, the user can start any application under Windows by selecting the Run command from the Start menu; by selecting an application from the Start menu's submenus; or by double-clicking a shortcut, document, or application icon on the desktop or in a folder window. Sometimes, however, you'll want to restrict access to a group of selected applications. For example, you might want your office manager to use only Microsoft Word for Windows and Microsoft Excel and your system administrator to be able to access all other applications, including Windows Explorer. Your system administrator can use the System Policy Editor to define these restrictions. Following are the steps to set restrictions for a single user:

1. Start the System Policy Editor, load the (local) Registry, and select the user whose access rights will be restricted. (For example, you can double-click Local User.)

2. Expand the *Windows 98 System\Restrictions* branch on the Local User Properties property sheet's Policies property page. This branch contains several options that restrict user access to the system (see Figure 4-41).

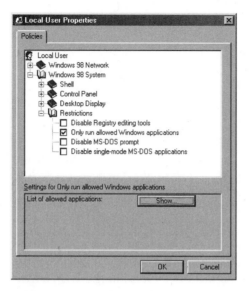

Figure 4-41.
Entries in the Windows 98 System\Restrictions branch.

3. Check the Only Run Allowed Windows Applications option on the Policies property page. You have to set the allowed applications manually, so click Show to display your options.

4. The Show Contents dialog box opens with a list of all allowed applications (see Figure 4-42). Edit this list by using the Add and Remove options.

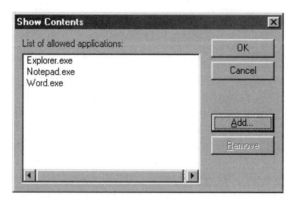

Figure 4-42.
List of applications that you can restrict access to.

5. Close the open dialog boxes by clicking OK, and save the settings in the Registry.

After you complete these steps, the Windows shell allows the current user to access only the specified applications. These restrictions are valid for all shell components (shortcuts on the desktop, icons in the Windows Explorer window, the Run command on the Start menu, submenu entries on the Start menu, and so on). The new restrictions take effect the next time the system is reset.

These access-restriction settings are stored in the Registry in the *HKEY_CURRENT_USER\Software\Microsoft\Windows\CurrentVersion\Policies\Explorer* branch. If the access to applications is restricted for the current user, the key contains the value *RestrictRun*, which is set to *0x00000001*. The names of the applications that can be accessed by this user are stored in the *RestrictRun* subkey. The entries in this subkey are numbered from *1* through *n*, and their values are strings containing the paths (optional) and names of the applications (see Figure 4-43). Only applications found in the *RestrictRun* subkey are accessible by the current user.

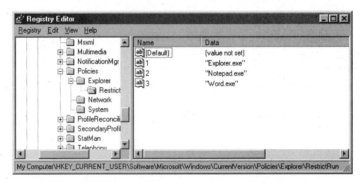

Figure 4-43.
Registry entries for RestrictRun.

To enable access, remove the *RestrictRun* value from the *Explorer* key or set the value for *RestrictRun* to *0x00000000*. The latter option is preferable if you use REG files to modify the Registry. (See the RESRUNOF.REG file in the \chapter 4 folder of the sample files.)

> WARNING: Be careful when you use this option. If you restrict access to several modules and only one profile for all users is enabled, you won't be able to restart the System Policy Editor to alter the *RestrictRun* settings. You'd have to edit the Registry with the Real Mode version of the Registry Editor and reset the *RestrictRun* option.

On network systems, you can use the System Policy Editor to set access rights for different user groups. Consult the *Microsoft Windows 98 Resource Kit* (Microsoft Press, 1998) to learn how to create and set remote system and user policies.

Restricting Access to the Registry Editing Tools

To prevent an experienced user from resetting Registry settings, set the Disable Registry Editing Tools option, which is available in the *Windows 98 System\Restrictions* branch of the System Policy Editor (see Figure 4-41 on page 207), and store it in the Registry. The flag *DisableRegistryTools* is then inserted in *HKEY_CURRENT_USER\ Software\Microsoft\Windows\CurrentVersion\Policies\System*. If this flag is set to *0x00000001*, the user can't launch the Registry Editor but the System Policy Editor is still executable.

It might seem advantageous to remove both the Registry Editor and the System Policy Editor from the local computer, but an experienced user can still create a simple REG file and import it into the Registry with a double-click. Surprisingly, a user can reset many Registry entries. (By the way, in Microsoft Windows NT, additional access privileges are required to access system components.) The *RestrictRun* feature offers you a way to construct a second barrier against users who try to use REG files to change the Registry. If the Registry Editor isn't included in the list of accessible applications, the user can't import a REG file by double-clicking the file's icon. The only remaining way to change the Registry would be to use a boot disk containing the Registry Editor and to alter values in Real Mode. If you accidentally lock yourself out, you can use this backdoor method to reset the Registry. The better approach, however, is to recover the Registry with your backup copy, which you created—I hope—before you began modifying the Registry in the first place.

Disabling the MS-DOS Prompt
and the Single-Mode MS-DOS Feature

Windows lets you invoke an MS-DOS window and execute old MS-DOS applications. This command is available from the Programs submenu of the Start menu, or you can create a shortcut on the desktop to the MS-DOS command window. You can disable the MS-DOS command prompt for the current user (or for a user group) by using the System Policy Editor. To disable the MS-DOS prompt from the Windows shell, follow these steps:

1. Start the System Policy Editor, load the local Registry, and select the user whose access rights will be restricted (for example, the Local User).

2. Expand the *Windows 98 System\Restrictions* branch on the Policies property page, and check the Disable MS-DOS Prompt option.

3. Close the open dialog box by clicking OK, and save the Registry settings.

The settings for disabling the MS-DOS command prompt are stored in the Registry in the *HKEY_CURRENT_USER\Software\Microsoft\Windows\ CurrentVersion\Policies\WinOldApp* branch. (This key will not exist until you set an option whose value is stored there.) If the MS-DOS command prompt is disabled, the key contains the entry *Disabled = 0x00000001*. Removing this value or setting it to *0x00000000* enables the MS-DOS command prompt again.

The other option you can disable with the System Policy Editor is the single-mode MS-DOS feature, which is available as an option in the Shut Down Windows dialog box. (To access this dialog box, click the Start menu and select Shut Down). To disable this mode under Windows 98, follow these steps:

1. Start the System Policy Editor, load the local Registry, and select the user whose access rights will be restricted (for example, the Local User).

2. Expand the *Windows 98 System\Restrictions* branch on the Policies property page, and check the Disable Single-Mode MS-DOS Applications option.

3. Close the open dialog box by clicking OK, and save the settings in the Registry.

After these steps are executed, the Restart In MS-DOS Mode option in the Shut Down Windows dialog box is hidden.

The settings for disabling the single-mode MS-DOS feature are stored in *HKEY_CURRENT_USER\Software\Microsoft\Windows\CurrentVersion\ Policies\WinOldApp*. When the single-mode MS-DOS feature is disabled, this key contains the *NoRealMode* entry set to *0x00000001*. Removing this value or setting it to *0x00000000* enables the single-mode MS-DOS option again.

NOTE: You can enter single-mode MS-DOS—despite the Registry settings—by rebooting the system and entering MS-DOS mode
or by using a boot disk.

Changing the Menu Delay

Clicking a menu item often invokes a submenu. You can increase or decrease
the speed with which Windows shows and hides these submenus. Although
Microsoft Windows 98 doesn't include a property page to change this option,
you can employ two methods to make this type of change. The simplest way is
to use the Mouse property page in Tweak UI (see Figure 4-44). Adjust the slider
to vary the menu speed, and right-click the test icon to see the effects of your
modifications.

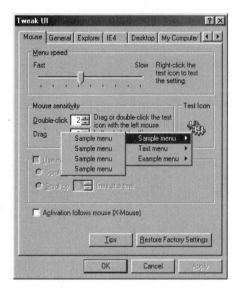

Figure 4-44.
Testing the menu delay in Tweak UI.

If Tweak UI isn't available, change the Registry settings by using the
Registry Editor. The value for menu speed is stored in the Registry key *HKEY_
CURRENT_USER\Control Panel\desktop*. If you use Tweak UI to change the
setting for the menu speed, there will be a value in the key *MenuShowDelay* that
can be set to a string value. A value of *"0"* represents the fastest response to a
mouse click; higher values represent a delay factor that slows down a menu's
appearance. In Windows 95, the *MenuShowDelay* value could be set from *1* to *10*.

Inspecting the Tweak UI settings reveals that Windows 98 recognizes settings from *"0"* through *"32767"* and from *"-32768"* through *"-2"*. After you restart the system, menu delay modifications take effect.

Changing the Update Mode

If you are connected to a network, policies for the local computer can be downloaded from the network when you log on. You can enable this feature with the System Policy Editor:

1. Start the System Policy Editor, and load the local Registry.

2. Open the Policies property page on the Local Computer Properties property sheet.

3. Select the *Windows 98 Network\Update* branch, and click the Remote Update option (see Figure 4-45).

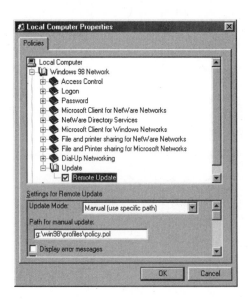

Figure 4-45.
Setting the Update Mode.

4. Here you can set the Update Mode to either Automatic (Use Default Path) or Manual (Use Specific Path).

5. If you select Manual (Use Specific Path), you must fill in the Path For Manual Update text box with the path containing the policy (POL) file from which you want the policies loaded.

6. Click OK to close the property sheet.

7. Store the values by using the Save function.

The Update Mode is stored in the Registry in the branch *HKEY_LOCAL_MACHINE\System\CurrentControlSet\control\Update* in the *UpdateMode* value. *UpdateMode* can be set to *0* (no update), *1* (automatic update), or *2* (manual update). The *NetworkPath* value in the same key contains the path to the policy file for manual updates.

> T I P : You can use the System Policy Editor to create a POL file and then add user entries to this file. Change the settings for each user on the User property page, and store these settings in the POL file. To overwrite these settings for the defined user, select Manual Update mode and set the path to the POL file (see Figure 4-45). Windows 98 will use the POL file settings to overwrite the Registry when the user logs on during the next system start. You can find further information on this topic in the *Microsoft Windows 98 Resource Kit* (Microsoft Press, 1998).

Resetting the Run MRU List

Windows maintains lists of the most recently used (MRU) files or commands for several shell functions. One list contains the last commands executed by the Run command from the Start menu; you can display it by clicking the open list arrow in the Run dialog box (see Figure 4-46).

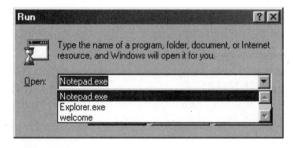

Figure 4-46.
The MRU list for the Run command.

This list is called the Run MRU list; it's maintained in *HKEY_CURRENT_USER\Software\Microsoft\Windows\CurrentVersion\Explorer\RunMRU*. The structure of the entries contained in this key is shown in Figure 4-47 on the next page. The entries define the order of the commands that show up in the list box and the appearance of the commands themselves.

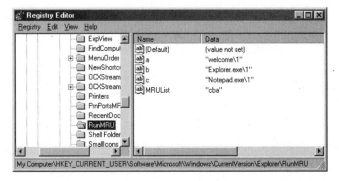

Figure 4-47.
The structure of the Run MRU list in the Registry.

Here are the attributes of the Run MRU list:

■ The *MRUList* value contains a string defining the order in which the other entries will appear in the list. In the example shown in Figure 4-47, the entry *"cba"* indicates that the first item that will be shown in the Run list (see also Figure 4-46) is Notepad.exe.

■ The commands themselves are stored as strings (terminated with the characters \1) in values with the names *a*, *b*, *c*, and so on. Twenty-six entries are possible.

This structure is used in several MRU lists. You can revise an MRU list by using a REG file to reset the values in the *RunMRU* key to empty strings. (You cannot remove the entries contained in the *RunMRU* key by using a REG file.) The following REG file (CLRRNMRU.REG, available in the \chapter4 folder of the sample files) will reset the Run MRU list after you import the file with a double-click.

```
REGEDIT4

[HKEY_CURRENT_USER\Software\Microsoft\Windows\CurrentVersion\   ↴
Explorer\RunMRU]

"a"=" "
"MRUList"=""
```

You could write a similar REG file resetting all 26 entries—*a*, *b*, and so on through *z*—to empty strings, but this isn't required. The REG file above shows you a simple trick: set only the first value, *a*, to an empty string, and clear the *MRUList* value. After the next restart, with the *MRUList* value empty, the shell won't be able to detect an order and thus will show an empty list box in the Run dialog box. The Run command line will also be empty.

NOTE: You can create a REG file to reset the Run MRU list, or you can create an INF file to remove the values *b* through *z* from the Registry and reset the *MRUList* value to *""*. Some users have reported problems when setting a value to *""* with a REG file. Therefore, I prefer using INF files to clear values. I'll discuss INF files at greater length in later chapters. Also, remember that some settings require a reboot before they become valid.

NOTE: On the IE4 property page in Tweak UI, there is a check box named Clear Document, Run, Typed-URL History On Exit. This check box sets the value *ClearRecentDocsOnExit* either to *01 00 00 00* or *00 00 00 00* in the key:

HKEY_CURRENT_USER\Software\Microsoft\Windows\ CurrentVersion\Policies\Explorer

You can also set this option by using the System Policy Editor with the SHELL98.ADM file template, contained in the folder \chapter7\adm of the sample files.

Resetting Other MRU Lists

In addition to the Run MRU list, there is a Find MRU list, which you can access by invoking the Find command. The Find MRU list is maintained in the *HKEY_CURRENT_USER* branch of the Registry in the key ...\Software\ Microsoft\Windows\CurrentVersion\Explorer\Doc Find Spec MRU. This key contains the same entries (that is, *MRUList*, *a*, *b*, *c*, and so on) as *RunMRU*.

The Any Folder function provided in the Power Toys package contains an MRU list maintained in the *HKEY_CURRENT_USER\Software\Microsoft\ Windows\CurrentVersion\Explorer\OtherFolder* key. The structure is identical to the other MRU lists, and you can use a REG file to reset this list.

The Registry key *HKEY_CURRENT_USER\Software\Microsoft\Windows\ CurrentVersion\Explorer\RecentDocs* contains an MRU list with the entries (15 maximum) shown in the Documents submenu of the Start menu. Setting the *MRUList* entry to *""* and resetting the shell empties the Documents submenu.

If the Have Disk button is enabled on the Windows Setup property page (available through the Add/Remove Programs icon in the Control Panel), the Install From Disk dialog box contains the Copy Manufacturer's Files From list box. Open this list to show the previously used paths during software setups. This MRU list is maintained in the Registry key *HKEY_CURRENT_ USER\InstallLocationsMRU*. The key also contains the values *MRUList*, *a*, *b*, *c*, and so on, as described for the other MRU lists.

Modifying Miscellaneous Keys Containing Shell Data

You might be interested to know about the other entries in the …*Software\Microsoft\Windows\CurrentVersion\Explorer* branch of the *HKEY_ CURRENT_USER* root key, such as the *Shell Folders* key, which specifies the paths to the folders used by the shell. The values contained in this key are listed in Table 4-13.

Values in the *Shell Folders* Key

Value Name	Description
AppData	Defines the path to user-specific application data (*"C:\WINDOWS\Profiles\Born\Application Data"*, for example)
Cache	Defines the path to temporary Internet files (*"C:\WINDOWS\Temporary Internet Files"*, for example)
Cookies	Defines the path to Internet cookies (*"C:\WINDOWS\ Profiles\Born\Cookies"*, for example)
Desktop	Defines the path to the desktop folder (*"C:\WINDOWS\ Desktop"*, for example)
Favorites	Defines the path to favorite Web sites and files (*"C:\WINDOWS\Favorites"*, for example)
Fonts	Defines the path to the font files (*"C:\WINDOWS\Fonts"*, for example)
History	Defines the path to the history of Web sites visited (*"C:\WINDOWS\Profiles\Born\History"*, for example)
NetHood	Defines the path to the Network Neighborhood definitions (*"C:\WINDOWS\Profiles\Born\NetHood"*, for example)

Table 4-13.
These values each define a path to a folder used by the shell.

Value Name	Description
Personal	Defines the path to the location where personal files are stored (*"C:\My Documents"*, for example)
PrintHood	Defines the path to printer folder items (*"C:\WINDOWS\ PrintHood"*, for example)
Programs	Defines the path that Windows follows for the Programs subfolder of the Start menu (*"C:\WINDOWS\Profiles\ Born\Start Menu\Programs"*, for example)
Recent	Defines the path to the folder that contains the links to the documents shown in the Start menu's Documents submenu (*"C:\WINDOWS\Profiles\Born\Recent"*, for example)
SendTo	Defines the path to the folder where the definitions for the Send To command, shown in Windows Explorer's context menu, are stored (*"C:\WINDOWS\SendTo"*, for example)
Start Menu	Defines the path to the Start Menu folder (*"C:\WINDOWS\ Profiles\Born\Start Menu"*, for example)
Startup	Defines the path to the Startup folder (*"C:\WINDOWS\ Profiles\Born\Start Menu\Programs\Startup"*, for example)
Templates	Defines the path to the folder where new templates for the New command in the shell's context menu are stored (*"C:\WINDOWS\ShellNew"*, for example)

These entries are updated by Windows each time a user logs on. (The original data is kept in the *HKEY_USERS* branch.) The key *HKEY_CURRENT_ USER\Software\Microsoft\Windows\CurrentVersion\Explorer\User Shell Folders* defines a second set of pointers defining the paths to the folders used by the shell. These values are set by default to match the values in Table 4-13. Enabling user profiles allows you to define separate locations for the Desktop, Programs, Start Menu, Startup, NetHood, and Recent folders. The names and locations of these folders are maintained in the *User Shell Folders* key and can be altered with the System Policy Editor—select Local User, and then Windows 98 System\Shell\Custom Folders.

Other entries are located in the key *HKEY_CURRENT_USER\Software\ Microsoft\Windows\CurrentVersion\Policies\Explorer*. If this key contains the value *NoStartMenuSubfolders* set to *0x00000001*, the Start menu's subfolders will be hidden. This option can be set within the System Policy Editor (in the *Windows 98 Shell\Restrictions* branch).

> NOTE: Other options for the Start menu and taskbar (such as the size of the icons) are stored in the *StreamMRU* key, which is contained in the *HKEY_CURRENT_USER\Software\Microsoft\ Windows\CurrentVersion\Explorer* branch. This list is updated dynamically. In the next chapter, I'll give you some information about the structures used in this key.

Disabling Save Settings

If the user somehow alters the desktop (for example, by opening a folder) and exits Windows, the settings will be saved permanently in the Registry. You can disable this save feature with the System Policy Editor by clicking the Don't Save Settings At Exit option in the *Windows 98 System\Shell\Restrictions* branch. If this option is set, the system's old settings will remain after the system is reset.

The System Policy Editor inserts the *NoSaveSettings* flag into the Registry key *HKEY_CURRENT_USER\Software\Microsoft\Windows\CurrentVersion\ Policies\Explorer*. If the flag is set to *0x00000001*, the settings are not saved upon exiting. A value of *0x00000000* saves the settings.

> NOTE: You might enable this option if you want to prevent the user from changing the desktop properties. However, disabling the save settings feature has one side effect. With the save settings feature enabled, if you close a shell window or the Windows Explorer window, the window's properties (for example, its size, position, icon size) are stored in the Registry. Windows stores the properties of the most recently opened folders in an MRU list, and if you reopen one of these folders, Windows tries to reuse the settings from the MRU list. If the save settings feature is disabled, the MRU list entries are used only for the current session; after the next restart, the settings are gone. I'll discuss the MRU list further in Chapter 5.

Customizing Windows Explorer and Shell Settings

In Chapter 3, we learned how to register new file types in Microsoft Windows 98. Registering file types affects features that are accessible with Windows Explorer, such as the context menu. In this chapter, we'll look at other ways to enhance and customize various Windows Explorer and shell functions, and we'll further examine the internals of the Registry. Among other things, we'll extend the context menu of the Windows Explorer window and thus the shell, change the icons for the shell, modify Shortcut arrow icons, and extend the templates for the New command of the shell's context menu.

Modifying Windows Explorer's Context Menu

As we saw in Chapter 3, extending a file type's context menu with a new command is fairly simple. When you register a new file type, the context menu for files of that type is extended. You can also register new commands for elements accessible through Windows Explorer other than file types, such as folders and drives, and extend their context menus. Inspecting the *HKEY_CLASSES_ROOT* branch of the Registry reveals keys such as *Folder*, *Drive*, and so on. If we restrict our view to the way the shell uses command extensions, the shell perceives no differences between a file, a folder, or a drive. So you can add extensions to the context menu of a folder or drive in basically the same way you register extensions for a file's context menu.

Adding the New Explorer Window Command

When you open a folder or drive in the Windows Explorer window, the contents of the selected item appear in that window. You can also right-click on a folder or drive and select Open and your selection will be opened in a shell window as if you had opened it from My Computer. From the My Computer window, you can opt to show the contents of the folder or drive in a second window by choosing the Open Each Folder In Its Own Window option in the Browse Folders As Follows section of the Custom Settings dialog box. First choose Folder Options from the View menu; select the Custom, Based On Settings You Choose radio button on the General property page; and then click the Settings button. (Despite the nomenclature of its options, this method does work for both folders and drives.)

Having two open windows on the desktop enables you to copy or move a file with a simple drag-and-drop operation. Wouldn't it be convenient to have the option to open two Windows Explorer windows? Well, that is possible. You can put a new command on the context menu that enables you to open a second Windows Explorer window with only a right mouse click. (See Figure 5-1.)

Figure 5-1.
The New Explorer Window context menu command.

Extending the shell with this new command is straightforward. If you know how to use the Registry Editor to register a new file type, you know how to extend the shell commands applicable to a folder or drive. Here are the steps you take to set the required entries in the Registry:

1. Open the key *HKEY_CLASSES_ROOT\Folder\shell*, which is where you can extend the context menu that appears when you right-click a folder. Commands stored in this key are also available from the context menus of drives and network devices (and from the Start button, because it is a part of the shell).

2. Add a subkey to the *shell* key for the verb you are adding to the key. You can use any name for this new key, but the name must be unique in the *Folder**shell* branch. (For example, you could name it *newWindow*.)

3. Set the *Default* value of the verb key to the string you want to see on the context menu—for example, *New Explorer &Window*. The ampersand (&) character defines the accelerator key used for the command on the context menu. (See pages 94–97 in Chapter 3 for details about the accelerator keys used on context menus.)

4. Add a *command* subkey to the verb key (*Folder**shell**newWindow*\\ *command*, for example), and set the subkey's *Default* value to the required Explorer command (*Explorer.exe*). Your Registry should look something like that shown in Figure 5-2.

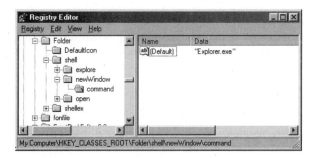

Figure 5-2.
New Registry entries for the New Explorer Window context menu command.

Immediately after you enter these values, the new context menu command is available. Right-click a folder or drive symbol (in the Windows Explorer window, in a shell window, or on the desktop) to see a new context menu like the one shown in Figure 5-1.

Defining the Command String

At least one question remains: how useful is it to define the command string invoking the second Windows Explorer window by using the method in the preceding steps? We used the command *Explorer.exe* as the *Default* value of the *HKEY_CLASSES_ROOT**Folder**shell**newWindow**command* key. (Remember that a path to the EXE file is not required because EXPLORER.EXE is contained in the Windows folder.) Using this command opens a Windows Explorer window showing the entire desktop hierarchy. We could live with this if our goal were simply to launch a second Windows Explorer window and we were too lazy to do so through the Start menu. (Obviously, you can also place a shortcut to Windows Explorer on the desktop, but the icon will be hidden most of the time by application program windows.)

But let's face it, a second Windows Explorer window showing the complete desktop hierarchy is not very convenient because you have to browse the directory structure in the new window to reach your desired folder. This is too cumbersome a task for a lazy person like me. When I select a folder and choose New Explorer Window from its context menu, I want to see the contents of this folder in the second window. So why not let Windows Explorer itself find the folder? We want the second Explorer window to open with the contents of the desired folder displayed, so let's invoke EXPLORER.EXE with the following command syntax:

```
<path>explorer.exe [/e] [,/root,<object>] [[,/select],<sub-objects>]
```

Using this command syntax in the *command* key's *Default* value allows us to control how the second copy of Windows Explorer is invoked. Let's look more closely at the command syntax before adding the entry.

First, all expressions included in square brackets ([ ]) or angle brackets (<>) are options and can be omitted depending on your purpose. The switches after the name of the EXE file work in the following ways:

- The */e* switch creates a Windows Explorer–style window with two panes. If you omit this switch and add some other option to the command line, a single pane window with the specified file list opens (following the shell style).

- The */root,<object>* option defines the root object you want shown in the new Explorer window (such as C:\Text in Figure 5-3).

- With the */select* switch, you can preselect defined sub-objects within an object. This allows you to select a subfolder or a file.

Example Commands for the Explorer

Windows Explorer's command syntax might seem a little complicated, so let's look at a few examples of the command. You can test these commands with the Run function, available from the Start menu. This is an example command for a selected sub-object:

```
Explorer.exe /e ,C:\Text
```

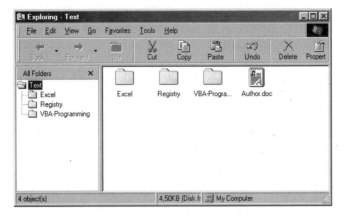

Figure 5-3.
The Windows Explorer window using C:\Text as the root.

This command opens the Explorer window, preselects the C:\Text folder, and shows the folder's contents in the window's right-hand pane.

Now try to use the following modified command, which was used to create Figure 5-3.

```
Explorer.exe /e ,/root, C:\Text\
```

Carefully place the commas and the backslash that terminates the path. This command opens the Explorer window with the \Text folder shown as the root folder in the left pane and with the folder's contents shown in the right pane. With this construction, you can't switch to the parent folder of C:\Text in the Windows Explorer window because C:\Text is the root.

A command without the /e switch invokes a shell-style window of a single pane. The command below shows the contents of C:\Text and the file AUTHOR.DOC selected in the single pane window.

```
Explorer.exe , C:\Text\ , /select , C:\Text\author.doc
```

> **NOTE:** In Windows 95 and Microsoft Windows NT 4, you can show the contents of a folder and select a file in the right pane with the following statement:
>
> ```
> Explorer.exe /e , C:\Text\ , /select , C:\Text\author.doc
> ```
>
> This context doesn't work in Windows 98. This command will display the contents of the folder in the right pane, but it won't select the file.

Adding Placeholders to the Command String

Within the Registry *command* key, you can't define a fixed folder. The Windows Explorer parameters depend on the folder selected by the user. To get around this obstacle, substitute the folder's name with a placeholder. The command line to invoke a copy of Windows Explorer can contain the following items:

```
Explorer.exe /e , /root, /idlist, %I
```

The placeholder for the folder currently selected with the right mouse-click is *%I*. If you insert this command into the Registry, the New Explorer Window entry on the context menu will invoke a second copy of Windows Explorer showing the contents of the preselected folder or drive.

Putting It All Together in an INF File

So far, so good. Now, how do you install this new shell extension into the Registry? Because it's difficult to correctly enter all the keys and settings manually, and because using a REG file creates a mess if the Windows path is different from the settings in the REG file, my preferred method is to use an INF file.

Following are the statements included in the INF file. All lines starting with a semicolon are comments—you'll find that I've added a lot of comments to help clarify the workings of the file. (You can find the EXPLORE1.INF file in the \chapter5 folder of the sample files.)

```
; File: Explore1.inf  (G. Born)
; !!! Works only in Windows 98
;
; Install script to extend the Explorer's context menu.
; If the user right-clicks a folder symbol in the
; Explorer's window or in a shell window, the
; "New Explorer Window" command appears on the context menu.
; Selecting this command opens a new Explorer window.
; This feature can be removed with the Control Panel
; Add/Remove Programs uninstall function.

[version]
signature="$CHICAGO$"
SetupClass=BASE

; During install, add something into the Registry and copy the
; INF file into the Windows 98 \INF folder. Copy is required
; because we need this file for the uninstall function.

[DefaultInstall]
AddReg = Explore.AddReg
CopyFiles = Explore.CopyFiles.Inf
```

```
; This section defines how to uninstall the feature
; (remove the Registry entries and delete the INF file).
; The section name is defined in the [Explore.AddReg]
; section in the UninstallString value

[Explore.AddReg]

;  Add the newWindow verb and the string for the context menu
;  contained in %COMMAND_STRING%
HKCR,Folder\shell\newWindow,,,"%COMMAND_STRING%"

;  Add the command to activate the Explorer
HKCR,Folder\shell\newWindow\command,,,%COMMAND%

;  Required to set up the Uninstall feature

HKLM,%UnKEY%,DisplayName,,"%EXPLORE_REMOVE_DESC%"
HKLM,%UnKEY%,UninstallString,,"RunDll32 setupapi.dll, ⇁
InstallHinfSection DefaultUninstall 132 Explore1.Inf"

; Here we are with the uninstall part (which is executed
; after selecting the uninstall feature).

[DefaultUninstall]

DelReg = Explore.DelReg
DelFiles = Explore.DelFiles.Inf

; This section removes keys from the HKEY_CLASSES_ROOT\Folder\shell
; for the shell extension.

[Explore.DelReg]

;  Remove the newWindow verb and the string for the context menu
;  contained in %COMMAND_STRING%
HKCR,Folder\shell\newWindow

;  Remove the newWindow key in Uninstall by adding this line

HKLM,%UnKEY%

; Define the files to be copied. (Source and
; destination directories are defined in the following sections.)

[Explore.CopyFiles.Inf]
Explore1.Inf
```

(continued)

continued

```
; Define the files to be deleted. (Source and
; destination directories are defined in the following sections.)

[Explore.DelFiles.Inf]
Explore1.Inf
Explore1.PNF

; Definition for the source (use the path where the INF file
; is activated; 55 is defined in the SourceDisksFiles section)

[SourceDisksNames]
55="New Explorer Window","",1

[SourceDisksFiles]
Explore1.Inf=55

; Specify the destination. 17 is the logical disk ID for the
; Windows 98 INF subfolder

[DestinationDirs]
Explore.CopyFiles.Inf = 17
Explore.DelFiles.Inf = 17

; Define miscellaneous variables with strings.
; These variables are used in the preceding commands.
; During install, the variable will be replaced by its
; string value.
;
; For this example we define the strings for the context menu
; entry and for the name in the uninstall component list.

[Strings]
; This section contains two COMMAND declarations, one of which
; must be commented out

; Command to invoke the Explorer window
COMMAND = "Explorer.exe /e,/root,/idlist,%I"
; Command to invoke a shell window
;COMMAND = "Explorer.exe ,/root,/idlist,%I"

; String for the context menu entry
COMMAND_STRING = "New Explorer &Window"

; String for the Uninstall entry
EXPLORE_REMOVE_DESC = "Remove Born's (Win 98) New Explorer Window"
```

```
; String containing the Uninstall key
UnKEY = →
"Software\Microsoft\Windows\CurrentVersion\Uninstall\newWindow"

; End ***
```

Right-clicking the file and selecting Install from the context menu modifies the Registry. After installing the extension, right-click a folder or drive to open the context menu and see the New Explorer Window command. Right-clicking a file won't show this new command.

NOTE: If you have trouble installing the file, be sure the folders in the path to the source disk do not contain long filenames; only eight-character format names will be found during the install.

If you don't like this context menu extension, you can uninstall it—in fact, the most interesting feature of this INF file is its uninstall function.

1. Double-click the Add/Remove Programs icon in the Control Panel, and select the Install/Uninstall property page. This page should show the Remove Born's (Win 98) New Explorer Window entry, as shown in Figure 5-4.

2. Click this entry and then click Add/Remove.

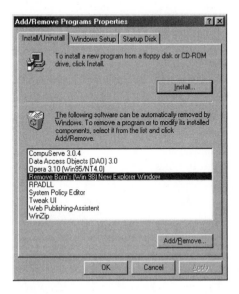

Figure 5-4.
The Install/Uninstall property page, which can be used to uninstall the new extension.

After you perform these steps, the extension will be removed; you can check this using the Registry Editor.

NOTE: You might have noticed that the EXPLORE1.INF program includes two Explorer command strings. The first string is the command to bring up a new Windows Explorer window. If you comment out this first string and uncomment the second string, the command brings up a shell window. The EXPLORE2.INF program in the \chapter5 folder of the sample files is the same as the EXPLORE1.INF program, but its shell window command is active and its Explorer window command is commented out.

EXPLORE1.INF file details   Although the INF file we looked at contains a lot of comments, I'd like to explain its details further. The file contains different sections, each beginning with a section head appearing in square brackets ([ ]), that define actions for the install and uninstall processes. The most important section is [Explore.AddReg], which contains the commands for entering the New Explorer Window function into the *HKEY_CLASSES_ROOT\ Folder\shell* key of the Registry. At least two lines are necessary in this section: one to add the *newWindow* key and the other to add the *command* subkey.

The rest of this section prepares the uninstall function. As noted earlier, Windows provides the Install/Uninstall property page so that you can uninstall software and clear the Registry of the software's related settings. Windows keeps the entries for this property page in the key *HKEY_LOCAL_MACHINE\ SOFTWARE\Microsoft\Windows\CurrentVersion\Uninstall*. Each application providing an uninstall function should add a subkey to this *Uninstall* key. The [Explore.AddReg] section of the INF file contains lines like the following, which adds the *newWindow* subkey to the *Uninstall* branch.

```
HKLM,Software\Microsoft\Windows\CurrentVersion\Uninstall\ ⟶
newWindow...
```

The lines start with the abbreviation for the root key—*HKLM*, in this case, which stands for *HKEY_LOCAL_MACHINE*. Parameters are separated by commas. The second parameter defines the subkey to be altered. In the sample lines above, you won't find *Software\Microsoft\Windows\...* as a second parameter. Instead, I've used the INF variable *%UnKEY%*, which contains this string. The variable is defined in the [Strings] section in the INF file. If the subkey defined by the second parameter doesn't exist, a new key is added. The third parameter defines the value's name, and the fourth parameter is left blank. The last parameter can contain the value for the name inserted in the key. The *newWindow* subkey in the *Uninstall* branch contains two entries:

- The first entry, *DisplayName*, contains the string shown on the Install/Uninstall property page. For our example, I used the text "Remove Born's (Win 98) New Explorer Window". This string is defined in the *%EXPLORE_REMOVE_DESC%* INF variable.

- The second entry in the *\Uninstall\newWindow* key has the name *UninstallString* and contains a command. This command will be executed when the user selects the entry from the Install/Uninstall property page and clicks Add/Remove.

Some application programs come with their own setup and uninstall programs; in these cases, the paths and filenames of the uninstall programs must be set in the *UninstallString* values (*C:\Windows\Unwise.exe\install.log*, for example). My INF file uses the poor man's approach: the command executes the Windows RunDLL32 program.

NOTE: At this point, history begins to create trouble for us. In Windows 95, we have to use RunDLL to call SETUPX.DLL. In Microsoft Windows NT 4.0 and Windows 98, we must employ RunDLL32 and call SETUPAPI.DLL. Thus, if we try to run a Windows 98 INF file under Windows 95, we hit a wall. For this reason, the EXPLORER1.INF file above has changed from the Windows 95 version that appeared in the previous edition of this book. Also, the explanations below are valid only for Windows 98. If you are interested in Windows 95 INF files, please consult *Inside the Registry for Microsoft Windows 95* (Microsoft Press, 1997).

The RunDLL32 program is an interface that calls other procedures in dynamic-link library (DLL) routines. All other entries in the command line are parameters, described below, for the DLL routine.

- The first parameter defines the name of the DLL file. (I used SETUP-API.DLL.)

- Further parameters are DLL-specific (and are documented in the Win32 SDK).

SETUPAPI.DLL needs several parameters, such as the name of the INF file that will be executed. In our example, this file is EXPLORE1.INF. For the INF file to be used for the uninstall, it must be located in the Windows INF folder, which is why we have to copy the INF file during the install process. [DefaultUninstall] is the name of the section in the INF file that contains the statements to be executed during the uninstall process. In EXPLORE1.INF, the

[DefaultUninstall] section contains a reference to the [Explore.DelReg] section and the DelReg keyword is used instead of AddReg, causing SETUPAPI.DLL to remove all Registry entries defined in the [Explore.AddReg] section.

> **NOTE:** For those of you familiar with the previous edition of this book, let me mention a few other facts. In the version of EXPLORER1.INF file created for Windows 95, I used only one section, [Explore.AddReg], for install and uninstall. This trick won't work in Windows 98. During testing, I found that the SETUPAPI routine left empty keys in the *Folder* branch, which causes faulty context menus. Therefore, I had to change the structure of the INF file to that shown in the version above. The new file cleans the Registry during uninstall in a predefined way. I also had to take care to delete the PNF file, created by Windows 98 during install, in the uninstall step. (Alas—sometimes it's hard to be a programmer.) Further details about Windows 98 INF file structures are discussed in Chapter 7.

Activating MS-DOS from Windows Explorer

Windows provides a great user interface, but sometimes I feel more comfortable running certain commands in the MS-DOS window. Copy, Rename, and Delete, for example, are faster in MS-DOS. Unfortunately, you have to click several commands to reach the MS-DOS window and then you have to use the *CD* (change directory) command to switch to the requested subfolder. Wouldn't it be more efficient to right-click a folder's icon and select an MS-DOS command, as shown in Figure 5-5, from the context menu?

All you need to do is hack a little bit in the Registry. At the very least, you have to add a new verb (such as *dos*) with a *command* subkey in the *HKEY_CLASSES_ROOT\Folder\shell* branch. The lines of the following REG file show the commands necessary to register the DOS command processor as a shell extension:

```
REGEDIT4

[HKEY_CLASSES_ROOT\Folder\shell\dos]
@="MS-DOS"

[HKEY_CLASSES_ROOT\Folder\shell\dos\command]
@="command.com"
```

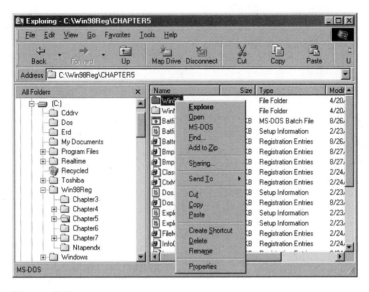

Figure 5-5.
The MS-DOS entry in the context menu.

Since you don't need to indicate a path to invoke the DOS command processor COMMAND.COM, you can use a REG file to extend the Registry without risk. The only disadvantage of this REG file solution is the missing uninstall feature. If you need this feature, use an INF file with the following statements:

```
; File: DOS.inf  (G. Born)
; Windows 98 Version !
;
; Install script to extend the Explorer's context menu
; with a DOS command
;
; If the user right-clicks a folder in the Explorer's
; window or in a shell window, the MS-DOS command
; will occur on the context menu. Selecting this
; command invokes the MS-DOS window and highlights the folder.


[version]
signature="$CHICAGO$"
SetupClass=BASE


; Add the extension into the Registry
```

(continued)

continued

```
[DefaultInstall]
AddReg = DOS.AddReg
CopyFiles = DOS.CopyFiles.Inf

; Uninstall part

[DefaultUninstall]

DelReg = DOS.DelReg
DelFiles = DOS.DelFiles.Inf

; This part adds the keys to the Registry. The feature
; is registered in HKEY_CLASSES_ROOT\Folder\shell.

[DOS.AddReg]

; Add the dos verb and the string for the context menu
; contained in %COMMAND_STRING%
HKCR,Folder\shell\dos,,,"%COMMAND_STRING%"

; Add the command to activate COMMAND.COM
HKCR,Folder\shell\dos\command,,,%COMMAND%

; *** This stuff is required to set up the Uninstall feature
; Attention: we have used RunDll32 SetupApi.dll ...
; instead of RunDll Setupx.dll ...
;
HKLM,%UnKey%,DisplayName,,"%DOS_REMOVE_DESC%"
HKLM,%UnKey%,UninstallString,,"RunDll32 setupapi.dll,
    InstallHinfSection DefaultUninstall 132 DOS.Inf"

[DOS.DelReg]

; Remove the command to activate COMMAND.COM
HKCR,Folder\shell\dos\command,,,%COMMAND%

; Remove the dos verb and the string for the context menu
; contained in %COMMAND_STRING%
HKCR,Folder\shell\dos

; Don't forget to remove the dos key in Uninstall.
; This is done by adding the following line.

HKLM,Software\Microsoft\Windows\CurrentVersion\Uninstall\dos
```

```
; Define the files to be copied, and define source and
; destination directories

[DOS.CopyFiles.Inf]
DOS.Inf

; Define the files to be deleted during uninstall

[DOS.DelFiles.Inf]
DOS.Inf
DOS.PNF

; Definition for the source (use the path where
; the INF file is activated; 55 is defined in SourceDisksFiles)

[SourceDisksNames]
55="MS-DOS","",1

[SourceDisksFiles]
DOS.Inf=55

; Now we have to specify the destination. 17 is the
; logical disk ID for the Windows INF subfolder.

[DestinationDirs]
DOS.CopyFiles.Inf = 17
DOS.DelFiles.Inf = 17
; Define miscellaneous variables

[Strings]
; Command to invoke COMMAND.COM
COMMAND = "command.com"

; String for the context menu entry
COMMAND_STRING = "MS-DOS"

; String for the Uninstall entry
DOS_REMOVE_DESC = "Remove Born's (Win 98) MS-DOS Shell Extension"

; String containing the Uninstall key
UnKEY = "Software\Microsoft\Windows\CurrentVersion\Uninstall\dos"

; End ***
```

This file sets the Registry entries for the shell extension and the uninstall feature. You can remove this extension by using the Install/Uninstall property page on the Add/Remove Program Properties property sheet.

NOTE: You will find the files DOS.REG and DOS.INF in the \chapter5 folder of the sample files. Go to Chapter 7 for further information about the uninstall feature used in Windows 98 INF files.

Printing a Directory List from Windows Explorer

Windows Explorer is a marvelous tool for working with features such as files, icons, and folders. But if you're like me, you get lost wading through a huge file list. I remember the good old MS-DOS days when I could use the command *DIR *.* >PRN:* to print the directory. I'd use the listing to check which files had to be altered, copied, deleted, and so on. Nothing comparable is available in Windows Explorer. (And I know such a feature is on the wish list of many users.)

What about using the MS-DOS window, which we looked at in the previous section? Couldn't we run the DOS.INF file to register this extension, right-click a folder or a drive, select MS-DOS from the context menu to get to the MS-DOS window, and then enter the *DIR >PRN:* command?

Well, we *could,* but why perform tasks if we can get Windows to perform them for us? Let's evaluate our options. Maybe we should try to use the *DIR *.* > PRN:* command in the Registry. The command makes sense, but I haven't figured out exactly how to get MS-DOS piping to work in a Registry command. So our solution is to store the command in a simple MS-DOS batch file and enter a command to execute this BAT file in the Registry. The BAT file solution is the best one because we also need a form feed at the end of the report to advance the last page. The following lines show the contents of a simple BAT file (PRNDIR.BAT, located in the \chapter5 folder of the sample files) that prints a directory.

```
@ECHO OFF
DIR %1 >PRN:
ECHO ^L >PRN:
ECHO ON
```

The form feed is sent by the *ECHO ^L>PRN:* line. The *%1* is the placeholder for the current directory, which is supplied by Windows Explorer when the BAT file is invoked.

NOTE: By the way, I used the MS-DOS program EDIT.COM to create the BAT file. Notepad won't allow you to enter the ^L character. Another tip: on PostScript printers, you can use the command *ECHO SHOW >PRN:* to advance one page. Also, *PRN* might not work if you're hooked up to a network printer, in which case you'd want to substitute the path to the printer for *PRN*.

Now all we have to do is register the BAT program as a new context menu command in the Registry. To do so, add a new verb in *HKEY_CLASSES_ROOT\Folder\shell* with a *command* subkey whose *Default* value defines the string that invokes the BAT file, like so:

```
HKEY_CLASSES_ROOT\Folder\shell\PrnDir = "Print Directory"
HKEY_CLASSES_ROOT\Folder\shell\PrnDir\command ="<Path>PRNDIR.BAT %1"
```

Notice that the *<Path>* parameter in the lines above is still undefined, so you can't use these lines in a REG file. The reason is simple. Let me explain where the BAT file is stored and what you need to know to use a BAT file.

Storing and Selecting Properties for the BAT File

The first issue we need to resolve is where we are going to store the BAT file for our planned shell extension. This information will be of interest if you plan to install other shell extensions too. The simplest solution would be to store it in the \Windows folder because the programs in this folder don't require a path description in a command—but don't do it! Essentially, storing software in your Windows folder spoils it with clutter; after you uninstall this kind of software, you'll have an extremely difficult time determining which files are superfluous and can be deleted. (Do not believe that the uninstall function will clear your hard disk—I have hundreds of files on my hard disk left there by uninstall programs and little idea which ones I can wipe out.) Well-designed software uses its own folder to store its files. Here are some appropriate locations for this purpose:

- An install program can create a new folder in the root directory of a drive (for example, C:\PRNDIR). If you distribute your application with such a program, the install routine will give the user a chance to select a new name for the destination directory. (But we can't use this approach, because I want to use an INF file to install the extension.)

- You can use the \Program Files folder, which is created by Windows, to store common Windows tools (such as WordPad). If you create your own subfolder here, you can easily clean it after uninstalling software.

■ You can create a subfolder with its own name in the \Windows directory, indicating that the program belongs to Windows.

I decided to create a Windows subfolder and name it \Born to make it clear who created the mess. I'll also use this subfolder to store other files discussed in this book.

The second issue we need to resolve is which properties we want to assign to the BAT file. We want this program to always run minimized as an icon on the taskbar, to run in the background, and to terminate after printing the directory. These options for an MS-DOS window can be controlled with its property sheet: right-click the BAT file, and select Properties from the context menu. Set the options required for the program to run minimized in the background. When you close the property sheet, a Program Information File (PIF) is created with the settings you selected. You can store this PIF file in the same folder as the BAT file. (See PRNDIR.PIF in the \chapter5 folder of the sample files.)

You can also set the DOS properties of your BAT program in the APPS. INF file, which is located in the Windows \INF subfolder. APPS.INF is used to register the properties of several MS-DOS applications, but I won't discuss this topic here.

Installing the Print Directory Extension

We need the BAT file, the PIF file, and an INF file to install the Print Directory extension.

NOTE: Programmers, you can write your own Windows application to print a directory list. And you can register your file with less overhead—no PIF file is needed—but you should still take a look at the discussion about file locations.

The following INF file contains the commands to register the Print Directory shell extension and copy the required files. (You'll find the PRNDIR.INF file in the \chapter5 folder of the sample files.)

```
; File: PrnDir.INF  (by G. Born)
; Windows 98 version
;
; Install Print Directory command on Explorer's
; context menu: Copy PRNDIR.BAT and PRNDIR.INF into the
; Windows folder \Born, and add the Registry keys.
; Right-clicking a folder (after installing the
; extension) shows the command.
; The command invokes the PRNDIR.BAT file, which runs
; minimized in the background and prints the directory.
;
```

```
; The INF file also provides an uninstall function to
; remove the Registry entries and files copied
; during install. The Windows subfolder \Born will
; not be removed. (It can be used for other extensions.)

[version]
signature="$Chicago$"

; During install: Keep the INF file for uninstall,
; copy BAT and PIF files, and update the Registry

[DefaultInstall]
CopyFiles = Explore.CopyFiles.Inf, Explore.CopyFiles.Bat
AddReg = Explore.AddReg

; During uninstall: Delete the INF/PNF file,
; the BAT and PIF files, and update the Registry

[DefaultUninstall]
DelReg = Explore.DelReg
; use a separate section to delete INF/PNF files
DelFiles = Explore.DelFiles.Inf, Explore.CopyFiles.Bat

; Update the Registry keys

[Explore.AddReg]
HKCR,Folder\shell\prnDir,,,"%EXPLORE_DESC%"
HKCR,Folder\shell\prnDir\command,,,"%10%\%MY_FOLDER%\%COMMAND%"

; Add uninstall stuff
HKLM,%UnKey%,DisplayName,,"%REMOVE_DESC%"
HKLM,%UnKey%,UninstallString,,"RunDll132 →
setupapi.dll,InstallHinfSection DefaultUninstall 132 PrnDir.inf"

; Execute the uninstall part

[Explore.DelReg]
HKCR,Folder\shell\prnDir

; Don't forget this key for the uninstall part
HKLM,%UnKey%

; INF file to be copied in the Windows INF subfolder

[Explore.CopyFiles.Inf]
PrnDir.Inf
```

(continued)

continued

```
; BAT and PIF files needed by the extension, copied
; into the Windows subfolder defined in %MY_FOLDER%

[Explore.CopyFiles.Bat]
PrnDir.bat
PrnDir.pif

; Files we must remove

[Explore.DelFiles.Inf]
PrnDir.Inf
PrnDir.PNF

[DestinationDirs]
Explore.CopyFiles.bat = 10,%MY_FOLDER%
Explore.CopyFiles.Inf = 17
Explore.DelFiles.Inf = 17

[SourceDisksNames]
55="Print Directory","",1

[SourceDisksFiles]
PrnDir.inf=55
PrnDir.bat=55
PrnDir.pif=55

; Strings with destination folders, commands, and
; context menu text

[Strings]
MY_FOLDER = "Born"
COMMAND = "PRNDIR.BAT %1"
Explore_DESC = "Print Directory"
REMOVE_DESC = "Remove Born's (Win 98) Print Directory"
UnKey="Software\Microsoft\Windows\CurrentVersion\Uninstall\prnDir"
; End ***
```

After running Install on the INF file, you should be able to print directory contents by right-clicking a folder and selecting Print Directory. To remove this shell extension, use the Install/Uninstall property page (available through the Add/Remove Programs icon in the Control Panel).

NOTE: The uninstall process will delete the files copied during the install but will leave the folder \Born in the Windows folder because the \Born folder can be used for other files.

Modifying Miscellaneous System Settings

When you open a folder, the shell opens a window that displays the folder's contents. By default, Windows Explorer opens only one window to show the contents of the selected folder. The shell can use one window to show the contents of only the most recently opened folder, or it can open a new window for each folder you open. You can change the settings of each folder window that is opened, and Windows will store these settings (such as window size, icon size, and so on) and reuse them the next time the folder is opened. You can also set options to hide or show file extensions and to exclude system files from Windows Explorer's view. Let's examine how the Registry supports these and other features.

Hiding and Showing System Files and Extensions

You can hide or show system files (such as DLL, SYS, and VXD files) as well as MS-DOS file extensions in both the shell and Windows Explorer windows. Set the global hide and show options on the View property page of the Folder Options property sheet (see Figure 5-6 on the following page), which is available by selecting Folder Options from Windows Explorer's View menu. Following are explanations of some of these hide and show options:

- The Hidden Files options—Do Not Show Hidden Or System Files, Do Not Show Hidden Files, and Show All Files control whether system files appear in the shell windows.

- The Hide File Extensions For Known File Types option hides (when checked) or shows (when unchecked) file extensions in the shell windows. The global status of this option can be overruled for certain registered file types through options that appear in the Add New File Type and Edit File Type dialog boxes (which both can be reached from the File Types property page on Windows Explorer's Folder Options property sheet). Two Registry values, *NeverShowExt* and *AlwaysShowExt*, control this option and exist (in mutually exclusive fashion) in the key *HKEY_CLASSES_ROOT\file type*, *file type* being the specific file type, such as *1STfile*. (See Chapter 3 for further details on this subject.)

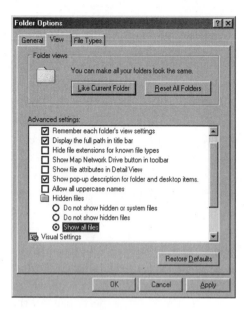

Figure 5-6.
The View property page.

Windows 98 includes other options to customize the shell and Windows Explorer views. All these settings are user-specific. Windows 98 keeps the options in the Registry key *HKEY_CURRENT_USER\Software\Microsoft\Windows\ CurrentVersion\Explorer\Advanced*. This key contains several values that control the settings on the View property page of the Folder Options property sheet. The options shown in Figure 5-6 are associated with their Registry values in the list that follows:

- Remember Each Folder's View Settings. Checking this box sets the value *ClassicViewState* to *0x00000000* and forces the shell to store the settings for each folder. Unchecking this value sets *ClassicView State* to *0x00000001*.

- Display The Full Path In Title Bar. This value is the only one in this list not stored in the ...*Explorer\Advanced* key. Checking this box sets the value *FullPath* in the ...*Explorer\CabinetState* key to *0x00000001* and makes the file path appear in the Windows Explorer and shell window title bars.

- Hide File Extensions For Known File Types. Checking this box sets the value *HideFileExt* to *0x00000001* and hides file extensions in the shell and Windows Explorer windows. Unchecking the box sets the value to *0x0000000*.

- Show Map Network Drive Button In Toolbar. Checking this box sets the value *MapNetDrvBtn* to *0x00000001* and shows the Map Network Drive button on the shell window toolbar and the Windows Explorer window toolbar. Unchecking the box sets the value to *0x0000000*.

- Show File Attributes In Detail View. Checking this box sets the value *ShowAttribCol* to *0x00000001* and shows the Attributes column in the Windows Explorer window when Detail view is selected.

- Show Pop-up Description For Folder And Desktop Items. This option controls whether QuickInfo tips for folders are shown. The option is associated with the value *ShowInfoTip*, which can be set to *0x00000000* (causing the tips to be shown) or *0x00000001*.

- Hidden Files. The three options available in this category are associated with the key's *Hidden* value, which can be set to *0x00000000* (the equivalent of selecting Do Not Show Hidden Or System Files), *0x00000001* (related to the Show All Files option), or *0x00000002* (related to the Do Not Show Hidden Files option).

- Hide Icons When Desktop Is Viewed As Web Page. Checking this box sets the value *HideIcon* to *0x00000000*. The value is set to *0x00000001* when the option is not selected.

- Allow All Uppercase Names. Checking this option sets the *DontPrettyPath* value to *0x00000001* and allows for files and folders to be displayed in all uppercase letters in Windows Explorer and shell views.

But take care, the text shown on the View property page and the values used for check boxes and radio buttons can be customized. The key *HKEY_LOCAL_ MACHINE\SOFTWARE\Microsoft\Windows\CurrentVersion\explorer\Advanced* is used to customize the entries for the options on the View property page (see Figure 5-7 on the following page).

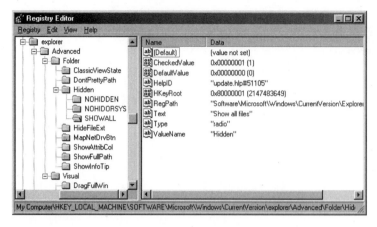

Figure 5-7.
Entries for customizing the View property page.

> **NOTE:** Other shell settings are stored as bit flags in the values stored in the key *HKEY_CURRENT_USER\Software\Microsoft\Windows\CurrentVersion\Explorer\Streams*.

In the General tab of the Folder Option property sheet (select Folder Options from the View menu in Windows Explorer), you can select the Windows Desktop Update mode. Selecting the option Custom, Based On Settings You Choose and clicking Settings opens the Custom Settings dialog box shown in Figure 5-8. Most of these options are stored in binary value streams. At least one of these options is going into the following key:

HKEY_CURRENT_USER\Software\Microsoft\Windows\CurrentVersion\Explorer\CabinetState

The fifth bit (counting from 0) of the fifth byte of the *Settings* value contains the Browse Folders state. If the bit is set, each folder will be opened in its own Window. If the value is *0*, each folder will be opened in the same window.

You can also set your click options from the Custom Settings dialog box. If you select Single-click To Open An Item, you're given two choices for the icon underline display. These choices are stored in the value *IconUnderline* in the key *HKEY_CURRENT_USER\Software\Microsoft\Windows\CurrentVersion\Explorer*.

A value of *02 00 00 00* sets the option Underline Icon Titles Only When I Point At Them. The value of *03 00 00 00* sets the option Underline Icon Titles Consistent With My Browser Settings.

Figure 5-8.
Custom settings for folder view.

Customizing a Few Shell Options

Now let's look at several more options that you can customize by using Registry settings. These options are not available through any of the standard Windows 98 property sheets, but I'll discuss below how you can load the SHELL98.ADM template to extend the System Policy Editor's Local User property page to access them.

Disabling the Shell's Context Menu

When you right-click on a drive, folder, file, or other desktop item, a context menu is displayed. During the last few years, I've received requests from system administrators asking whether there is a way to disable these context menus in the shell. Well, here's a simple way to control context menus in Windows 98. Previously in this chapter, we've looked at the following key, which contains several values that control shell options.

HKEY_CURRENT_USER\Software\Microsoft\Windows\CurrentVersion\ Policies\Explorer

If the value *NoViewContextMenu* is set to *0x00000001*, the context menu will be hidden. Removing this value or setting it to *0x00000000* brings the context menu back. (You must reset the shell, by logging off and logging back on, for example, to turn the context menu back on.)

NOTE: Use the files NOCTXMEN.REG and CTXMENON.REG in the \chapter5 folder of the samples files to hide and show, respectively, the shell's context menu. Or you can use the System Policy Editor with the SHELLM.ADM template, located by default in the Windows\INF folder, to customize this option.

Removing the File Menu

The Shell and the Windows Explorer windows have a File menu with several menu options such as New, Close, and so on. Sometimes system administrators want to prevent users from accessing this menu. This can be done by adding the value *NoFileMenu* to the following key:

HKEY_CURRENT_USER\Software\Microsoft\Windows\CurrentVersion\ Policies\Explorer

A value of *0x00000001* hides the File menu after the next system startup. (See Figure 5-9.) Removing this value or setting it to *0x00000000* and then resetting the shell (by logging off and logging on again) brings the File menu back.

NOTE: Use the files NOFILEMN.REG and FILEMNON.REG in the \chapter5 folder of the sample files to disable and enable, respectively, the File menu. After the next logon, the changes will take effect.

TIP: System administrators can customize the settings discussed in this section by using the System Policy Editor. This topic will be discussed in the section "Customizing the Shell Settings By Using the System Policy Editor," beginning on the next page.

Disabling the InfoTip Window

Moving the mouse pointer over some desktop or shell items opens a small window containing InfoTip text (see Figure 5-9). I have mentioned in earlier chapters that the *InfoTip* value (which is set in several keys) is used to define this InfoTip text.

If you want to disable these InfoTip windows, add the *ShowInfoTip* value set to *0x00000001* to the key *HKEY_CURRENT_USER\Software\Microsoft\ Windows\CurrentVersion\Explorer\Advanced*. If the value is removed or set to *0x00000000*, the InfoTips are shown again.

NOTE: You can use the files NOINFO.REG and INFOON.REG in the \chapter5 folder of the sample files to disable and enable, respectively, the InfoText window. Or you can use the System Policy Editor with the SHELL98.ADM template to customize this option.

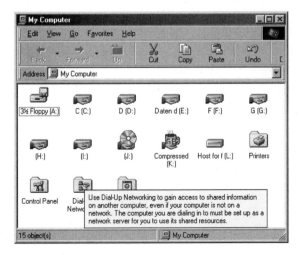

Figure 5-9.
Shell window showing InfoTip text and a hidden File menu.

Customizing the Shell Settings by Using the System Policy Editor

Installing the System Policy Editor doesn't automatically enable all policies available for Windows 98. The \chapter7\adm folder of the sample files contains templates (ADM files) for the System Policy Editor. Policy templates can be used to define policies from within the System Policy Editor. Use the following steps to load a template:

1. Copy the ADM file to your hard disk.

2. Start the System Policy Editor, and select Policy Template from the Options menu. The Policy Template Options dialog box is opened.

3. Use the Add button to select the path and filename of the ADM file you want to add. (Use SHELL98.ADM to get the template with the shell options, for instance.)

4. Close the Policy Template Options dialog box.

After you perform these steps, the System Policy Editor contains new options. You can see these new options by opening the local Registry (select Open Registry from the File menu) and selecting Local User Properties. You will find new entries on the Policies property page, as shown in Figure 5-10 on the following page.

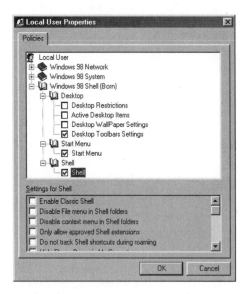

Figure 5-10.
Extended Local User Properties for the Windows 98 shell.

Below I will discuss a few additional Registry entries that you can use to customize Shell and Windows Explorer options.

Force Classic Style View

Windows Explorer contains menu entries, such as Go and Favorites, that reflect the new Web features of Windows 98. If you don't use these features and don't want to see them, you can force Windows to use a classic style for the shell and Windows Explorer windows by adding the value *ClassicShell* set to *0x00000001* to the following key:

HKEY_CURRENT_USER\Software\Microsoft\Windows\CurrentVersion\ Policies\Explorer

After the next login, the Web features in the menu bar and the options Web Style and Custom, Based On Settings You Choose on the General property page of the Folder Options dialog box are hidden or disabled. Removing this value or setting it to *0* enables the new Web-based features.

NOTE: Use the files CLASSICVIEW.REG and NEWVIEW.REG in the \chapter5 folder of the sample files to switch between both modes. Or you can use the file SHELLM.ADM delivered with the System Policy Editor to add this option to the Local User property page. (See Figure 5-10.)

Disable Customization of Folders

In the shell and in Windows Explorer, you can customize the appearance of individual folders. These custom settings are stored on the hard disk and require a lot of space on the system. To control whether the command Customize This Folder in the View menu is shown or hidden, use the value *NoCustomizeWebView* in this key:

HKEY_CURRENT_USER\Software\Microsoft\Windows\CurrentVersion\ Policies\Explorer

A value of *0x00000001* in *NoCustomizeWebView* hides this command.

Defining the Column Settings of the Windows Explorer Window

When you select the Details mode from the View menu in Windows Explorer, the file list in the right pane of the Explorer window is shown with five columns: Name, Size, Type, Modified, and Attribute. To change the width of these columns, drag the column separator left or right. The information about the most recently used column size is kept in the Registry key *HKEY_CURRENT_ USER\Software\Microsoft\Windows\CurrentVersion\Explorer* in the *Directory ColsX* value. This binary value consists of WORDs, described in Table 5-1, that define the initial size of each column.

Column Settings in the *Explorer* Key

WORD	Definition
0	Width of Windows Explorer's Name column
1	Width of Windows Explorer's Size column
2	Width of Windows Explorer's Type column
3	Width of Windows Explorer's Modified column
4	Width of Windows Explorer's Attribute column

Table 5-1.
Coding of the DirectoryColsX *value.*

Other values in this key—*NetDomainColsX*, *NetServerColsX*, and *Doc FindColsX*—also contain byte streams with the initial column sizes for the Workgroup folder, the Entire Network folder, and the Find window.

N O T E : The shell window (that is, My Computer) uses a similar construction, which is discussed in the following sections.

Removing Shortcut Symbols

When you create a shortcut to an item (such as a document, folder, drive, and so on), a small arrow is displayed in the lower left corner of the item's icon, as in the icons shown in Figure 5-11.

PrnDir   PrnDir.inf

Figure 5-11.
You can determine whether an item is a shortcut by looking for an arrow on the icon.

The icons for PIF files also appear with this small arrow. You can remove this shortcut symbol from the icons for shortcuts and for PIF file types. The information about the shortcut is stored in the *HKEY_CLASSES_ROOT* branch of the Registry: shortcuts are registered in the *lnkfile* key; PIF files are registered in the *piffile* key. If these keys contain the value *IsShortcut*, the arrow will be shown. *IsShortcut* is always set to *""*. Deleting this entry from a key will remove the Shortcut arrow after the screen is refreshed.

> NOTE: The *NeverShowExt* flag in the *lnkfile* and *piffile* keys suppresses the display of file extensions in the Windows Explorer and shell windows. Remove this flag and the extensions LNK and PIF are shown. In either case, the LNK extension isn't shown on the desktop in an icon title because the extension for the file or application associated with the LNK file is shown instead ("Shortcut to Winword.exe", for example).

You can use the Registry Editor to strip out the *IsShortcut* values, but using the following INF file is more convenient. (You can find SHORTCUT.INF in the \chapter5 folder of the sample files.)

```
; File: Shortcut.INF
; Windows 98 Version
;
; Remove the Shortcut arrow shown for shortcuts on the shell.
;
; The INF file also provides an uninstall function to
; recover the factory settings.

[version]
signature="$CHICAGO$"
SetupClass=BASE
```

```
; During install: Remove IsShortcut entries, set uninstall
; information

[DefaultInstall]
CopyFiles = Shortcut.CopyFiles.Inf
DelReg = Shortcut.Remove.Reg
AddReg = Shortcut.AddReg

; During uninstall: Delete the INF file,
; the BAT and PIF files, and update the Registry.

[DefaultUninstall]
AddReg = Shortcut.Remove.Reg
DelReg = Shortcut.DelReg
DelFiles = Shortcut.DelFiles.Inf

; Remove the IsShortcut flags

[Shortcut.Remove.Reg]
HKCR,lnkfile,IsShortcut,,""
HKCR,piffile,IsShortcut,,""

; Set uninstall keys

[Shortcut.AddReg]
; Add uninstall stuff
HKLM,%UnKey%,DisplayName,,"%REMOVE_DESC%"
HKLM,%UnKey%,UninstallString,,"RunDll32          ⤵
setupapi.dll,InstallHinfSection DefaultUninstall 132 Shortcut.inf"

[Shortcut.DelReg]
; Don't forget to uninstall this key
HKLM,SOFTWARE\Microsoft\Windows\CurrentVersion\Uninstall\ ⤵
IsShortcutOn

; INF file to be copied to the Windows INF subfolder

[Shortcut.CopyFiles.Inf]
Shortcut.Inf

[Shortcut.DelFiles.Inf]
Shortcut.Inf
Shortcut.PNF

[DestinationDirs]
```

(continued)

continued

```
Shortcut.CopyFiles.Inf = 17
Shortcut.DelFiles.Inf = 17

[SourceDisksNames]
55="Shortcut Remove","",1

[SourceDisksFiles]
Shortcut.inf=55

[Strings]

REMOVE_DESC = "Restore (Win 98) Shortcut arrow (Born)"

UnKey= ↴
"SOFTWARE\Microsoft\Windows\CurrentVersion\Uninstall\IsShortcutOn"
; End ***
```

Right-clicking the INF file and selecting Install from the context menu removes the Shortcut arrows. You can restore the default settings by clicking the Restore (Win 98) Shortcut Arrow (Born) option on the Install/Uninstall property page (select Control Panel and then Add/Remove Programs).

Removing the Shortcut To Prefix from the Icon Title

When you create a shortcut, the text *Shortcut to* is attached to the filename as a prefix and used to build the shortcut's icon title (for example, *Shortcut to EXPLORER.EXE*). Tweak UI provides a function to hide this prefix. Follow these steps:

1. Start Tweak UI (available through the Control Panel), and select the Explorer property page.

2. Uncheck the Prefix Shortcut To On New Shortcuts option in the Settings group (see Figure 5-12).

A system reset might be necessary to activate this modification. The *Shortcut to* prefix is controlled by the *link* value, which is available in several Registry keys. One of these keys is *HKEY_USERS\xxxx\Software\Microsoft\Windows\CurrentVersion\Explorer*, where *xxxx* stands for the user name (or for *.Default*). If this key doesn't contain the *link* value or the value is set to *00 00 00 00*, the prefix is hidden.

> NOTE: The *link* value in the *HKEY_CURRENT_USER* key is sometimes used as a counter that is incremented each time a shortcut is created. Modifying this value isn't required, because a system restart will rebuild the whole branch from *HKEY_USERS* anyway.

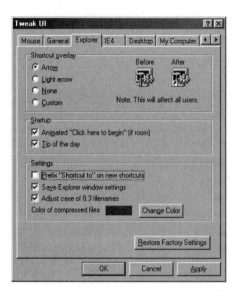

Figure 5-12.
The Tweak UI Explorer property page.

How the Shell Window Settings Are Saved

You can specify unique characteristics for any folder window opened in shell mode (such as My Computer)—for example, you might display large icons for one folder and a file list for another. In most cases, when you close the window and reopen it later, the settings you specified remain.

How does this work? As long as your computer is not in View As Web Page mode, the settings for the folder windows are saved in the Registry in the same way that the settings for the Windows Explorer window are saved, except that Windows uses a behind-the-scenes construction comparable to a "cache" to save the settings for more than one window at a time. When you open a folder, Windows checks whether the settings for that folder are still in the cache. If Windows finds the settings in the Registry, those settings are used to open the folder window. If Windows finds no settings, it uses the default settings. When a folder window is closed, one record is written to the cache with the settings for that particular window configuration. In Windows 95 and Windows NT 4.0, the settings for up to 28 different window configurations could be stored. As far as I can tell, Windows 98 supports up to 99 different folder windows plus the desktop. If Windows has stored the settings for 99 windows and you close a window with a group of settings not yet stored in the cache, the record of the settings for that window overwrites one of the existing records in the cache.

Windows uses a key construction for storing such records in the cache that is similar in construction to the MRU lists discussed in Chapter 4. The key *HKEY_CURRENT_USER\Software\Microsoft\Windows\CurrentVersion\ Explorer\StreamMRU* contains values named *0, 1, 2, 3*, and so on up to *99*. Each entry stores a byte stream containing several flags with some of the status information for the folder. The *MRUListEx* value in this key defines the order of the 99 entries.

The rest of the data for each of the 99 folders is stored in a second subkey: *HKEY_CURRENT_USER\Software\Microsoft\Windows\CurrentVersion\ Explorer\Streams*. This key contains subkeys with the names *0, 1, 2*, and so on that define the streams carrying the data for all folders. For each entry in *StreamMRU*, you will find a corresponding subkey in *Streams*. The mapping between the *StreamMRU* values and the subkeys in *Streams* is set to the following: value *0* corresponds to the subkey *\Streams\0*, value *2* corresponds to the subkey *\Streams\1*, and so on.

A *Streams* subkey can have two values: *CabView* and *ViewView2*. Both entries are byte streams defining options for the folder's window. (But the exact coding of each byte isn't clear to me.) The only exception is the *Desktop* key, which can also contain a *Taskbar* value and a *Toolbars* value.

Modifying Miscellaneous Network Keys

Windows 98 provides several keys to control the network options available in the shell. I discuss these options and their related keys in the sections that follow.

Recent and Persistent Network Connections

The association of a drive letter to a network service is stored in the key *HKEY_CURRENT_USER\Network\Persistent*. This key contains subkeys named after each drive and printer associated with a persistent network device (*G, H, I*, and *LPT1*, for example). Each key contains several values defining the network settings, as listed below:

- *ProviderName* defines the name of the service provider (*"Microsoft Network"*, for example).

- *UserName* stores the user name.

- *RemotePath* contains a string with the network path in UNC conventions (*"\\C486-1\C486"*, for example).

The key *HKEY_CURRENT_USER\Network\Recent* stores a list of the recent network connections made by the computer. Each connection is stored in its own subkey (named, for example, *./../C486-1/C486*). Each of these subkeys contains the values *ProviderName, UserName,* and *ConnectionType* (a binary value) storing the particular connection's data. The keys are updated each time the user changes a network connection in the shell.

Clear Last User Name in Logon Window

Windows 98 shows the name of the last user logged on to the system in the Welcome To Windows dialog box. For security purposes, system administrators often hide this name so that the dialog box appears as it does in Figure 5-13.

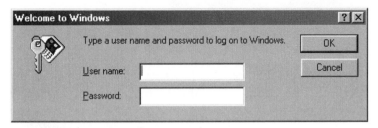

Figure 5-13.
The Welcome To Windows dialog box with the last user name hidden.

Tweak UI provides an option on the Paranoia property page called Clear Last User At Logon that controls whether the last user name is shown in the Welcome To Windows dialog box. Windows keeps this option in the key *HKEY_LOCAL_MACHINE\SOFTWARE\Microsoft\Windows\CurrentVersion\ Winlogon*. If this key includes a value *DontDisplayLastUserName* set to *"1"*, Windows won't show the last user name during logon. Setting this value to *"0"* or deleting it forces Windows 98 to show the name of the last user logged on to the system.

> **N O T E :** Use the file LOGON.REG in the \chapter5 folder of the sample files to set *DontDisplayLastUserName*. This feature won't work if you use the Microsoft Family Logon feature, a service that can be installed through the Network Properties property sheet.

Registering a New Template for the New Command

You can create a new document by using the shell's New command, accessed by right-clicking an empty space on the desktop and selecting New from the context menu. The New command contains a submenu with a list of optional document formats. (See Figure 5-14 on the following page.) You can modify this list by registering your own document templates.

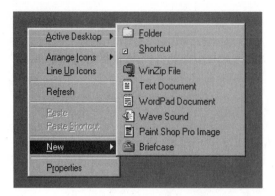

Figure 5-14.
The New command on the shell's context menu.

The Tweak UI property sheet contains a property page named New—Templates in previous versions of Tweak UI—that lets you register a new template with a simple drag-and-drop operation. However, when you ship a software package, you'll want your install program to register the new template type, and you can't use Tweak UI. So the best way to register a new document template is by following these steps:

1. Use your application program to create a document template in the required format, and store this template file in the Windows subfolder \ShellNew.

2. Search for the file extension key (*.bmp*, for example) in the *HKEY_CLASSES_ROOT* branch, and extend this key with a *ShellNew* subkey.

3. Insert an entry with the name *NullFile* into the *ShellNew* key, and set the value to an empty string. The New command will create an empty file with the file extension used in the Registry (a BMP file, for example). This can also be done for text files.

4. To use your template for the new file, insert an entry with the name *FileName* instead of the name *NullFile* and set the value for this item to the template's filename.

The next time the system is reset, you should find the new file type in the New command's submenu. The following REG file statements will register a new template for an empty BAT file type. (BATTEMPL.REG is in the \chapter5 folder of the sample files.) The *HKEY_CLASSES_ROOT\.bat* key is already registered in Windows 98, so no path definitions are necessary.

```
REGEDIT4
```

```
[HKEY_CLASSES_ROOT\.bat\ShellNew]
"Nullfile"=""
```

After you register this file by double-clicking it, the New command's sub-menu should contain a new MS-DOS Batch File entry. Most of the templates preinstalled by Windows 98 use a *NullFile* entry.

The following INF file copies a template file (BATFILE.BAT) into the *ShellNew* folder and registers the new template in *HKEY_CLASSES_ROOT\ .bat\ShellNew*.

```
File: Batfile.INF
;
; Windows 98 Version
;
; Enter the BAT template to the New command.
;
; The INF file also provides an uninstall function to
; recover the factory settings.

[version]
signature="$CHICAGO$"
SetupClass=BASE

; During install: Copy the template
; batfile.bat into the Windows subfolder ShellNew,
; copy the INF file for uninstall purposes,
; add the ShellNew key to \.bat, and set the uninstall feature

[DefaultInstall]

CopyFiles = Bat.CopyFiles.Bat, Inf.CopyFiles.Inf
AddReg = Bat.AddReg

; During uninstall: Delete the INF file and
; the template file, and delete the Registry entries

[DefaultUninstall]
DelReg = Bat.DelReg
DelFiles = Inf.DelFiles.Inf, Bat.CopyFiles.bat

; Add the ShellNew key into the .bat key
[Bat.AddReg]
HKCR,.bat\ShellNew,,,
HKCR,.bat\ShellNew,FileName,,"Batfile.bat"
```

(continued)

continued

```
; Add uninstall stuff
HKLM,%UnKey%,DisplayName,,"%REMOVE_DESC%"
HKLM,%UnKey%,UninstallString,,"RunDll32          →
setupApi.dll,InstallHinfSection DefaultUninstall 132 Batfile.inf"

; Don't forget this key for the uninstall part
HKLM,SOFTWARE\Microsoft\Windows\CurrentVersion\Uninstall\battempl,,,

[Bat.DelReg]
HKCR,.bat\ShellNew

; Don't forget this key for the uninstall part
HKLM,SOFTWARE\Microsoft\Windows\CurrentVersion\Uninstall\battempl

; INF file to be copied in the Windows INF subfolder

[Inf.CopyFiles.Inf]
Batfile.Inf

; INF file to be removed in the Windows INF subfolder

[Inf.DelFiles.Inf]
Batfile.Inf
Batfile.PNF

; BAT template file to be copied to the Windows ShellNew subfolder
[Bat.CopyFiles.Bat]
Batfile.bat

[DestinationDirs]

Bat.CopyFiles.Bat = 10,ShellNew
Inf.CopyFiles.Inf = 17
Inf.DelFiles.Inf = 17

[SourceDisksNames]
55="Batfile Template","",1

[SourceDisksFiles]
Batfile.inf=55
Batfile.bat=55

[Strings]
REMOVE_DESC = "Remove BAT (Win 98) template (Born)"

UnKey="SOFTWARE\Microsoft\Windows\CurrentVersion\Uninstall\battempl"
; End ***
```

After you install the INF file by right-clicking the icon and selecting the Install entry from the context menu, the MS-DOS Batch File item should be available on the New command's submenu.

> **N O T E :**   The files BATFILE.BAT and BATFILE.INF are available in the \chapter5 folder of the sample files. Alter this INF file to register other templates. If the settings won't take effect, try restarting your system.

Occasionally, more than one application will register a template for a particular file type. This is the case for the DOC file type (see Figure 5-15 on the following page). Windows scans the Registry for *ShellNew* entries and adds all matches into the New command's submenu, but because there can be only one *ShellNew* key used for a particular file type, the name of the template that will be used must be set in the parent key of the *ShellNew* subkey. In the *Default* value of the parent key, you will find the key name of the application currently used to open a file of that type. For example, the *Default* value of the *.doc* key shown in Figure 5-15 is set to *"WordPad.Document.1"*, so the template registered in the …*WordPad.Document.1\ShellNew* subkey is used.

Additional Information About the *ShellNew* Key

I mentioned that *ShellNew* contains the values *NullFile* and *FileName*, but this is only half the truth. Here are all the entries that you can use in this key.

- *Nullfile = ""*   Creates an empty file with the extension of the registered file type. Using this option requires that your application open a file with a zero length.

- *Data = Binary value*   Creates a file with the registered extension and fills it with the specified binary values.

- *FileName = "Name"*   Searches for the Name file in the Windows \ShellNew subfolder and creates a copy in the destination folder.

- *Command = "<Path>application.exe parameters"*   Contains a command to execute an application (such as a wizard) that will create the new file.

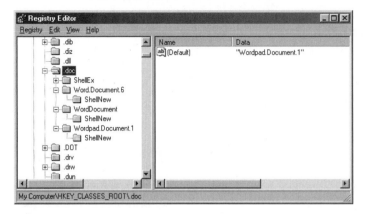

Figure 5-15.
The .doc *key in* HKEY_CLASSES_ROOT.

Modifying the Shell Icons

The shell comes with a large set of predefined icons for folders, printers, file types, and so on. The icon used for a file type is defined in the Registry in the *HKEY_CLASSES_ROOT* branch that defines the file type's properties (for example, in the *HKEY_CLASSES_ROOT\ascfile* key for the ASC file type). As we've seen in Chapters 3 and 4, the *DefaultIcon* subkey of each of these keys sets the icon for the file type. But the many other icons that the shell uses are registered differently. The following sections discuss how you can customize the shell icons.

How the Shell Icons Are Stored

The icons used by the shell are contained in the file SHELL32.DLL, which is in the Windows\System folder. Icons for shell components are preset and, at first glance, appear unalterable. (Maybe you noticed the *DefaultIcon* key in the branch *HKEY_CLASSES_ROOT\Folder*; unfortunately, changing this entry has no effect on the icons used for a folder.) You could use one of those special tools available to modify icons contained in a DLL file, but that's a dangerous approach—you could inadvertently change a critical component of a module. Is there any other way?

Well, I've got good news—a solution that was previously undocumented and difficult to find and that I'm happy to let you in on. I came across it while working with Tweak UI: you can use one optional key in the Registry to redefine the settings for the shell icons. The key belongs to the Registry branch *HKEY_LOCAL_MACHINE* (because these settings are relevant to the whole machine) and is located in the branch *SOFTWARE\Microsoft\Windows\Current Version\explorer\Shell Icons*.

The *Shell Icons* key is not available by default. You will see it in your Registry only if you have used tools like the Microsoft Plus package or Tweak UI to modify the shell icon settings. If you have modified the icon settings, you'll see entries like those shown in Figure 5-16. The entry shown in Figure 5-16 was created after I changed the Shortcut arrow icon with Tweak UI's Explorer property page.

Icons used by the shell can be remapped in the *Shell Icons* key. An entry consists of a value name, which is a number from *0* through *n*, and its associated data. The number is fixed for each shell icon. For example, the *29* value always affects the Shortcut arrow icon. (You will find the numbers for the most common entries in Appendix A, beginning on page 381.) The data for an entry contains a pointer to the icon source and the icon index. The statement in Figure 5-16 uses the index *2* (which is the third icon because the index starts with *0*) and points to TWEAKUI.CPL.

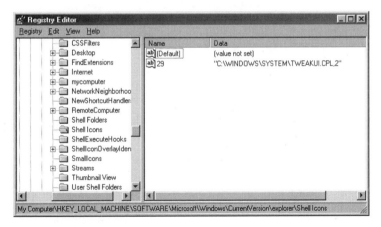

Figure 5-16.
An example of a Registry entry for a shell icon.

If when you inspect the Registry the *Shell Icons* key is not available, you can create this key. Then you can insert an entry, set the value name to a number, and set the pointer to an icon source as a value. Use your own DLL file as an icon source, or redirect the pointers to icons in SHELL32.DLL. (If the *Shell Icons* key is already available and contains some entries, you should back up this key before you alter any settings. You can use the Registry Editor export function, as described in Chapter 2, for this purpose.)

The icons shown in Appendix A are used by the shell in different places, and SHELL32.DLL contains more icons than are shown in the table (for example, the Windows flag and additional Recycle Bin icons). You can reassign most of the icons used by the shell to some of these other icons contained in SHELL32.DLL (or in another DLL file) by adding the number shown in the first column of Appendix A as a value name in the *Shell Icons* key. The data for this entry must be set to the icon source.

Icon Size and Color Depth

You need to pay attention to icon size and colors. In Windows 98, several icon sizes are used, with the following pixel sizes:

- 16 × 16
- 32 × 32
- 48 × 48

The 32 × 32 pixel icons are shown on the desktop and as large icons in folder windows. The 16 × 16 pixel icons are shown as small icons. A DLL library should contain an icon image for both of these resolutions. You can set other sizes for the desktop icons by using the Appearance property page of the Display Properties property sheet. Because Windows must rescale the 32 × 32 pixel image of the icon to the new size you set, "damaged," or altered, icons are displayed on the desktop.

You can also modify icon colors in Windows 98. Icons can be stored with 16 or 256 colors. And you can store icons with High or True color (that is, 16 bits or 24 bits per color). You must create at least one icon for each color scheme in each of the three sizes listed above and store them in an icon file. If you create icons, make sure that your icon editor supports this feature. (One such tool is Microangelo, which is offered in various online forums.) For most of your needs, creating a 32 × 32 16-color icon will be sufficient.

Note that icons are stored in ICO files, in CPL files, in EXE files, or in DLL files. Be aware, if you use ICO files as icon sources, that Windows often has problems refreshing icons created from ICO files. Also, here's a trick that you can use to create an icon: Start a program like Microsoft Paint, create a 32 x 32 pixel image, and save the image as a 16-color or 256-color BMP file. Then use

Windows Explorer to rename the file extension from BMP to ICO. Surprisingly, Windows will display the contents of this file as an icon (although the file is still stored in the BMP format). When using this "pseudoicon," Windows has the same problems refreshing this icon as it does refreshing icons taken from any other ICO file.

Activating Your Icon Changes

You need to know under which circumstances your changes in *Shell Icons* will take effect—simply restarting Windows won't work in every case. You might have noticed that when you use Tweak UI to change the Shortcut arrow icon or when you use the Appearance property page of the Display Properties property sheet to change the size of desktop icons, icon entries you have redefined in the *Shell Icons* key will also take effect.

Both of these changes cause a reset of the shell (that is, the shell is reloaded), but often you need to perform one more step for your changes to be visible. The Windows folder contains a file named SHELLICONCACHE. Windows keeps a copy of all icons used by the shell in this cache file. You must delete this file first and then restart the system. During the system restart, the SHELLICONCACHE file is rebuilt with the icons defined in the Registry. After the system restart, the new icons will be used by the shell.

Keeping SHELLICONCACHE to a Manageable Size

Windows keeps several icons used by the shell in the file SHELLICONCACHE. If you change the shell settings frequently, the size of the file will grow. Deleting SHELLICONCACHE from time to time will reduce its size. You can also restrict the size of the icon cache by setting an optional entry in the Registry key *HKEY_LOCAL_MACHINE\SOFTWARE\Microsoft\Windows\CurrentVersion\explorer*. Insert the value *Max Cached Icons* to set a limit. By default, this value does not appear in the *explorer* key.

> NOTE: I have read about cases in which icons suddenly show up as black spots on the desktop. This can happen after you change something in the system's graphics adapter or tamper too much with the *Shell Icons* key. Most of the time, these spots will disappear when you delete the SHELLICONCACHE file and restart the system.

Tips for Customizing Other Shell Icons

We've looked at several techniques for changing the icons used by the shell in this chapter and in Chapter 4, but a few additional tips will help you further customize parts of the shell.

Showing BMP Files as Icons

When you open a folder, each file is shown as an individual icon; many of these icons are defaults and thus are predefined for registered file types. When you open a folder containing icon files (that is, files stored in the ICO format), the contents of the ICO files are used to represent the files themselves. Setting the Large Icon option shows you the contents of the icon files as thumbnails. You can also force the shell to show the contents of BMP files as thumbnails by using the Registry key *HKEY_CLASSES_ROOT\Paint.Picture\DefaultIcon*.

The key's *Default* value is set to something like *"C:\xxxx\MSPAINT. EXE,1"*, where *xxxx* is the path to the MSPAINT.EXE file. This example value defines the second icon stored in MSPAINT.EXE as the icon source. If you set the *Default* value of the *DefaultIcon* key to *%1*, BMP files will be shown in a folder as thumbnails, like those shown in Figure 5-17. You can use the files BMPON.REG and BMPOFF.REG in the \chapter5 folder of the sample files to turn this option on and off.

Figure 5-17.
BMP and ICO files shown as thumbnails.

Maybe you already know this trick, but I bet you don't know why it works with BMP files. Here's the scoop: The Registry contains the entries for registered file types in *HKEY_CLASSES_ROOT*. A file type entry might have a *DefaultIcon* key, which defines the icon source for that file type. In Chapter 4,

I mentioned that a registered file type can have the placeholder *%1* in the *DefaultIcon* key, which enables the icon handler to set an individual icon for each file instance. The ActiveX handler for BMP files implements this *%1* placeholder feature. (BMP and ICO are file formats used internally in Windows.) If the *%1* placeholder is found, the handler reads the content of the BMP file, rescales it, and displays it as an icon symbol. (By the way, you will get the best results when the BMP file is 32 × 32 pixels in size.) The ICO file handler functions the same way. If other handlers that support the *IExtractIcon* interface are already installed, you can use this feature for other file types.

> **NOTE:** You can also register the CLSID of a separate *IconHandler* in the *shellex* branch of a registered file type and add to it the value *DefaultIcon = %1*. The application must provide its own icon handler to implement the *IExtractIcon* interface, which is used by the shell to retrieve icons.

Changing the Icon of a Drive

When you open a window containing local or remote drives, the drive symbols are shown. The shell provides default symbols for each drive type, but you can change the icon for a drive type in the *Shell Icons* key. Add the appropriate icon index number as a value into this key, set the string to a new icon source, delete the SHELLICONCACHE file, and reset the computer. All drives of the type you changed will be shown with the new symbol. (See Figure 5-18.)

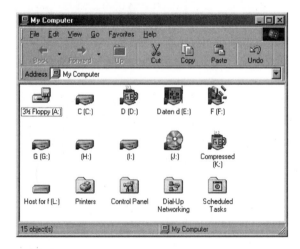

Figure 5-18.
Folder with the new drive symbols.

Is there a simpler way? Can you assign individual icons to selected drives without hacking in the Registry? Yes, you can. I discovered this trick a few years ago while creating a CD-ROM. If you insert a CD-ROM into a drive, the default icon for the CD-ROM drive will be substituted with another icon. The reason is fairly simple: The CD-ROM contains in its root directory a file with the name AUTORUN.INF, which can be used to start an application when the CD-ROM is inserted into the drive. An AUTORUN.INF file can contain, for example, the following statements:

```
open=Start.exe
icon=BornIcon.dll,10
```

The first line defines the name of the executable application that will be invoked after the CD-ROM is inserted into the drive. The second line defines the name of the icon file used for the drive's symbol. Double-clicking the CD-ROM symbol activates the *open* command defined in the INF file. As a result, the Registry settings are temporarily overwritten.

It's possible to store an AUTORUN.INF file containing only the following line in the root directory of a hard disk drive.

```
icon=BornIcon.dll,11
```

But you must also store an icon source on this drive. (You can store the source in either the root or a subfolder such as \Icons\BORNICON.DLL.) The result will be visible the next time the screen refreshes—the drive gets its own icon. If you don't want to store an icon file on each drive, assign the same icon index in the icon statement of AUTORUN.INF to the other drives. Windows will cache this icon in SHELLICONCACHE. If you delete the AUTORUN.INF file, the old drive symbol is shown after the next system start.

> **NOTE:** You can also use an EXE file as an icon source. For example, the *icon=c:\Windows\Explorer.exe,0* command displays the first icon stored in Windows Explorer.

Windows 98 keeps an *AutoRun* key in the *HKEY_CLASSES_ROOT* branch. This key is updated during each system start or whenever the shell is refreshed, and it contains a subkey for each drive having an AUTORUN.INF file in its root. As you can see in Figure 5-19, the *DefaultIcon* key contains the path to the icon source.

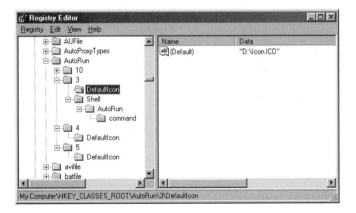

Figure 5-19.
The HKEY_CLASSES_ROOT\AutoRun *entry, used to set up the drive icons.*

AutoRun for CD-ROM

If you insert a CD-ROM into a drive and the CD-ROM contains an AUTORUN.INF file in its root directory, Windows 98 executes the command appearing in the run line of this INF file. Many software packages take advantage of this AutoRun feature. If you would like to disable the feature, open the Registry Editor and search for this key:

> *HKEY_CURRENT_USER\Software\Microsoft\Windows\ CurrentVersion\Policies\Explorer*

You'll find that the key contains a value named *NoDriveTypeAuto-Run* set to *95 00 00 00*. Setting this value to *b5 00 00 00* disables the AutoRun feature after the next system start. You can also use the Paranoia property page in Tweak UI to set this option.

Changing the Shortcut Symbol

You can change the Shortcut arrow icon in two ways. The first way is to define a pointer to a new icon source in the *Shell Icons* key (see Figure 5-16 on page 259), delete the SHELLICONSCACHE file, and restart the computer.

The more efficient way is to use Tweak UI for this task. If you invoke Tweak UI and select the Explorer property page, you should see the Shortcut Overlay section containing options to customize the shortcut icon. (See Figure 5-12 on page 251.)

Selecting the Custom option button opens a Change Icon window showing all icons in the SHELL32.DLL file. Within this window, you can select a new icon and apply the settings. Tweak UI then handles all the details.

Miscellaneous Registry Settings

The Registry contains many entries that control internal Windows 98 settings. Some of these entries influence various parts of the shell; others affect only the Windows kernel. In this chapter, I'll discuss a wide range of miscellaneous Registry entries.

Sound Events in the Registry

If you've installed a sound card or the SPEAKER.DRV driver, you can assign different sounds to different Microsoft Windows events, such as the execution of the Start Windows and Close Program commands. You can also link sounds to various events in application programs. For example, you can link a sound event to the receipt of a message in Microsoft Exchange. In this section, we'll look at how to set up sound events and at how Windows handles the related Registry values. (Remember that to be able to survey and manipulate sound events, you must first have a sound device installed on your system.)

Where Sound Events Are Registered

Sound events are user-specific, and users can define their own sounds if user profiles are enabled on their systems. Sound events are registered in the *HKEY_CURRENT_USER\AppEvents* key, in the *EventLabels* and *Schemes* subkeys. (See Figure 6-1 on the following page.) Copies of sound event settings are also stored in *HKEY_USERS* under the key named after the current user. In most cases, you have to set options in only the *HKEY_CURRENT_USER* key because Windows automatically updates the other branches when you shut down the system. If no user profiles are set, copies of these settings are stored in the key *HKEY_USERS\.Default*.

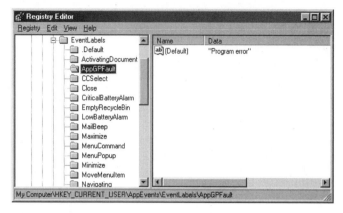

Figure 6-1.
Sound event settings registered in the EventLabels *subkey.*

The *EventLabels* Key

The subkeys of the branch *HKEY_CURRENT_USER\AppEvents\EventLabels* (for example, *.Default*, *AppGPFault*, *Close*, *Open*, and so on) define the events available in Windows. The default value of each of these subkeys contains the string (as in the Data column in Figure 6-1) that is shown in the Events list of the Sounds property page, which is available by double-clicking the Sounds icon in the Control Panel. The Sounds property page is shown in Figure 6-2.

Where Can I Edit Sound Events?

You can change the sound associated with an event by selecting options on the Sounds property page or by modifying settings in the Registry Editor. The Sounds property page is the least risky and most convenient tool available for such editing.

If you want to distribute software with sounds associated with specific events, you should use INF files to register the sound files and events. By default, Windows 98 uses the subfolder \Media in the \Windows folder to store the WAV files used for sound events. Therefore, you could use a REG file rather than an INI file, but remember: Folder names can be changed from the default. In that case, the REG file won't work.

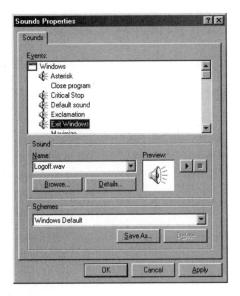

Figure 6-2.
The Sounds property page.

To customize a string shown in the Events list, redefine the *Default* value of the subkey associated with the event. Table 6-1 gives a brief overview of some of the subkeys you'll find in *HKEY_CURRENT_USER\AppEvents\EventLabels*.

Keys in *HKEY_CURRENT_USER\AppEvents\EventLabels*

Key	Description
.Default	Defines the "Default sound" event
ActivatingDocument	Activates when a document is loaded
AppGPFault	Activates when a program error occurs
CCSelect	Activates when a Cc function in an e-mail editor is selected
Close	Executes before a program is closed
CriticalBatteryAlarm	Executes when the battery is in critical condition
EmptyRecycleBin	Activates when the Recycle Bin is emptied
LowBatteryAlarm	Activates when the battery is low
MailBeep	Activates when mail arrives
Maximize	Activates when a window is maximized

Table 6-1.
Keys for registering sound events.

(continued)

269

Keys in *HKEY_CURRENT_USER\AppEvents\EventLabels* *continued*

Key	Description
MenuCommand	Activates when a menu command is clicked
MenuPopup	Activates when a menu pops up
Minimize	Activates when a window is minimized
Open	Executes during the opening of a program
RestoreDown	Activates when a window is restored to its default size after being maximized
RestoreUp	Activates when a window is restored to its previous size after being minimized
ShowBand	Activates when a user moves a toolbar band (of the Active Desktop)
SystemAsterisk	Used for the system's asterisk events, such as when an error message box appears
SystemExclamation	Used in a message box with an exclamation mark icon
SystemExit	Executes before Windows exits
SystemHand	Activates when the system's hand cursor is shown, to imply a critical stop
SystemQuestion	Used in a message box with a question mark icon
SystemStart	Executes during each Windows startup

The *Schemes* Key

A sound scheme is a set of sounds that a user defines for particular applications to mark events in those applications, such as opening or closing an application. You can define a sound scheme on the Sounds property page or register it in the subkeys of *HKEY_CURRENT_USER\AppEvents\Schemes*. The *Default* value for the *Schemes* key is set to the name of the scheme currently being used (such as *Born0*), and the *ControlIniTimeStamp* value is used internally by Windows. The *Schemes* subkey *Apps* contains the applications registered for sound events, and the subkey *Names* contains the names of schemes defined for sound events.

The *Apps* subkey   Applications registered for sound events are listed in the *Apps* subkey, which is shown in Figure 6-3. Notice the *.Default* subkey, which contains the keys for Windows events, and the subkeys for additional applications such as Windows Explorer or Media Player. Each program's EXE file is used as the subkey's name. To register sound files for a particular application, add a key named after the application's EXE file. We'll look at this process in more detail later in the chapter.

Keys for applications such as Windows Explorer contain subkeys named after the verbs of the possible sound events, such as *Open* and *MenuCommand*. (These names are defined in the *EventLabels* key, as we learned earlier.) Take a look at Figure 6-3 and notice the *EmptyRecycleBin* subkey of the *Explorer* branch. It contains three subkeys with the names of available schemes: *.Current*, *.Default*, and *Born0*. The *Default* value of each of these subkeys contains the path to a particular sound file. Windows uses the WAV file format by default; these files are stored in the Windows subfolder \Media. Notice in the Data column that I used the DING.WAV file for Windows Explorer's EmptyRecycleBin event. Since the Born0 scheme is the active scheme, this file is also stored in the *.Current* subkey of the *EmptyRecycleBin* key, which means that the sound will be played each time the Recycle Bin is emptied. If I wanted to hear a sound, for example, whenever Windows Explorer terminates, I'd need to add the *Close* key and its sound scheme subkeys to *Explorer* and define a path to the particular sound file. Windows can do a lot of this setting up for you; we'll look at how it does so later.

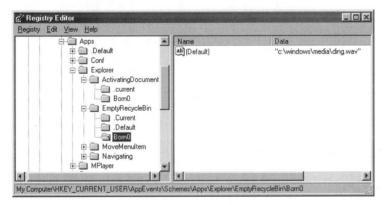

Figure 6-3.
Subkeys of the Apps *subkey.*

The *Names* subkey The *Names* subkey contains only the names of the schemes defined for sound events and always contains the following two subkeys: *.Default* and *.None*. Any sound modifications that the user makes and then stores as a new scheme on the Sounds property page is added to *Names* as a new key. The key name is restricted to seven characters and always terminates with a digit. If a new entry matches an existing key, Windows changes the last digit from *0* to *1* (or from *1* to *2*, etc.) until there's no longer a match. The name that the user gives this new scheme is stored in the *Default* value of the key, as shown in Figure 6-4 on the following page.

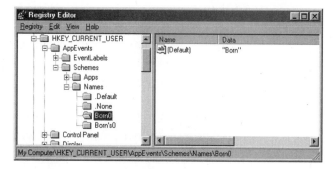

Figure 6-4.
Subkeys of the Names *subkey.*

The *Names* key and its subkeys are used by the Sounds property page. When you save a new scheme, the scheme's name is inserted as a key into the *...\Apps\application name\event name* subkey for each of the registered applications' events affected by the sound scheme. For example, look at Figure 6-3 again. You can see that *Born0* has been added as a subkey to the *Apps\Explorer\ EmptyRecycleBin* key. Also, the *Default* value data from the *.Current* key of each *...\Apps\application name\event name* branch is copied into each occurrence of the new key. In other words, the *Default* value of *Born0* in the *EmptyRecycleBin* key contains the same information as the *Default* value of the *.Current* key (*"c:\windows\media\ding.wav"*).

The name of the active scheme is defined in the *Default* value of the *HKEY_ CURRENT_USER\AppEvents\Schemes* key. This is different from the way in which Windows stores color schemes, for example, and it might be a little difficult to use the Registry Editor to maintain the Registry entries for a sound scheme. Therefore, I advise you to use the Sounds property page to fine-tune sound settings and to leave it to Windows to ensure that the right settings will be used.

> NOTE: Sound events can be helpful to people with disabilities, enabling them to use their computers more efficiently. Sound events are also a great gimmick, but having too many of them can slow down your system considerably because an action will not occur until its associated sound is played. It's a good idea to limit sound events to critical actions.

Registering a Sound Event for an Application

The method you employ to set up a sound event for an application depends on whether that application is registered. If the application is registered, you can associate sounds with particular application events by using the Sounds property page. Double-click the Sounds icon in the Control Panel, and follow these steps:

1. Search for the entry with the application name.

2. Click the entry for the event (Open or Close, for example), and associate one of the available sound files. Repeat this step, as desired, for other events available for this application.

3. If you want to keep both the original settings and your new settings, click Save As to save the settings as a new scheme. (See Figure 6-5.)

4. Click OK to apply the changes, and close the property sheet.

The last step generates all necessary subkeys to define the sound events in the *Apps* subkey. If Windows detects missing subkeys (in the *Open* and *Close* branches, for example), these keys are added automatically.

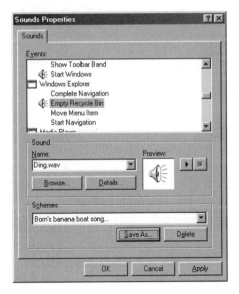

Figure 6-5.
Entries for an application's sound events.

If the application isn't yet registered, you won't be able to find the application name in the Events list of the Sounds property page and you'll need to add the filename of the application to the following key:

HKEY_CURRENT_USER\AppEvents\Schemes\Apps

Suppose, for example, that you want to extend the Registry with and assign sounds to the Open and Close events for the Notepad text editor. To register the events, follow these steps:

1. Extend the *HKEY_CURRENT_USER\AppEvents\Schemes\Apps* key with a *Notepad* subkey. Notepad is the name of the EXE file, so the Windows Session Manager should recognize the application when it loads it into memory.

2. Add the *Open* and Close subkeys to *HKEY_CURRENT_USER\ AppEvents\Schemes\Apps\Notepad*. Both subkey names are already registered in the *HKEY_CURRENT_USER\AppEvents\EventLabels* key as global system events. The new subkeys enable you to supersede the global settings with individual parameters for this application.

Steps 1 and 2 prepare the system for the new sound event by registering the application and the events. You could also register the application and events by using a REG file. At this point, we can use a REG file because we don't need paths for the Registry settings and we don't have to ensure, yet, that sound files are available. Here's the SOUND.REG file (located in the \chapter6 folder of the sample files):

```
REGEDIT4

[HKEY_CURRENT_USER\AppEvents\Schemes\Apps\Notepad]
@="Windows Notepad"

[HKEY_CURRENT_USER\AppEvents\Schemes\Apps\Notepad\Open]

[HKEY_CURRENT_USER\AppEvents\Schemes\Apps\Notepad\Close]
```

Now the system is aware of the new open and close events, but no sounds are associated with them. (This is the default for most events.) You've still got to tell Windows which sounds you want to hear when the events occur. You could do this by messing around in the Registry, but it would be difficult for several reasons. First, you'd have to be sure that the WAV files were in the correct folder (the \Windows\Media subfolder by default). Sound files are optional components in the Windows 98 Setup, so if you didn't intend to create your own sound files you would have to be sure the Windows 98 sound files were installed. Second, you'd have to know the status of schemes already defined in the *Apps* subkeys. You'd need to define a subkey with an associated sound file for each existing sound scheme.

You could handle only about half this job with a simple INF file by adding a fixed subkey name to the scheme (for example, *Open*\\.*Default*). The entries would be updated when the user saved a new scheme by using the Sounds property page. As a result, you'd want to be careful using the .*Current* scheme to store your new settings, because these settings could get lost if the user didn't save the new scheme after changing the entries on the Sounds property page.

So as you can see, hacking the Registry is probably not the best way to associate sounds with events. Your best bet, once you've registered an application, is to define the sound events on the Sounds property page.

Establishing a Sound Event for an Empty Recycle Bin

If you inspect the *HKEY_CURRENT_USER\\AppEvents\\Schemes\\Apps* branch, you'll find the *Explorer* key containing an *EmptyRecycleBin* subkey. (See Figure 6-3 on page 271.) The EmptyRecycleBin event occurs when the user empties the Recycle Bin, and you can associate a sound file to this event.

1. If the *EmptyRecycleBin* subkey is not available, use a REG file (such as BINSOUND.REG, located in the \\chapter6 folder of the sample files) or the Registry Editor to add this entry into the *HKEY_CURRENT_USER\\AppEvents\\Schemes\\Apps\\Explorer* branch.

2. Invoke the Sounds property page (by opening the Control Panel and selecting Sounds). Select the Empty Recycle Bin entry in the Windows Explorer branch, and associate a sound file.

After you close the property sheet by clicking OK, the new sound event is registered. If you right-click the Recycle Bin icon and select the Empty Recycle Bin command from the context menu, a sound notification is sent to your sound device.

Setting Up Application Paths in the Registry

A path defines where program files (EXE files) and dynamic-link libraries (DLL files) are located. In Windows 98, you can define a path in two ways. One way is to define a global path in the MS-DOS PATH environment variable, which is set by the AUTOEXEC.BAT file during system startup. This solution isn't state-of-the-art, however, because AUTOEXEC.BAT is used only for compatibility purposes with old application programs. The PATH environment variable set in AUTOEXEC.BAT defines a global path used for all applications, so if you use many applications that have their own folders the PATH command gets too long to fit into the environment variable. The more efficient option, then, is to define paths in the Registry. The Registry contains a key in which application programs can register their own paths.

Entries in the *App Paths* Key

An application that conforms to the standards set in the *Windows Interface Guidelines for Software Design* (Microsoft Press, 1995) stores files in different folders: the EXE file of an application is located in a subfolder named after the application (for example, the BornTool application is stored in the ...\BornTool subfolder), and the DLL and HLP files are located in a system folder (for example, in ...\BornTool\System). This file structure is contained in the following Registry key:

> *HKEY_LOCAL_MACHINE\SOFTWARE\Microsoft\Windows\
> CurrentVersion\App Paths*

A setup program for an application adds a new subkey to this branch. The subkey's name is defined by the EXE file. For example, if the application is executed with the BORNTOOL.EXE file, the following key is added to the Registry:

> *HKEY_LOCAL_MACHINE\SOFTWARE\Microsoft\Windows\
> CurrentVersion\App Paths\BornTool.exe*

This new key can contain two values with path strings:

- ■ The *Default* value   The *Default* value of the key must be set to the path and filename of the EXE program. Windows uses this string to load the application into memory. If the application program BORNTOOL.EXE is stored in the folder C:\Born\, the *Default* value of the key is set to *C:\Born\BornTool.exe*. This value can also contain additional parameters to control the application.

- ■ The *Path* value   If the application uses DLL files, an optional *Path* value can be inserted into the key. The *Path* value contains the paths to the folders required by the application. It can include several path definitions separated by semicolons (for example, "*C:\Born; C:\Born\System;*").

The following lines show the *App Paths* entry for the Internet Connection Wizard program ISIGNUP.EXE.

```
REGEDIT4

[HKEY_LOCAL_MACHINE\SOFTWARE\Microsoft\Windows\CurrentVersion\ ⇥
AppPaths\ISIGNUP.EXE]
@="C:\\Program Files\\Internet Explorer\\Connection Wizard\\ ⇥
ISIGNUP.EXE"
"Path"="C:\\Program Files\\Internet Explorer\\Connection Wizard\\;"
```

The *Default* value points to the \Program Files\Internet Explorer\Connection Wizard folder, which contains the file ISIGNUP.EXE. The *Path* value uses the same path to direct Windows 98 to the folder where the DLL and data files will be found.

> NOTE: If you start an application by typing the name of the EXE file—without a path—in the Run dialog box accessible from the Windows Start menu, Windows will look for the file in the current directory. If the file is not in the current directory, Windows will look at the *Default* value in the appropriate *EXE* subkey of the *App Paths* key.
>
> Although some people have tried to use the *Path* value in the Registry to define paths for a program, as far as I know it's not possible to use the *Path* value to force Windows to use this access path for an application. However, the application itself can look up the value to determine where to find the requested libraries.

Entries in the *SharedDLLs* Key

When an application shares DLL files with other programs, the install program creates a new value entry in the following key:

> *HKEY_LOCAL_MACHINE\SOFTWARE\Microsoft\Windows*
> *CurrentVersion\SharedDLLs*

The value name is set to the path and filename of the shared DLL file. The value's data is a binary counter. Each install program will increment this value if the installed application uses this shared DLL file. If the application is removed, the uninstaller should decrement this value by 1. If the counter reaches the value *0*, the user can remove the Registry value and the DLL file. Figure 6-6 on the following page shows example entries in the *SharedDLLs* key. Most of the DLL routines shown in Figure 6-6 are currently used by only one application each.

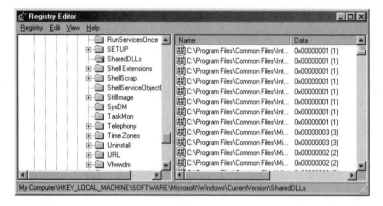

Figure 6-6.
Keys for shared DLL routines.

NOTE: An uninstall routine removes all of an application's files, including the DLL files. When files are shared, the uninstall routine does not remove the files because they might be used by other applications. So it's a good idea to use the values in *SharedDLLs* to determine whether a shared DLL file can be removed. If the value has been decremented to *0*, you can safely remove the DLL file.

Keep in mind that poorly written install and uninstall programs might cause a problem. A good install program detects when a user tries to install the same application several times and does not increment the value for the shared DLL. If this were not the case, you wouldn't be able to remove the DLL files after uninstalling all other applications. Likewise, a good uninstall program detects when a user tries to uninstall a program more than once and so decrements the counter only once. If the uninstall feature did not detect this, the counter would be decremented to zero and the file would be removed, disabling the other applications relying on that DLL.

Entries in the *Shared Tools* Key

Some Microsoft application programs share software tools that enable them to perform certain functions. For example, Microsoft Word, Microsoft Excel, and Microsoft Access share graphics filters that allow them to import a variety of file formats. Filter modules are installed from application setup programs and stored in folders. For example, when Windows 98 is installed, the MSPAINT.EXE program is installed in the \Program Files\Accessories folder. This folder also contains a PCX graphics filter required by MSPaint. When you install Microsoft

Office components, other graphics components are copied onto the hard disk and stored in folders.

Information about shared software components that are already installed is stored in the following Registry key:

HKEY_LOCAL_MACHINE\SOFTWARE\Microsoft\Shared Tools

This key can contain subkeys that define the location of shared tools provided by Microsoft applications. Graphics filters are located in the subkey *Graphics Filters\Import*, as shown in Figure 6-7, with each graphics file type (such as JPEG or PCX) getting its own subkey. Each subkey has three values:

- *Extensions*, which contains the file extensions for the file types that use the graphical filter interface

- *Name*, which contains the name of the filter

- *Path*, which contains the path to the filter file

Other applications can access this information from the Registry to use existing filter interfaces. Some of the file type subkeys, such as the *JPEG* key in Figure 6-7, have additional subkeys specifying APIs and other options.

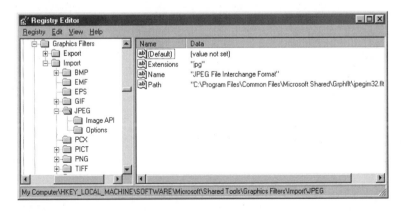

Figure 6-7.
Entries in the Shared Tools branch.

Other subkeys of ...*SOFTWARE\Microsoft\Shared Tools* (such as *Text Converters*, *MSInfo*, and others) contain information about other shared components available in Windows 98. A related key, *HKEY_LOCAL_MACHINE\ SOFTWARE\Microsoft\Shared Tools Location*, is used by Microsoft Office products to find the path to the folder that contains additional shared modules specific to Office.

Miscellaneous Application Settings

The Registry contains several keys that store system and application settings. These keys are described in the following sections.

HKEY_LOCAL_MACHINE\SOFTWARE

Application programs insert subkeys defining machine-specific settings into this key. Microsoft uses a key named *Microsoft* to store such settings for all Microsoft products. If you've installed different software packages, you'll see other subkeys in *HKEY_LOCAL_MACHINE\SOFTWARE* as well, such as the *SCC* key and the *ODBC* key for ODBC driver settings. (See Figure 6-8.) The names and contents of these subkeys are vendor-specific.

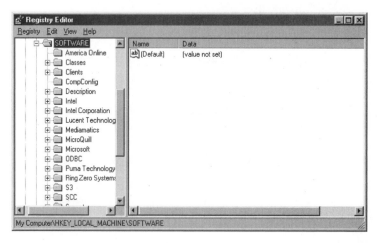

Figure 6-8.
Entries in the HKEY_LOCAL_MACHINE\SOFTWARE *branch.*

The *Microsoft* branch contains many entries related to Microsoft products (shipped as add-ons to Windows 98 or installed separately). The *Active Setup* key is used by the Active Setup installation of Microsoft Internet Explorer 4.0. The subkey *Advanced INF Setup* contains entries provided by advanced INF files. (See Chapter 7 for more information on this matter.) The *Code Store Database* key contains many entries required by Internet Explorer 4.0 to support the Java machine. Internet Explorer 4.0 keeps its own settings in the branch *Internet Explorer*.

Windows system programs store information in the subkeys of the ...\SOFTWARE*Microsoft**Windows**CurrentVersion* branch. For example, Backup stores backup configurations and the flag denoting whether a tape drive is detected in the ...*Applets\Microsoft Backup* key. ScanDisk stores information about the status of its error-checking in the ...*Applets\Check Drive* key. (You can access these tools on the Tools property page of a drive's Properties property sheet. Right-click the drive symbol, and select Properties.) Other keys, such as ...*explorer\LastOptimize* and ...*explorer\LastCheck*, are used by ScanDisk and Defrag to store information about the time at which the user last ran the optimize and check procedures.

HKEY_CURRENT_USER\Software

An application's user-specific settings are stored here. Windows stores the settings for all registered users in the *HKEY_USERS* branch upon each system exit, unless the No Save Settings On Exit option is enabled.

HKEY_USERS\xxxx\Software\ Microsoft\Windows\CurrentVersion\Applets

This key contains subkeys that are inserted by application programs to store settings for the specific user *xxxx*. For example, MSPaint and WordPad each keep a *Recent File List* key (for example, ...*Applets\WordPad\Recent File List*) and other application-specific information under this key, and you can find user-specific data for ScanDisk in the *Check Drive* subkey. (None of the values used by ScanDisk should be altered by the user; the tool maintains the data during each check-and-optimize process.)

Launching Programs During Windows Startup

You can have Windows automatically start applications for you during Windows startup by putting a shortcut to the application in the \Windows\Start Menu\Programs\Startup folder. This works well for users, but when a developer creates an application that needs to run at Windows startup, the most reliable method is for the application's setup program to store the startup information in the Registry. This is where the *Run* keys come in.

Registry Keys for Launching Applications and Services

The five Registry keys that launch applications and services are located in the branch *HKEY_LOCAL_MACHINE\SOFTWARE\Microsoft\Windows\Current Version*. These *Run* keys are shown in Figure 6-9 on the next page and are described in the following sections.

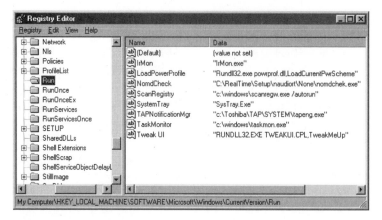

Figure 6-9.
The Run *keys launch applications during system startup.*

Run

Applications registered in the *Run* key are executed during each Windows 98 startup. Each entry in this key consists of a value named after an application and string value data. This string value contains the path and the filename of the application to launch. Look at Figure 6-9 again to see entries such as *Scan Registry* and *Tweak UI* in the *Run* key.

RunOnce

The *RunOnce* key contains values with the names and paths of applications that will be executed only once during a Windows startup; Windows removes the entries in this key after the system successfully starts. If an install program must execute a reset, it can enter its own name and the required options into this key and force a Windows restart. After a successful restart of Windows, the install program is executed and can continue the install process.

RunOnceEx

The *RunOnceEx* key has the same function as the *RunOnce* key but allows for more options to be specified for the startup, such as the order in which applications should execute.

RunServices

The *RunServices* key is used to launch network or system services during a Windows startup. Entries are structured in this key as they are in the *Run* key: each entry comprises a value with the name of the service and a string pointing to the name of the program to execute.

RunServicesOnce

The *RunServicesOnce* key can be used by the setup programs of network components to execute a network service only once during the next Windows startup.
After a successful restart, the entries in this key are removed.

Modifying the *Run* Keys

You can modify these five Registry keys by using the Registry Editor, a setup
program, an INF file, or the System Policy Editor, which contains a few modification options in the Windows 98 System branch. (See Figure 6-10.) To modify
the keys by using the System Policy Editor, follow these steps:

1. Start the System Policy Editor, and open the Registry by selecting
   Open Registry from the File menu.

2. Double-click the Local Computer icon.

3. Select one of the *Run* key check boxes (that is, Run, Run Once,
   or Run Services) from the \Windows 98 System\Programs To Run
   branch, and then click Show.

4. Edit the list of applications in the Show Contents window.

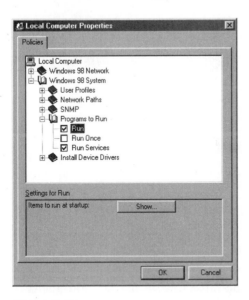

Figure 6-10.
Entries in the System Policy Editor to set the Run, RunOnce, *and*
RunServices *keys.*

NOTE: Not only is it easy for a setup program to modify these keys during a software installation, but you can also use these keys in an INF file. The *Run* keys also enable you to launch an application without the user knowing about it. If you use the Startup folder instead, there's a chance that the user will accidentally delete these entries.

Settings for Signature Checking and Error Logging

Windows 98 provides the capability to verify the digital signatures of device drivers and to log all faults occurring on the system. The keys described below are used for these purposes.

Digital Signature Check for Device Drivers

Look at Figure 6-10 again and you'll see the *Install Device Drivers* branch, which includes a check box option to establish a digital signature check for installed drivers by setting the *Policy* value in the *HKEY_LOCAL_MACHINE\ SOFTWARE\Microsoft\Driver Signing* key. Selecting this box reveals a list box with the following entries:

- Allow Installation Of All Drivers. This entry sets the *Policy* value to *0*.

- Warn Installation Of Non-Microsoft Signed Drivers. This entry sets the *Policy* value to *1*.

- Block Installation Of Non-Microsoft Signed Drivers. This entry sets the *Policy* value to *2*.

The *Policy* value contains DWORD data.

Error Logging in Windows

Windows 98 supports error logging. To enable error logging, you must set the *LogFile* value in the following key:

HKEY_LOCAL_MACHINE\SOFTWARE\Microsoft\Windows\ CurrentVersion\Fault

LogFile value is of type String and must contain the path and filename of the log file. You can set the entry by using the Paranoia property page in Tweak UI.

Settings for the File System

The Windows 98 file system features long filenames, a tool for remapping long filenames to standard DOS 8.3 names, and other options (such as caches). This section examines Registry entries that relate to file system settings.

Disabling Long Filenames

If your network environment is not fully compatible with the long filenames of Windows 98, you can disable the long filenames feature and thus force Windows 98 clients to generate filenames in the 8.3 format only. The settings for the file system are kept in the following Registry branch:

> HKEY_LOCAL_MACHINE\System\CurrentControlSet\control\
> FileSystem

NOTE: This key contains several subkeys and values containing the file system settings used on hard disks and floppy disks. (See the *Microsoft Windows 98 Resource Kit* [Microsoft Press, 1998] for information about the architecture of the Windows modules used by the file system.)

The information about long filenames is kept in a value named *Win31 FileSystem*. The value is set to *00* by default. If you set the value to *01* and restart the computer, the old DOS and Windows 3.1 file system with 8.3 filenames will be used.

You can use the Registry Editor to change this flag, but a better way is provided by the System Policy Editor. Click the Local Computer icon, select Microsoft Client For Netware Networks under the Windows 98 Network branch, and check the Support Long File Names option.

Modifying the Mapping of Alias Names

For reasons of compatibility with older applications, Windows 98 provides a function that generates 8.3 aliases from long filenames. The alias name is created from the beginning characters of the long filename (typically, the first six), a tilde (~), and a numerical tail (as in BORNJA~1.DOC). If two alias names match in a folder, Windows distinguishes one from the other by modifying one of the numerical tails, thus generating a new alias. In the best case, the result is a six-character name. However, you can force Windows 98 to use eight characters for the alias name by entering the value *NameNumericTail = 0* in the following key:

> HKEY_LOCAL_MACHINE\System\CurrentControlSet\control\
> FileSystem

This can be done with the Registry Editor or with the following REG file:

```
REGEDIT4

[HKEY_LOCAL_MACHINE\System\CurrentControlSet\control\FileSystem]
"NameNumericTail"=hex:00
```

After you reboot the system, the feature that maps the long filenames to the alias names will use eight characters whenever using these eight characters doesn't create duplicate filenames. The ALIASOFF.REG file is located in the \chapter6 folder of the sample files.

Setting Miscellaneous Options in the *FileSystem* Key

The *FileSystem* key contains additional entries for configuring the file system. All of these entries can be set through the Hard Disk, CD-ROM, and Troubleshooting property pages of the File System Properties property sheet. This property sheet is available by clicking the System icon in the Control Panel and then clicking File System on the Performance property page. If there are no values for these entries in the *FileSystem* key, Windows uses the default setting.

LastBootPMDrvs

This flag is set to the number of the last boot driver.

ReadAheadThreshold

This value defines a threshold for the read-ahead buffer. When an application requests data, Windows automatically reads ahead, in increments, up to the threshold value. *ReadAheadThreshold* is set with the Read-Ahead Optimization slider, available on the Hard Disk property page. This property page is available through the File System Properties property sheet.

DriveWriteBehind

This value enables and disables the write-behind caching for all drives, ensuring that data is continually flushed from caches to the hard disk. You can set this value by using the Disable Write-Behind Caching For All Drives check box on the Troubleshooting property page. Selecting this option sets the value to *00 00 00 00*; deselecting this option sets it to *FF FF FF FF*. By default, the flag is deselected and *DriveWriteBehind* is not displayed in the Registry.

AsyncFileCommit

This value is set to *00* by default, which enables a synchronous commit of buffers to disk. Setting this value to *01* enables an asynchronous file commit. The flag is affected by the setting of the Disable Synchronous Buffer Commits option, which is available from the Troubleshooting property page, as shown in Figure 6-11.

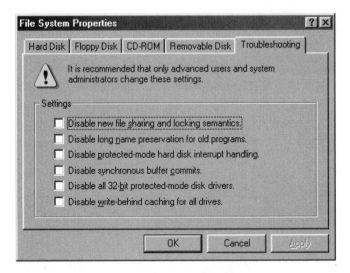

Figure 6-11.
The Troubleshooting property page.

PreserveLongNames

This value enables and disables the Windows 98 feature that preserves long filenames even after a file has been opened and saved by an application that does not support long filenames. Set the value by using the Disable Long Name Preservation For Old Programs option on the Troubleshooting property page. Deselecting this option sets *PreserveLongNames* to *FF FF FF FF*; selecting it sets the value to *00 00 00 00*. By default, the option is deselected and *PreserveLong Names* is not displayed in the Registry.

ForceRMIO

If this flag is set to *01*, the real mode disk IO is forced. (In other words, 32-bit access is disabled.) You can set this flag by using the Disable All 32-Bit Protect-Mode Disk Drivers option, available on the Troubleshooting property page. By default, this flag is set to *00*.

VirtualHDIRQ

Enabling this option prevents Windows 98 from terminating interrupts from the hard disk controller. Set this flag by using the Disable Protected-Mode Hard

Disk Interrupt Handling check box, available on the Troubleshooting property page. A value of *0* enables this feature; a value of *1* (the default) disables this feature.

SoftCompatMode

This value enables and disables the rules for file sharing and locking and can be set when you use the Disable New File Sharing And Locking Semantics option on the Troubleshooting property page. Selecting this option sets the value to *00*; deselecting it sets the value to *01* (the default).

Compression Settings

If you use the DriveSpace 3 tool (available from the Start menu by selecting Programs/Accessories/System Tools/DriveSpace) to compress files on disk volumes, several entries are kept in the *FileSystem* key. These entries can be set from the Disk Compression Settings dialog box, shown in Figure 6-12. To open this property page, select Settings from the Advanced menu in the DriveSpace 3 utility.

Figure 6-12.
The Disk Compression Settings dialog box.

- *AutoMountDrives* If this value is set to *"1"* in the *FileSystem* key, removable compressed media will be automounted. Use the Automatically Mount New Compressed Drive check box (see Figure 6-12) to alter this value.

■ *CompressionAlgorithm* This value defines the compression algorithm (*3*=HiPack, *2*=Standard, *1*=No compression unless disk is full, *0*=No compression at all) used in DriveSpace. Use the option boxes in Disk Compression Settings (see Figure 6-12) to set the value.

■ *CompressionThreshold* This value sets the percentage of free space (of the disk's capacity) required to start the compression. The value is calculated as 100 percent minus the value set in the % text box in the Disk Compression Settings dialog box.

Drive Spin Down Settings

Other entries, such as *ACDriveSpinDown* (alternate current drive spin down) and *BatDriveSpinDown*, specify the amount of time after which the hard disks will be powered off. (But I haven't found a way to set these values by using the Power Management Properties property sheet.)

NOTE: The Search For New Floppy Disk Drives Each Time Your Computer Starts check box shown on the Floppy Disk property page of the File System Properties property sheet is associated with the following key:

HKEY_LOCAL_MACHINE\Config\000x\Enum\BIOS*PNP0700\0B

This key contains a value named *FloppyFastBoot*, which can be set either to *0x00000001* or *0x00000000*. If the value is set to *0*, Windows will start faster because it doesn't check whether a new floppy drive is available.

The *CDFS* and NoVolTrack Subkeys

The *CDFS* subkey contains the entries *CacheSize*, *PrefetchTail*, and *Prefetch*, which control the CD-ROM cache settings. You can set or view these entries on the CD-ROM property page of the File System Properties property sheet.

The *CacheSize* value defines the size of one cache buffer block. The *Prefetch Tail* value defines the number of cache buffer blocks. Multiplying these two values gives you the size of the physical memory used by Windows to read CD-ROM data. That size is shown on the CD-ROM property page. (See Figure 6-13 on the following page.) The *Prefetch* value, which is set in the Optimize Access Pattern For list box, specifies the speed of the CD-ROM drive.

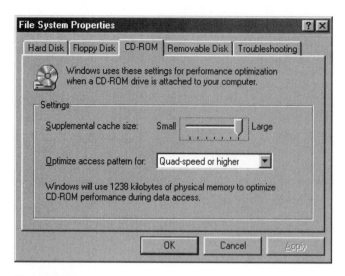

Figure 6-13.
Set the values for the CD-ROM cache.

NOTE: Other settings for the CD-ROM driver, including *Required Pause Tolerance* and *Desired Lru1 Percentage*, are located in *HKEY_LOCAL_MACHINE\SOFTWARE\Microsoft\Windows\CurrentVersion\CD-ROM*.

The *NoVolTrack* subkey contains values for devices that don't have a volume track, such as ROM disks.

NameCache and *PathCache*

On the File System Properties property sheet's Hard Disk property page, which is shown in Figure 6-14, you can define the role of the machine you are using by selecting Desktop Computer, Mobile Or Docking System, or Network Server. Your role selection here determines the size of the *NameCache* and *PathCache* values.

How does this feature work? Windows 98 stores and retrieves the paths and filenames of the last files read in caches. The *NameCache* entry defines the size of the cache used to buffer filenames. The *PathCache* entry defines the size of (that is, the number of entries in) the path cache. Both caches are implemented in the Windows 98 system heap. Table 6-2 shows the sizes of the values for each machine "role."

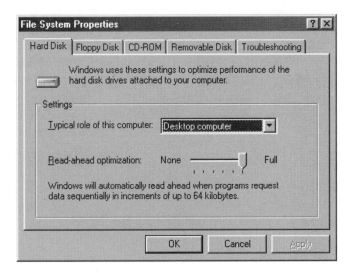

Figure 6-14.
On the Hard Disk property page, you determine the role of the computer you are using.

NameCache and *PathCache* Values

Machine Role	Cache	Value Data
Desktop Computer	*NameCache*	*677*
	PathCache	*32*
Mobile Computing	*NameCache*	*337*
	PathCache	*16*
Network Server	*NameCache*	*2729*
	PathCache	*64*

Table 6-2.
The entries define the size of the values for each machine role.

These cache settings are stored in the *Desktop, Mobile,* and *Server* subkeys of the following Registry key:

*HKEY_LOCAL_MACHINE\Software\Microsoft\Windows\
CurrentVersion\FS Templates*

The *Default* value of the *FS Templates* key contains the name of the selected file system template (for example, *Desktop*). The *Default* value of each subkey contains the related name shown in the list box on the Hard Disk property page. If the *PathCache* and *NameCache* values are not shown in the *Desktop* key's settings, the default values in Table 6-2 are used.

You can define your own profile and fine-tune the cache size. To do so, insert a new subkey into the *FS Template* key, insert a text string into the added key's *Default* value, and then define the values *NameCache* and *PathCache*. (In Figure 6-15, I defined the new profile *Born* with my own settings.) After you define the new subkey and its values, the subkey will be shown as an entry in the Settings group list box on the Hard Disk property page.

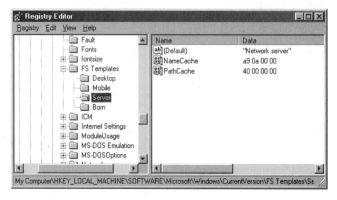

Figure 6-15.
Entries defining the file system templates.

System Properties in the Registry

The Registry contains the settings for the system properties. Most of these settings are defined during Windows setup and during the installing and uninstalling of hardware components. You can alter some of these properties on the System Properties property sheet. (Open the Control Panel and select System.) In this section, we'll look at how the information for hardware profiles and device manager data is stored.

Hardware Profiles

Windows detects the hardware components currently available for dockable computers. You can create profiles for the current configuration on the System Properties property sheet's Hardware Profiles property page, as shown in Figure 6-16.

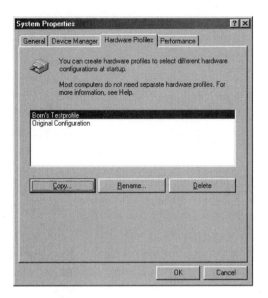

Figure 6-16.
Create profiles on the Hardware Profiles property page.

If you have a mobile computer with different docking stations, you might want to create a hardware profile for each configuration and set a unique name for each profile. You can do this by clicking Copy, which saves the current settings in a separate hardware profile. During the next system startup, you'll see a menu asking which hardware profile should be used, and you'll be able to select the appropriate configuration.

Windows uses two Registry keys, described in the following list, to store information about the hardware profiles.

- *HKEY_LOCAL_MACHINE\System\CurrentControlSet\control\ IDConfigDB* stores global information about the profiles. The *CurrentConfig* value defines the name of the profile currently used. The value is set to a string, such as *"0001"*, which is just a pointer to a subkey of this name that is contained in the *HKEY_LOCAL_ MACHINE\Config* branch. An entry such as *FriendlyName0001* contains profile names, as shown in Figure 6-16.

- *HKEY_LOCAL_MACHINE\Config* stores the hardware profile itself. This key has an additional subkey for each defined hardware profile. These profile subkeys are named *0001, 0002,* and so on. The current profile is indicated by the *CurrentConfig* value mentioned in the preceding bullet. A profile subkey contains the subkeys *Display, Software, System,* and *Enum.*

The *HKEY_LOCAL_MACHINE\Config* key's *Display* subkey contains the subkeys *Fonts*, storing the font properties used by the system, and *Settings*, storing the screen settings. The *Settings* key contains data about the screen resolution, metrics, and other screen attributes. Changing the Hardware Acceleration slider on the Advanced Graphics Settings dialog box affects some of the entries in the *Settings* key. (The Advanced Graphics Settings dialog box is available by clicking Graphics on the Performance property page of the System Properties property sheet.) By default, the Hardware Acceleration slider is set to Full. Moving the slider to the left adds values to the *Settings* key. For example; moving the slider one notch to the left adds a value named *SwCursor* set to *1*, which indicates that the hardware cursor support in the display driver is disabled. Setting the slider to None sets the entries *Advanced=0* and *SwCursor=1*.

The *Software* subkey contains a few subkeys with Internet settings used for this profile. The *System* subkey contains the *CurrentControlSet* subkey with additional subkeys that define the names of the printer drivers.

The *Enum* key contains subkeys with information about the hardware-specific strings used in this profile.

Storing and Manipulating Hardware Component and Plug & Play Information

The *HKEY_LOCAL_MACHINE\Enum* key and the device manager allow you to view the status of and customize your system components. Specifically, *Enum* stores information about the hardware and Plug & Play (PnP) components of your system, and the device manager enables you to manipulate the device configuration. The device manager uses the information stored in the *Enum* key.

Values in the *Enum* Key

The *Enum* key contains subkeys for the specific hardware components used by the computer. Windows uses this information to allocate resources, such as IO addresses and interrupts, for the devices. All values in the *HKEY_LOCAL_MACHINE\Enum* branch are vendor-specific and device-specific, so specific information about parameters is not available. The following list briefly describes entries contained in the *Enum* key, which is shown in Figure 6-17 on page 297.

■ *BIOS* This subkey contains entries for PnP components of the BIOS (which includes timers, controllers, and DMA chips). Each subkey of *BIOS* starts with the string **PNP* and is followed by a four-digit number that represents a particular class of PnP components. Table 6-3 on the following page lists some of the PnP component codes. Each *PNPxxxx* key has subkeys (such as *00* and *01*) that contain the data (such as class name, device description string, driver name, and hardware ID) for the device configuration.

- *ESDI*　This subkey contains the configuration data of the ESDI controller used for hard disk drives and other devices.

- *FLOP*　This subkey contains the configuration data of the floppy disk controllers used in the system.

- *HTREE*　This subkey is reserved for use by Windows.

- *INFRARED*　This subkey is used for infrared devices.

- *ISAPNP*　Contains entries for PnP equipment used on an Industry Standard Architecture (ISA) bus system.

- *MF*　Defines manufacturer-specific information about hardware components.

- *MODEMWAVE*　Stores vendor-specific information for installed modem wave drivers.

- *Monitor*　This subkey contains information about the monitor used in the system. If the setup can't detect the monitor type, the selection is set by the user.

- *Network*　Contains information about the network (redirectors, services, NetBEUI, and so on). The network adapter is specified in the …*Enum\Root\Net* subkey.

- *PCI*　Contains entries for PnP equipment used on a Peripheral Component Interconnect (PCI) bus system.

- *Root*　Contains *PNPxxxx* entries for old non–Plug & Play hardware (such as the CPU, BIOS, network adapters, and printer drivers).

- *SCSI*　Contains the configuration data of the SCSI controllers used in the system.

- *VIRTUAL*　This subkey contains the configuration data for virtual PCI bus PnP devices.

Values for PnP Components

Value Name	Description
PNP0000–PNP0004	Interrupt controllers
PNP0100–PNP0102	System timers
PNP0200–PNP0202	DMA controllers
PNP0300–PNP0313	Keyboard controllers
PNP0400–PNP0401	Printer ports
PNP0500–PNP0501	Communication ports
PNP0600–PNP0602	Hard disk controllers
PNP0700	Standard floppy disk controller
PNP0800	System speaker
PNP0900–PNP0915, PNP0930–PNP0931, PNP0940–PNP0941	Display adapters
PNP0A00–PNP0A04	Expansion buses
PNP0B00	CMOS real-time clock
PNP0C01	System board extension for PnP BIOS
PNP0C02	Reserved
PNP0C04	Numeric data processor
PNP0E00–PNP0E02	PCMCIA controllers
PNP0F01	Serial Microsoft mouse
PNP0F00–PNP0F13	Mouse ports
PNP8xxx	Network adapters
PNPA030	Mitsumi CD-ROM controller
PNPB0xx	Miscellaneous adapters

Table 6-3.
PnP codes are contained in the ...\Enum\BIOS key.

As I mentioned above, PnP components are grouped in classes according to their four-digit code. Further information about the Plug & Play standard can be found in different specifications, which are located on the Microsoft FTP site ftp.microsoft.com in the /developr/drg/Plug-and-Play/Pnpspecs/READ-ME.TXT file and related subdirectories.

Modifying the Device Configuration

You can view and manipulate the device configuration used on your computer through options on the System Properties property sheet's Device Manager property page, shown in Figure 6-18, which is available by clicking the System icon in the Control Panel. This property page lists all the devices recognized by Windows to be on the system (and registered in the Registry) as well as any hardware conflicts. Device conflicts and the current status of each device in the configuration are stored in the Registry key *HKEY_DYN_DATA\Config Manager\Enum*.

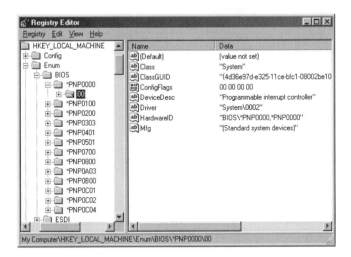

Figure 6-17.
The Enum *key.*

Figure 6-18.
Modify the device configuration by using the Device Manager property page.

297

To inspect or change device properties, you need to access the Properties property sheet. (Click the desired entry on the device list, and then click the Properties button. A property sheet opens with a General tab and other tabs appropriate for the specific device.) You can use these property pages to modify device settings (such as drive letter, I/O range, and Interrupts). All settings are device-specific.

Changing CD-ROM Drive Letters

The drive letters for hard disks and CD-ROMs are defined by Windows 98. Some application programs rely on CD-ROM drives having a specific drive letter. This can cause trouble if the hard disk is partitioned (using FDISK) and drive letters are reassigned. Each partition gets its own drive letter (that is, two partitions will use the drive letters C: and D:), and the CD-ROM is assigned a new drive letter (E:, for example). Some device drivers allow you to reassign the drive letter used by the devices.

Select the drive (under CDROM or Disk Drives, for example) from the device list in the Device Manager, and click Properties. A property sheet opens containing a property page that shows the drive letters available for this device. For a CD-ROM drive, you can alter the range of possible drive letters (for example, E: through H:).

The drive letters used by a particular controller are stored in the drive controller's subkey of the *HKEY_LOCAL_MACHINE\Enum* branch. Each of these subkeys contains the *CurrentDriveLetterAssignment* value set to the name of the assigned drives. (See Figure 6-17 for a list of *Enum* subkeys and controller values.) The assignment of a drive letter to a specific piece of hardware involves vendor-specific information, so you need detailed advice from the vendor about how to change a drive letter.

The *AutoInsertNotification* value controls Windows notification regarding whether a CD-ROM is inserted into a drive. A value of *01* enables notification.

Local System Properties: *HKEY_LOCAL_MACHINE\System*

The *HKEY_LOCAL_MACHINE\System* key contains only one subkey, *CurrentControlSet*, which defines the system properties of the local machine. *CurrentControlSet* has two subkeys: *control* and *Services*.

The *control* Subkey

The *control* subkey contains all the settings necessary for the current Windows configuration. In it you'll find a list of keys storing information about installed system files, file system settings, passwords, and service providers, among other things. The *control* key contains one value besides *Default*, named *Current User*, which contains the name used during logon. Here is a short overview of *control*'s subkeys.

- ▥ *ASD*   This key contains two subkeys, *List* and *Prob*, which store settings used internally by Windows.

- ▥ *ComputerName*   This key contains a subkey also named *ComputerName*. The last key in this hierarchy contains the value *ComputerName*, which defines the computer name of the local machine used for identification in a workgroup. You can alter this name on the Identification property page of the Network property sheet (available by selecting Network in the Control Panel).

- ▥ *DeviceClasses*   This key contains several keys describing device classes.

- ▥ *FileSystem*   This key contains settings for the file system. (See pages 285–290 for a description of this key.)

- ▥ *GroupOrderList*   This key contains a value named *Base* that stores a binary byte stream defining the group order.

- ▥ *IDConfigDB*   This key contains the friendly names for hardware profiles set on the System Properties property page. (See page 293 for further description.)

- ▥ *InstalledFiles*   This key contains a list of the system files (VXD, SPD, DLL) already installed in Windows. This is one of the lists that uninstallers use to detect unused files that can be removed from the \System subfolder.

- ▥ *keyboard layouts*   This key identifies subkeys named for the country code used for international settings in Windows. Subkeys are named like this: *00000409*. Each subkey contains two values: *layout file* (such as "*kbdus.kbd*") and *layout text* (which contains a readable text string such as "*United States*").

- ▥ *MediaProperties*   This key contains subkeys with the properties for Joysticks and MIDI schemes.

- ▥ *MediaResources*   The resources for multimedia devices are defined in this key. This key contains subkeys with the data for audio compression (the *acm* subkey), image compression (the *icm* subkey), the media mapper, a filter list, etc. The data in the *MediaResources* key is controlled by the Multimedia Properties property sheet (select

Control Panel and then Multimedia). The Devices property page of this sheet contains a list of the multimedia devices; from this list you can select an entry to modify. Selecting a device and clicking Properties enables you to view and change the device's settings.

- *NetworkProvider*   This key contains the name and the order of the network providers used on the local machine.

- *Nls*   The *Nls* key contains the definition for national language settings (names of the code pages and the mapping between the country codes and the country names).

- *NTKern*   This key contains one entry, *NextLUID*, specifying the next LUID (logical User ID) to use.

- *PerfStats*   This key contains configuration information for the System Monitor (available from the System Tools submenu of the Accessories menu) and is used to show performance values of memory usage, system components such as the kernel, and other system-related information. The information contained in *PerfStats* is static. Use the key entries to customize the options shown in the Add Item dialog box of the System Monitor. The entries in the Category list are defined by the *Name* value of keys such as *KERNEL*, *VFAT*, etc. The *Name* entry in each subkey defines the string shown in the Item list of the System Monitor. The *Description* value contains the string that will be shown in a message box if you select an item and click the Explain button in the Add Item dialog box. Dynamic data for the system monitor is collected in the *HKEY_DYN_DATA\PerfStats* key.

- *Print*   The print key contains several subkeys (*Environments, Monitors, Ports, Printers, Providers*) that define the data for the installed printers.

- *PwdProvider*   All services needing an access password (such as the screen saver and network services) store the options for the password provider here.

- *SecurityProviders*   This key specifies the DLL files of the security provider.

- *ServiceGroupOrder*   This key contains entries that specify the order of several service groups.

- *ServiceProvider*   This key contains information about service providers used in Windows 98.

■ *SessionManager* Windows uses a session manager to control all applications and routines loaded into memory. Microsoft keeps in the *SessionManager* key information that controls applications. The data in these *SessionManager* subkeys, listed below, should be modified only by Microsoft, in cooperation with affected software vendors, and distributed with Windows and software upgrades.

❑ *AppPatches* This key contains the names of applications and the patch data that forces these applications to run under Windows 98.

❑ *CheckBadApps* This key contains the names and versions of application programs (each filename is also a key name) that cause trouble in Windows 98. If the user tries to load such an application in Windows, a message box with a warning occurs. The *CheckBadApps400* key contains similar entries.

❑ *CheckVerDLLs* This key contains a list of DLL routines whose versions are checked during loading.

❑ *HackIniFiles* This key contains information for modifying the INI files of applications so that they run properly in Windows 98.

❑ *Known16DLLs* This key contains the names of all 16-bit DLL routines installed in Windows 98. (If you add a driver in SYSTEM.INI, for instance, it will be shown in the list.)

❑ *KnownDLLs* This key contains a list of 32-bit DLL routines.

❑ *WarnVerDLLs* Loading a DLL included in *WarnVerDLLs* results in a warning during loading.

❑ *Shutdown* This key contains data relevant to a shutdown process (*Fast Reboot="1"*, for instance).

NOTE: There is also a key named *Session Manager* (notice the space that differentiates it from the *SessionManager* key) containing the *Power* subkey. This key contains two values defining the AC and DC power policies.

■ *TimeZoneInformation* This key contains the settings for the current time zone. Some of its entries are used on the Date/Time Properties property sheet (available by double-clicking the current time display on the Windows taskbar).

■ *Update* This key, which contains the values *NetworkPath* and *UpdateMode*, specifies how Windows is updated: *UpdateMode=0* (no update), *UpdateMode=1* (automatic update, use network path),

UpdateMode=2 (manual update, requests a path). The values *UpdateMode*, *NetworkPath*, and the optional flags *LoadBalance* and *Verbose* can be altered with the System Policy Editor (select Local Computer and then the path *Windows 98 Network**Update*).

■ *VMM32Files* This key contains a list of all VXD files installed in Windows 98.

■ *WebPost* This key is used by the Web Publishing Wizard.

The *Services* Subkey

HKEY_LOCAL_MACHINE*System**CurrentControlSet**Services* contains a list of Windows 98 services. The content of this list depends on the software installed under Windows 98.

■ *Arbitrators* This key contains other subkeys with specific data (denoting reserved resources, for instance) for the bus arbitrators (address, DMA, IO, IRQ).

■ *Class* This key contains device data organized by class (adapter, USB, CDROM, disk drivers, display, and keyboard, among others).

■ *Inetaccess* This key contains settings (such as cache parameters) for Internet access.

■ *MSNP32* This key contains parameters for the Microsoft Network.

■ *NcpServer* This key contains the NCPServer parameters.

■ *NPSTUB* Stub with empty keys for NP protocol.

■ *NWNP82* This key defines the network provider for group policies in Novell Networks.

■ *ProtectedStorage* This key contains settings for the Microsoft Authenticode storage protection of downloaded ActiveX components.

■ *RemoteAccess, MSNP32, NcpServer, Winsock* These keys contain information specific to optional services. These keys contain valid data only if the service is already installed. *RemoteAccess* is used to allow remote access to the local Registry through the System Policy Editor. *Winsock* is necessary if you use the TCP/IP protocol to establish, for example, an Internet connection with Microsoft Internet Explorer.

■ *SNMP* This key contains subkeys storing information related to the Simple Network Management Protocol.

- *UPDATE*   This key contains entries related to the Intel Update Driver.

- *VXD*   This key contains the names of all VxD drivers loaded during Windows startup.

- *WDMFS*   This key contains entries related to the Windows File System Mapper.

- *WebPost*   This key contains entries for the Web Publishing Wizard.

- *WinSock*   This key contains Windows Sockets parameters.

- *WinSock2*   This key contains more Winsock parameters.

Settings for System Software

Information about installed fonts, settings for starting an MS-DOS window, and other install information is controlled by keys in the Registry.

Installed Fonts

By default, fonts are stored in TTF files in the \Windows\Fonts folder, but they can also be stored in other folders on the local system. Information about the fonts available in Windows 98 is stored in the following key:

HKEY_LOCAL_MACHINE\SOFTWARE\Microsoft\Windows\CurrentVersion\Fonts

Names of the values for this key are the same as the font names, and each value's data is a text string containing the name of the TTF file.

To take a look at a list of the currently installed fonts, open the Fonts folder. (Open the Control Panel, and then click Fonts.) If you want to add any fonts to this list, you can do so through the Add Fonts dialog box. (Open the File menu, and select Install New Font.) Windows 98 allows you to install approximately 1000 fonts; this limit exists because Windows 98 can read keys with a maximum size of 64 KB. (In Microsoft Windows NT, the size of a key is limited to 1 MB.) Here are some tips for installing fonts efficiently.

- If you can, install all fonts in the \Windows\Fonts folder. Font files take up space on the hard disk and can slow the system down, so you don't want duplicate fonts on your system.

- If an application requires its fonts to be stored in a separate folder, you can still ensure that there are no duplicates by creating a shortcut (a LNK file) from the \Fonts subfolder to the folder in which the font file is stored. Do this by deselecting the Copy Fonts To Fonts Folder option in the Add Fonts dialog box when you add the font. Fonts are stored in a font cache (TTFCACHE) and are loaded during the system startup.

Besides the TrueType fonts kept in the *Fonts* key, there are also settings for raster fonts. These settings are stored in the key *HKEY_LOCAL_MACHINE\ Config\000x\Display\Fonts*. Definitions for the small and large fonts are stored in the branch *HKEY_LOCAL_MACHINE\SOFTWARE\Microsoft\Windows\ CurrentVersion\fontsize*. The *120* subkey defines large fonts, and the *96* subkey defines small fonts.

User-Supplied Install Information

During the Windows install process, Setup asks you to enter the owner name, the organization, the CD key, and so on in a series of dialog boxes. These settings are then used in several other dialog boxes and message boxes. What if some of this information has changed? Do you need to reinstall Windows 98? No—using the Registry Editor, you can modify these types of settings, which are all stored in the following single key:

> *HKEY_LOCAL_MACHINE\SOFTWARE\Microsoft\Windows\ CurrentVersion*

In this key, you'll find interesting information about installation parameters and other miscellaneous settings, some of which are described here:

- *ConfigPath* This value defines the path to the \config subfolder, which contains the file GENERAL.IDF, which is used for MIDI instruments.

- *DevicePath* This value points to the \INF subfolder, which contains the INF files for the uninstall feature.

- *MediaPath* This value defines the path where the media files (such as WAV, AVI, and MDI files) are stored.

- *ProductId* This value contains the CD-ROM key code that you must enter during the install process.

- *RegisteredOrganization* This value names the organization for which the installed Windows 98 copy is registered.

- *RegisteredOwner* This value names the registered owner for the installed Windows 98 copy.

Besides these values, you'll find other entries that contain the installation date, the Windows version number, and the path of the old Windows folder.

If you must change the name of the owner/organization, you can use the following statements in a REG file:

```
REGEDIT4

[HKEY_LOCAL_MACHINE\SOFTWARE\Microsoft\Windows\CurrentVersion]
"RegisteredOwner"="xxxxx"
"RegisteredOrganization"="yyyyy"
```

These lines are in the OWNER.REG file in the \chapter6 folder of the sample files. Insert the relevant names in place of *xxxxx* and *yyyyy*, and then save the lines in a REG file. After you double-click the REG file, the information is added to the Registry. You can check whether the values have taken effect by double-clicking the System icon in the Control Panel. The General property page of the System Properties property sheet should show the new entries.

Applets

The ...*CurrentVersion\Applets* key contains the Applets settings (for Check Drive and Defrag, for example).

Controls Folder

The ...*CurrentVersion\Controls Folder* key contains a binary data stream of data that is used to create the Control Panel folder.

ICM

The ...*CurrentVersion\ICM* key has subkeys containing information related to integrated color management.

Internet Settings

The ...*CurrentVersion\Internet Settings* key contains the settings for Microsoft Internet Explorer 4.0. You can alter many of these settings by using the Internet Explorer property sheet.

ProfileList

The ...*CurrentVersion\ProfileList* key contains the names of the user profiles used on the computer. If you want to remove one user profile, delete the entry for the particular user in this key.

Setup Data

The following key contains several subkeys that control the Windows 98 Setup process and that are used to install and remove optional components:

HKEY_LOCAL_MACHINE\SOFTWARE\Microsoft\Windows\ CurrentVersion\SETUP

The values in the key's various subkeys are set by Windows, so you shouldn't modify them. The subkeys are as follows:

- *BaseWinOptions*. This key can contain the names of INF files that are used to configure the basic Windows options. An entry like *msmail.inf* can be set to *0x00000001* to indicate that Windows should use the INF file for the settings.

- *EBD*. This key contains subkeys that control the keyboard settings and locale settings in AUTOEXEC.BAT and CONFIG.SYS.

- *NetSetup*. This key contains parameters related to network setup.

- *OptionalComponents*. This key contains a value for each optional component; each value identifies the name of a component. For example, the value name *CharMap* identifies the Character Map program. The value data associated with a value name is set to the component's name (for example, *"CharMap"*). For each value in *Optional Components*, you'll find a subkey under *OptionalComponents* named after the component's value name. For example, if the key includes the value *CharMap = "CharMap"*, you'll also find the subkey ...*OptionalComponents\CharMap*. The entries in the *CharMap* subkey define whether the optional component is installed.

- The value *INF* defines the name of the INF file used to install or remove the optional component (such *as "appletpp.inf"*).

- The *Installed* entry indicates whether an optional value is installed. A value of *"1"* in *Installed* indicates that the optional component is already installed. A value of *"0"* indicates that the component isn't installed yet.

- The *Section* entry defines the section in the INF file that is used to install the optional component.

- *SetupX*. This key contains information related to the INF files, catalog files, and certifications stored on the system.

- *VarLDID*. This key contains entries related to the LDID (logical disk ID) of several installed Internet components.

■ *WinbootDir.* This key contains the entry *devdir.* The value is set to the Windows subfolder (for example, *"C:\Windows").*

Setting Keyboard Speed and Delay

When you press down on a single keyboard key for an extended period of time, the keyboard eventually generates the character repeatedly. You can control keyboard delay (that is, the time it takes the system to begin generating the letter) and keyboard speed (that is, how quickly the character repeats) on the Speed property page of the Keyboard Properties property sheet, which is available by selecting the Control Panel and clicking the Keyboard icon. Set such values by using the Repeat Delay and Repeat Rate slider settings. When you set these values and click Apply, a new *Keyboard* subkey is generated in the *HKEY_USERS\ xxxx\Control Panel* key and the values *KeyboardDelay* and *KeyboardSpeed* are added. (The characters *xxxx* stand for the user's name or for *.Default.* The *Keyboard* key is not available by default.)

NOTE: The value for the cursor blink rate is stored in the *Cursor BlinkRate* value, which can be found in the *HKEY_CURRENT_ USER\Control Panel\desktop* key.

Settings for the MS-DOS Mode

Windows offers an MS-DOS window that allows you to run old DOS application programs. The following key contains the subkeys *MS-DOS Emulation* and *MS-DOSOptions*:

HKEY_LOCAL_MACHINE\SOFTWARE\Microsoft\Windows\ CurrentVersion

MS-DOS Emulation contains the *DisplayParams* value, which defines the display properties of the MS-DOS window. It also contains several predefined subkeys with settings for certain MS-DOS applications. (Users cannot alter these subkeys.)

You can also run each MS-DOS application in single MS-DOS mode. You can configure the options for this mode with the following steps:

1. Right-click the MS-DOS file, and select Properties to open the file's Properties property sheet.

2. Click the Program tab, and then click Advanced. This invokes the Advanced Program Settings dialog box. (See Figure 6-19 on the following page.)

3. Check the MS-DOS Mode option, and then select Specify A New MS-DOS Configuration.

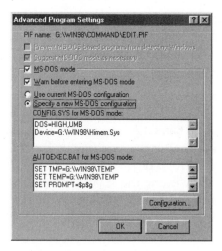

Figure 6-19.
The Advanced Program Settings dialog box.

4. Click the Configuration button to invoke the Select MS-DOS Configuration Options dialog box. (See Figure 6-20.) You can set different options for MS-DOS mode in this dialog box.

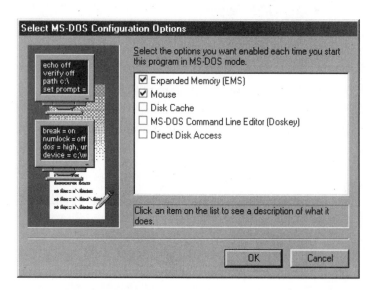

Figure 6-20.
The MS-DOS configuration options.

When you check one of the options in the Select MS-DOS Configuration Options dialog box and click OK, Windows generates the statements for CONFIG.SYS and AUTOEXEC.BAT to support the selected feature (for example, Disk Cache, EMS, etc.).

The options for the single MS-DOS mode are stored in the following key:

HKEY_LOCAL_MACHINE\SOFTWARE\Microsoft\Windows\ CurrentVersion\MS-DOSOptions

If you open this key in the Registry Editor, you'll see several subkeys containing the settings for various options. (See Figure 6-21.)

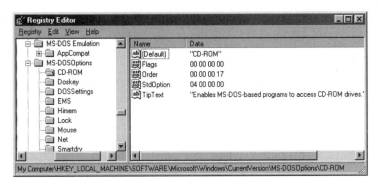

Figure 6-21.
The MS-DOSOptions *key.*

Each subkey of *MS-DOSOptions* can contain several values that set the options for the feature defined by the subkey. Table 6-4 on the following page contains brief descriptions of these values.

You can change the settings in the *MS-DOSOptions* subkeys. Use the strings in the *Autoexec.Bat* and *Config.Sys* values to customize the commands for your computer. For example, you can overwrite the settings of your old MS-DOS configuration files, such as the commands to include the CD-ROM driver and MSCDEX.EXE, which are commented out by the Windows Setup program. The same occurs with network and mouse statements.

When you click OK, Windows takes the *Autoexec.bat* and *Config.sys* values in the *MS-DOSOptions* subkey and inserts their data strings in the Advanced Program Settings window. If you miss a command necessary to run the MS-DOS application in *Autoexec.bat* or *Config.sys*, you can add the line manually into the Advanced Program Settings window. However, this requires that you know which command is needed, its order in the configuration file, and all parameters or options requested for this command.

Values for the Subkeys of the *MS-DOSOptions* Key

Value Name	Description
Default	The *Default* value of each key contains the string shown in the Select MS-DOS Configuration Options window, shown in Figure 6-20 on page 308. You can change the string to customize the option.
Autoexec.Bat	This value contains a string with the statement inserted in AUTOEXEC.BAT (*"LoadHigh %WINDIR%\Command\ DOSKey"*, for example). The placeholder *%WINDIR%* defines the Windows folder.
Config.Sys	This value contains a string value with the command line that must be inserted into CONFIG.SYS.
Flags	This is a binary value that can be set to the following (hex) values: *00* Disable the key *02* Show this option; uncheck the box *07* Hide this option; select option by default *1B* Show this option; check the box The values *01* and *40* disable the option. The *Flags* value is stored sometimes as a binary value and sometimes as a DWORD value.
Order	The statements in AUTOEXEC.BAT and CONFIG.SYS must be ordered. Windows uses this DWORD value to order the lines in the *Autoexec.Bat* or *Config.Sys* values. If several entries use identical *Order* values, Windows arranges these lines as it reads them from the Registry. If you want one entry to precede another, set its *Order* value to a number lower than that of the entry you want it to precede.
StdOption	This value is used internally by Windows 98.
TipText	The string found in this value is shown in the Select MS-DOS Configuration Options dialog box in the footer "tip" box when you click the entry. (See Figure 6-20.) Consider this string help text showing the user additional information about the selected option.

Table 6-4.
Values that set the options for the feature defined by a subkey of
MS-DOSOptions.

Wouldn't it be nice to extend the options available in the configuration window? This would allow you to simply check an option to make Windows use the Registry to change the command. (You need to set the option for the

MS-DOSOptions subkey only once.) To extend the *MS-DOSOptions* key, you must add a subkey and set the values defined in Table 6-4. This can be done with a simple REG file:

```
REGEDIT4

[HKEY_LOCAL_MACHINE\SOFTWARE\Microsoft\Windows\CurrentVersion\ ⇥
MS-DOSOptions\Born]
@="NumLock off (Born)"
"TipText"="Switch off the Numlock key."
"Flags"=hex:02,00,00,00
"Order"=hex:00,00,00,13
"Config.sys"="NUMLOCK=OFF"
```

After you double-click the REG file, you will find the new *Born* subkey in the Registry, as shown in Figure 6-22. You can find the MSDOS.REG file in the \chapter6 folder of the sample files.

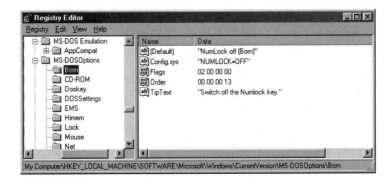

Figure 6-22.
The new Born *subkey for* MS-DOSOptions.

The entries shown in Figure 6-22 create a new option, NumLock Off (Born), in the Select MS-DOS Configuration Options window, as shown in Figure 6-23 on the following page. When you check this option, Windows inserts the NUMLOCK=OFF command into CONFIG.SYS, which switches off the NumLock key after a system startup.

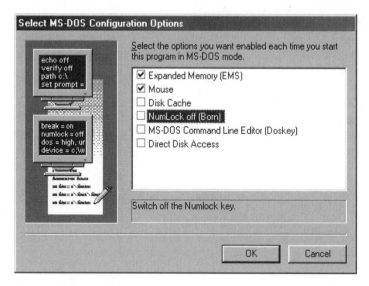

Figure 6-23.
A new option in the configuration window.

> NOTE: If you want to offer a remove option for these options, you must create an INF file that adds the uninstall commands for the new subkeys. Examples of such INF files are given in other chapters.

Modem Registry Keys

Installed modem drivers keep their information in the following key:

> *HKEY_LOCAL_MACHINE\System\CurrentControlSet\Services\
> Class\Modem*

Each installed modem has its own subkey, which is named *0000, 0001*, etc. The *Init* subkey contains the string to initialize the modem before Windows 98 uses it. The coding of the modem keys is discussed in the *Microsoft Windows 98 Resource Kit* (Microsoft Press, 1998) and in detail in the *Windows 98 Device Development Kit*.

TCP/IP Keys

Configuration settings for the TCP/IP protocol are stored in several Registry keys. You can find some of these settings in the following branch:

> *HKEY_LOCAL_MACHINE\System\CurrentControlSet\Services*

This branch contains the keys *VXD**MSTCP*, *VXD**MSTCP**ServiceProvider*, *VXD**MSTCP**NodeType*, and *Class**NetTrans**000x*, all of which contain multiple TCP/IP settings. Further information about these settings can be found in the *Microsoft Windows 98 Resource Kit*.

CHAPTER SEVEN

Programming Issues

Throughout this book, we've looked at how software components can be registered using different techniques. If you are writing software that will be distributed to end users, using the Registry Editor to register components is appropriate only for test purposes—you can't distribute modifications to end users. REG files, setup programs, and INF files offer more convenient and safer methods for customizing the Registry, and they provide more practical methods for distributing those modifications.

If you write your own software, this chapter will be especially relevant to you. We address in more detail how and where you register software components, how you can use a program to update the Registry, and how you can use INF files more extensively. We will also take a quick look at how to build your own templates for the System Policy Editor.

Registering Version and Status Information

Some software information is inserted into the Registry by the software's setup program; other information is stored later by the application. An application stores this information in the *Software* key of these two root keys:

- *HKEY_LOCAL_MACHINE* Settings that pertain to the software, such as a version number, are stored here.

- *HKEY_CURRENT_USER* Settings that are user-dependent, such as the most recent file list, are stored here.

If you are writing software, your application must enter its settings in the appropriate keys. Let's look at an example to determine where certain kinds of information would be stored. Suppose your software had multiple versions, one version designed for the typical end user and one for the experienced professional user. This information is pertinent to your machine and would therefore be stored in *HKEY_LOCAL_MACHINE*. Your setup program would add the following entries—generic names are used in this example—in the Registry:

HKEY_LOCAL_MACHINE\SOFTWARE\company\product\settings

For the first two subkeys under the *SOFTWARE* key, use your actual company and product names. For example, Microsoft inserts the key ...*SOFTWARE\\Microsoft*, which contains entries for Microsoft products, such as Microsoft Windows, Microsoft Word, and Microsoft Excel, as well as entries for system extensions such as SCC viewers. You can use your own structure following the *product* key. You might, for example, want to insert all settings relevant to all users as values in the *product* subkey. Note that Windows uses the *CurrentVersion* subkey of the *Windows* product key to separate miscellaneous entries. Take a look at the key structure of other software programs to learn how to build your own.

You've also got to build a structure for user-dependent settings. As we've seen, they're stored in the *HKEY_CURRENT_USER\Software* branch. This branch also has a key structure that includes the vendor and product names: ...*company\product\settings*. What you've got to decide now is which entries should be keys and which entries should be values. Let's assume you want to store a recent file list for the current user. I don't recommend that you use subkeys such as *File*, *File1*, and *File2*. Rather, you should create a subkey with a name like *Recent Files* and then add values with names such as *File*, *File1*, and *File2*.

Remember that a key's name cannot be changed without using the Registry Editor. If you want to change the name of a key, you'll have to delete the key and add its entries under a new key name.

> **NOTE:** The distinction between the *HKEY_CURRENT_USER* branch and the *HKEY_USERS* branch is important. The *HKEY_CURRENT_USER* branch is built during each Windows startup, after the user logs on to the system. This branch contains all data relevant for the current user.
>
> Windows collects the settings for all registered users in the *HKEY_USERS* branch. Therefore, you'll find subkeys such as *.default* and *Born* in *HKEY_USERS*. If you change a setting in *HKEY_CURRENT_USER*, that change is immediately reflected in *HKEY_USERS* in the current user's subkey.
>
> You should update all values in the *HKEY_CURRENT_USER* branch, not in the *HKEY_USERS* branch. If you want to apply the settings to all users, you can do so in *HKEY_LOCAL_MACHINE*.

Application-Specific Registry Entries

If you are a developer writing software that will be installed under Microsoft Windows 98, you'll want your setup program to set specific Registry entries.

Registering a New File Type

If you want your application to start automatically when a file of a given file type is double-clicked, you'll need to register the file type and associate it with your application. Also, if you want to extend the context menu of the file type, you'll need to add a few entries to the Registry. You'll probably also want to register a unique icon for this file type. Windows 98 stores this information in the *HKEY_CLASSES_ROOT* tree. (The *HKEY_LOCAL_MACHINE\ SOFTWARE\Classes* branch contains a copy of this branch.) Each file type should have two keys in *HKEY_CLASSES_ROOT*, signified here as *.ext* and *identifier*:

```
HKEY_CLASSES_ROOT
  .ext = "identifier"
  ⋮
  identifier = optional text string
  ⋮
    DefaultIcon = "path to icon source"
    shell
      verb
        command = command string
```

See Chapter 3 for details on where in the Registry this information belongs.

Registering an Icon Handler

Some applications provide their own icon handlers. These handlers must be registered in the *shellex* subkey, as shown below:

```
identifier
  DefaultIcon = "%1"
  ⋮
  shellex
    IconHandler
      {xxxxxxxx-xxxx-xxxx-xxxx-xxxxxxxxxxxx}
      ⋮
```

The characters in the key *{xxxxxxxx-xxxx-xxxx-xxxx-xxxxxxxxxxxxxx}* stand for the Class ID code (CLSID) of this handler. (The CLSID code is a unique number for each ActiveX component, and there is a *CLSID* subkey in the *HKEY_CLASSES_ROOT* branch to register additional ActiveX components. Chapter 3 contains some additional information about this CLSID code.) The *DefaultIcon* key contains the name of the icon source. If an application supports its own icon handler for a file type, setting the value for *DefaultIcon* to *%1* means that the icon handler can show different icons for each file instance of this file type.

Registering a Context Menu Handler

Some applications provide handlers for their own application-specific context menus. For instance, the Recycle Bin handler contains its own context menu handler. If you right-click on the Recycle Bin icon, a context menu containing entries specific to the Recycle Bin is shown. Context menu handlers must be registered in the *shellex* subkey as follows:

```
identifier
  ⋮
  shellex
    ContextMenuHandlers
      {XXXXXXXX-XXXX-XXXX-XXXX-XXXXXXXXXXXXXX}
```

The characters in the key *{xxxxxxxx-xxxx-xxxx-xxxx-xxxxxxxxxxxxxx}* stand for the CLSID code of the handler.

Registering a Property Sheet Handler

An application can provide its own handler for property sheets. For example, if you invoke a property sheet for a drive or for a BAT file, the property sheet will contain property pages specific to the selected item. The property sheet handler must be registered in the *shellex* subkey, as shown here and in Figure 7-1.

```
identifier
  ⋮
  shellex
    PropertySheetHandlers
      {XXXXXXXX-XXXX-XXXX-XXXX-XXXXXXXXXXXXXX}
        ⋮
```

The characters in the key *{xxxxxxxx-xxxx-xxxx-xxxx-xxxxxxxxxxxxxx}* stand for the CLSID code of this handler.

Figure 7-1.
Property Sheet handler entry in the Registry.

> **NOTE:** The Control Panel contains entries that include their own property sheets. Extending those property sheets with property pages of your own choosing requires an extension of the Registry.

Registering Other Handlers

An application can provide its own data handler to support data in the clipboard. This handler must be registered in the *shellex* subkey as follows:

```
identifier
  ⋮
shellex
  DataHandler
    {XXXXXXXX-XXXX-XXXX-XXXX-XXXXXXXXXXXX}
    ⋮
```

If the application supports its own drag and drop function, the drop handler also must be registered in the *shellex* subkey:

```
identifier
  ⋮
shellex
  DropHandler
    {XXXXXXXX-XXXX-XXXX-XXXX-XXXXXXXXXXXX}
    ⋮
```

The characters in the key *{xxxxxxxx-xxxx-xxxx-xxxx-xxxxxxxxxxxx}* stand in both cases for the CLSID code of this handler.

A Few Remarks About Registering ActiveX Components

For each ActiveX component (formerly called an OLE component) registered on a machine, the Registry contains a subkey in the *HKEY_CLASSES_ROOT\ CLSID* branch. This key is named for the Class ID number associated with the component. The key can contain an *InfoTip* value, and it contains one or more of the following subkeys, which designate the different parts of the component that are registered. (See Figure 7-2.)

- *LocalServer32*   This key is optional and contains the path and filename of the local 32-bit out-of-process server (an EXE program with any command-line arguments).

- *InProcServer32*   The default value defines the path (which is optional) and the filename of a 32-bit in-process server (which is a 32-bit DLL). The *ThreadingModel* value defines the threading for the component and will contain data such as *Apartment*.

- *InProcHandler32*   Registers the path and filename of a 32-bit DLL handler used for this object type.

NOTE: Above I have listed only 32-bit components. A programmer who intends to support old 16-bit handlers can also add *LocalServer*, *InProcServer*, and *InProcHandler* entries to the Class ID number key under the *CLSID* key.

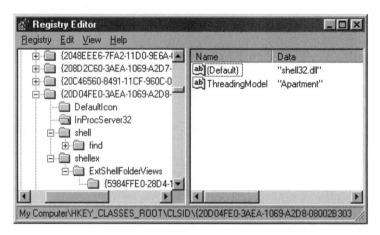

Figure 7-2.
The InProcServer32 *entry in the Registry.*

There are other subkeys in the *HKEY_CLASSES_ROOT* branch containing additional settings for registered ActiveX components.

■ *Interface* This subkey contains the interface identifiers, such as *IUnknown* and *IClassFactory*, for the COM interface.

■ *TypeLib* This subkey contains the ClassID codes of type libraries that are used to store information about ActiveX classes, interfaces, and data structures.

NOTE: If your application relies on data in specific paths, you need to register these paths. See Chapter 6 for details on Registry locations. Also, every application designed for Windows 98 should have an uninstall feature. You must add your application to the Registry to make this feature available through the Add/Remove Programs Properties property sheet (which is available from the Control Panel). See Chapter 5 for more information on using the Registry with the uninstall feature.

NOTE: Some details about OLE are discussed in Charles Petzold's book *Programming Windows* (Microsoft Press, 1998). The basics about OLE can be found in the book *Inside OLE, 2nd Edition,* by Kraig Brockschmidt (Microsoft Press, 1995).

Using a Program to Access the Registry

If you use a programming tool such as Microsoft Visual Basic (VB) or Microsoft Visual C++, you can write your own setup routine to perform the install process. This setup routine copies the required files and updates the Registry entries. Microsoft programming language packages are shipped with setup wizards and install programs (such as InstallSHIELD) that provide you with functions to install and uninstall the software packages you create. You can find further information about these tools in the online reference shipped with the compilers.

In some cases, you must access the Registry from a program to read settings or store specific settings for the next session. Windows 98 provides a set of API functions for accessing the Registry. Table 7-1, on the next page, contains an overview of some of the API functions provided by Windows (or, more precisely, by Win32). Both Win16 and Win32 API functions are supported by Windows 98.

API Functions Supported by Windows 98

Function	Description
RegCloseKey	A Win16 API function that closes the defined key.
RegCreateKey	A Win16 API function that creates the specified key. New Win32 applications should use the Win32 *RegCreateKeyEx* function.
RegCreateKeyEx	A Win32 API function that creates the specified key. If the key already exists in the registry, this function opens it.
RegDeleteKey	A Win16 function that deletes a defined key by removing the key and all its values. It cannot delete a key that contains subkeys.
RegDeleteValue	A Win32 function that deletes a named value from a specified key.
RegEnumKey	A Win16 API function that enumerates subkeys of the given open Registry key. The function retrieves the name of one subkey each time it is called. Win32 applications should use *RegEnumKeyEx*.
RegEnumKeyEx	A Win32 API function that enumerates the subkeys of a given open key.
RegEnumValue	A Win32 API function that enumerates all values of a given open key.
RegFlushKey	Writing information to the Registry can take several seconds before the cache is flushed onto the hard disk. An application can use the Win32 *RegFlushKey* function to force Windows to write the buffers to the hard disk, but this function uses many system resources and should be called only when necessary.
RegOpenKey	A Win16 function that opens a key. *RegOpenKey* does not create the specified key if that key does not exist in the Registry. *RegOpenKey* is provided for compatibility with Microsoft Windows 3.1. New Win32 applications should use the *RegOpenKeyEx* function.
RegOpenKeyEx	A Win32 API function that opens a specified key.

Table 7-1.
*These API calls are supported by Windows 98 and can be used to read
and change the settings in the Registry.*

Function	Description
RegQueryInfoKey	A Win32 API function that delivers information about a key.
RegQueryValue	A Win16 API function that retrieves the value associated with the unnamed value for a specified open key in the Registry. New Win32 applications should use the *RegQueryValueEx* function.
RegQueryValueEx	A Win32 API function that returns the value of an entry associated with a given open key.
RegSetValue	A Win16 API function that sets a value of a given key. New Win32 applications should use the *RegSetValueEx* function, which allows an application to set any number of named values of any data type.
RegSetValueEx	A Win32 API function that sets the value in the specified key.

NOTE: The Win32 API functions are defined for Windows 95, Windows 98, and Microsoft Windows NT. Windows NT contains additional attributes (security attributes) for Registry keys. You can find a detailed description of the API calls in the Win32 SDK.

The application must open the Registry key by using *RegOpenKey* or *RegOpenKeyEx* before a value is read or stored. Both API functions deliver a handle to the key; that handle will be used in other API calls. *RegCreateKey* and *RegCreateKeyEx* create a new subkey for an already open key. *RegCloseKey* closes an open key and writes the data to the Registry. The data is cached, and you can use *RegFlushKey* to flush the cache to the hard disk.

A Visual Basic Example

The commands needed to read/write information to the Registry depend on the language platform you use. Visual Basic 4.0 and later, for example, provide built-in functions such as *SaveSetting*, *GetAllSettings*, and *GetSetting* for reading and writing Registry entries, and you don't need any commands at all to open or close the Registry. (The Registry is opened and closed in the run-time library.) Beginning on the following page is a simple Visual Basic for Applications (VBA) procedure that accesses application settings in the Registry.

```
Sub Registry()
'
' Visual Basic Code (by G. Born)
'
' Sample program to show how to access application
' settings in the Registry with Visual Basic

Dim Settings As Variant
Dim Response As Integer
Dim Version As String

' Create a new key "G_Born\Init" in:
' HKEY_CURRENT_USER\Software\VB and VBA Program Settings
'
' Command: SaveSetting appname, section, key, setting
'
' All four parameters are required, all string expressions:
' appname  containing the application or project name
' section  containing the section name
' key      containing the name of the key
' setting  containing the value

' An error occurs if the key setting can't be saved
'


Response = MsgBox("Add keys?", vbYesNo + vbQuestion _
           + vbDefaultButton2, "Registry access")
If Response = vbYes Then        ' User chose Yes
' Add the new keys with fixed values
    SaveSetting appname:="G_Born", Section:="Init", _
                Key:="Version", setting:=1.3

    SaveSetting "G_Born", "Init", "LRUFile", "C:\Text\Born.doc"

    SaveSetting "G_Born", "Init", "Author", "G. Born"
End If

' Try to read the version number back

Version = GetSetting(appname:="G_Born", Section:="Init", _
                     Key:="Version", Default:="Key not found")

' Show the result in a message box
Response = MsgBox("Key: Version = " + Version, _
           vbOKOnly + vbInformation, "Key value")
```

```
' Test to see whether the key exists--
"Version" is set to "Key not found"
If Version <> "Key not found" Then
    crlf = Chr(10) + Chr(13)
    test = ""                          ' Clear string

    ' Now try to list all subkeys in Init

    Settings = GetAllSettings(appname:="G_Born", Section:="Init")
    For Count = LBound(Settings, 1) To UBound(Settings, 1)
        test = test + Settings(Count, 0) + ": " _
                + Settings(Count, 1) _
                + crlf
    Next Count

    Response = MsgBox(test, vbOKOnly + vbInformation, "Key values")

    ' Ask before deleting the key
    Response = MsgBox("Delete key?", vbYesNo + vbQuestion _
                + vbDefaultButton2, "Registry access")
    If Response = vbYes Then          ' User chose Yes
        ' Remove the section "Init" and all its settings
        ' from Registry.
        ' The key "G_Born" can't be removed!
        DeleteSetting "G_Born", "Init"
    End If
End If

End Sub
```

This code creates a *G_Born* subkey under the key *HKEY_CURRENT_USER\Software\VB and VBA Program Settings* and adds to it the *Init* subkey with the values *Version*, *LRUFile*, and *Author*. Different message boxes control the program flow to access, show, and delete the *G_Born* key's Registry settings.

When you access the Registry through Visual Basic 4.0 or later, you must use the 32-bit version—16-bit code will create INI files instead.

NOTE: You can find this procedure in the REGISTRY.BAS file in the \chapter7\VBASample folder of the sample files. This procedure can be used with Visual Basic 4.0 or later, and the file can be imported into Microsoft Office 97 VBA. If you use Microsoft Word for Windows 95, WordBasic provides the GetPrivateProfileString and SetPrivateProfileString commands to alter the Registry. (You'll find an example of how to access the Registry with WordBasic in the RegOptions macro in the MACROS7.DOT file, located by default in the MSOffice\WinWord\Macros folder.)

Extended Registry Access in Visual Basic

Using the SaveSetting and GetSetting functions supported in VB limits you to the *HKEY_CURRENT_USER\Software\VB and VBA Program Settings* key in the Registry. But often Visual Basic and VBA programs need to access other Registry keys. Below I'll show you how to use the API calls from Table 7-1 to access Windows 98 Registry keys. To keep this task as simple as possible for the Visual Basic programmer, all modules are encapsulated in simple VB functions. Therefore, Registry access requires nothing more than a simple function call (that is, all internals are hidden in the called function).

To call API functions from VB modules, we need to add Declare statements for the API function calling interface as well as declarations for a few constants used in the API calls. The listing below shows these declarations. (Most of these declarations can be found in C header files or in VB API declaration files.)

```
' Constants for Registry keys
Public Const HKEY_CLASSES_ROOT = &H80000000
Public Const HKEY_CURRENT_USER = &H80000001
Public Const HKEY_LOCAL_MACHINE = &H80000002
Public Const HKEY_USERS = &H80000003
Public Const HKEY_PERFORMANCE_DATA = &H80000004
Public Const HKEY_CURRENT_CONFIG = &H80000005
Public Const HKEY_DYN_DATA = &H80000006


' Other constants used in API calls
Public Const KEY_QUERY_VALUE = &H1
Public Const KEY_SET_VALUE = &H2
Public Const KEY_CREATE_SUB_KEY = &H4
Public Const KEY_ENUMERATE_SUB_KEYS = &H8
Public Const KEY_NOTIFY = &H10
Public Const KEY_CREATE_LINK = &H20
Public Const KEY_READ = KEY_QUERY_VALUE Or _
            KEY_ENUMERATE_SUB_KEYS Or KEY_NOTIFY
Public Const KEY_WRITE = KEY_SET_VALUE Or KEY_CREATE_SUB_KEY
Public Const KEY_EXECUTE = KEY_READ
Public Const KEY_ALL_ACCESS = KEY_QUERY_VALUE Or _
            KEY_SET_VALUE Or KEY_CREATE_SUB_KEY Or _
            KEY_ENUMERATE_SUB_KEYS Or __
            KEY_NOTIFY Or KEY_CREATE_LINK
Public Const ERROR_SUCCESS = 0&
Public Const REG_NONE = 0      ' No value type
Public Const REG_SZ = 1        ' Unicode null terminated string
Public Const REG_EXPAND_SZ = 2 ' Unicode null terminated string
                               '(with environment variable
                               ' references)
```

```
Public Const REG_BINARY = 3     ' Free form binary
Public Const REG_DWORD = 4      ' 32-bit number
Public Const REG_DWORD_LITTLE_ENDIAN = 4 ' 32-bit number
                                         ' (same as REG_DWORD)
Public Const REG_DWORD_BIG_ENDIAN = 5    ' 32-bit number
Public Const REG_LINK = 6                ' Symbolic Link (unicode)
Public Const REG_MULTI_SZ = 7            ' Multiple Unicode strings
Public Const REG_OPTION_NON_VOLATILE = &H0
Public Const REG_CREATED_NEW_KEY = &H1


' Declare API calls for Registry access
Declare Function RegOpenKeyEx Lib "advapi32.dll" _
                Alias "RegOpenKeyExA" ( _
                ByVal hKey As Long, _
                ByVal lpSubKey As String, _
                ByVal ulOptions As Long, _
                ByVal samDesired As Long, _
                phkResult As Long) As Long
Declare Function RegCloseKey Lib "advapi32.dll" _
                (ByVal hKey As Long) As Long
Declare Function RegQueryValueEx Lib "advapi32.dll" _
                Alias "RegQueryValueExA" ( _
                ByVal hKey As Long, _
                ByVal lpValueName As String, _
                ByVal lpReserved As Long, _
                lpType As Long, lpData As Any, _
                lpcbData As Any) As Long
Declare Function RegCreateKeyEx Lib "advapi32.dll" _
                Alias "RegCreateKeyExA" ( _
                ByVal hKey As Long, _
                ByVal lpSubKey As String, _
                ByVal Reserved As Long, _
                ByVal lpClass As String, _
                ByVal dwOptions As Long, _
                ByVal samDesired As Long, _
                ByVal lpSecurityAttributes As Any, _
                phkResult As Long, _
                lpdwDisposition As Long) As Long
Declare Function RegFlushKey Lib "advapi32.dll" ( _
                ByVal hKey As Long) As Long
Declare Function RegSetValueEx_String Lib "advapi32.dll" _
                Alias "RegSetValueExA" ( _
                ByVal hKey As Long, _
                ByVal lpValueName As String, _
                ByVal Reserved As Long, _
```

(continued)

327

continued

```
                ByVal dwType As Long, _
                ByVal lpData As String, _
                ByVal cbData As Long) As Long
Declare Function RegSetValueEx_DWord Lib "advapi32.dll" _
                Alias "RegSetValueExA" ( _
                ByVal hKey As Long, _
                ByVal lpValueName As String, _
                ByVal Reserved As Long, _
                ByVal dwType As Long, lpData As Long, _
                ByVal cbData As Long) As Long
Declare Function RegDeleteKey Lib "advapi32.dll" _
                Alias "RegDeleteKeyA" ( _
                ByVal hKey As Long, _
                ByVal lpSubKey As String) As Long
Declare Function RegDeleteValue Lib "advapi32.dll" _
                Alias "RegDeleteValueA" ( _
                ByVal hKey As Long, _
                ByVal lpValueName As String) As Long
```

After declaring all API functions and the required constants, we are ready to access the API functions from a Visual Basic (or VBA) procedure. When you declare these functions, you must be very careful to use the correct data types for the function arguments. Also, the API calls must be handled in a predefined way. These are advanced programming tasks that are often beyond the grasp of most VB programmers.

So I have defined some VB functions, such as ExistKey, CreateKey, GetValue, and DeleteKey, that simplify the task of accessing Registry values. You can call these functions from an application module to identify, set, get, and delete a Registry entry. These functions (developed to hide the API calls) are shown in the following listing:

```
Option Explicit
' Here are the functions to access the Registry
' using Win API calls.
'
Function ExistKey(Root As Long, key As String) As Boolean
' Check whether a key exists.
Dim lResult As Long
Dim keyhandle As Long

    ' Try to open the key...
    lResult = RegOpenKeyEx(Root, key, 0, KEY_READ, keyhandle)
    ' If the key exists, close it (because it's just a test)
    If lResult = ERROR_SUCCESS Then RegCloseKey keyhandle
```

```
    ' Return the value True or False
    ExistKey = (lResult = ERROR_SUCCESS)
End Function

Function GetValue(Root As Long, key As String, Field As String, _
                Value As Variant) As Boolean
' Read a value from a specified key
' The key is set as: Root, key, and name (Field)
Dim lResult As Long
Dim keyhandle As Long
Dim dwType As Long
Dim zw As Long
Dim bufsize As Long
Dim buffer As String
Dim i As Integer
Dim tmp As String

    ' Open the key
    lResult = RegOpenKeyEx(Root, key, 0, KEY_READ, keyhandle)
    GetValue = (lResult = ERROR_SUCCESS) ' Success?
    If lResult <> ERROR_SUCCESS Then Exit Function
    ' Key doesn't exist
    ' Get the value
    lResult = RegQueryValueEx(keyhandle, Field, 0&, dwType, _
                              ByVal 0&, bufsize)
    GetValue = (lResult = ERROR_SUCCESS) ' Success?
    If lResult <> ERROR_SUCCESS Then Exit Function
    ' Name doesn't exist

    Select Case dwType
        Case REG_SZ         ' Zero terminated string
            buffer = Space(bufsize + 1)
            lResult = RegQueryValueEx(keyhandle, Field, 0&, dwType, _
                              ByVal buffer, bufsize)
            GetValue = (lResult = ERROR_SUCCESS)
            If lResult <> ERROR_SUCCESS Then Exit Function ' Error
            Value = buffer

        Case REG_DWORD      ' 32-Bit Number    !!!! Word
            bufsize = 4     ' = 32 Bit
            lResult = RegQueryValueEx(keyhandle, Field, _
                              0&, dwType, zw, bufsize)
            GetValue = (lResult = ERROR_SUCCESS)
            If lResult <> ERROR_SUCCESS Then Exit Function ' Error
            Value = zw
```

(continued)

continued

```
        Case REG_BINARY        ' Binary
            buffer = Space(bufsize + 1)
            lResult = RegQueryValueEx(keyhandle, Field, 0&, _
                                        dwType, ByVal buffer, _
                                        bufsize)
            GetValue = (lResult = ERROR_SUCCESS)
            If lResult <> ERROR_SUCCESS Then Exit Function ' Error
            Value = ""
            For i = 1 To bufsize
                tmp = Hex(Asc(Mid(buffer, i, 1)))
                If Len(tmp) = 1 Then tmp = "0" + tmp
                Value = Value + tmp + " "
            Next i
            ' Here is space for other data types
    End Select

    If lResult = ERROR_SUCCESS Then RegCloseKey keyhandle
    GetValue = True

End Function

Function CreateKey(Root As Long, newkey As String, _
                    Class As String) As Boolean
Dim lResult As Long
Dim keyhandle As Long
Dim Action As Long

    lResult = RegCreateKeyEx(Root, newkey, 0, Class, _
            REG_OPTION_NON_VOLATILE, KEY_ALL_ACCESS, _
            0&, keyhandle, Action)
    If lResult = ERROR_SUCCESS Then
        If RegFlushKey(keyhandle) = ERROR_SUCCESS Then _
            RegCloseKey keyhandle
    Else
        CreateKey = False
        Exit Function
    End If
    CreateKey = (Action = REG_CREATED_NEW_KEY)

End Function

Function SetValue(Root As Long, key As String, Field As String, _
                    Value As Variant) As Boolean
Dim lResult As Long
Dim keyhandle As Long
Dim s As String
Dim l As Long
```

```
    lResult = RegOpenKeyEx(Root, key, 0, _
                        KEY_ALL_ACCESS, keyhandle)
    If lResult <> ERROR_SUCCESS Then
        SetValue = False
        Exit Function
    End If

    Select Case VarType(Value)
        Case vbInteger, vbLong
            l = CLng(Value)
            lResult = RegSetValueEx_DWord(keyhandle, _
                    Field, 0, REG_DWORD, l, 4)
        Case vbString
            s = CStr(Value)
            lResult = RegSetValueEx_String(keyhandle, _
              Field, 0, REG_SZ, s, Len(s) + 1) ' +1 for trailing 00

    ' Here is space for other data types
    End Select

    RegCloseKey keyhandle
    SetValue = (lResult = ERROR_SUCCESS)

End Function

Function DeleteKey(Root As Long, key As String) As Boolean
Dim lResult As Long

    lResult = RegDeleteKey(Root, key)
    DeleteKey = (lResult = ERROR_SUCCESS)
End Function

Function DeleteValue(Root As Long, key As String, _
                    Field As String) As Boolean
Dim lResult As Long
Dim keyhandle As Long

    lResult = RegOpenKeyEx(Root, key, 0, _
            KEY_ALL_ACCESS, keyhandle)
    If lResult <> ERROR_SUCCESS Then
        DeleteValue = False
        Exit Function
    End If

    lResult = RegDeleteValue(keyhandle, Field)
    DeleteValue = (lResult = ERROR_SUCCESS)
    RegCloseKey keyhandle
End Function
```

These procedures can be used in Visual Basic 4.0 or later, and the file can be imported into Microsoft Office 97 VBA.

NOTE: Be aware that the functions shown above don't support all handling to update Registry values. For instance, updating Binary entries isn't implemented. But it should be no major problem to add this functionality to the functions.

You can find both the APIDECLARATIONS.BAS file and the REGISTRYACCESSFUNCTIONS.BAS file in the folder \chapter7\ VBASample of the sample files.

Using the New Functions to Alter the Registry in Visual Basic

The procedures introduced above can be used in a Visual Basic module to update any Registry key. To demonstrate how to use these functions, we'll use a simple Visual Basic program. The program should add the key *HKEY_CLASSES_ ROOT\.1G_Born*, and it should add the value *Test="Hello World"* to this key. The value stored in the Registry key will be read back; and finally we are given the options to remove the value and the key. Each of these steps must be confirmed by the user, as shown in Figure 7-3.

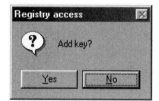

Figure 7-3.
Dialog box with user confirmation in the Registry sample program.

These confirmation dialog boxes allow the user to inspect the Registry by using the Registry Editor after processing a step. The sample program itself uses the Visual Basic code shown below:

```
' Module to demonstrate Registry access
' through API functions using VB4/VB5/VBA5-
' !!!No warranty of any kind, use at your own risk!!!
'


Sub Registry()
'
' Visual Basic Code (by G. Born)
'
' Sample program to show how to access application
```

```
' settings in the Registry with Visual Basic.

Dim Settings As Variant
Dim s As String
Dim Response As Integer
Dim Root As Long
Dim key As String
Dim valx As String

    ' Create a new key ".1G_Born" in:
    ' HKEY_CLASSES_Root\

    Root = HKEY_CLASSES_ROOT
    key = ".1G_Born"
    valx = "Test"

    Response = MsgBox("Add key?", vbYesNo + _
              vbQuestion + vbDefaultButton2, _
              "Registry access")
    If Response = vbYes Then     ' User chose Yes
    ' Add the new key
        If CreateKey(Root, key, " ") Then
            MsgBox "Key created"
        Else
            MsgBox "Key not created"
        End If

        ' Now set a value Test = "Hello"

        s = "Hello"
        If SetValue(Root, key, valx, s) Then
            MsgBox "Value created"
        Else
            MsgBox "Value not created"
        End If
    End If

    ' Try to read the Value back
    ' First test whether the key exists
    If ExistKey(Root, key) Then
    ' Key exists - > get the value
        If GetValue(Root, key, valx, Value) Then
            MsgBox "Value " + valx + ": " + CStr(Value)
        Else
            MsgBox "Value unknown"
        End If
```

(continued)

continued

```
    Else
        MsgBox "Key doesn't exists"
    End If

    ' Ask before deleting the value

    Response = MsgBox("Delete value?", _
                vbYesNo + vbQuestion + _
                vbDefaultButton2, "Registry access")
    If Response = vbYes Then      ' User chose Yes
        If DeleteValue(Root, key, valx) Then
            MsgBox "Value deleted"
        Else
            MsgBox "Value not deleted"
        End If
    End If

    ' Ask before deleting the key

    Response = MsgBox("Delete key?", _
                vbYesNo + vbQuestion + _
                vbDefaultButton2, "Registry access")
    If Response = vbYes Then      ' User chose Yes
        If DeleteKey(Root, key) Then
            MsgBox "Key deleted"
        Else
            MsgBox "Key not deleted"
        End If
    End If
End Sub
```

As you can see, accessing the Registry is now as simple as using GetSetting and SaveSetting in the previous example. Instead of using the built-in VB functions, call the functions ExistKey, CreateKey, ReadKey, DeleteValue, and DeleteKey. Further details about the functions and their arguments can be found in the listings shown above.

The file REGISTRYVBAEXAMPLE.BAS can be found in the \chapter7\ VBASample folder of the sample files and can be imported into a Visual Basic project. For all of you using Microsoft Word 97 or Microsoft Excel 97, I've placed two files, REGISTRY.DOC and REGISTRY.XLS, in the same folder. Each of these files contains the whole project, including all declarations and function libraries. Both files also contain two simple forms that let you access and read Registry entries from within Word 97 or Excel 97. These forms,

RegistryEdit and RegistryShow, demonstrate how to use the functions discussed previously to alter Registry entries. (See Figure 7-4.)

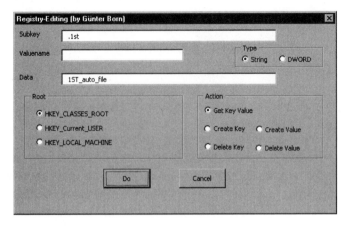

Figure 7-4.
Sample VBA form to access Registry entries.

Using the Windows Scripting Host to Alter the Registry

Windows 98 provides a new feature, the Windows Scripting Host (WSH), that enables you to automate several functions. The WSH supports two script languages: Visual Basic Script and Microsoft JScript (the Microsoft equivalent of JavaScript). Microsoft has added methods to both languages for accessing Registry keys by using the WshShell object. Creating a new key or setting a value takes just a simple statement like this one:

```
WshShell.RegWrite "HKCR\.1G_BORN\", ""
```

This line uses the RegWrite method to create a subkey named *.1G_BORN* in *HKEY_CLASSES_ROOT.* The RegWrite method uses the first parameter to indicate whether a key or a value should be inserted into the Registry. If the string ends with a backslash (\), a key is inserted. Should the key named by the method already exist, nothing will happen. If the string ends with a name (for example, *"HKCR\.1G_BORN\Test"*), RegWrite creates a value in the Registry (the value *Test*, in this case, appearing in *HKEY_CLASSES_ROOT\.1G_BORN*).

The second parameter in the statement contains the data for the value created by the first parameter, while a third parameter defines the type of the value added into the key. Take a look at the following line:

```
WshShell.RegWrite "HKCR\.1G_BORN\Test", "Hello World", "REG_SZ"
```

335

This statement creates a value *Test* in the key *HKEY_CLASSES_ROOT\ .1G_Born* and sets the value to the string *"Hello World"*. The value's data type is set with the third parameter: "REG_SZ". (Other data types include REG_EXPAND_SZ, REG_DWORD, and REG_BINARY. Windows 98 supports only REG_SZ, REG_DWORD, and REG_BINARY.)

To read a key value, use the RegRead method, as shown in the following statement:

```
sregval = WshShell.RegRead ("HKCR\.1G_BORN\Test")
```

This method requires the full key and the value name as input and returns the value data. If the key doesn't exist, a run-time error occurs.

NOTE: I haven't found a way to check whether a key exists. Maybe future documentation will describe ways to realize the error handling.

You can remove a key or a value with the RegDel method. The command is shown below:

```
WshShell.RegDelete "HKCR\.1G_BORN\Test"
```

The parameter can contain either a value name or a key name (if the string ends with a backslash \, a key name is assumed). If the key contains subkeys or values, the whole subbranch is deleted. The listing shown below demonstrates how to use a Visual Basic Script (VBS) file to alter the Registry. Each step requests a user confirmation to allow you to check the Registry Editor to see how the Registry is altered.

```
' Windows Script Host Sample Script
' (by Günter Born)
' Module to demonstrate Registry access (in VBScript)
' !!!No warranty of any kind, use at your own risk!!!
'

' Set a few variables
Root = "HKEY_CLASSES_ROOT"
key = "\.1G_Born\"
valname = "Test"
valx ="Hello World"

' Set Object for the Shell
Dim WSHShell
Set WSHShell = WScript.CreateObject("WScript.Shell")

' Ask the user whether the key should be created
```

```
Response = MsgBox("Add key?", vbYesNo + vbQuestion _
           + vbDefaultButton2, "Registry access")

If Response = vbYes Then              ' User chooses Yes
    WSHShell.RegWrite Root+Key, ""    ' Create key without value
                                      ' Use popup to show success
    WSHShell.Popup "Key " + Root + Key + " created"
End If


' Ask the user whether the value should be created

Response = MsgBox("Add value?", vbYesNo + vbQuestion _
           + vbDefaultButton2, "Registry access")

If Response = vbYes Then      ' User chooses Yes
                              ' Create a string entry
    WSHShell.RegWrite Root+Key+valname, valx, "REG_SZ"
    WSHShell.Popup "Key " + Root + Key + valname + " set"

    ' Try to read the value back
    sregval = WSHShell.RegRead (Root + Key + valname)
    MsgBox "Value " + valname + ": " + sregval
End If


' Ask before deleting the value

Response = MsgBox("Delete value?", vbYesNo + vbQuestion + _
                  vbDefaultButton2, "Registry access")
If Response = vbYes Then      ' User chose Yes
    WSHShell.RegDelete Root + Key + valname
    MsgBox "Value " + valname + " deleted"
End If


' Ask before deleting the key

Response = MsgBox("Delete key?", vbYesNo + vbQuestion + _
                  vbDefaultButton2, "Registry access")
If Response = vbYes Then      ' User chose Yes
    WSHShell.RegDelete Root + Key
    MsgBox "Key " + key + " deleted"
End If
' *** End ***
```

NOTE: The file REGISTRY.VBS can be found in the \chapter7\ WSHScript folder of the sample files. Double-clicking this file invokes the Windows Scripting Host, which executes the script.

Same Steps as in JScript

Do you prefer to write scripts using JavaScript (or JScript as it is called in its Microsoft implementation)? If you do, you can use the same methods described in the example above to access the Registry in JScript. But the syntax of JScript statements is slightly different from that of VBScript. Below you'll find a similar sample JScript program that adds the key *.1G_Born* and the value *Test* to the Registry, reads the value back, and deletes the new entries. Each step requires user confirmation. Further details can be found in the listing shown below:

```jscript
// Windows Script Host Sample Script
// (by Günter Born)
// Module demonstrates Registry access in JScript
// !!!No warranty of any kind, use at your own risk!!!

var vbOKCancel = 1;
var vbInformation = 64;
var vbCancel = 2;

// Set a few variables
var Root = "HKEY_CLASSES_ROOT";
var key = "\\.1G_Born\\";
var valname = "Test";
var valx ="Hello World";
var result;

// Create the WshShell object

var WSHShell = WScript.CreateObject("WScript.Shell");

{
// Ask the user whether the key should be created
    result = WSHShell.Popup("Add value?",
                            0,
                            "Registry access",
                            vbOKCancel + vbInformation );
    if (result != vbCancel)
    {   // Use "REG_SZ" or "REG_BINARY" or "REG_BINARY" as type

        WSHShell.RegWrite(Root + key + valname, valx, "REG_SZ");
        WSHShell.Popup("Added: " + Root + key + valname);

        // Try to read the value back
        sregval = WSHShell.RegRead (Root + key + valname);
        WSHShell.Popup("Value: " + sregval);
    }
```

```
    // Ask before deleting the value
    result = WSHShell.Popup("Delete value?",
                            0,
                            "Registry access",
                            vbOKCancel + vbInformation );
    if (result != vbCancel)
    {
        WSHShell.RegDelete(Root + key + valname);
        WSHShell.Popup("Deleted: " + Root + key + valname);
    }

// Ask before deleting the key

    result = WSHShell.Popup("Delete key?",
                            0,
                            "Registry access",
                            vbOKCancel + vbInformation );
    if (result != vbCancel)
    {
        WSHShell.RegDelete(Root + key);
        WSHShell.Popup("Deleted: " + Root + key);
    }
}
// END
```

NOTE: The file REGISTRY.JS can be found in the \chapter7\ WSHScript folder of the sample files. Double-clicking this file invokes the Windows Scripting Host, which executes the script.

More About INF Files

We've looked briefly at INF files and used them throughout this book to perform such tasks as registering file types, customizing the Recycle Bin icon, and adding commands to the Windows Explorer window. In this section, we'll look at INF files in more detail to help you begin to write your own. We'll use them to create a Components list for the Have Disk dialog box, and I'll show you how to run an INF file during each system start to reset the Run MRU list.

Advantages and Disadvantages of Using INF Files

Windows 98 offers the INF file format to run an automatic install script that allows you to copy, rename, and delete files; to update INI files; and to control the entries in the Registry. You can use placeholders for path descriptions and specify what will happen to a new value if a duplicate entry exists.

But writing such an INF file is complicated. You must know the INF file format, and you must create the complete install script. Windows 98 doesn't provide a debug tool for testing an INF file step-by-step. When a problem occurs, Windows doesn't automatically tell you what's wrong with the file. (Later on, we'll look at how to squeeze some debug information out of the setup process.) Another disadvantage is that INF files do not provide commands for detecting special conditions. If you use shared libraries, for instance, you must programmatically increment the counter that indicates how many installed applications rely on the module. You cannot increment the counter by using an INF file.

Still, although you can't use INF files for all purposes, in many cases an INF file is a good choice if the setup is not too complicated and you don't want to ship a separate install program.

Details About the INF File Structure

INF files provide information that is used by Windows 98 to install software and hardware devices. The primary purpose of the INF file is to support hardware devices. The INF file format is based on the Windows 3.*x* INI file format, described here:

- The file is divided into sections.

- Each section name must be unique within the INF file. A section name is enclosed in brackets. An INF file contains predefined section names (such as [Version]) and user-defined section names ([Born], for example).

- Each section contains one or more keywords. These keywords do not have to be unique, but their order within a section is significant.

Defining an INF Header in the [Version] Section

The [Version] section is simply a header of the INF file. It identifies whether the INF file is valid and defines whether the INF file is used for Plug & Play components or for some other purpose. The following lines define entries for the [Version] section.

```
[Version]
Signature="$Chicago$"          ; Identify the INF file
SetupClass=BASE
```

For a Windows 98 program, the *Signature* keyword of your INF file must be set to the value *"$Chicago$"*, as shown in the preceding lines of code. The *SetupClass* keyword indicates that the INF file will be loaded by the setup program. The *Class* keyword, not shown in our example, is optional. *Class* indicates that the file is used for Plug & Play. If both the *Class* and *SetupClass* keywords are missing, the file will not be loaded by the setup program. If you install software that has nothing to do with a hardware device, set the *SetupClass* value to *BASE*.

Another optional keyword is *LayoutFile=filename*. This keyword defines the name of a second file that contains information about the layout of the distribution media. If you omit this keyword, you must insert the sections [SourceDisksNames] and [SourceDisksFiles] in the INF file to define where the files come from.

Other optional keywords include *ClassGUID* (with which you record the device GUID stored in the Registry for a device installed by the INF file) and *Provider* (with which you give the name, usually a company name, of the INF file creator).

NOTE: Windows 98 also supports advanced INF files, which use the keyword *AdvancedINF=2.5* (where 2.5 stands for the version of the Advanced INF Installer [ADVPACK.DLL]to be checked). You'll find further information about such files in the section "Advanced INF Files," beginning on page 366, and in Appendix E.

Creating a Components List for the Have Disk Dialog Box

For some of your software purposes, you'll find it helpful to offer a list of optional components that users can install. Take a look at the Components list on the Windows Setup property page shown in Figure 7-5 on the next page. (You can access this page by double-clicking the Add/Remove Programs icon in the Control Panel and then selecting the Windows Setup property page.) Hardware-related components offered by Microsoft and those that are available on the system are automatically included in this list.

To ensure that you don't haphazardly modify this list, Microsoft requires third-party vendors to supply the INF file for each new hardware component installed on a computer running Windows 98. (This INF file is typically supplied on a disk. For example, if you're going to install a new graphics card, you should receive a driver's disk from the manufacturer.) You must install these components to make them appear in the Components list. First you click Have Disk on the Windows Setup property page to invoke the Install From Disk dialog box, shown in Figure 7-6, which contains a text box for the path to the INF file. Then you enter the path manually or click the Browse button to select the appropriate path. If you have a disk or a directory containing an INF file, you can specify the path to this location. After you click OK, the INF file is read. (If the directory or disk contains several INF files, the first entry in the file list is used. You'll see the filename when you click Browse and select the directory in the Open dialog box.) If the hardware vendor supports several hardware components, all options will appear in the Components list.

Figure 7-5.
Optional Windows 98 components.

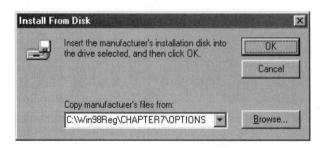

Figure 7-6.
Enter the path to an INF file.

Wouldn't it be a perk to provide an identical feature for installing software components? Figure 7-7 shows a simple example of a Components list containing four entries. These four entries add or remove keys in the Registry. (This is just an example to show the technique.) All you need to do to add the first two entries to *HKEY_CURRENT_USER\Software* is click the check boxes next to the entries and then click the Install button. Selecting the last two entries and clicking Install removes the keys.

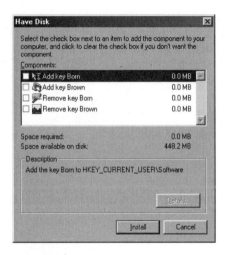

Figure 7-7.
New options added to the Components list.

The INF file that created the Components list shown in Figure 7-7 contains the following lines:

```
; File: Options.inf  G. Born
;
; Demonstrates how to create a Components list with
; optional entries in the Have Disk dialog box.
; Checked components will be included in the install
; process.

[version]
signature="$CHICAGO$"
Provider=%author%
SetupClass=Base

[DestinationDirs]
; This section is left empty in this example
```

(continued)

continued

```
;*******************************************************
; Here we define all components for the Components list
;*******************************************************

[Optional Components]
Born                     ; Optional components sections
Brown
BornUninst
BrownUninst

[Born]
; For the Born option, you can add keywords
; like DelReg, CopyFiles, and DelFiles.
; In this example, I will add an option into the Registry.

AddReg = Born.AddReg

; Here is the optional information shown in the
; Have Disk dialog box

OptionDesc  = %Option1_DESC%    ; Define the entry
Tip         = %Option1_TIP%     ; Define the tip text
InstallType = 0                 ; Allow manual only
IconIndex   = 45                ; Windows Logo mini icon for dialogs

[BornUninst]
; BornUninst removes the key added in [Born]

DelReg = Born.AddReg

; Here is the optional information shown in the
; Have Disk dialog box

OptionDesc  = %Option3_DESC%    ; Define the entry
Tip         = %Option3_TIP%     ; Define the tip text
InstallType = 0                 ; Allow manual only
IconIndex   = 46                ; Windows Logo mini icon for dialogs

[Brown]
AddReg = Brown.AddReg

OptionDesc  = %Option2_DESC%    ; Define the entry
Tip         = %Option2_TIP%     ; Define the tip text
```

```
InstallType  = 0              ; Allow manual only
IconIndex    = 47             ; Icon

[BrownUninst]
DelReg = Brown.AddReg

OptionDesc   = %Option4_DESC% ; Define the entry
Tip          = %Option4_TIP%  ; Define the tip text
InstallType  = 0              ; Allow manual only
IconIndex    = 48             ; Icon

; Information about Registry keys (used in AddReg, DelReg)

[Born.AddReg]
HKCU,Software\Born,,Test,"Hello there"

[Brown.AddReg]
HKCU,Software\Brown,,Test,"Hello there"

[Strings]
; Localizable strings
author = "Born"
Option1_DESC = "Add key Born"
Option1_TIP = "Add the key Born to HKEY_CURRENT_USER\Software"

Option2_DESC = "Add key Brown"
Option2_TIP = "Add the key Brown to HKEY_CURRENT_USER\Software"

Option3_DESC = "Remove key Born"
Option3_TIP = "Remove the key Born from HKEY_CURRENT_USER\Software"

Option4_DESC = "Remove key Brown"
Option4_TIP = "Remove the key Brown from HKEY_CURRENT_USER\Software"

; *** End
```

The important part of this code, the part that creates the Components list, is the [Optional Components] section. In this section, you can insert the names of other sections, which are scanned by the install routine. In my example, I inserted the section names [Born], [Brown], [BornUninst], and [BrownUninst]. These sections contain other INF commands with which you can copy files, add keys to the Registry, etc. (I'll discuss the required commands later on.) In each section, you can also set additional information for the Have Disk dialog box by using the keywords on the following page.

■ *OptionDesc*   This keyword specifies the string displayed for the option in the Components list of the Have Disk dialog box.

■ *Tip*   This keyword defines the string shown in the Description section of the Have Disk dialog box.

■ *InstallType*   This keyword specifies the type of installation for Windows 98 Setup. Valid values are *0* (compact), *1* (typical), *2* (portable), and *3* (custom). The default value is *1*.

■ *IconIndex*   This keyword defines the mini-icons shown in the Components list. (See Figure 7-8.)

You can also add other keywords that define the install options, such as the required disk space.

NOTE: You can find further information about keywords in Appendix E, "The Windows INF File Format," and in the *Windows 95 Software Development Kit*. You'll find the file OPTIONS.INF in the \chapter7\Options folder of the sample files.

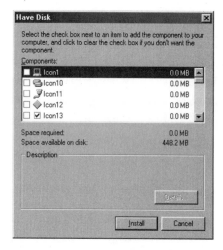

Figure 7-8.
Mini-icons for the Have Disk dialog box.

TIP: To examine the icon index, use the file ICONS.INF contained in the \chapter7\Icons folder of the sample files. Opening this folder from the Install From Disk dialog box reveals a list of the first 30 icons. (See Figure 7-8.) Because indexing starts with 0, the *IconIndex* value used in the INF file is always one less than the number shown in the Have Disk dialog box's Components list. You can extend the ICONS.INF file to show the other mini-icons provided by the Windows Setup routines.

Installing and Uninstalling Files

During a software installation, you need to copy files from the install disk to the destination directories of the computer. Some files go into the Windows directories; others must be copied into new folders. And some of these files must be deleted from the hard disk after they perform their functions. For example, temporary files must be deleted after installation, and an uninstall feature must remove all files for an application from the hard disk. You can accomplish all of these jobs with a simple INF file. The next sample file copies two files: the sample file itself, FILECOPY.INF, and TSTFILE.TXT. The file FILECOPY.INF is copied into the \Windows\INF subfolder. This file is needed later on for the uninstall feature. The file TSTFILE.TXT is copied into the \Windows\Born subfolder. (If this subfolder doesn't exist, the INF file will create it. If you don't want this subfolder to be created, you can designate an existing subfolder.)

The sample file also provides an uninstall feature. After you run this file, you'll find the option Remove Testfile (Born) on the Install/Uninstall property page. (Access this property page by invoking the Add/Remove Programs Properties property sheet, which is available from the Control Panel.) This entry allows you to remove the INF and TXT files—which were copied during the install process—from the hard disk.

```
; File: Filecopy.INF
;
; Demonstrate how to copy and delete files in Windows 98
;
; This INF file provides an uninstall function to
; remove the files

[version]
signature="$CHICAGO$"
SetupClass=BASE

; This is the install part. Here we copy the files,
; but you can add other commands as well.
```

(continued)

continued

```
[DefaultInstall]

CopyFiles = Tst.CopyFiles, Inf.CopyFiles
AddReg=Tst.AddReg              ; Add uninstall entries

; This is the uninstall section. We use the DelFiles keyword
; to remove the files. The destination section is the same as
; for the CopyFiles section, so Windows will do the job.

[DefaultUninstall]

DelReg=Tst.AddReg              ; Remove uninstall entries
DelFiles = Inf.CopyFiles, Tst.CopyFiles

; Add the uninstall stuff to the Registry

[Tst.AddReg]

HKLM,SOFTWARE\Microsoft\Windows\CurrentVersion\Uninstall\tst,  ⤍
DisplayName,,"%REMOVE_DESC%"
HKLM,SOFTWARE\Microsoft\Windows\CurrentVersion\Uninstall\tst,  ⤍
UninstallString,,"RunDll setupx.dll,InstallHinfSection          ⤍
DefaultUninstall 4 Filecopy.inf"

[Tst.DelReg]
; Remove the key for the uninstall part
HKLM,SOFTWARE\Microsoft\Windows\CurrentVersion\Uninstall\tst

; INF file to be deleted from the Windows\INF subfolder
[Inf.DelFiles]
Filecopy.Inf
Filecopy.PNF

; INF file to be copied in the Windows\INF subfolder

[Inf.CopyFiles]
Filecopy.Inf

; Test file to be copied in the Windows\Born subfolder
[Tst.CopyFiles]
Tstfile.txt

[DestinationDirs]
```

```
Tst.CopyFiles = 10,Born          ; Create new subfolder
Inf.CopyFiles = 17               ; INF subfolder
Inf.DelFiles = 17                ; INF subfolder

[SourceDisksNames]
55="Testfile Disk","",1

[SourceDisksFiles]
Filecopy.inf=55
Tstfile.txt=55

[Strings]
REMOVE_DESC = "Remove Testfile (Born)"

; End ***
```

I kept the contents of this INF file simple to illustrate my points. The first section, [Version], contains the signature for an install file. The [DefaultInstall] and [DefaultUninstall] sections, which come next, contain the following commands for copying and deleting files:

- To copy one or more files, you must insert the *CopyFiles* keyword in a section. After the equal sign, list the names of the sections that identify which files will be altered.

- To delete a file, insert the *DelFiles* keyword into the section. The equal sign is followed by a list of sections that describe the files to manipulate.

In our example, the [DefaultInstall] section contains the *CopyFiles* keyword designating the [Tst.CopyFiles] and [Inf.CopyFiles] sections, which contain information about the files to be copied. You can define the names of these sections as you see fit—the only requirement is that each section name be unique within the INF file.

The next issue in our example concerns the files that will be copied. This information is contained in the sections referenced in the *CopyFiles* line. Notice in our sample that the [Tst.CopyFiles] section contains only one entry, *Tstfile.txt*, which is copied from the source to the destination. We'll take a closer look at source and destination information in a moment.

A Pitfall of Using CopyFiles and DelFiles

When using the CopyFiles and DelFiles commands in an INF file, you need to remember that each section can contain only one CopyFiles command and one DelFiles command. Take a look at the following lines of code:

```
[DefaultInstall]
CopyFiles = Inf.CopyFiles    ; copy INF files into INF folder
CopyFiles = Bat.CopyFiles    ; copy a BAT file into Born folder
AddReg=Tst.AddReg            ; Add uninstall entries
```

Looks fine? Looks as if you've got a quick overview of which files will be copied. Unfortunately, this code won't work. (I was caught in this same trap by a sample file I shipped with the first version of this book. After testing the INF file, I split the CopyFiles statement into two lines of code to make the listing more readable.) Windows will process such an INF file without an error message, but only the first CopyFiles statement will be executed. Windows ignores all the CopyFiles lines following the first statement within the section. As a result, some files aren't copied. (In my case, I had no chance to detect this failing because the files were already on my hard disk. A few weeks later, I began to receive feedback from my readers telling me that the INF file wouldn't work.) However, the solution is pretty simple—just write the code as shown here:

```
[DefaultInstall]
CopyFiles = Inf.CopyFiles, Bat.CopyFiles
AddReg=Tst.AddReg
```

This simple trick has a significant effect: Windows detects the CopyFiles statement and processes all the sections listed.

Details About the Uninstall Feature

The file FILECOPY.INF contains a section named [DefaultUninstall]. This section name implies it might have something to do with an uninstall feature provided by the Install/Uninstall property page, but this is only partially true—[DefaultUninstall] is just a section name. You could name this section [Born] and you'd get the same results. The uninstall feature offered by Windows 98 requires that you add a key to the following branch:

HKEY_LOCAL_MACHINE\SOFTWARE\Microsoft\Windows
CurrentVersion\Uninstall\xxxx

You can use the program's EXE name instead of the subkey *xxxx* to create a unique subkey. This subkey must contain two values: *DisplayName* and *UninstallString*. *DisplayName* defines the string shown on the Install/Uninstall property page. *UninstallString* contains the command for removing all settings provided during the install process. (I've discussed these topics in the examples shown in Chapter 4 and Chapter 5.) The *UninstallString* value can contain, for example, the following command that activates RUNDLL.EXE.

```
"RunDll32 setupapi.dll, InstallHinfSection DefaultUninstall 4  ⟶
    Filecopy.inf"
```

As mentioned in previous chapters, RUNDLL32.EXE is a stub program that calls other DLL routines. The line above activates the Windows SETUPAPI.DLL routine, which reads the INF file. Therefore, the INF file must be located in the \Windows\INF subfolder. SETUPAPI.DLL uses this syntax:

```
SetupApi.dll, InstallHinfSection <section> <reboot-mode> <inf-name>
```

The following list describes the SETUPAPI.DLL parameters:

- The first parameter is always set to the string *InstallHinfSection*.

- The next parameter defines the name of the INF file section that will be executed. (In my examples, I've named this section [DefaultUninstall]. If you prefer a different section name, you must also alter the entry in the *UninstallString* value.)

- The third parameter defines the reboot mode. This value is a little bit mysterious because in some INF files you'll find it set to *4* and in other INF files you'll find it set to *132*.

- The last parameter is always set to the name of the INF file used to uninstall the settings. In most cases, the INF file used for the install is also used for the uninstall. (In these cases, you could use the same structures in *CopyFiles* and *DeleteFiles*, *AddReg* and *DelReg*, and so on.)

The possible values for the reboot mode are defined in Table 7-2.

Reboot Mode Values

Value	Description
0	*NeverReboot* The PC will not be rebooted. It is up to the client program to determine whether the PC should reboot. The setup program must add entries to the WININIT.INI file or create a new WININIT.INI file and copy it to the \Windows folder to ensure that settings will be initialized at the next reboot.
1	*AlwaysSilentReboot* The PC will always reboot without prompting the user.
2	*AlwaysPromptReboot* The user will always be asked to respond to a Reboot The Machine, Yes/No dialog box. Setup does not attempt to determine whether a reboot is necessary.
3	*SilentReboot* If Setup determines the need for a reboot, the PC is rebooted without prompting the user.
4	*PromptReboot* If Setup determines the need for a reboot, the setup program prompts the user with a Reboot The Machine, Yes/No dialog box.

Table 7-2.
The reboot mode is the third parameter of SETUPAPI.DLL.

Some Remarks About Uninstalling in Windows 95

Windows 95 uses the same scheme to register an uninstall feature. Unfortunately, this operating system version doesn't support the RUNDLL32.EXE and the SETUPAPI.DLL programs. Instead you must use the following call to invoke the uninstall part:

```
"RunDll setupx.dll, InstallHinfSection DefaultUninstall 4  ⟶
    Filecopy.inf"
```

This statement won't work under Windows 98 and Windows NT 4.0, but it is necessary under Windows 95. There are also some other slight differences in Windows 95. For instance, in Windows 95 you can use the AddReg section in an INF file during the uninstall steps to remove the Registry entries; you don't need a separate DelReg section. And Windows 95 doesn't create PNF files in the INF folder. For those interested in the old Windows 95 INF file settings, I have provided a Windows 95 version of the FileCopy example in the folder \chapter7\Filecopy\Win95.

If the parameter <inf-name> specifies your INF file instead of a Windows 98 INF file, you must add the value *128* to the values shown in Table 7-2. If you install optional components, you should add *128* to the value *4*, resulting in a reboot value of *132*. (I also used the value *4* successfully.) I recommend that you use *4* or *132* as the reboot value. If you add *128* to the reboot mode value, all the files that your installation program is installing must be in the same directory on the installation disk as the INF file.

> **NOTE:** Many other commands can be included in INF files. For a complete overview of INF file options, see Appendix E, "The Windows INF File Format."

Defining the Source and Destination

How do we define the files' source and their destination? This is a little bit tricky in an INF file.

Defining the source   The source must be either the source disk or a folder that contains the files. This information is provided in the [SourceDisksNames] section. Each entry in this section, like the one shown here, specifies a disk containing the files to be copied:

```
55="Testfile Disk","",1
```

The number *55* is a disk ordinal used in the [SourceDisksFiles] section. This number is associated with a specific filename or with several filenames. The string after the equal sign is the name of the source disk. This text is displayed in a message box if the file cannot be found. The second parameter after the equal sign—empty in the example entry above—defines the disk label, and the last parameter is used for the serial number of a disk.

Defining the destination   The destination directories are defined in the [DestinationDirs] section of the INF file. The syntax of a line contained in the section is as follows:

```
section name=destination directory
```

The section name, which identifies the section that contains the files that will be copied, must be defined in the INF file. In our example, we used three section names: [Tst.CopyFiles], [Inf.CopyFiles], and [Inf.DelFiles]. Each of these entries defines a separate destination directory.

Now let's have a look at the destination directory. INF files are designed to install a device driver into the Windows folders, so Microsoft has defined

Logical Disk IDs (LDIDs) that allow you to specify a destination directory. Table 7-3 lists the LDID values for the most often used predefined directories.

LDID Values for INF Files

LDID	Destination Directory
10	Windows
11	System
12	IOSubsys
13	Command
14	Control Panel
15	Printers
16	Workgroup
17	INF
18	Help
20	Fonts
30	Root directory of the boot drive
31	Root directory of the host drive (of a virtual boot drive)
32	Old Windows
33	Old MS-DOS

Table 7-3.
Use the LDID codes to specify predefined destination directories for INF files. These codes are defined by Microsoft.

If you wanted to copy the files defined in the [Tst.CopyFiles] section into the Windows folder, you would use the following line:

```
Tst.CopyFiles = 10
```

Because I wanted to copy the files in [Tst.CopyFiles] to the subfolder \Born, I added the Born subpath after the LDID in our example. You can add other subfolder names after the LDID number. Adding 30\MyProgram, for example, creates the folder \MyProgram on the boot drive.

The *DelFiles* keyword is handled in the same way as the *CopyFiles* keyword. You have to use the defined sections to specify the names of the files to be deleted and the destination directory. With Windows 95, you can use a simple trick. The sections [Inf.CopyFiles] and [Tst.CopyFiles] already contain the information about the files copied during the install process, so you need to add only the following line of code to the [DefaultUninstall] section.

```
DelFiles = Inf.CopyFiles, Tst.CopyFiles
```

Windows 95 recognizes the *DelFiles* keyword and uses the information in [Inf.CopyFiles] and [Tst.CopyFiles] to remove the files. This method won't work in Windows 98 or in Windows NT 4.0 because each of these operating systems creates in the INF folder a separate PNF file (with the same name as the INF file) that must also be removed during uninstall. (Also, as I'll discuss in a moment, the *DelReg=Tst.RegAdd* entry won't work.)

Therefore, I added a separate uninstall and delete file section to the INF file. Still, I was left with a problem that I couldn't solve: the subfolder \Born, which was created during the install process, can't be removed through the use of INF file commands.

NOTE: You can find the files TSTFILE.TXT and FILECOPY.INF in the \chapter7\Filecopy folder of the sample files. Right-clicking the INF file and selecting Install copies both files included in the folder onto the hard disk. If you use the Install/Uninstall property page, you can remove the files with the Remove Testfile (Born) option.

WARNING: Don't install the Windows 95 version contained in the subfolder \chapter7\Filecopy\Win95 under Windows 98. The files will be copied and the Registry entries will be set, but the uninstall feature won't work (for the reasons mentioned above) and the Registry will contain unnecessary keys.

Adding and Deleting Registry Entries

An INF file can contain the *AddReg* keyword to add a new key or value into the Registry and *DelReg* to delete a key or value. The FILECOPY.INF file we've been looking at (on pages 347–349) contains both keywords. The following line of code defines the [Tst.AddReg] section in the INF file:

```
AddReg=Tst.AddReg
```

This [Tst.AddReg] section contains all information necessary to add an entry into the Registry. It was common in Windows 95 to use the information in the [Tst.AddReg] section with the line of code appearing at the top of the next page to remove entries.

```
DelReg=Tst.AddReg
```

In Windows 98, the *DelReg* keyword forces the SETUPAPI.DLL routine to remove the keys mentioned in the specified section. Unfortunately, the routine won't work in exactly the same way as the Windows 95 SETUPX.DLL program. If you use the [Tst.AddReg] section to remove keys, the uninstall won't work properly. Therefore, I always create a separate uninstall section in the INF file, [Tst.DelReg] in our example, to remove the Registry entries and to delete the files copied during install.

We looked briefly in Chapter 3 at the syntax for a line of code that enters a key into the Registry, but let's review it again here:

```
root-key, [subkey], [value name], [flag], [value]
```

You must first enter the root key in this line—the root key is inserted as an abbreviation. (See Table 7-4.) Parameters included in brackets are optional and can be left blank, and they must be separated by commas.

Abbreviations for Root Keys

String	Meaning
HKCC	HKEY_CURRENT_CONFIG
HKCR	HKEY_CLASSES_ROOT
HKCU	HKEY_CURRENT_USER
HKDD	HKEY_DYN_DATA
HKLM	HKEY_LOCAL_MACHINE
HKU	HKEY_USERS

Table 7-4.
When you enter a key into the Registry, you must first enter the appropriate root key abbreviations in the line.

The root key name is followed by a string specifying the subkey (*\Software\Microsoft*, for example). The third parameter defines the name of the value entry in the subkey. If this parameter is empty, Windows sets the *Default* value. The fourth parameter contains an optional flag defining the insertion mode for data. This flag is defined in Table 7-5. (The sample files in this book do not set this flag, so the default value *0* is set.)

Flag Codes

Value	Meaning
0	Default. Use an ANSI string for the value, and replace the key's value if it exists.
1	Use a HEX record, and replace the key's value if it exists.
2	Use an ANSI string. Don't replace an existing key's value.
3	Use a HEX record. Don't replace an existing key's value.

Table 7-5.
Optional flags for the fourth parameter.

The last parameter in the line is also optional and defines the value data that the value in the third parameter is set to. This value can be an ANSI string or a hexadecimal representation of a binary record in Intel format (least significant byte first). Binary value entries can be extended beyond the 128-byte line limit with a backslash (\) appended to each line. Look at the following statement:

```
HKLM,SOFTWARE\Born, MyEntry,,"Hello I was there"
```

This statement creates the key *HKEY_LOCAL_MACHINE\SOFTWARE\ Born*, adds the value *MyEntry* to the key, and inserts the string *"Hello I was there"* as the data for this value. The fifth parameter can also contain a command comprising a path and filename, such as this one:

```
"C:\WINDOWS\Notepad.exe %1"
```

If the path is changed by the user (for example, the user might rename the Windows folder during Setup), you can use one of the LDID numbers shown in Table 7-3 (appearing on page 354) as a placeholder. You can also write the previous command like this:

```
"%10%\Notepad.exe %1"
```

Windows will substitute the *%10%* placeholder with the current Windows folder name.

The INF section pointed to by the *DelReg* keyword contains a similar command:

```
root-key, subkey, [value name]
```

The root key parameter here also uses the abbreviations shown in Table 7-4 on page 356. The subkey is required for a *DelReg* statement, but the value name is optional. If you omit the value name, the subkey and all its values will be removed.

> NOTE: As you can see in Table 7-5, an INF file doesn't contain a flag value for adding a DWORD value into the Registry. But you can enter a DWORD value as a 4-byte binary value. In that case, you must make sure that the code that reads the value either ignores the value data type returned or accepts both binary and DWORD values.

Putting It All Together in an INF File

Let's put all these details about INF files to work in an INF file that copies a new icon library to the hard disk and sets the icons for the Recycle Bin. (This situation should sound familiar—we dealt with the Registry key for setting the Recycle Bin icon and looked at RECY98-0.INF and RECY98-1.INF in Chapter 4.) Our INF file will also support the uninstall feature so that we can recover the default system settings. The following code handles these requirements:

```
; File: Recycle.INF
;
; Redefine the icons used by the Recycle Bin in Windows 98
;
; This INF file provides an uninstall function to
; remove the files and recover the factory settings.

[version]
signature="$CHICAGO$"
SetupClass=BASE

; This is the install part. Here we will copy the files.

[DefaultInstall]

CopyFiles = DLL.CopyFiles, Inf.CopyFiles
AddReg=Bin.AddReg             ; Add uninstall entries

; This is the uninstall section. We use the DelFiles keyword
; to remove the INF file.

[DefaultUninstall]
DelReg=Bin.DelReg                  ; Remove uninstall entries
AddReg=BinOld.AddReg               ; Reset factory values
DelFiles = Inf.DelFiles, DLL.CopyFiles ; Delete INF file
```

```
; Set new icons and add the uninstall stuff to the Registry

[Bin.AddReg]
; Use HKEY_CURRENT_USER\Software\Classes\CLSID\
; Set "Full" to icon number 5 in BornIcon.dll
HKCU,Software\Classes\CLSID\{645FF040-5081-101B-9F08-00AA002F954E}\→
DefaultIcon,Empty,,"%10%\Born\BornIcon.dll,0"
HKCU,Software\Classes\CLSID\{645FF040-5081-101B-9F08-00AA002F954E}\→
DefaultIcon,Full,,"%10%\Born\BornIcon.dll,5"


; Here comes the uninstall stuff ...

HKLM,SOFTWARE\Microsoft\Windows\CurrentVersion\Uninstall\bin,  →
DisplayName,,"%REMOVE_DESC%"
HKLM,SOFTWARE\Microsoft\Windows\CurrentVersion\Uninstall\bin,  →
UninstallString,,"RunDll32 setupapi.dll,InstallHinfSection      →
DefaultUninstall 132 Recycle.inf"


[Bin.DelReg]
; Don't forget to remove this key for the uninstall part
HKLM,SOFTWARE\Microsoft\Windows\CurrentVersion\Uninstall\bin


[BinOld.AddReg]
; Reset factory settings in HKEY_CLASSES_ROOT\CLSID
HKCU,Software\Classes\CLSID\{645FF040-5081-101B-9F08-00AA002F954E}\→
DefaultIcon,Empty,,"%11%\\shell32.dll,31"
HKCU,Software\Classes\CLSID\{645FF040-5081-101B-9F08-00AA002F954E}\→
DefaultIcon,Full,,"%11%\\shell32.dll,32"


; INF file to be copied to the Windows\INF subfolder

[Inf.CopyFiles]
Recycle.Inf


; INF file to be deleted from the Windows\INF subfolder

[Inf.DelFiles]
Recycle.Inf
Recycle.PNF


; Test file to be copied in the Windows\Born subfolder
[Dll.CopyFiles]
BornIcon.dll


[DestinationDirs]
```

(continued)

359

continued

```
Dll.CopyFiles = 10,Born        ; Create new subfolder
Inf.CopyFiles = 17             ; INF subfolder
Inf.DelFiles = 17              ; INF subfolder

[SourceDisksNames]
55="Set folder to: \Win98Reg\chapter7\recycle","",1
56="Set folder to: \Win98Reg\chapter4","",1

[SourceDisksFiles]
Recycle.inf=55
BornIcon.dll=56                ; Icon source in ...\chapter4

[Strings]
REMOVE_DESC = "Reset Recycle Bin icons (Born)"

; End ***
```

These lines copy the BORNICON.DLL file from the \chapter4 subfolder into the Windows subfolder named \Born. The Registry is also updated with the new icon settings for the Recycle Bin and for the uninstall feature. The INF file is copied into the \INF subfolder to support the uninstall feature.

> **NOTE:** The file RECYCLE.INF is in the \chapter7\Recycle folder of the sample files. Right-click the INF file, and select the Install option from the context menu. During installation, you will be prompted to change the disks. Set the new path to \chapter4 to continue the file copy operation. After installing the file, you must change the contents of the Recycle Bin window before the new icons will be visible. Recovering the factory settings requires using the Install/ Uninstall property page. (Select Control Panel, and then double-click Add/Remove Programs.) Select the Reset Recycle Bin Icons (Born) option, and then click Add/Remove. The old icons return after the next change occurs in Recycle Bin (such as the deletion of a file).

Executing and Testing an INF File

We've seen that you have two ways in which to execute an INF file and force Windows to process the commands it contains. You can right-click the filename and select Install from the context menu, or you can use the Windows Setup property page, which enables you to select the path to the INF file on the Install From Disk dialog box.

The advantage of the first option is that you can select any INF file and let Windows process it; the disadvantage of this option is that it does not show a dialog box with a Components list. The second option is preferable if the INF file supports options shown in the Have Disk Components list; its disadvantage is that only the first INF file of a source is processed.

The progress of the INF file's copy operation is shown in a progress bar in the Copying Files window, as shown in Figure 7-9. This window is visible only if you have defined several files to be copied.

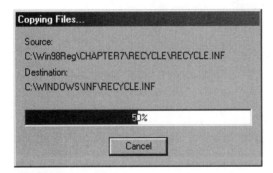

Figure 7-9.
Progress bar shown during the copy operation.

If a file defined in the [Inf.CopyFiles] section of the INF file cannot be found on the source disk or in the source folder, Setup invokes the dialog box shown in Figure 7-10. You must either change the path shown in the Copy Files From text box or click Skip File to omit the file.

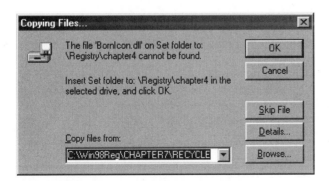

Figure 7-10.
Asking for a new source path.

Debugging an INF File

One big source of mistakes in INF files are typing errors, especially in section names, and the errors can be hard to detect. Unfortunately, Windows does not offer a method for debugging your INF files during processing, so if an INF file contains the wrong instructions you won't receive an error message stating that the section with the error was not processed. What do you do? Let's take a look at some lines of code that contain an error and then figure out how to track it down.

```
[DefaultInstall]
CopyFiles = Tst.CopyFiles, Inf.CopyFiles

[CopyFiles.Inf]
Filecopy.Inf
```

The *CopyFiles* line in the [DefaultInstall] section includes a reference to the [Inf.CopyFiles] section. This section, however, doesn't exist because of a typing error in the name of the section (that is, [CopyFiles.Inf]). Thus it's never processed, and the FILECOPY.INF file isn't copied into the destination folder. You won't be able to detect this until you try to uninstall the feature—uninstalling reveals that FILECOPY.INF is missing in the \INF subfolder. Windows removes the uninstall entry on the Install/Uninstall property page, but all other keys and files remain.

I was caught in this trap while creating the first version of the FILECOPY.INF example in my Windows 95 Registry book. How did I detect such a problem? I inspected the Registry entries and folders and also tested the features, but to no avail. So I came to the conclusion that something must be wrong in the INF file itself. I printed it and had a look (a very long look) at the listing—not a very efficient way to test huge INF files.

What we need is a kind of breakpoint to insert in the INF file in several places to check whether this point is reached. Unfortunately, no breakpoint command exists in the INF file syntax to allow us to do this. Still, if you haven't got a tool to create and check INF files, you can use this simple (and dirty) trick to debug the INF files:

1. Insert the name of a nonexistent file into the section that is used to copy files. If you insert several file names into the INF file (for example, TEST0.TST, TEST1.TST, etc.), you can inspect several sections in an INF file. When Windows detects the missing file, a dialog box showing the filename is invoked. (See Figure 7-10.) Now you know that Windows has reached the section containing this so-called breakpoint.

2. Click Details to invoke the message box shown in Figure 7-11, which has information about the source and destination paths. Click Skip File (see Figure 7-10) to skip the breakpoint and continue the setup process.

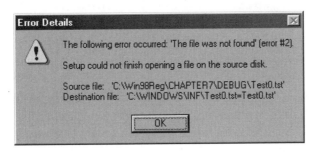

Figure 7-11.
The Error Details message box contains information about the missing file.

Following are some lines of code I prepared for test purposes:

```
[Inf.CopyFiles]
Filecopy.Inf
Test0.tst                 ; *** Breakpoint 0

; Test file to be copied in the Windows\Born subfolder
[Tst.CopyFiles]
Tstfile.txt
Test1.tst                 ; *** Breakpoint 1
```

NOTE: You'll find the tweaked file FILECOPY.INF in the \chapter7\Debug folder of the sample files. If you try to execute the file (by right-clicking it and selecting Install from the context menu), you'll see the messages mentioned.

Using INF Files to Master Your MRU Lists

We have already discussed several aspects of INF files, and we now know a lot about the Registry. I have mentioned that Windows keeps several MRU lists. The System Policy Editor gives the user the option to force Windows 98 to delete these MRU lists during system exit. But this is an all-or-nothing option. Wouldn't it be nice to reset only the MRU list of the Start menu Run command? In Windows 95, you could do this with a REG file. You can use the same REG file in Windows 98, but Windows 98 asks for user confirmation before the REG file content will be imported. So why not use an INF file instead?

I have mentioned the following key:

HKEY_LOCAL_MACHINE\SOFTWARE\Microsoft\Windows\ CurrentVersion\Run

The entries in this key are executed each time the system starts. We can add a value to this key containing a command such as this one:

```
RunDll32 setupapi.dll,InstallHinfSection MRUExecute 132 MRUclear.inf
```

Each time Windows 98 starts, the MRUExecute section in the file MRUCLEAR.INF is processed. This section contains commands for resetting the Run MRU list. The code listing below shows the INF file that does this job.

```
; File: MRUclear.INF (by Günter Born)
;
; Shows how to clear the Run MRU list during each
; system start in Windows 98
;
; This INF file provides an uninstall function to
; remove the file and restore the Registry settings.

[version]
signature="$CHICAGO$"
SetupClass=BASE

[DefaultInstall]
; This is the install section.

CopyFiles = Inf.CopyFiles    ; Copy INF file
AddReg=MRU.AddReg            ; Add Registry entries

[DefaultUninstall]
; This is the uninstall section.
DelReg=MRU.DelReg            ; Remove Registry entries
DelFiles = Inf.DelFiles      ; Delete files

[MRUExecute]
; Executed during each system startup

AddReg=MRU.ClearReg          ; Clear Run MRU entry

[MRU.AddReg]
; Add the run and uninstall stuff to the Registry
; Enter the run command into the Registry in
; HKLM\Software\Microsoft\Windows\CurrentVersion\Run
```

```
HKLM,Software\Microsoft\Windows\CurrentVersion\Run,MRUDel,,    →
"RunDll32 setupapi.dll,InstallHinfSection MRUExecute 132       →
MRUclear.inf"

; Here comes the uninstall stuff ...

HKLM,SOFTWARE\Microsoft\Windows\CurrentVersion\Uninstall\MRUclear,  →
DisplayName,,"%REMOVE_DESC%"
HKLM,SOFTWARE\Microsoft\Windows\CurrentVersion\Uninstall\MRUclear,  →
UninstallString,,"RunDll32 setupapi.dll,InstallHinfSection         →
DefaultUninstall 132 MRUclear.inf"

[MRU.DelReg]
; Remove the Run entry
HKLM,Software\Microsoft\Windows\CurrentVersion\Run,MRUDel

; Don't forget to remove this key for the uninstall part
HKLM,SOFTWARE\Microsoft\Windows\CurrentVersion\Uninstall\MRUclear

[MRU.ClearReg]
; Clear the Run RunMRU list in
; HKCU\Software\Microsoft\Windows\CurrentVersion\Explorer\RunMRU

HKCU,Software\Microsoft\Windows\CurrentVersion\Explorer\RunMRU,  →
MRUList,,"a"
HKCU,Software\Microsoft\Windows\CurrentVersion\Explorer\RunMRU,a,,""

[Inf.CopyFiles]
; INF file to be copied to the Windows\INF subfolder

MRUclear.Inf

[Inf.DelFiles]
; Files to be deleted from the Windows\INF subfolder

MRUclear.Inf
MRUclear.PNF

[DestinationDirs]

Inf.CopyFiles = 17          ; INF subfolder
Inf.DelFiles = 17           ; INF subfolder

[SourceDisksNames]
55="MRUDisk","",1
```

(continued)

continued

```
[SourceDisksFiles]
MRUclear.inf=55

[Strings]
REMOVE_DESC = "Remove Born's (Win 98) MRUclear"
            ; *** Breakpoint 0
; End ***
```

Most parts of the INF file are used to improve usability. Right-clicking this INF file and selecting Install from the context menu installs the whole thing. The INF file is copied into the Windows\INF folder, an uninstall part is added to the Registry, and the Run entry that executes the INF file during each system start is set in the *Run* key of the Registry. Each time Windows 98 starts, the *Run* key is scanned and the command in the *MRUDel* value is executed. This command forces Setupapi to scan the MRUExecute section in the INF file. This section contains commands for setting the data in the *MRUList* value of the key *HKEY_CURRENT_USER\Software\Microsoft\ Windows\CurrentVersion\Explorer\RunMRU* to *"a"* and the data in the key's *a* value to *""*. As a result, the Run dialog box (displayed by selecting Run in the Start menu) contains only a shortened MRU list with one empty entry. To uninstall this feature, the user must select the Remove Born's (Win 98) MRUclear entry in the Install/Uninstall property page (Control Panel, Add/ Remove Programs entry) and click Add/Remove. The uninstall part of the INF file deletes the *MRUDel* value from the *Run* key and removes the uninstall entry in the Registry.

NOTE: You will find the file MRUCLEAR.INF in the folder \chapter7\MRUclear in the sample files. Further details can be found in the above listing.

Advanced INF Files

Windows 98 supports the advanced INF file format. This format requires the Advanced INF Installer, which is located in the file ADVPACK.DLL. The extensions found in the advanced INF file format can perform tasks such as prompting a user for a destination directory, installing files to a directory specified in the Registry, and checking for mandatory applications before performing an upgrade. At the time this book was written, little information about the advanced INF file format was available. In the coming sections, I'll give you some information about this new format and explain how to use it.

How to Call an Advanced INF File

Using the features in an advanced INF file requires more than right-clicking an INF file and selecting Install from the context menu. The Install command invokes the RunSetupCommand function in SETUPAPI.DLL, which executes only the old INF keywords. If you want to execute the advanced INF file keywords, you must invoke ADVPACK.DLL with the following command:

```
rundll32.exe advpack.dll,LaunchINFSectionEx,   →
C:\Win98Reg\chapter7\advancedinf\test1.inf,DefaultInstall
```

The RUNDLL32.EXE program calls the ADVPACK.DLL library, which executes the LaunchINFSectionEx function. This function launches a specified section of a specified INF file. The second parameter specifies the name and location of the INF file. If this isn't the Windows \INF folder, you must include the path. The third parameter defines the section within the INF file to be executed. In the sample above, the DefaultInstall section will be processed. If this parameter is omitted, DefaultInstall will be assumed.

An optional fourth parameter for flags can be appended. This parameter defines how the install part should be applied. Table 7-6 shows the codes that are available for the flag.

Flag Codes

Value	Meaning
4	Quiet Mode
8	No GrpConv
16	Force Self-Updating on User's System
32	Backup Data Before Install
64	Rollback to Previous State
128	Validate the Backup Data
256	Bypass Building File List
512	Force Delay of OCX Registration

Table 7-6.
Optional flags for the fourth parameter.

The following command executes the [DefaultInstall] section in the file TEST1.INF in the Windows 98 \INF folder.

```
rundll32.exe advpack.dll,LaunchINFSectionEx, %17%\test1.inf,,12
```

The flag indicates that the installation should be done in Quiet mode without GrpConv.

NOTE: It's also possible to use the command

```
rundll32.exe advpack.dll,LaunchINFSection ⌐
C:\Win98Reg\chapter7\advancedinf\test1.inf,DefaultInstall
```

to launch the advanced INF file. In this case, only the flag values *1* and *2* are allowed, *1* representing Quiet Mode and *2* representing No GrpConv. A sample demonstrating how to back up the Registry is shown in the section "Using an Advanced INF File to Back Up the Registry," beginning on page 371.

The Advanced INF File Format

An advanced INF file must contain the *AdvancedINF* entry in the [Version] section. This entry has the following syntax:

AdvancedINF=xx, "text"

where *xx* stands for a version of the ADVPACK.DLL. If the requested version isn't found, the text will be shown in a message box, as you can see in Figure 7-12.

Figure 7-12.
The Advanced INF Install message box indicating that the requested version isn't installed.

The following lines of code show the beginning of an advanced INF file:

```
[version]
Signature= "$CHICAGO$"
AdvancedINF= 2.5,"You need a new version of advpack.dll"

; This is the install part.
[DefaultInstall]
CopyFiles = Tst.CopyFiles
```

The *AdvancedINF* keyword specifies that version 2.5 of ADVPACK.DLL must be installed. (Because Windows 98 comes with version 2.5, I set this version number to 4.5 to display the message box shown in Figure 7-12.)

The following code demonstrates how to use some of the features contained in advanced INF files. To execute this INF file, you must use the Rundll32 command (previously discussed) in the Start menu Run dialog box. Also notice that I used absolute path settings—C:\Win98Reg\chapter7\AdvancedINF—in the file. If you use a different drive or a different folder, you must edit the paths in the Run command to test the file.

```
; File: Test2.INF
;
; Demonstrate how to use an advanced INF file
; Use the Run command with the following line:
; rundll32.exe advpack.dll,LaunchINFSection
; C:\Win98Reg\chapter7\advancedinf\test2.inf,DefaultInstall
; to execute the advanced INF file.

[version]
Signature= "$CHICAGO$"
AdvancedINF= 2.5,"You need a new version of advpack.dll"

; This is the install part.
[DefaultInstall]

CopyFiles = Tst.CopyFiles    ; Just a dummy
AddReg=Tst.AddReg            ; Add test entries
RunPreSetupCommands=Tst.PreSetup
RunPostSetupCommands=Tst.PostSetup

BeginPrompt=Tst.PromptBegin  ; Prompt before install
EndPrompt=Tst.PromptEnd      ; Prompt after install

; Demonstrate how to launch programs during install
[Tst.PreSetup]
calc.exe                     ; Launch Calculator before install

[Tst.PostSetup]
explorer.exe                 ; Launch Explorer after install

[Tst.AddReg]

HKCR,.1G_Born,Test,,"Hello World"  ; Add a key
```

(continued)

continued

```
; Test file to be copied to the Windows\Born subfolder
[Tst.CopyFiles]
Test1.tst                ; *** Breakpoint 1

[DestinationDirs]

Tst.CopyFiles = 10,Born        ; Create new subfolder

[SourceDisksNames]
55="Testfile Disk","",1

[SourceDisksFiles]
Tstfile.txt=55

[Tst.PromptBegin]
Prompt="Begin with installation"
ButtonType=[YESNO | OKCANCEL]
Title="Test INF Install"

[Tst.PromptEnd]
Prompt="Finish with installation"

[Strings]
REMOVE_DESC = "Remove Testfile1 (Born)"
; End ***
```

Processing this INF file by using the Rundll32 command mentioned above shows a dialog box before the installation starts and after the installation ends. These dialog boxes are created using these commands:

```
BeginPrompt=Tst.PromptBegin  ; Prompt before install
EndPrompt=Tst.PromptEnd      ; Prompt after install

[Tst.PromptBegin]
Prompt="Begin with installation"
ButtonType=[YESNO | OKCANCEL]
Title="Test INF Install

[Tst.PromptEnd]
Prompt="Finish with installation"
```

The keyword *Prompt* specifies the string shown in the dialog box. The *ButtonType* keyword is used to set the buttons available in the message box, but I haven't found a way to determine which button the user clicked. If you want to launch a program before the installation starts or after the installation is finished, you must use the following commands:

```
RunPreSetupCommands=Tst.PreSetup
RunPostSetupCommands=Tst.PostSetup
[Tst.PreSetup]
calc.exe                        ; Launch Calculator before install

[Tst.PostSetup]
explorer.exe                    ; Launch Explorer after install
```

The *RunPreSetupCommands* keyword defines a section within the INF file containing some commands to be executed before the INF file is processed. The commands shown above start the Windows Calculator before the INF file is processed; Windows Explorer is launched after the installation is finished.

N O T E : You will find the two files, TEST1.INF and TEST2.INF, in the folder \chapter7\AdvancedINF of the sample files. Remember that you must use the Run command in the Start menu to execute the "Rundll32.exe advpack.dll" command discussed above to use the advanced INF file features.

Using an Advanced INF File to Back Up the Registry

As you can see in Table 7-6 on page 367, an advanced INF file gives you the option to back up a Registry key during installation. You can also roll back the Registry settings. Unfortunately, it's a little bit difficult to find out how to force such a backup. After playing around a while, I found a way to back up and roll back Registry entries. You need an advanced INF file, and you must use the correct commands to execute this INF file. Let's assume the advanced INF file REGBACK.INF is located in the folder C:\Win98Reg\chapter7\advancedinf. To force a backup, you need to invoke the file with the following command:

```
Rundll32.exe advpack.dll,LaunchINFSectionEx   →
C:\Win98Reg\chapter7\advancedinf\RegBack.inf,DefaultInstall,,32
```

There are two things I need to mention. You must use the *LaunchINF-SectionEx* function, and you must append the value *32* (Backup Data Before Install, as indicated in Table 7-6) to the command. You can't use the *LaunchINFSection* function because the flag value *32* isn't allowed.

The advanced INF file used to back up a Registry key is similar to the files shown above.

```
; File: RegBack.INF (G. Born)
;
; Demonstrate how to use an advanced INF file to back up
; a branch in the Registry (and restore it later)
;
; Run the following command to invoke the INF file:
;
; rundll32.exe advpack.dll,LaunchINFSectionEx <path>regback.inf, ⮑
; DefaultInstall,,flag
;
; <path> must be set to the drive and path of the INF file.
; The flag must be set to:
; 32 - Backup or 64 - Rollback
;
; Use at your own risk!

[version]
Signature= "$CHICAGO$"
AdvancedINF= 2.5,"You need a new version of advpack.dll"

; This is the install part.
[DefaultInstall]

; Inform the user about beginning and end of execution
BeginPrompt=Tst.PromptBegin
EndPrompt=Tst.PromptEnd

; Just to demonstrate that it works
RunPreSetupCommands=Tst.PreSetup
RunPostSetupCommands=Tst.PostSetup

; Now set the component name and version. (These settings
; are used to create the Registry entry.)
ComponentName="BornG"
ComponentVersion=4.0

; This is my Backup section
BackupReg=Tst.BackupReg
BackupPath=%10%\BornG

; Can be executed before Rollback
PreRollBack=GenInstallSection

; Removing the next semicolon forces Windows to reboot
;Reboot=1
```

```
; #### Backup Registry section in the BackPath ####
[Tst.BackupReg]
; Try to save the "*" entry in HKCR
; After processing the INF file, the user can
; alter this key (for instance, rename it to "*1")
HKCR,"*"

[GenInstallSection]
; This section is still empty

[Tst.PreSetup]
calc.exe        ; Just for test purposes

[Tst.PostSetup]
; For test purposes
Explorer.exe       ; Inspecting Backup folder in the Windows folder

[Tst.PromptBegin]
; Inform the user that we're starting
Prompt="Begin with installation?"
ButtonType=[YESNO | OKCANCEL]
Title="Test INF Install"

[Tst.PromptEnd]
Prompt="We are finished with the installation"
; End ***
```

This file contains a lot of extra code for several purposes. For instance, I've used the *RunPreSetupCommand* to run the Windows Calculator. This is a means of informing the user that the advanced INF file is executing. The important parts of the file that are used for backing up a Registry entry are listed below:

```
ComponentName="BornG"
ComponentVersion=4.0
BackupReg=Tst.BackupReg
BackupPath=%10%\BornG

[Tst.BackupReg]
HKCR,"*"
```

ComponentName is used to identify the backup entries stored in the Registry. After executing the advanced INF file by using the Rundll32 command shown above, you'll see two new entries in the Registry. The first entry,

> HKEY_CURRENT_USER\Software\Microsoft\Advanced INF Setup\
> BornG

contains only the empty subkey *RegBackup*. The second entry,

HKEY_LOCAL_MACHINE\SOFTWARE\Microsoft
Advanced INF Setup\BornG

contains value names—*BackupFileName*, *BackupPath*, *BackupRegistry*, and so on—with values that are required for rolling back the old settings. The *BackupRegistry* flag, for instance, indicates whether backup values are available for a rollback. *BackupPath* defines the path where Windows has stored the backup data. This path is set in the BackupPath entry in the advanced INF file. The Registry branch that will be saved in the backup is defined in the [Tst.BackupReg] section of the INF file. For the current sample, I backed up only the wildcard key *HKEY_CLASSES_ROOT**.

> NOTE: After executing the advanced INF file by using the Rundll32 command shown above, you can inspect the Registry for the entries described in the previous paragraph. Also, the Windows folder should have the subfolder *BornG* containing the backup data. To demonstrate the rollback effect, change something in the *HKEY_CLASSES_ROOT** key, such as renaming the ...* key to ...*1 or adding a subkey to ...*).

You can invoke the rollback with the following command:

```
Rundll32.exe advpack.dll,LaunchINFSectionEx,    →
C:\Win98Reg\chapter7\advancedinf\RegBack.inf,DefaultInstall,64
```

This is the same command we used to back up the Registry, except that the flag value is now set to *64* (Rollback to Previous State). After you execute this command, the previous Registry settings in the *HKEY_CLASSES_ROOT** key will appear.

> NOTE: You'll find the file REGBACK.INF in the folder \chapter7\ AdvancedINF of the sample files. Remember that you must use the Run command in the Start menu to execute the "Rundll32.exe advpack.dll" command discussed previously that allows you to use the advanced INF file features. To simplify my tests, I created two short-cuts to this INF file on my desktop and I set the commands to execute each of them on the property page of the INF file.
>
> There is still one problem: how do we force Windows 98 to use the advanced INF features on a user's machine? If the user right-clicks on the INF file and selects *Install*, the advanced commands aren't executed. But you can use a trick in your INF file: add the

Rundll32 command to execute the advanced INF file to the *HKEY_LOCAL_MACHINE\SOFTWARE\Microsoft\Windows\ CurrentVersion\RunOnce* key, and then force a system restart.

Creating Policy Editor Template Files

The System Policy Editor uses template files (ADM files) to customize the property pages for Local User and Local Computer. You can create your own templates to customize the options available in the properties pages. We have used this strategy in previous chapters. (See "Customizing the Shell Settings by Using the System Policy Editor" in Chapter 5 for how you can add such a template to the System Policy Editor.)

The ADM Template File Structure

ADM files are stored as simple text files. You can use any of the Windows editors, such as Notepad or WordPad, to alter such files. Each file contains a structure describing the options that will be available in the property page, as shown in Figure 7-13.

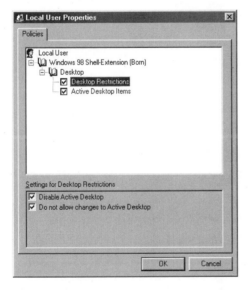

Figure 7-13.
The Local User Properties property page showing the options from a custom template.

```
CLASS type
  CATEGORY name
    POLICY name
      KEYNAME key
      definition of policy
    END POLICY
  END CATEGORY
```

The *CLASS* keyword specifies which class of the System Policy Editor the options will be displayed in. A type of USER specifies the Local User Properties property page, while MACHINE specifies the Local Computer Properties property page. The *CATEGORY* keyword defines a name that will be shown as the category on a property page. For example, in Figure 7-13, the category is Windows 98 Shell-Extension (Born). For each *CATEGORY* keyword, you must have a closing *END CATEGORY* keyword.

The *POLICY* keyword defines the entries for the requested policy. These are the entries that display a check box under each category name. For example, Desktop Restrictions, shown in Figure 7-13, is a policy. Each occurrence of the *POLICY* keyword must have a closing *END POLICY* keyword.

> NOTE: If the parameter following the keywords is preceded by the characters !!, the string that follows is a variable name.

The Registry key used for this policy is defined with the *KEYNAME* keyword. You can define the options for a policy with the *PART* keyword. These options are shown in the footer of the property page (for example, Disable Active Desktop in Figure 7-13). This keyword must be terminated with an *END PART* keyword.

The keyword *CHECKBOX* instructs the System Policy Editor to display a check box next to the option defined with the *PART* keyword. You can assign the following values to a check box:

- **ACTIONLISTON** Specifies actions that take place when the check box is on.

- **ACTIONLISTOFF** Specifies actions that take place when the check box is off.

- **DEFCHECKED** Sets the check box to be checked by default.

- **VALUEON** Specifies the Registry value when the check box is checked.

- **VALUEOFF** Specifies the Registry value when the check box is unchecked.

The keyword COMBOBOX instructs the System Policy Editor to display a combo box option. You can assign the following values to a combo box:

- DEFAULT value   Denotes the default string that is entered in the combo box.
- MAXLEN value   Specifies the maximum length for an entry (1 to 255).
- REQUIRED   If set, the user must alter the option.
- SUGGESTIONS   Specifies a list of suggestions in the combo box.

The keyword DROPDOWNLIST instructs the System Policy Editor to display a drop-down list option. You can assign the following values to a drop-down list:

- ITEMLIST   Defines a list of items to be shown in the drop-down list.
- REQUIRED   If set, the user must alter the option.

The keyword EDITTEXT instructs the System Policy Editor to display a text field option. You can assign the following values to a text field:

- DEFAULT value   Defines the value shown in the text field.
- MAXLEN value   Sets the maximum length of a text entry.
- REQUIRED   If set, the user must alter the option.

The keyword LISTBOX instructs the System Policy Editor to display a list box option. You can assign the following values to a list box:

- ADDITIVE   The list box value will overwrite the Registry value.
- EXPLICITVALUE   Indicates that the user must specify the name and the value of an entry.
- VALUENAME   Defines the name for the list box.
- VALUEPREFIX name   Defines the prefix name for an entry (such as File in File1).

The keyword NUMERIC instructs the System Policy Editor to display a text field for numeric input. You can assign the values on the following page.

- **DEFAULT value**   The default value shown in the text box.
- **MAX value**   The maximum value for the entry.
- **MIN value**   The minimum value for the entry.
- **REQUIRED**   If set, the user must alter the option.
- **SPIN value**   Enables a spin control and specifies the increments for the control. A value of *0* removes the spin control.
- **TXTCONVERT**   Inserts values as strings into the Registry.

The keyword TEXT creates a simple label and won't affect any Registry entries.

NOTE: Further information and samples about the ADM file format can be found in the *Microsoft Windows 98 Resource Kit*.

The following sample file defines the options shown in Figure 7-13.

```
; Born.adm
; This file customizes the Local Users Properties
; in the System Policy Editor of Windows 98.
; The file contains settings for a few shell features.
;
; Warning: This file is provided AS IS WITHOUT WARRANTY OF ANY
; KIND AND IS PROVIDED WITHOUT ANY IMPLIED WARRANTY OF FITNESS
; FOR PURPOSE OF MERCHANTABILITY. Use this template entirely
; at your own risk. Please back up your system to avoid problems
; with your Registry settings.


; The entries will go into the Local User branch
;;;;;;;;;;;;;;;;;;;;
CLASS USER ;;;;;;;
;;;;;;;;;;;;;;;;;;;;

; Add the new category Born. The string displayed
; in the Local User Properties property page is defined in the
; [String] section at the end of this file.

CATEGORY !!Born

    CATEGORY !!Desktop
        KEYNAME Software\Microsoft\Windows\CurrentVersion\  ⮑
                Policies\Explorer
```

```
     POLICY !!DesktopSub
         PART !!NoActiveDesktop CHECKBOX
             VALUENAME NoActiveDesktop
         END PART

         PART !!NoActiveDesktopChanges CHECKBOX
             VALUENAME NoActiveDesktopChanges
         END PART

     END POLICY

     POLICY !!ActiveDesktop_Title
     KEYNAME "Software\Microsoft\Windows\CurrentVersion\   ⬎
             Policies\ActiveDesktop"
         PART !!sz_ATC_NoComponents CHECKBOX
             VALUENAME "NoComponents"
         END PART
         PART !!sz_ATC_DisableAdd CHECKBOX
             VALUENAME "NoAddingComponents"
         END PART
         PART !!sz_ATC_DisableDel CHECKBOX
             VALUENAME "NoDeletingComponents"
         END PART

         PART !!sz_ATC_DisableEdit CHECKBOX
             VALUENAME "NoEditingComponents"
         END PART
         PART !!sz_ATC_DisableClose CHECKBOX
             VALUENAME "NoClosingComponents"
         END PART
     END POLICY
   END CATEGORY
END CATEGORY

; Now we have to define the strings used for the variables above

[strings]
; These are the entries for the upper level of the branch
Born="Windows 98 Shell-Extension (Born)"
Desktop="Desktop"

;
DesktopSub="Desktop Restrictions"
ActiveDesktop_Title="Active Desktop Items"

; Strings shown for the check boxes
```

(continued)

continued

```
NoActiveDesktop="Disable Active Desktop"
NoActiveDesktopChanges="Do not allow changes to Active Desktop"

; Here we have several Active Desktop subitems

sz_ATC_NoComponents="Disable ALL desktop items"
sz_ATC_DisableAdd="Disable adding ANY desktop items"
sz_ATC_DisableDel="Disable deleting ANY desktop items"
sz_ATC_DisableEdit="Disable editing ANY desktop items"
sz_ATC_DisableClose="Disable closing ANY desktop items"


; End
```

This file uses string values to define the values for several keywords and uses a nested CATEGORY scheme.

NOTE: You can inspect other ADM files shipped with Windows 98 to find out more about system policies and how to customize Windows 98 by using Registry entries. All keys used in a system policy will be found in the ADM file. The file BORN.ADM shown above is located in the folder \chapter7\ADM of the sample files. This folder also contains a second ADM file that you can use to customize the Windows 98 shell.

Conclusion

I have discussed most of the Registry entries relevant to Windows 98 settings and a lot of topics relevant to dealing with the Registry. There are still many things to say about INF files and other Registry topics, but it was never my goal to address all these topics—just some of the more critical issues. Use the references listed throughout the book to find more information.

Icons Contained in SHELL32.DLL

This appendix contains two tables. The first table describes the standard icons used by Microsoft Windows 98. The second table lists other, less frequently used icons that you can use as you like.

> TIP: The second column lists negative values. Each of these values is the resource identifier of a particular icon. You can also use these resource identifiers to define icons. The advantage of using a resource identifier value instead of an icon index value is that resource identifiers are compatible between Windows 95, Microsoft Windows NT 4.0, and Windows 98, while icon index schemes are dependent on particular Windows versions.

Common Icons Used by Windows 98

Icon Index	Icon Resource	Icon	Description
0	-1		Default used for unregistered file types and for files for which no icon is available.
1	-2		Default used for files with the extension DOC. As I discussed in Chapters 3 and 4, you can redefine this icon by using the *DefaultIcon* subkey in the *docfile* key of the Registry.

(continued)

Common Icons Used by Windows 98 *continued*

Icon Index	Icon Resource	Icon	Description
2	-3		Used for executable programs that have no icon, such as MS-DOS, EXE, and COM files. (This icon can be overwritten by PIF file settings.) To change the icon, click Change Icon on the Program property page of the file's Properties property sheet.
3	-4		Used by the shell (comprising the Microsoft Windows Explorer, desktop, Start menu, and shell windows) to indicate a closed folder. This icon must be redefined in the *Shell Icons* key.
4	-5		Used by the shell to indicate an open folder. This icon must be redefined in the *Shell Icons* key.
5	-6		Used by the shell for a 5¼" floppy disk drive. This icon must be redefined in the *Shell Icons* key.
6	-7		Used by the shell for a 3½" floppy disk drive. This icon must be redefined in the *Shell Icons* key.
7	-8		Used by the shell for a removable drive. This icon must be redefined in the *Shell Icons* key.
8	-9		Used by the shell for a hard disk drive. You can redefine this icon in the *Shell Icons* key, or you can use the AUTORUN.INF file method described on page 264.
9	-10		Used by the shell for the drives associated with a network device (that is, a folder or drive). You can redefine this icon in the *Shell Icons* key.
10	-11		Used by the shell if the connection to an associated network device is broken. You can redefine this icon in the *Shell Icons* key.
11	-12		Used by the shell for a CD-ROM drive. You can redefine this icon in the *Shell Icons* key, but this icon is always temporarily overwritten when a CD-ROM contains an AUTORUN.INF file with an icon definition. (See Chapter 5.)

Icon Index	Icon Resource	Icon	Description
12	*-13*		Can be used for RAM drives or for hardware settings. (I see no need to redefine this icon.)
13	*-14*		Used in the Network Neighborhood window to show the Entire Network. (I see no need to redefine this icon in *Shell Icons*.)
14	*-15*		Another icon for a network connection. (I haven't found the place where this icon is used by the shell.)
15	*-16*		Used in the Network Neighborhood window to show workgroup computers. (The icon is defined in the *HKEY_CLASSES_ROOT\CLSID* key of the network ActiveX server.) This icon belongs to one of the shell's namespace objects. (See Chapter 4.)
16	*-17*		Used for local printer drivers in the Printers folder, and used in links that you create in folders or on the desktop. (This icon can't be redefined.)
17	*-18*		Used by the shell for the Network Neighborhood. This icon belongs to the shell's namespace objects. (See Chapter 4 to learn how to change this icon.)
18	*-19*		Used in the Entire Network window to show a workgroup entry. (The icon can't be redefined in *Shell Icons*.)
19	*-20*		Used for the Programs entry on the Start menu and for the entries of the program groups in the submenus. The icon also represents program group entries in the window of the Start Menu folder and subfolders (such as Accessories, Startup, and so on).
20	*-21*		Used for the Documents entry on the Start menu.
21	*-22*		Used for the Settings entry on the Start menu.
22	*-23*		Used for the Find entry on the Start menu and other places.

(continued)

Common Icons Used by Windows 98 *continued*

Icon Index	Icon Resource	Icon	Description
23	-24		Used for the Help entry on the Start menu. (The symbol shown for help files is defined in *HKEY_CLASSES_ROOT\hlpfile* and is contained in WINHLP32.EXE.)
24	-25		Used for the Run entry on the Start menu.
25	-26		Used for Suspend mode if the computer supports a power-saving feature.
26	-27		Used for computers with a docking station.
27	-28		Used for the Shut Down entry on the Start menu. The icon can be changed in the *Shell Icons* key.
28	-29		Used in combination with other icons (of drives, folders, and printers) to represent sharing within a workgroup. Any icon you substitute for this one must have a transparent background.
29	-30		Superimposed over other icons (of drives, folders, printers, and files) to indicate a shortcut (or a PIF file). You can suppress this icon by removing the *IsShortcut* entry in the *lnkfile* and *piffile* keys. (This topic is discussed in Chapter 5.) If you want to use a substitute for this arrow, use an icon with a transparent background. Tweak UI offers a feature to suppress the Shortcut arrow or to set another icon (such as the light arrow icon).
30	-31		Can be superimposed over other icons to indicate shortcuts (or PIF files). The icon has a transparent background. Tweak UI provides an option to use this icon as a Shortcut symbol.

Icon Index	Icon Resource	Icon	Description
31	*-32*		The standard icon used to represent an empty Recycle Bin. This icon is set in the *DefaultIcon* key of the ActiveX server in the *CLSID* branch. (See Chapter 4 for further information.)
32	*-33*		The standard icon used to represent a Recycle Bin that isn't empty. This icon is set in the *DefaultIcon* key of the ActiveX server, in *CLSID*. (See Chapter 4 for further information.) Other icons that can be used to represent a Recycle Bin that contains elements are located in the SHELL32.DLL file.
33	*-34*		Used by the dial-up networking function. (You have the option to install this in Microsoft Windows 98.) This icon is set in the *CLSID* key of the ActiveX server.
34	*-35*		Used in the shell for the Desktop entry (Windows Explorer window) and for the Show Desktop option on the taskbar.
35	*-36*		Used for the Control Panel folder. This icon can be shown or hidden on the desktop. (See Chapter 4.)
36	*-37*		Used to represent the large icons for the program group folders on the Start menu.
37	*-38*		Used for the Printers folder. This icon can be shown or hidden on the desktop. (See Chapter 4.)
38	*-39*		Shown for the Fonts folder in the Control Panel.
39	*-40*		The Microsoft Windows symbol with a button.
40	*-41*		Icon used for the CD Player utility that comes with Windows 98.

Other Icons Available for General Use

Icon Index	Icon Resource	Icon	Description
41	-42		Tree symbol.
42	-43		Explore computer and folder symbol.
43	-44		Favorites folder symbol.
44	-45		Log Off symbol.
45	-46		Find in folder symbol.
46	-47		Update Windows 98 symbol.
47	-133		Multiple documents symbol.
48	-134		Find files and folders symbol.
49	-135		Find computers symbol.
50	-136		Shut-down Windows symbol.
51	-137		Control Panel folder symbol.
52	-138		Printer folder symbol.
53	-139		Add new printer symbol.
54	-140		Network printer symbol.
55	-141		Print to file symbol.

Icon Index	Icon Resource	Icon	Description
56	-142		Recycle Bin full symbol.
57	-143		Recycle Bin full symbol.
58	-144		Recycle Bin full symbol.
59	-145		Document symbol.
60	-146		Document copy symbol.
61	-147		Rename folder symbol.
62	-148		Copy (system files) symbol.
63	-151		Document file (INI file) symbol.
64	-152		Document file (text) symbol.
65	-153		Executable program symbol.
66	-154		System file (DLL, SYS, and so on).
67	-155		(Bitmap) Font symbol.
68	-156		TrueType font symbol.
69	-157		Adobe Type Manager font symbol.

(continued)

Other Icons Available for General Use *continued*

Icon Index	Icon Resource	Icon	Description
70	-160		Run application symbol.
71	-161		Send file symbol.
72	-165		Backup symbol.
73	-166		ScanDisk symbol.
74	-167		Defragment symbol.
75	-168		Default printer symbol.
76	-169		Default network printer symbol.
77	-170		Print to disk by default symbol.
78	-171		Folder tree symbol.
79	-173		Favorites folder symbol.

Values for the *International* Key

Listed in this table are the possible values contained in the following Registry key: *HKEY_CURRENT_USER\Control Panel\International.* You can set these values by clicking Regional Settings in the Control Panel and then selecting the appropriate property page. If the default for a given value is selected, the value will not be shown in the *International* key.

Value Name	Description
Number Settings	
sDecimal	Decimal symbol for numbers.
iDigits	Number of digits after the decimal. The value can be *0* through *9*.
sThousand	Digit grouping symbol. An example of the format is 1,000.
sGrouping	Number of digits in a group. The value is *x;0*.
sNegativeSign	Negative sign symbol.
iNegNumber	Negative number. The following list shows the value and the format, respectively: *0* (1.1) *1* −1.1 *2* − 1.1 *3* 1.1− *4* 1.1 −
iLZero	Display leading zeros. The following list shows the value and the format: *0* .7 *1* 0.7

(continued)

continued

Value Name	Description

Number Settings *(continued)*

iMeasure	Measurement system. The following list shows the value and the format: *0* Metric *1* U.S.
sList	List separator.

Currency Settings

sCurrency	Currency symbol.
sMonDecimalSep	Decimal symbol.
iCurrDigits	Number of digits after decimal. The value can be *0* through *9*.
sMonThousandSep	Digit grouping symbol.
sMonGrouping	Number of digits in group. The value is *x;0*.
iCurrency	Position of currency symbol. The following list shows the value and the format: *0* $1.1 *1* 1.1$ *2* $ 1.1 *3* 1.1 $
iNegCurr	Negative number format. The following list shows the value and the format: *0* ($1.1) *1* -$1.1 *2* $-1.1 *3* $1.1- *4* (1.1$) *5* -1.1$ *6* 1.1-$ *7* 1.1$- *8* -1.1 $ *9* -$ 1.1 *10* 1.1 $- *11* $ 1.1- *12* $ -1.1 *13* 1.1- $ *14* ($ 1.1) *15* (1.1 $)

Value Name	Description
Time Settings	
iTime	Time format. The following list shows the value and the format: *0* 12 hours as 1:30 *1* 24 hours as 13:30
iTLZero	Display leading zeros in time. The following list shows the value and the format: *0* 9:15 *1* 09:15
sTimeFormat	Time style (*h* represents 1 through 12, *H* represents 0 through 23). The following list shows the value in the left-hand column and the AM and PM formats in the middle and right-hand columns: *h:mm:ss tt* 1:15:00 AM 1:15:00 PM *hh:mm:ss tt* 01:15:00 AM 01:15:00 PM *H:mm:ss* 1:15:00 13:15:00 *HH:mm:ss* 01:15:00 13:15:00
sTime	Time separator.
s1159	AM symbol.
s2359	PM symbol.
Date Settings	
sLongDateL	Long date style with date and weekday(*M* is month, *d* is day). *M:* month as 1–12. *MM:* month as 01–12. *MMM:* month as Jan–Dec. *MMMM:* month as January–December. *d:* day as 1–31. *dd:* day as 01–31. *ddd:* day as Mon–Sun. *dddd:* day as Monday–Sunday. The following list shows the value and the format: *dddd, MMMM dd, yyyy* Wednesday, January 01, 1998 *MMMM dd, yyyy* January 01, 1998 *dddd, dd MMMM, yyyy* Wednesday, 01 January, 1998 *dd MMMM, yyyy* 01 January, 1998

(continued)

continued

Value Name	Description
Date Settings *(continued)*	
sShortDate	Short date style (only day, month, and year).
	M/d/y 1/1/98
	M/d/yyyy 1/1/1998
	MM/dd/yy 01/01/98
	MM/dd/yyyy 01/01/1998
	yy/MM/dd 98/01/01
	dd-MMM-yy 01-Jan-98
sDate	Date separator.
iDate	Date style. The list below shows the value and the format:
	0 USA
	1 Europe
	2 Japan
sLanguage	Language code for sorting and ordering.
Locale	Windows 95 country code (USA is 409).

The Registry in Windows NT 4.0 Workstation

Microsoft Windows NT 4.0 Workstation and the server version both include the Microsoft Windows 95 shell (which is similar to the Windows 98 shell) and a Registry, so it would be safe to assume that the Windows NT Registry and the Windows 98 Registry are compatible in some ways. A brief look at the Windows NT Registry shows us that several of the topics we addressed regarding the Windows 95 and Windows 98 Registries are likely to be relevant to the Windows NT Registry.

But there is a limit to the similarities—Windows NT 4.0 Workstation *is* a different operating system, and in many ways its Registry is remarkably different from the Windows 98 Registry. I can't address all the Windows NT–specific topics in detail in this book, but I can provide you with some important insights that will help you with your work. (An examination of the Windows NT Registry really requires its own book. Perhaps I'll write it!)

> NOTE: You can find further information about the Windows NT 4.0 Registry in the file REGENTRY.HLP, which is provided on the CD shipped with the *Microsoft Windows NT 4.0 Workstation Resource Kit*. The resource kit also contains printed information about several Registry keys.

The Role of INI Files

As discussed in Chapter 1, Windows 98 still supports the old INI files for compatibility reasons. In Windows NT, however, the Registry is used in place of most of the INI files—Windows NT doesn't use the INI files at all. So when you install Windows NT 4.0 Workstation over Windows 3.*x*, all entries in the INI files will be moved into the Registry and those entries will be deleted from the INI files. After the install is complete, a few INI files will remain in the

Windows NT folder, including WIN.INI and SYSTEM.INI. These files contain a small number of entries that aren't compatible with the Windows NT Registry and are maintained only for compatibility with 16-bit Windows software (and that will be used by only those programs).

> **NOTE:** For additional information about the mapping of the Windows 3.*x* INI file entries into the Windows NT 4.0 Registry, take a look at the *Microsoft Windows NT 4.0 Workstation Resource Kit.*

The Windows NT Registry Architecture

Like the Windows 98 Registry, the Windows NT 4.0 Registry is structured as a hierarchical database. The information stored in this database is organized in keys; each key contains one or more values and perhaps one or more subkeys. (See Chapter 1 for details about this type of structure.) The difference between Windows 95/Windows 98 and Windows NT 4.0 Workstation is in the root keys.

The Five Root Keys in the Windows NT Registry Structure

The Windows NT 4.0 Registry consists of only five root keys that reflect different parts of the configuration data—user data and machine-dependent settings. (The sixth root key in the Windows 95/Windows 98 Registry, *HKEY_DYN_DATA*, is not available, as explained in the Note on page 396.) Related information about a particular aspect of the system (for example, about the user, the hardware, the application, and so on) is grouped together in a key, or branch. Each root key, named *HKEY_xxxx*, is followed by several subkeys. The root keys are displayed when you start the Registry Editor. (See Figure C-1.)

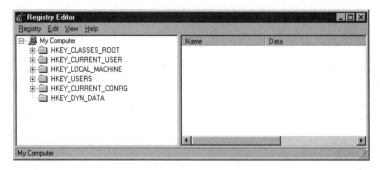

Figure C-1.
The Windows NT 4.0 Registry Editor.

The following sections describe the contents of the five branches within the Registry. These branches are discussed in more detail later in this appendix in the section "Windows NT 4.0 Workstation Registry Entries," beginning on page 414.

HKEY_CLASSES_ROOT

This branch contains all data used in Windows NT for OLE and drag-and-drop operations, including the names of all registered file types and their properties. All entries in this branch can also be found in the key *HKEY_LOCAL_MACHINE\SOFTWARE\Classes*. You can use Windows Explorer's File Types property sheet (invoked by selecting View and then Options) to change the file type associations. The entries and steps explaining how to change these entries are discussed in Chapters 3 and 4.

HKEY_USERS

In Windows NT, more than one user can log on to a single computer, and each of those users can have unique settings for the desktop, application software, etc. Information about each of these users (as well as settings for the desktop, Start menu, application defaults, and so on) is located in the *HKEY_USERS* key. Default values for new users logging on to the system are stored in the *.DEFAULT* subkey of *HKEY_USERS*. The information in the *.DEFAULT* subkey is also used when no user is logged on to the system. Unlike Windows 98, which employs a user's name as a subkey, Windows NT uses the user's Security ID string as the subkey.

HKEY_CURRENT_USER

Settings for the current user are stored in this key. This information is built from *HKEY_USERS* during the logon process.

HKEY_LOCAL_MACHINE

Configuration data for the local computer that is not user-dependent is stored in this key. This information is used by applications, drivers, and the Windows NT system. Some parts of this key are built during each system startup. (We'll examine this process more closely later in this appendix.)

HKEY_CURRENT_CONFIGURATION

This branch is new to Windows NT 4.0 and contains the configuration data for the hardware profile currently used in the computer. This branch was added for compatibility with Windows 95, which means that the application can use this branch to run under Windows 95, Windows 98, and Windows NT 4.0.

NOTE: A close look at Figure C-1 reveals a sixth key, *HKEY_ DYN_DATA*. This key is actually not available—you will see it in the REGEDIT.EXE program only. If you try to open this key, the Registry Editor displays an error message.

What Are Hives?

In Windows 98, the Registry is stored in only two files: USER.DAT and SYSTEM.DAT. In Windows NT 4.0, Registry entries are saved in a more atomized structure. (This strategy is related to the security concept used in Windows NT.) A single component of this atomized structure is called a "hive."

As we know, some Registry keys are rebuilt dynamically during each system startup, and other keys are essential for Windows NT 4.0 and must be available during each system startup. A hive is one of those essential keys. It is a permanent Registry key. The values for each hive are stored in a separate file in the Windows NT folder. Table C-1 contains a brief overview of these hives and files. You can find the names and directory locations of hives on a computer in the Registry's *HKEY_LOCAL_MACHINE\SYSTEM\ CurrentControlSet\Control\hivelist* key.

Windows NT 4.0 Hives

Hive	Description
HKEY_LOCAL_ MACHINE\SAM	Stores information for the security access manager in the \System32\Config subfolder in the files SAM, SAM.LOG, and SAM.SAV. This key can't be inspected by the user.
HKEY_LOCAL_ MACHINE\SECURITY	Stores security information in the \System32\Config subfolder in the files SECURITY, SECURITY.LOG, and SECURITY.SAV. This key can't be inspected by the user.
HKEY_LOCAL_ MACHINE\SOFTWARE	Stores information in the \System32\Config subfolder in the files SOFTWARE, SOFTWARE.LOG, and SOFTWARE.SAV.
HKEY_LOCAL_ MACHINE\SYSTEM	Stores information about the hardware profiles of this subkey in the \System32\Config sub folder in the files SYSTEM, SYSTEM.LOG, and SYSTEM.SAV.

Table C-1. *(continued)*
Hives, keys, and their associated files.

Windows NT 4.0 Hives *(continued)*

Hive	Description
HKEY_CURRENT_CONFIG	Stores information about the *System* subkey of this hive in the \System32\ Config subfolder SYSTEM.SAV, and SYSTEM.ALT.
HKEY_USERS\ .DEFAULT	Stores information for a new user who is logged on to the system. The information for this hive is stored in the \System32\Config subfolder in the files DEFAULT, DEFAULT.LOG, and DEFAULT.SAV.
HKEY_CURRENT_USER	Stores information for the current user under the \Profiles subfolder in the files NTUSER.DAT and NTUSER.DAT.LOG.

The Registry Database

The Windows NT 4.0 Registry is spread over several files, which you can inspect using Windows Explorer. See Table C-1 for a detailed description of these hives and files.

Files in the \Profiles Subfolder

The files that support the entries in *HKEY_CURRENT_USER* are stored in the \Profiles subfolder of the Windows NT folder. Selecting this subfolder in Windows Explorer shows the All Users and Default User subfolders as well as a subfolder for each user with an account under Windows NT. All subfolders except All Users contain the files NTUSER.DAT and (sometimes) NTUSER.DAT.LOG. The file NTUSER.DAT contains the user profile for the current machine. The file NTUSER.DAT in the Default User subfolder contains the hive for each new user. When a new user logs on to the system for the first time, the data in the NTUSER.DAT file in the Default User subfolder is copied to a file in the user's subfolder.

Files in the \System32\Config Subfolder

The other supporting files for the hives are stored in the Windows NT subfolder \System32\Config. Some of these files, such as SAM, DEFAULT, and SOFT-WARE, do not contain an extension but do contain a copy of the hive content. All files with the extension SAV, such as DEFAULT.SAV and SOFTWARE.SAV, contain a copy of the hive file. This copy is made at the end of the text-mode

Setup. All changes made to a key in a hive are recorded in a file with the extension LOG (such as SAM.LOG). The file SYSTEM.ALT contains a copy of the critical hive *HKEY_LOCAL_MACHINE\SYSTEM*.

> **NOTE:** The USERDIFF file in the Windows NT subfolder \System32\Config does not contain a hive. It is used only for compatibility reasons with older Windows NT versions. When a user logs on to the system for the first time, the settings from the old user profile will be read from USERDIFF and incorporated into the Registry.

Recovery in the Windows NT Registry

Windows NT 4.0 uses a strategy different from that of Windows 95 and also from that of Windows 98 to record all changes in the Registry and allow a recovery. After you modify a Registry entry, the changed data is written by the system to the hive's LOG file and the value is stored on the hard disk when the next flush operation occurs. This flush operation can occur within a few seconds automatically, or it can occur when an application forces it to.

During this flush, the first sector of the LOG file is marked to indicate that a Registry transfer is under construction. After the flush, the changed data is also written to the actual hive file. If this transfer operation is successful, the hive file and the LOG file are marked as complete. If the system crashes during the transfer, the system detects the incomplete transaction (the mark in the LOG file is still available) and recovers the hive from the previous value recorded in the LOG file.

The *SYSTEM* hive is processed a little bit differently. After Windows stores the changed data in the hive and LOG files, the SYSTEM.ALT file is updated in the same manner. If Windows restarts with a *SYSTEM* hive still under construction, the contents of SYSTEM.ALT will be used.

> **NOTE:** Backing up, recovering, and restoring the Windows NT Registry is discussed on pages 410–414.

Data Types Used in the Windows NT Registry

In earlier chapters, we examined the data types available for the Windows 95/Windows 98 Registry: string, DWORD, and binary. If you use the Registry Editor REGEDIT.EXE to modify entries, you can use these three data types. In Windows NT 4.0, you can also use the Registry Editor REGEDT32.EXE (see "Tools for Accessing the Windows NT Registry," beginning on page 400) to use additional data types to define a key's value. Table C-2 contains an overview of these data types.

Data Type	Description
REG_BINARY	This type describes raw binary data as a byte stream. The data type is named binary in REGEDIT.EXE.
REG_DWORD	An entry of this data type represents a 4-byte (or 32-bit) number. This data type is also available as DWORD in REGEDIT.EXE.
REG_SZ	Values for this data type can contain a sequence of characters (a string) that are easily understood by a user. (We've seen many of these strings in the previous chapters.) This data type is also supported as the string data type by REGEDIT.EXE.
REG_EXPAND_SZ	Windows NT recognizes expandable data strings, which are not supported in Windows 95 or Windows 98. Such a string contains a variable that can be expanded when an application is called. For example, you can insert the variable *%SystemRoot%* into an expandable data string and the variable will be replaced by the name of the Windows NT directory (for example, *%SystemRoot%\NOTEPAD.EXE*). This data type can be created by a program or by REGEDT32.EXE.
REG_MULTI_SZ	This value describes a multiple string that contains several user-readable entries separated by NULL characters. This data type is also supported only by a program or by REGEDT32.EXE.

Table C-2.
Data types available for Windows NT Registry values.

As Table C-2 points out, keys containing some data types can be created only by a program or by your using the REGEDT32.EXE Registry Editor. A Windows NT Registry key entry can be as long as 1 MB—a lot longer than a Windows 95 Registry key, which is restricted to a length of 64 KB. (In Windows 98, this limit no longer exists.) However, a Registry full of long values will result in very large Registry hive files, and a lot of memory is required to load such large files. So Microsoft recommends storing entries longer than 2048 bytes in separate files and storing the paths and filenames of these files in the Registry key. A key name can be up to 16,000 Unicode characters long. One important fact regarding Windows NT is that key names are case-sensitive, unlike in Windows 95 or in Windows 98.

NOTE: Other data types might be added by various programs, but this data can't be edited by the Registry Editor.

Tools for Accessing the Windows NT Registry

Because the Windows NT 4.0 Registry file structure is different from the Windows 98 Registry file structure, you need special tools to access and modify it. These tools include the two Registry Editors, both REGEDIT.EXE and REGEDT32.EXE, as well as a diagnostics tool, Windows Explorer, the Control Panel, and REG and INF files.

REGEDIT.EXE

After you install Windows NT 4.0 Workstation, you will find in the Windows NT folder the REGEDIT.EXE file. REGEDIT.EXE is the new style of Registry Editor provided by Windows NT. The Windows NT Registry Editor has the same functionality and structure as the Windows 95/Windows 98 Registry Editor, so you can use it in the same way. (See Chapter 2 of this book for details about using the Registry Editor.) The disadvantage of this Registry Editor is that it doesn't support the extended data types defined for Windows NT. (These data types are listed in Table C-2.)

REGEDT32.EXE

Windows NT 4.0 Workstation is shipped with a second Registry Editor, REGEDT32.EXE, which is available in the Windows NT subfolder \System32 after you install Windows NT. This second Registry Editor is based on older versions of Windows NT, so its user interface is different from the REGEDIT.EXE interface. Context menus are not available, and the Registry keys are displayed in separate windows, as shown in Figure C-2. The menu bar in the Registry Editor's window contains commands for viewing, editing, and storing Registry data.

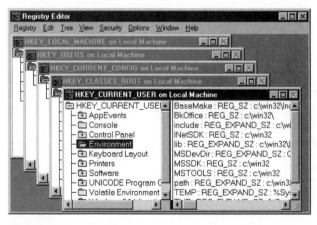

Figure C-2.
The Registry structure shown in REGEDT32.EXE.

Registry Menu Commands

Registry menu commands available to you with REGEDT32.EXE include the Save Subtree As command, which allows you to save a selected subkey to a text file, commands for printing a subkey (or "subtree"), and commands for loading and unloading a hive.

Loading and unloading a hive   The Load Hive and Unload Hive options are available from the Registry menu only if you select a subkey that is actually a hive. These options enable you to load a copy of another computer's hive files into the Registry Editor and modify them. The hive files of the current machine are loaded when you start REGEDT32.EXE. To load another computer's hives, select the *HKEY_LOCAL_MACHINE* key or the *HKEY_USERS* key and click the Load Hive command on the Registry menu. The Load Hive dialog box opens, which allows you to select another computer's hive from a file copied to a floppy disk. After you select the hive file, you can modify it, save it back to the original computer, and restart Windows NT.

> NOTE: To export a key into a hive file, select the key and use the Save Subtree As command. To import the hive file, click the key and select the Restore command from the Registry menu of the Registry Editor. After these steps, you can select the name of the hive file. As you can see, this export and import process is different from the export and import process used for REG files that are provided by REGEDIT.EXE.

View and Options Menu Commands

The View menu contains a Find Key command that allows you to search for a key. (REGEDIT.EXE also allows you to search for a key, as well as for a key's value.) Luckily, the Options menu offers the Read Only Mode command. This is a great function because it allows you to inspect the Registry without the risk of inadvertently modifying it.

The Security Menu's Permissions Command

Each key in the Windows NT Registry contains an access permission attribute. The system administrator can use REGEDT32.EXE to limit a user's access to any key to prevent that user from modifying the key. The Permissions command on the Security menu of the Registry Editor allows you to set the access permission to Read, Full Control, and Special Access. The Special Access command allows users to modify specific values of a key.

> WARNING: Be careful when you restrict access permission to system keys—you might inadvertently restrict people such as the system administrator from modifying them. Always back up the Registry

before changing any access privileges, and let the system administrator "own" all keys. You can find further information about this topic in the *Microsoft Windows NT 4.0 Workstation Resource Kit.*

Windows NT Diagnostics

You can use the Windows NT Diagnostics tool WINMSD.EXE to inspect important system settings. This file is available in the Windows NT subfolder \System32. After you invoke WINMSD.EXE (by clicking the Start menu and then selecting Programs, Administrative Tools, and Windows NT Diagnostics), you'll see a property sheet with several property pages, as shown in Figure C-3.

Through these property pages, you can view various system components. (Each component corresponds to a property page.) This diagnostic tool allows only Read access, which prevents you from accidentally changing something in the Registry.

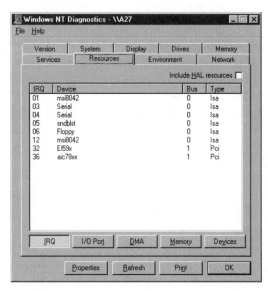

Figure C-3.
The Windows NT diagnostics program.

Windows Explorer

You can use Windows Explorer to change file type associations by selecting the Options command from the View menu. The File Types property page contains the settings for all registered file types. You can change these settings as explained in Chapter 3.

Control Panel

When you want to change the system settings in the Registry, *always go through the Control Panel first.* To open the Control Panel window, click the Start menu, select Settings, and then select Control Panel. Double-click the desired icon to open its property sheet. On the property sheet, you can safely inspect and modify the settings. We examined how to do this for Windows 98 in earlier chapters, and you can use the same steps for Windows NT 4.0.

Windows NT includes the functions of the Windows 95 Plus! Pack, which simplify some tasks, such as changing desktop icons for My Computer, Recycle Bin, and Network Neighborhood. All you have to do is invoke the Display Properties property sheet, which you can do from the Control Panel, and select the Plus! property page, which contains options for changing the desktop icons. (See Figure C-4.) This page is similar to the Effects property page in Windows 98. Clicking a desktop icon on this property page and then clicking Change Icon allows you to select a new icon source.

Figure C-4.
Changing the desktop icons on the Plus! property page.

> NOTE: Be aware that Windows NT 4.0 and Windows 98 handle Registry entries differently. As I discussed in earlier chapters, Windows NT 4.0 uses the Windows 95 scheme to store the CLSID entries in the Registry.

> NOTE: The Policy Editor for Windows 95 and Windows 98 isn't available in Windows NT 4.0 Workstation. POLEDIT.EXE is shipped only with Windows NT 4.0 Server and the *Microsoft Windows NT 4.0 Workstation Resource Kit.*

REG Files

You can use a valid REG file to import a key into the Windows NT 4.0 Registry by double-clicking the filename. The REG file must be stored in the same format as a REGEDIT.EXE export file. (We looked at this format in Chapter 2.) Importing with a REG file has its risks and disadvantages—the same ones we noted for Windows 95 and Windows 98. If you use REG files created under Windows 95 or Windows 98, you must carefully check the paths and keys before you import those files into Windows NT 4.0. Although Windows NT 4.0 uses different paths to store the files and the Registry structure is somewhat different from that in Windows 95 and Windows 98, you can try to customize the Windows NT 4.0 shell by using some of the REG files described in the previous chapters. (See also the \NTApendx folder in the sample files for Windows NT 4.0 versions of REG and INF files.)

INF Files

A better solution for accessing the Registry is provided by INF files, which allow you to add placeholders for the path description. In Chapter 7, we examined how to manipulate the Windows 98 Registry by writing and using INF files. Using similar INF files, you can modify the Windows NT 4.0 Registry, but you must understand how the Registries and their file structures differ (described further in the next section). Also keep in mind that Windows NT flushes the internal write buffers to the hard disk only occasionally. If you change a setting in the Registry (by using a Registry Editor, a REG file, or an INF file), several seconds might pass before the new data is stored to all locations on the hard disk. (See page 410 for an explanation of how Windows NT saves information to the hive files.)

What Should I Know About Using INF Files Under Windows NT 4.0?

Before you use INF files, you need to be aware of several differences between Windows 95, Windows 98, and Windows NT 4.0. As long as you accommodate these differences, you can use INF files in Windows NT 4.0 in the same way we have used them throughout the book.

NOTE: Are you using the INF files provided for Windows 95 or for Windows 98? For your convenience, I've ported several INF files from Windows 95 to Windows NT 4.0 Workstation. These are located in the \NTApendx subfolder of the sample files.

Take care if you use Windows 98 INF files. Windows NT 4.0 doesn't support the Advanced INF files provided by Windows 98. There are also several differences in the way Windows 98 handles Registry entries for shell features. I've discussed these differences in previous chapters.

Placeholders   First of all, your INF file should start with these lines of code:

```
[version]
signature="$Windows NT$"
```

Next you should be aware of the different ways that Windows 95/Windows 98 and Windows NT use placeholders in an INF file. In Chapter 7, we examined how to use the placeholders *%10%* and *%11%* in a statement. These placeholders are also used in Windows NT. As in Windows 95 and Windows 98, these placeholders stand for the Windows folder and the system subfolder and are replaced when the INF file is processed. If you inspect a Registry entry you've set using these placeholders, you will find the name of the current drive and folder containing the Windows NT system files. If you omit these placeholders, you should keep in mind that the Windows 95/Windows 98 system subfolder is named System whereas the Windows NT system subfolder is named System32. (Windows 98 has also the \System32 subfolder for driver compatibility purposes.)

Another placeholder that can be used in a Windows NT Registry command is *%SystemRoot%*. This placeholder is not converted to a path when the INF file is installed; it is inserted as a string value directly into the Registry. Windows NT 4.0 recognizes the *REG_EXPAND_SZ* data type, which allows you to insert variables into a command. During the execution of a command, Windows NT will replace *%SystemRoot%* with the name of the current Windows folder.

Keys for identical tasks differ   Windows 95 and Windows NT 4.0 use the same shell (which is also used, with some extensions, in Windows 98), but only some Registry structures are similar in both operating system versions. Unfortunately, you can be easily misled by these similarities. For example, let's take a closer look at our trick for changing the desktop icons (discussed in Chapter 4). Can we use the INF file RECYCLE1.INF (in the chapter4\Win95 folder) to change the Recycle Bin icon? The INF file itself can be used, but the keys you need to modify are different. Under Windows 95, the entries for the Recycle Bin icons are stored in the key at the top of the following page.

HKEY_CLASSES_ROOT\CLSID\{645FF040-5081-101B-9F08-00AA002F954E}\DefaultIcon

This key is also available in Windows NT 4.0, but it's not the key you want to modify to affect the Recycle Bin icons on the desktop. In Windows NT 4.0, the Recycle Bin icons are defined in a different key:

HKEY_CURRENT_USER\Software\Classes\CLSID\{645FF040-5081-101B-9F08-00AA002F954E}\DefaultIcon

(This is similar to the way Windows 98 stores shell values in keys.) If you modify the entries in the INF file, you can change the desktop icon for the Recycle Bin as you would in Windows 95. Following are the statements contained in an INF file that sets a new icon for the Recycle Bin under Windows NT 4.0.

```
; File: Recycle1.INF (Windows NT 4.0)
; by Guenter Born
;
; Set the Recycle Bin Full icon to a new symbol
[version]
signature="$Windows NT$"

[DefaultInstall]
AddReg = Recycle.AddReg

[Recycle.AddReg]
; Use HKEY_CURRENT_USER\Software\Classes\CLSID
; Set "Full" to icon no 54 in shell32.dll
HKCU,Software\Classes\CLSID\{645FF040-5081-101B-9F08-00AA002F954E} ⮕
\DefaultIcon,Empty,,"%11%\\shell32.dll,31"
HKCU,Software\Classes\CLSID\{645FF040-5081-101B-9F08-00AA002F954E} ⮕
\DefaultIcon,Full,,"%SystemRoot%\\system32\\shell32.dll,53"
; End ***
```

The file that resets these icons must have a similar structure. Other desktop icon entries (such as My Computer and Network Neighborhood) are also stored in this branch.

32-bit versions of programs and libraries must be used   Another difference is that you must always use the 32-bit version of programs and libraries, so you can't take advantage of the Windows 95 uninstall commands. Instead, you must use similar commands as described for Windows 98 in Chapter 7. Although the *Uninstall* subkey is still available in the Windows NT 4.0 Registry, you can't use RUNDLL.EXE (that is, the Windows 95 version library) to invoke other libraries. Instead, Windows NT provides the RUNDLL32.EXE program to call other DLL libraries. The library SETUPX.DLL isn't available under Windows NT 4.0, so you must insert the library SETUPAPI.DLL, which has the same calling interface as SETUPX.DLL. (This is equivalent to the way Windows 98 handles uninstall parts.)

Following are INF file statements that install the MS-DOS Window as a shell extension. This INF file also provides an uninstall feature that can be invoked in the Install/Uninstall property sheet. (You can access this property sheet by selecting Settings from the Start menu, then Control Panel, and then Add/ Remove Programs.)

```
; File: DOS.inf (c) G. Born ** Windows NT 4.0 Version
;
; Install script to extend Windows Explorer's context menu
; with a DOS command under Windows NT 4.0
;
; If the user right-clicks a folder symbol in the
; Explorer's window or in a shell's window, the command
; "MS-DOS" will appear on the context menu. Selecting this
; command invokes the MS-DOS window and selects the folder.


[version]
signature="$Windows NT$"
SetupClass=BASE


; Add the extension into the Registry


[DefaultInstall]
AddReg = DOS.AddReg
CopyFiles = DOS.CopyFiles.Inf


; Uninstall part


[DefaultUninstall]

DelReg = DOS.AddReg,
DelFiles = DOS.DelFiles.Inf


; This part adds the keys to the Registry. The feature
; is registered in HKEY_CLASSES_ROOT\Folder\shell.


[DOS.AddReg]

; Add the DOS verb and the string for the context menu
; %COMMAND_STRING%
HKCR,Folder\shell\dos,,,"%COMMAND_STRING%"
; Add the command to activate command.com
HKCR,Folder\shell\dos\command,,,%COMMAND%
; *** This stuff is required to set up the uninstall feature.
; *** Attention: The UninstallString is different from Windows 95!!!
```

(continued)

```
continued
HKLM,SOFTWARE\Microsoft\Windows\CurrentVersion\Uninstall\dos, ⟶
DisplayName,,"%DOS_REMOVE_DESC%"
HKLM,SOFTWARE\Microsoft\Windows\CurrentVersion\Uninstall\dos, ⟶
UninstallString,,        ⟶
"RunDll32 setupapi.dll,InstallHinfSection DefaultUninstall 4 DOS.Inf"

; Don't forget to remove the newShellWindow key in Uninstall
; by adding the following line:
HKLM,SOFTWARE\Microsoft\Windows\CurrentVersion\Uninstall\dos

; Here we define the files to be copied. Source and
; destination directories are defined in the following sections.

[DOS.CopyFiles.Inf]
DOS.Inf

; Files to be deleted
[DOS.DelFiles.Inf]
DOS.Inf
DOS.PNF

; This is the definition for the source. (Use the path where
; the INF file is activated; 55 is defined in SourceDisksFiles.)
[SourceDisksNames]
55="MS-DOS","",1

[SourceDisksFiles]
DOS.Inf=55

; Now we have to specify the destination. The
; logical disk ID for the Windows subfolder INF is 17.

[DestinationDirs]
DOS.CopyFiles.Inf = 17
DOS.DelFiles.Inf = 17

; Define miscellaneous variables

[Strings]
; Command to invoke command.com
COMMAND = "command.com"

; String for the context menu entry
COMMAND_STRING = "MS-DOS"

; String for the Uninstall entry
DOS_REMOVE_DESC = "Remove Born's Win NT 4.0 MS-DOS Shell Extension"
; End ***
```

Modifying the Registry Size

The Registry data is kept in an area of physical memory that is used for system data. This data area is flushed from time to time to the hard disk. The Registry size is limited by default to 25 percent of the paged memory pool. You can set this limit within the *RegistrySizeLimit* value in this Registry key:

HKEY_LOCAL_MACHINE\SYSTEM\CurrentControlSet\Control

The *RegistrySizeLimit* value is defined as a DWORD. The size for the paged memory pool is kept in the *PagedPoolSize* DWORD value in the *HKEY_LOCAL_MACHINE\SYSTEM\CurrentControlSet\Control\Session Manager\Memory Management* key. If the Registry grows, you must either increase the memory limits or remove unused hives.

Removing Unused Registry Parts

As mentioned in the other chapters of this book, you should keep the Registry up to date. After using Windows NT 4.0 for a while, you'll probably be able to find some unused Registry entries. If you do nothing about these unused entries, eventually the Registry will become too large to back up, so you should clean it up from time to time.

You can use the Registry Editor to delete unused keys in the Registry. However, although doing this keeps the Registry clean, it won't reduce the Registry's size significantly. On the other hand, cleaning up user profiles can have an impact on the size of the Registry. Each user who has an account on a workstation gets his or her own Registry profile, which is stored in the *HKEY_USERS* branch. Viewing the *HKEY_USERS* branch of the Registry with the Registry Editor shows the *DEFAULT* key and a key with the name of each user's Security ID string. During a system startup, Windows NT loads into memory the entries in the *HKEY_USERS\.DEFAULT* key. Pressing the Ctrl-Alt-Del key combination invokes the logon dialog box. If the user enters a name and password, Windows NT uses the user's Security ID string to load the associated branch from *HKEY_USERS*. This means that Windows NT keeps only the data for the current user in the memory pool.

Nevertheless, for each user with an account under Windows NT, the operating system keeps a profile in the file NTUSER.DAT. If many unused user accounts exist, it is always a good idea to remove the corresponding profiles from the computer. This can be done in Windows NT Setup by clicking the Delete User Profiles option on the Options menu. (For further information, take a look at *Microsoft Windows NT 4.0 Workstation Resource Kit.*)

Backing Up and Recovering the Windows NT 4.0 Registry

Before you modify a setting in the Registry, you should back it up. This will ensure that you can recover a clean Registry if the one you are working on is corrupted. Because Windows NT 4.0 uses a different Registry file structure than Windows 95 does, you can't use the Windows 95 tools to create a backup. In the following sections, we'll take a look at some tips for creating a backup of the Windows NT 4.0 Registry.

Backing Up

You have several options for backing up your Windows NT 4.0 Registry, and Windows NT 4.0 comes with a few utilities that support the backup process. The most convenient way, however, is offered by the tools shipped on the CD available with the *Microsoft Windows NT 4.0 Workstation Resource Kit.*

Using the Backup Program to Save the Hives

We know that permanent Registry information is stored in hives. Those hives are mapped into files, which are located in several folders on the hard disk so that you can create a backup of them. The recommended way to create a backup of your Windows NT Registry is to use the Backup program provided with Windows NT, but you've got to have a tape drive to use it. The Backup program is available after you install Windows NT. Here's what to do:

1. Click Start on the taskbar, and then select Programs, Administrative Tools (Common), and Backup.

2. Once the program has started, click Backup on the Operations menu to open the Backup Information dialog box.

3. Select the Backup Local Registry option. This option saves all the local hive files necessary for the Registry.

Using the Repair Disk Utility

If you don't have a tape drive available under Windows NT 4.0, you can try to save the hive files on a floppy disk as long as your Registry isn't too big. Windows NT 4.0 comes with a tool called Repair Disk Utility that can be used for this purpose. You start this tool by running the RDISK.EXE file, located in the Windows NT subfolder \System32.

RDISK.EXE allows you to update the repair information for Windows NT stored on your hard disk. You can also create an Emergency Repair Disk that

410

can be used for the reconstruction of the system files if they are damaged. After starting this tool, you will see the dialog box shown in Figure C-5. Here's an overview of the dialog box options:

- The Update Repair Info button enables you to update the repair information on the hard disk. This information is stored in the Windows NT subfolder \repair, which contains the system files in a compressed version. These system files are necessary to create an Emergency Repair Disk.

- The Create Repair Disk button invokes a function that uses the information stored in the \repair subfolder to create an Emergency Repair Disk. The function formats a 1.44-MB floppy disk and copies the files onto the disk.

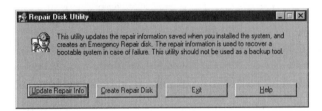

Figure C-5.
The Repair Disk Utility.

If you invoke RDISK.EXE by double-clicking the file's icon, the program will back up only the hive files for the system and software. You can force RDISK.EXE to also back up the SAM and security hives by activating the tool with the command RDISK -s. But be aware of space requirements when you use this switch: if a lot of user accounts are on the system, more space than is available on a floppy disk might be required for the SAM and security hives.

> **NOTE:** During system installation, Setup creates a file set in the \repair subfolder. This file set contains the image of the system files after the first successful system startup. If you create an Emergency Repair Disk, you will get the postinstall system configuration. To keep an up-to-date copy of your system configuration files, you should use the Update Repair Info button before you use the Create Repair Disk function.

Other Backup Methods

Depending on your system, you can use other methods, described below, to create a backup of your system files.

- If Windows NT uses a FAT partition, you can start MS-DOS or Windows 95/Windows 98 on that machine and then copy the files contained in the Windows NT subfolder \System32\config to a backup medium. This enables you to use tools such as WinZip or PKZIP to squeeze the files onto a floppy disk.

- If you have already installed a second version of Windows NT, you can use the process described in the first bullet to access the \System32\config folder on an NTFS partition and save the files on backup media.

- If you have access to the *Microsoft Windows NT 4.0 Workstation Resource Kit* CD, you can use the program REGBACK.EXE to create a backup of the Registry files.

- You can use the Registry Editor REGEDT32.EXE to save parts of the Registry in hive files. Then you can copy these hive files onto a floppy and load them into the Registry later with REGEDT32.EXE. This approach enables you to share parts of the Registry between two computers.

All these methods require that you keep track of your files. You should note that it is not possible to copy a hive file under Windows NT Explorer or with the DOS copy command because the file is locked by the operating system.

Recovering the Registry

There are several ways to recover a corrupted Registry and restore an old version. If you have already created a backup of your Registry, you can use this backup copy to recover the Registry. In this section, we'll briefly examine some strategies for recovering the contents of the Registry.

Using the Last Version

The Registry Editors provided with Windows NT do not support an Undo function. When you delete a key, the Registry is updated and the results are stored after a few seconds in the hive files on the hard disk. You get a chance to recover a key deleted in *HKEY_LOCAL_MACHINE\SYSTEM\CurrentControlSet* if you restart your computer with Windows NT. During the system startup (in the character-based setup), the "Press Spacebar To Invoke Hardware Profile" message is displayed. If you press the spacebar immediately when this message appears, you can go back to the Last Known Good Registry configuration by pressing the L key.

Restoring the Backup Files

If your Registry is corrupted, Windows NT might not be able to start up successfully. If you have the Windows NT Startup disk and the Emergency Repair Disk, you can use them to restore the system. The Emergency Repair Disk recovers the image of the Registry saved in the \repair subfolder—this is the image created during the first installation of the Registry or during the last Update Repair Info process. Once you restore the data from the Emergency Repair Disk and successfully start Windows NT, you can try to restore more of the Registry settings in several ways, which are briefly described in the following sections.

Reloading a hive file after startup   If you have a copy of a hive file (created with REGEDT32.EXE), you can reload it into the Registry after a successful Windows NT 4.0 startup. This approach is very problematic, however. Windows NT requires a ReplaceKey operation for active parts of the Registry, but this operation isn't supported by the Registry Editor. For inactive parts of the Registry, you can do the following:

1. Invoke the REGEDT32.EXE program, and select the hive or key you want to update.

2. Open the Registry menu, and click Load Hive.

3. Select the hive file in the Load Hive dialog box, and click the Open button. The Registry Editor loads the hive into the selected key.

Using a backup set   The best method of recovering your Registry is to use a backup set created with the Windows NT 4.0 Backup program. Also, if you have a backup tape, you can use the Backup option to restore the Registry.

Starting your computer with a different operating system   If you created a backup manually by copying files, you can't copy the hive files from the backup set to the hard disk because Windows NT locks the system files currently in use. So you have to start your computer with a different operating system (such as MS-DOS) and copy the backup files to your hard disk (in the Windows NT subfolder \System32\config and in the \Profiles subfolders). Then you must restart your computer and hope that Windows NT will boot in a proper manner.

Using REGREST.EXE   If you have access to the *Microsoft Windows NT 4.0 Workstation Resource Kit* CD, you can use the program REGREST.EXE to restore a backup created with the REGBACK.EXE tool, which is included with the CD.

> N O T E :   You can find additional information about backing up and recovering the Registry in the *Microsoft Windows NT 4.0 Workstation Resource Kit*.

Windows NT 4.0 Workstation Registry Entries

Many of the Windows 98 Registry entries examined in this book are also available in the Windows NT 4.0 Registry, but some branches in Windows NT are not available under Windows 98, and some information that both Registries share is contained in different branches. In this section, we'll take a look at the branches and entries in the Windows NT Registry.

HKEY_CLASSES_ROOT

As noted earlier in this appendix, this branch contains all data that is used for OLE and drag-and-drop operations in Windows. You can use the procedures throughout this book to identify and modify entries in this branch, which is mirrored in the *HKEY_LOCAL_MACHINE\SOFTWARE\Classes* key.

HKEY_USERS

This branch and the Windows 98 *HKEY_USERS* branch contain similar information. In Windows NT, this branch stores information about the user profiles for each user account. The *.DEFAULT* key contains the profile used by Windows NT if no user is logged on to the system. Every other key directly under *HKEY_USERS* contains the data for a particular user. As in Windows 98, the information about the current user is copied into the *HKEY_CURRENT_USER* branch.

HKEY_CURRENT_USER

When a user logs on to the system, Windows NT copies the user profile into this key from *HKEY_USERS*. *HKEY_CURRENT_USER* contains several subkeys, described in the following sections. The profiles of these Windows NT 4.0 subkeys are similar to their Windows 98 counterparts, so you can find additional information about them in the preceding chapters of this book.

AppEvents

This subkey contains paths to sound files that are loaded for particular system events (for example, when an error message occurs). The structure of this key is similar to the same key in Windows 98.

Console

Available only in Windows NT, this subkey defines the options and the window size for the console. (The console is the DOS window interface that is used for character mode applications.) The value names used in this key are self-explanatory. You can change the settings of this key by using the property sheet for the console. This property sheet can be invoked in two ways: in the console window (select Programs from the Start menu and then Command Prompt) by right-clicking the title bar and selecting Properties from the context menu, or by opening the Control Panel and double-clicking the Console icon.

Control Panel

Data that can be altered in the Control Panel window (such as screen settings) is contained in this subkey. (Most of its entries are similar to those you'll find in …*Control Panel* under Windows 98, so take a look at the previous chapters in this book to find out more about them.) In this subkey, you'll also find the settings for the screen savers installed under Windows NT. Screen saver options are set on the Display Properties property sheet on the Screen Saver property page.

Environment

This subkey contains the names of Environment variables (such as *TEMP*). To set Environment variables or change their values, open the Environment property page through the System Properties property sheet. You can access this property sheet by opening the Control Panel window and double-clicking the System icon.

Keyboard Layout

This subkey contains information about the language used for the keyboard layout. You can change keyboard layout settings on the Input Locale property page, which is available from the Keyboard Properties property sheet. Access this property sheet by opening the Control Panel and double-clicking the Keyboard icon. The options in the Switch Locales group set the *Hotkey* value in the …*Toggle* subkey to *1*, *2*, or *3*. These values correspond to the three option boxes. (The value *3*, for example, stands for the None option.)

Printers

Information about the installed printer drivers for the current user is stored in this subkey. You can change the settings of a printer by using the property sheet of the printer driver. Open the Printers folder in the Control Panel, right-click the desired printer, and then select Properties from the context menu.

Network

This subkey is no longer supported in Windows NT 4.0. Windows 98 and previous versions of Windows NT use this key to store persistent network connections. In Windows NT 4.0, the information about persistent network connections has moved to the following branch of *HKEY_CURRENT_USER*:

> ...\Software\Microsoft\Windows NT\CurrentVersion\Network\Persistent

Software

This subkey describes the properties of user-installed software. This subkey refers to the *HKEY_LOCAL_MACHINE* branch, in which applications store their settings. If both *HKEY_CURRENT_USER\Software* and *HKEY_LOCAL_MACHINE\SOFTWARE* contain similar data for a particular subkey, the entry in *HKEY_CURRENT_USER* takes precedence over the *HKEY_LOCAL_MACHINE* value. This allows you to override some machine-specific settings with user-specific settings.

UNICODE Program Groups

This subkey isn't used in Windows NT 4.0 because the Windows NT shell no longer uses GRP files.

Windows 3.1 Migration Status

This subkey exists only if Windows NT 4.0 is set up as an upgrade to Windows 3.1. These entries contain information about whether INI and GRP files have been converted successfully.

HKEY_LOCAL_MACHINE

This branch defines all specific information for the local machine, such as drivers, installed hardware, port mappings, software configuration, and so on. This information is valid for all users logged on to the system. *HKEY_LOCAL_MACHINE* is divided into several subkeys, which are described here.

HARDWARE

This key contains the settings for the hardware used by the current computer. Figure C-6 shows the structure of this key.

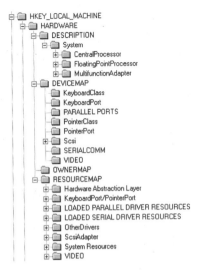

Figure C-6.
Contents of the HARDWARE *key.*

The following sections describe the subkeys contained in *HKEY_LOCAL_ MACHINE\HARDWARE.*

DESCRIPTION   This subkey contains information about the hardware. All entries are built from the firmware information contained in the computer. This information is detected by the NTDETECT.COM program and the Windows NT Executive during each system startup. The *System* subkey contains information about numeric processors and multifunction adapters (for serial and parallel ports and for disk controllers).

DEVICEMAP   This subkey contains a subkey for each device; that subkey stores values specifying where in the Registry device-specific information is located.

OWNERMAP   This subkey appears only on machines having a PCI bus. It contains data to associate a PCI driver with PCI devices installed on the bus.

RESOURCEMAP   This subkey maps the device drivers to resources that the drivers use. This data is stored in raw binary format and describes I/O addresses, DMA channels, interrupts, and so on. The contents of this branch are built during each system startup, so it wouldn't make sense to write data into the keys contained here.

SAM

This branch belongs to the Security Account Manager and contains information about user accounts. It cannot be directly accessed or changed. This key is mapped to the *HKEY_LOCAL_MACHINE\SECURITY\SAM* key.

SECURITY

This branch contains security information and belongs to the Security Account Manager. The keys in this branch cannot be accessed through the Registry Editor.

SOFTWARE

All information about the software installed on the machine is stored in this branch, the structure of which is shown in Figure C-7.

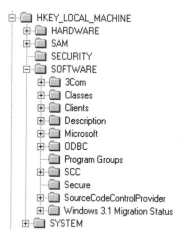

Figure C-7.
Contents of the SOFTWARE *branch.*

The following sections describe some of the subkeys you'll find in the *HKEY_LOCAL_MACHINE\SOFTWARE* branch.

Classes   This subkey contains the registered filename extensions and the Class ID subkeys for Component Object Model objects (CLSID codes). All entries contained in this subkey are mapped into the *HKEY_CLASSES_ROOT* branch of the Registry. You can find further information about the entries in this branch in Chapter 3.

Description This subkey stores the names and versions of software installed on the local computer. The entries in the *Description* subkey must be stored as ...*Company**Product**Version*. After Windows NT is installed, the *Description* subkey contains only one entry, ...*Microsoft**Rpc*, which defines data for remote procedure calls.

Microsoft Configuration settings for Microsoft programs installed on the local machine are contained in this subkey. The ...*Microsoft**Windows**CurrentVersion* subkey contains information used by the Windows NT 4.0 shell. The entries in the ...*Microsoft**Windows**CurrentVersion* subkey are similar to the subkeys of the same name in Windows 95 / Windows 98. The subkey ...*Microsoft**Windows NT**CurrentVersion* contains information about services built into Windows NT.

ODBC Settings for any ODBC drivers installed on the local machine are contained in this subkey.

Program Groups In previous versions of Windows NT, this subkey stored program group information. In Windows NT 4.0, the Start menu Programs folder structure stores program group information. The *Program Groups* subkey now contains only the *ConvertedToLinks* value. A value of *1* in this entry indicates a successful conversion of old program group files (GRPs) to the new folder structure.

Secure Application information can be stored in this subkey. Only a system administrator can modify the subkeys of *Secure*. This subkey is empty after Windows NT Setup.

Windows 3.1 Migration Status Information about the migration status of INI and GRP files is stored in this subkey. It contains valid data only if Windows NT is installed over Windows 3.1.

SYSTEM

This branch contains all system-specific data, which is needed during startup and which might not be configured by detection software. This branch is mapped into the *SYSTEM* hive. Figure C-8 on the next page shows the structure of *HKEY_LOCAL_ MACHINE**SYSTEM*.

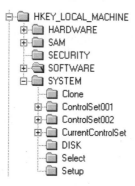

Figure C-8.
Contents of the SYSTEM key.

The following sections describe the subkeys and contents of *HKEY_LOCAL_MACHINE\SYSTEM*.

Clone   This subkey is not accessible in the Registry Editor. It contains the last control set used for the system startup.

Control sets   Data necessary during the system startup is grouped in control sets. Multiple control sets are stored in the *SYSTEM* key (usually two with the numbers 001 and 002). The *Microsoft Windows NT 4.0 Workstation Resource Kit* contains further information about typical values found in this subkey. Each of these control sets has a number and contains four subkeys, described here:

- *Control*   This subkey always contains configuration information (for example, computer name, file system, etc.).

- *Enum*   Hardware configuration information (data for devices and drivers loaded in Windows NT) is stored here.

- *Hardware Profiles*   This subkey contains configuration data needed for drivers and devices that are used in hardware profiles. If the configuration for a specified hardware profile differs from the standard configuration, that information is stored in this subkey.

- *Services*   This subkey contains subkeys for driver, file system, service program, and virtual hardware used by Windows NT. The data in these subkeys is used to load the corresponding services.

DISK This subkey contains entry information with a binary data stream value that defines information about the disk. *DISK* will be available only after you have run Disk Administrator at least once. You can run Disk Administrator from the Start menu by selecting Programs, then Administrative Tools, and then Disk Administrator.

Select This subkey stores information about the status of the Registry. If the system starts, the control set stored in the *Clone* subkey is used. Following is a description of values stored in the *Select* subkey.

- *LastKnownGood* This value contains the number of the control set that is known as good for a system startup.

- *Default* This value defines the control set that is used for a default system startup.

- *Current* This value is the name of the control set used during startup. The user can change this value by selecting a control set at system startup. (Press the spacebar in the character-based startup process when the message "Press spacebar..." appears.)

- *Failed* This value is a flag indicating that a system startup has failed.

Setup This subkey is left over from the Windows NT system setup program.

HKEY_CURRENT_CONFIG

Added to provide compatibility between Windows 95 and Windows NT, this branch is new in Windows NT 4.0 and contains the current hardware configuration for computers with varying hardware profiles (docking stations). Although application programs can run under both operating systems, the hardware data in Windows NT and Windows 95/Windows 98 is stored differently. So these application programs cannot alter the Registry. Instead, the programs use the Config Manager API to access information in the *HKEY_CURRENT_CONFIG* key. The entries in this key are stored separately from the entries in this branch:

HKEY_LOCAL_MACHINE\SYSTEM\ControlSetxxx\Hardware Profiles

If the user selects a hardware profile during system startup, this profile is set in the *HKEY_CURRENT_CONFIG* key.

Canonical Verbs

The following table contains a few canonical verbs used in Windows 95, Windows 98, and Windows NT 4.0.

Verb	Context menu entry	Description
explore	*Explore*	Opens the object and displays its component in a Windows Explorer window.
find	*Find*	Opens the Find dialog box.
open	*Open*	Opens the object and displays its component in a shell window.
openas	*Open With...*	Opens the Open With dialog box.
print	*Print*	Prints the selected file; uses an application to print the file.
printto	---	Prints the dragged file; does not create a context menu entry.

The Windows INF File Format

This appendix describes the structure for the setup information files (INF) used to configure devices and networking components in Microsoft Windows 95. This format is used under Windows 98, Microsoft Windows NT 4.0, and Windows NT 5.0.

This information is of particular use if you are creating custom setup scripts, either manually as described in this book or by using tools such as BATCH.EXE (located in the tools\reskit\batch folder on the Windows 98 CD) or the INF Installer (INFINST.EXE). This description of the INF file format will help you read the information in the Windows INF files to find the values to be provided in MSBATCH.INF. The general format is also used for statements in the [*Install*] section of MSBATCH.INF.

Windows 95 Device Information Files Overview

Device information (INF) files provide information used by Windows 95, Windows 98, Windows NT 4.0, and Windows NT 5.0 to install software that supports a given hardware device. When hardware manufacturers introduce new products, they must create INF files to explicitly define the resources and files required for each class of device.

The format of the INF files is based on Windows 3.*x* INI files:

- Section names are enclosed in brackets ([ ]) and must be unique within an INF file.

- Keys within a section do not have to be unique, but the order of keys within a section is significant.

- Private sections in an INF file are not evaluated by Windows.

The operating system detects the unique ID of each device installed. For the device identified, a specific section of the INF file provides information on that class of device; the following section, "General INF File Format," describes the information contained in a typical INF file section.

NOTE: As you've seen in previous chapters, INF files are also handy for installing small software packages or extending Windows 98 features.

General INF File Format

An INF file is organized in several sections that define information that Setup and the hardware detection process use to determine the resource needs of the hardware device and to install software for that device or for other purposes. An INF file is organized by hardware, with each class of device described in its own section. Within each device section, the following general organization applies.

[Version] Section

The [Version] section contains a simple header that identifies the INF file and the class of device this file supports.

[Manufacturer] and [*Manufacturer Name*] Sections

The [Manufacturer] and [*Manufacturer Name*] sections list all the individual manufacturers of the devices identified in this file and all the devices built by each manufacturer. These entries are displayed directly to the user and used to generate the appropriate Registry entries. There must always be at least one manufacturer section unless the INF file is used to install a software package or function that has nothing to do with hardware.

[*Install*] Section

The [*Install*] section describes the device driver and physical attributes of the hardware device. It also identifies the names of all the [*Install*] sections that contain information and instructions for installing this device. This section is also used during the software install process, as shown in previous chapters.

[ClassInstall] Section

The [ClassInstall] section defines a new class for the hardware device. The section is optional and is not used in INF files for software installation.

Miscellaneous Control Sections

The miscellaneous control sections specify how a device is handled by the Windows user interface.

[Strings] Section

Defines all localizable strings used in the INF file.

[Optional Components] Section

Lists [*Install*] sections defining optional components that can be installed separately from the regular setup process for the application.

Section Formatting

Each section contains one or more entries. The typical entry consists of a key and a value separated by an equal sign. Keys within a section do not have to be unique, but the order of keys might be significant depending on the purpose of the section. An INF file can include comments—any string of text, up to the end of the line, that starts with a semicolon. A comment can start anywhere on a line. For example:

```
Key=value    ; comment
```

A basic INF file will have the following sections; more complex INF files can include additional sections.

Section	Meaning
[Version]	Version information for validating the INF file.
[DefaultInstall]	Installation section that is executed by default (in SETUPX.DLL or SETUPAPI.DLL). This section has pointers to other sections specifying files to copy and delete, Registry updates, INI file updates, etc.
[OtherInstall]	Optional. Uses the same format as the [DefaultInstall] section but must be explicitly called. Useful for defining how a component should be uninstalled.

(continued)

427

continued

Section	Meaning
[DestinationDirs]	Specifies the destination on the drive where files will be copied, deleted, or renamed (that is, Windows directory, Windows\System directory, etc.)
[Copy, Delete, Rename Section(s)]	These sections list files to be copied, deleted, or renamed.
[RegistryUpdate Section(s)]	Specify Registry additions or deletions.
[IniFileUpdate Section(s)]	Allow updates to INI files.
[SourceDisksNames]	Lists disks that contain the files to be copied.
[SourceDisksFiles]	Lists the specific disk that each file is on.
[Strings]	Lists localizable strings to be used in other sections.

NOTE: For complete details about the syntax and use of statements in Windows 95 INF files, see the *Win32 Software Development Kit for Windows 95 and Windows NT*.

[Version] Section

Syntax

```
[Version]
Signature="$Chicago$"
Class=class-name
Provider=INF_creator
LayoutFile=filename.inf
```

The [Version] section defines the standard header for all Windows INF files.

Signature   Defines a signature for the operating version. The string must be "$Chicago$" for Windows 95 and for Windows 98. In Windows NT 4.0 and Windows NT 5.0, I've used the signature "$Windows NT$" instead. Signature-string recognition is case-insensitive, so "$Chicago$" and "$CHICAGO$" are equivalent.

class-name   Defines the class in the Registry for any device installed from this INF. The following are some examples of class names:

Adapter	Hdc	Monitor	PCMCIA
Cdrom	Keyboard	Mouse	Ports
Display	MCADevices	MTD	Printer
EISADevices	Media	NetNetService	SCSIAdapter
Fdc	Modem	Nodriver	System

filename.inf   Names the INF file that contains the layout information (source disks and files) required for installing this driver software. Typically, for Windows 95 components, this is LAYOUT.INF. This line is optional. If not given, the [SourceDisksNames] and [SourceDisksFiles] sections must be given in this INF file.

This example shows a typical [Version] section:

```
[Version] ·
Signature="$Chicago$"
Provider=%MSFT%
Class=Adapter
LayoutFile=LAYOUT.INF
```

> **NOTE:**   The entries Provider and Class are of no relevance if the INF file is used for software installation, as you can see in the sample files used in the previous chapters.

[Manufacturer] Section

Syntax

```
[Manufacturer]
manufacturer-name | %strings-key%=manufacturer-name-section
```

The [Manufacturer] section identifies the manufacturer of the device and specifies the name of the [*Manufacturer Name*] section that contains additional information about the device driver.

manufacturer-name   Name of the manufacturer. This name can be any combination of printable characters, but it must uniquely identify the manufacturer and must be enclosed in double quotation marks.

strings-key   Name of a string as defined in a [Strings] section.

manufacturer-name-section   Name of the [*Manufacturer Name*] section. This name can be any combination of printable characters, but it must uniquely identify the manufacturer name.

The following example shows a typical [Manufacturer] section in which a string key, *%M1%*, is used to identify the manufacturer. In this example, the [*Manufacturer Name*] section is APEXD.

```
[Manufacturer]
%M1%=APEXD     ; Strings key for this manufacturer
```

NOTE: This section is required for hardware device installation only; it is superfluous in software installation INF files.

[*Manufacturer Name*] Section

Syntax

```
[manufacturer-name]
device-description=install-section-name, device-id  ⮑
    [,compatible-device-id]...
```

The [*Manufacturer Name*] section gives the device description and identifies the [*Install*] section for this device. The *manufacturer-name-section* name must be defined in the [Manufacturer] section.

device-description   Description of the device to install. This can be any combination of printable characters or a Strings key.

install-section-name   Name of the [*Install*] section for this device.

device-id   Identifier for this device.

compatible-device-id   Identifier of a compatible device. More than one identifier can be given, but each must be preceded by a comma.

The following example shows a typical [*Manufacturer Name*] section. The name of the [*Install*] section for this device is SuperSCSI. This device-id is *PNPA000, and its compatible device identifier is *PnPA001.

```
[APEXD]
%DevDesc1% = SuperSCSI, *PNPA000, *PnPA001
```

For each driver installed using this INF file, Setup uses the information in these [*Manufacturer Name*] sections to generate Driver Description, Manufacturer Name, DeviceID, and Compatibility list entries in the Registry.

NOTE: This section is required for hardware device installation only; it is superfluous in software installation INF files.

[*Install*] Section

Syntax

```
[install-section-name]
LogConfig = log-config-section-name[,log-config-section-name]...
Copyfiles=file-list-section[,file-list-section]...
Renfiles=file-list-section[,file-list-section]...
Delfiles=file-list-section[,file-list-section]...
UpdateInis=update-ini-section[,update-ini-section]...
UpdateIniFields=update-inifields-section[,update-inifields-section]...
AddReg=add-registry-section[,add-registry-section]...
DelReg=del-registry-section[,del-registry-section]...
Ini2Reg=ini-to-registry-section[,ini-to-registry-section]...
UpdateCfgSys=update-config-section
UpdateAutoBat=update-autoexec-section
Reboot | Restart
```

The [*Install*] section identifies the additional sections in the INF file that contain descriptions of the device and instructions for installing files and information needed by the device drivers. The *install-section-name* must be defined in a [*Manufacturer Name*] section and consist of printable characters.

> NOTE: For software installation, the [DefaultInstall] section always defines the *install-section-name* because the [*Manufacturer Name*] section isn't used.

Not all entries in this section are needed or required. If an entry is given, it must specify the name of a section. (An exception to this is the CopyFiles entry.) Only one of each type of item can be used in any one [*Install*] section. More than one section name can be given for each entry, but each additional name must be preceded by a comma. For instance, look at the following lines:

```
[DefaultInstall]
; Copy my files
CopyFiles = Explore.CopyFiles.Inf
CopyFiles = Explore.CopyFiles.bat
```

The second line is never executed. If you need two or more sections to copy different files, use the following lines instead:

```
[DefaultInstall]
; Copy my files
CopyFiles = Explore.CopyFiles.Inf, Explore.CopyFiles.bat
```

The exact format and meaning of the corresponding entry depends on the entry type and is described in later sections. Each [*Install*] section should include the creation date of the driver set.

The Reboot or Restart entries can be added to the [*Install*] section to force the system to either restart or to reboot the machine after performing the commands in the [*Install*] section.

This example shows a typical [*Install*] section for a hardware device. It contains a LogConfig entry that identifies two logical configuration sections for this device. It also contains CopyFiles and AddReg entries that identify the sections containing information about which files to install.

```
[SuperSCSI]
; Apex Drivers Model 01 - SuperSCSI+
Log_Config = With_Dma, WithoutDMA
CopyFiles = MoveMiniPort, @SRSutil.exe
AddReg = MOD1
```

The CopyFiles entry provides a special notation that allows a single file to be copied directly from the copy line. An individual file can be copied by prefixing the filename with an @ symbol. The destination for any file copied using this notation will be the DefaultDestDir as defined in the [DestinationDirs] section. The following example shows how to copy individual files:

```
CopyFiles=FileSection1,@myfile.txt,@anotherfile.txt,LastSectionName
```

The next example shows an INF file's [DefaultInstall] section that adds an entry to the Registry and copies the INF files.

```
; install script
[DefaultInstall]
AddReg = Explore.AddReg
CopyFiles = Explore.CopyFiles.Inf
```

[*Logical Configuration*] Sections

Syntax

```
[log-config-section-name]
ConfigPriority = priority-value
MemConfig = mem-range-list
I/OConfig = io-range-list
IRQConfig = irq-list
DMAConfig = dma-list
```

A [*Logical Configuration*] section defines configuration details, such as IRQs, memory ranges, I/O ports, and DMA channels. An INF file can contain any number of [*Logical Configuration*] sections, as many as are needed to describe the device dependencies. However, each section must contain complete details for installing a device. The *log-config-section-name* must be defined by the LogConfig entry in the [*Install*] section.

Not all entries are needed or required. If an entry is given, it must be given appropriate values as described in the subsequent sections.

Each entry can specify more than one resource. However, during installation only one resource from an entry is used. If a device needs multiple resources of the same type, multiple entries must be given. For example, to ensure two IRQs for a device, two IRQConfig entries must be given. If a device does not require an IRQ, no IRQConfig entry should be given. For each entry, Setup builds binary logical configuration records and adds these to the driver section of the Registry.

NOTE: This section is required for hardware device installation only; it is superfluous in software installation INF files.

[*Update AutoExec*] Section

Syntax

```
[update-autoexec-section]
CmdDelete=command-name
CmdAdd=command-name[,command-parameters]
UnSet=env-var-name
PreFixPath=ldid[,ldid]
RemOldPath=ldid[,ldid]
TmpDir=ldid[,subdir]
```

The [*Update AutoExec*] section provides commands to manipulate lines in the AUTOEXEC.BAT file. The *update-autoexec-section* name must appear in an UpdateAutoBat entry in the [*Install*] section.

Not all entries are needed or required. The section can contain as many CmdAdd, CmdDelete, and UnSet entries as needed, but only one entry for PreFixPath, RemOldPath, and TmpDir can be used per file.

Setup processes all CmdDelete entries before any CmdAdd entries.

For information about LDID values, see the "[*Update INI*] Section" beginning on page 437.

[*Update Config*] Section

Syntax

```
[update-config-section]
DevRename=current-dev-name,new-dev-name
DevDelete=device-driver-name
DevAddDev=driver-name,configkeyword[,flag][,param-string]
Stacks=dos-stacks-values
Buffers=legal-dos-buffer-value
Files=legal-dos-files-value
LastDrive=legal-dos-lastdrive-value
```

The [*Update Config*] section provides commands to add, delete, or rename commands in CONFIG.SYS. The *update-config-section* name must appear in an UpdateCfgSys entry in the [*Install*] section.

Not all entries are needed or required. This section can contain as many DevRename, DevDelete, and DevAddDev entries as needed, but the other commands can be used only once per section. When processing this section, Setup processes all DevRename entries first, all DevDelete commands second, and all DevAddDev commands last.

[*CopyFiles*] Section

Syntax

```
[CopyFiles-section-name]
destination-file1-name[, source-file1-name][, temporary-file1-name]
    [, flag]
destination-file2-name[, source-file2-name][, temporary-file2-name]
    [, flag]
    ⋮
```

The [*CopyFiles*] section contains a list of the names of files to be copied from a source disk to a destination folder. The source disk and destination directory associated with each file are specified in other INF file sections. The name of the [*CopyFiles*] section must appear in a Copyfiles item in the [*Install*] section.

You can specify the copying of a single file in the CopyFiles item of the [*Install*] section itself, without building a [*CopyFiles*] section. (Use the special character "@" to force a single file copy.) Copying a single file in this way is somewhat limiting because the source and destination filenames must be the same and you cannot use a temporary file.

destination-file-name   Name of the destination file. If no source filename is given, this is also the name of the source file.

source-file-name   Name of the source file. If the source and destination filenames for the file copy operation are the same, this is not required.

temporary-file-name   Name of a temporary file used during the file copy operation. The installer copies the source file but gives it the specified temporary filename. The next time the operating system starts, it renames the temporary file to the destination filename. This is useful for copying a file to a destination that is currently open or in use by Windows.

   If the file is not in use by Windows, use a flag value of 8 to force the copy operation to use the temporary name. This method will work only if the file already exists in the target folder. To get around this restriction, first copy the file into the folder and then use flag 8 to copy it again.

flag   Optional parameter used to perform special actions during the installation process. Multiple flags can be used by adding the values to create the combined flag. The following valid flags can be used.

Value	Meaning
1	On CopyFiles: Warn if user tries to skip file.
1	On DelFiles: If file is in use, queue up delayed delete in WININIT.INI. If this flag is not set, an in-use file will not be deleted.
2	Setup Critical: don't allow user to skip file.
4	Ignore version check and always copy file. This will overwrite a newer file.
8	Force Rename (trick engine into thinking that file is in use). NOTE: Only happens if file already exists on target.
16	If file already exists on target, don't copy.
32	Suppress version conflict dialog, and don't overwrite newer files.

The following example copies three files.

```
[CopyTheseFilesSec]
file11 ; copies file11 from source as file11 to destination
file22,, file23,8 ; copies file22, temporarily naming it file23
file31, file32    ; copies file32 to file31
```

All the source filenames used in this example must be defined in a [SourceDisksFiles] section, and the logical disk numbers that appear in the [SourceDisksFiles] section must have been defined in a [SourceDisksNames] section. As an alternative, you can use a LAYOUT.INF file so as to supply this information.

You also must define the destination directory for each [*CopyFiles*] section by using the [DestinationDirs] section. More than one destination directory requires more than one [*CopyFiles*] section.

> NOTE: Take care to use 8.3-format filenames in a [*CopyFiles*] section. Long filenames won't be copied in the [*CopyFiles*] section. You can use temporary filenames to copy files with 8.3-format filenames and rename them later on.

[*RenameFiles*] Section

Syntax

```
[RenameFiles-section-name]
new-file-name, old-file-name
    ⋮
```

Lists the names of files to be renamed. The name of the section must appear in a Renfiles item in an [*Install*] section of the INF file.

new-file-name   New name of the file.

old-file-name   Old name of the file.

The example below renames the files file42 to file41, file52 to file51, and file62 to file61 in the system folder.

```
[DefaultInstall]
RenFiles=RenameOldFilesSec

[RenameOldFilesSec]
file41, file42
file51, file52
file61, file62

[DestinationDirs]
RenameOldFilesSec=11
```

The folder where all the old filenames are stored must be defined in a [DestinationDirs] section, as shown in the above example.

[*DeleteFiles*] Section

Syntax

```
[DeleteFiles-section-name]
file-name[,,,flag]
   ⋮
```

Lists the names of files to be deleted. The section name must appear in the Delfiles item of an [*Install*] section.

file-name   Identifies a file to be deleted.

flag   Optional parameter used to force Windows to delete the *file-name* file even if it is in use during the installation process. Set the *flag* parameter value to 1 to cause Windows to queue the file-deletion operation until the system has restarted. If a file marked with the *flag* equal to 1 cannot be deleted because it is in use, a system restart will occur after the device installation is complete.

   If you specify a *file-name* parameter but do not set the *flag* parameter value to 1, if that file is in use when the [*DeleteFiles*] section is executed it will not be deleted from the system.

   The example below deletes three files in the system folder.

```
[DefaultInstall]
DelFiles=DeleteOldFilesSec

[DeleteOldFilesSec]
file1
file2
file3,,,1   ;delete file, even if it is in use

[DestinationDirs]
DeleteOldFilesSec=11
```

[*Update INI*] Section

Syntax

```
[update-ini-section]
ini-file, ini-section, [old-ini-entry], [new-ini-entry], [flag]
   ⋮
```

Replaces, deletes, or adds entries in the given INI file. The *update-ini-section* name must appear in an UpdateInis entry in the [*Install*] section.

ini-file   Name of the INI file containing the entry to change.

ini-section   Name of the section in the INI file containing the entry to change.

old-ini-entry   Optional. Usually in the form Key=Value.

new-ini-entry   Optional. Usually in the form Key=Value. Either the key or value can specify replaceable strings. For example, either the key or value specified in this parameter can be *%String1%*, where the string that replaces *%String1%* is defined in the [Strings] section of the INF file.

flag   The optional action flag can be one of these values:

0   Default. Matches Value of old-ini-entry Key, ignores its value. If Key is present, replaces with new-ini-entry. If old-ini-entry is NULL, the new-ini-entry is added unconditionally. If new-ini-entry is NULL, the old-ini-entry is deleted.

1   Matches both Key and Value of old-ini-entry. Update is done only if both Key and Value match. If both Key and Value of old-ini-entry exist in an INI file entry, that entry is replaced with new-ini-entry. Note that both the Key and Value of the old-ini-entry parameter and the INF file entry must match for the replacement to be made.

   (This is in contrast to using a flag value of 0, where only the Key must match for the replacement to be made).

2   Conditional and matches only the Key of old-ini-entry. If Key in old-ini-entry already exists, no operation is performed on the INI file. If the Key in the old-ini-entry parameter and the key in the new-ini-entry parameter both exist in INI file entries, the INI file entry that matches the Key in the new-ini-entry parameter is deleted and the Key of the INI file entry that matches the old-ini-entry parameter is replaced with the key in the new-ini-entry parameter. If the key in the old-ini-entry parameter exists in an INI file entry and the key in the new-ini-entry parameter does not exist, an entry is added to the INI file made up of the Key in the new-ini-entry parameter and the old Value.

   Note that the match of the old-ini-entry parameter and an INI file entry is based on Keys alone, not on Keys and Values.

3   Conditional and matches both Key and Value of old-ini-entry. If the Key=Value of old-ini-entry exists, do not replace with new-ini-entry. (See also flag value 2.)

The wildcard character (*) can be used in specifying the Key and Value, and they will be interpreted correctly.

The *ini-file* name can be a string or a Strings key. A Strings key has the form *%strkey%*, where *strkey* is defined in the [Strings] section in the INF file. In either case, the name must be a valid filename.

The name should include the name of the directory containing the file, but the directory name should be given as a logical directory identifier (LDID) rather than as an actual name. Setup replaces an LDID with an actual name during installation.

An LDID has the form *%ldid%*, where *ldid* is one of the predefined identifiers or an identifier defined in the [DestinationDirs] section. For LDID_BOOT and LDID_BOOTHOST, the backslash is included in the LDID, so %30%BOOT.INI is the correct way to reference BOOT.INI in the root of the boot drive.

The following examples illustrate entries in this section.

```
%11%\sample.ini, Section1,, Value1=2   ; adds new entry
%11%\sample.ini, Section2, Value3=*,   ; deletes old entry
%11%\sample.ini, Section4, Value5=1, Value5=4  ; replaces old entry
```

[*Update IniFields*] Section

Syntax

```
[update-inifields-section]
ini-file, ini-section, profile-name, [old-field], [new-field], [flag]
```

Replaces, adds, or deletes fields in the value of a given INI entry. Unlike the [*Update INI*] section, this section replaces, adds, or deletes portions of a value in an entry rather than the whole value. The *update-inifields-section* name must appear in an UpdateIniFields entry in the [*Install*] section.

ini-file   Name of the INI file containing the entry to change.

ini-section   Name of the section in the INI file containing the entry to change.

profile-name   Name of the entry to change.

old-field   Field value to delete.

new-field   Field value to add, if not already there.

flag   Specifies whether to treat *old-field* and *new-field* parameters as if they have a wildcard character.

Value	Meaning
0	(Default) Treat "*" character literally when matching fields and not as a wildcard character. Use a blank (" ") as a separator when adding a new field to an entry.
1	Treat "*" character as a wildcard character when matching fields. Use a blank (" ") as a separator when adding a new field to an entry.
2	Treat "*" character literally when matching fields and not as a wildcard character. Use a comma (",") as a separator when adding a new field to an entry.
3	Treat "*" character as a wildcard character when matching fields. Use a comma (",") as a separator when adding a new field to an entry.

Any previous comments in the line are removed because they might not be applicable after changes. When looking in the INI file for fields in the line, spaces, tabs, and commas are used as field delimiters. However, a space is used as the separator when the new field is appended to the line.

[*Add Registry*] Section

Syntax

```
[add-registry-section]
reg-root-string, [subkey], [value-name], [flag], [value]
    ⋮
```

Adds subkeys or value names to the Registry, optionally setting the value. The *add-registry-section* name must appear within an AddReg entry in the [*Install*] section.

reg-root-string Abbreviation for the Registry root key name, which can be one of these values:

HKCR = HKEY_CLASSES_ROOT
HKCU = HKEY_CURRENT_USER
HKLM = HKEY_LOCAL_MACHINE
HKU = HKEY_USERS
HKR = Means relative from the key passed into GenInstallEx

subkey Optional. Identifies the subkey to set, in the form *key1\key2\key3....* This parameter can be expressed as a replaceable string (for example, *%Subkey1%*), where the *%Subkey1%* is defined in the [Strings] section of the INF file.

value-name Optional. Defines the value name for an item added to the subkey. If the *value-name* parameter is left empty for string type, the value for the subkey specified in the *subkey* parameter is set to a NULL string. Note that the *value-name* parameter can be expressed as a replaceable string (for example, *%Valname1%*), where the string must be defined in the [Strings] section of the INF file.

flag Optional. Determines both the value type and whether the Registry key is replaced if it already exists.

Value	Meaning
0	(Default) Value is an ANSI string. Replace key if it exists.
1	Value is a hexadecimal number. Replace key if it exists.
2	Value is an ANSI string. Do not replace key if it exists.
3	Value is a hexadecimal number. Do not replace key if it exists.

NOTE: As you can see in the table above, there is no way to create a DWORD value entry. Instead, you must use a binary value (such as 01 00 00 00) to store such a value.

value Optional. Value to set. Can be either an ANSI string or a number in hexadecimal notation and Intel format. Any item containing a binary value can be extended beyond the 128-byte line maximum by using a backslash (\) character. A string key of the form *%strkey%* can also be given. The *strkey* must be defined in the [Strings] section of the INF file. To include a % character in the line as part of the string, use %%. At least two fields in the above command are required. However, one can be NULL; thus, at least one comma is required when using this form.

The two items in the example AddReg-type section below add two value names to the Registry. Note that *%25%* will be expanded to the machine's Windows directory.

```
[Test.AddReg]
HKLM,Software\MyApp,ProgramName,,"My Application"
HKLM,Software\MyApp,"Program Location",,"%25%\MyApp.exe"
```

[*Delete Registry*] Section

Syntax

```
[del-registry-section]
reg-root-string, subkey, [value-name]
  ⋮
```

Deletes a subkey or value name from the Registry. The *del-registry-section* name must appear in a DelReg entry in the [*Install*] section. This section can contain any number of entries. Each entry deletes one subkey or value name from the Registry.

reg-root-string   Registry root name. Can be one of the values HKCR, HKCU, HKLM, HKU, and HKR mentioned in the section, beginning on page 440, related to [*Add Registry*].

subkey   Identifies the subkey to delete, in the form *key1\key2\key3*.... This parameter can be expressed as a replaceable string (for example, *%Subkey1%*), where the string is defined in the [Strings] section of the INF file.

value-name   Optional. Identifies the value name for the subkey. Note that the *value-name* parameter can be expressed as a replaceable string. For example, you could use *%Valname1%*, where the string to replace *%Valname1%* is defined in the [Strings] section of the INF file.

[*Ini to Registry*] Section

Syntax

```
[ini-to-registry-section]
ini-file, ini-section, [ini-key], reg-root-string, subkey, flag
  ⋮
```

Moves lines or sections from an INI file to the Registry, creating or replacing an entry under the given key in the Registry. The *ini-to-registry-section* name must appear in an Ini2Reg entry in the [*Install*] section.

ini-file   Name of the INI file containing the key to copy.

ini-section   Name of the section in the INI file containing the key to copy.

ini-key   Name of the key in the INI file to copy to the Registry. If *ini-key* is empty, the whole section is transferred to the specified Registry key.

reg-root-string Registry root key name abbreviation, which can be one of the values HKCR, HKCU, HKLM, HKU, and HKR mentioned in the section earlier related to [*Add Registry*].

subkey Identifies the subkey to receive the value, in the form *key1\key2\key3....*

flag Indicates whether to delete the INI key after transfer to the Registry and whether to overwrite the value in the Registry if the Registry key already exists. The possible *flag* values can be found in the table below.

Value	Meaning
0	(Default) Do not delete the INI entry from the INI file after moving the information in the entry to the Registry. If the Registry subkey already exists, do not replace its current value.
1	Delete the INI entry from the INI file after moving the information in the entry to the Registry. If the Registry subkey already exists, do not replace its current value.
2	Do not delete the INI entry from the INI file after moving the information in the entry to the Registry. If the Registry subkey already exists, replace its current value with the value from the INI file entry.
3	Delete the INI entry from the INI file after moving the information in the entry to the Registry. If the Registry subkey already exists, replace its current value with the value from the INI file entry.

For example, suppose the following entry exists in the WIN.INI file:

```
[Windows]
CursorBlinkRate=15
```

If a *CursorBlinkRate* subkey does not exist under ...*Control Panel\Desktop*, the following item in an [*Ini to Registry*] section creates the subkey, sets the value of the subkey to 15, and leaves the original line in WIN.INI unchanged:

```
win.ini,Windows,CursorBlinkRate,HKCU,"Control Panel\Desktop"
```

If the subkey already exists, the INF file item sets the value of the subkey to 15 and leaves the original line in WIN.INI unchanged.

[DestinationDirs] Section

Syntax

```
[DestinationDirs]
file-list-section=ldid[,subdir ]
   ⋮
DefaultDestDir=ldid[,subdir ]
```

The [DestinationDirs] section defines the destination directories for the given [*File-List*] sections and optionally defines the default directory for any [*File-List*] sections that are not explicitly named.

file-list-section   Name of a [*File-List*] section. This name must have been defined in a Copyfiles, Renfiles, or Delfiles entry in the [*Install*] section.

ldid   A logical disk identifier (LDID), which can be one of these values:

00	NULL LDID; this LDID can be used to create a new LDID
01	Source drive:\ pathname
02	Temporary Setup directory; this is valid only during Windows 98 Setup
03	Uninstall directory
04	Backup directory
10	Windows machine directory; maps to the Windows directory on a server-based setup
11	SYSTEM directory
12	IOSUBSYS directory
13	COMMAND directory
14	Control Panel directory
15	Printers directory
16	Workgroup directory
17	INF directory
18	Help directory
19	Administration
20	Fonts
21	Viewers
22	VMN32
23	Color directory
24	Root drive containing the Windows directory
25	Shared directory

26	Winboot
27	Machine specific
28	Host Winboot
30	Root directory of the boot drive
31	Root directory for host drive of a virtual boot drive
32	Old Windows directory if it exists
33	Old MS-DOS directory if it exists

subdir   Name of the directory, within the directory named by *ldid*, to be the destination directory.

The optional DefaultDestDir entry provides a default destination for any Copyfile entries that use the direct copy notation (@filename) or any [*File-List*] section not specified in the [DestinationDirs] section. If DefaultDestDir is not given, the default directory is set to LDID_WIN.

This example sets the destination directory for the [MoveMiniPort] section to the Windows IOSUBSYS directory and sets the default directory for other sections to be the BIN directory on the boot drive:

```
[DestinationDirs]
MoveMiniPort=12
; Destination for MoveMiniPort Section is windows\iosubsys
DefaultDestDirs=30,bin  ; Direct copies go to Boot:\bin
```

[*File-List*] Section

A [*File-List*] section lists the names of files to be copied, renamed, or deleted. Entries in this section have three forms, depending on the type of entry in the [*Install*] section that defines the section name.

A [*File-List*] section for a Copyfiles entry has this form:

```
[file-list-section]
destination-file-name,[source-file-name],[temporary-file-name]
```

The *file-list-section* name must appear in the Copyfiles entry.

destination-file-name   Name of the destination file. If no source filename is given, this is also the name of the source file.

source-file-name   Name of the source file. Required only if the source and destination names are not the same.

temporary-file-name   Name of the temporary file for the copy. Setup copies the source file but gives it the temporary filename. The next time Windows 98

445

starts, it renames the temporary file to the destination filename. This is useful for copying files to a destination that is currently open or in use by Windows.

The following example copies three files:

```
[CopyTheseFilesSec]
file11                      ; copies file11
file21, file22, file23      ; copies file22 to file21, temporarily
                            ; naming it file23
file31,file32               ; copies file32 to file31
```

A [*File-List*] section for a Renfiles entry has this form:

```
[file-list-section]
new-file-name,old-file-name
    ⋮
```

The *file-list-section* name must appear in the Renfiles entry.

This example renames the files FILE42, FILE52, and FILE62 to FILE41, FILE51, and FILE61, respectively:

```
[RenameOldFilesSec]
file41,file42
file51,file52
file61,file62
```

A [*File-List*] section for a Delfiles entry has this form:

```
[file-list-section]
filename
    ⋮
```

The file-list-section name must appear in the Delfiles entry.

This example deletes three files:

```
[DeleteOldFilesSec]
file1
file2
file3
```

In the preceding examples, the given filenames are assumed to have been defined in the [SourceDisksFiles] section and the logical disk numbers are assumed to have been defined in the [SourceDisksNames] section.

[SourceDisksFiles] Section

Syntax

```
[SourceDisksFiles]
filename=disk-number[, subdir][, file-size]
    ⋮
```

Names the source files used during installation and identifies the source disks that contain the files.

filename   Name of the file on the source disk.

disk-number   Ordinal of the source disk that contains the file. This ordinal must be defined in the [SourceDisksNames] section and must have a value greater than or equal to 1. (Zero is not a valid disk-number parameter value.)

subdir   Optional parameter that specifies the subdirectory on the source disk where the file resides. If this parameter is not used, the source disk root directory is the default.

file-size   Optional parameter that specifies the size of the file, in bytes.
   This example identifies a single source file, SRS01.386, on the disk having ordinal 1:

```
[SourceDisksFiles]
SRS01.386 = 1
```

[SourceDisksNames] Section

Syntax

```
[SourceDisksNames]
disk-ordinal="disk-description",disk-label,disk-serial-number
```

Identifies and names the disks used for installation of the given device drivers.

disk-ordinal   A unique number that identifies a source disk. If there is more than one source disk, each must have a unique ordinal.

disk-description   A string, enclosed in double quotation marks or a Strings key, that describes the contents or purpose of the disk and that is displayed by the installer to the user to identify the disk.

disk-label   Volume label of the source disk that is set when the source disk is formatted.

disk-serial-number   Unused. Value must be 0.
   This example identifies one source disk and assigns it ordinal 1. The disk description is given as a Strings key:

```
[SourceDisksNames]
1 = %ID1%, Instd1, 0000-0000
```

[ClassInstall] Section

Syntax

```
[ClassInstall]
Copyfiles=file-list-section[,file-list-section]...
AddReg=add-registry-section[,add-registry-section]...
Renfiles=file-list-section[,file-list-section]...
Delfiles=file-list-section[,file-list-section]...
UpdateInis=update-ini-section[,update-ini-section]...
UpdateIniFields=update-inifields-section[,update-inifield-section]...
AddReg=add-registry-section[,add-registry-section]...
DelReg=del-registry-section[,del-registry-section]...
```

The [ClassInstall] section installs a new class for a device in the class section of the Registry. Every device installed in Windows has a class associated with it (even if the class is "UNKNOWN"), and every class has a class installer associated with it. Setup processes this section if one of the devices defined in this INF file is about to be installed and the class is not already defined. Not all entries are needed or required.

The following example specifies the class entry for Setup to create in the Registry (AddReg=SampleClassReg) and specifies a normal [*Install*] section in [SampleClassReg]. In this example, the Class description is required and the relative key (HKR) denotes the class section. This example creates the class Sample and registers the description, installer, and icon for the class.

```
[ClassInstall]
Addreg=SampleClassReg
CopyFiles=@Sample.cpl

[SampleClassReg]
HKR,,,,%SampleClassDesc%
HKR,,Installer,,Sample.cpl
HKR,,Icon,HEX,00,00
```

[Strings] Section

Syntax

```
[Strings]
strings-key=value
  ⋮
```

The [Strings] section defines one or more Strings keys. A Strings key is a name that represents a string of printable characters. Although the [Strings] section is generally the last section in the INF files, a Strings key defined in this section can be used anywhere in the INF file that the corresponding string would be used. Setup expands the Strings key to the given string and uses it for further processing. Using a Strings key requires that it be enclosed in percent signs (%). The [Strings] section makes localization easier by placing all localizable text in the INF file in a single section. Strings keys should be used whenever possible.

strings-key   A unique name consisting of letters and digits.

value   A string consisting of letters, digits, or other printable characters. It should be enclosed in double quotation marks if the corresponding Strings key is used in an entry that requires double quotation marks.

The following example shows the [Strings] section for a sample INF file.

```
[Strings]
MSFT="Microsoft"
M1="APEX DRIVERS"
DevDesc1=APEX DRIVERS SCSI II Host Adapter
ID1="APEX DRIVERS SuperSCSI Installation disk"
```

[Optional Components] Section

Syntax

```
[Optional Components]
install-section-name
(install-section-name)
    ⋮
```

Lists [*Install*] sections that are displayed when the user selects the INF file from the "Have Disk..." button in the Windows Setup tab on the Add/Remove Programs Properties property sheet. The [*Install*] sections show up as choices in the list of check boxes. (See Chapter 7.)

> NOTE: The [Optional Components] section is ignored during the execution of an INF file when you right-click the INF file and select Install. When you execute an INF file in this manner, the [DefaultInstall] section is executed. The [Optional Components] section is also ignored if the INF file is being executed via the SETUPAPI.DLL InstallHinfSection entry point. When you execute an INF via the SETUPAPI entry point, the [*Install*] section specified as a parameter to the entry point is executed.

The [*Install*] sections follow the same format as described previously, and the following additional keys can be added to the [*Install*] section to drive the UI in the Have Disk dialog box.

```
OptionDesc=option-description
Tip=tip-description
InstallDefault=0 | 1 ; Whether to install this component by default.
               ;   1=Yes, 0=No.
IconIndex=icon-index
Parent=install-section-name
Needs=install-section-name, (install-section-name)
Include=inf-file, (inf-file)
```

option-description   String value that is used as the component name in the Components list box. The *option-description* parameter can be *%String1%*, where the string that replaces *%String1%* is defined in the [Strings] section of the INF file.

tip-description   String value that is displayed in the Description box when the component is selected in the Components list box. The *tip-description* parameter has a 255-character limit and can be *%String1%*, where the string that replaces *%String1%* is defined in the [Strings] section of the INF file.

icon-index   Numeric value that determines the mini-icon that is displayed next to the component name in the Components list box. Valid values include the following.

Value	Icon
0	Machine (base and monitor)
1	Integrated circuit chip
2	Monitor
3	Network wires
4	Windows flag
5	Mouse
6	Keyboard (3 keys)
7	Phone
8	Speaker
9	Hard disks
10	Comm connector

Value	Icon
11	Diamond (default value)
12	Checked box
13	Unchecked box
14	Printer
15	Net card
16	Same as 0
17	Same as 0 with a sharing hand underneath
18	Question mark
19	Modem
20	Grayed check box
21	Dial-up networking
22	Direct cable connection
23	Briefcase
24	Exchange
25	Partial check
26	Accessories group
27	Multimedia group
28	Quick View
29	MSN
30	Calculator
31	Drive converter
32	Generic document
33	Drive space
34	Solitaire
35	HyperTerminal
36	Object Packager
37	Paint
38	Screen saver
39	WordPad
40	Clipboard viewer
41	Accessibility
42	Backup
43	Bitmap document
44	Character map

(continued)

continued

Value	Icon
45	Mouse pointers
46	Net Watcher
47	Phone Dialer
48	System Monitor
49	Help book
50	Globe (international settings)
51	Audio compression
52	CD Player
53	Media Player
54	Sound scheme
55	Video clip
56	Video compression
57	Volume control
58	Musica sound scheme
59	Jungle sound scheme
60	Robotz sound scheme
61	Utopia sound scheme
62	Check box
63	Minesweeper

***Parent* Item**   The optional components displayed in the Components list box can have sub-levels. You access these sub-levels, or child components, by selecting the parent component and clicking the Details button. If the optional component is a child, the *Parent* keyword defines the [*Install*] section for the parent.

***Needs* Item**   If this component has dependencies on other components, this item defines [*Install*] sections that are required by this component. If the component is selected, the user will be warned that the component requires the component(s) described in the [*Install*] section(s) listed on the *Needs=* line.

NOTE: The [*Install*] sections listed in the *Needs=* line must be in the same INF file unless you've specified the external INF files in the *Include=* line.

***Include* Item**   The *Include* item enables you to specify INF files that Setup must also load into memory when it loads your INF file. These INF files contain sections that must be run in addition to the install sections in your INF file. The *Needs* item specifies the names of the sections you intend to run in the included INF file(s).

The following example defines two optional component install sections, and each install section uses the additional entries to specify UI elements and dependencies.

```
[Optional Components]
InstallGame1
InstallGame2

[InstallGame1]
OptionDesc=%My_DESC%
Tip=%My_TIP%
IconIndex=35 ;Phone mini-icon for dialogs
Parent=MailApps
Needs=MSMAIL, MAPI, MicrosoftNetwork
Include=mos.inf, msmail.inf
CopyFiles=Game1Files
UpdateInis=Game1Links
AddReg=Game1RegItems

[InstallOtherApps]
OptionDesc=%Other_DESC%
Tip=%Other_TIP%
IconIndex=4 ;Windows mini icon for dialogs
CopyFiles=OtherFiles
UpdateInis=OtherLinks
AddReg=OtherRegItems

[Strings]
My_DESC="Mail Utilities"
My_TIP="Mail utilities"
Other_DESC="Disk Utilities"
Other_TIP="Calculator"
```

Sample INF Files

This example assumes a fictitious piece of hardware, a SCSI II Host Adapter built by a company named Apex Drivers. The board requires four I/O ports that can be based at 180H, 190H, 1A0h, or 1B0h. The board requires one exclusive IRQ chosen from 4, 5, 9, 10, or 11. The board can use a DMA channel if one is assigned.

```
;SCSI.INF
;
; Standard comment

[Version]
Signature="$Chicago$"
Provider=%MSFT%
HardwareClass=SCSIAdapter

[Manufacturer]
%M1%=APEXD  ; Strings key for this manufacturer

[APEXD]
%DevDesc1% = SuperSCSI, *PNPA000, *PnPA001

[SuperSCSI]
; Apex Drivers Model 01 - SuperSCSI+
Log_Config = With_Dma, WithoutDMA
Copyfiles=MoveMiniPort, @SRSutil.exe
AddReg=MOD1

[With_DMA]
; Primary Logical Configuration
ConfigPriority = NORMAL
I/OConfig = 4@180-1B3%fff0(3:0:)
; Allocate 4 ports at base 180,190,1A0 or 1B0, device decodes
; 10 bits of I/O address and uses no aliases.
IRQConfig = 4,5,9,10,11  ; Allocate Exclusive IRQ 4, 5, 9, 10, or 11
DMAConfig = 0,1,2,3  ; Allocate DMA Channel 0, 1, 2, or 3

[Without_DMA]
; Secondary Logical Configuration
ConfigPriority = SUBOPTIMAL
I/OConfig = 4@180-1B3%fff0(3:0:)
IRQConfig = 4,5,9,10,11

[MOD1]
HKR,,DevLoader,,I/OS
HKR,,Miniport,,SRSmini.386

[DestinationDirs]
MoveMiniPort=12
; Destination for MoveMiniPort Section is windows\iosubsys
DefaultDestDirs=30,bin  ; Direct copies go to Boot:\bin
```

```
[SourceDiskSFiles]
SRS01.386 = 1

[SourceDisksNames]
1 = %ID1%, Instd1, 0000-0000

[MoveMiniPort]
SRS01.386

[Strings]
MSFT="Microsoft"
M1="APEX DRIVERS"
DevDesc1=Apex Drivers SCSI II Host Adapter
ID1="Apex Drivers SuperSCSI Installation disk"
```

The following example extends Windows Explorer's context menu in Windows NT 4.0. It's a typical example of an INF file used to install additional software features.

```
; File: Explore3.inf  (G. Born) Windows NT 4.0
; Platform: Windows NT 4.0 Workstation (Server)
;
; This INF File extends Windows Explorer's context menu
; with a "DOS-Window" command.
;
; To install this new command, right-click on the
; INF file and select Install on the context menu.
;
; To reset the factory settings:
; - open the Control Panel
; - double-click on the Add/Remove Programs icon
; - select the Install/Uninstall property page
; - click the entry "Remove DOS-Windows in Explorer - Born"
; - click the Add/Remove button
;
;**************************************************
; Warning: The file is provided free for your     *
;          personal use. The material may not be  *
;          distributed for commercial use or with *
;          any other commercial material without  *
;          my permission. The file is provided    *
;          AS IS and comes with NO WARRANTY OF ANY*
;          KIND. The ENTIRE RISK arising out of   *
;          the use remains with you. In no event  *
;          shall the author be liable for any     *
;          damages or losses whatsoever.          *
;                                                 *
```

(continued)

continued

```
; Additional information about the Registry      *
; entries used in this file (and about INF files *
; and the Windows NT Registry) may be found in:  *
;                                                 *
; Günter Born: "Inside the Microsoft Windows 98  *
;                 Registry" (Microsoft Press, 1998) *
; This book is also available in German and French*
;**************************************************
;

[version]
signature="$WINDOWS NT$"
SetupClass=Base

; install script
[DefaultInstall]
AddReg = Explore.AddReg
CopyFiles = Explore.CopyFiles.Inf

; uninstall part
[DefaultUninstall]

DelReg = Explore.AddReg,
DelFiles = Explore.DelFiles.Inf

; adds the keys to register the new extension

[Explore.AddReg]
HKCR,Folder\shell\DOS-Fenster,,,"%EXPLORE_DESC%"
HKCR,Folder\shell\DOS-Fenster\command,,,"%10%\system32\COMMAND.COM"
HKLM,Software\Microsoft\Windows\CurrentVersion\Uninstall\DOSWin, →
DisplayName,,"%Explore_REMOVE_DESC%"
HKLM,Software\Microsoft\Windows\CurrentVersion\Uninstall\DOSWin, →
UninstallString,,"RunDll32 setupapi.dll,InstallHinfSection      →
DefaultUninstall 132 Explore3.Inf"

HKLM,Software\Microsoft\Windows\CurrentVersion\Uninstall\DOSWin

; files to be copied
[Explore.CopyFiles.Inf]
Explore3.Inf

; files to be deleted during uninstall
[Explore.DelFiles.Inf]
Explore3.Inf
Explore3.PNF
```

```
; definition for the source
[SourceDisksNames]
55="DOS-Window","",1

[SourceDisksFiles]
Exploree.Inf=55

[DestinationDirs]
Explore.CopyFiles.Inf = 17
Explore.DelFiles.Inf = 17

[Strings]
; English strings
Explore_DESC = "&DOS-Window"
EXPLORE_REMOVE_DESC = "Remove DOS-Windows in Explorer - Born"
; German strings
;Explore_DESC = "D&OS-Fenster"
;EXPLORE_REMOVE_DESC = "DOS-Fenster im Explorer entfernen (Born)"
author="Born"
; End ***
```

Advanced INF Files

The Advanced INF Installer (ADVPACK.DLL) includes INF extensions that can perform tasks such as:

- Prompting a user for a destination directory

- Installing files to a directory specified in the Registry

- Checking for mandatory applications before performing an upgrade

The Advanced INF Installer is supplied by Microsoft Internet Explorer 4. This section describes the syntax of the Advanced INF Installer and how to perform routine tasks by using its features.

Syntax

```
[Version]
Signature="$Chicago$"
AdvancedINF=2.5, "You need a newer version of advpack.dll."
; Error message if setup can't find a proper version of
; advpack.dll to use.
```

(continued)

continued

```
[InstallSection]
CustomDestination=CustomDestinationSection

[CustomDestinationSection]
CustomLDIDNumber=CustomLDIDSection, <Flag>

[CustomLDIDSection]
'<Root Key>','<Sub Key>','<Value Name>','<Message>','<Default to use>'
```

> **NOTE:** Single quotes should be used instead of double quotes in the above syntax so that the INF file meets the Windows NT 4.0 INF processing requirements.

Parameters

The parameters mentioned in the items above are defined as follows.

Parameter	Description
<Flag>	A number that determines how the value of the custom LDID is determined. This number can be constructed by summing appropriate values from the table on the next page.
<LDID Value>	The LDID value to which a value is assigned. It must be an integer value of at least 49000 and less than 50000. This is to avoid other reserved LDIDs in Windows NT.
<Root Key>	A root key of a Registry entry. Same format as [AddReg] and [DelReg] INF file sections.
<Sub Key>	A subkey of a Registry entry. Same format as the [AddReg] and [DelReg] INF file sections.
<Value Name>	A subkey of a Registry entry. Same format as the [AddReg] and [DelReg] INF file sections. The default value for a key can be a NULL string (two double quotes).
<Message>	A message that can be displayed to the user.
<Default>	A string that is used as a default value if no LDID value can be obtained from Registry entries.

Flag Values

Flag Value	Description
1	Default: Make a Registry subkey the value of custom LDID. Return branch name.
	Set: Make Registry value the value of the custom LDID. Return a value in the branch.
2	Default: If none of the Registry entries in the CustomLDIDSection exist, use the default as the LDID value.
	Set: Fail the installation if none of the Registry entries exist. Upon failure, show the user the message specified on the last line of the CustomLDIDSection.
4	Default: Display a dialog box prompting the user to enter a destination directory. Prompt the user with the message string corresponding to the Registry entry, if found, or to the default value. Fill the edit box with either the Registry value or the default value.
	Set: Do not prompt the user. Use either the Registry value, if found, or the default value as the LDID value.
8	Default: Strip a semicolon from the end of the custom LDID value if one is there.
	Set: Do not strip a semicolon from the LDID value.
16	Default: Before assigning a Registry value or subkey to an LDID, check to see if the Registry value is a valid directory on the user's system.
	Set: Do not check the Registry value to see if it is a valid directory.
32	Default: No effect on other flags.
	Set: Has to be used in conjunction with flag value 2. Fails the install if any of the Registry keys searched for exists. Reverses logic of flag value 2.

NOTE: If flag value 1 is not set, Internet Express (IExpress) will not confirm that a Registry value it looks for is a valid directory. (You'll get the same results if flag value 16 is set.) Replaceable strings from the [Strings] section can be used in Advanced INF Installer sections. Standard LDIDs can also be used. Previous versions of IExpress could not create c:\myapp\samples\LFNDIR. This is no longer a limitation. Also, under Windows NT 4.0, any value assigned to an LDID must be in the form of a directory, otherwise the Windows NT 4.0 Setup engine (SETUPAPI.DLL) will attempt to convert it to a valid directory name. Setup will not fail if a conversion cannot be made, but the string represented by the LDID probably will not remain intact.

The only time that you are safe in using the contents of an LDID under Windows NT 4.0 is when the LDID is assigned to a valid directory name. Attempting to set the LDID to a Registry branch (flag = 0) will rarely produce the expected result.

Using RunDLL32 to Launch Advanced INF Files

The LaunchINFSection function in ADVPACK.DLL can be used to launch advanced INF files using RunDLL32. This feature is useful for uninstalls and for testing advanced INF files. The syntax for LaunchINFSectionEx is:

```
(inf filename) [,section name] [,cab name] [,flags] [,smart reboot]
```

The flags are:

4 = Quiet Mode

8 = No GrpConv

16 = Force Self-Updating on User's System

32 = Backup Data Before Install

64 = Rollback to Previous State

128 = Validate the Backup Data

256 = Bypass Building File List

512 = Force Delay of OCX Registration

To start ADVPACK.DLL by using rundll32 in the file MYINF.INF, use the following command:

```
rundll32 advpack.dll,LaunchINFSection myinf.inf,,12
```

This command installs MYINF.INF with [DefaultInstall] section (because the section parameter is left blank) in Quiet Mode with no GrpConv (because the flags parameter is set to 12, Quiet Mode 4 plus No GrpConv 8).

inf filename   The name of an INF file, relative to the current directory.

section name   A section in the INF file to launch.

cab name   The name of the CAB file that contains the files you want to install on the user's system.

When ADVPACK.DLL is called, it executes the specified section of the INF file in the same manner as if it were called using RunSetupCommand, except that the dialog title is extracted from the [BeginPrompt] section of the INF file.

Uninstalling Via LaunchINFSectionEx

The following command creates an entry for the uninstall key in the Registry.

```
HKLM,SOFTWARE\Microsoft\Windows\CurrentVersion\Uninstall\IExpress, ⇥
"DisplayName",,"My Application Name"
HKLM,SOFTWARE\Microsoft\Windows\CurrentVersion\Uninstall\IExpress, ⇥
"UninstallString",,"RunDll32 advpack.dll,LaunchINFSectionEx %17%\ ⇥
<inf file>, <UninstallSection>"
```

The parameters mean the following:

inf file   The name of your INF file. Use an LDID other than 17 if the INF is not in the INF directory.

UninstallSection   The section of the INF file to launch.

> NOTE: To uninstall using the LaunchINFSectionEx function, ADVPACK.DLL, W95INF16.DLL, and W95INF32.DLL must all be present on the user's system at uninstall time. These files should be copied to the system directory as part of the install process. IExpress might do this automatically in the future.

Advanced INF File Options

The advanced INF file contains the sections described above and the following extensions.

AdvancedINF

The [Version] section defines the standard header for all Windows 95, Windows 98, or Windows NT INF files. Advanced INF files contain an extra command line in the [Version] section:

```
AdvancedINF=2.5, failure-dialog-string
```

Identifies the version of ADVPACK.DLL that Internet Explorer 4.0 must load to parse this INF file. In this case, version 2.5 is required. If the version of ADVPACK.DLL is not found, the *failure-dialog-string* is presented to the user.

RequiredEngine

Syntax

```
RequiredEngine=<Value>,%ErrorString%
```

There are two values that can be assigned to a *RequiredEngine* parameter:

<Value>	Description	Usage
SETUPAPI	32-bit version of Setup engine (ADVPACK.DLL)	Windows 95/Windows 98 is forced into 32-bit install or displays an error dialog box. Standard Windows NT Setup engine.
SETUPX	16-bit version of Setup engine	Cannot be used with Windows NT; forces Windows 95 and Windows 98 into 16-bit install.

For more information about SETUPAPI, check out setupapi.h in the Microsoft Platform Software Development Kit.

SmartReboot

Syntax

```
SmartReboot=<parameter>
```

SmartReboot lets you choose whether to ask a user to reboot his or her system. The install engine determines if a reboot is necessary. The parameter can be set as follows.

Parameter	Meaning
N	Never reboot.
AS	Always reboot without asking.
IS	Reboot if needed without asking.
A	Always ask user to reboot.
I	If a reboot is needed, ask user to reboot.

NOTE: *SmartReboot* is ignored unless the INF file is executed via *LaunchINFSection*.

Cleanup

Syntax

`Cleanup=1`

This parameter, located in an [*Install*] section, is useful for when you want to delete your INF when you uninstall, but you need your INF to finish uninstalling.

In the case where you need a reboot to finish deleting or unregistering a file because it is in use, your INF might still be needed. This function causes your INF to be deleted when it has finished the uninstall.

CheckAdminRights

Syntax

`CheckAdminRights=<flag>`

Checks whether the user has the right to access the Registry entry. (Rights are supported only in Windows NT.)

Flag	Function
0	Don't check rights—anyone can install.
1	Verify that the user has the rights to install.

ComponentName

Syntax

```
ComponentName="My Component"
```

This parameter is used by LaunchINFSectionEx to perform the rollback feature. The name "My Component" does not need to be localizable because the user will never see it; it is used only within the INF file.

PreRollBack

Syntax

```
PreRollBack=GenInstallSection
```

When using the rollback function in the Advanced INF Installer, the [GenInstallSection] section can be called before the rollback is executed. This allows the use of a separate [*Install*] section to prepare the user's machine before the rollback happens.

BackupPath

Syntax

```
BackupPath=%11%\MyText
```

If you want to back up your files for rollback into a directory other than the default, you can specify a path with this command.

PerUserInstall

Syntax

```
[InstallSection]
PerUserInstall=PerUserInst

[PerUserInst]
DisplayName=%WebInteg%
Version=5.0.0311.0
IsInstalled=1
ComponentID=IE4Shell_WIN
GUID={89820200-ECBD-11cf-8B85-00AA005B4395}
Locale=en
```

```
StubPath=rundll32.exe advpack.dll,LaunchINFSectionEx →
%11%\myinst.inf,UserStub,,36

[Strings]
WebInteg = "MyComp Update"
```

For each Active Setup–enabled component, this option defines the component's states, version, locale and per-user stubpath under the HKLM\SOFTWARE\ Microsoft\Active Setup\Installed Components\ClassID Registry key. When the user logs on for the first time after installing the component, the command specified in StubPath will be executed if the designated version of the component per-user stub has not been run for the user.

> N O T E : The StubPath data can be any command line launched by CreateProcess.

CustomDestination

Syntax

```
CustomDestination=CustomDestinationSection

[CustomDestinationSection]
49001=DestA,1 ;<1=prompt user, 5=no prompt>
```

Use this section to either ask the user for a custom destination for your files to be copied to, or obtain the destination from a Registry key.

RegisterOCXs

Syntax

```
RegisterOCXs=RegisterOCXSection
```

Use this command to properly register OCXs after installation. You can also unregister your OCXs before they are deleted upon uninstall.

```
[Version]
Signature="$Chicago$"
AdvancedINF=2.5

[DefaultInstall]
RegisterOCXs=RegisterOCXSection
```

(continued)

465

continued

```
[Uninstall]
UnRegisterOCXs=RegisterOCXSection

[RegisterOCXSection]
%<LDID>%\<subdir>\<OCX filename>,<flag,<parameter>>
```

Flag	Description
I	Call *DllRegisterServer* and *DllInstall*.
N	Do not call *DllRegisterServer*, only *DllInstall*.

parameter   This becomes available when a flag is used. You can pass a string as a parameter for *DllInstall*.

DelDirs

Syntax

```
[DefaultInstall]
DelDirs=DelDirsSection

[DelDirsSection]
%11%/FolderX
```

This command allows you to delete folders on a user's system. DelDirs will work only if the folder you specify in the [DelDirsSection] section is empty. The last line in the above syntax would delete the empty folder FolderX from the System folder.

RunPreSetupCommands

Syntax

```
[InstallSection]
RunPreSetupCommands=CmdSection1[:flag][,CmdSection2[:flag]

[CmdSection1]
Notepad.exe
Explorer.exe

[CmdSection2]
Calc.exe
```

You can launch any number of commands before an INF [*Install*] section is executed. Standard LDIDs can be used in preinstall command sections, but Custom LDIDs cannot. The flag is defined as follows.

Flag	Meaning
1	Quiet
2	No wait

The default value for the flag is not quiet and wait for the command to return.

NOTE: The sections specified in the *RunPreSetupCommands* command are executed after the [BeginPrompt] section.

RunPostSetupCommands

Syntax

```
[InstallSection]
RunPostSetupCommands=Section1[:flag][,Section2[:flag]]

[Section1]
Notepad.exe
Explorer.exe

[Section2]
Calc.exe
```

You can launch any number of commands after an INF section is executed. Both standard and custom LDIDs can be used in postinstall command sections.

Flag	Meaning
1	Quiet Mode
2	No Delay
4	Delay Command

The delayed commands will be added to either the *RunOnceEx* branch or the *RunOnce* branch based on the same logic as the delayed register OCXs method.

The system checks for the EXPLORER.EXE version or the presence of IERNONCE.DLL to determine where to add the values. If the commands are added to *RunOnceEx*, the starting subkey that the commands will be stored under is *990*.

Keep in mind that on Windows 95 systems that don't include the IERNONCE.DLL file, all of the delayed commands will be added to the *RunOnce* branch. Due to RegEnum limits, the order in which the commands will be performed under Windows 95 cannot be guaranteed, so it is recommend you use this feature only if you have Internet Explorer 4.0 installed.

> **NOTE:** The sections specified in the *RunPostSetupCommands* line are executed immediately before the [EndPrompt] section.

BeginPrompt and EndPrompt

Syntax

```
[InstallSection]
BeginPrompt=BeginPromptSection
EndPrompt=EndPromptSection

[BeginPromptSection]
Prompt="<Prompt>"
ButtonType=<ButtonType>
Title="<Title>"

[EndPromptSection]
Prompt="<Prompt>"
```

You can pop up a confirmation box before executing an INF so the user can decide whether he or she wants the INF to execute. You can also use a dialog box to inform users that an install/uninstall was completed.

Parameter	Description
<Prompt>	String that is displayed in dialog box
<ButtonType>	YESNO = Buttons are Yes/No
	OKCANC = Buttons are OK/Cancel
<Title>	Title displayed on all dialog boxes only if ADVPACK.DLL is called via LaunchINFSection

NOTE: Since the <Title> parameter in the [BeginPrompt] section is used for error dialog box titles and in the [EndPrompt] section dialog box, you must add a [] section to your INF with only a <Title> parameter so that your dialog boxes are displayed properly. Both prompt sections are executed only if the INF is launched via *LaunchINFSection* or *LaunchINFSectionEx*.

BackupReg

Syntax

```
[DefaultInstall]
BackupReg=BackupRegSection

[BackupRegSection]
HKLM,"SOFTWARE\Microsoft\Active Setup"
```

This is a normal Registry section similar to *AddReg* or *DelReg*. *BackupReg* is useful for saving the state of a Registry key before performing an install/rollback.

Sample Advanced INF

This example shows an INF file containing the Advanced INF items.

```
[Version]
Signature="$CHICAGO$"
AdvancedINF=2.5,%BadAdvpackVer%

[SourceDisksNames]
10="testDisk",,0

[SourceDisksFiles]
newfile.txt=10
inseng.dll=10
adv.inf=10

[DefaultInstall]
;existing gen install INF options
Copyfiles=CopyFilesSection
RenFiles=RenFilesSection
DelFiles=DelFilesSection
UpdateInis=UpdateInisSection
```

(continued)

continued

```
UpdateIniFields=UpdateIniFieldsSection
AddReg=AddRegSection
DelReg=DelRegSection
Ini2Reg=Ini2RegSection
UpdateCfgSys=UpdateCfgSysSection
UpdateAutoBat=UpdateAutoBatSection

;advanced INF options
RequiredEngine=[SETUPAPI | SETUPX],%BadSetupEngineVer%
CustomDestination=CustomDestinationSection
RegisterOCXs=RegisterOCXsSection
UnregisterOCXs=RegisterOCXsSection
BeginPrompt=BeginPromptSection
EndPrompt=EndPromptSection
RunPreSetupCommands=RunPreSetupCommandsSection
RunPostSetupCommands=RunPostSetupCommandsSection
SmartReboot=[I | A | N]
DelDirs=DelDirsSection
Cleanup=1
CheckAdminRights=[1 | 0]

;advanced INF options needed for save/rollback only
ComponentName=%Name%
ComponentVersion=4.0
BackupReg=BackupRegSection
PreRollBack=GenInstallSection ;optional parameter
BackupPath=%49000%\%UninstallData% ;optional
;Per User install options
PerUserInstall=PerUserInst

[PerUserInst]
DisplayName=%WebInteg%
Version=5.0.0311.0
IsInstalled= [1==installed | 0==uninstalled]
ComponentID=IE4Shell_WIN ;ComponentID in ActiveSetup .CIF file
GUID={89820200-ECBD-11cf-8B85-00AA005B4395}
Locale=en
StubPath=rundll32.exe advpack.dll,LaunchINFSectionEx ⤶
%17%\inst.inf,InstSec,,36

[DestinationDirs]
CopyFilesSection=11
DelFilesSection=17
RenFilesSection=17
```

```
[CustomDestinationSection]
49000,49012,49011,49010=DestA,1

[DestA]
HKLM,SOFTWARE\Test,TestLoc,"%Prompt1%",%17%
;HKLM,SOFTWARE\test2,"Blah",'%Prompt2%',"c:\test"
;HKLM,SOFTWARE\Microsoft\test3,,'%Prompt3%',"%11%"

[RegisterOCXsSection]
@%inat%
%11%\textfxr.ocx
%11%\inseng.dll
%11%\adesktop.dll
%11%\shdocvw,I,shell
or
%11%\shdocvw,I,web

[AddRegSection]
HKLM,"SOFTWARE\Microsoft\Active Setup\Installed Components\ ⮑
%GUID%",,,"My Component"
HKLM,"SOFTWARE\Microsoft\Active Setup\Installed Components\ ⮑
%GUID%","IsInstalled",1,01,00,00,00
HKLM,"SOFTWARE\Microsoft\Active Setup\Installed Components\ ⮑
%GUID%","Version",,"4,72,1605,0"

[DelRegSection]
HKLM,"SOFTWARE\Microsoft\Active Setup","SteppingMode","Y"
[DelDirsSection]
%49000%

[RunPreSetupCommandsSection]
calc.exe

[RunPostSetupCommandsSection]
DelFile c:\windows\inf\inseng.dll

[BeginPromptSection]
Prompt=%BeginPrompt%
ButtonType= [YESNO | OKCANCEL]
Title="Test INF Install"

[EndPromptSection]
Prompt=%EndPrompt%

[CopyFilesSection]
inseng.dll,,,16
adv.inf
```

(continued)

continued

```
[RenFilesSection]
newfile.txt,oldfile.txt

[DelFilesSection]
oldfile.txt,,,1

[UpdateInisSection]
win.ini,iniSection

[UpdateIniFieldsSection]
system.ini,iniSection,profile

[Ini2RegSection]
system.ini,iniSection,,HKLM,subkey

[UpdateCfgSysSection]
Buffers=40

[UpdateAutoBatSection]
TmpDir=C:\Temp

[BackupRegSection]
HKLM,"SOFTWARE\Microsoft\Active Setup"

[GenInstallSection]
AddReg=NewGenAddRegSection
DelReg=NewGenDelRegSection

[Strings]
BadAdvpackVer="Incorrect version of advpack.dll. ⇁
Please get new version from our Web site."
BadSetupapiVer="Setupapi.dll is required to install on this system."
BadSetupEngineVer=                                        ⇁
"Advpack.dll is required to install on this system."
BeginPrompt="Are you sure you want to proceed with install?"
EndPrompt="Install has completed successfully. NEW"
Prompt1="1: Is App's location right?"
Prompt2="2: Where would you like to install?"
Prompt3="3: Where would you like to go today?"
UninstallData="Uninstall Information"
GUID="MyGuid"
```

INDEX

SPECIAL CHARACTERS

& (ampersand), 94–97

<> (angle brackets), 56

* (asterisk), 115

@ (at sign), 27, 81, 432, 434

\ (backslash), 81, 89

{} (curly brackets), 59

\\ (double backslash), 81

!! (exclamation marks), 376

% (percent sign), 449

%1 placeholder, 57, 58–59, 78, 263

%10% placeholder, 86, 357, 405

%11% placeholder, 155, 405

%I placeholder, 224

" " (quotation marks), 18, 19, 27, 73, 81, 89

; (semicolon), 224, 427

[] (square brackets), 1, 27, 81, 340

16-bit components, 11–13, 128, 320

32-bit components, 320, 406–8

A

abbreviations for root keys, 86, 356

accelerator keys, 94–97

access, remote. *See* remote access

access, restricting

  to display properties, 191–93

  for execution of applications, 206–9

  to network properties, 193–94

access, restricting, *continued*

  to passwords properties, 194–95

  to printer properties, 195

  to Registry editing tools, 209

  to Registry keys, 401–2

  to system properties, 196

Active Desktop

  disabling, 140–41

  disallowing changes, 182–86

  enabling Web Page view, 139–40 (*see also* Web Page view)

  settings, 180–82

  wallpaper, 175–82

ActiveX components

  BMP handlers, 263

  Briefcase, 162

  context menu handlers, 318

  Control Panel (*see* Control Panel)

  data and drop handlers, 319

  as folders, 163–64

  icon handlers, 263, 317–18

  importing Registry data using, 26–27

  My Documents, 146

  Network Neighborhood, 141–43

  property sheet handlers, 318–19

  Recycle Bin (*see* Recycle Bin)

  registering, 319–21

  Registry entries, 131–34

  retrieving CLSID codes for, 60

ActiveX components, *continued*
   shell extensions and, 59–61
   shell items, 131
   viewers, 114
add-on utilities, 54
advanced INF files, 366–75, 457–72. *See also*
   INF files
   backing up Registry, 371–75
   executing, 367–68
   file format, 368–71
   launching, using RunDLL32, 460–61
   options, 461–69
   overview, 457–60
   sample, 469–72
   settings, 280
   signature, 341, 368, 462
   Windows NT 4.0 Workstation and, 405
Advanced INF Installer, 341, 366, 457
Advanced Power Management
   settings, 188–90
alias names, mapping of, 285–86
ampersand (&), 94–97
angle brackets (<>), 56
animated minimize feature, disabling, 170
API functions, 9, 321–23, 326–35
applets, 305
applications. *See also* programming issues;
   software settings
   changing associations with file types, 66
   creating optional components list for
      installation, 341–47
   default settings, 5–6
   installation INF files, 340, 455–57
   install programs, 54
   launching, at startup, 281–84
   Microsoft (*see* Microsoft software)
   Open With list (*see* Open With list)

applications, *continued*
   path settings (*see* pathnames)
   property sheets, 54
   registering several file types for single, 101–5
   registering single file type for several, 87–91
   registering sound events for, 272–75
   Registry and installation of, 9
   restricting execution of, 206–9
   shared DLLs, 277–78
   shared tools, 278–79
   status information, 315–16
   using, as viewers, 114–15
   utilities (*see* utilities)
   Win16, settings for, 11–13
associations. *See* file types, registered
asterisk (*), 115
at sign (@), 27, 81, 432, 434
ATTRIB.EXE program, 34, 36–37
attributes
   changing file, 34, 36–37
   Windows NT 4.0 Workstation
      Registry, 401–2
AUTOEXEC.BAT, 35, 37, 43, 275–76,
   309, 433
AUTORUN.INF
   changing drive icons, 264
   disabling, for CD-ROMs, 265

B

background options, desktop, 175–77
backing up and recovering Registry
   backing up Windows NT 4.0 Workstation
      Registry, 410–12
   booting system with startup disk, 37–38
   choosing methods, 49
   by exporting data, 29–32

backing up and recovering Registry, *continued*
   manually, 36–37
   recovering Registry in MS-DOS real mode,
     34–35
   recovering Windows NT 4.0 Workstation
     Registry, 398, 412–14
   using advanced INF file, 371–75
   using Microsoft Backup, 44–48
   using Registry Checker, 38–44
   Windows 95 tools, 36
backslash (\), 81, 89
Backup, Microsoft, 44–49, 410, 413
BAT files
   AUTOEXEC.BAT, 35, 37, 43, 275–76,
     309, 433
   changing file attributes, 36–37
   document template, 254–58
   executing, from Windows Explorer context
     menu, 234–38
   file type keys, 56
   property sheet for, 59–61
Beep On Errors, 171
binary data types, 18, 19–20, 21–22
BMP files as icons, 260–61, 262–63
boot driver setting, 286
booting. *See* rebooting
brackets, angle (<>), 56
brackets, curly ({}), 59
brackets, square ([]), 1, 27, 81, 340
breakpoints, INF file, 362–63
Briefcase, 162

C

/C option of Registry Editor, 34–35
CAB files, 37, 41–44

caches
   CD-ROMs, 289–90
   machine role and, 290–92
   shell icon file, 261
   shell window settings, 251–52
   write-behind, 286
canonical verbs, 92, 95, 97, 117, 423
CD-ROMs
   cache settings, 289–90
   changing drive letters, 298
   device drivers on startup disk, 38
   disabling AutoRun, 265
   Windows 98, 33, 49
CFGBack utility, 36
characters, valid, 17
$Chicago$ signature, 341, 428
classic style view, 246
ClassInstall section, INF files, 426, 448
cleaning Registry, 230
CLSID codes. *See also* ActiveX components
   for ActiveX handlers, 59, 131–34
   retrieving, for ActiveX components, 60
   Windows 95 vs. Windows NT 4.0, 403
color
   color schemes and custom colors, 172
   icon color depth, 260
   integrated color management, 305
   for Windows elements, 172
column settings, Windows Explorer, 247
commands
   context menu (*see* context menu)
   DDE, for file types, 78–79
   file type, 55–56, 57–59, 70–73 (*see also*
     verbs)
   Windows Explorer strings and
     syntax, 221–24

comments, INF files, 224

components, ActiveX. *See* ActiveX components

compression

  disk, 288–89

  file, 36

CONFIG.SYS, 37, 43, 309

configuration settings, Windows, 298–303

Confirm Open After Download, 76

console settings, 415

context menu

  commands for unregistered file
    types, 117–18

  creating folders for desktop, 163

  disabling shell, 243–44

  handlers, 149, 318

  Recycle Bin, 149

  registered file type (*see* context menu,
    registered file type)

  Windows Explorer (*see* context menu,
    Windows Explorer)

context menu, registered file type

  command accelerator keys, 94–97

  command names, 91–94

  command sequencing, 99

  commands for all file types, 115–17

  default commands, 97–99

  merging REG files into Registry, 26–27

  Open With dialog box and, 67

  Print command, 76–78

  Print To command, 99–100

  verbs, 58, 92, 423

context menu, Windows Explorer, 219–38

  adding placeholders to command strings, 224

  defining command string, 221–22

  disabling, 243–44

context menu, Windows Explorer, *continued*

  example command syntax, 222–23

  installing extensions with INF files, 224–30,
    236–38, 455–57

  MS-DOS command, 230–34

  New Explorer Window command, 219–30

  Print Directory command, 234–38

Control Panel

  adding cascading menu for, to Start menu,
    197–98

  adding folder icon for, to desktop, 162–63

  contents of, 196

  editing Registry settings, 13–14, 54

  folder settings, 305

  international settings, 190–91

  for Windows NT 4.0 Workstation, 403–4,
    415

CopyFiles command, 349, 350, 431–32,
  434–36

curly brackets ({}), 59

current configuration settings, 8

current user settings, 6–7

cursor parameters, 173–75

cursor schemes, 173

custom colors, 172

D

DAO files, 10, 44

database, Registry

  Windows 95, 10, 44

  Windows 98, 3–9

  Windows NT Workstation, 397–99

data handlers, 319

data types, 18, 398–99

DDE commands for file types, 78–79

debugging
   INF files, 362–63
   Windows NT Diagnostics, 402
default commands for registered file
      types, 97–99
default settings, 5–6, 17
default values, REG file, 27, 81
delay
   keyboard, 307
   menu, 211–12
DelFiles command, 349, 350
design of Registry, 2–3
desktop. *See also* shell
   Active Desktop settings (*see* Active Desktop)
   adding Control Panel folder, 162–63
   adding Printers folder, 164
   adding Recycle Bin icon to My Computer
      window, 164–66
   adding Registry Editor shortcut, 16
   Advanced Power Management
      settings, 188–90
   background options, 175–77
   Beep On Errors settings, 171
   color schemes and custom colors, 172
   colors for elements, 172
   cursor schemes, 173
   default settings, 5–6
   disabling animated minimize feature, 170
   disabling save settings, 218
   drag parameters, 175
   hiding all items, 138–39
   hiding and showing special items, 161–62
   hiding icons in Web Page view, 139–40
   international settings, 190–91
   metrics and visual effects, 166–69

desktop, *continued*
   mouse and cursor parameters, 173–75
   My Computer settings, 129–38
   My Documents settings, 146–48
   Network Neighborhood settings, 141–45
   Recycle Bin settings, 148–61
   restricting access to display properties,
      191–93
   restricting access to network properties,
      193–94
   restricting access to passwords properties,
      194–95
   restricting access to printer properties, 195
   restricting access to system properties, 196
   screen saver options, 186–88
   smooth scrolling settings, 170
   system icons as folders, 163–64
   user preferences for visual effects, 171
   Web Page view settings, 177-82
Desktop Computer role, 290–92
destination LDID values, 353–55
device configuration settings, 294–98
device drivers
   boot, 286
   CD-ROM, on startup disk, 38
   digital signature checking, 284
   INF files and, 426
   modem, 312
   settings, 7
   Windows NT 4.0 Workstation, 417
device information files. *See* INF files
Device Manager, 8, 296–98
digital signature checking, 284
directories. *See* folders
directory lists, printing, 234–38

disabilities, sound events and, 272
disks
    Emergency Repair Disk, 410–11, 413
    LDID values, 353–55
    real mode I/O, 287
    startup, 37–38
display properties
    Active Desktop settings and, 186
    Advanced Power Management
      settings, 188–90
    background options, 175–77
    changing Network Neighborhood icon, 141
    color schemes and custom colors, 172
    colors for Windows elements, 172
    disabled Active Desktop and, 186
    metrics for desktop items, 166–69
    My Computer settings, 129–30
    restricting access to, 191–93
    screen saver options, 186–88
    Web desktop settings, 177–82
Display Properties property sheet, 13–14,
    166–96. *See also* display properties
DLLs, shared, 277–78
dockable stations, 8, 421
Documents command, disabling, 204
document templates, 253–58
double backslash (\\), 81
double-clicking, 5
drag-and-drop settings, 5, 99–100, 175, 319,
    395, 414
drivers. *See* device drivers
drives
    CD-ROM (*see* CD-ROMs)
    changing icons, 263–65
    disk (*see* disks)

drives, *continued*
    hiding icons, 134–38
    Recycle Bin and, 157
    settings, 286–90
DriveSpace 3 settings, 288–89
drop handlers, 319
DWORD data type, 18, 20–21, 21–22
Dynamic Data Exchange commands for file
    types, 78–79
dynamic link libraries (DLLs), shared, 277–78
dynamic status information, 8

E

EDIT.COM, 121–23, 235
editing Registry
    with Registry Editor (*see* Registry Editor)
    safest methods, 13–14
    with System Policy Editor (*see* System Policy
      Editor)
    tools for, 53–54
edit options, register file types, 56, 106–8
emergency boot disks, 37–38
Emergency Repair Disks, 410–11, 413
Environment variables, 415
error logging, enabling, 284
Error Recovery Utility, 36
errors
    Beep On Errors settings, 171
    conflicting parameters between INI files and
      Registry, 13
    CopyFiles command, 350
    debugging INF files, 362–63
    DelFiles command, 350
    error logging, 284
    file type associations, 100–105
    importing and exporting Registry entries,
      30–32

errors, *continued*
    phantom applications, 123–25
    refreshing ICO file icons, 152, 260–61
    REG files, 82–85
    Registry Checker codes, 41
    removing file types, 68
    restricting execution of applications, 208
    uninstalling applications, 278
    Windows NT Diagnostics, 402
events. *See* sound events
exclamation marks (!!), 376
Explorer. *See* Windows Explorer
exporting Registry data, 26, 28–32,
    34–35, 401
extensions, filename. *See also* filenames
    hiding and showing, 75–76, 108–10, 239–43
    registered (*see* file types, registered)
    subkeys and, 5
extensions, shell, 59–61. *See also* shell
EzDesk, 159

F

Favorites command, disabling, 204
File menu, removing, 244
filenames
    CopyFiles command and, 436
    disabling long, 285
    extensions (*see* extensions, filename)
    long, containing blanks, 73, 81
    modifying mapping of aliases, 285–86
    pathnames (*see* pathnames)
    preserving long, 287
files
    application paths (*see* pathnames)
    BAT (*see* BAT files)
    BMP, as icons, 260–61, 262–63

files, *continued*
    CAB, 37, 41–44
    changing permissions, 34, 36–37
    compression, 36
    file system settings (*see* file system settings)
    hiding and showing system, 239–43
    HTML, as wallpaper, 175–82
    icon source, 75, 134, 143, 260–61, 264
    INF (*see* advanced INF files; INF files)
    INI (*see* INI files)
    installing and uninstalling, 347–55
    most recently used (*see* MRU lists)
    opening, after download, 76
    PIF, 236, 248
    sharing and locking, 288
    shell icon cache, 261
    REG (*see* REG files)
    template (*see* templates)
    Windows 95 Registry database, 10, 44
    Windows 98 Registry database, 10–11, 34
    Windows NT Registry database, 397–99
File System Properties property sheet, 286–90
file system settings, 285–92
    configuration settings, 286–90
    disabling long filenames, 285
    machine role settings, 290–92
    modifying alias mapping, 285–86
file types, registered, 55–118, 317
    changing associations with applications, 66
    command accelerator keys, 94–97
    command name on context menu, 91–94
    command sequence on context menu, 99
    commands for all, 115–17
    commands for unregistered files, 117–18
    DDE options, 78–79
    default command, 70–73, 97–99

file types, registered, *continued*

default icon, 56–57, 73–75

file description, 65, 69–70

hiding and showing file extensions, 108–10

HKEY_CLASSES_ROOT and, 5, 55–62

phantom applications and, 123–25

registering, using applications, 317

registering, using INF files, 85–87

registering, using Open With dialog box, 63–67

registering, using REG files, 61–62, 80–85

registering, using Registry Editor, 80

registering, using Windows Explorer, 69–76

registering several, for single application, 66, 101–5

registering single, for several applications, 87–91

removing, 67–68

Print command, 76–78

Print To command, 99–100

problems with file type associations, 100–101

protecting settings, 106–8

Quick Viewers, 111–15

shell actions, 57–59

shell extensions, 59–61

tools for adding and changing, 53, 62

file types, unregistered, commands for, 117–18

File Types property page, 53, 65, 125–26

filters, graphics, 278–79

Find command, disabling, 202–3

finding Registry information, 23–24, 401

Folder Options property sheet, 108–10, 239–43

folders. *See also* pathnames

ActiveX components as, 163–64

adding Control Panel, to desktop, 162–63

folders, *continued*

adding Printers, to desktop, 164

BAT files and installed files, 235–36

Briefcase, 162

Control Panel (*see* Control Panel)

creating, using desktop context menu, 163

deleting, with advanced INF files, 466

disabling customization, 247

fonts, 303–4

INF files, 351

locations of Registry database files, 10–11, 34, 37

My Documents, 146–48

name of Windows, 84–85

placeholders, 86, 155, 357

Printers, 198

printing directory lists, 234–38

Registry Checker backups, 41–42, 43

Registry Editor, 15

Registry shell settings for, 216–17

sound files, 268

system icons as, 163–64

Windows NT Workstation Registry database, 397–99

fonts, installed, 303–4

G

global local machine settings, 9, 136

graphics filters, 278–79

H

handlers. *See* ActiveX components

hardware. *See also* system properties

component and Plug & Play settings, 294–98

installing INF files, 340, 453–55

hardware, *continued*

    profiles, 292–94, 420, 421

    settings, 7–8

    Windows NT 4.0 Workstation settings, 416–17

hardware profiles, 292–94, 420, 421

Have Disk dialog box, 341–47

hexadecimal values, 18, 19–20

hiding and showing

    all desktop items, 138–39

    desktop icons in Web Page view, 139–40

    drive icons in My Computer window, 134–38

    file extensions, 75–76, 108–10, 239–43

    My Documents icon, 147–48

    Network Neighborhood icons, 143–45

    Recycle Bin icon, 158–61

    special desktop items, 161–62

    system files, 239–43

hives, Windows NT Workstation

    backing up, 410

    keys and files of, 396–97

    loading and unloading, 401

    reloading, after startup, 413

HKEY_CLASSES_ROOT, 5, 55–62, 113, 131, 395, 414

    HKEY_LOCAL_MACHINE and, 5, 9, 128, 395, 414

HKEY_CURRENT_CONFIG, 8, 421

HKEY_CURRENT_CONFIGURATION, 395–96

HKEY_CURRENT_USER, 6–7, 8, 9, 133, 134, 281, 315–16, 395, 414–16

    HKEY_LOCAL_MACHINE and, 8, 9

    HKEY_USER and, 9, 316

HKEY_DYN_DATA, 8, 394, 396

HKEY_LOCAL_MACHINE, 5, 7–8, 9, 280–81, 292–303, 315–16, 395, 416–21

    HKEY_CLASSES_ROOT and, 5, 9, 128, 395, 414

    HKEY_CURRENT_CONFIG and, 8

    HKEY_CURRENT_USER and, 8, 9

HKEY_USERS, 5–6, 9, 281, 395, 414

    HKEY_CURRENT_USER and, 9, 316

HTML files as wallpaper, 175–82

I

ICM settings, 305

ICO files, 152, 260

icons

    activating changes, 261

    adding Control Panel folder, to desktop, 162–63

    adding Printers folder, to desktop, 164

    adding Recycle Bin, to My Computer window, 164–66

    BMP files as, 262–63

    changing, for drives, 263–65

    changing, for My Computer, 129–34

    changing, for Network Neighborhood, 141–43

    changing, for Recycle Bin, 151–52

    changing shortcut symbol, 265–66

    creating, 260–61

    default, for file types, 56–57, 73–75

    handlers, 317–18

    hiding and showing My Documents, 147–48

    hiding and showing Recycle Bin, 158–61

    hiding desktop, in Web Page view, 139–40

    hiding drive, in My Computer, 134–38

    hiding Network Neighborhood, 143–45

icons, *continued*

how shell, are stored, 258–61

ICO file, 152

managing cache file for, 261

modifying shell, 258–66

registered file, and Open With dialog box, 67

removing shortcut symbols, 248–51

removing Shortcut To prefix, 250–51

resource identifiers, 57

size and color depth, 260

sources, 75, 134, 143, 152, 260–61, 264

standard Windows, for registered file types, 63

system, as folders, 163–64

identical keys in different branches, 9

importing Registry data, 25–28, 31–32, 34, 401

INF file format, 228–30, 425–72. *See also* INF files

advanced (*see* advanced INF files)

ClassInstall section, 448

general structure, 426–28

Install section, 431–47

Manufacturer Name section, 430

Manufacturer section, 429–30

Optional Components section, 449–53

Strings section, 448–49

Version section, 428–29

Windows 95, 425–26

INF files, 54, 339–66

activating MS-DOS from Windows Explorer, 231–34

adding and deleting Registry entries, 355–60

advanced (*see* advanced INF files)

advantages and disadvantages, 339–40

INF files, *continued*

AUTORUN, 264–65

changing drive icons, 263–65

changing Recycle Bin, 155–56

changing Recycle Bin icons, 358–60

comments, 224

creating software components list for installation, 341–47

debugging, 362–63

defining source and destination, 353–55

deleting Recycle Bin from My Computer, 166

executing and testing, 360–63

format (*see* INF file format)

file structure, 340–41

hiding and showing Recycle Bin icon, 160–61

INI file settings during Setup, 11

installing and uninstalling files, 347–55

installing MS-DOS as shell extension, 407–8

installing Print Directory extension, 236–38

installing shell extensions, 224–30, 236–38

pitfall of CopyFiles and DelFiles commands, 350

registering document template for New command, 255–58

registering file types, 85–87

registering sound events, 268

removing shortcut symbols, 248–51

resetting Run MRU list, 215, 363–66

sample hardware installation, 453–55

sample software installation, 455–57

signature, 341, 428

uninstall details, 350–53

Windows 95 uninstall feature, 352

Windows NT 4.0 Workstation, 404–8

InfoTip window, 147, 150, 244–45
INI files
    conflicting parameters between Registry and, 13
    INF files and, 437–40, 442–43
    Registry and, 1–3, 11–13
    Registry Checker, 42–43
    Windows NT 4.0 Workstation, 393–94
Inside OLE, 2nd Edition (Brockschmidt), 60, 321
Inside the Registry for Microsoft Windows 95 (Born), 10, 229
installation
    installing and uninstalling files, 347–55
    optional application components list, 341–47
    REG files, INF files, and, 123
    Registry settings and application, 9, 54
    Remote Registry service, 33
    scripts (*see* INF files)
    System Policy Editor, 49–51
    user-supplied information, 304–5
    Windows (*see* setup process)
Install section, INF files, 426, 431–47
    Add Registry section, 440–41
    CopyFiles section, 434–36
    DeleteFiles section, 437
    Delete Registry section, 442
    DestinationDirs section, 444–45
    File-List section, 445–46
    Ini to Registry section, 442–43
    Logical Configuration sections, 432–33
    RenameFiles section, 436
    SourceDisksFiles section, 446–47
    SourceDisksNames section, 447
    syntax, 431–32
    Update AutoExec section, 433

Install section, INF files, *continued*
    Update Config section, 434
    Update IniFields section, 439–40
    Update INI section, 437–39
integrated color management settings, 305
international settings, 190–91
Internet Explorer 4.0, Microsoft, 70–71, 180–82, 280, 305, 457
Internet settings, 70–71, 305, 312–13

J

JScript, Microsoft, 338–39

K

keyboard layout, 6, 415
keyboard speed and delay, 307
keys, accelerator, 94–97
keys, Registry, 3–9
    abbreviations, 86, 356
    adding new values or new, 21–22
    changing values, 18–21
    default value, 27, 81
    deleting, 22–23
    displaying values, 17–18
    finding, 23–24
    identical, in different branches, 9
    printing, 25
    renaming, 23
    root, 4–9, 86, 356
    subkeys and, 3–4
    Windows 95 vs. Windows NT 4.0 Workstation, 405–6
    Windows NT 4.0 Workstation root, 394–96

L

LDID (Logical Disk ID) values, 353–55, 444–45

loading and unloading hives, 401, 413

Local Computer Properties property sheet, 51–52

local machine settings, 7–8, 9, 280–81

Local User Properties property sheet, 51–53, 245–46, 375

Logical Disk ID (LDID) values, 353–55, 444–45

Logitech mouse middle button, 175

Log Off command, disabling, 203

logon window, clearing last user name in, 253

long filenames
    containing blanks, 73, 81
    CopyFiles command and, 436
    disabling, 285
    preserving, 287

M

machine role settings, 290–92

machine-specific settings, 280–81

manually backing up Registry, 36–37

Manufacturer Name section, INF files, 426, 430

Manufacturer section, INF files, 426, 429–30

mapping of alias names, 285–86

menus
    adding cascading Control Panel, to Start menu, 197–98
    adding cascading Printers, to Start menu, 198
    changing menu delay, 211–12
    context (*see* context menu)

menus, *continued*
    removing File, 244
    Start (*see* Start menu)

merging REG files into Registry, 26–27

metrics for desktop items, 166–69

Microsoft PowerToys, 137

Microsoft software
    Backup, 44–49, 410, 413
    Internet Explorer 4.0, 70–71, 180–82, 280, 305, 457
    JScript, 338–39
    Office 97 VBA, 325, 332
    Remote Registry service, 32–33
    settings, 6, 9, 280–81, 316, 419
    shared tools, 278–79
    Visual Basic 4.0 and Visual Basic for Applications, 323–35
    Visual Basic Script, 335–37
    Windows 3.*x*, 1–2, 416, 419
    Windows 95 (*see* Windows 95, Microsoft)
    Windows 98 (*see* Windows 98, Microsoft)
    Windows Explorer (*see* Windows Explorer, Microsoft)
    Windows NT (*see* Windows NT 3.51, Microsoft; Windows NT 4.0, Microsoft; Windows NT 4.0 Workstation Registry, Microsoft)
    Word for Windows 95, 325

Microsoft Windows 95 Resource Kit, 36

Microsoft Windows 98 Resource Kit, 53, 136, 199, 213, 285, 312, 313, 378

Microsoft Windows NT 4.0 Workstation Resource Kit, 404, 410, 412, 414, 420

MIME file types, 70–71

minimize, disabling animated, 170

Mobile Computing role, 290–92

modem settings, 312

modules. *See* ActiveX components

MORICONS.DLL, 75

most recently used lists. *See* MRU lists

Mouse Properties property sheet, 173–75

MRU lists

    resetting, 215–16

    resetting Run command, using INF files, 363–66

    resetting Run command, using REG files, 213–15

MS-DOS

    activating, from Windows Explorer context menu, 230–34

    configuration settings, 307–12

    disabling access, 209–11

    Registry access in real mode, 34–35

    Registry Checker and, 38, 39, 40

multiple hardware configuration computers, 8, 421

My Computer

    adding Recycle Bin icon, 164–66

    changing icon for, 129–34

    finding and modifying Registry entries, 131–34

    hiding drive icons, 134–38

My Documents, 146–48

N

naming

    clearing last user name, 253

    filenames (*see* filenames)

    pathnames (*see* pathnames)

    Recycle Bin, 148–50

    renaming Registry keys, 22, 23

    Windows folder, 84–85

Network Neighborhood, 141–45

    changing icon for, 141–43

    hiding icon for, 143–44

    hiding icons in, 144–45

network properties

    changing update mode, 212–13

    clearing last user name in logon window, 253

    machine role settings, 290–92

    Network Neighborhood, 141–45

    recent and persistent connections, 6, 252–53

    remote access to Registry, 6, 32–33

    restricting access to, 193–94

    user-login, 8

    Windows NT 4.0 Workstation, 416

Network Server role, 290–92

New command, registering template for, 253–58

O

OCXs, registering, 465–66

Office 97 VBA, Microsoft, 325, 332

OLE, 2, 5, 321, 395, 414

Open With dialog box, 63–67

    applications list (*see* Open With list)

    changing associated application of file type, 66

    changing registered file type settings, 53

    disadvantages, 67

    registered file type context menu command for, 117–18

    registering new file type, 63–64

    using, to add application to Open With list, 121–22

    verifying new file type, 65

Open With list, 119–28. *See also* shell
  adding applications, 121–23
  how applications are inserted by shell, 120
  removing applications, 123–28
Optional Components section, INF files, 427, 449–53

P

parameters, conflicting, 13
passwords properties, restricting access to, 194–95
pathnames, 275–81
  application settings, 280–81, 321
  file structure information, 276–77
  omitting, 152, 154
  placeholders, 85–87 (*see also* placeholders)
  in REG files, 81, 84–85
  search order, 277
  shared DLL file information, 277–78
  shared software tools information, 278–79
percent sign (%), 449
permissions
  changing file, 34, 36–37
  Windows NT 4.0 Workstation Registry, 401–2
phantom applications, removing, 123–25
PIF files, 236, 248
PIFMGR.DLL, 75
placeholders
  %1, 57, 58–59, 78, 263
  %10%, 86, 357, 405
  %11%, 155, 405
  adding, to command strings, 224
  %I, 224
  for pathnames, 85–87

placeholders, *continued*
  %SystemRoot%, 405
  in Windows NT 4.0 Workstation, 405
Plug & Play settings, 8, 294–98
Print command, 76–78
printers
  adding cascading menu for Printers folder to Start menu, 198
  adding icon for Printers folder to desktop, 164
  restricting access to properties, 195
  Windows NT 4.0 Workstation settings, 416
Printers folder, 164, 195
printing
  adding Print command to file type context menu, 76–78
  adding Print To command to file type context menu, 99–100
  directory lists from Windows Explorer, 234–38
  Registry information, 25
Print To command, 99–100
profiles. *See* hardware profiles; user profiles
programming issues, 315–80. *See also* applications; software settings
  API functions for accessing Registry, 321–23
  creating System Policy Editor template files, 375–80
  INF files (*see* advanced INF files; INF files)
  REG files (*see* REG files)
  registering ActiveX components, 319–21
  registering context menu handlers, 318
  registering data and drop handlers, 319
  registering icon handlers, 317–18
  registering new file types, 317 (*see also* file types, registered)

programming issues, *continued*

registering property sheet handlers, 318–19

registering version and status information, 315–16

Visual Basic Registry access examples, 323–35

Windows Scripting Host Registry access examples, 335–39

Programming the Windows 95 User Interface (Cluts), 18, 60, 84, 114, 132

Programming Windows (Petzold), 321

Programming Windows 95 (Petzold), 60, 149

programs. *See* applications; programming issues; software settings

property sheets/pages

BAT file, 59–61

changing Registry settings with applications, 54

Display Properties, 13–14, 166–96

File System, 286–90

File Types, 53, 65, 125–26

Folder Options, 108–10, 239–43

handlers, 318–19

Local Computer Properties, 51–52

Local User Properties, 51–53, 245–46, 375

Mouse Properties, 173–75

Recycle Bin Properties, 156–58

System Properties, 196, 292–303

protecting registered file type settings, 106–8

Q

QuickInfo window, 147, 150

Quick Viewers, 111–15

applications as viewers, 114–15

defining standard QuickView properties, 112–14

Quick Viewers, *continued*

enabling, 75

information about, 114

quotation marks (""), 18, 19, 27, 73, 81, 89

R

read-ahead buffer setting, 286

real mode, accessing Registry in MS-DOS, 34–35

real mode disk I/O, 287

rebooting. *See also* startup

advanced INF files and, 462–63

with Emergency Repair Disk, 410–11, 413

INF files and, 351–52

resetting shell without, 201–2

with startup disks, 37–38

recovering Registry. *See* backing up and recovering Registry

Recycle Bin, 148–61

adding icon for, to My Computer window, 164–66

changing, with INF files, 155–56

changing, with Recycle Bin Properties property sheet, 156–58

changing, with REG files, 153–54

changing icons, 151–52

changing icons with INF file, 358–60

defining sound event for emptying, 275

hiding and showing icon, 158–61

renaming, 148–50

user-specific settings, 150

Windows REG file versions and, 154

Windows NT 4.0 Workstation icons, 406

REGBACK.EXE and REGREST.EXE tools, 412, 414

REGEDIT32.EXE and REGEDIT.EXE, 15, 34, 35, 400–402, 412. *See also* Registry Editor

REG files, 54

  activating MS-DOS from Windows Explorer, 230

  adding applications to Open With list, 122–23

  adding Recycle Bin to My Computer, 165

  changing mapping of alias names, 285–86

  changing Recycle Bin with, 153–54

  combining Registry branches into, 61–62

  defining command accelerator keys, 96–97

  defining context menu command name, 92–93

  disabling options, 202

  exporting, 28–32, 34–35

  extending MS-DOS options, 311

  format, 27

  hiding drive icons, 138

  importing, 25–28, 34

  registering document templates for New command, 254–55

  registering file types, 80–85

  registering Quick Viewer for, 111–14

  registering several file types for single application, 103–5

  registering single file type for several applications, 88–89

  registering sound events for applications, 274

  resetting Run MRU list, 214–15

  risks of, 82–85

  signature, 27, 28, 83

  Windows 3.*x*, 2, 3

  Windows NT 4.0 Workstation, 404

  Windows versions and, 28, 154

registered file types. *See* file types, registered

Registry, 1–14

  accessing, 9

  accessing, with programming languages, 321–39 (*see also* programming issues)

  application launch during startup, 281–84

  application pathnames, 275–81

  architecture, 3–9

  backing up and recovering (*see* backing up and recovering Registry)

  combining branches of, into REG files, 61–62

  conflicting parameters between INI files and, 13

  database files, 10–11

  design of Windows 95, 2–3

  desktop settings (*see* desktop)

  editing, 13–14, 53–54 (*see also* Registry Editor; System Policy Editor)

  exporting data, 28–32

  file system settings, 285–92

  file type settings (*see* file types, registered)

  importing data, 25–28

  INI files and, 1–3, 11–13

  Open With lists, 119–28

  registering file types with, 80

  remote access to, 32–33

  shell settings (*see* shell)

  signature checking and error logging, 284

  sound events, 267–75

  Start menu settings, 197–216

  system properties, 292–303

  system software settings, 303–13

  this book's example entries, 14

  when to edit, 13

  Windows Explorer settings (*see* Windows Explorer)

  Windows NT 4.0 Workstation (*see* Windows NT 4.0 Workstation Registry)

Registry Checker, 38–44
   choosing, for backups, 47, 49
   creating and maintaining Registry backups
      with, 41–44
   undoing deletions, 23
   using, 39–41
   versions, 38–39
Registry Editor
   accessing Registry, 9
   accessing Registry in MS-DOS real mode,
      34–35
   adding keys or values, 21–22
   changing values, 18–21
   deleting entries, 22–23
   disabling, 139
   displaying key values, 17–18
   exporting Registry data, 28–32
   extending shell commands, 220–21
   finding Registry information, 23–24
   hiding and showing Recycle Bin icon,
      159–60
   importing Registry data, 26
   as last resort, 14
   locating, 15
   printing Registry information, 25
   remote Registry access, 32–33
   removing Open With list entries, 127–28
   renaming keys or values, 22, 23
   restricting access, 209
   starting, 15–16
   window elements, 16–17
   Windows NT 4.0 Workstation, 400–402,
      412
Registry Editors, Windows NT 4.0 Worksta-
      tion, 400–402, 412
Registry settings, miscellaneous, 267–313

remote access
   to INI files, 2
   to Registry, 6, 32–33
Remote Registry service, Microsoft, 32–33
renaming Recycle Bin, 148–50
renaming Registry keys, 22, 23
Repair Disk Utility, 410–11, 413
resource identifiers, 57
restricting access. *See* access, restricting
rollback, Registry, 371–75, 464
root keys
   abbreviations, 86, 356
   Windows 98 Registry, 4–9
   Windows NT 4.0 Workstation, 394–96
Run command
   application search path, 277
   disabling, 201–2
   resetting MRU list, using INF files, 363–66
   resetting MRU list, using REG files, 213–15
RUNDLL32.EXE and RUNDLL.EXE, 117,
      229, 351, 352, 367, 406, 460–61
Run keys, 281–84

S

save settings, disabling desktop, 218
SAV files, 397–98
SCANREG.EXE and SCANREGW.EXE. *See*
      Registry Checker
SCANREG.INI, 42–43
SCC viewer, 75, 111, 114
screen saver settings, 186–88
scripts, altering Registry using, 335–39
scrolling, smooth, 170
section heads
   INF file, 228, 426–28
   INI file, 1

security settings, 8, 401–2, 418

semicolon (;), 224, 427

sequencing context menu commands, 99

services

   configuration settings, 302–3

   launching, at startup, 281–84

   Windows NT 4.0 Workstation, 420

Settings submenu, removing entries from, 199–200

SETUPAPI.DLL and SETUPX.DLL, 229, 351–52, 406–7, 462

SETUPC.INF, 11

setup process. *See also* installation

   creating components list for, 341–47

   information files (*see* INF files)

   INI files and, 11–13

   settings, 304–5, 306–7

   SYSTEM.DAT and, 44

shared DLL settings, 277–78

shared files, 288

shared tool settings, 278–79

shell, 119

   activating icon changes, 261

   changing drive icons, 263–65

   changing shortcut symbol, 265–66

   clearing last user name in logon window, 253

   desktop (*see* desktop)

   disabling CD-ROM AutoRun, 265

   disabling context menu, 243–44

   disabling folder customization, 247

   disabling InfoTip window, 244–45

   extensions, 59–61

   file type commands, 57–59

   forcing classic style, 246

   hiding and showing system files and extensions, 239–43

   how applications are inserted in Open With lists, 120

shell, *continued*

   how icons are stored, 258–61

   how window settings are saved, 251–52

   icon size and color depth, 260

   managing icon cache file, 261

   miscellaneous settings, 216–18

   modifying icons, 258–66

   modifying miscellaneous system settings, 239–52

   modifying network settings, 252–53

   Open With list (*see* Open With list)

   registering a new template for New command, 253–58

   removing File menu, 244

   removing shortcut symbols, 248–51

   removing Shortcut to prefix from icon titles, 250–51

   resetting, without rebooting, 201–2

   showing BMP files as icons, 262–63

   using System Policy Editor to change settings, 245–47

   Windows Explorer (*see* Windows Explorer)

SHELL32.DLL, 56–57, 75, 134, 143, 152, 154, 258–60

SHELL98.ADM, 243, 244, 245–47

shell extensions, 59–61. *See also* shell

SHELLICONCACHE file, 261

SHELLM.ADM, 246

shortcut symbols

   changing, 265–66

   removing, 248–51

Shortcut To prefix, removing, 250–51

showing. *See* hiding and showing

Shut Down command, disabling, 204–5

signature

   advanced INF file, 341, 368, 462

   checking digital, 284

   $Chicago$ signature, 341, 428

signature, *continued*
  INF file, 341, 428
  REG file, 27, 28, 83
  $Windows NT$ signature, 405, 428
  Windows NT 4.0 Workstation INF files, 405
single-clicking, 5
single-mode MS-DOS feature, disabling, 209–11
size
  icon, 260
  INI files, 2
  Registry key values, 17
  Windows 98 Registry, 3
  Windows NT 4.0 Workstation Registry, 399, 409
smooth scrolling, 170
software settings. *See also* applications; pathnames; programming issues
  Microsoft, 6, 9, 280–81, 316, 419
  shared DLLs, 277–78
  shared tools, 278–79
  system software (*see* system software settings)
  user-installed, 7
  Windows NT 4.0 Workstation, 416, 418–19
sound events, 267–75
  Beep On Errors settings, 171
  defining, for emptying Recycle Bin, 275
  editing, 268
  event labels, 268–70
  registering, for applications, 272–75
  settings, 267–72
  sound schemes, 270–72
  Windows NT 4.0 Workstation, 415
Sounds property page, 268–69, 272–74
source LDID values, 353–55
speed, keyboard, 307
spin down settings, 289

square brackets ([ ]), 1, 27, 81, 340
Start menu
  adding cascading Control Panel menu, 197–98
  adding cascading Printers menu, 198
  adding Registry Editor, 16
  changing options, 197–216
  default settings, 5
  disabling Documents command, 204
  disabling Favorites command, 204
  disabling Find command, 202–3
  disabling Log Off command, 203
  disabling miscellaneous settings, 205–6
  disabling MS-DOS prompt and single-mode MS-DOS feature, 209–11
  disabling Run command, 201–2
  disabling Shut Down command, 204–5
  menu delay settings, 211–12
  network update mode settings, 212–13
  removing entries from Settings branch, 199–200
  resetting MRU lists, 215–16
  resetting Run MRU list, 213–15
  resetting shell without rebooting, 201–2
  restricting execution of applications, 206–9
startup
  application launch at, 281–84
  disks, 37–38
  in MS-DOS mode, 211
  rebooting (*see* rebooting)
  recovering Windows NT 4.0 Workstation Registry at, 412–13
  Registry Checker and (*see* Registry Checker)
  settings, 10
status information, application, 315–16
storage of shell icons, 258–61
string data types, 18, 19, 21–22
Strings section, INF files, 427, 448–49

subkeys, 3. *See also* keys, Registry

subscribed Web channels, 181–82

SYSTEM.1ST, 44

SYSTEM.DAO, 44

SYSTEM.DAT, 10, 34, 36–37, 41, 44

system files, hiding and showing, 239–43

SYSTEM.INI, 11–13, 41

System Policy Editor, 49–53

changing desktop settings, 183–86

changing network update mode, 212–13

changing shell settings, 243–47

digital signature check, 284

disabling Find command, 202–3

disabling long filenames, 285

disabling MS-DOS prompt and single-mode MS-DOS feature, 209–11

disabling Run command, 201–2

disabling save settings, 218

disabling Shut Down command, 204–5

disabling Start menu settings, 205–6

editing Registry, 13–14

editing shell settings, 245–47

enabling user profiles, 50–51

hiding all desktop items, 138–39

hiding drive icons in My Computer, 134–38

hiding Network Neighborhood icon, 143–44

installing, 49–51

launching applications at startup, 283–84

removing entries from Settings submenu, 199–200

resetting Run MRU list, 215

restricting access to display properties, 191–93

restricting access to network properties, 193–94

restricting access to passwords properties, 194–95

System Policy Editor, *continued*

restricting access to printer properties, 195

restricting access to Registry editing tools, 209

restricting access to system properties, 196

restricting execution of applications, 206–9

templates, 183–84, 203, 205, 243–47, 375–80

using, 51–53

Windows NT 4.0 Workstation and, 404

system properties

device configuration settings, 294–98

hardware profiles, 292–94

local Windows configuration settings, 298–302

restricting access to, 196

Windows services lists, 302–3

System Properties property sheet, 196, 292–303

%SystemRoot% placeholder, 405

system software settings, 303–13

applets, 305

Control Panel folder, 305

installed fonts, 303–4

integrated color management, 305

Internet Explorer, 280, 305

keyboard speed and delay, 307

modem drivers, 312

MS-DOS mode, 307–12

setup process, 306–7

TCP/IP protocol configuration, 312–13

user profiles, 305

user-supplied install information, 304–5

Windows configuration settings, 298–302

Windows services settings, 302–3

system-specific desktop elements, 129

system-specific settings, 128, 419–21

T

TCP/IP protocol settings, 312–13

templates
document, for New command, 253–58
System Policy Editor, 183–84, 203, 205, 243–47, 375–80

testing INF files, 360–63

text values, 19, 21–22

third-party utilities, 13–14

toolbar settings, 185

tools, shared, 278–79

Tweak UI, 54
Beep On Errors settings, 171
changing desktop items into folders, 164
changing menu delay, 211–12
changing shortcut symbol, 265–66
clearing last user name in Logon window, 253
disabling Active Desktop, 140–41
disabling animated minimize, 170
disabling Documents command, 204
disabling Favorites command, 204
disabling Log Off command, 203
disallowing Active Desktop changes, 182–86
enabling error logging, 284
hiding and showing Control Panel entries, 158–59
hiding and showing desktop items, 161–62
hiding and showing Recycle Bin icon, 158–59
hiding drive icons, 137–38
hiding Network Neighborhood icon, 144
mouse settings, 175
registering document templates for New command, 254
removing Shortcut to prefix, 250–51

Tweak UI, *continued*
resetting Run MRU list, 215
smooth scrolling settings, 170
user preferences for visual effects, 171

types. *See* data types; file types, registered

U

uninstalling
applications and, 321
deleting INF file after, 463
shared DLLs and, 278
using advanced INF files, 461
using INF files, 227–28, 230, 231–34, 238, 347–55
in Windows 95, 252

unregistered file types, commands for, 117–18

Update Mode, changing, 212–13

upgrades to Windows 98, 11–13

USER.DAO, 10, 44

USER.DAT, 10–11, 34, 36–37, 41

user-installed software, 7

user name, clearing, from logon window, 253

user profiles, 10, 395, 414
enabling, 50–51
settings, 305
USER.DAT and, 37
Windows NT Workstation, 397, 409

user-specific settings
application, 281
folder options, 239–43
INI files and, 2
install information, 304–5
Recycle Bin, 150
Registry keys, 5–7, 9
USER.DAT and, 10–11, 34, 36–37
visual effects, 171

utilities
add-on, 54
Registry recovery, 36
third-party, 13–14
Tweak UI (*see* Tweak UI)

V

verbs. *See also* commands
canonical, 92, 95, 97, 117, 423
file type, 58
sound, 271
verifying new registered file type, 65
version information, 315–16
Version section, INF files, 426, 428–29
viewers. *See* Quick Viewers
views. *See* classic style view; Web Page view
Visual Basic 4.0 and Visual Basic for
Applications, Microsoft, 323–35
accessing application settings in Registry,
323–25
extended Registry access calling API
functions, 326–35
Visual Basic Script, altering Registry using,
335–37
visual effects, user preferences for, 171. *See also*
display properties

W

wallpaper settings, 175–82, 185
WAV files, 268, 271
Web browsers, 70–71
Web Page view. *See also* Active Desktop
background options, 175–77
desktop settings, 177–82
disabling, 246
enabling, 139–40
hiding desktop icons in, 139–40

wildcard extensions, 115
Win16 applications settings, 11–13
Win32 API functions, 321–23, 326–35
*Win32 Software Development Kit for
Windows 95 and Windows NT*, 428
windows
activating MS-DOS, from Windows Explorer,
230–34
clearing last user name from logon, 253
defining column settings for Windows
Explorer, 247
how shell settings are saved, 251–52
InfoTip, 147, 150, 244–45
opening second Windows Explorer, 219–30
Registry Editor, 16–17
Windows 3.*x*, Microsoft, 1–2, 416, 419
Windows 95, Microsoft
CLSID entries, 403
deleting files with INF files, 354–55
icon settings, 154
INF files overview, 229, 425–26
REG files, 28, 82, 154
Registry database files, 10, 44
Registry design, 2–3
Registry key value size, 17
Registry recovery tools, 36
Registry structure, 5
uninstalling in, 352
Windows 95 Software Development Kit, 346
Windows 98, Microsoft
API functions, 9, 321–23, 326–35
configuration settings, 298–303
folder name problem, 84–85
icon settings, 154
INI files, 11–13, 229 (*see also* INI files)
My Computer, 129
Recycle Bin settings, 150 (*see also*
Recycle Bin)

Windows 98, Microsoft, *continued*

REG files, 28, 82, 154 (*see also* REG files)

Registry (*see* Registry)

Setup (*see* setup process)

shell (*see* shell)

startup disks, 37–38

Windows Explorer (*see* Windows Explorer, Microsoft)

Windows 98 Device Development Kit, 312

Windows API functions, 9, 321–23

Windows Explorer, Microsoft, 67–79. *See also* shell

adding Print command to registered file types, 76–78

assigning commands to file types, 70–73

column settings, 247

context menu (*see* context menu, Windows Explorer)

directory hierarchy, 4

disabling folder customization, 247

enabling Confirm Open After Download, 76

enabling file extension display, 75–76

enabling QuickView command, 75

forcing classic style view, 246

hiding and showing system files and extensions, 239–43

miscellaneous system settings, 239–52

registering MIME file types, 70–71

registering new file types, 69–76

removing File menu, 244

removing Open With list entries, 125–26

removing registered file types, 67–68

resetting shell without rebooting, 201–2

setting icons for file types, 73–75

using DDE option for registered file types, 78–79

Web Page view (*see* Web Page view)

for Windows NT 4.0 Workstation, 402

Windows Interface Guidelines for Software Design, 276

Windows NT 3.51, Microsoft, 5

Windows NT 4.0, Microsoft

icon settings, 154

My Computer, 129

REG files, 28, 82, 154

Registry structure, 5

Windows NT 4.0 Workstation Registry, Microsoft, 393–421

architecture, 394–99

backing up, 410–12

branches and entries, 414–21

Control Panel, 403–4

database files, 397–99

hives, 396–97

INF files and, 404–8

modifying size of, 409

recovering, 412–14

REG files and, 404

Registry Editors, 400–402

role of INI files, 393–94

root keys, 394–96

tools for accessing, 400–409

Windows Explorer and, 402

Windows NT Diagnostics and, 402

Windows NT Diagnostics, 402

$Windows NT$ signature, 405, 428

Windows Scripting Host, altering Registry using, 335–39

WIN.INI file, 1–2, 11–13, 41, 128

Word for Windows 95 WordBasic, 325

write-behind caching, 286

About the Author

Günter Born holds an engineering degree in physics and has studied information science and electrotechnics. He began working as a software developer and project engineer in the German spacecraft and chemical industries in 1979, managing software development groups and consulting on several international projects with Japan, Thailand, and Europe. Currently he works as an independent writer and translator.

Born started his work with computers as a student when one of his professors encouraged him to work through a series of equations for mechanical systems. Too poor to buy a pocket calculator and too lazy to do the calculations by hand, Born turned to an IBM 370 computer, which had to be fed with punched cards. An incorrect FORTRAN statement resulted in a long listing and wasted time, but after the program was finally running the computer saved Born a lot of time and provided a lot of free paper, which he used for classroom notes.

His publishing career started with some mistakes. In 1987, he failed to publish an article he wrote about an 8085/Z80 Dissembler implemented in BASIC—nobody wanted to read about Basic. So he decided to learn Pascal. He borrowed an old IBM PC/XT with a Borland Pascal compiler, spent a weekend porting his dissembler to Pascal, exchanged the Basic listings with Pascal source code, and succeeded at last, publishing his article in a computer magazine. Born wrote his first book to get the money to buy a PC. (The royalties, as it turned out, barely covered the cost of the PC.)

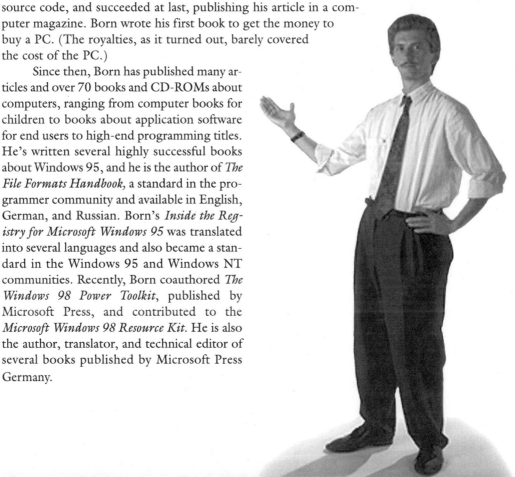

Since then, Born has published many articles and over 70 books and CD-ROMs about computers, ranging from computer books for children to books about application software for end users to high-end programming titles. He's written several highly successful books about Windows 95, and he is the author of *The File Formats Handbook,* a standard in the programmer community and available in English, German, and Russian. Born's *Inside the Registry for Microsoft Windows 95* was translated into several languages and also became a standard in the Windows 95 and Windows NT communities. Recently, Born coauthored *The Windows 98 Power Toolkit,* published by Microsoft Press, and contributed to the *Microsoft Windows 98 Resource Kit.* He is also the author, translator, and technical editor of several books published by Microsoft Press Germany.

The manuscript for this book was prepared and submitted to Microsoft Press in electronic form. Text files were prepared using Microsoft Word 97. Pages were composed by Microsoft Press using Adobe PageMaker 6.52 for Windows, with text in Galliard and display type in Helvetica bold. Composed pages were delivered to the printer as electronic prepress files.

Cover Graphic Designer
Tim Girvin Design, Inc.

Cover Illustrator
Glenn Mitsui

Interior Graphic Artist
Joel Panchot

Principal Compositor
Elizabeth Hansford

Principal Proofreader/Copy Editor
Teri Kieffer

Indexer
Shane-Armstrong Information Systems

Microsoft Windows 98 advances *the* **desktop.** Here's how to advance with it.

U.S.A. **$69.99**
U.K. £64.99 [V.A.T. included]
Canada $100.99
ISBN 1-57231-644-6

The MICROSOFT® WINDOWS® 98 RESOURCE KIT provides you with all of the information you need to plan for and implement Windows 98 within your organization. In fact, this 1792-page reference book—with electronic book text as well as tools, utilities, and accessory software provided on CD-ROM—is the most complete source of professional-level information on Windows 98 available any-where. Details, discussions, explanations, and insights on installing, configuring, and supporting Windows 98 will save you hours of time and help you get the most from your computing investment. This exclusive Microsoft publication, written in cooperation with the Windows 98 development team, is the perfect technical companion for network administrators, support professionals, systems integrators, and computer professionals.

Microsoft®Press

Microsoft Press has titles to help everyone— from new users to seasoned developers—

Step by Step Series
Self-paced tutorials for
classroom instruction or
individualized study

Starts Here™ Series
Interactive instruction
on CD-ROM that helps
students learn by doing

Field Guide Series
Concise, task-oriented
A–Z references for
quick, easy answers—
anywhere

Official Series
Timely books on a wide
variety of Internet topics
geared for advanced
users

All User Training

All User Reference

Quick Course® Series
Fast, to-the-point
instruction for new users

Running Series
A comprehensive
curriculum alternative to
standard documentation
books

At a Glance Series
Quick visual guides for
task-oriented instruction

start faster and go farther!

The wide selection of books and CD-ROMs published by Microsoft Press contain something for every level of user and every area of interest, from just-in-time online training tools to development tools for professional programmers. Look for them at your bookstore or computer store today!

Professional Select Editions Series
Advanced titles geared for the system administrator or technical support career path

Microsoft® Certified Professional Training
The Microsoft Official Curriculum for certification exams

Best Practices Series
Candid accounts of the new movement in software development

Microsoft Programming Series
The foundations of software development

Professional   Developers

Strategic Technology Series
Easy-to-read overviews for decision makers

Microsoft Press® Interactive
Integrated multimedia courseware for all levels

Microsoft Professional Editions
Technical information straight from the source

Solution Developer Series
Comprehensive titles for intermediate to advanced developers

Microsoft® Press

mspress.microsoft.com

mspress.microsoft.com

Microsoft Press Online is your road map to the best available print and multimedia materials—resources that will help you maximize the effectiveness of Microsoft® software products. Our goal is making it easy and convenient for you to find exactly the Microsoft Press® book or interactive product you need, as well as bringing you the latest in training and certification materials from Microsoft Press.

MICROSOFT LICENSE AGREEMENT

(Inside the Microsoft Windows 98 Registry - Book Companion CD)

IMPORTANT—READ CAREFULLY: This Microsoft End-User License Agreement ("EULA") is a legal agreement between you (either an individual or an entity) and Microsoft Corporation for the Microsoft product identified above, which includes computer software and may include associated media, printed materials, and "on-line" or electronic documentation ("SOFTWARE PRODUCT"). Any component included within the SOFTWARE PRODUCT that is accompanied by a separate End-User License Agreement shall be governed by such agreement and not the terms set forth below. By installing, copying, or otherwise using the SOFTWARE PRODUCT, you agree to be bound by the terms of this EULA. If you do not agree to the terms of this EULA, you are not authorized to install, copy, or otherwise use the SOFTWARE PRODUCT; you may, however, return the SOFTWARE PRODUCT, along with all printed materials and other items that form a part of the Microsoft product that includes the SOFTWARE PRODUCT, to the place you obtained them for a full refund.

SOFTWARE PRODUCT LICENSE

The SOFTWARE PRODUCT is protected by United States copyright laws and international copyright treaties, as well as other intellectual property laws and treaties. The SOFTWARE PRODUCT is licensed, not sold.

1. **GRANT OF LICENSE.** This EULA grants you the following rights:

   a. **Individuals.** If you are an individual person, this EULA grants you the right to install and use one copy of the SOFTWARE PRODUCT on a single computer. The primary user of the computer on which the SOFTWARE PRODUCT is installed may make a second copy for his or her exclusive use on a portable computer.

   b. **Entities.** If you are a corporation, limited liability company, limited partnership or other legal entity, this EULA grants you, your subsidiaries and affiliates (collectively, the "Organization") the right to install and use an unlimited number of copies of the SOFTWARE PRODUCT, for the Organization's internal purposes only, on personal computers, workstations or similar devices which are owned or otherwise possessed and used by and for the benefit of the Organization, provided that: (i) each copy shall be a true and complete copy, including all copyright and trademark notices, except that, the foregoing notwithstanding, no right is granted herein to copy or distribute within the Organization the portions, if any, of the SOFTWARE PRODUCT that are designated as not redistributable in the Readme.txt file that forms a part of the SOFTWARE PRODUCT; (ii) each copy shall be subject to the terms of this EULA; and (iii) no copy shall be offered for resale.

   c. **Sample Code.** Solely with respect to portions, if any, of the SOFTWARE PRODUCT that are identified within the SOFTWARE PRODUCT as sample code (the "SAMPLE CODE"):

   i. **Use and Modification.** Microsoft grants you the right to use and modify the source code version of the SAMPLE CODE, *provided* you comply with subsection (d)(iii) below. You may not distribute the SAMPLE CODE, or any modified version of the SAMPLE CODE, in source code form.

   ii. **Redistributable Files.** Provided you comply with subsection (d)(iii) below, Microsoft grants you a nonexclusive, royalty-free right to reproduce and distribute the object code version of the SAMPLE CODE and of any modified SAMPLE CODE, other than SAMPLE CODE (or any modified version thereof) designated as not redistributable in the Readme.txt file that forms a part of the SOFTWARE PRODUCT (the "Non-Redistributable Sample Code"). All SAMPLE CODE other than the Non-Redistributable Sample Code is collectively referred to as the "REDISTRIBUTABLES."

   iii. **Redistribution Requirements.** If you redistribute the REDISTRIBUTABLES, you agree to: (i) distribute the REDISTRIBUTABLES in object code form only in conjunction with and as a part of your software application product; (ii) not use Microsoft's name, logo, or trademarks to market your software application product; (iii) include a valid copyright notice on your software application product; (iv) indemnify, hold harmless, and defend Microsoft from and against any claims or lawsuits, including attorney's fees, that arise or result from the use or distribution of your software application product; and (v) not permit further distribution of the REDISTRIBUTABLES by your end user. Contact Microsoft for the applicable royalties due and other licensing terms for all other uses and/or distribution of the REDISTRIBUTABLES.

2. DESCRIPTION OF OTHER RIGHTS AND LIMITATIONS.

- **Limitations on Reverse Engineering, Decompilation, and Disassembly.** You may not reverse engineer, decompile, or disassemble the SOFTWARE PRODUCT, except and only to the extent that such activity is expressly permitted by applicable law notwithstanding this limitation.

- **Separation of Components.** The SOFTWARE PRODUCT is licensed as a single product. Its component parts may not be separated for use on more than one computer.

- **Rental.** You may not rent, lease, or lend the SOFTWARE PRODUCT.

- **Support Services.** Microsoft may, but is not obligated to, provide you with support services related to the SOFTWARE PRODUCT ("Support Services"). Use of Support Services is governed by the Microsoft policies and programs described in the user manual, in "on-line" documentation, and/or in other Microsoft-provided materials. Any supplemental software code provided to you as part of the Support Services shall be considered part of the SOFTWARE PRODUCT and subject to the terms and conditions of this EULA. With respect to technical information you provide to Microsoft as part of the Support Services, Microsoft may use such information for its business purposes, including for product support and development. Microsoft will not utilize such technical information in a form that personally identifies you.

- **Software Transfer.** You may permanently transfer all of your rights under this EULA, provided you retain no copies, you transfer all of the SOFTWARE PRODUCT (including all component parts, the media and printed materials, any upgrades, this EULA, and, if applicable, the Certificate of Authenticity), **and** the recipient agrees to the terms of this EULA.

- **Termination.** Without prejudice to any other rights, Microsoft may terminate this EULA if you fail to comply with the terms and conditions of this EULA. In such event, you must destroy all copies of the SOFTWARE PRODUCT and all of its component parts.

3. COPYRIGHT.
All title and copyrights in and to the SOFTWARE PRODUCT (including but not limited to any images, photographs, animations, video, audio, music, text, SAMPLE CODE, REDISTRIBUTABLES, and "applets" incorporated into the SOFTWARE PRODUCT) and any copies of the SOFTWARE PRODUCT are owned by Microsoft or its suppliers. The SOFTWARE PRODUCT is protected by copyright laws and international treaty provisions. Therefore, you must treat the SOFTWARE PRODUCT like any other copyrighted material **except** that you may install the SOFTWARE PRODUCT on a single computer provided you keep the original solely for backup or archival purposes. You may not copy the printed materials accompanying the SOFTWARE PRODUCT.

4. U.S. GOVERNMENT RESTRICTED RIGHTS.
The SOFTWARE PRODUCT and documentation are provided with RESTRICTED RIGHTS. Use, duplication, or disclosure by the Government are subject to restrictions as set forth in subparagraph (c)(1)(ii) of the Rights in Technical Data and Computer Software clause at DFARS 252.227-7013 or subparagraphs (c)(1) and (2) of the Commercial Computer Software—Restricted Rights at 48 CFR 52.227-19, as applicable. Manufacturer is Microsoft Corporation/One Microsoft Way/Redmond, WA 98052-6399.

5. EXPORT RESTRICTIONS.
You agree that you will not export or re-export the SOFTWARE PRODUCT, any part thereof, or any process or service that is the direct product of the SOFTWARE PRODUCT (the foregoing collectively referred to as the "Restricted Components"), to any country, person, entity, or end user subject to U.S. export restrictions. You specifically agree not to export or re-export any of the Restricted Components (i) to any country to which the U.S. has embargoed or restricted the export of goods or services, which currently include, but are not necessarily limited to, Cuba, Iran, Iraq, Libya, North Korea, Sudan, and Syria, or to any national of any such country, wherever located, who intends to transmit or transport the Restricted Components back to such country; (ii) to any end user who you know or have reason to know will utilize the Restricted Components in the design, development, or production of nuclear, chemical, or biological weapons; or (iii) to any end user who has been prohibited from participating in U.S. export transactions by any federal agency of the U.S. government. You warrant and represent that neither the BXA nor any other U.S. federal agency has suspended, revoked, or denied your export privileges.

DISCLAIMER OF WARRANTY

NO WARRANTIES OR CONDITIONS. MICROSOFT EXPRESSLY DISCLAIMS ANY WARRANTY OR CONDITION FOR THE SOFTWARE PRODUCT. THE SOFTWARE PRODUCT AND ANY RELATED DOCUMENTATION IS PROVIDED "AS IS" WITHOUT WARRANTY OR CONDITION OF ANY KIND, EITHER EXPRESS OR IMPLIED, INCLUDING, WITHOUT LIMITATION, THE IMPLIED WARRANTIES OF MERCHANTABILITY, FITNESS FOR A PARTICULAR PURPOSE, OR NONINFRINGEMENT. THE ENTIRE RISK ARISING OUT OF USE OR PERFORMANCE OF THE SOFTWARE PRODUCT REMAINS WITH YOU.

LIMITATION OF LIABILITY. TO THE MAXIMUM EXTENT PERMITTED BY APPLICABLE LAW, IN NO EVENT SHALL MICROSOFT OR ITS SUPPLIERS BE LIABLE FOR ANY SPECIAL, INCIDENTAL, INDIRECT, OR CONSEQUENTIAL DAMAGES WHATSOEVER (INCLUDING, WITHOUT LIMITATION, DAMAGES FOR LOSS OF BUSINESS PROFITS, BUSINESS INTERRUPTION, LOSS OF BUSINESS INFORMATION, OR ANY OTHER PECUNIARY LOSS) ARISING OUT OF THE USE OF OR INABILITY TO USE THE SOFTWARE PRODUCT OR THE PROVISION OF OR FAILURE TO PROVIDE SUPPORT SERVICES, EVEN IF MICROSOFT HAS BEEN ADVISED OF THE POSSIBILITY OF SUCH DAMAGES. IN ANY CASE, MICROSOFT'S ENTIRE LIABILITY UNDER ANY PROVISION OF THIS EULA SHALL BE LIMITED TO THE GREATER OF THE AMOUNT ACTUALLY PAID BY YOU FOR THE SOFTWARE PRODUCT OR US$5.00; PROVIDED, HOWEVER, IF YOU HAVE ENTERED INTO A MICROSOFT SUPPORT SERVICES AGREEMENT, MICROSOFT'S ENTIRE LIABILITY REGARDING SUPPORT SERVICES SHALL BE GOVERNED BY THE TERMS OF THAT AGREEMENT. BECAUSE SOME STATES AND JURISDICTIONS DO NOT ALLOW THE EXCLUSION OR LIMITATION OF LIABILITY, THE ABOVE LIMITATION MAY NOT APPLY TO YOU.

MISCELLANEOUS

This EULA is governed by the laws of the State of Washington USA, except and only to the extent that applicable law mandates governing law of a different jurisdiction.

Should you have any questions concerning this EULA, or if you desire to contact Microsoft for any reason, please contact the Microsoft subsidiary serving your country, or write: Microsoft Sales Information Center/One Microsoft Way/Redmond, WA 98052-6399.